CHARLIE'S ODYSSEY

Charlie's Odyssey

Lloyd J. Guillory

The Book Guild Ltd
Sussex, England

The Book Guild Ltd.
25 High Street,
Lewes, Sussex

First published 1995

Set in Meridien
Typesetting by Raven Typesetters, Chester, Cheshire

Printed in Great Britain by
Antony Rowe Ltd.
Chippenham, Wiltshire.

A catalogue record for this book is
available from the British Library

ISBN 0 86332 980 2

1

Adelle nervously fingered her martini (her third) as she looked around the bar, avoiding eye contact with the many unattached males who either stared at her, or made repeated attempts to get her attention as they passed in front of her table, as she sat alone awaiting her husband. She smiled inwardly. They reminded her of bantam roosters parading before the flock of hens, trying to arouse their interest. She hated being nervous, especially while waiting for a man she had been married to for the past four years. But this was no normal day, nor a normal meeting. No! This would be one meeting they would both remember for the rest of their lives – a day she had been rehearsing for months. Her nervousness made her perspire, and she could feel the moisture accumulating in her armpits, and that made her more nervous as she shifted her arms to help the situation.

She was thirty-three years old, of medium height, with brown hair and green eyes. Her hair, usually straight, had a short curl in it. She was an attractive woman – no beauty, although she had been voted one in college, but then who can account for the taste of over-libidinous college boys. She was of reasonable intelligence, she had decided in her second year of college . . . no more . . . no less, and she had further decided that she would have to make a good marriage if she were to succeed at all, and that was how Charles Alexander Forester 'Charlie', had come into her life. He was the son of the man who had founded Alexander Forester, Inc., a large real estate firm which now owned and managed shopping malls, office buildings and the like. She had gone to work in the firm as a combination secretary/receptionist, and soon, with some female provocation and body language, had caught the eye of Charlie, the boss's son. His imperious mother and pompous father had warned him against dating an employee of the firm, but love will not be denied and Charlie fell in love with Adelle.

As she slowly raised her glass to her lips, she saw her husband coming through the entrance to the bar which they and their friends frequented regularly. He paused as the maitre d'hotel pointed out his wife to him by waving in her direction. He smiled as he saw her. He adored Adelle. He always had since the first time he saw her smiling at him over the receptionist's desk. This had been only moments after she had been told that Charlie was the boss's son. She had been told this by a frustrated secretary who had, herself, made an ill-fated attempt to capture him, but she lacked the ammunition that Adelle had in profusion.

Adelle forced a smile as he bent over to kiss her cheek, as she tilted her head to offer him her face.

'Adelle, darling, you look so lovely, but then, you always do.'

Over the years, he had been generous in his praises of her to the point they meant very little to her as they had been diluted with repetition. She expected them and the only emotion she displayed was disappointment on those rare occasions when he neglected to mention them.

She smiled weakly as she responded, 'Thank you, Charlie . . . you look lovely, too.'

This was her stock reply, which had also been diluted with monotonous repetition. A waitress stood by, solicitously, waiting for his drink order.

He pointed to his wife's drink . . . 'The same.'

'Well, my dear, you said you wanted to see me. I can't imagine what is so important that it could not have waited until I got home from work.'

He could see that she had had a few drinks already, and he found that strange. She was really not a drinker.

'But,' he added, 'I am at your disposal, my love.' He

looked at her, expectantly, as the waitress placed his drink before him.

Adelle waited until the waitress had left and, as she took a sip from her drink, she said softly . . . 'Charlie, I want a divorce.'

The words struck him like a thunderbolt. They had been married for four years – happily, he thought. At least, he had been happy. He knew she had experienced periods of depression, but when questioned by him, her reply had been, 'It's only some silly female problem you would not understand.'

As she waited for the words to sink in, he looked at her to see if she was smiling. This had to be some sort of joke. But she was not smiling. She had looked directly into his eyes as she said it, but now she avoided his gaze. Her eyes, as far as he could tell, showed no signs of jesting or regret.

He managed a very weak smile as he looked directly at her eyes. 'Is this some kind of joke? If it is . . it is not very funny!'

She gave him a steely look. 'No, Charlie, it is not a joke. I want a divorce, and I want it now!'

'But . . . but,' he stammered, ' we're happily married! Why would you want a divorce?'

'No, Charlie,' she replied coolly, 'you are happily married! I am miserably married . . .'

'But,' he interrupted, 'only last night, while we were making love, you said. . . ."I love you, Charlie." '

'I lied. I've been lying to you for the past two years, and I can't go on any longer . . . living a lie, that is.'

'Two years? Two years, you say? We've been married for four years! What of the other two?' he demanded.

She raised her glass to her lips as she formed her answer. She shook her head as she replied. 'The first year was one of trying . . . the second one was one of pretending, and the last two were ones of lying. That is as honest an answer as I can give you.'

'Honest! You have been living a lie for the past four years, and you talk of honesty!'

His voice rising in anger, as his mind became inflamed with the reality of the situation. It was only beginning to register on him that this was no joke – it was real – this woman to whom he had been married for the past four years was now telling him it was all a lie – a farce. It was an empty as a hollow log. Anger was building up in him. His face was now red, and his eyes were ablaze.

She could see it as she counselled, 'Please, Charlie, don't make a scene. People are staring . . . '

He grabbed her arm above the wrist, holding her tightly. 'You think I give a good goddamn what people in this crummy bar think right now? You have just driven a spike through my heart,' and he looked around the room, lowering his voice, 'and you want me to remain calm!'

'Yes . . . please do. I was hoping we could settle this like civilized people . . . '

He laughed. 'Like civilized people? Haven't I heard that line in a Bette Davies movie? Or was it Joan Crawford? What does it matter?'

She ignored the reference, saying, 'Yes, if you don't try to be too difficult, we can resolve this amicably. My attorney says . . . '

He raised his head. 'Your attorney? D'ya mean to tell me you have already seen an attorney about this?'

'Well . . . of course, Charlie, I've seen an attorney. I knew damn well that you and your family, with all that money and those company lawyers, would be all over me like flies on a dead carcass . . . me . . . a poor defenceless woman, so I naturally needed protection and advice.'

He sat there mesmerized, for a while, trying to collect his thoughts, going over the past four years of their marriage and two years of courtship. She had loved him. He was sure of it! His mind resurrected those countless nights when they had held each other in a passionate embrace, and after passions had subsided, continued embraces filled with tender words of love and devotion until their bodies succumbed to slumber.

He reminded her of all these things, even mentioning some particular occasion, when for some reason, now unremembered, that had been especially tender and warm.

'What of them?' he asked, plaintively. 'Were you simply acting out your little drama?'

She shook her head. 'No, Charlie at first they were real, or, at least, I tried to make them so. I thought I was in love with you. . . . I tried to be . . . I swear I tried, but it became more and more difficult as time went on, and then what had once been affection turned to disaffection, and then to resentment, and I was forced to look elsewhere for,' and she searched for the right word . . . 'fulfilment.'

His eyes widened. 'So, that is it! There is another man! That is what this is all about . . . isn't it?' he demanded.

She had not intended to get into this. She had almost decided to say 'Yes, it is another man,' but that would have piled lies on top of lies, and she felt she had lied to him enough, so she said, quietly, 'No, Charlie, there is no other man. There is another woman.'

His glass slipped from his hand, crashing to the floor. The waitress rushed up, exclaiming, 'Now don't you worry about that little ole mess, Mr Forester, we'll have that cleaned up in a jiffy, and in the meantime I'll bring you another one. How about you, Mrs Forester . . . another one?'

Adelle nodded, grateful for the interruption as she mustered the courage to go on with her blockbuster admission.

'Yes, Charlie, I am in love with another woman! Men don't hold any particular fascination for me, but women do, especially this one particular woman . . .'

'Who?' he demanded.

'I don't think any purpose would be served by my telling you her name. You don't know her. I met her at the country club. At first we just seemed attracted to each other . . . you know . . . girl to girl, but as time went on, we both realized it was more. Actually, she seduced me. I didn't have the guts, or the experience to attempt it. But, I must confess to you that I didn't resist it . . . I wanted it. It took some time for me to sort out my real feelings, but that is where they are, and I know that is what I have to do. Please try to understand, Charlie.'

He was incredulous. He did not understand, nor did he want to. He had never understood the lesbian thing. He had read about it, but to the best of his knowledge he had never even met one, and now he was married to one.

'Do you mean to tell me that you are capable of switching, for want of a better word, from an affection for a male to the same kind of affection for a female?, just like that!' and he snapped his fingers.

'No, it's not quite that simple. I had a lesbian experience in college, but I thought it was wrong, unnatural, so I tried to overcome it. I was determined to. After college, before I met you, I had a few brief affairs with men, mostly I guess to prove to myself that it could be done, but the old desires were always there. Then I went to work in your office, and there you were . . . the boss's son . . . good looking . . . rich, and a pretty nice guy. I thought it would work, Charlie . . . I really did, but,' and she emitted a sob, 'it's not working. I'm miserable, and in time I'll make you miserable, too.'

He shrugged. 'You have already achieved that, I assure you. Why weren't you honest with me up front, before I married you?'

She shrugged, as she looked into his eyes. 'Would you have married me . . . if you had known . . . If I had levelled with you?'

'No, I guess not.'

She began to cry softly, and as he looked at her, he wondered, 'Is she acting now?' How could he tell? He no longer trusted her.

'Adelle, what do you want from me?'

'I told you, Charlie, I want a divorce. I don't want to be a greedy bitch, but I have no family to fall back on . . . no real money, and I'm not the world's greatest secretary. I want some security, Charlie, so I can start a new life . . .'

'With her?' he interrupted.

'I don't know where that is going. She is married, too, but she doesn't want to divorce her husband. He is quite wealthy, Charlie . . . richer than you are.'

He grunted at that, as she continued, 'She wants security as well as love.'

He laughed a cruel laugh. 'Hell, Adelle, everyone wants that! How much security are you looking for . . . in hard currency, that is. I presume that is what we are talking about. I'm sure you realize I could tear your ass up in court with all that lesbian business. You see, my dear, I have never been unfaithful to you . . . not once! Yet, during all those years in which I have been faithful, you have not given me one moment of sincerity. Our entire marriage has been one big goddamm joke. Thank God we did not have children to make this disaster worse than it already is.'

At the sound of those words, she gave him a contrite look, as she said meekly, 'I guess I should tell you that I have had two abortions. Yes, Charlie, you and I should be the proud parents of at least two snotty-nosed brats by now, but I couldn't bear it . . . I'm sorry . . .'

He shrugged his sagging shoulders, looking down at his drink, fingering it. 'Jesus, two of my babies . . . murdered, and you hid it all. I'll say one thing for you, Adelle, in addition to being a first class shit, you are a damn good little actress, too. You ought to be in Hollywood.'

'I'm sorry about the abortions, Charlie . . . I really am. I wish I had kept at least one of them so you would have something to show for four years of marriage . . .'

'You worthless bitch! Do you really believe I would want anything that is a part of you? No, by God, I wouldn't!'

'You're being cruel, Charlie. There is no excuse for that.'

He shoved his drink away. 'I've had enough of this farce, Adelle. All you are entitled to, and I am being overly generous, considering I don't owe you anything – not even respect – is one half of the property we've accumulated since our marriage. It is worth every penny of it to be rid of you. You are not entitled to any of the family business since it is not community property, so that leaves you with half a house, half of some stock and a bank account and two automobiles. I figure that should come to about three hundred thousand dollars all together, and your half would come to one hundred fifty thousand dollars. Accept that, or take your chances in court. Your lover will be subpoenaed, I assure you, and if you believe she can't be located, you are very naive. I will brand you the lesbian bitch that you are, believe me.'

'Do you hate me because I am a lesbian?'

'No! That is your privilege! I hate you because you lied to me about the whole thing. A little truthfulness would have avoided all this. Do you understand?'

She nodded, not answering him audibly. 'Well,' she countered, 'then you should be glad to be rid of me. Are you willing to write me a cheque for one hundred and fifty thousand dollars? If so, I'll be on my way.'

He cut her off. 'You know damn well I can't write you a cheque for that amount. Our holdings have to be liquidated so I can pay you.'

'Don't you want to keep the house . . . to live in?'

He sneered at her. 'I don't want anything to remind me of you . . . nothing! If I ever date another woman, which is rather doubtful just now, I don't want her to have the same perfume as you. I have had enough of deceitful females to last me a long time. If I want affection, I will buy it.' He laughed. 'Come to think of it, that is precisely what I have been doing for the past four years. I'm sure I can find it cheaper some other place.'

'Then, can I live in the house in the meantime?'

'No! I want you out tonight. It will go on the market tomorrow!'

'But, what will I do in the meantime? Where will I live?'

He gave her a cruel sneer as he replied, 'I know this phrase will sound familiar to you, but, frankly, my dear, I don't give a damn!'

He rose to leave, and from force of habit, reached for his wallet to leave money for the drinks, but he caught himself, and returning his wallet to its pocket, he told her, 'No, I see no reason why I should pay for the drinks. The one who gets screwed should never pay for the drinks.' He turned to leave.

'Charlie . . . I'm really sorry. What will you do, now?'

'Adelle, I intend to spend the rest of my life trying to forget you,' and as an afterthought, 'and all other women like you.'

2

Agatha Forester stared at her son with the same imperious look which had so intimidated him as a child, the only difference was that they were now both thirty years older, but the stare remained unchanged.

'What else could you expect, Charles?' (She had never called him Charlie and frowned at those who did, including her husband) 'You marry a little trollop from out of the office force, with no family to speak of . . . no background! What else could you expect?'

'Now, Mother' (she had never let him call her Mama as he wanted to), 'how do you know she had no family background? Everyone has a family background, for better or worse,' he teased.

'Please do not be flippant with me, Charles. You know precisely what I mean.'

'Now, Agatha,' interrupted Alexander Forester, as he stood at the fireplace, sipping a glass of wine, 'you know very well that she seemed a perfectly respectable young lady at the time of the wedding. You had no reservations about her at the time. . . . '

'That is not true, Alex! I had plenty of reservations at the time.'

'Why didn't you voice them, then, my dear?'

'Well, in retrospect, I should have, but I was more concerned with the happiness of my son. He seemed to love her so. Men,' she exclaimed, 'you are never able to see past the derriere and the bosom where young females are concerned. . . . . '

Alexander Forester laughed. He tried never to take his imperious wife too seriously. 'But, my dear, those were the first two attributes that attracted me to you. . . .'

'Don't be vulgar, Alex! You know how I hate vulgarity . . . especially in my own home.'

While this exchange was taking place, Charlie sat there in his family's library, in an overstuffed chair, sipping his wine and looking down at the floor. He knew there were things he should be saying, but . . .

His mother had recoiled in horror when he told her her of the meeting with Adelle, and as the facts unfurled, she was in a state of apoplexy, with hands to the throat, exclamations of, 'Oh, Alex . . . did you hear that? A lesbian . . . my God! What is wrong with these young people these days? Can't they even decide what they are in this life? Why, I never even heard the word until I was in my twenties, in college, and then I was shocked beyond belief!'

Alexander Forester looked at his wife, shaking his head. He had long ago chosen the path of either acquiescence or total disregard where his wife was concerned, depending on his proximity to her at the time.

She had come from a wealthy family, and she had had a splendid liberal arts education at a prestigious all-girls school, and she had had a sheltered life, but, in their nearly forty years of marriage, she had tried his patience on too many occasions to enumerate. It was her family money that had bankrolled him in his first real estate ventures, and even as he grew more and more successful on his own, she made sure he never forgot where the seed money came from.

'Now, Agatha, it will serve no useful purpose to chastise Charlie for his poor choice of a wife. How was he to know of her unnatural sexual preferences if she deceived him at the time. They don't have an external look about them which tells the general public what they are. If she had been perfectly honest with him, this would not have happened . . . '

'I am not trying to rewrite history, Alex! I am practicing what you refer to as damage control. Can you imagine what this will do to our reputation in this town when the word gets out that our son married a les . . . oh, God! I can't even say the word without shivers going down my spine!'

'Really, Mother,' broke in Charlie, 'no one needs to know about that! I doubt seriously that Adelle will spread it, and you two are the only ones I intend to tell. How will the town find out?'

Being of a suspicious nature, and having had the dubious distinction of being one of the town's leading gossips, whose details of marital infidelities were often the highlight of her bridge club luncheons, the mother responded, 'You'll see!'

'That is not what bothers me at this time, Agatha! Charlie, did you and Adelle discuss any kind of property settlement? Thank God you received the company stock in your name before your marriage. She can't touch that? But, what of your community property . . . did you discuss that? I'm sure she will want her share, even though I'm sure we can break her in court, and give her nothing!'

Charlie related the discussion he and Adelle had had on the settlement.

The father shook his head. 'You were too generous with the little bitch . . . oh, excuse me, my dear . . . you should never make an offer in the heat of battle, Charlie! You know I've always told you that . . . '

'Look, I don't give a damn . . . oh, excuse me Mother . . . about the money! I just want to get rid of her and go on with my life.'

Agatha brought her handkerchief up to her eyes, daubing them lightly, as she sighed. 'And what of the rest of your life, Charles? Oh, my poor darling! Please don't let this ruin your life. Find another girl to marry. I will help you look this time. . . . '

Charles shuddered at the mere thought of it, and he turned to his father, who had placed his glass of wine on the mantel, and placed his hand on his son's shoulder, asking, 'What will you do, now, son? Do you want of go away for awhile? We can cover for you in the office. Why don't you take a trip . . . a long trip . . . go far away . . . try to forget her! Do you still love her? Will that be a problem for you?'

He shook his head as he pondered his father's question. His mother looked up, waiting for his reply to the question no one had bothered to consider . . . not even Charlie! Did he still love Adelle? He had, just five minutes before she dropped the verbal bomb on him. Can love be forgotten in so short a time? Can love turn to hate, or even indifference, in the blink of an eye? He turned the question over in his mind, not knowing the real answer, himself . . . not an honest answer.

He looked first at his mother, then at his father, responding, 'Whatever feelings I have for Adelle, or, had for her, will be dealt with by me in the months and years to come . . . '

The father came up to the son, solicitously, 'Charlie, do you need any money to do all this? You know you can count on me . . . for anything . . . '

He placed his arm around his father, smiling at him warmly. 'I know that, Dad, but money is not what I need just now. What I need, money can't buy . . . not at any price!'

His mother, believing that money could solve just about any problem known to the human race, inquired, 'What do you mean, Charles?'

'I mean, Mother, that I need to reacquire some faith in the human race, especially the female side of it. I have just been deceived by a woman whom I loved, and who I was foolish enough to believe, loved me. I found out her alleged love for me was just a sham . . . not more than a joke really . . . '

She rose and rushed to her son, exclaiming to her husband, 'You see, Alex, just what I feared has happened! He is now bitter! Not just to women, but to the entire human race. Oh, he will be scarred for life . . . I know it!'

'Oh, Agatha, shut up for once, will you! If he has not been scarred by this traumatic turn in his life, he will damn sure be scarred by your amateurish psychological evaluation . . . '

Stunned, she made no reply and sat down, gently sobbing.

Her son went to her, placing his arm around her shoulders. 'Now, now, Mother, I assure you this will not scar me for life! For a few months, perhaps, but I will recover. After all, I have your genes in me . . . that should count for something.'

She sat upright, squared her shoulders, dabbed her eyes with a linen handkerchief and managed a smile, saying nothing, since she agreed completely with the accolade her son had just emitted.

The father, not equally impressed, asked, 'What will you do next, Charlie?'

'Well, Dad, I think I'll take you up on your suggestion. I do believe an extended trip would do me some good. I want to get away from this town for a while. I don't want to have to face the same people I have faced for the past four years. You know how it is . . . maybe they don't know, but you always think they do, and you react accordingly . . . know what I mean?'

The father nodded, 'Yes, I know what you mean. What do you want me to do?'

'Since the divorce will be uncontested if Adelle keeps her word, all we have to do is sign some papers and go before a judge and it's all over . . . is that right?'

'Well, I'm no lawyer, but that is the way I see it!'

'Then, why can't I just sign a power of attorney and let the company lawyers handle the whole thing. I've read where some celebrities are not present at the actual court proceedings, so why should I be!'

'I think we can handle it that way. And, with the company lawyers handling it, we can keep it in the family, so to speak. Why don't we meet with the attorneys in the morning and see if we can do it without your being present.'

'Good! Let's do it. Oh, Mother, I need a place to sleep tonight. I never want to spend another night in that house . . . '

She never let him finish as she jumped up . . . 'Oh, Charles, this is still your home! You know that! Why, your room is exactly the same as when you left it. It would warm my heart to have you under our roof, again,' as mother and son embraced.

As father and son walked out of the library and out of earshot of the mother who had gone upstairs to see to her son's comfort, the father asked, 'What if Adelle balks at the terms after you've left town . . . you know what I mean . . . reneges on the verbal agreement you made with her. What do you want me to do?'

'If she wants more than the hundred and fifty we agreed on, don't even call me where I am . . . just turn the dogs loose on her! Know what I mean?'

The father smiled. This was the kind of language he understood from the hardball world of real estate negotiating, as he replied, 'Don't worry about a thing, son . . . I'll take care of it. Just go have yourself some fun!'

The son smiled in return, saying nothing.

He lay awake a long time that night as he looked around the room in which he grew up. Had he been really happy here? What is real happiness when one is growing up? A good home . . . loving parents . . . food on the table . . . clothes in the closet . . . friends to run with? Yes, he concluded, he had had a good childhood, but now – what of now? He had told his parents he would go on a trip. Where? He had not the slightest idea where he wanted to go. What of his friends? What would he tell them? How much would he tell them?

He had to have a plan of action, he knew that. Tomorrow he would look into it, but for now. . . .

* * *

After leaving the office of the company attorneys he went to the garage where all the executives had covered parking spaces, got into his Jaguar and headed out. His first impulse was to go out to the country club for lunch, but he thought of Adelle. She often went to the country club. Was it not there that she met the woman who was now one of the causes of all his troubles? No! No country club. He decided on the yacht club. Adelle never went to the yacht club without him, so there would be no chance of running into her there.

As he turned into the parking lot, he saw the Cadillac of his old college chum, Arnold Broadhurst, better known as Arnie in their younger days. Arnie was an accountant – a CPA no less, and he had a large and prosperous firm – large enough and prosperous enough to enable him to not only belong of the yacht club, but to also reach that pinnacle of all yacht club habitués, the proud owner of a fifty foot ketch – a true blue-water sailing yacht with three staterooms, all with private baths.

As he entered the dining room, he saw Arnie sitting at a table near the window overlooking the harbour and marina. There were several people at the table and as he turned to go, he saw Arnie wave in his direction, beckoning him to come over. He was really not in the mood for company just now, but Arnie was a good friend, and what choice did he have as he saw Arnie coming towards him.

'Charlie, my boy . . . we were just discussing you . . . '

Oh, my God, he thought. Have they heard, already? 'Discussing me? What about?'

'Come over to the table! We're just getting ready to order lunch . . . join us! There is something we want to talk to you about. Come on, and I'll introduce you to Kate Russell – she is the only one you don't know. She is engaged to Bill Morton – you know Bill, don't you – he works in our office as a tax attorney – can't live without one these days . . . '

'Oh, look, Arnie, I don't want to break in on your party. I just want a quick bite and I have to be on my way. I'm getting ready to leave town soon . . . '

'But, I was getting ready to call you. Our discussion involves you . . . and Adelle. Come on.'

He allowed himself to be led. Arnie's comment concerning Adelle convinced him that Arnie knew nothing as yet. 'Well, OK, but just a quick lunch and then I have to run.'

'After you hear what we have to say, you might not want to run, except to where we're running to . . . '

'Oh?' He was interested after all.

As they neared the table, those who knew each other, smiled and waved, making the usual innocuous comments . . . 'Hi . . . How are ya? . . . Good to see ya!'

Arnie motioned to Kate Russell, a lovely thing with dark brown hair, good complexion, nice teeth and great eyes-young, probably no more than late twenties.

'Charlie,' said Arnie, 'This is the fiancée of our boy,

Bill Morton, and tell me, is he not to be envied? Kate Russell, meet Charles Alexander Forester, better known as Charlie. He's married to Adelle, who is not present at this time, but . . . '

Charlie smiled at Kate, who gave him a very warm smile, extending her hand. 'Hi, Charlie, glad to meet you.'

'Same here! May I compliment Bill on his flawless taste,' Charlie said, without heart, for was this not a woman, and did he now not hate anyone of the feminine species?

'Oh, how sweet, Charlie. May I compliment the absent Adelle on her choice of a husband,' she replied, returning the compliment.

The words burned in Charlie, but he said nothing, just smiling an abstract smile as he completed his greetings. He kissed Peggy Broadhurst on the cheek. He had stood in their wedding and they had stood in his and Adelle's.

That made the matter all the more painful at this time, especially when Peggy asked, 'Where's Adelle? We need her for this discussion we're about to have.'

He knew this was not a good time to mention his trouble. He knew if this kept up, he would have to. He mumbled some innocuous excuse to Peggy about Adelle's absence, and it was accepted without further comment.

Arnie rapped his water glass for attention, and clearing his throat as if about to address a joint session of Congress, he began, 'Ladies and gentlemen, before we get started on ordering lunch, let us discuss the matter at hand. All of us, Charlie, have discussed this briefly among ourselves, but believe me, you and Adelle have been part of this from the start . . . huh gang?' to which all responded with a nodding of heads.

Charlie was not comfortable at all. 'What the hell are you talking about?'

'The cruise, Charlie . . . the cruise! We are planning a cruise on my trusty craft to Ambergris Cay . . . '

Charlie looked perplexed, as he asked, 'What's Ambergris Cay?'

'Oh, you've heard me mention it before. That is

where I have been going fishing the past few years. It is in Belize, and for the benefit of you less erudite people, you might remember Belize from your high school geography as British Honduras . . . '

Charlie nodded. 'Yes, I remember you showing me snapshots of the big barracuda you caught down there, but you always flew down there, didn't you? Are you telling me you intend to take your boat down there?'

Arnie nodded, as did the rest.

'That is precisely what I am telling you. We . . . all of us at this table are going to take the *Polaris* down to Belize on her own bottom, as they say in nautical circles, and you and Adelle are invited to come along too. Before you answer, good buddy, I have to tell you this is Dutch treat . . . everyone will have to pay his own way, but the amount is nominal, and I am sure that Charles Alexander Forester would have no trouble coming up with the loose change.'

'How loose?' asked Charlie, out of curiosity.

His first reaction had been very negative, for obvious reasons, but this was beginning to appeal to him, if only he could settle the Adelle problem.

'Well,' responded Arnie, 'each couple will be asked to chip in two grand, but that will be for both people . . . you and Adelle.'

Charlie swallowed hard, as he looked around the table.

He raised his hands for attention. 'Look . . . you will find out about this sooner or later, and it would be best from me, but, you see, Adelle and I have split. We're going to be divorced. . . . '

There were groans and moans from all present, with Peggy taking the lead. 'Oh, Charlie, but you and Adelle were so happy! At least, you seemed so . . . what happened . . . oh, I'm sorry! I have no right to ask that! I apologize, Charlie . . . '

He figured he had best put the matter to rest, now, as he looked around. 'Look, I don't intend to go into the details of the matter just now. Just accept the cold hard fact that Adelle and I are finished, so I guess you had better try to find someone else to make the third couple.

It will definitely not be me and Adelle.'

'But, Charlie, we have to have you . . . with or without Adelle.'

'What do you mean by that?'

'Well, don't take this wrong, Charlie. This is not the only reason we invited you, but . . . well . . . you see, you are one of the few people in this town who know celestial navigation. We need to have a navigator on board . . . '

Charlie interrupted him. 'Aw, come on, Arnie . . . that expensive floating toy of yours has all kinds of sophisticated navigational equipment on board, including Sat-Nav which will give you your position within a hundred feet of anywhere. You must admit that.'

Arnie became serious as CPA's are prone to do when they are getting ready to tell you of your income tax liability, as he replied. 'Only a fool would leave the dock without a back–up system of navigation in case the electronics go out. You know that, Charlie, and I am no fool . . . not in that regard,' as the others around the table grunted in agreement.

Arnie continued. 'You always said you learned celestial navigation in case some friend asked you to go on a world cruise, someday, and this is it. It may not be a world cruise, but, Charlie baby, Belize is nothing to sneeze at. We have to pass through the Yucatan Channel, right next to Cuba, and I don't want any trespassing trouble with those Commies, believe me.' Once again, there were grunts of assent from those around the table.

Charlie sighed. 'I would be really interested in this thing if it were not for two complications.'

'What complications?' asked the entire group.

'Well, to begin with,' Charlie responded, 'Adelle damn sure will not be going, and besides, I am leaving tomorrow on an extended trip, which may last several weeks . . . maybe, a month? Who knows? . . . the mood I'm in!' There were sympathetic groans from the women and nods of assent from the men.

'But,' asserted Arnie, 'that will work out just fine. We don't intend to leave for at least a month. It will take us that long to`make preparations for an extended trip like this. You go ahead and make your trip . . . no problem.'

'But, shouldn't I be here to help you with the planning and logistics?' protested Charlie.

"Uh-uh! We don't need you. Just leave a cheque with us for half the amount to cover some up-front costs. We'll take care of everything.'

'But . . . what about a roommate for me? How will we take care of that?' asked a concerned Charlie.

Peggy Broadhurst chimed in. 'Now don't worry about a roommate, Charlie, I'll find you one.'

'OK, but make sure he doesn't snore too much,' laughed Charlie in response.

'Then it's all settled? You'll come with us? We can count on you, Charlie?'

'Uh-huh! Count me in. Now let's eat.'

3

His preparations being all completed, Charlie was saying goodbye to his parents the last night he would spend with them.

His mother, ever solicitous of her thirty-six year old son, cautioned, 'Charles, please drive carefully, and remember, do not pick up hitchhikers. You can't trust anyone these days, and please, dear, call me every night or so to let me know how you're doing . . . and Charles . . . do try to forget that little trollop who has nearly ruined your life.'

'Yes, Mother! Oh, Dad, do you mind if I take that new Jeep Cherokee from the office? I would like to have four wheel drive, in case I want to get off the beaten track.'

'Sure, son, it's been recently serviced. Just fill the tank and take it. When are you coming back? . . . not that I'm trying to hurry you . . . I'm not. . . . you take your time.'

'I'm not sure, but it cannot be more than a month. I promised Arnie Broadhurst I would take a cruise with him to Ambergris Cay, an island off the coast of Belize . . . '

'Oh, my God' exclaimed his mother. 'Belize? . . . isn't that a primitive place?'

He laughed. 'Not as primitive as you think, Mother. They had an advanced civilization hundreds of years before this country was even settled.'

'Oh dear . . . are you sure?'

His father laughed it off, and shaking his son's hand, replied, 'Go and have some fun. If you need anything . . . well, just call me. Good luck.'

* * *

Even as he headed out on Interstate 10, he had no idea where he was going. He just headed west with a full tank of gas in the Cherokee, ten thousand dollars worth of travellers cheques in his wallet and a broken heart in his bosom. He tried not to think of Adelle as he drove, but it was hard not to. He was still shocked. Just a week ago he was a married man, happily married he had thought, and now he felt he was a man betrayed. Why had she deceived him so? If only she had been honest with him. Maybe, if she had told him the truth up front, they might have been able to work it out . . . perhaps some kind of therapy. No! Those longings cannot be changed. Are they in the body or in the mind?

He shook his head, trying to get her out of his mind. Instead, he thought of the cruise to Belize. That should be fun! Several weeks of just water and sky. He thought of the group who would go . . . Arnie and Peggy. They were old friends . . . he liked them! He thought of Bill Morton and Kate Russell, the engaged couple. That Kate . . . what a beauty! He hoped Kate was a real woman . . . not like Adelle.

'There I go again . . . Adelle! And what of my roommate on the cruise. Hope Peggy finds some man who is compatible with me. I'd hate to spend several weeks with some obnoxious ass in the tight confines of a small stateroom. Hope he doesn't snore. Adelle snored when she slept on her back.'

He thought of Adelle on her back, and bitter memories came back. Once more he shook his head to clear it of memories of her. His mind went back to the cruise. 'I wonder if I'll have any trouble with my celestial navigation . . . good thing I brought along my books so I can brush up on it. I hope I can remember the rules of algebra when I get to the spherical trigonometry problems . . . oh well, we'll see.'

Not much will be said of the crossing of Texas for what can be said of a day and a half of seeing nothing but land and sky, sky and land, the concrete ribbons of the Interstate boring through the state with monotonous regularity. His interest was aroused in the surroundings as he climbed Raton Pass, New Mexico and entered Colorado. At Pueblo, he turned west towards the Rockies, feeling that the thin clear and cool air of the mountains would have a cleansing effect on his bruised mind and ego. Yes, his ego had been badly bruised. What man would not be offended by losing out to a woman? Another man . . . that was acceptable . . . manly . . . fair fight, and all that . . . but . . . another woman. How do you combat that? The equipment is not even the same.

He reached some quaint old mining town about sundown. He had been driving twelve hours that day and he was tired. He looked for a place to stay for the night. Not much of a choice, really. Just a little ten-room motel that advertised, proudly, that they had TV. He grinned . . . big deal . . . TV! Across the street was a combination restaurant and bar. What more could he want, he thought as he pulled in to the motel office. The old neon sign blinked. . . . VACANCY. . . . but not continuously.

He went into the lobby/office and looked around. Old . . . cheap and old . . . worn furniture lined the walls of the lobby. The usual painting of Custer's Last Stand hung on the wall behind the counter. An old timer with a week's growth of whiskers sat impassively behind the counter, his wife on one side and his dog on the other. She didn't look up, but the dog did, as he stood at the desk. The old timer looked him up and down, thought about it for awhile, and then asked, 'Ya want ah room, do ya?'

'Well yes, but,' and he looked at the couple sheepishly, 'I'd like to take a look at it first.'

He had a mischievous look in his eye as he asked, 'Why'd ya want to do that? It's just a room with a bed and a dresser in it.'

'Well, does it have a private bath?'

The old timer laughed a raucous laugh. 'You must think we still got cowboys and Indians running 'round heah . . .'course it's got a bathroom . . . toilet flushes too, but you gotta wipe yo'self,' and he and the old woman both laughed. It seemed to Charlie that the dog was smiling too.

The old timer seemed offended as he said, 'Iffen ya gotta see the room . . . aw'right, but Ma'll have to go with ya . . . Ah can't leave the desk on one of mah busy nights.'

Saying nothing, the old woman picked up an axe handle which was leaning against the wall, motioned to the dog by snapping her fingers and walked towards the door, saying to Charlie, 'Nah don ya git no funny ideas when we git in that room . . . ah got mah axe handle 'n ah got mah dawg.'

Charlie could not help but smile as he replied . . . 'No ma'am, you have nothing to worry about . . . I swear.'

The room was surprisingly clean – actually spotless, which she proudly pointed out to him, as she bent over the bath tub to pick up a human hair she had missed in her cleaning. Saying nothing else, she looked at him for acceptance . . . or rejection, and then asking . . . 'Well?'

He smiled, 'Looks fine . . . I'll take it.'

She made no reply as she headed back to the lobby, axe handle in hand, and dog in tow.

Charlie walked up to the desk, saying . . . 'I'll take it.'

The old timer smiled, 'Good thing, young fella . . . ain't nuthin else fo the next fifty miles 'n these heer mount'ns git cold at night. 'Iffen ya wants some gal to keep ya warm, why ya kin git one at that bar 'cross the street . . . ain't cheap, though. Some of them foolish men pay as high as fifty dollars for one of them Denver whores who come through here eva now 'n then. This is a big weekend . . . big rodeo in town . . them Denver whores will be heah in droves . . . '

The old woman shifted in her chair . . . 'Iffen ya bring one of them whores inta ya room, why that'll be ten dollars extra for the room . . . extra cleaning, ya know . . . '

Charlie smiled . . . 'I understand,' and he placed his gold credit card on the counter.

The old timer looked at it, and said, 'We don't take plastic. That'll be twenty-five dollars . . . cash!' Charlie smiled . . . took out the cash . . . paid, and left. The dog raised his head as he went by.

After a good hot shower and a change of clothing,

Charlie decided he was hungry. He looked out of the window at the restaurant/bar across the street and went out, his expectations not too high as to the quality of the food.

The place was crowded, much more than he expected – evidently some of the rodeo crowd had come into town a few days early. The bar was crowded with a mixture of men and women, some attached and some quasi-attached, with the women moving from one bar stool to another, working the crowd, or so it seemed. Perhaps, they were just friendly country girls spreading goodwill among the transients.

He walked out of the bar side and into the restaurant side, and seeing an empty booth, took it and sat, waiting for the waitress. He watched her walk over, glass of water in one hand and menu in the other. She was not very young, probably forty at most. She had been pretty at one time, but the trials and tribulations of life had left a pattern of fatigue on her face. She looked tired as she put the glass before him. Her hair had little life in it, for it, too, was tired from misuse. But her eyes attracted him the most. They were sky blue and in spite of her apparent fatigue they still had a shine in them.

She managed a smile with reasonably good teeth showing. 'Even'in cowboy . . . want a minute to make up your mind, or do you know what you want . . . spec'l of the day is beefalo steak, with coleslaw and French fries . . . six ninety-five . . . drinks is extra.'

Charlie gave her a warm smile. 'Sounds good . . . I'll take it. And, incidentally, I'm not a cowboy . . . just passing through.'

She smiled. 'Ah call every man cowboy . . . no offence.'

He watched her walk away. She had a trim figure with exceptionally good legs. No doubt due to hard work, he thought, as his gaze followed her to the door into the kitchen. He walked to the bar and ordered a beer to kill time until the food was ready. He exchanged glances with several of the young women as he walked along the bar. Some of the glances were of the innocent, curious type, but one of the women gave him an inviting glance. He smiled in return, as he remembered he now hated all women, thanks to Adelle. As he got back to his booth the waitress was arriving with the food, waiting for him to enter the booth.

'That was fast,' he said.

She laughed. 'It was already fixed. It's what most people order, so it's ready to go. Hope ya enjoy it.'

And enjoy it he did. He was surprised. The beefalo was delicious . . . tasty . . . not as fat as pure beef. The coleslaw was not good . . . too watery . . . the French fries were tolerable. All in all, not a bad meal for six ninety-five plus tax.

As he sat fingering his third beer, watching the crowd become more intoxicated, more boisterous, he became more morose, as he remembered he was supposed to be sad. After all, he had come on this trip to forget Adelle, and the only way he could forget Adelle was to remember how she had wronged him. It is known as self pity and is practised by the whole human race on occasions, when it serves one's purpose to do so.

The waitress came up with the bill, and handing it to him, asked. 'Can Ah git you anything else before I go off duty?'

He looked at her, finally noticing her name tag. Her name was Meagan.

'Are you Irish, Meagan?' he asked as she handed him the bill.

She looked tired as she sighed. . . . 'Yes, my Ma, bless her soul, came from the old country when she was a young girl, and she named me after an old aunt of hers.'

He really didn't want to get personal with her, or any other woman for that matter but for some reason he could not fathom, he asked, 'You look tired Meagan, why don't you sit with me awhile when you go off duty . . . just to talk . . . '

She laughed. 'Mista, if you're looking for love and comfort, you're talking to the wrong girl. I ran out of love and comfort a few years back. Found out it didn't pay with the man I was married to. The more love and comfort I gave him, the more abuse he gave me.'

He realized she had taken it the wrong way. 'No . . . no, I swear, Meagan, I just want company . . . someone to talk to.'

She laughed. 'That's what they all say, cowboy,' and she turned to leave, but he took her hand, saying 'But, I swear I mean it. All I want is company. You can get up and leave anytime you want to . . . what will it hurt?'

She realized that this man was begging, and for what? . . . just company? Could this be true? Could a man who looked as prosperous as he did really have to beg for company?

She looked at him with the same compassion one would give a wounded animal. 'What's your name?'

'Charlie.'

She looked around to see if anyone was watching and she slipped into the booth, saying, 'Look, Charlie, if it is love and affection you're looking for, ya see that little filly in the white blouse and red skirt, the one with the big boobs, standing next to the man with the cowboy hat, well, she is available. Ah don't know what she charges, but Ah hear whatever it is, she is worth every penny. You see, she is young and not tired and she does that for a liv'in. Ah'm old and tired and Ah don't do that for a liv'in. Ah don't even do it for love anymore, because Ah don't believe in love,' and she added as an after thought, 'anymore.'

She got up to leave.

'Don't you understand? If I wanted her, or, someone like her, I would be asking her to sit with me. I'm not interested in her . . . '

As she stood there, she added, 'Well, if she's not your type, the peroxide blonde just com'in through the front door is also available . . . '

He was getting angry. 'Dammit woman . . . that is not what I want . . . '

'What are you looking for, Charlie? Do you know?'

He shook his head. 'No . . . I don't.'

As she walked off, he turned back to his beer, feeling ashamed of himself, ashamed that he, Charles Alexander Forester had virtually begged a worn-out, over-the-hill, overly-tired waitress, to sit and talk to him. Women! Damn them! Who the hell do they think they are? All I asked her was for a little conversation, that's all. That is their main problem! Think every man is after their bodies. That's their problem!

He sipped his beer and looked at his watch. It was only nine o'clock. He felt tired from the driving, but not sleepy. What did he have to look forward to? Going back to that dingy but clean room, alone, undress, get into bed, and look at the ceiling. Damn that Adelle! If only she had been 'straight'. They would be lying in their bed, now, probably making love . . . that's what they would be doing about now. Probably!

His beer was getting empty, and he was getting up to get another one when Meagan appeared, asking, 'Can Ah get you another beer, cowboy? Ah'm off duty, now, but Ah'll do that fer you since you left me a heck of a big tip for the meal. You're not try'in to buy mah affections, are you cowboy?'

He smiled. 'No, I have always been taught that good service deserves a good tip. That's all.'

'Well, if you promise to be a good boy, Ah'll sit with you while you drink the beer, but, Ah'm go'in home after that.'

'I promise to be a good boy,' he jested as he watched her walk off to get the beer.

She looked back and smiled, but said nothing.

She returned with the beer, but only one, which prompted him to ask. 'Aren't you having one with me? I hate to drink alone while you're watching me.'

'Ah promised to sit with you while you drank. Ah didn't promise to have onc with you.'

'Something tells me that you are a hard woman, Meagan.'

She looked at him without smiling, replying, 'Ah kin be as hard as Ah got to be, 'specially with men.'

'You don't like men?'

'It's hard to say. Ah ain't hardly eva met a nice one, so's Ah can't tell if Ah'd like a nice one or not, cowboy.'

'My name is Charlie. Why don't you call me that instead of cowboy, since I'm not a cowboy.'

'What do you do, Charlie, when you're not running away from whateva you're running away from?'

'How do you know I'm running away from anything?'

She smiled. 'Charlie, when you bin waitress'n as many years as Ah have, you learn to read people. I bin reading you all night, 'n you're running away from something, but, don't get me wrong . . . Ah don't want to know what it is . . . got enough troubles 'o mah own. Sure do,' she emphasized.

He looked at her, seriously, 'I guess you're right. Everyone has problems of some sort.'

'Uh huh,' she agreed. 'You ain't told me what you do, Charlie. Do you have some kind 'o job?'

He was not sure how to answer her. Something told him not to give her all the facts of his family holdings, so he replied, 'Well, I'm sort of into real estate.'

'What kind 'o real estate? Like selling houses and such?'

'Yes, something like that.'

'Ah ain't try'in to git personal, Charlie. It's just that what a man does tells something about him, 'n it gives us something to talk about while we sit here. Ah got to be goin in a minute.'

'But tomorrow is Sunday,' he protested. 'You don't have to work on Sunday, do you?'

'No, but Ah got to go somewhere tomorrow . . . Ah go every Sunday,' and she became sombre.

'Where do you go, if I'm not getting too personal?'

'Well, you are. Ain't none 'o your business where Ah go,' but she smiled at him to indicate that she was not really angry at his question.

She got up to leave. 'Ah'm going home, Charlie . . . good night.'

He arose. 'Wait. Where do you live? I'll see you home.'

'No! That ain't necessary. This here town ain't no jewel, but it's still safe for a girl to walk the street. Besides, Ah kin take care of myself . . . believe me. Ah only live two blocks from here.'

'Look, Meagan, I'm on my way back to the motel. I don't mind walking two blocks to your home with you . . . '

She laughed. 'It ain't no home. Just an apartment

over a garage . . . nothing fancy.'

'Come on, let me walk you home.'

'Oh come on, but don't git no ideas that Ah'll invite you in. If you expect that, you'll be disappointed. And don't expect no goodnight kiss just 'cause you gave me a big tip.'

He looked to see if she was smiling, but she was not.

He helped her on with her coat, and it was easy to tell she was not accustomed to receiving any help from any male, nor did she expect it.

The night was clear and cool. A sign on the newspaper office next door to the cafe/bar gave the elevation as 7,680 feet. The bar patrons were still ingressing and egressing the watering hole, and he remarked to her, 'The drinking crowd is still doing business, I see.'

She shrugged. 'It's Saturday night. All there is to do in this town on Saturday night is drink and . . . ' she hesitated, 'you know what Ah mean.'

He laughed. 'Yes, I think I know what you mean.'

He was surprised that she would even hint at . . . you know! He was fascinated with her. He had never met any woman like her. She was completely without guile . . . honest to a fault. Everything was black and white – right or wrong – honest or dishonest.

She looked up at him from her five-foot-five level and gave him a smile. 'So, Charlie, where did you say you were from?'

'I didn't say. From the Gulf coast . . . the Deep South.'

He didn't care to give her his home town. After all, he knew nothing about this woman. If she ever came to his home town, it would not be too difficult to find Charles Alexander Forester. The Forester name was plastered on buildings all over town, buildings that the family owned and/or managed. His father and mother had even donated the land and most of the funds for the town library, and their name was on it: THE AGATHA AND ALEXANDER FORESTER wing. It was one of his mother's most cherished possessions, for she felt it was truly hers, not the town's.

She knew his answer was evasive. She was accustomed to getting evasive answers from men, so she let the matter drop, as she pointed to a two story building a block away. 'There's mah home . . . right there over the garage.'

He was not impressed, but she showed no chagrin at showing him the decrepit place in which she lived.

'So, you're staying at the Elk Motel, huh, Charlie. How're you git'n along with Elmo and Blanche?' and she laughed.

He laughed back. 'So that is their names. Oh, we get along all right.'

And he told Meagan of Blanche's threat against his person if he had gotten fresh with her as he viewed his room.

She laughed. 'Poor Blanche. Does she really believe that any man but Elmo would be interested in . . . ' and once again she stopped, not completing the obvious phrase.

'Quite frankly, I liked the dog the most. He had the best personality of the three,' Charlie joked.

She laughed, as she stopped at the stairs leading to the upstairs apartment. The garage was closed, and the place was deserted. She turned and extended her hand. Charlie said, more in jest than real intent, 'Sure that I can't come up for a nightcap before we bring this fabulous evening to a close.'

'You know what Ah tole you, Charlie . . now don't give me a bad time. Ah had you pegged as a nice man . . . don't make me change my mind. Where are you head'in in the morning? Are you running to the east or the west, or,' and she smiled at him . . . 'just running?' Before he could answer, she extended her hand. 'Goodnight, Charlie.'

'Goodnight, Meagan. I enjoyed your company. Thanks for the time you spent with me.'

'Same here, Charlie. If you eva come back through this place, you know where to find me.'

'Yeah, sure. I'll be sure to look you up. Goodnight.'

He watched her climb the stairs. At the top landing, she put her key into the lock and went in without looking back.

4

As he lay in bed that night, he thought of Meagan and women like her. He didn't know any details of her life, but he bet it was hard. She obviously had no man in it, or she would have said so. She didn't mention children. She was not well educated, he could tell that. Probably had not even finished high school. Her speech was that of the mountain people, and her demeanour was one of a real tough gal. But, he was impressed mostly by her honesty. Meagan would never lie to you, not as Adelle did to him. No, she would have levelled with him . . . in everything. He realized, now, just how much lying Adelle had done to him in their marriage. Bitch! Meagan would never lie to him. He may not like what she had to say, but it would be the truth . . . the unvarnished truth!

He picked up his celestial navigation books and began to study them. He thought of the upcoming cruise. He tried to picture Ambergris Cay. He studied some of the navigation maps Arnie had given him of the place. There it was, just below the Mexican border on the Yucatan peninsula. He felt sure he could find it from the ocean as they approached it from the Yucatan channel separating Mexico from Cuba. He'd better, or he would never live it down. But, why was he worried, the *Polaris* had all the most modern and sophisticated navigation equipment. No problem! The intricacies of celestial navigation soon made him drowsy, and he dropped off to sleep.

* * *

He awoke early the next morning, and the Sunday

morning quiet was broken only by the barking of the dog. He showered, packed and went out to start the Cherokee. He had decided to forego breakfast in this one-horse town and try to reach Aspen in time for lunch. It was mid-summer, so the skiers would not be crowding the highways as they did in ski season. He threw the bags in the back of the Jeep and climbed in. He turned the key in the lock and the Jeep tried to start, but it was not catching. He realized that he should have had the engine set for high altitude before he left the gulf coast, but he had left in such a hurry. He gave it a new turn and the starter turned over once again, and then, it began to grind, and then, he saw smoke coming up from under the hood.

'Oh, shit! Trouble! I don't need this. Not in this little town and on a Sunday morning.'

He climbed out and raised the hood. Sure enough, smoke was coming from the starter. He had a burnt starter. No doubt about that. He was not going anywhere . . . not today, anyway. He looked around to see if there was any possibility of help from anybody. The town was beginning to stir. He had not checked out of his room yet, so he went into the motel lobby. As usual, Elmo and Blanche and the dog were there.

He told Elmo of his suspected troubles, and he laughed. 'You're in big trouble son,' the old timer said, 'ain't nothing open today, 'n iffen thar was, you ain't neva gonna git no Jeep parts in this town . . . not on a Sunday, or any other day . . . no siree!' he emphasized.

Charlie looked disgusted. 'I hope you can reserve my room for me for at least one more night . . . maybe two, until I can get this thing fixed,' he lamented.

Elmo gave him his most discerning look, as he replied, 'Whal, Ah had that room reserved for tonight . . . some Denver people, but seeing as you're a regular customer, whal, Ah kin let you have it. 'Course, Ah'll have to charge you mah Sunday rates.'

'And what is that?' asked a perturbed Charlie.

'Whal, you see, that thar room is our best room, 'n on Sunday, it is used by a lot of them travellers for what they call "quickies", and Ah rent that room three 'o four times in one day. Make good money on it, too. That's why Ah'll have to charge you double fer it. That's fifty dollars.'

Charlie was in no mood to put up with Elmo's mercenary tactics, and he said 'Screw you! I'll sleep in that goddam Jeep before I give you fifty dollars for that room.'

'How 'bout forty?'

'Screw you!' and he stormed out.

As he got outside, he saw the Greyhound bus pull into the Texaco garage, which also served as its depot. He saw Meagan get on the bus, carrying a little duffel bag. She had on what he felt sure was her best clothes. She looked nice, he thought. As the bus pulled out, he could see her in the window, and as she recognized him, she waved and smiled. He gave her a weak smile in return.

He spent the entire morning trying to find someone, anyone, who could remedy his situation, but Elmo was right: even if he had found a garage open, and a mechanic available, they would not, and could not, change his starter for him. There was not a Jeep dealer between there and Denver.

He was miserable as he pondered his options. Damn that Adelle! If it were not for her treachery, he would not be here now, and his hatred found new ground. He knew he needed a room for the night which he was sure he would be spending in that little town, so he looked around. In addition to Elmo's Elk Motel, he could see two other motels of sorts. In normal times, he would not have given either of them a second glance, but, he concluded, these were not normal times.

His attempt to get a room in either place met with failure . . . 'You know we got this rodeo in the county this week, and well, them cowboys has got all the rooms in this county booked up all week. Nah, iffen ya will'n to pay Elmo's Sunday rates, why, he might be able to fix you up . . . '

He was adamant! 'No, thank you.'

He knew he was stuck in this town for today, tomorrow, and maybe even Tuesday, depending on how soon they could get a new starter out of Denver. Today was Sunday, they couldn't even order it until tomorrow. Damn that Adelle! He locked his Jeep and began to walk around the town. Not much to see. He found the rodeo area and spent the afternoon watching the tryouts for the big show. He ate hot dogs and drank beer all afternoon. He was bored. He started to call his mother and father, but what could he tell them that would brighten their day.

Instead he called Arnie and Peggy . . . 'Yeah, he was having a great time watching the rodeo in this fabulous rustic mountain community which the tourists had not discovered, yet.'

And to the question, 'Have you found me a roommate yet?', Peggy replied, 'Not yet, but I'm working on it.'

When the time had come for his evening meal, he sauntered on down to his favourite cafe/bar.

He found the same booth empty, and he slipped into it. He had not been in it more than a few minutes when a sultry looking thing came over, smiling all the way. He recognized her as the one Meagan had pointed out the night before. She slid into the booth, not even asking permission to do so. Her lack of good manners offended him, but these were not normal times, and he felt he needed a friendly face to talk to, and this was a friendly face, as she gave him the warmest of smiles.

'How ya, cowboy, mind if I sit a spell and shoot the breeze?'

Is this not an original and charming way to break the ice between two humans? Charlie smiled. He was amused, and he needed some amusement about now. He motioned her to the seat, which she had already occupied, and asked her, 'Would you like something to drink?'

'Well, I really don't drink, but, perhaps a little beer, just to moisten the throat. The dry air in these mountains are hard on a little girl from the farmlands of

Nebraska.'

He noticed her misuse of the pluralized 'are', but he smiled at it. He needed some amusement.

It did not take her long to get to the matter at hand, as she asked him what his plans were for the evening. His mind was working fast. If she was a real professional she would have a place to sleep, and he badly needed a place to sleep. His mind quickly calculated that Elmo's Sunday rates were probably cheaper than hers, but he also ciphered in the entertainment factor. Blanche, even in her most charming moments, could not equal, much less surpass the charms of this professional.

'I had not really made any plans for the evening. I'm wide open, so to speak.'

These were words that warmed the cockles of her heart, for availability was one of the requirements of her negotiations, exceeded only by money.

'Why, what did you have in mind?' he teased, knowing very well what she had in mind.

She became demure, as if the words she was about to say offended her sensitivities, as she fingered her beer, 'Well, you see, I am a professional escort. I provide company to the cowboys during this rodeo week,' and she giggled, lightly, as she added, 'and amusement of sorts.'

He was enjoying this. As much as he hated women nowadays, he was enjoying this. He asked, 'And you get paid for this, I would imagine?'

She seemed offended that he should have to ask. 'Well, sure! This is what I do for a living. I'm a professional escort.'

'And this would be for the entire night?'

She smiled, feeling that she was making headway. 'That's up to you, honey. My services go by the hour, the day, or the night, but the nights are more expensive, of course.'

'Of course! And for the nights . . . would that include a place to sleep . . . for the night, that is?'

She giggled. 'Sleep? Oh, of course, after? Sleeping accommodations are available . . . it is all included in the nightly price. Well, it depends how much amusement you'd want.'

She extracted a printed sheet from her purse and handed it to him. His eyes widened considerably as he perused it. It was graphic, in great detail, illustrating the various services available, and the cost of each.

He smiled. 'Sort of like a menu in a restaurant, isn't it?'

She giggled, pleased at the comparison.

He mentally calculated the range of complete services, from Alpha to Omega, and it came to quite a bit of money.

He whistled as he commented. 'Could run into a lot of money, couldn't it?'

'Well, no one has ever taken everything. You simply take which ones you want. I'm not sure you could take everything . . . in one night, that is . . . it is very tiring. Now, the weekly rate would probably be your best buy . . . '

He did not hear her last words because he saw the Greyhound bus pull into the Texaco station, and he saw Meagan alight from it.

The lady in his booth, seeing his moment of distraction and feeling she was loosing her grip on the situation, said, 'Of course, all these prices are negotiable . . . '

He saw Meagan headed for the cafe and he would not have liked her to see them together, so he said. 'Look, I have some things to check on, first. Do you have a business card to give me? I may want to contact you later.'

He felt sure she had none, but he was surprised as she handed him an engraved card, with her photo on it, tastefully done, but risqué.

She arose, saying, 'OK, but if you wait too late, you may miss out. This is a busy week.'

'I know! If you don't hear from me in an hour . . . well, make other arrangements . . . '

She seemed offended as she turned, but being a good businesswoman, she turned and smiled at him . . . a warm smile.

He quickly took her empty beer bottle and moved it to an adjacent table as Meagan came through the door. She looked around and immediately saw him, and walked over to him, shaking her head.

'Well, well, Charlie, you love this little town so much you can't tear yourself away to leave it. Or, is it that you and Blanche have finally hit it off?'

He smiled as he rose to greet her, motioning to her to sit, which she did, dropping her weight in the seat, as if she were exhausted.

'Whew . . . that is a hard day's work. Riding that ole bus all the way there, and then, all the way back . . . whew!'

'Where did you go?'

She became serious. 'I told you last night it was none 'o your business, Charlie!'

'I'm sorry. I wasn't trying to pry. I just wondered what you had done to make you so tired.'

'I live tired. I'm tired into the future,' and she gave him a weak smile. 'So, I'm waiting to hear why you're still in our little town. You told me you were leaving here this morning. What happened?'

He related to her his misfortunes of the day, and his rebuff of Elmo's outrageous price gouging.

She shook her head. 'That Elmo, someday, somebody's gonna shoot him, 'n it will be good riddance to bad rubbish. So, you have no place to sleep tonight?'

'Well, I wouldn't say that, exactly.' He then told her of the hooker's approach, and her offer of the evening.

She looked offended as she replied, 'Well, don't let me interfere with your evening of pleasure, Charlie . . . good luck,' and she rose to leave.

He grabbed her arm and pulled her back into the booth. She allowed herself to be pulled back.

He looked into her eyes. 'Do you really think I would pay her outrageous prices for a place to sleep . . . '

She smiled. 'Oh, Ah'm sure she would give you more than a place to sleep, 'specially at those prices,' as she perused the sheet he showed her. She seemed offended, as she threw the sheet back at him. 'Ah've seen this filthy thing before.'

He realized then just how prudish she really was. She was not joking. She really was offended by what he thought would be amusing to her. He thought she must have come from an old fashioned family . . . highly moral mother and father. He continued to be interested in her. He had never known anyone like her. All the women he had met all his life were, for the most part, wealthy, spoiled, sophisticated. Their true feelings were hard to ascertain through that veneer of contrived sophistication. But here was a creature free from those contrived veneers, stripped of pretension, willing to stand in the bright glare of sunlight and tell the world . . . 'here I am . . . take it or leave it, 'cause it ain't gonna git no betta.'

'Did you really believe that I would take her up on it?'

She looked directly in his eyes. 'Hell, yes! you're a man, Charlie, and men ain't got no sense when it comes to women.'

He thought of Adelle, and he felt he could not take issue with her logic, so he decided to change the subject, asking, 'What brings you to your place of employment on a Sunday evening? I can't believe you eat here on your days off.'

'Lord, no! Ah can't afford to eat out, even here where Ah kin git ten percent off the bill. No . . . Ah'll go home and open a can of soup for my supper. Ah jus came by to pick up mah mail. Ah git mah mail here at work. The postman won't climb those steps to mah apartment. He's got arthritis real bad in his knees, poor fella. Ah forgot to pick up mah mail last night with all your foolishness about walking me home,' she blushed.

He hesitated. 'Meagan . . . if you haven't eaten, stay and eat with me . . . please! I'd love to have you be my guest for supper.'

She shook her head. 'Ain't no reason fer you to buy me suppa! Ah ain't done nuthin fer you. Men don't do nuthin fer women without being paid in kind.'

He shook his head in disbelief. Was this how she really felt? In her world, did men really expect to be paid for any act of kindness?

He took her hand without thinking, asking, 'Meagan, do you really feel that way? Do you think if I bought you a meal, that I would expect you to do something for me in return? What about when you were growing up? If your date took you to a dance and bought you a hamburger and a coke, did he expect you to sleep with him?'

'Iffen he thought he could . . . yes. He'd expect a kiss fer sure!' She withdrew her hand, looking around to see if anyone was looking.

'Hasn't any man ever done anything for you for nothing?'

'Nobody 'ceptin mah Pa, 'n he died when Ah was young. Since then no man has eva done nuthin fer me fer nuthin,' and she spat the words out with vehemence.

He asked, quietly, 'You hate men, don't you, Meagan?'

She looked away, first, then, directly in his eyes, 'Ah ain't got much use fer them.'

He started to comment when he saw the hooker trying to get his attention from across the cafe. She gave him a questioning look, pointed to her watch, then raised her hands. He saw Meagan look in her direction, so he shook his head at the hooker. She gave him a disgusted look and turned away.

Meagan smiled as she asked, 'Sure Ah'm not keeping you from a warm bed, Charlie? You still don't have a place to sleep.'

'I'll worry about that later. For now, will you have supper with me, Meagan . . . please. I would appreciate your company.'

She hesitated for a moment. 'OK, Charlie, but I want you to understand, this won't get you noth'in but friendship and appreciation . . . that's all . . . understand?'

He nodded. 'I understand. That's all I want.'

Old habits die hard as she got up and went to the menu rack and walked back with two menus.

He was amused but not pleased, as he took the menu, saying, 'Meagan, this is your night off. Let the waitress do the work. You're a customer here, tonight, just like I am. OK?'

She looked embarrassed, and looked down sheepishly, saying, softly, 'I guess it's a habit . . . Charlie. These other gals don't move fast enough fer me. Why, she shoulda bin here already, asking if we needed anything . . . can't git good help like you used to,' she smiled.

'Well, tonight, put up with the bad service. I'd like you to relax and enjoy your meal OK?'

She gave him a mischievous smile. 'OK'

He was highly amused as she perused the menu as if she had never seen it before. It should be ingrained in her mind, he thought as she squinted her eyebrows and wrinkled her forehead.

He volunteered, 'How about the beefalo steak. I had one last night and it was good . . . remember?'

She looked aghast. 'You know what that will cost for two people? If you was rich, Charlie, you wouldn't be eat'in in this place. You'd be in Aspen or Vail where the rich are.'

'Do you have a problem with rich people?'

'Ah sure do!'

'What?'

'Because they got money 'n Ah ain't, that's all,' she smiled.

'Let's not worry about money tonight, Meagan. Let's live like we have all the money we need to enjoy the evening.'

'Ah wouldn't know how to act like that. Ah have to watch every penny Ah make. It takes all Ah can get my hands on to pay my rent, buy my groceries, and go every Sunday to . . . ' She gave him a sheepish look and let it die.

He talked her into getting a big beefalo steak, mashed potatoes, green beans, and garlic bread. He was amused how she gave the young waitress implicit instructions as to how she wanted the steaks prepared and served on a heated plate. He was further amused as he watched her eat like she had not eaten in twelve hours or so, for she had not.

Unknown to him, she had had juice and toast at six that morning. She had not eaten in thirteen hours, and it showed, but she indicated no embarrassment as she went through all the food without doing much talking, except to say, 'Gee, this is good. You're not hungry, Charlie? You just playing with your food. If Ah had cooked this supper for you, Ah'd be mad as a wet hen 'bout the way you're playing with all that good food.'

'Well, you see, I spent the afternoon at the rodeo and I ate three hot dogs, and . . . '

'All that trash is not good fer you. Why, mah pore ole Mama, God rest her soul, she never would let me eat trash . . . no siree,' as she swallowed a huge bite, 'She made me eat my vegetables. Ah guess that's why Ah'm so healthy, with good teeth 'n all, 'cause we ate good on the farm. Neva had any money, but we ate good.'

He even talked her into dessert, in which she seldom indulged for two reasons. She couldn't afford to waste money on such frills, and, 'They ain't good fer your teeth.'

As she finished, she wiped her mouth and leaned back in her seat, moaning, 'Oh, Charlie, Ah'm so full,' and she got a mischievous look in her eye as she said, 'Thank God I ain't got to sleep with you, tonight . . . you know what Ah mean.'

He was mildly offended but curious as he asked, 'Why?'

She signed. 'Oh, Charlie, it's so hard on a full stomach.'

He was highly amused as she blushed at her own risqué remark. The remark surprised him, but he made no follow up to it, so she let it die. She seemed to be deep in meditation for a moment, and finally, she looked at him. 'Charlie, you still need a place to sleep. Tell you what Ah have to offer you, and you'd betta not take this wrong if you know what's good fer you. Ah have two bedrooms in that place of mine. It ain't no palace, but it's no worse than the Elk Motel.'

He was startled at her suggestion, as he replied, 'Oh, Meagan, I could not impose on your generosity like that. I have a sleeping bag, and I can bunk down in the Jeep.'

'You wouldn't be imposing, Charlie, you'd be paying. Ah would charge you the same price as the Elk Motel. But I have a bonus to offer you.'

His eyes lit up in libidinous interest. 'A bonus?'

'Now, now, Charlie, don't you let them hormones 'o

yourn git to running loose. The bonus Ah'm talking 'bout is a good hot breakfast 'o bacon 'n eggs . . . that's mah bonus. Ah only got one bathroom so you'll have to share that, 'n Ah don't want you to pee all ova the seat, so raise the seat 'fore you go 'n put it down when you're finish. Is it a deal? But, 'fore you answer, you'd betta remember one thing! All you're gitt'in is bed and breakfast. A clean bed and a warm breakfast, but your breakfast is the only thing warm you're gonna git. Ah kin use the extra money 'n it ain't a bad deal fer you for only one or two nights. What'dya say?'

He thought about it for awhile. 'You sure you want to do this? What about your reputation? What will the neighbours say?'

'Charlie, Ah ain't got no neighbours, 'n iffen Ah did, Ah don't care what they say. Your friends know what you're really like, 'n your enemies don't count, my ole Mama used to say.'

To Charles Alexander Forester, this seemed like an interesting social experiment. He was definitely interested in seeing how she lived in her own element. She was unlike any female he had ever known in his sheltered life, and he was intrigued, and . . . he did need a place to sleep, and . . . the price was not bad when breakfast was taken into consideration.

As they left the cafe/bar to the stares of the habitués and hookers, they were oblivious to the thoughts going on in the minds of all. It could best be described in the terms of the bartender who commented, 'Ah ain't neva seen Meagan leave heer with no man 'fore,' and he shook his head in amazement.

The spurned hooker gave them a look of astonishment as she commented, 'I'd like to see her brochure and price list.'

5

Meagan seemed to be in a good mood as they walked to her apartment. She was careful not to walk too close to Charlie, making sure she did not send the wrong signals, and doubly sure he did not receive any.

As they reached her door, she placed her key in the lock, and turning to him, said, 'Now, ah want to warn ya, this ain't no palace, Charlie, but it's home to me, 'n it's clean,' she remarked proudly.

He tried not to be condescending as he replied, 'I'm sure it will be just fine, Meagan. I don't need a palace to be happy.'

She led him into what was a combination parlour, dining room, and kitchen. It was a fairly large room, probably twelve by twenty-four . . . maybe thirty. The furniture was old and worn as he expected, but the smell of pine oil permeated the air. The place was spotless, as she had said.

She turned to him, 'Give me a few minutes to straighten up the bath and your bedroom. Ah didn't know when Ah left there this morning that Ah'd be bringing company home with me tonight. 'Scuse me for a few minutes. Make yo'self at home as we used to say in the country,' and she disappeared into the small hall which separated the two bedrooms.

He turned to look at the room. He saw an old black and white television set sitting on an even older radio console from the forties or fifties. There were photographs on a bureau against one wall. He moved over to look at the several framed photographs. He saw one of Meagan as a young girl. Then, he saw one which drew his attention. There was one of Meagan with a baby in her arms, then one of Meagan with a child of eight or ten at her side, and then, one of a very attractive young woman of eighteen, maybe. She resembled Meagan as a young woman and he was not sure if it were she or not.

As he stood there, staring, wondering, she came up, saying softly, 'She's a beauty ain't she . . . my baby?'

He turned to her, amazed. 'She is your daughter?'

She became very solemn, as she replied, 'Yes, she's my daughter . . . my beautiful baby girl, and now . . . '

He did not know if he should ask or not, but he felt he should. If he said nothing, it would be an indication of disinterest, and she seemed to want him to be interested, so he asked, 'Where is she?'

She didn't answer right away. She turned to a couch and she sat down, staring at the photograph which she had picked up, and she began to sob, softly. She turned her head to hide her tears.

He was surprised to see this tough little woman cry, and he was embarrassed to be there, so he said to her, 'I'm so sorry if I've opened something painful to you Meagan. Would you prefer that I leave?'

She shook her head. 'No, it's nothing you did, Charlie. It's something another man did.'

'I'm sorry. I'm trying to understand, but I don't and I don't mean to pry, but, please, tell me. I really want to know. Perhaps, whatever it is that is hurting you, I can fix it.'

She shook her head. 'Ah'm afraid you can't fix this, Charlie. Nobody kin . . . not now.'

'Is she dead?'

She shook her head. 'No, but she might as well be . . . where she is.'

He hated to press, but he had to. 'Where is she?'

She shuddered as she replied, 'The Colorado State Prison For Women,' and she added . . . 'in Canon City.'

'My God . . . what did she do?'

'She killed the bastard . . . that's what. Iffen she hadn't Ah would have, after what he did to her . . . the bastard.'

These were the first words of profanity he had ever

heard her say, not even hell or damn, and she said them with all the vehemence she could. Whoever he was, she hated him, that was certain.

He inquired, 'Who is this bastard?'

She had stopped crying. 'He was my husband at the time.'

'Was he her father?'

She shook her head. 'No, her stepfather. Ah guess that is why he could do what he did to her.'

'Megan . . . tell me, for God's sake. What did he do?'

'He raped her . . . my baby . . . she was just seventeen . . . a virgin too,' and she began to sob, again.

'Then . . . then,' and he hesitated. . . 'you've been married twice?'

She shook her head. 'No, just once. Ah got pregnant in high school. When the boy found out, he dropped me like a hot potato. When my Mama found out, she kicked me out of the house, telling me Ah had disgraced the family. It wasn't her fault! That's the way it was in my family. There I was, out on my own at sixteen, pregnant, broke . . . no place to go.'

Then, she hung her head and placed her hands in her lap, embarrassed, saying, 'I don't have any right to burden you with all my problems. I'm sorry. Just forget all this, Charlie. Let's talk about something else.

He gave her a discerning look. The hard exterior which she had exhibited at their first meeting in the cafe had disappeared. Now, as she sat there with her hands in her lap, looking down at the floor, she seemed like any other hurt and scared person, not sure of herself anymore. She looked at him and smiled meekly, waiting for him to say something.

He was mesmerized. He had only heard stories like this in movies or on television. No one of his acquaintance ever got into this kind of mess. They simply had an abortion. He tried to take her hand, but she mildly withdrew it, giving him a meek smile of embarrassment.

He withdrew his hand. 'Please tell me the rest, if you feel like talking about it. I don't mean to pry, though.'

She shook her head. 'I need to talk to someone about

it,' she murmured. 'Ah've had this thing bottled up inside me for a long time.'

She sighed as she continued, 'well, like Ah said, he raped mah baby while Ah was at work. He was mah husband . . . Ah trusted him with mah baby. He betrayed me! When Ah got home, my daughter, Erin . . . that's her name. . . . Erin told me what he had done. She said he'd been drink'in. He started drink'in heavy afta he lost his job . . . said he didn't feel like a man anymore.' She smirked. 'Ah guess he had to prove he was still a man,' she said sarcastically.

'What happened? How did she kill him?'

She took a deep breath as she continued. 'He was gone when she told me about the rape. Ah was so mad Ah wanted to kill him, so Ah took a butcher's knife from the kitchen 'n was goin out the door to look fer him at the pool hall. Ah figgur'd he was there. 'Bout that time, he comes through the door. We got into a hell of a fight. He saw the butcher's knife and he tried to take it away from me. We rassl'd fer it, 'n he finally got me down on the floor,' and she shuddered as she went on, 'n he was ready to drive that knife into my heart when she drove those scissors into his back, into his lungs.

'He fell on me, blood coming out of his mouth, all ova me. Erin was hysterical, 'n Ah was hysterical. We was both screaming 'n crying. People heard it. Soon, there was people all ova here . . . police 'n everything. Next thing we knew me and Erin was both in jail. They said they'd keep us both there 'til they learned the truth, 'cause we both said we'd killed him. Ah begged Erin to let me take the blame, but she wouldn't. She kept to her story that she'd killed him. They gave us those lie detector tests. She passed 'n Ah failed, so she's in jail 'n Ah'm here with you, now. Ya see, Charlie, you walked into a real mess of a place. If you want to leave now, Ah'll understand. Ah didn't plan on bringing you here tonight. Iffen Ah did, those pictures would've been moved, 'n we'd be talking about something more pleasant 'bout now,' and she managed a weak smile.

'Meagan, is that where you go every Sunday? To Canon City?'

She nodded. 'Uh, huh, Ah go to see mah baby.'

'How long is she in for?'

'They gave her ten years for manslaughter.'

'But, she is not guilty. Why, any good criminal lawyer could get her out of that.'

'Maybe so, Charlie, but them boys don't work for noth'in. Ah ain't got money, as you kin see. That is why Ah hate the rich . . . they got money. Iffen Ah had money, mah baby'd be out of that horrible place. Can you imagine what those bull dikes do to a pretty little thing like Erin,' and she began to cry, uncontrollably, as she got up, saying, 'Oh, Charlie, Ah didn't want you to hear all this . . . maybe you'd better go and sleep in your Jeep, after all.'

He got up and went to her, putting his arms around her, saying, 'If you don't mind, I would like to stay here tonight with you.'

She sniffed. . 'If that is what you want . . . all right,' and she walked into the bathroom. She was gone for nearly thirty minutes. She was smiling as if nothing had happened as she said, 'I'm through in the bathroom. You kin have it now, but remember what Ah said about the potty . . . raise the seat. Ah know how messy you men kin be. Ah'll see ya in the morn'in. Your bedroom is all ready fer you. Goodnight, Charlie. Breakfast at seven. Ah have to be at work at noon. Thank God Ah don't have to work that breakfast shift.'

He waved her a goodnight as she closed her bedroom door. He went into the bedroom and he smiled as he saw the bed had been turned down. As he looked more closely, he smiled again as he saw a mint had been placed on the pillow.

'At least,' he thought, 'she has not lost her sense of humour. Good thing. Poor woman! So, this is how the other half lives.'

He threw himself down on the bed, fully dressed, just staring up at the ceiling. He thought of his world – so different from Meagan's. He thought of all the spoiled women he knew – his mother for starts, and then his thoughts went to Adelle. Adelle was as different from Meagan as night is from day – their only similarity was the fact that they both belonged to the female species, and in Adelle's case, even that was a matter for conjecture.

As he reviewed the events of the evening he said to himself, 'My God, forty-eight hours ago I had never seen this woman before, and now I seem to be drawn into her life as if in a whirlpool. The smart thing for me to do would be to get out of here in the morning, say goodbye and good luck, and get the hell out of town by any means possible, even to getting on a Greyhound bus.'

'But,' he reasoned, 'I can't let her down. She is a miserable and tormented soul. I feel there must be some way to help her without getting too involved . . . but how?'

He didn't sleep well that night. He tossed. He turned. He thought. It was a combination of too hard a mattress and too soft a mind, he felt. He awoke to the smell of bacon frying, and there is something about the frying of bacon, high in the mountain air that stirs a man to action.

He leaped out of bed and tiptoed to the bedroom door. He could hear her in the kitchen – dishes rattling – refrigerator door opening and closing, so he went into the bathroom in his bathrobe. He smiled as he saw the old pedestal type bathtub with the hose and nozzle remote shower head. He smiled, again, as he raised the toilet seat to relieve himself, carefully lowering it when he finished.

He took a quick shower, not lingering too long, for he was anxious to get started on his Jeep repair problem. He dressed in a plaid flannel shirt and Sans-a-belt blue jeans, proud that he could still wear size 34 trousers, thanks to a lifestyle of tennis and more tennis. He walked into the kitchen area of the combination parlour, dining, and cooking area.

She looked up as she saw him walk in, smiled, saying, 'Good morning, Charlie. Did you sleep well?' as she poured his juice, adding, 'You just sit yourself down and you'll get your bonus that you can't git at the Elk Motel.'

He smiled at her, returning her good morning, jokingly saying as he sat down, 'My women usually kiss me good morning.'

'Oh, yeah, well then, good morning, Charlie,' and she kissed him on the head, smiling as she did. Then she added, 'Charlie, I would just as soon you forget what we talked about last night, you know . . . about Erin . . . just forget it. It ain't none 'o your affair . . . OK?'

He nodded, as she placed his eggs and bacon before him, and then returned with a cup of steaming coffee. She then brought her cup to the table and smilingly asked, 'Want me to keep you company while you eat, or do you want me to do what Ah do in the cafe . . . go away?'

'I'd like you to sit with me. You don't have to go to work before noon. What do you usually do all morning?'

She laughed. 'That's when Ah go to the beauty parlour to have mah hair done! What do you think Ah do? That's the only time Ah got to clean this place, to do mah laundry, to do mah grocery shopping, to . . . '

He interrupted . . . 'OK, I got the idea, but this morning, just spend it with me. I want to know more about you. Meagan, I don't even know your last name.'

She gave a disgusted look at that, replying, 'Mah last name is the same as the bastard who raped mah Erin, 'cause ah was married to him, legal and all, and ah ain't got the money to have it changed. It's Lewis . . . L.E.W.I.S. Ah wish Ah could change it to mah maiden name . . . Mahoney. Meagan Mahoney. Has a nice ring to it, don't it?'

'Uh huh, it does,' as he ate his eggs and bacon. 'You know it doesn't cost that much to have your name changed . . . only a few hundred dollars, I've heard . . . '

Her laugh cut him off. . . . 'Charlie it might as well be a few thousand dollars. Ah have to put off buying groceries on the days when Ah have to go to the dentist, and you want me to spend good money on changing mah name. Ah neva put off going to the dentist, 'cause Ah like good teeth, 'n Ah got good ones . . . see,' and she displayed a fine set of even teeth.

He nodded, not wanting to show indifference to her teeth, and he was secretly embarrassed at his lack of sensitivity to her financial plight. He was just not accustomed to this side of life, he felt.

He sipped his coffee, asking of her 'Speaking of money . . . how do you want me to pay you for the room and board?'

'Oh, cash will do . . . each morning. Ah don't take plastic, eitha,' she joked.

He reached for his wallet, and extracted twenty-five dollars, and then, on second thought, he placed fifty dollars on the table.

She watched him closely. 'What's the fifty dollars for? Ah tole you it was the same as Elmo's . . . twenty-five dollars a night."

'Well, there is no doubt that I will be here again tonight, so I am paying for both nights.'

'Oh! Well, Ah guess that's OK . . . long as you ain't trying to give me charity. Ah don't like charity, Charlie, less'n it's me giving it.'

He ignored the warning. 'Could I have another cup of coffee, Miss?', as if he were in a cafe.

'Oh, yes, sir . . . right away sir!' as she jumped up.

Returning to the table, she said 'It worked out fine, didn't it, Charlie? You staying here last night? And, Ah appreciate you being a good boy. You know . . . not trying anything. Some men would'a bin knocking on may door all night . . . being as how some men are . . . you know what Ah mean. Not that Ah'm a prize worth fight'n for,' she said, looking down at the floor.

'Meagan, you're more of a prize than you know, compared to most of the women I've known in my life.'

'Now, don't you start sweet talking me, Charlie . . . Charlie? You ain't told me your last name, Charlie!'

'It's Forester.'

'That's a nice name. Charlie, you still ain't tole me what you're doing here . . . where you're going. Are you hid'in anything? You ain't running from the police, are you?'

He laughed. 'I'm running, Meagan, but it's not from

the police. It's from women. You see, just now in my life . . . I hate women.'

'So, that's it. Want to talk about it? Ah tole ya all mah troubles . . . now, you kin unload on me,' she jested.

He shook his head. 'Not now. Perhaps later. I've got to get out of here and see about getting my Jeep fixed. I guess you won't see me until later today. Tell you what, I'll be at the cafe about seven to eat, and I'll hang around to walk you home, if that is alright with you.'

She smiled. 'That'll be fine. Oh, do you think you will have to git back in here while Ah'm at work? Ah kin give you a key . . . Ah trust you.'

'No! I'll be gone all day. I'll see you tonight.'

'OK. Take care of yo'self, Charlie, and stay clear of them hookers from Denver. Ya might ketch something,' she teased.

He merely smiled as he went out of the door and down the steps, and headed for the Texaco garage to see if they had a mechanic who could repair the Jeep. They did, but all that could be done now was to call Denver and have a new starter put on the bus to be delivered to them later that day or, more probably, the next day, Tuesday. He found that unacceptable.

'Is there a car rental agency here in town?'

'Sure is,' the garage man answered proudly, 'you're looking at him. See that little Chevy Geo over there, well, that is mah rental car. You can rent it by the day or the week.'

'I'll take it for the day. I'll drive to Denver and get the starter, myself, and bring it back. I'll be back later today, and your man can put it in first thing in the morning. OK?'

'Why, sure, if that is the way you want to do it. I'll give you the name and address of the dealer so's you don't waste all day looking for it in that big town. But, that shouldn't take all day.'

'I have other things I want to do in Denver. I'll be gone all day.'

6

He entered the doors of the law firm of Henshaw, Morten, and Dervish, and asked for the name of a criminal lawyer he could talk to.

The receptionist asked, 'Do you have an appointment, sir?'

'No, I don't, but this will not take long. I just want to have something looked into, and we can make future appointments at that time.'

She leafed through the appointment book, dialled a number, talked for a moment, and said to him, 'Mr Brownlow will see you for a few moments . . . third door on the right.'

The attorney was waiting for him at the door, saying as he extended his hand, 'Good morning, Mr Forester, I'm sorry I can't spend more than a few moments with you. I have an appointment in fifteen minutes . . . but come in, please . . . '

'I don't need much of your time, Mr Brownlow. I want you to look into something for me. It concerns a female prisoner in the state penitentiary for women. Her name is either Erin Mahoney or Erin Lewis. I would like you to review her case with regard to having it brought back into court for retrial.'

The attorney seemed confused, asking, 'I could better decide on how to advise you if I knew what you were trying to accomplish with regard to that young lady.'

'Well,' he hesitated, not sure of his own intentions, 'I have reason to believe she was incarcerated unfairly, without adequate defence, and I would like her case reviewed with regard to having her sentence reduced, or set aside completely. I have reason to believe she was unjustly treated by the system. Do you have enough information to go on?'

'Yes, for now,' as he took notes. 'We have our contacts who can follow through on this.'

He cleared his throat, looked at Charlie's casual dress with some professional disdain and suspicion as he said, 'This will involve some money, and since you are a stranger to us . . . '

Charlie nodded. 'I understand,' and he withdrew his pack of traveller's cheques from his jacket. The attorney's eyes widened as he endorsed one thousand dollars worth of cheques, saying, 'I will call you in a day or so to check in with you. If you will let me know how much money is needed for now, I will send a bank draft to your account. I only need a day's notice to accomplish that.'

The attorney handed him a business card, and Charlie, not to be outdone, handed him his. The attorney read the card – Charles A. Forester, Vice-President of The Forester Companies, but then, thought the attorney, anyone can have any type of card printed that he chooses. They shook hands and parted.

By the time he had found the Chrysler Jeep dealer in Denver and secured the starter, the afternoon was half gone. He felt he had to make good time to get back to the cafe for seven, and the little Geo strained climbing the mountainous roads back to the small town high in the Rockies.

As he walked into the cafe thirty minutes late, Meagan saw him and her face lit up. She was genuinely glad to see him, saying as she placed the ubiquitous glass of water before him, 'Ah thought you had run out on me, Charlie! Not that Ah'd blame ya.'

'Why would I do a thing like that?'

'Oh, Ah was just kidd'in. Ah guess you already ate, huh, see'in as how you're so late.'

'No. I went to Denver to pick up the starter. They told me if they shipped it, it would be tomorrow before it would get here.'

'And Ah guess you're in a hurry to leave here, huh?' she said rather sadly, looking in his eyes for his response.

'Well, I did have a schedule I wanted to keep, but, we'll see how things turn out.'

She became professional. 'What'll you have? The spec'l fer today is fried chicken, potato salad, and some chowder of some kind for soup. Six ninety-five.'

'That'll be fine.'

As they walked back to her apartment at nine-thirty, she noticed the package under his arm, in a brown paper bag.

'What's in the package, if Ah ain't gitt'in too personal?'

'It's a bottle of good wine I brought from Denver. I though you and I would kill it tonight. You like wine?'

'Ain't had much of it. Cost too much. But, Ah remember it makes me loose when Ah drink it. You not trying to git me drunk, are you, Charlie?' she teased as she slipped her arm in his.

'You know what they're saying at the cafe . . . 'bout us, Ah mean? They say you're mah boy friend. Embarrassed me to tears, that did. But, Ah don' care what they say. You know that Denver hooker in the white blouse and red skirt? You know she had the nerve to come ova and ask me, "how was it?" You know what Ah mean, Charlie?'

He was silently amused. 'Uh huh, I know exactly what she meant. She still has her feelings hurt that I turned her down.'

'Maybe, you missed out on a lot of fun, Charlie,' she said, waiting for his response. 'Ain't you sorry, now?'

He patted her shoulder as they walked. 'I have no regrets.'

'Well, here we are,' as she climbed the stairs, looking back at him as she did.

He sensed she was in a different mood this evening. Her tough veneer had vanished. She seemed softer . . . warmer, as she smiled going through the door.

She headed for the bathroom, saying, 'Make ya self at home, as usual, Ah'll be right back.'

He went to the kitchen, looking for a corkscrew for the wine. He found one, much to his surprise, but it was one of those found on can openers from the old days. He smiled as he finally got the cork out of the bottle. He took two water glasses out of the cabinet after seeing she had no wine glasses. He poured two glasses full to the top and went to the couch, waiting for her to return.

She did, eventually. She had obviously bathed, put on her pyjamas and a housecoat and, as she walked to the couch, said, 'Ah hope you don't mind me being in my P.J.'s and robe. It's the way Ah live everyday when Ah'm alone. When Ah get home, ah take mah bath 'n dress for bed. Ah hope you don't mind.'

He shook his head, as he handed her the glass of wine, motioning her to sit by him on the couch. She sat at the opposite end, bringing her feet up under her. She raised the glass of wine to her lips and she smiled at him as she sipped it.

She cooed, 'Oh, that's good. What kind is it, not that Ah'd know the difference?'

'It's a Rhine wine, made of a Riesling grape . . . my favourite grape . . .'

She sipped it once more, studying him. 'Charlie, do you have money? You must have if you know about wine. Poor boys just know about beer, not wine! Are you rich?'

'What's your definition of rich?'

She thought about it for a while. 'Having more money than you need to live. Having money left over at the end of the month after you'd paid all your bills. That's rich to me.'

He smiled at her. 'Then, I guess I'm rich because I always have a few dollars left over at the end of the month,' and he laughed as he added, 'that is when Adelle didn't go crazy with the bills that month.'

She looked at him for an explanation, and when none came forth, she asked, 'Who's Adelle. Is she your wife? Are you married, Charlie?'

He shook his head. 'Not any more. Adelle is who I am running away from,' and he looked down at the floor.

'Want to tell me about it?'

He didn't really, but she looked at him with those big

questioning eyes, full of sincerity. Would she understand about Adelle? How could she? He didn't understand. But, he took a long sip of wine and he told her everything he could remember of that fateful night. He even went back further than that. He gave her a recap of his whole marriage to Adelle. She said nothing the whole time.

Only once did she interrupt him, asking him if he wanted another glass of wine. He handed her his glass without comment as he continued his narration. She returned to the couch, still at the opposite end, her legs still tucked up under her. As he finished, he raised his hands in a futile gesture, indicating it was all over.

'Geez . . . ' she said, shaking her head. 'Ah heard of women like her, but Ah ain't never run into one. Erin says they're all over that prison. She says if you ain't one when you go in, you damn sure will be one when you come out, whether you want to or not.'

She shuddered as she looked at him. 'Poor, Charlie . . . . you and me got a lot in common. You bin betrayed by a woman 'n Ah bin betrayed by a man. You was married to the one who betrayed you. 'Ah was married to the one who betrayed me. Don't say much fer marriage, does it?' She asked with profound conviction.

She looked at him, and as he looked into her eyes, he could see the effect of the wine as she asked, 'You hurt'in Charlie, ain't you?'

He smiled at her, amused that the wine, which she was not used to, had this effect on her so soon, answering, 'I don't guess I'm hurting any more than you are.'

'But, Ah'm used to hurt, Charlie. You ain't. Ah kin tell by the way you act . . . you ain't used to it.'

She got up, saying, 'Ah got to tinkle. This wine goes right through me,' and he watched her half stagger to the bathroom. He felt ashamed of himself, allowing her to get drunk like this. He should have known she was not used to the fruit of the vine, and he should have known better than to allow her to drink so much of it.

He smiled as she returned to the couch, and she now sat closer to him, within touching distance. She didn't say anything for a while, just sipping her wine, and looking at him.

She slid over closer to him, putting her hand on his, and she hesitatingly asked, 'Charlie . . . if you're really hurt'in, Ah know that men like to make love when they're hurt'in, 'n well, iffen it'll make ya feel better, then Ah'm will'in to . . . you know,' and she blushed, looking away.

He was torn between desire and responsibility. He knew she was half drunk, and he was well on his way, himself. He was feeling a little mellow. That was no regular sized bottle for wine. It was a large bottle, and they had consumed nearly all of it. He thought over her invitation. She had looked away, waiting for his response. He took her hand in his, searching for the right words to guide his response, for he was sure she would regret her actions in the morning, knowing her as he did.

He brought her hand to his lips, and she now looked at him, as he softly asked, 'Meagan, I'm sure you have just made an offer out of sympathy, did you not?'

She half giggled. 'Sure, but you will enjoy it just as much, I promise you . . . you won't know the difference.'

He asked, 'Have you had a man since the . . . the accident?'

She turned away, shaking her head. 'No,' she replied. 'I hated men so much Ah didn't have any desires for 'em. Ah took pleasure in turning them down . . . seeing the desire burning in their eyes . . . damn them.'

'That is what I thought.'

'But, you're different, Charlie! You're nice 'n kind 'n . . . oh, Ah don't know . . . Ah'm confused, Charlie.'

'I know you are.'

He pulled her close to him and she came willingly. He stroked her hair and she melted into him like a child seeking affection. It was obvious that she had had no real affection shown to her for a long time, and she responded like a child, burying her head in his chest, as she sobbed.

He continued to stroke her hair, as he whispered, 'Let's just hold each other tonight. Some other time, when you have not been drinking, and you get some real feelings for . . . you know (he mimicked her) well, then, we'll do it the way it should be done . . . the right way.'

She groaned. 'OK' and she snuggled closer.

That was the way they went to sleep that night, until he carried her to her bed in the middle of the night. She moaned as she turned over, saying nothing else as he tiptoed out of the room.

* * *

She showed no embarrassment the next morning as she greeted him with a cheery, 'Good morning, Charlie . . . sleep well?'

But, as he finished his breakfast and was having his second cup of coffee, she joined him as usual.

She looked at him, smiling an embarrassed smile, saying, 'Charlie . . . thanks fer last night . . . you were right. It was sympathy . . . 'n Ah was a little drunk. It was not a good idea. You'll be leaving here today 'n with mah luck, you'd leave me pregnant,' and she laughed, 'and at mah age, that is all Ah need . . . a baby,' and she looked away.

He was sure there were tears in her eyes, but she quickly recovered, asking, 'Well, Ah guess this is goodbye, huh, Charlie? Ah guess Ah won't see you afta today. Good thing we didn't do nuth'in last night . . . Ah don't need anymore heart aches.'

He became solemn. 'Meagan, if you don't mind, I need to stay another day or so. I've got some business to do in Denver. It may take some time. I can't leave before it's finished. Do you mind?'

Her face lit up. 'No . . . you kin stay as long as you want. Well . . . at least 'til Ah git tired of you,' she smiled. 'And, Charlie, ya don't have to pay me anymore . . . you kin be just like company, OK?'

'We'll see about the money later. I would have to be paying someone, and it may as well be you.'

'But, Ah feel bad 'bout taking your money . . . speci'lly afta last night . . . you know . . .'

He laughed . . . 'Yes, I know. Look, I have to go and tend to my jeep. I'll be gone all day. I'll see you at the cafe at seven as usual . . . OK?'

She nodded, hesitated, then went to him, turned her

face up to him, asking, 'Kiss me goodbye, Charlie . . just a little one. We didn't even kiss last night. We almost . . . you know, but we didn't kiss . . . isn't that funny?'

He kissed her lightly on the lips. She had her eyes open and she was smiling the whole time. He was fascinated.

Within a couple of hours he had the Jeep running and purring once again. That made him happy. An American male without wheels is like a duck out of water. He is only a half person.

He smiled as he headed out of the garage after paying the bill which killed another traveller's cheque of one-hundred dollar denomination. At this rate, he thought, he would have to send for more money, and he thought of the attorneys in Denver.

He used the car phone in the Jeep to call the attorneys. 'Have you made any headway in the matter we discussed yesterday?'

'Yes we have, Mr Forester. The girl in question was incarcerated under the name of Erin Mahoney, which is what she was christened at birth.' (Figures, he thought . . . she was not married at the time) The attorney continued . . . 'It would appear at a cursory glance that she was not very well represented during her trial, as you suspected. The public defender assigned to her, as is so often the case, was a young and inexperienced lawyer, and he did not handle her case well at all. We have read a transcript of the trial and we believe, as you intimated, that we can do her some good.'

'Oh, that is good news! Do you need any more money just now?'

He was shocked by the reply. 'Not now . . . stay in touch.'

His spirits were high as he went to the cafe that night to eat and see Meagan, and his attitude showed it.

She sensed it, too. 'Well, you must have had a good day, Charlie. You're actually smiling, tonight.'

'Are you telling me I don't smile enough?'

'Uh huh, that is what I'm telling you.' As she handed him the menu, she grinned. 'The special tonight is curried lamb, baked potato, green salad. All for six ninety-five . . . '

He laughed. 'It's always six ninety-five . . '

'Well, sir . . . that is the going price these days. Do you want it or not, sir?' she teased.

'Oh, what the hell . . . bring it.'

* * *

As they walked to the apartment, she once again placed her arm in his as they started. She walked a little closer than she did last night, and he noticed it, but he said nothing.

She looked at him, smiling. 'I don't see any bag with wine in it . . . thank God! Charlie, I had a hangova this morn'in 'n it's all your fault,' she teased.

'My fault?' I didn't get you drunk last night. You got yourself drunk. You're lucky you were out with a gentleman or you would have lost your temporary virginity.'

She cuddled close to him. 'Ah know! Ah appreciate it, too. Are you sorry, now?'

'Uh huh, I was sorry all night.'

She laughed . . . 'Oh, Charlie!'

After she had taken her usual bath, she returned to the living area and, once again, sat at the far end of the couch. He noticed it, and teased, 'I thought after last night that you might sit a little closer to me, tonight.'

She smiled. 'Ah have to tonight, for a different reason. This morning, Ah started mah monthly curse, so you see, we have noth'in to say about it this time.'

'Oh, hell. That ruins my whole day, and things were going so well.'

'You're just teasing me 'n you know it. Ah probably can't even hold a candle to the women you're used to . . . huh?'

'You're only half right, Meagan.'

'What do you mean?'

'They can't hold a candle to you. Most of the women I've known . . . not all, but most, are so egocentric, so self-serving, that they are not capable of real spontaneous affection, as I think you are.'

She looked embarrassed. 'What's egocentric?'

He smiled at her lack of erudition. She fascinated him. 'It means they believe that the world revolves around them.'

'Was Adelle egocentric, or, whatever it is?'

He could not help but laugh aloud. 'Egocentricity was only one of her problems.'

'But, you married her, and you're not stupid, Charlie. What happened to ruin it?' and she giggled as she added, 'Besides the fact that she liked other women.'

'Isn't that enough?'

'Was she good in bed? You know what I mean?'

'I don't have much to compare her to. I was not a very promiscuous man . . . you know what I mean.'

She poked him in the ribs. 'You're making fun of me 'cause Ah don't like that horrible word.'

He pulled her close and she came without any protest, except, 'Remember what Ah told you, Charlie, tonight won't be the night,' and she snuggled into his chest.

'I'm not worried about that just now. Meagan . . . if you had any wish in the world that could be granted to you right now, what would you wish?'

She sat up, thinking about it, replying, 'Ah'd wish fer my baby to come home to me. That's what Ah want more'n anything in this world. Ah would give mah life for it, iffen Ah could spend some time with her before Ah had to go.'

He sat up, too, and taking both her hands in his, said, 'I want to tell you something, Meagan, but please don't get too excited right away before I finish.'

She waited with wide-eyed anticipation as he continued. 'Maybe, something will come of this, and,' he lowered his voice, 'maybe it won't. I don't want you to get your hopes up. I don't want you to be disappointed if it doesn't pan out,' and he told her of his talk with the Denver attorneys.

Her hands went to her throat. She gasped. 'Oh, Charlie . . . please don't play games with me! Is this real? Oh, God! My baby free!' and she smothered him with kisses, laughing, crying, and then, she sat down. 'Ah better settle down, huh? Maybe, this will not happen, after all. Ah better not git mah hopes up, huh?'

'It would be better if you realized that it might not happen, but the attorneys seemed optimistic.'

Her eyes widened. 'The lawyers? They cost a lot of money. How will Ah pay fer them. Ah'll do anything Ah kin, 'ceptin sell mah body, to git mah baby outa that prison. Maybe, even that,' she shuddered.

'Don't worry about the money. It is all taken care of. It will cost you nothing, and you won't have to sell your body, either.'

'Oh, Charlie, why are you doing this fer me? You don't hardly know me! You don't owe me this, much as Ah want it to happen. Kin you really afford this? The money Ah mean!'

He smiled at her. 'I can afford it. You see, I'm doing it because I am selfish.'

'Selfish?'

'Yes, I want to be happy. I am looking for happiness, just now, and helping you makes me happy.'

She moved into his arms. 'Oh, Charlie, you picked a bad night for this. I want to take you to bed and love you to pieces right now.'

'As much as I would like that, it would be an act of repayment, wouldn't it?'

'Well, maybe, but you would enjoy it, believe me!'

'I don't want to sound like a sanctimonious saint, but last night would have been an act of pity and tonight would be an act of gratitude. Some night, when you have real feelings for me . . . and for Meagan . . . let me know, and then we'll . . . you know.'

She laughed as she cuddled once again. 'Oh, Charlie, Ah love you.'

The words grabbed him. Did she mean it, or, were they just words of the moment, to fulfil the needs of the moment? If she meant them, was he leading her down the wrong path. He held her close. He had no answers just now.

After a while, he held back from her, looking at her. 'Meagan, can you get the day off, tomorrow? I want you to come to Denver with me to meet the lawyers. It is important that you know them so that when I leave here in a day or two, you can complete the negotiations on your own. Besides, they need information that only you can give.'

She sat up, saying, sadly, 'That's right! You will be leaving here in a day or two . . Ah almost forgot about that,' and she began to wring her hands, as if in despair, as she continued . . . 'Ah guess Ah kin git the day off iffen Ah find somebody to take mah place. There's a little girl . . . she's married now. She takes mah place now 'n then. When are we coming back?'

'Probably, in a day or two. Don't worry about the money you will lose. I'll make it up for you.'

'Oh, Charlie, you've done so much fer me, 'n Ah ain't had the chance to do anything fer you . . . yet . . you know what ah mean.'

'There you go again. Don't you feel that your friendship is worth something?'

'Ah ain't neva found anybody, yet, who thought so,' she lamented.

'You sell yourself too short, Meagan.'

'Ah ain't neva thought Ah was worth any more than what you see in front of you, now.'

He drew her close to him, again. 'We'll worry about that later . . . now, let's go to bed.'

'The last time a man told me that, Ah slapped his face,' she teased, as she kissed him, warmly, passionately, and then she broke lose and ran to her bedroom. He laughed, shaking his head. He was fascinated by her.

7

As she climbed in the Jeep the next morning, she looked around at the plush interior . . . the car phone. 'Whew! When you told me you had a Jeep, Ah thought you meant one of them war surplus things all the cowboys back in the hills want. Ah said to mahself, ''No wonder the starter went out . . . that thing must be fifty years old.''

He laughed. 'No it's only a year old, and the starter should not have gone out.'

As they approached Denver on I-70, she was as excited as a child.

He watched her with amusement. 'Have you ever been to Denver, before?'

'Oh, sure . . . two or three times, but Ah was a little girl.'

'And you haven't been since?'

'No! Seems like something always happened to keep me from it. Are we gonna stay in a hotel, tonight?'

'Uh huh. Does that bother you?'

'Same room?'

'Uh huh, unless that bothers you.'

She pondered it for a while. 'No, but maybe you'd betta git two beds . . . you know . . . consider'in mah condition. But, the one room is OK. Ah trust you, Charlie'

He smiled at her childlike simplicity. 'And I would never do anything in this world to violate that trust, Meagan.'

She smiled in return.

He watched her eyes, wide with excitement as he drove up to the Airport Stouffer Hotel, with its sloping sides, and as they entered the huge atrium she stared, open mouthed.

He had called ahead for reservations, and as they entered the glass front elevator, she took hold of his hand. She had dressed in what she considered her best dress, and it was not bad, but Charlie tried to picture her after a visit to a good beauty parlour and in a new high-priced outfit. He felt her trim figure could do real justice to a beautiful, well-fitted dress. He made a mental note to follow up on it later.

'Why are we staying here? It is out of town, isn't it?'

'Yes, a little, but it is close to the attorney's offices.'

'Oh!'

As she entered the suite, she walked around open-mouthed, and after the bellhop left, she asked, 'Is this our room? Ah thought it was still part of the lobby,' she joked.

He laughed. 'Sometimes, I think you are pulling my leg.'

'You finally caught on, huh? Ah was beginning to think you were slow, Charlie,' she teased.

'Do you know what couples usually do when they first get to a hotel room?' he asked.

'Uh huh! Ah may be green as grass, but Ah ain't that green, but it ain't gonna happen that way . . . not today, anyhow,' as she poked him in the ribs. 'Ah got to tinkle . . . hope they got flushing johns in this high-price joint,' and she disappeared into the bath.

As she came out, he was on the telephone, saying, 'Yes, Dad, I know I was supposed to be farther west by now, but that damn Jeep you lent me broke down, and I have to spend two days in a small town way up in the Rockies waiting to get a replacement starter . . . no, Dad, I don't need anything else. Give my love to mother . . . yes . . . goodbye.'

'Your dad, huh? Ah hope you didn't tell him Ah was in this hotel room with you!'

He smiled. 'What difference would that make? He doesn't know you from Eve.'

'Well, that's true, but your daddy wouldn't be proud to know you had a woman in your hotel room . . . you know that.'

'That's true,' he agreed. Now, get your self together so we can go to the attorney's office to discuss the case.'

* * *

As they drove along the crowded streets in the city traffic, she put her hands to her cheeks, shaking her head.

'What's wrong? Don't you feel well?'

'Oh, Ah feel OK, but, I'm nervous, Charlie. . . . Ah don't like talking to lawyers. They make me nervous.'

He patted her hand. 'You have nothing to be worried about. These lawyers are on your side. They want to help you. I want you to go over in your mind all the details of that day, because that is what they want to go over with you.'

She nodded, not looking at him, and as he drove on he could see her wince, twitch and frown, as she relived those traumatic moments again.

After a while, she smiled at him, saying. 'OK, Ah did it. Ah remember it all.'

They were led into the office of Everett Brownlow, who was standing by his desk when they entered, and after greeting him Charlie introduced Meagan. When the attorney heard the name of Lewis, he gave them a quizzical look. Charlie explained the difference of names, and the story embarrassed Meagan, but she made no comment as she quietly sat in the chair offered her.

The attorney asked if he could offer them some refreshments, and Meagan requested a soda, saying her throat was dry, which made Charlie pat her hand for reassurance.

The attorney looked at Charlie, saying, 'I took the liberty of looking up the Forester firm in Dun and Bradstreet. . . . very impressive, I must say. It is unusual in this time of S & L failures to see a real estate company so healthy.'

Charlie nodded. 'That's because we were smart enough not to try to swim in the sea of junk bonds and leveraged buyouts. We kept doing business with our local banks. That keeps you out of big trouble when you stay away from the New York boys.'

The attorney smiled. 'Especially when the local bank is owned by your mother's family, huh?'

Charlie nodded and smiled back. 'It helps to keep it in the family.' Meagan merely forced a smile at all this. She understood none of it.

'But, we are digressing,' said the attorney. 'Let me bring you up to date on where we are. We have a lady attorney in the firm . . . I must warn you she is a flaming liberal and a rabid feminist, but that is precisely what you need in this case. The deeper she dug into this matter, the more incensed she became, and when Monica de la Rosa gets angry, the establishment learns about it. She finished Harvard Law School, Magna Cum Laude. We were happy to get her. She feels that Mrs Lewis' daughter had her civil rights violated so she is going into federal court with this.

'She doesn't want to run the risk of the State court's sympathy for their own system to be a hindrance to a fair hearing, but, let me bring her in and she will take over from here on. Just one more thing, Mr Forester, and I'm sure this will be good news to you. Our firm takes on a certain percentage of cases each year, Pro Bono, for the public good, so to speak, and Miss de la Rosa has asked the managing partners to accept this one as such, and they have agreed. It seems she plans to present a paper on this perceived injustice at the next national convention of the ABA.'

It should be noted here that those with good hearing would have heard a slight wisp of air escaping from Charlie's lips, and a smile appeared on his face.

The lawyer continued. 'If you will allow your retainer to go towards covering out-of-pocket expenses, I believe this case will cost you nothing more . . . is that fair?'

'Quite fair! I appreciate the gesture and I'm sure Mrs Lewis does, too.'

Meagan had gotten the drift of that exchange, and she, too, smiled, saying softly, 'Oh, thank you, sir.'

The attorney picked up his telephone, punched a number, saying, 'Miss de la Rosa, would you come in please. The folks are here on the Erin Mahoney case . . . yes . . . thank you.'

There was a perfunctory knock at the door and a woman with dark hair, less than medium in height, and wide of hips, walked in. Her Roman nose confirmed her Italian heritage. She smiled as she entered, going up to Meagan, first, offering her hand, saying, 'I am so happy to meet you Mrs Lewis,' and then to Charlie, 'the same to you, Mr Forester.'

Everett Brownlow turned to the woman lawyer, saying, 'Monica, if you have no further need of me, why don't you take these folks into your office to hear Mrs Lewis's version of the accident.' Charlie took notice of the word 'accident'.

'Why, yes, of course. Won't you folks follow me, please.'

Charlie lagged behind, thanking Everett Brownlow for his and the firm's effort.

The attorney placed his hand on Charlie's shoulder, replying, 'I'm optimistic about this thing.'

Charlie nodded. Pointing to a departing Meagan, 'Poor woman, she needs a break . . . she deserves a break. Goodbye.'

Charlie watched from a distant chair as Monica de la Rosa led Meagan through her version of the day of the murder. She sobbed from time to time as the awful moments came to life again, especially the lurid details of the scissors going into her husband's back and lungs, the look in his eyes, the blood pouring forth from his mouth. The attorney went to her, put her arms around her, consoling her, but leading her on, relentlessly.

He heard words like . . . 'I'll be going to the prison in a day or so to talk to Erin. I have to get her version of what happened. Your stories have to jibe. Then, I'm going to try to get a federal judge to have her paroled immediately, pending a new hearing. If what you've told me is correct, that child has no business being in prison . . . not one more day!'

He heard Meagan ask, 'When will my baby be able to get out of that horrible place?'

'I can't say for sure, but, I'm hoping soon . . . real soon.'

Meagan responded . . . 'Oh, praise God! Ah hope so.'

* * *

Meagan was euphoric as they returned to the Jeep. Her hopes were high. Maybe, too high, Charlie felt, and he told her so in these words, 'Now, Meagan, don't let your hopes run away from you. I don't want you to go off the deep end if this does not pan out . . . '

She protested, 'Ah believe that woman kin do anything she sets her mind to . . . she's tough, Charlie . . . tougher than me.'

'I know. She is hell on wheels. I wonder if de la Rosa is her maiden name. Is she married? Do you know?'

'She ain't married. Ah kin tell, 'n she ain't had no ring on, eitha.'

'Well, let's get our minds off this thing and go have some fun in this big town. Meagan, I want to propose something to you, but don't be offended by it . . . '

She placed her hand on his arm as he drove, replying, 'Ah don't believe Ah could get offended at you, Charlie, not afta what you went and done for me and Erin. What do you want to do?'

He hesitated. He knew he might be opening a hornet's nest, but he went on. 'Well, I thought you might like to go to a beauty parlour first, and then, we'll go shopping for some new clothes for you . . . '

But he never go to finish, as she questioned him in an offended tone. 'You're not satisfied with me the way Ah am, Charlie? Ah know Ah ain't no society lady, with hair all arranged and fancy clothes, 'n Ah know Ah don't talk too good, but, this is me, Charlie . . . this is how Ah am. Iffen you don't like me like Ah am . . . then Ah'm sorry. Ah know Ah embarrass you when we git in front of edjicat'd people like them lawyers, 'n Ah'm sorry. Yaw'll said words Ah neva heard of before, but Ah know that's mah fault, but Ah can't help it.

'Ah bet them people ain't bin out on their own since they was sixteen, with a baby in their belly, 'n no one to turn to. Iffen it hadn't bin fer them nuns taking me in, well, Ah don't know what I'da done,' and she began to cry, as she continued, 'makes me so damn mad when Ah cry in front of a man . . . Ah don't like no man to see me cry, so don't look at me, Charlie!'

He smiled at her, feeling she had vented her anger, as he tried to reason with her. 'Why do you feel if I suggest some ways to improve your appearance that I am unhappy with how you look now. If you were married to me, I would have no reservations about saying the same things I just told you.'

'Oh, yeah, 'n what iffen your wife didn't like it anymore than Ah did . . . what then, huh?'

'Adelle would have said . . . "blow it out, Charlie!"

'You know Ah don't like to use dirty words like that.'

'I'm sure you can think up some words of your own to tell me the same thing.'

'But, Ah like Adelle's better. So, blow it out, Charlie!' and she poked him in the ribs.

She was quiet for a while, but, finally, she asked, 'What would you want me to do iffen Ah did go to a beauty parlour?'

'I have no idea. I'd suggest you let the operator propose some things to you, and if you like them, she'd do it to you. I know they show photos of models sometimes, and women say . . . "Yes, I want to look like that."'

'Then, if Ah don't like it, Ah don't hafta do it, huh?'

'That's right. I wouldn't try to make you do something you don't want to do, would I?'

'You ain't bin able to do it, yet,' she teased. 'OK, Charlie, Ah'm willing to go 'n try it . . . just to please you. Ah guess Ah owe you that. Ah hope you ain't gonna sit there 'n watch me as she does it to me . . . Ah'd be embarrassed.'

'Lord no! You couldn't pay me to stay and watch. I'll drop you off and go to movie or something . . . I'll find something to do.'

She pondered that for a while, and finally said, 'OK, Ah'll do it. Ah guess you know you'll have to pay fer this, but, Ah promise Ah'll pay you back. Ah want you to keep track of all the money you're spending on me. Ah promise Ah'll pay you back,' and she added . . .'someday . . . some way!'

He stopped at a gas station to fill up with gas, and

looked up the location of some beauty shops in town in the yellow pages.

As he leafed through the pages with Meagan looking over his shoulder, he could hear the voice of his mother saying . . . 'looking for a beauty parlour in the yellow pages. . . . are you insane, Charlie? Why, you would need references . . . what about cleanliness? Oh, my God . . yellow pages . . . how horrible,' but Meagan did not say that.

She merely nodded as he pointed to one with a large ad, 'See, when a company takes out this large an ad, that usually means they're good, or, large, or something.'

'OK, Charlie, what do Ah care.'

He agreed to pick her up in two hours, being assured by the owner of the shop that that was sufficient time.

That was after she had inquired, indelicately, 'What do you want us to do with her?'

'Make her look great!' he responded.

She was waiting for him when he drove up, and she was not smiling as she came out and got into the Jeep. She had an expectant look on her face as she got in, sheepishly glancing at him for comment. He sat mesmerized as he viewed her with a fairly short hairdo, so stylish these days among professional women. Meagan had worn her hair long, and since it was straight as nails, it was usually stringy. While at work, she would put it into the same ponytail hairdo she had used for the past twenty years.

He looked into her eyes, filled with expectation, saying, 'Gee, you look great!'

She smiled a broad smile. 'Yeah, Ah do, don't I? Ah love it,' and then the excitement which had lain dormant broke forth. 'You know how we did it, Susie 'n me . . . that's her name . . . Susie. Well, Susie started flipping through this book filled with gorgeous models with all kinds of hairdo's, 'n then, she turned to a woman with mah colouring . . . but lots prettier . . . 'n then Ah put mah finger on that page, 'n said, 'That's the one. Kin you make me look like this?' 'n she said, "Honey" . . . that's what she called me . . . "Ah kin make you look like a movie star iffen you got the time 'n money'', so you know what Ah tole her? Well, Ah said Ah had the time 'n my boyfriend had the money. Hope you don't git mad that Ah called you mah boyfriend . . . Ah was just joking, anyhow.'

He shook his head, laughing, replying, 'The way you look now, I'd be proud to be your boyfriend.'

She smiled happily. 'What are we gonna do now? This is fun.'

He smiled at her, happily watching her basking in her newfound pleasures of indulgence. She was happy and he was happy that she was happy.

'Meagan, I want to take you out to dinner, tonight, to a beautiful place up in the foothills. It overlooks Denver, and at night it is a beautiful sight to see the entire city spread out before you, with lights twinkling like all the stars in the universe. I was there, once, several years ago.'

She was pensive. 'Were you there with a woman?'

'As a matter of fact, yes, I was there with Adelle. We had come to a real estate convention, and we went up there to eat.'

'How was she dressed?'

'I don't remember. Why?'

'Ah was just wondering.'

'You know what is next on the list of things to do? We're going to buy you some clothes . . . '

She groaned. 'Oh, Charlie, Ah feel like a kept woman, with all this money you're spending on me, 'n you ain't collect'in your share of the bargain . . not yet, anyhow.'

'I didn't know we had a bargain. Do you feel that you have to provide me with sex to repay me for everything I do for you?'

'Isn't that the way it works?' she asked, innocently.

'That's the way prostitution works, Meagan . . . money for sex. Do you consider yourself a prostitute?'

She became inflamed. 'Don't you insult me, Charlie Forester! You know Ah ain't no prostitute. Ain't neva bin 'n neva will be! Iffen Ah don't love a man, Ah don't do it!'

'I didn't say you were. I'm just trying to make a

point. Why can't I buy you things if I want to, if there are no strings attached, and there are none . . . you know that.'

'Ah didn't mean to rile you, Charlie, it's just . . . it's hard to take charity when ya proud, 'n even though Ah ain't got nuthin, Ah'm proud, 'n don't you eva forgit it.'

He smiled at her. 'And you're sassy too. Now, are you going to let me buy you a dress for tonight?'

'Iffen you want to. Ah want to look good . . . for you, Charlie. Ah want you to be proud of me when we walk in that restaurant.'

She tried on several new outfits while Charlie was sitting there watching her each time she came out of the dressing booths. She would stand in front of the mirror, turning around, and then she would look from Charlie to the salesperson. It took a consensus of all three heads nodding before she would say, 'Ah'll take it.'

When they got back to the hotel, she excused herself to go into the bathroom, muttering, 'Damn period! You picked a fine time to show up.'

He yelled at her, 'You'd better get started with bathing and dressing. We have only one bathroom in this suite, and I have to bath, too.' She yelled back at him, 'OK.'

She came out of the bathroom some time later with her bathrobe on, and as she removed it to dress, she had on only panties and a bra. She had turned her back to him, but he was surprised she had allowed this bit of immodesty. Then, he remembered she had not taken any of her dress clothes into the bathroom. She had no choice.

He had never seen her in any state of undress and he could not help but notice what a lovely trim figure she had. He felt his emotions stir within him as he looked at her, and he heard her say, softly, 'Like what you see, Charlie?'

'I have to admit that I do . . . you have a lovely figure, Meagan.'

She turned to him, smiling. 'Be patient, Charlie, it won't be long, now . . . its winding down, if you know what Ah mean.'

He picked up his clothes to go into the bathroom, passing by her, he whispered, 'I know what you mean.'

When he came out of the bathroom she was standing there waiting for him, fully dressed in new clothes from the skin up, new hairdo, and a new ambience.

She smiled, proudly. 'How do you like it, Charlie? Was it worth all that money you spent?'

He reached for her hand and as she extended hers, he brought her to the full-length mirror, with him standing behind her.

He put his arms around her and said, 'The important thing is . . . how do you like it, Meagan?'

She continued to admire herself. She placed her arms on his which encircled her, and she swayed back and forth as she replied, 'Ah love it. Ah think Ah look great. What do you think?'

'You look so good that when we walk into that restaurant, tonight, up on the side of that mountain, every man in the place will fall in love with you, and every woman will hate you out of pure envy.'

She smiled. 'Oh, Charlie, you really know how to make a woman feel good about herself.'

She turned around and kissed him, passionately, and when she was done, said, 'Now, Ah got to fix mah lipstick all ova, agin. We'd betta git outta here 'o we won't be going at all, Ah swear.'

The higher they climbed on the road to the restaurant, the more she looked back and 'ooed'. 'Oh, Charlie, it's beautiful! Just like you said it would be.'

'Have I ever lied to you?' he joked.

She took the joke seriously, as she replied, seriously, 'No! Ah'd trust you with mah life . . . Ah swear. You bin good to me, Charlie. Ah ain't neva had no man treat me like you do. You treat me like Ah'm a queen.'

He smiled. 'You are a queen, Meagan, in your kingdom.'

'But, not in yours, huh?'

He found her remark strange. 'What do you mean by that?'

She laughed. 'Noth'in! Don't pay any attention to me. Let's just have fun, tonight, before my dream ends.'

* * *

He had called ahead for reservations, asking that they be seated out on the half-enclosed balcony, and the view was spectacular from there. She looked in all directions like a child in a candy store, but she was discreet in her exclamations. She had promised herself to try to be a lady. She had even resolved to improve her English. It was not that she did not know better grammar, it was just that in an attempt to fit in with the small town mountain crowd, she did just that . . . try to fit in, and soon, it became a habit.

She spoke in moderate tones as she remarked, 'That view is quite remarkable, isn't it, Charles?'

He smiled, seeing her mischievous grin. 'Yes, Meagan, it defies human speech to describe it adequately.'

She kicked him under the table. 'Don't push your luck.'

They lingered long over the dinner. She was not sure of her table manners, so she watched his every move. Quite obviously he finished before she did, for she did not start a course until he had picked up the correct utensil. She smiled at him, and their eyes exchanged words as surely as if they were audibly spoken.

When he suggested another bottle of wine, she gave him a knowing grin, shaking her head. 'No, thank you.'

'Are you ready to return to your castle, Cinderella?'

'No, I want to stay here, for ever . . . 'pronouncing her 'r's. Then she said, 'All right, Charles. I knew this would not last for ever,' and she grinned at him.

As the Jeep wound down the curves she allowed her body to rub up against his. Finally, she moved over to his side, placing her head on his shoulder, whispering, 'So this is how women live in your world, huh?'

'Well, no . . . not exactly. We don't go out and do this every night.'

'How often did you eat out?'

'Oh, maybe three or four times a week.'

'Was Adelle a good cook?'

'I beg your pardon! Did you ask if Adelle was a good cook?'

'Uh, huh.'

He thought about it. 'I couldn't really say. I can't recall her ever cooking a meal.'

She bolted up, looking at him. 'You gotta be kidd'in. She neva cooked?'

'Do you call opening a can and heating it, cooking?'

'Lord, no! Ah mean real cook'in . . . you know . . . pots 'n pans, 'n stuff like that.

He shook his head, ashamed he had to tell her this. 'We had a cook to cook for us.'

She looked at him, incredulously. 'Jesus!' and she sat back down, saying nothing else for a while, and then, 'You know something, Charlie, you 'n me come from different worlds. Tell the truth . . . Ah don't belong in your world 'n you don't belong in mine.'

'Do you want me to get out of yours?'

She held his right arm closely. 'No . . . not yet . . . let me dream for a while longer. Do you want me to git outa yours?'

He smiled. 'Not for a while. I want to dream a little longer, too.'

She smiled, bent over and kissed him, lightly.

When they had gotten to the hotel room, she looked at him, asking, 'What'll we do now? . . . watch TV?'

She had a demure look on her face that could not be concealed. She acted like all the females of the lower species do when they come into oestrus, and search out the male of the species. He just sat on the chair by the window looking at her as she stood in the middle of the room.

'Do you want to watch TV?' he asked.

'N'oo. Ah'm not in the mood for TV.'

'What do you feel like doing?'

'Ah feel like going to bed.'

'Are you sleepy?'

'No . . . not in the least.'

'Well, I think I will go in and put my pyjamas on if that is alright with you, or, do you want the bathroom first.'

'No,' she responded quickly. 'You go first. Ah may be a while.'

After he came out in his pyjamas, she had already slipped out of her clothes, and once again stood before him in her panties and bra. This time she was facing him. She held her bathrobe in front of her as if to shield her body, but not entirely. She wanted him to see, and he looked. She said nothing as she went into the bathroom.

He heard the shower running, again. 'The second time in four hours . . . clean woman,' he thought.

When she appeared again, she stood for a moment at the bathroom door. She was wearing only a sheer nightgown which he had not seen before, and as she stood in the doorway her body was perfectly silhouetted by the lights behind her. It had the desired effect on Charlie as he lay in bed looking at her, and his emotions were now definitely stirring.

He thought to himself, 'She may act green as grass, but she is still a woman and all women are experts at this.'

She stood there long enough for the view to serve its intended purpose.

Still standing there, leaning against the door, she said, softly. 'Charlie, remember you said that if one day, Ah had real feelings for . . . you know . . . well, Charlie, Ah got them real bad . . . and if you got them, too . . . '

'But, what about your problem?'

'It's all ova . . . trust me.'

'Oh, I trust you,' and he motioned her to come to him.

She walked slowly towards his side of the bed, and as he pulled back the sheets to let her in, she slid next to him. He held her close, and she snuggled next to him. In time, their bodies became as one as long pent-up emotions in both of them burst forth in a torrent of passion. For Meagan, it was a release from years of forced self-denial against the male of the species, enforced by the tender display of a sensitive man, which she had never experienced in her entire life.

So hungry for love and affection was she, that she responded with all her being in a fashion which could only be termed as animalistic, and one which she felt embarrassed to express, at times, but unable to alter as her pent-up emotions poured forth like a Niagara of passion.

For Charlie, it was a first . . . the first time that a woman had ever given herself to him, completely, without reservation or guile, and he reached levels of euphoria unknown to him. He felt guilty, at times, as he compared Meagan's passion to Adelle's.

He was able to smile as he said to himself, 'No comparison! So this is what it is like to be with a really unselfish woman . . . a woman truly interested in pleasing you . . . only you.'

Their passion spent, they lay on their sides holding each other, their arms entwined and their hearts beating in unison. There were terms of endearment whispered, and in time, she could hear his regular and deep breathing, but she remained awake, for she was a troubled woman. As her mind went over the passionate moments just past she remembered each word spoken by both. She remembered that at the moment of sweet delight, as her arms held him close, she had whispered, 'Oh, Charlie, I love you,' to which he had responded, 'Oh, Meagan.'

He did not utter the words, 'I love you,' and she was aware of it. Was it merely an oversight on his part, the words obscured in the mist of passion, or, did he not love her, at least, not enough to tell her so?

She turned this over in her mind, still holding him, still hearing him breathe the deep breathing of sleep. She was not a dumb woman in spite of her unsophisticated country background. On the contrary, she was of better-than-average intelligence, and she embarked on a psychological study of the situation, although she would not have recognized it from that viewpoint. As she pondered his words of omission, those words so sacred to a woman, she wondered, why should she even believe that he loved her?

Simply because he had been kind and generous and solicitous of her welfare, that was not true love. You could be those things with a perfect stranger whom you had just met. Yet, he had indicated to her in so many small ways that he cared for her a lot, but, then, that is not love either. Had she misread the signals? She felt she loved him. He had filled a huge vacuum in her life that was just waiting to be filled. But, did he have a vacuum in his life? How could he? Only two weeks ago he was in love with another woman, or, he thought he was.

No man can go from one love to another in just two weeks. If he can, he is not worth loving, for he could switch his emotions again in two more weeks. No, he is not ready for love, again . . . not yet . . . not to her, or anyone else.

That is what she thought as her brain sought out some sort of rationale to explain the matter. What could she do but hold on to the tenuous cord which bound them? She knew that once he climbed into that Jeep and headed out of town, her dreams would go with him . . . unless, he came back some day.

And with her rationalization now complete, she, too, began the heavy breathing of deep sleep, as she tightened her grip on his arms. At least, she consoled herself, I have him now. In his sleep, he responded. She smiled as a tear slipped from her eyes and found refuge on her pillow, and she held him closer.

8

In keeping with her country habits she was awake first in the morning. She wanted a cup of coffee, and looking around in what she thought would be a futile search, she saw the coffee kit on the built-in room refrigerator and microwave. She carefully slipped out of bed, but not before she stood for a moment looking at her sleeping lover. She smiled. If only she could have him for keeps . . . she wanted him for her own.

In a few moments the perking of the coffee pot awakened her lover and he moaned, 'What time is it?'

She went to the bed and sat by him, leaning over him, whispering, 'It's time to get up . . . there is plough'in to be done on the back forty . . . '

He held her close. 'You plough it . . . I'm going to stay in bed for a while.'

'If you don't get outta bed Ah'm coming in with you,' she teased. He dragged her in, and coffee was delayed for quite some time.

As they sat in the hotel coffee shop having a well-deserved heavy breakfast, she began to play with her food towards the end, and he noticed it, so he asked, 'What's on your mind? You seem to be deep in thought.'

'Oh, Ah was jus think'in. You'll be leaving here in a day 'o two, 'n Ah'll neva see you agin . . . ' and her voice trailed off. 'Can't ya stay fer a while longer?' she pleaded.

He had never mentioned the cruise to Ambergris Cay to her. As a matter of fact, other than Adelle, he had mentioned nothing to her of his real life, so he spent two cups of coffee, time wise, to tell her of the trip, of his friends, and the fact he did not have a roommate, as yet, as far as he knew.

She listened in silence, and as he finished, she said, wistfully, 'Sounds like real fun.'

His eyes lit up, and he said, excitedly, 'Why don't you come with us? You be my roommate . . . come on, Meagan.'

She smiled, shaking her head. 'No'oo! Ah don't think that would be a good idea . . . besides. Ah hafta work fer a liv'in. Ah cain't git off like them rich lady friends 'o yurn.'

He picked his words carefully. 'Meagan, I'll fix it so you won't lose any money by not working . . . I can do it.'

'Charlie, Ah'm beginn'in to feel more and more like a prostitute . . . the more you talk . . . the more Ah feel. 'Sides, Ah would be embarrassed to be with yore edjicated friends, you know that, 'n Ah don't enjoy be'in embarrassed. Ah got mah pride. Maybe, the best thing you kin do is to git in that Jeep 'n go outta mah life 'fore mah heart gits broken in two. When Ah git mah baby back, Ah'll be all right, Charlie.'

* * *

She was unusually quiet on the trip back to Mountain View and her world. Her euphoria over the anticipated release of her daughter, Erin, was dampened by the certain loss of her friend and, now, lover. He made a few attempts to engage her in conversation, but he failed, for she was deep in thought.

Finally, she asked, 'What else do Ah hafta do with those lawyers so Ah kin git mah daughter back? Just tell me 'n Ah will do it. Ah don't want to bother you any more, Charlie. You bin real good to me 'n Ah appreciate it. Ah jus wish Ah could do more for you, but,' and she smiled at him, 'you got all Ah got to give . . . there ain't no more.'

He pulled the Jeep off the narrow two-lane road and stopped on the shoulder. She sat on the opposite side, tears coming down her face, and she turned away so he could not see her cry, saying, 'Ah tole ya not to look at me when Ah'm crying, Charlie.'

He pulled her over, and she came willingly. She knew she had no more fight in her where he was concerned.

There had been total capitulation on her part.

He put his arm around her and she cuddled close to him, crying, 'What's go'in to happen to me, Charlie? Ah cain't seem to git mah life in order. Just when Ah should be the happiest woman in the world, Ah'm gitt'in more and more miserable.'

He did not answer. What could he say? He held her close for a long time while she sobbed softly. The tough and mean woman he had met just a week ago was now a soft, tender, and vulnerable female. She was right. It would have been better if he had never entered her life . . . but . . . he had not planned it.

'Damn that Adelle! She is to blame for this.'

He stroked her hairdo . . . her new, stylish hairdo, of which she was so proud. He tilted her face up and he said, 'Meagan, I wish there was something I could offer you, now, but,' he said soulfully, 'there isn't. Can't we just let it ride for a while . . . maybe something will develop . . . who knows?'

She sat upright, looking him in the eye. 'What are you try'in to say? Are you tell'in me that something might develop. What does that mean, Charlie? That you might fall in love with me? You know, Ah don't know if you were pay'in attention, or not, but last night, Ah tole you that Ah loved you. That wasn't just passion talking, Charlie . . . it was real talk . . . honest talk.'

He answered softly, 'I was paying attention, Meagan . . . I heard it, and I wish I could have said the words you wanted to hear, but I can't . . . not now, anyway. Jesus Christ, just two weeks ago, I thought I was in love with another woman. My feelings are still bruised. I'm not sure of anything just now . . . '

She held him close. 'Ah know . . . Ah understand . . . Ah'm will'in to settle for what Ah've got now. At least, when you leave, Ah'll have some pleasant memories. For the past few years, Ah ain't had nuthin but misery memories . . . that's all.'

'I wish I could give you more,' he repeated.

She moved back to the other side. 'Let's go, Charlie . . . Ah got to git back 'n see if Ah still have a job.'

He drove off and for a long time, said nothing, then, 'Meagan, you have to get a telephone in that apartment so I can call you from time to time . . . '

'Ah don't want to talk to you after you leave here. Once you leave, Ah got to git started on forgit'in you, Charlie. 'Sides, it's just another expense. Ah don't need a telephone! There ain't nobody Ah want to talk to.'

'Yes, there is. The attorneys will have to talk to you from time to time, to give you progress reports . . . to ask information, to give you the date of Erin's release so you can be there to meet her . . . '

She bolted up. That got her attention. 'You're right, Ah guess, but Ah'll pay fer it, not you . . . some way.'

He smiled at the resurgence of her independence. 'How do you know I don't want to call you now and then?'

'To tell me what? How much fun you 'n yore rich friends are having in Amber . . . whatever that place is . . . '

'How do you know it won't be to tell you how much I miss you?'

She looked at him, sharply. 'You've never lied to me, yet, Charlie . . . don't start now.'

'You think I won't miss you? You're wrong, Meagan.'

She became pensive. 'Ah had a puppy dog when Ah was young. He died. Ah missed him, too. Thirty days after you leave here, Charlie, you won't even remember mah name . . . you'll say Ah sure had a good time in that hotel in Denver with . . . what's her name? She was a good lay . . . she sure was . . . wish Ah could remember her name . . . maybe Ah'll go back to Mountain View someday 'n visit that little filly agin . . . '

He was sharp with her. 'Stop it, Meagan! That is not the way it is, and you know damn well it isn't!'

'If you say so, Charlie,' and she became quiet.

They had arrived in Mountain View in time for her to go on her shift at twelve noon. She hated to go, but she had to. She knew there would be stares at the new hairdo . . . questions about . . . 'Where ya bin . . . have fun?'

She toughened up, replying, 'Ah ain't had so much fun in all mah life.'

* * *

Charlie showed up at seven for the evening meal. She smiled as she saw him come in. She had lectured to herself all day. Why should she be angry with him . . . just because he had not fallen in love with her as she had with him. He had been honest with her. Are there any more insidious words on this planet than, 'I love you,' not said in earnest . . . from the heart?

She picked up the glass of water, put a professional smile on her face and walked over to his booth.

'Evening, sir. The spec'l fer today is chicken fried steak, mashed potatoes with brown gravy, and a crappy, dried up salad. Six ninety–five'

He smiled at her. 'Sounds good to me.'

As usual, he waited for her until she got off at nine, and they walked to her apartment. He was surprised. She put her arm in his, but not saying much.

He could see she was reflective, so he asked, 'How did it go today?'

'It was OK. The otha girls loved the hairdo. Some of them love you too, Charlie. They tole me when Ah finished with you, to send you to them.'

'And what did you say to that?'

She smiled, mischievously. 'Ah tole them when Ah finished with you, there wouldn't be much left to fight ova.'

'Is that true?'

'Just wait until we git in that apartment . . . you'll see. Ah figure Ah might as well enjoy you while Ah got you, Charlie. Ah guess you'll be leav'in in the morn'in, huh?'

'Not necessarily.'

'No?'

'Not unless you want me to.'

'Ah jus tole you Ah intend to enjoy you while ah got you. Why should Ah run you off?'

As she entered the apartment, she started to go to the bathroom for her nightly ritual, but she heard a telephone ring in her apartment. She looked at the newly installed phone, and then, at Charlie, and she looked again at the telephone. Who could be calling her?

No one knew she had a phone, so she said, 'You'd betta answer that phone. It cain't be fer me,' and she proceeded into the bathroom.

She could hear him talk to someone . . . she didn't know who, but he mentioned things about the boat trip, so she assumed he had called his friends and given them the new number. She turned on the shower and could hear no more of the conversation, nor did she want to. It was not of her world.

As they were having a glass of wine from the newly-acquired stock brought from Denver, she said, 'You know, Charlie, this wine is beginning to grow on me. Ah may turn into a wine head afta you leave. Funny how easy it is to form a habit. Same thing about having a man in mah bed. Ah forgot how much fun it was . . . guess Ah'll have to find me a replacement when you leave . . . ' and she waited for the response.

These were not careless words, emitted without design . . . no, they were one of the main tools in the female arsenal . . . jealousy! And, the words had the desired effect on him, for they burned in the part of the brain reserved for jealousy. The thought of another man in bed with her offended him greatly. He said nothing for a while, for he was forming a response which they could both live with.

'Are you trying to get me mad?'

'Why should that make you mad? Ah'm not yore wife! You have no hold on me. Do you expect me to be faithful to you? Will you be faithful to me? For how long? A week . . . or two,' and she coolly sipped her wine, as she looked at him over the glass.

'All I know is, the thought of another man with you makes me mad as hell . . . just the thought of it.'

She smiled. 'You men! Got to feel like you own it, don't you?'

'Yes, that's the way we are.'

She smiled at him. 'Ah guess Ah don't hafta explain to you, Charlie, there's only one way a man kin own it . . . '

He nodded, looking at the floor. 'Yes, I see your point.'

She emptied her glass. 'Well, ah'm going to bed . . . coming?'

'You bet your life.'

It should be noted that only one week had elapsed since he first arrived in the little village, tired from a long day's drive and looking for a place to rest his weary head. It was fate, he thought, as well as hunger, that led him to the cafe/bar where Meagan worked as a waitress. Little did he know how soon and how deep he would be enmeshed in her life and she in his, so fast does the fickle finger of fate work. He had begun this odyssey as a means of purging any and all memories of Adelle from his mind, conscious and subconscious, and to that extent, the odyssey had been a success. Only in rare moments of pent-up frustration and anger, did he still curse Adelle for her treachery.

While he lay in Meagan's arms during those moments of sheer delight, he blessed Adelle in absentia, for if she had not practised her treachery, well, he would not be enjoying the fruits of his misfortune, and he told Meagan of this, while exchanging terms of endearment, during those tender moments. She nodded in agreement, knowingly, secure in the knowledge that each day he spent with her only made the parting more difficult for him, so sure was she now of her quarry.

He begged her once again to consider going on the cruise with him, and once again, she refused. The cruise was enemy territory to her. It was not of her world. She would not be in control, and here, in her world, she was in control of her man.

To the questions from his father and mother as to the progress being made to expunge Adelle from his mind, he replied that he was making considerable progress. It was true. He hardly thought of her anymore.

'How much longer do you think you will be gone?' asked his mother.

'Not too much longer. Perhaps a week,' he responded. 'I need to get back soon to prepare for the cruise.'

Meagan heard all these conversations. From the conversations, alone, she was able to piece together what was going on in his world . . when he would be leaving, and she spun her web accordingly. Her love was growing deeper day by day, to the point that she knew she could never forget him, and that concerned her. She did not have him for her own . . . not yet! She knew that. He had still not mentioned the magic word as yet, although in moments of passion she felt sure it was forthcoming, but she did not want to hear it then. Many men said that . . . then! She was smart enough to know that. She wanted to hear it in the cool light of dawn, but she didn't.

She was ecstatic when Charlie ran to the cafe that day to tell her that Monica de la Rosa had called with great news. Erin would be allowed out from prison, on parole, while her case was being appealed . . . the appeal her public defenders should have filed for her, but didn't. Meagan could not suppress a scream of delight as he informed her of the call.

'But, when? How soon? Oh, Charlie! Mah dreams have come true.'

'It will still be a month or so. Miss de la Rosa said it would take that long for the paperwork to go through the system.'

'A month? Oh, well! Ah bin wait'in fer years. Ah kin wait another month . . . but . . . oh, Charlie, you won't be here when Erin comes home . . . oh, you have to wait fer that . . . you gotta.'

He shook his head. 'I'm sorry, but I can't . . . I'm sorry.'

'But, she's got to thank you in person, Charlie.'

'I'll come back to see her . . . and you . . . I promise.'

'You gotta come back, Charlie . . . you just got to.'

'I told you I promise I will.'

'Ah'm holding ya to that promise. It's the only thing Ah ever made you swear to. You swear, Charlie?'

'I swear it.'

There! It was done. She now knew that he would come back to see her . . . and Erin. He was a man of his word. He would not lie to her. He would enter her world, again, someday. She was content to wait, hoping that nature would take its course.

The remainder of the week was spent towards that end. Never had a man been treated so well by a woman. She saw to that. She waited on him hand and foot. She fed him. She washed his clothes. She gave him love. If this seems natural to those to whom this is a way of life, remember, in his world, no woman, not even his wealthy, aristocratic mother, had ever cooked his meals, washed his clothes, and loved him without reservation, withholding nothing. He felt this was the way it should be in both worlds, but then . . .

* * *

Meagan became more sombre as the appointed day came close. Even his solemn promise to return did not help. Her man was leaving her. She was now deeply in love. There was no turning back. If she could not have him, she wanted no other. She felt that at her age she could live without a man as she had done for the past few years. She would devote her life and her efforts to helping Erin rebuild her shattered life. Hopefully, Erin would find some good man who could accept her as she was. She was still a beauty. Some man would love her, and then, children . . . her grandchildren. Sure, that was it. She would not have time for a man in her life. She had to take care of her grandchildren.

But, for now, on the last night, she had asked Charlie to take her back to Denver. She wanted to relive those magic moments, again.

'You've done so much fer me, Charlie . . . just do this one more thing fer me.' She became coquettish . . . 'Ah promise ya you won't regret it,' she said, seductively.

'I thought you told me, before, that you had no more to give,' he teased.

'Oh, girls always have some secrets they keep fer the big battle,' she cooed.

He found her term 'big battle' interesting. 'Is this the big battle?'

'Charlie . . . ah'm fight'in fer mah life.'

'But, how will you get back home?'

'Ah'll take the bus.'

* * *

Their last night together was a mixture of rapture and sadness, and each party knowing that it might very well be just that . . . their last night together. Meagan, filled with love and apprehension, tried to offer a profusion of the first and a concealment of the latter, and she did a good job of it.

Over coffee the next morning their attentions were turned to the practical and realistic side of life.

'We have to talk money, Meagan. I can see that our involvement will cost you some money, money you can't afford to spend. You've got to let me help you financially . . . you've got to . . . '

She shook her head. 'There you go agin, Charlie . . . making me feel more 'n more like a prostitute. Ah don't intend to be a kept woman . . . not yourn 'o anybody else's. Ah ain't sell'in it, Charlie . . . Ah did it 'cause ah love you . . . that's why!'

'Please don't take it that way. I'm talking about things like the telephone bills, the bus fare. You'll need money, extra money, when Erin comes home. She will need clothes and things like that.'

She became pensive. 'Ah'll make out on mah own, but thanks, anyway.'

'Dammit, Meagan, I won't take no for an answer! You can't stop me from sending you money . . . you stubborn little . . . '

'And you cain't make me take it, you stubborn ole male. . . . '

He could not be deterred. 'I'll send you a thousand dollars a month. I save more than that by not being married to Adelle.'

'Ah'll just send it back!'

As promised, he would mail her a cheque each month for one thousand dollars. Each month she mailed back to him a cheque for eight hundred dollars. It is strange about money. It is difficult to look it in the face and ignore it.

As they stood in front of the bus station that morning,

oblivious to the stares of passers by, they embraced without shame. Their goodbyes were soft and tender, each promising to remember the other, no matter what happened in their lives.

As they made their final parting, with outstretched hands, she said, with tears blurring her vision, 'Remember, Charlie, Ah love you . . . for real.'

He replied . . . 'I'll remember . . . I promise.'

And so we leave them on the last day of this part of the odyssey. As she had planned, the web was spun even tighter and her quarry was even more confused than he thought he was. His mind played with all kinds of scenarios as he thought of ways to keep her in his life, with his mind going from the ridiculous to the sublime, even to practising the words, 'Mother, I would like you to meet my wife, Meagan. 'Oh, my God, he thought to himself . . . 'that would be interesting.'

9

Charlie had driven straight through back to his home, making no attempt to call Meagan on her newly-acquired telephone. He purposely did not call her. He wanted time away from her to think the thing out. As his mind reviewed the happenings of the past few weeks, he was incredulous at his actions. Not only had he become involved with another woman just days after he swore he hated all women, worse than that, he was enamoured of her. She was in sharp contrast to all the other women he had ever known – perhaps that was the answer, he thought. In her earthy way, with her unpolished demeanour, she had charmed him, unwittingly he felt, for he was convinced she could have gone on living without him. She never really pursued him, not at first, and he had not intended to pursue her, even now; he was not sure he wanted to. Was it fate? Are there some forces beyond our control which arrange these little scenarios for us mortals, to test our mettle? He wondered. He was sure of one thing, though . . . he missed every bone in her earthy, unpolished body, and that perplexed and distressed him.

What would come of that relationship if he did allow it to develop? Could she ever fit into his life. He pictured those evenings in his parents' home, with his mother and father seated at the huge dining room table, and he and Meagan sitting there with them, partaking of the evening meal, with all its formal amenities. And as the conversation turned to the arts, or to music, or even the innocuous events of the day, what would Meagan do to participate in the discussions? Would she just sit there . . . embarrassed for herself, and could he just sit there embarrassed by her, and for her? He could see his mother staring her imperious stare at the unpolished creature before her, her social sensitivities stretched to the breaking point. And his father . . . more realistic than the wife, attempting to engage the poor girl in some conversation commensurate with her level.

He shuddered as he thought of these things. It was an impossible situation, he concluded, as he entered the private drive to his parent's stately home, the place he had called home for so many years.

His mother and father were delighted to see him, and the mother was most anxious to resume her psychological examination of him to determine if he had exorcised Adelle from his mind as yet, and she began hardly before he had seated himself in the library where they had convened for his home-coming.

'Charles, dear . . . how have you been? I've been so worried about you . . . your state of mind . . . '

The father, always the mediator, cautioned, 'Now, now, Agatha, please let the boy relax for a while before you start delving into his mind. Did you enjoy yourself, Charlie? See anything interesting? Oh, don't even bother to answer that . . . just making conversation,' and he smiled at his son, while looking for traces of strain in his eyes.

Knowing he had to give some account of where he had been and what he had been doing for the past three weeks, he gave them a rambling and disjointed account of his odyssey, of his stay in that quaint little mountain village, of the colourful characters he had met. He told them of his encounter with Elmo and Blanche and the dog.

Even his mother laughed when he told them of Blanche's threat against his life if he made any amorous advances towards her. 'Oh, Charles, I can't believe she could have been so presumptuous to even think . . . how quaint those people must be! It is difficult to believe they live in the same country as we do.'

Those words burned in him, as he thought of Meagan. She was one of those quaint people.

He turned to his father, asking, 'Have I been missed at the office. I really hate taking all this time off, and after the cruise, I intend to . . . '

His mother, at the sound of the word 'cruise', exclaimed, 'Oh, Charles, I almost forgot, Arnie Broadhurst wanted you to call him as soon as you got back . . . please do, so he won't think that I have forgotten to tell you.'

He rose, excusing himself, saying, 'I'll call him right now, Mother,' and he headed upstairs to use the phone, with his father calling after him, 'You could use the phone here in the library. It would not bother Mother and me. We're leaving, anyway, and Charlie, don't worry about the office. We've assigned those projects you were working on to Bill Hudson. He's a good man . . . he can handle them. Go on your cruise . . . enjoy yourself, and when you get back, well, then . . . '

He stopped his father as his mother went out of the room, and he sheepishly asked, 'Have you heard anything from Adelle? Did the legal matter work out OK?, or did she change the rules in the middle of the game? She's famous for that!'

The father shook his head. 'No, she settled for what you two had agreed on, so we concluded the matter. She did ask me how you were,' he added.

Charlie snickered. 'As if she cares . . . the bitch!'

The father put his arms around his son. 'Try not to be too bitter, Charlie. Remember the old adage – "hate can consume the vessel containing it." '

He shrugged. 'I'll remember.'

He looked at his watch as he entered his bedroom, intending to use the telephone there. He wanted privacy, for he intended to call Meagan . . . just to see how she was. He had made up his mind to be casually objective with her . . . nothing gushy or intimate . . . no! The phone rang seven or eight times, and then he remembered she was at work. He started to call her at the cafe, but he knew this would embarrass her, so, instead he dialled the number of Arnie Broadhurst.

'Hello,' from Peg Broadhurst.

'Hi, Peg . . . Charlie Forester . . . I'm back.'

'Oh, Charlie, I'm so glad to hear from you . . . we have to talk.'

'I know Arnie is looking for me, my mother tells me.'

'Uh, huh, he is, he wants to go over the details of the cruise with you, but I need to talk to you about your roommate.'

'What about him? Who is he?'

'Charlie I don't want to talk about this over the phone. I want to be able to look you in the eye to test your reaction.'

'What are you talking about, Peg?'

'Not now, Charlie! Besides, Arnie isn't here now. He has called for a meeting of the group for tomorrow . . . lunch at the yacht club . . . can you make it?'

'Well, sure . . . tomorrow . . . at noon?'

'Uh huh . . . see you then, and . . . Charlie . . . try to have an open mind about this . . . '

'About what?'

'See you at noon, tomorrow . . . bye.'

As he hung up the phone, he said to himself, 'Damn, but that Peg is being evasive about something.'

It was nearly ten thirty in the evening before he had gotton back to his bedroom. His mother and father had lingered long after dinner, and as they had more than the usual cup of coffee, they continued to ask him details of his trip. He supplied them with innocuous answers, but never did he give them any hint of Meagan, and to his mother's query . . .' What did you do with your evenings?' he replied, 'Practised my celestial navigation in preparation for the cruise.'

That was half true, but his mother exclaimed, 'That doesn't sound too much like fun,' and in her usual end – run type of interrogation, she got to the main thrust of her interrogation, 'Did you meet any young women?'

He could not lie to her. Not a bald face lie, anyway, so he offered, 'Yes, a few, but all of the local genre . . . quite colourful, too.'

He did not usually speak in stilted terms, but he knew his mother did, and he did it for her sake. Then, in an attempt to bring the conversation to a close, he volunteered the story of the Denver hooker who had hustled him, including a description of her price list.

His father howled, asking, 'Did you bring one of the price lists home with you? I'd love to see it!'

The mother exclaimed, 'Alexander! Please!' and turning to her son, 'Charles, I certainly hope you did not consort with such common trash.'

He smiled. 'I assure you, Mother, I did not avail myself of her services . . . she was much too expensive.'

'Oh, Charles . . . how tacky of you!' she laughed.

* * *

He looked at his watch, again. Ten thirty-five. Allowing for the one hour time difference, it would be nine thirty-five in her little apartment. He felt she must be home by now – 'Probably taking her bath,' he mused, He dialled her number.

'Hello . . .'

'Meagan, it's Charlie.'

'Oh, Charlie . . . Ah'm so glad you called.'

'You sound short of breath.'

'Ah know . . . Ah was in the bathroom. Ah thought it might be you, so Ah ran to answer it.' She laughed. 'Ah'm standing here in mah bathrobe, half dripping . . .'

'Do you have anything under the bathrobe?'

'Uh uh . . . just wet skin.'

'Oh, God . . . Meagan . . . I miss you.'

'Ah miss you, too . . . Ah'm miserable, Charlie. Iffen it wasn't fer mah baby comin' home, soon, Ah'd die from loneliness.'

'Have you heard from Erin, or, the attorneys?'

'Yeah . . . she will be out in about two weeks.'

'That's good. I know you're happy about that.'

'Oh, yes. Iffen you was here with me, Ah'd be in heaven, Charlie, Ah swear.'

'I wish we were together right now. I miss you, Meagan.'

'Charlie . . . do you miss me, or it? You know what Ah mean?'

'I miss you both . . . you and it!'

She giggled. 'Normally, Ah'd git mad iffen a man tole

me that, but Ah'm not mad at you, Charlie. Ah don't know iffen Ah could git mad at you, anymore . . . Ah love you so much, but don't push your luck 'cause Ah won't let no man mistreat me . . . never agin!'

'I have no intention of mistreating you, Meagan.'

'All Ah ask of you, Charlie, is . . . be honest with me. Don't lie to me about how you feel.'

'I've never lied to you about that. If I were a liar, I could easily have told you I loved you just to get you into bed.'

She laughed. 'You didn't have to. Ah took care 'o that. When will Ah see you, agin? Are you still com'in when Erin gits out of prison?'

'I promised you I would come, but not at the moment she gets out. I will probably be on the cruise . . . '

'Oh, Charlie. Ah won't be able to talk to you when you're on that ole boat.'

'Sure, you can. That boat has a satellite phone on it. I can call you from it.'

'Will you? You promise?'

'I promise. Now, it is time for bed, for you and me, so I'll sign off. Meagan?' he asked, softly.

'Yeah?'

'I miss you . . . I really do.'

'Charlie . . . ah love you . . . Ah really do.'

'I know, Meagan . . . goodnight.'

'Goodnight, Charlie.'

He placed the receiver down gently on the base, and so did Agatha Forester as she placed hers down. She shuddered from remorse of conscience at having listened to her son's phone call and from the words she had heard from this uncultured person on the other end. She could justify her listening in under the guise of a 'mothers duty', but the words she had just heard had shocked her into near apoplexy, as her husband walked out of his dressing room just as she replaced the receiver.

'Who was that? I didn't hear the phone ring.'

She thought fast. 'I called for the right time. I wanted to set my alarm clock,' and she picked up the clock.

He looked at her. 'You look pale. Do you feel alright, my dear?'

'I did have a weak spell for a moment, but I am all right, now.'

'Can I get you anything?'

'Perhaps . . . an asprin. I think I will have a difficult time going to sleep tonight.'

And she did. Agatha Forester had heard words that distressed her no end. She might be imperious, she might be haughty, but she was still a mother, and she loved her only child, Charles, and the conversation she had just intruded on gave her reason for concern . . . deep concern. Who was this creature who talked like a hillbilly? What was she to her son. The references to 'it' distressed her, for she was not sure what 'it' was, although she thought she did, and it made her shudder. Had her son been intimate with this wench? She could forgive him for that, for, after all, he was a man . . . a man who had just been through a traumatic experience caused by another wench, although a more erudite one. She began to question her son's ability to distinguish wenches from nice girls.

No wonder in days of old, marriages were arranged. Marriage was far too serious a business to leave to people who were merely in love, or, thought they were. Did family background not count anymore? Were not genes more important than passion? She thought of herself. Why, she had descended from generations of cultured, accomplished people . . . solid as a rock. People with character.

This consoling thought helped her relax to the point that she felt she could sleep. She could hear her husband snoring in the next bedroom. They had long ago, in a moment of mutual abandonment, gone their separate ways in that part of their lives. He convinced her he had no more interest in sex and since she never had, they both accepted the arrangement with grace. She felt it would be best for their marriage. Since he had gotten all he had bargained for in the union, he readily agreed, and he would search for fulfilment in other places and in other ways.

As she pulled her satin sheets up to her chin, she resolved to keep the stolen conversation she had just monitored to herself, not even divulging it to her husband, for he would only chastise her for her deceit, and she could not stand being chastised by anyone.

His reaction would have been characteristic of him. 'Surely, you don't begrudge the boy a roll in the hay, after what he's been through.' And, besides he would not understand her concern . . . only mothers understood these matters.

* * *

Charlie walked into the yacht club feeling rather chipper. He felt his conversation with Meagan had gone fairly well. She had professed her love for him, while he had merely told her he missed her. He did, too, but the words, 'I love you' were not in his vocabulary just now. He saw the group already at table. The men were in business suits and the ladies were in more casual dress, since none of them worked. He saw a blonde woman sitting next to Peg Broadhurst, a gorgeous woman. He looked at her open-mouthed, as he got closer. She was a truly beautiful woman, with eyes as blue as the sky, full lips, and perfect complexion. Her hair was long and flowing, the kind models have who advertise expensive shampoos.

She smiled as she saw him coming, and Peg motioned to him to come to her, as she introduced them, 'Amanda Winters . . . Charlie Forester,' and as she extended her hand, Charlie felt a thrill at the touch of her cool skin.

'Charlie,' said Peg, 'You sit next to Amanda so you two can get to know each other, since you will be roommates on the cruise.'

Charlie was not sure he had heard correctly, so he, without thinking, turned to Peg, 'I bet your pardon . . . '

Peg said, proudly, 'That is what I wouldn't tell you on the phone, yesterday. Amanda has agreed to come on the cruise with us, and I thought you would be delighted to share a stateroom with a former third runner-up in the Miss America pageant . . . '

Charlie smiled a weak smile. What could he say . . . now? But, he thought plenty, 'That Peggy Broadhurst must be crazy. She has done some way out things in her time, but, this . . . '

As Arnie went over the details of the trip, Charlie was forced to concentrate on the details being discussed, but every minute or so he would look at the beautiful woman sitting at his side, and say to himself, 'Geez . . . I can't believe this is happening to me.'

Kate Russell, the young engaged girl rose, and looking at the other two women, asked, 'Anybody going to join me in the little girl's room?' to which Amanda Winters responded, 'Yes, I think I will,' and as Peg rose to join them, Charlie kicked her under the table motioning her to stay.

The two women were hardly out of earshot, when he turned to Peg in a fit of distemper, asking, 'Are you crazy? Have you lost your mind, Peg Broadhurst?' Arnie smiled, saying to his wife, 'I told you he would not take this well.'

The tax lawyer, the young engaged man, Bill Morton, looked sheepishly at Peg and Arnie for some response.

'Now, Charlie, what's the big deal? I thought it would work out well. You're in the process of getting a divorce, and so is Amanda. You can commiserate together . . . '

'But, two people of the opposite sex . . . two complete strangers, sharing the same small stateroom . . . are you crazy? Did she agree to this?' demanded an outraged Charlie.

'Charlie, I'm not suggesting you two cohabitate, for God's sake. This is the twentieth century, not Victorian times. Do you mean to tell me that you can't overcome your Neanderthal yearnings just for two or three weeks. Amanda is not bothered by this. Why should you be? After all, you have a private bath.'

The two women were returning from their sojourn to the john, and Peg motioned for Charlie to desist, with, 'We can thrash this out, later.'

The meeting continued with all the logistical details being put in place by the skipper, Arnie.

'We'll work in two-person shifts, eight hours at a time. Of course, the logical assignments would be for each couple to be the active crew for that shift. That means we have to work as a team. Now, my ketch is not all that complicated to sail, since all the winches are mechanical . . . '

Amanda raised her hand, 'What does that mean?'

Arnie looked a little exasperated as he explained, 'It means you won't have to strain one of your pretty little muscles . . . the winches are all electric . . . '

'Oh! That's nice' she cooed.

Arnie continued. 'We'll spend all the spare time we have in the next week preparing for the trip. That means we'll go out sailing every chance we get so each couple can learn working together as a team. It is essential that you know what everything is and how it works. Charlie and Bill . . . you two guys have sailed her before, so you know what to do. The SAT – NAV will give us ongoing readouts of longitude and latitude, so you will always know where you are at any time . . . '

Amanda gave her best little girl look, asking, 'What are longitude and latitude?'

Arnie gave her an exasperated look. 'You don't need to know that, now. Charlie will explain that to you later.'

She gave Charlie a warm smile. 'Charlie, I guess I have to depend on you for guidance.'

He gave her a weak smile.

Arnie spoke up. 'OK, gang. That is it for now. Everybody be at the boat at four o'clock. We're going sailing.

As they walked out, Peg tugged Charlie's arm, taking him off to the side. 'See, Charlie . . . it won't be so bad. and, let's face it, most men would gladly give up one testicle to spend a couple of weeks with her in a small stateroom. What do you have to complain about?'

He shook his head, answering, 'Why do I feel like this is going to be a disaster?'

Peg laughed. 'That's up to you, boy. I've done all I can to help you over your trauma. The rest is up to you. If Amanda can't help you get over Adelle, who the hell can?'

'I don't recall asking you for any help.'

Peg smiled and gave no answer, just throwing him a pursed-lip kiss as she got into her car.

Charlie drove to the company office for a few hours of work, but he could hardly concentrate so upset was he by Peg's foolish act, as he viewed it. He decided to call Arnie to get his version of the matter before he made his decision about the trip.

'Now, Charlie, ole buddy, don't blame me for that hair-brained idea. I learned years ago that my woman could come up with some wild schemes now and then. Why, I could tell you some things that happened in our bedroom that would curl your hair . . . '

'But, damn it, Arnie, you're still the captain of the boat, are you not?'

'Sure, I am,' he laughed, 'when Peg is not on board. Aw, come on , Charlie . . . it's just a two week trip at most. As Peg said, we're not telling you and Amanda you have to have a lovey-dovey relationship . . . keep it business. As a matter of fact, Amanda had stipulated that there will be no hanky-panky. She hates men right now as much as you hate women. You should be perfectly compatible in an inverse way,' he joked.

Charlie said goodbye, and as he put the phone down, he lamented, 'Hell, I feel like cancelling I can't see sharing that little stateroom for two weeks with a spoiled, self-centred, egotistical, beautiful, desirable, gorgeous creature that I hate. but, if I did, who would navigate for them if the electronics went out. I promised Arnie I'd go, so . . . I guess I'll go.'

'But, I don't even know this woman. I've only spent one hour with her. What is she really like? I would really like for us to get to know each other better before we leave on this cruise. I guess I'll ask her out to dinner so we can get acquainted. That's it. I'll call her. What's her number? Where does she live? Guess, Peg has her number,' which she did.

As he dialled the number, he cleared his throat. He was a little nervous. He hadn't called a girl for a date in years. He didn't even remember how to go about it.

After the fourth ring, he heard a soft voice say, 'Hello.'

'Amanda?'

'May I ask who is calling, please?'

He responded, cheerfully, 'It's Charlie Forester . . . '

'Well, well, I was wondering how long it would take you to call me, Charlie.'

'What do you mean? I don't understand.'

'Never mind. What can I do for you?'

'Well, I was thinking it would be a good idea if we got to know each other better before the cruise. I was wondering if you would like to go out to dinner tonight? We could either eat at the yacht club after we get through sailing, or, we can get dressed and make it a little more formal . . . '

'No, thank you. I think you had better understand one thing, Charlie . . . this trip is going to be platonic . . . no cootchy-cootchy, do you understand, so if that is what you have in mind, forget it. I think if I agreed to have dinner with you, it might send the wrong signals, and I would not want you to get the wrong signals. I hope you understand . . . goodbye, Charlie.'

He was incensed. Never in his entire life had any woman turned him down for a date with such lack of feeling and compassion. After all, there was a proper way to do that, and most women were good at it.

They were taught so by their mothers at puberty, with the words, 'The ability to say no to a boy and still keep him interested is one of the greatest weapons in the female arsenal.'

Charlie was so angry that when a young secretary came into his office with a routine question, he was rude to her, and she left in tears. He hated all women now, again . . . damn that Adelle . . . damn that Amanda. He thought of Meagan . . . dear unpolished, countrified Meagan . . . so sincere . . . so true.

He was tempted to call Peg and tell her of her friend's actions, but he was embarrassed to do so. He hated women even more than ever.

10

Charlie could hardly wait until that day's practice session. He was anxious to see how Amanda would react to him after her insulting rejection of him earlier in the day. As the group walked to the marina slip, he could see Amanda and Peg walking together, laughing and joking, with Arnie, Bill, and Kate bringing up the rear.

Upon seeing him it was Amanda who first spoke, smiling a warm smile in Charlie's direction, and telling the group, 'There's my bunkmate, Charlie. Ready to hit the blue waters, Charlie?'

He was amazed at her complete personality reversal from a few hours earlier. To add insult to injury, as the old adage goes, she had the temerity to place her arm in his as they walked to the boat.

Peg smiled to herself, and walking over to her husband, observed, 'See Arnie, they seem to be hitting it off. Amanda told me she thought Charlie was a real nice guy.'

Arnie nodded. 'Uh huh.'

The small diesel engine was turned over and with a cloud of blue smoke emitting from the exhaust as the cylinders cleansed themselves of latent fuel, the crew cast off and the ketch left the harbour for the greenish waters of the gulf.

The crew was instructed, and practised, raising and lowering the sails, the principal of reefing, coming about, tacking, fair wind, close haul, and a myriad of nautical terms baffling to the mind of the lay person.

Amanda fell in that category. She tried not to look confused as the sailing terms were mentioned, and to Arnie's admonition, 'Don't forget this . . . or . . . don't forget that.' She would give her beautiful head a toss, smile, and say, 'Charlie, I hope you will remember all this . . . I'm counting on you,' and she bestowed on him a warm smile that all the others could see. Peg nodded, approvingly.

Feeling that his crew had absorbed all they were capable of for the day, Arnie suggested, 'Let's go to the club for a quick one, and then, Peg and I gotta go.'

They had adopted a standard seating pattern since their first meeting, with Charlie and Amanda seated side by side. She smiled at him as they sat, and then her beautiful smile was bestowed on the others as they gave the waitress the drink orders.

It was Peg who said, 'Well, I think we are making great progress! I can hardly wait for the big day,' and turning her gaze to Amanda, she asked, 'And how are you and Charlie getting along, Mandy? Think you can stand each other for a few weeks?'

Amanda gave them a dazzling smile, and turning to Charlie, replied, 'I'm sure Charlie and I will get along famously.'

Charlie merely nodded . . . confused. He had met several women in his lifetime who were enigmas, and as the time went on they became more enigmatic, and he said to himself, 'I believe she may be the most enigmatic of all.'

He was determined to find out more about her. He had to if he had to survive the next few weeks with her.

As the one drink party broke up and they were leaving, he sauntered over to Peg, saying softly, 'I need to talk to you, Peg.'

'Sure, Charlie,' as she moved closer to him.

'No! Not here. I want to talk to you in private.'

'Gee, this sounds serious. Are you finally ready to profess your love for me after all these years,' she kidded.

'Come on, woman, get serious for once.'

'OK, when do you want to talk, and where?'

'Can I come over to your house, tonight? I want Arnie to be there when I talk to you.'

'Aw, shucks . . . why do all men tell me that? How

about eight-thirty? No! Why don't you come over for supper at seven? I'll have to bust my butt to get it done, but I can do it, if you don't expect anything too fancy.'

'I didn't want to put you to any trouble . . . just talk.'

She shook her head. 'Charlie, Charlie, Charlie! You are not trouble, and you are not company . . . not after all these years. Supper at seven . . . OK?'

'OK . . . see you at seven.'

During the meal, Peg kept waiting for him to bring up the subject matter, but he didn't.

As the meal ended, Charlie looked at them, as they looked at him, with the irrepressible Peg asking, 'well, Charlie?'

He nodded. 'I have to talk to you about Amanda . . . '

'Oh, Charlie, don't tell me we have a problem . . . '

'No! At least I don't think so, but . . . well . . . I can't figure her out,' and he related the phone conversation of the afternoon.

Peg laughed. 'Hell, Charlie, if the girl didn't want to go out with you tonight what's the big deal? Maybe she's got PMS . . . who knows? You know how complicated we females are.'

'No, you don't understand. It's not the refusal to go that bothered me . . . I've been refused before, but it was the brutal way she did it. That is hardly the way to begin a relationship of close living for the next few weeks . . . ' and his voice trailed off.

Then, he asked,'Where does she come from? How well do you know her, Peg?

'Oh, I can't say I know her real well . . . at least, not anymore. We were sorority sisters in college. Believe me, she was the campus queen. Nature was overly generous with her in all respects, and I am speaking as one who has seen her in the shower on many occasions. Well, with her beauty, it was not long before a modelling career beckoned, but not before she won her state title and went on to the Miss America pageant, where, as I have previously mentioned, she came out third runner-up, which ain't bad, considering the competition.'

Peg sipped her coffee, as she continued. 'Then, she

got married to a guy with lots of money, and well, something happened to the marriage. I'm not sure she would want me to elaborate on this.'

He was curious. 'How did your paths cross again? How did she end up on the cruise?'

Arnie spoke up. 'I guess I can answer that better than Peg. I also knew Amanda in college, since we all were there at the same time, except you, Charlie,' he laughed. The University of Texas was not good enough for you. You had to go to that smart-ass school . . . A & M,' he teased. Charlie shrugged.

'Well,' continued Arnie, 'Peg had come to Dallas with me on business one time, and it seemed Amanda was staying in the same hotel we were. She didn't know we were there and we didn't know she was either.

'I get on this elevator one day and I see this gorgeous creature standing there with some wimpy looking guy. She looks at me and I look at her. She says, "excuse me, but would you be Arnie Broadhurst by any chance?" I say, "I could be, depending on who's asking" . . . I heard that line in a movie, once, and it's kind of catchy, so I used it. She smiled a smile that could melt steel, and she grabs me and says, "Arnie . . . it's me . . . Amanda Winters" . . . that's her maiden name. We hugged as old college chums will. She says . . . "how's Peg? I heard you guys got married." Then, I say, "Peg is here with me", and she screams in delight, so . . . one thing led to another . . . '

Peg barged in, 'We met and talked and talked . . . Arnie had gone off to meet some business people. To make a long story short, she was miserable. The wimpy guy she was with was her attorney, and they were in the midst of a property settlement with her rich husband. She came out with plenty because of the nature of the breakup . . . '

That caught Charlie's attention. 'What nature?'

Peg, who seldom was embarrassed by anything, blushed, and smiling, replied, 'It appears he liked men more than he did women.' She laughed. 'Can you imagine what that did to Amanda Winters' self esteem? Most men would, as I have so tackily explained to you, before, gladly surrender their best testicle for her, and here is the man she is married to preferring the company of men . . . well!'

Charlie laughed at the irony of it all. 'Well, well, it seems that Amanda and I are kindred spirits after all . . . ' and he caught himself.

Peg . . . sharp-eyed Peg, caught it though. She retorted, 'It would appear that your ex-spouses, Charlie, had the same problem.'

'I don't understand what you mean,' he lied.

'Oh, come on, Charlie, I knew about Adelle long ago. Lots of people did. Your friends respected your privacy, while talking behind your back.'

He looked forlorn, knowing his secret was no longer a secret. 'I see, and you never told me. What kind of friends are you?'

Peg became uncommonly serious, for her, taking his hand, looking into his eyes, replying, 'There are some things good friends do not talk about, and that is one of them. Besides, I knew it was just a matter of time before Adelle's and Miriam's secret got out . . . '

'Miriam? Charlie asked.

'Yes . . . Miriam Baxter. I thought you knew.'

'No I didn't.'

Peg sighed. 'To continue with the story. Amanda was miserable, and she told me so. She said she had to get away from Dallas for a while, and you know me with my big mouth. I told her about the cruise and her eyes lit up, and I was looking for a roommate for you, and you know how my wild imagination works, and the first thing I thought of was that in a bizarre sort of way, you two might be good for each other,'

And she shook her head, saying, 'Maybe I screwed up, Charlie . . . I don't know. Would you like me to talk to Amanda?'

'And say what? That I don't like the way she acted. That would be kind of wimpy, wouldn't it?'

'Well, I could tell her what a nice guy you are, and to not be so bitchy with you.'

'No, thank you. Let it alone. I will handle it on my own.'

'I don't want you two fighting the whole while. That won't be any fun for you or us,' Peg warned.

Remembering the way she was warm and solicitous in front of the others, he replied, 'I don't think it will happen that way.'

'Well, if you're sure you can handle it, I'll keep quiet, which is unusual for me,' she laughed. 'How about a drink before you go . . . a real drink?'

'No, thank you. I've got some phone calls to make after I get home, and I don't want to call these people too late, so I'll say goodnight.'

'Goodnight, Charlie,' and she hugged and kissed him on the cheek, as Arnie patted his back.

As he entered the home of his parents, his mother, quite perturbed, asked, 'Charles . . . where have you been? I was quite concerned about you when you did not show up for dinner. Your father and I waited nearly an hour.'

He was embarrassed. 'I'm sorry, Mother, I really am. We have been busy practising for the cruise, and then, Arnie and Peg invited me for supper, but that is no excuse . . . I should have called.'

She drew herself up, just a little indignantly, as she responded, 'It would have been proper to do so.'

The father laughed it off, saying, 'Your mother will not ever get used to the idea that you are a grown man, Charlie, and are not accountable to us for your actions.'

She became a little more indignant. 'That is not quite true, Alex! When one lives in the home of another . . . even within the family unit, good manners dictate . . . '

'Oh, Agatha, get off your high horse just for once! You're talking to your son . . . your thirty-six year old son, for God's sakes!'

Charlie was anxious to bring this to an end, so he went to his mother, kissing her on the cheek, saying, 'I'm sorry for the breach of manners, Mother, I'll try to do better in the future,' and he winked at his father who could not conceal a wide grin.

The mother seemed pleased. Charlie made a mental note to move into an apartment as soon as he got back from the cruise.

His father stood up. 'Now that we have weathered that crisis, how about a glass of sherry with us, son?'

He hesitated, 'Sure, but just one. I have some telephone calls to make before going to bed.'

He did not notice the raising of his mother's eyebrows as he said that.

He made his way up the stairs to the second floor bedroom area, thinking of the call he would make to Meagan. He had called her every night since he had left her at the bus station in Denver. He wondered if that was wise or foolish. He was not sure. Was he sending strong signals to her? Stronger than he wanted to? He wasn't sure. All he knew was, he wanted to hear her voice. He dialled her number.

'Hello . . . Charlie?'

'Yes, Meagan, it's me. How are you? I miss you.'

She sighed. He could not see as she lowered herself into a chair, as she whispered, 'Ah miss you, too . . . so much.'

'What have you been doing with yourself? The usual?'

'Oh, no, Charlie! Mah whole life has changed.'

He did not expect this. 'Oh? What's happened? Has Erin come home?'

'No . . . not yet, but it won't be long. No! Guess what Ah'm do'in now, Charlie?'

He laughed. 'You mean at just this minute?'

'No . . . silly! Ah mean what do you think ah'm do'in to change mah life?'

'I have no idea.' He didn't either, as he pondered what she could be doing in her tight little world to change her life.

'Ah'm go'in to school, five nights a week.' She said this with great excitement in her voice.

'But, how can you do that and still work?'

'Ah switched to the morn'in shift, much as Ah hate it, but it's the only way Ah kin go to school at night. Ah make less money on that shift 'cause the big tips come from the even'in meal, but with the extra money you send me . . . well, Ah kin make it. What do ya think?'

'I think it is a great idea, but what prompted you to go back to school?'

'Ah want you to be proud of me, Charlie. Ah want to talk right. Ah don't want to embarrass you iffen Ah eva git . . . ' and she did not finish the sentence.

'Meagan . . . have I ever given you the impression that you have embarrassed me in any way?'

She hesitated. 'No . . . not in so many ways, but Ah know what Ah'm like Charlie . . . Ah'm no fool.'

'How do you know I don't like you the way you are?'

'How am Ah?'

'Sweet, pure, simple, uncomplicated, honest . . . '

'Maybe, Ah want to be more complicated, Charlie.'

'Why?'

'Ah think men find complicated women more interesting.'

He thought of Amanda. ''I'm not too sure of that, but regardless, Meagan, I am proud of you for wanting to go back to school. I think that is a commendable endeavour.'

'See what Ah mean, Charlie. Ah don't understand those words, 'n well, Ah want to be able to say words that people don't understand, too. Ah want to talk like you.'

He laughed to himself at her simplistic reasoning, but he was proud of her. 'When do you think Erin will come home?'

'Ah think it will be in a week or so. She is so excited, Charlie. She calls you her guardian angel She says God sent you to me so you could help her. Ah believe that, too. You're mah guardian angel, too.'

'The real guardian angel is Monica de la Rosa. I hope you will tell her so some day.'

'Oh, Ah will! Ah intend to bake her a cake . . . a big one, too, but Ah want Erin to help me so's it will come from us both. Ah'm go'in to make it from scratch, too. Real stuff.'

He smiled to himself. He thought of Adelle and Amanda and what their approach would be to this act of thanksgiving, if ever the thought crossed their minds.

They would call the florist and order an arrangement ... probably some exotic tropical arrangement ... expensive, and then when asked what the card should read, reply, 'Thanks. No, you sign it!'

He replied to her proud intentions, 'I think she would like that very much.'

She seemed doubtful. 'You really think so?'

'Yes, because it came from the heart . . . yours and Erin's. That's why.'

She answered, solemnly,'It would, too.'

'Well, I guess I had better sign off, now, so the schoolgirl can get some rest. Incidentally . . . what are you wearing, right now?'

She giggled. 'Just mah bathrobe.'

'Nothing else?'

She said, demurely, 'Uh uh . . . noth'in else.'

'Do you have any idea how much I would like to be there with you just now?'

'No! Tell me.'

'I am so tempted that if I thought I could get a flight out tonight and be in Denver in a couple of hours, I would do so without hesitation.'

She signed. 'You sure know how to git a gal excited, Charlie. Now, how do'ya 'spect me to go to sleep?'

'Do you have any wine?'

'Uh huh! Ah bought some.'

'Well, pour yourself a glass, then climb into bed . . . lean back on your pillow, and think of me.'

'If Ah do that, the wine will be mixed with tears. Ah love you, Charlie . . . Ah really do. This is no joke with me.'

He thought for a while. 'I'm not joking, either, Meagan. I think I'm beginning to fall in love with you.'

At the sound of those words, her heart skipped a beat. She had longed to hear them, but without any reservations. 'When you know fer sure, Charlie, let me know.'

'You will be the first to know . . . I promise. Goodnight.'

'Goodnight, Charlie.'

* * *

As he twiddled his fingers while sitting at his desk the next morning, he thought over his near declaration of love to Meagan the night before, and he wondered if he had done the right thing. He had told her the truth. He thought he loved her, but he was not sure if it was real love, or merely fascination with a type of woman he had never met before. Then he thought of Amanda. His conversation with Arnie and Peg had shed some light on the strange and beautiful creature, but, yet? He thought about her rejection of his invitation to dinner. Perhaps Peg was right. Maybe, he had caught her on a day of PMS, or some other quirk which makes humans act in the inexplicable manner they do.

He decided, more out of devilment than anything else, to give her another chance to right that wrong. He would call her again. She had moved from Dallas to Corpus Christi to be near them until the cruise started and in the meantime, with her newly acquired wealth from the marriage settlement, she could afford to stay in an expensive, completely furnished condo overlooking the marina.

He dialled her number. The same soft voice he had now become accustomed to said, 'Hello.'

'Amanda, this is Charlie, your bunkmate, as you've been referring to me down on the boat . . . remember me?'

She replied, coolly, 'Oh, sure, I remember you. How may I help you?'

This was the type of response one got from a salesclerk in a good department store . . . not a bunkmate!

He said, in jest, 'I thought I'd give you an opportunity to right the wrong you perpetrated against me last week.'

'Oh . . . I was not aware that I had wronged you, Charlie. What wrong are we referring to?'

He felt sure she was playing with him. Damn her. 'The wrong when you turned me down for dinner. I thought I'd give you a chance to rectify that by accepting another one.'

'You men,' she sighed, 'You never give up, do you?

When I turned you down, I thought I made it perfectly clear that I did not want any personal relationship between us to act as a . . . how shall I say this . . . a catalyst . . . between us, since we will be forced to live in close proximity for several weeks under what could be described as provocative conditions.'

She was proud of herself, feeling that she had chosen her words carefully, and that they had conveyed the message she intended.

He thought that over for a moment or two, replying, 'Then, I guess the answer is . . . no!'

'You've got it, Charlie.'

'Then, your choice is for me to be as cold to you as you have been to me, unless, of course, we are in the presence of others, and then, you can go into your act.'

She seemed offended by his perception, but, she could not argue with its accuracy . . . he had found her out.

She responded, once again, 'You've got it!'

When he hung up this time, he was not angry with her as he had been the first time. He now caught on to the game she was playing with him, but he didn't know the details. Whether she was genuinely afraid of a close relationship for the reasons she had given, or whether she now hated all men for the time being, he was not sure. He knew one thing: she suffered from the same disease he did. They had both been rebuffed in their marriages for the same reason . . . they had lost out to the wrong sex. Peg was right! It did not do much for building self-esteem in one's prowess as a lover.

He made up his mind he would play the game. He, too, would be civil and sweet to her in the presence of others, but in the confines of the stateroom, he could, and would, be as bitchy as she. He decided to guide his actions by hers. 'I'll play her like a piano . . . by ear.'

In the subsequent meetings they were forced into as the crew continued to train for the cruise she continued to be sweet and courteous in the company of others, but to present a cold side whenever alone.

He didn't care anymore. 'What the hell! I can be as obnoxious as she can . . . probably more so!'

To Peg's constant queries of, 'How are things going between you and Mandy?', he would reply, 'Great!'

She would give him a disbelieving look . . . more of a smirk, as he smiled. One day, after the question had been asked, he added, 'Peg, when this is over, you will owe me one!

She looked confused. 'Why will I owe you one? Any reason in particular?'

'For putting up with your schizophrenic friend during an entire cruise, a cruise on which I went to forget my schizophrenic wife.'

Peg thought about it for awhile, replying, 'I guess you're right, sweetheart . . . I owe you one, but, only one,' and she got a mischievous look like only she could get, adding, 'but, you'll have to wait until my husband is out of town.' They both laughed at this, as only old and close friends can.

* * *

It was the night before the start of the cruise and Charlie had, out of filial duty, agreed to spend the evening with his parents, much to his mother's delight. They lingered long after the meal, talking of many things, and Charlie could not help but feel that his mother had something on her mind. She kept looking at him as mothers are prone to do when they feel that their child has been mischievous, but can't quite put their finger on the actual deed.

The father began to yawn, signalling that his day had come to an end, and turning to the two, he smiled. 'You two seem to be hell bent on talking all night, so I ask to be excused.' He patted his son on the shoulder as he went by, saying, 'Have a good time on the cruise, Charlie. Don't worry about anything in the office. We can manage without you for a while,' and going to his wife, kissed her on the cheek, a nightly ritual, saying, 'Sleep well, my dear.'

She had raised her cheek to him, also a nightly ritual, replying, 'You, too, my love.'

Charlie smiled with satisfaction. He was well aware that his parent's marriage was not one 'made in heaven', but they had reached an accommodation, and was not that the way of most modern marriages.

His mother took a deep drag on her cigarette, which she smoked with an unusually long holder of silver and mother-of-pearl, a gift from her cigar smoking husband, who was not allowed to smoke his cigars anywhere but in his study which had been equipped with special electronic air filters. She smiled at her son, looking at him through the smoke.

'May I get you another brandy, Mother?'

'No, thank you, dear. I'm ready to say goodnight as soon as you answer one question which I feel I must ask. It is my motherly duty.'

Those words startled him, for each and every time in his entire life that his mother had spoken those words it had been traumatic to him in some manner.

He smiled. 'Ask me anything you wish, Mother. I only hope my answer can be as sincere as your question.'

She smiled. 'Who is Meagan?'

He was absolutely startled at her question, and he groped for a response, as she looked at him, no longer smiling.

He asked, 'How could you possibly know about Meagan?'

She looked down at the floor, avoiding his gaze. 'I'm too embarrassed to tell you, ' and for the first time in his life, she seemed to be on the defensive with him.

'I think you had better tell me, Mother.'

She looked in his eyes, sadly. He even thought he detected a hint of a tear, but he was not sure, as she continued, 'I picked up the telephone in my room . . . to make a call for the correct time . . . I swear to you, Charles . . . and I heard you talking to someone you called Meagan.'

'And, I'm sure you immediately placed the receiver back on the base,' he said with some confidence.

She shook her head. 'No! That is what good manners and correct social graces would have dictated, but, oh, Charles, I could not! I listened to your entire conversation with this Meagan person.'

He became alarmed. He was not sure which night she had listened in, so he asked, 'And what did you hear that has apparently upset you?'

She looked too embarrassed to continue, but, finally, she sighed, saying, 'You talked of "it". I'm not sure what you meant by that, but, really, Charles, I am not a child.' And then she paused for a moment, gaining momentum, 'Then that person mentioned something about someone dear to her in prison,' and she began to cry.

'Oh, Charles, what have you gotten yourself into? Perhaps, if you have been involved with this person, we could have our attorneys approach her for some kind of settlement. These women of her type are usually looking for a handout . . . '

He cut her off. He stared at her. The roles were now reversed. It was he who had the imperious stare and she the recipient, but she still looked defiant, her head held high. He tried to hold his temper as he shook his finger at her – something he had never done in his entire life.

'First, you had no right to listen in on our conversation.' She nodded, head down. 'Secondly, I would appreciate it if you would not refer to Meagan as "that person" as if she were from outer space. She is a woman I met on my journey. She is uncultured, I admit, by your standards, but she is one of the warmest, most honest, most sincere people I have ever met, which I think you will agree is an improvement for me in my choice of acquaintances.'

'That is all well and good if you were involved in social work, but, tell me this . . . truthfully . . . what is she to you?' the mother asked in motherly fashion, as she added, 'Please tell me the truth'.

He looked at her, solemnly, raising his hands in despair. 'I can't tell you what she is to me because I honestly don't know. She loves me from what she tells me and knowing the simplistic honesty of her nature, I would have to believe her. As for me, I am definitely attracted to her. She is unlike any other woman I've ever known. She is very uncomplicated . . . everything is black and white to her . . . right or wrong . . . good or evil. She is the complete opposite of Adelle.'

The mother tried hard to understand her son, as she

took hold of his hands, saying softly, 'Perhaps, you are confusing love with fascination. After all, Charles, you were in love with another woman only a month ago . . . '

'I know, Mother, I've thought of that.'

'Where do you intend to go with this affair?'

'I don't view it as an affair in the usual sense of the word. I'm not playing games with Meagan.'

The mother looked concerned. 'And what of this prison business? That horrifies me, Charles. Tell me, please.'

And so he related the entire story of his meeting Meagan, leaving out nothing but the intimate details which he implied and she perceived.

She was not mollified even now that she knew . . . on the contrary, she was more concerned than ever.

'Do you really believe you could ever have a real life with this Meagan? You come from two different worlds. She could never fit into yours and I can't believe you would want to fit into hers. Oh, Charles be realistic. Give this woman up. Get her out of your mind and out of your life.'

'I don't know that I can,' and he paused . . . I don't know that I want to. Tomorrow, I'll leave on the cruise which will last two or three weeks, and,' he sighed, 'I'll give this matter a lot of thought and make a decision with regard to her.'

She nodded, rising, 'Thank you for being truthful with me, and please forgive me for listening in on your phonecall . . . I am truly sorry. Goodnight, Charles.'

He rose. 'Goodnight, Mother.'

As he climbed the stairs to his bedroom, he wondered what he would say to Meagan on this his last call to her before leaving for the cruise. His feelings were very ambivalent after his conversation with his mother. He had never had an opposing view concerning Meagan except those he imposed on his own brain, and that could hardly be considered objective. He sat on his bed as he dialled her number.

'Oh, Charlie . . . it's late! I-thought-you-would-never-call-this-evening. '

He wrinkled his brow. 'You don't sound the same, Meagan. Why are you speaking so slowly?'

She laughed. 'It's the way I have to talk if I want to speak correctly, so I can pronounce the words correctly.' And she laboured slowly through that also.

He laughed. 'How long do I have to put up with this? It takes you an hour to complete a sentence,' he teased.

'Oh, Charlie, don't tease me . . . Ah'm do'in this fer you,' as she lapsed back into character.

'I know, and I appreciate it, too. Meagan, tomorrow we leave for the cruise so it will be a few days before you hear from me, again.'

'Oh, Charlie, Ah'm so depressed ova that. Ah think Ah'll go crazy missing you.'

'Do you miss me that much?'

'Uh, huh! More than you'll eva know. Ah love you so much.'

'What did you do before I came into your life?'

'Ah tole you Ah was so filled with hatred fer men that Ah wanted noth'in to do with them. You were so kind and gentle with me when we met . . . not like those cowboys who tried to hassle me in the cafe. And then, my yearnings got to churning around as we got friendlier, and then, well, you know what happened, and after that . . . Ah was gone . . . mah goose was cooked as far as you were concerned, Charlie.'

He could not help but smile at what could be the most charming and unique declaration of love he had ever heard.

He pressed on determine to learn the depth of her feelings. 'Suppose I had not gone into that cafe that night, hungry and tired . . . suppose you had not met me. Do you think you could ever have gotten interested in some other man?'

'Ah don't now. Why are you asking me all that?'

'I'm just trying to learn if you are really in love with me, or, is it that we are fascinated with each other . . . for different reasons.'

She was quiet for a while finally saying, softly, 'So, you think it's fascination, huh, Charlie? You didn't believe me all the times that Ah said, Ah love you?' She began to cry softly. 'What's happening, Charlie? Ah don't understand. But, if you're ready to git rid 'o me just say so! Ah ain't begg'in no man to love me . . . no siree! Just say goodbye right now, Charlie. Ah'll git ova you . . . someday.'

'Oh, Meagan . . . please don't! I'm not trying to get rid of you! I'm trying to sort out my feelings for you.'

'You might have to sort out your feelings, Charlie, but don't try to sort out mine . . . they're already sorted out,' she replied with justifiable indignation.

He was distressed. The conversation was not going the way he wanted. His mother's admonitions were obviously affecting his thinking, and he resented that. Damn women.

'Meagan, please don't get excited . . . stay calm . . . '

'Ah'm not excited, Charlie. Ah'm just try'in to be treated right by a man Ah love . . . that's all. Seems like Ah've had to fight all mah life fer love . . . someth'in so simple, Charlie. It should be easy as as fall'in off a log, but you're mak'in it complicated. No wonder your love life is a mess.'

Her words burned in his brain. She was right. Love should not be complicated. It should be simple. It is simply a case of two people caring for each other more than they care for anyone else in the world.

He conceded the point. 'You know something, Meagan, you're absolutely right. I am trying to complicate it, but I promise you it will get untangled in a few weeks. Will you give me that much time?'

'Sure, Charlie. Mah love fer you ain't go'in nowhere. It's yours that's meandering all ova the place. Go on yore trip . . . have fun! If you find another woman you like more'n me . . . pick her, but just one more thing, Charlie . . . make damn sure she loves you more'n Ah do. Goodnight, Charlie.'

She had not waited to hear his goodnight. He knew she was highly upset and he was truly distressed. This was their first lover's quarrel. He learned one thing from the exchange. She might be in love with him, but she would tolerate no crap from him.

He could not sleep. He realized that if his mother had not intervened the conversation with Meagan would have gone differently. He felt sorry for her, and as he twisted and turned in his bed, it ate into him to the point that he picked up the receiver to call her, again. It was late . . . he shouldn't, but he had to.

He could tell the voice was sleepy as she anxiously said, 'Hello?'

'Meagan . . . I had to call you back to tell you I love you! Don't be upset with me. Just remember I love you. Bear with me for a few weeks more, that's all I ask you.'

She paused for a while, trying to absorb the magic words she heard through a sleepy brain, as she replied, 'Charlie, did Ah hear you right? You said you loved me?'

'Yes, that is what I said.'

'And you didn't say I think I love you?'

'No, Meagan I left out the word think.'

'Oh, Charlie . . . Ah think Ah'm dream'in.'

'No! you're not dreaming . . . I said it. I said it!'

'Oh, Charleeee . . . Ah want you here right now!'

'That's where I want to be right now! Be patient. Goodnight, Meagan.'

She was smiling as she cooed, 'Goodnight, Charlie.'

As he placed the phone down he was more pleased with himself. He had done it, and it didn't hurt half as much as he thought it would. He was now able to go to sleep.

11

As the exuberant crew boarded the beautiful fibreglass sailing yacht the air was filled with anticipation of a long and relaxing ocean voyage . . . an odyssey. She was of a typical ketch design with one larger mast forward and a smaller mast aft, but forward of the rudder post, resulting in three sheets of sail, counting the jib.

Arnie had forsaken the huge spinnaker for the trip, declaring, 'Hell, we're not a racing boat. The women will have a hard time fighting a spinnaker on a typical two person shift.'

She was a luxurious craft of fifty feet, an interior of oiled Burmese teak, with three staterooms, all with private head (toilet). Except for the master stateroom which had a fibreglass tub and shower, the other two heads boasted a small, combination toilet, lavatory, and shower-combination type head. The type in which one had to sit on the potty to take a shower, but . . . it was private.

As each crew partnership retreated to their own stateroom to stow the luggage, it should be noted that there was little or no friction caused by the living accommodations of two of the couples but Amanda was not happy with the cramped accommodations of the small stateroom, spoiled, self-centred creature that she was, and she registered her feelings to Charlie in very clear terms.

'Look . . . we have to live in this tiny, cramped, space for the next few weeks. Let's get a few basic rules straight between us, Charlie. It will be, as I've explicitly stated, previously, platonic . . . very platonic! That means if there is ambiguity in my words . . . no physical contact whatsoever. I will dress and undress in the bathroom and I expect you to do the same. Speaking of bathrooms (she had said she will not refer to it as a head), you will please raise the toilet seat when you urinate, and, you will kindly replace it when you are finished. I am well aware of how dirty you men can be.'

Then, looking at the upper and lower bunks, she gave Charlie an imperious glance, reminiscent of his mother's as she decided, 'You take the top bunk and I will take the lower,' and gave him a cold shrug, adding . . . 'I'm sure that some primeval urge will be satisfied by your being on top and I on the bottom.'

Charlie took it all with amusement. He was beginning to enjoy her verbal thrusts, and he could not help replying, 'Oh, I don't know! I've met many women who did not insist on that time honoured tradition.'

She gave him a hard look. 'Please spare me the lurid details of your intimate life.'

He smiled again. 'I thought we'd spend a lot of these lonely hours on deck, during our watch, exchanging titbits on our intimate lives.'

She gave him a toss of her beautiful head, replying in a huff, 'Not hardly!'

She went to the small built-in closet, nestled in the curvature of the hull, opened the louvered doors, and exclaimed, 'I can't live with this! There is not enough room in here for both of us to hang our clothes. I have to talk to Arnie about this!'

He made a magnanimous gesture. 'Take it all. I can live out of this duffle bag for a couple of weeks.'

She looked at the duffle bag with disdain.

'How primitive, but, if that is what you want,' and she proceeded to place her designer clothes in the closet.

Charlie smiled, thinking, 'This is going to be more fun than I thought.'

The first day out all three crews worked together to sharpen their sailing skills, those which needed sharpening, and Amanda was in that category. She tried, as she put on designer gloves to handle the lines and shrouds, afraid that the nylon ropes would blister her sensitive skin.

The low land mass of the Texas gulf coast began to disappear as the *Polaris* headed southeast towards the Yucatan Peninsula, some six hundred miles away, which had to be rounded to reach Belize.

Arnie had been tempted to follow the Mexican coastline, 'For safety' . . . but, 'aw, what the hell . . . the weather forecasts for the next couple of weeks are good, so we'll save quite a bit of time if we cut across.'

The boat's speedometer was showing a not-too-good six knots since the boat was heading into a southeast wind and had to tack all day, with Arnie commenting, 'Geez, I wish this wind would shift to the northwest, but I guess that is too much to hope for.'

To celebrate their first day at sea they had decided on a big formal meal, the kind one sees in the advertisements for luxury yachts where everyone is sitting on the fantail in black tie tuxedos, glass of wine in hand, with Asian-looking men and women serving exotic foods and everyone smiling at each other. The women had prepared the food the day before so it was simply a matter of heating it.

For most of the trip, when they had settled down to a regular routine, it would be the task of the off crew for that shift to prepare the food, but for tonight, they all chipped in. Happiness prevailed as if it were a county fair. They laughed . . . they ate . . . they drank, and as the sun began to set in the west, a slight breeze came up out of the east, hitting the boat broadside on port and starboard tacks.

The lovely yacht began to develop a slight roll on either tack. Arnie smiled at Peg . . . Bill smiled at Kate . . . Charlie smiled at Amanda, since he felt he owed her that. She smiled in return. She felt she owed them all that. As time went on the full moon made its entrance in the darkening eastern sky. This was no accident of nature . . . No! The irrepressible Peg had insisted that their departure coincide with the most beautiful of nature's displays, and the most romantic . . . a full moon.

She had explained to her husband, 'No telling to what heights I can be moved with a full moon shining through the porthole.'

Bill Morton and Kate Russell would have the first working shift from 1600 to 2400. The engaged couple volunteered for that shift, for them it had many advantages. They would be on deck during the early hours of the evening as the moon and stars were at their loveliest. Is this not appropriate for an engaged couple? How better to be inspired in the exchange of terms of endearment? And the added benefit . . . when they did retire after midnight, all the others on the boat with the exception of the working crew would be asleep. This would give them the solitude needed to fulfil those feelings that had developed all through the evening.

Charlie was not happy with the shift he and Amanda had from 2400 to 0800, but then, he would not have been happy with the other two either. It forced them to be in their stateroom very early, trying to get a few hours sleep before they went on at midnight but, of course, this was impossible on their first night out for the partying went on much later than usual.

As they ate and drank, the boat continued to roll. Arnie and Peg were at the helm, but food and drink were taken to them on a regular basis. Arnie, being the owner of the craft and the signer of the note at the bank, vowed to stay sober, and so did Peg, as she drank his share. Bill and Kate drank sparingly, for their minds were on other things.

Charlie also drank sparingly, as he watched Amanda drink more than a normal share of wine. He assumed there would be some fun before the night was over and he wanted to be sober enough to enjoy it. The more she drank the more voluble she became, and, the more voluble she became the more Peg winked at Arnie, and the more Arnie winked at Charlie. Charlie just smiled. The boat was in a good solid rolling mode, the kind that induces sea sickness in the uninitiated. Amanda began to lose her volubility and she actually became quiet. She didn't look too good, either, as her beautiful face took on a grey pallor. She no longer tossed her tresses. She would look at the others over her wine glass, and then she put that down, excusing herself, saying she was going into the cabin.

Sensing she might need assistance, Charlie asked, 'Would you like me to help you?'

'Certainly not!' she retorted, as she disappeared down the ladder.

A considerable amount of time elapsed and she still did not reappear on deck.

Peg was concerned, 'Charlie, do you think Amanda is OK . . . she should have been back by now.'

Charlie shrugged. 'I don't know if she is coming back. Perhaps, she turned in. We have to go on at midnight, you know.'

'I can't believe she would have done that without saying goodnight, do you?'

He gave Peg a smile. 'She's capable of it.'

'Oh, come on, Charlie, go and check on your roommate.'

He rose to get up, 'If you insist.'

As he neared the door to their stateroom he could hear her vomiting in the head. He smiled as he opened the door and eased in. She was coming out of the bath, wiping her mouth. Her hair was a mess and she looked sick . . . real sick.

'Are you all right, Amanda?'

'No, I'm not all right . . . I'm sick. Just go away and leave me alone . . . get out . . . get out!' she screamed at him.

'Perhaps you've forgotten . . . I live here.'

She ignored him, going to her bunk, flopping in on her back, wet wash cloth on her face . . . moaning.

He tried once again. 'Are you sure I can't get you some medication? We have several things on board to help you.'

'All I want you to do is get Peg for me . . . please!'

He turned to the door. 'OK.'

In a few moments he was back with Peg in tow. She wrinkled her nose at the sour smell coming from the bathroom, shaking her head, as she sat on the bunk next to the sick woman. Amanda pointed to Charlie, and then to Peg, 'Ask him to get out!' Peg motioned to Charlie and he left.

It was quite some time before Peg came out on deck, smiling a weak smile.

'She is some sick, folks. She wants to die. Charlie, she doesn't want you in the room, tonight, so I guess you'd better sleep in the lounge . . . on the couch. I'm sorry, but she is so upset . . . '

'With me?' he asked, incredulously.

Peg shook her head. 'No . . . with herself. Her self esteem has been shattered again . . . poor kid. Do you mind bunking on the lounge couch for tonight?'

Charlie shook his head. 'Amanda and I were supposed to go on duty at midnight . . . she won't be able to.'

'No! Either Arnie or I will substitute for her. We'll make out.'

She laughed, and nodding her head at the young engaged couple, 'We shouldn't break up their routine.'

Charlie smiled. 'I agree. Let the lovers be,' and with that he descended the ladder to the lounge.

He looked at the couch, shaking his head, thinking, 'I paid good money for this? I could be in that little apartment of Meagan's right now . . . drinking wine with her . . . talking of things . . . holding her close.'

And as he put his weary body down on the couch his thoughts were of Meagan, and not of the sick woman in the stateroom. He finally dozed off for an hour or two, awakened by Peg as she headed for her stateroom.

Arnie was at the helm when he came up on deck, shaking his head as Charlie approached.

'What a hell of a way to start a romantic cruise, huh?' Charlie smiled and nodded.

They talked of many things as they sailed, business, money, politics,women . . . Amanda.

Arnie confided to Charlie, 'Something tells me she can be real bitchy, when she wants to . . . '

Charlie nodded. 'I bet she can.'

Amanda did not put in an appearance on deck the next

morning, nor was she visible at noon.

Peg went to check on her at intervals, returning to say, 'She's feeling better. She'll be out later in the afternoon.'

And she was, putting in a very meek appearance at 1435. She smiled, weakly, at all in sight, making no apologies for her indisposition of the night before, not that any were required by social graces, especially at sea.

To the queries, 'Are you feeling better?' she merely shook her head, 'I can't imagine why I got sick. I've never been seasick before so I'm sure it was something I ate.'

Oh, how many times have those words been uttered the morning after since the dawn of seafaring man!

Charlie had taken out his sextant and was 'shooting the sun', that mysterious science whereby man can, with certain mathematical calculations, tell where he is on this planet.

Arnie saw him, asking, 'How's the SAT-NAV doing, Charlie? Are we where we're supposed to be?'

'Give me a few minutes to work the math and I'll let you know.

Within ten minutes, Charlie said, proudly, 'If I didn't screw it up, we should be near north latitude 26.5 and west longitude 95, more or less,' he laughed.

Arnie looked at the SAT-NAV which showed a position of 95 degrees 45 minutes, west, and 26 degrees 43 minutes north.

'Not bad, ole buddy . . . not bad at all. I'm proud of you.'

He smiled. 'It's not hard when the sea is calm enough to get a good shot, but in a pitching sea that is a different story.'

Arnie nodded. 'Well, take care of that sextant. We may need it yet.'

Amanda, looking on with some interest, asked, 'What do you do when there is no sun?'

Charlie responded, 'You don't do anything, but keep on doing dead reckoning, and hope for the best.'

As their second day at sea came to a close Charlie yawned as the evening meal ended, and, having had very little sleep the night before, excused himself, saying, 'I need some sleep after last night,' and turning to Amanda, he smiled, 'try not to wake me when you come in, no matter how strong your urges are,' which brought titters and laughter from the others, but from Amanda, 'Don't flatter yourself. My urges could never get that strong.'

This raised eyebrows among the others, even though it was now common knowledge among all that Charlie and Amanda had not hit it off.

'Too bad,' lamented Peg to Arnie, in private. 'It could have been a hell of a relationship.'

'Yeah,' echoed her husband, 'There is nothing like a mad woman in the sack, if she is mad at someone else.'

'How would you know?' demanded his wife.

'I read the letters in *Playboy* magazine . . . that's how.'

Eyebrows were raised again, when just ten minutes later, Amanda, too, exclaimed. 'I think I'll turn in, too, if I have to work the night shift with Mr Charming.'

As Peg watched her go, she whispered to the others, 'Wouldn't you pay good money to listen to that pillow talk for just one night?'

Charlie was just coming out of the shower when Amanda came into the room. He was just wearing a towel around his middle.

Amanda gave him a dirty look, saying, 'I told you that we would dress in the bathroom! Not in the bedroom. Can you not, at least, agree to that small bit of civility?'

'I'm sorry. I thought you were still out on deck.'

'Well, I'm not as you can see. Please do so in the future.'

'OK.' And he returned to the head with his clothing, then, dressed in his pyjamas, he climbed up into the top bunk.

She said nothing more as she picked out her night clothes and went into the head. He smiled as he heard her tinkle in the fibreglass potty.

'Well, wouldn't that set her off if she knew of the

audio I'm hearing right now. Oh, well, I can hardly wait until she hears me. That should invoke a lecture in acoustics.'

He could then hear the shower going, and he pictured her sitting on the potty with the water coming down over that gorgeous body, and he had to admit he was titillated. He could hear the noise as she squirmed in the narrow confines of the small bathroom to dress, hearing now and then, 'Ouch . . . damn.'

She emerged looking quite lovely, he had to admit. She had put her hair up for the shower, and she left it up. She was fully clothed, including a bath robe.

The boat was air conditioned, but the room was humid from the shower steam. She was perspiring, and he could see it. He said nothing as they exchanged glances, and he turned back to his book. This was a unique experience for both. It was safe to assume that neither had ever shared a room with an adult of the opposite sex without other intentions in mind than what they had. It was awkard and they both knew it.

She removed her bathrobe as she gave him a quick glance. She was wearing a teddy, which surprised him, for teddies were usually reserved for intentions other than what they had. She saw him glance at her but she said nothing as she let herself down into the lower bunk. He had returned to his reading, still enjoying the mental image of her in the teddy.

He could hear her toss and turn as she sought the right position for slumber. After a moment of silence, she said, softly, 'Charlie?'

'Yes?'

'I guess I owe you an apology for last night . . . you know . . . asking you to leave the room. After all, you paid for the right to be here just as I have, and you had as much right to be here as I did, but, I was ill, and I didn't want anyone to see me . . . so, I'm sorry.'

'It's OK . . . no harm done.'

He expected some more conversation now that the ice was broken, but he was wrong. She said nothing else, and soon, he could hear her steady breathing.

He raised his head and looked over the edge of the

bunk. She looked gorgeous as she lay there on her side. She had loosened her hair and it spilled out over the pillow. He sighed as he placed his head back on the pillow, and his thoughts went to Meagan. He compared them. They were as different as night from day. Amanda was far more beautiful on the outside, but Meagan was far more beautiful on the inside, and with that profound thought in his mind, he went to sleep.

By the end of the third day the position locater indicated that they had come a little over three hundred miles - half way to the tip of the Yucatan Peninsula at which time they would turn the point and head south for Belize. They had planned on a stop off at Cancun for a day or two on shore. They would check into one of the luxury hotels for a real bath, some real food, some clean laundry, and, a good night's sleep. They all looked forward to that.

Their fourth night out Charlie retired at what had become his regular time. As usual, Amanda would give him time to get out of the bathroom, and then she would follow him to bed. He smiled as he heard all her same actions and motions, again unknown to her, for she was always behind him in time. He was sure, as proud as she was, she would have been mortified to know he heard her tinkle each and every time. If she ever heard him in the middle of the night, she had never said and he frankly did not care.

He was reading, as usual, as she climbed into her bunk.

She asked, 'What are you reading?'

'Madame Bovary. Are you familiar with it?'

'No, what's it about?'

'It's a great love story. Takes place in France in the last century. Some experts claim that Gustave Flaubert invented the modern novel with this book.'

'Really?' She did not seem interested.

The was a period of silence, then . . . Charlie?'

'Yes?'

'Peg told me that your marriage just broke up.'

He was surprised she wanted to get personal. He responded, 'Yes, that's true.'

'She also told me that you had the same problem with your wife that I had with my husband.'

He smiled, teasing her, 'No, my wife liked girls. I hear your husband liked boys . . . '

'Don't be a smart-ass! You know what I mean.'

'Yes, Amanda, I know what you mean.'

'Do you hate her?'

'Which one?'

'Your wife, silly.'

'Yes, I hate her.'

'Because she was a lesbian?'

'No, because she deceived me, that's why.'

'I know what you mean. I hate my ex-husband, too.'

He thought he saw an opening into her mind. 'Do you hate all men?'

'For the time being, yes. I guess when I have time to sort out my feelings . . . and the old urges come back, I'll return to the game.'

'What game?'

'The boy-girl game, Charlie. How about you? Will you return some day?'

He wanted to say, 'I've already returned,' but he didn't, instead, replying, 'Yeah, I guess so.'

'Goodnight, Charlie.'

'Goodnight, Amanda.'

As she became quiet, he said to himself, 'Well, well, what do you know? I do believe she is human after all, but what hatred and resentment lies within that beautiful body.'

The next night, following the usual routine, she removed her bathrobe, and apparently forgetting something in the bathroom, she went back to retrieve it without putting her robe back on. He watched her walk away, the lilting sway of her hips showing under the satin finish of the teddy, and he was still looking as she returned.

She saw him looking, and, surprisingly, she smiled.

'Like what you see, Charlie?'

'Yes, I'd be lying to you if I said I didn't. You're a very lovely, woman, Amanda . . . very lovely.'

'Thank you,' she said softly, 'but don't let yourself get too worked up, Charlie . . . nothing's going to happen.'

He was perturbed at her presumption as he replied, 'What makes you so damn sure I want it to happen?'

She went up to his bunk, looking him in the eye. 'Because I know men. If there is one thing I know and understand, it's the way you guys think and feel. Right now, Charlie, you would sell your soul to be able to climb into that bunk with me, wouldn't you? Tell the truth,' and she gave him a seductive smile.

'I don't know about my soul, that's pretty expensive, but I might be willing to pay the going price . . . '

She backed off, sneering. 'You son-of-a-bitch.' She retired to her bunk, saying nothing more for a while, then, 'Don't you think you owe me an apology. That was pretty low, comparing me to a prostitute . . . '

'I did not!' he exclaimed.

'Well, you implied it!'

'I did not.'

'Oh, go to sleep, Charlie. I should have known better than to expect civility from you.'

He was incensed. 'After the way you've treated me?'

'Go to sleep! . . . male chauvinist.'

'To hell with you . . . man hater.'

Well, he thought, at least we're making progress . . . we're talking.

As she lay back on her pillow and her anger subsided, she thought, 'Maybe, I've been too hard on him. He's really not a bad guy. Under different circumstances, I could get interested in him. Oh, well . . . we'll see.'

12

They arrived off the coast of Isla de Cozumel on the evening of the sixth day at sea. The joy of a long extended cruise wears thin after a while as the confines of a small boat begins to grate.

The relationship between Charlie and Amanda had not sweetened to any great extent. Simply because of its bad beginning, each felt he or she owed it to the other not to be congenial. The acrimony had subsided to some extent, but the idea of actually being warm to the other was alien to both. They, more than the others, welcomed the sight of Cozumel and its luxury hotels.

Since they had arrived late in the day they knew it would do no good to contact the Mexican customs officials to clear them for entry, so they anchored offshore and planned a quiet evening aboard the boat.

After supper and drinks had lost their interest, the three couples looked at each other expectantly.

Arnie gave Peg a look very familiar to her as he, with a lascivious gleam in his eye, said, 'Well, baby, what do you say we turn in. This is the first night since leaving the good ole USA that I will be able to concentrate on what I'm doing.'

She looked at him with the uninterested look women have cultivated in response to lustful proposals from their mates, while in the company of other women, replying, 'Not tonight, Arnie. Tomorrow night we'll be in a large air-conditioned suite . . . a real play pen . . . relax.'

And he was then rewarded with a light kiss and a look which held great promise. Since he had not had a full night's sleep in a week, he accepted the postponement with grace.

The engaged couple, Bill and Kate, merely looked at each other and smiled.

And what of our special couple, Charlie and Amanda? They were driven by different forces. They simply wanted a night away from each other – a night free from sarcasm and spite. Charlie had another reason. He was deeply remorseful at not having called Meagan once since they had left Corpus Christi . . . not once! On the first night he had heard the others use the satellite phone, calling family and friends, the conversations could be heard all over the boat.

He concluded to himself, 'How can I call Meagan from this boat. I could not be myself. I could not say I love you, Meagan, nor could I even utter the very basic I love you without naming a name.' He was most anxious to get to the privacy of a hotel room where he could express his love to her in proper fashion.

Next day they went through the embarrassment of a thorough custom check by an over-zealous inspector who was suspicious of all luxury yachts. He poked into every nook and cranny,.

The indignities over, they were free to dock the *Polaris* and head towards the Hotel Caribbe and attempt to obtain rooms. It took a great deal of persuasion and the ever-present display of American dollars to convince the clerk that he did, indeed, have three rooms available.

'Three rooms?' exclaimed a disgruntled Amanda. 'We need four rooms! I insist on a room of my own!'

The over coaxed clerk, feeling he had extended his purchased generosity as far as he could go, replied, as he raised his hands in a futile gesture and flashed a beautiful Latin smile, 'Ah eem so sorrry, senorrita . . . eet ees imposseeb.' And then he added, proudly, 'Tomorrow night, she ees OK!'

The looks on Amanda's and Charlie's faces were those of deep regret and dismay. They both wanted privacy badly, for different reasons. Charlie gave her a futile gesture look, and she returned one of complete disgust, turning her beautiful, unkempt head and stormed to the elevator, with Charlie in tow.

All six entered the elevator at the same time. Four of the six were in high spirits as they looked forward to a comfortable night of good food, good accommodations, and . . . romance.

The other couple said nothing, for disappointment was great in each. They entered their room with an air of dejection.

Amanda threw her bags on the bed . . . the one king-sized bed, as she looked aghast, exclaiming, 'One bed in this miserable room? All hotel rooms have two beds nowadays. How the hell are we going to make out with one bed?'

Charlie was as disappointed as she was, but he would not let this opportunity pass, so he countered with, 'I guess we'll have to share this one bed . . . '

She cut him off, 'You wish, Charlie . . . you just wish! And, you can keep on wishing. You can sleep on the floor over there, and I'll sleep in the bed for the first part of the night. Then, I'll set the clock for two or three and then, we'll switch places. That's all I'm agreeable to. Damn this place.'

He smiled. 'OK with me.'

She started to unpack her bags, saying, 'I'll be in the bathroom a long time, so you'd better go first, do you mind?'

He thought of the chance to call Meagan and he gladly replied, 'No, you go first . . . go ahead . . . take your time.'

Making sure she had gone into the bathroom for good, he picked up the telephone and dialled Meagan's number . . . no answer. He looked at his watch – only 1435 and he tried to visualize the time zones. Then he remember her new schedule. She went to work at six, but what time did she get off? Was she still working? And he uttered an unrepeatable expletive as he looked to make sure no one was listening. The phone call would have to wait. He began to unpack his duffel bag.

In a fit of anger on the boat when Amanda had complained about the small closet, he had thrown all his clothes in the large duffel bag, including his dress slacks and blazers. Now, he deeply regretted his generosity, because the hotel party tonight was to be a dressy affair, complete with dress clothes. He went back to the phone and called room service to remedy that situation, and having solved that problem he let himself down on the fully made bed to rest.

He dozed off real fast, long before Amanda had finished in the bathroom and by the time she came out, in her bathrobe, he was snoring. She gave him a mean look as she walked over to wake him, and as she got to the side of the bed, she paused, looking at him sleeping, and then she smiled as she stood there for a while, watching him. Then, she picked up her dress clothes and began to dress on one side of the room. Just as she had disrobed down to her bra and panties and was ready to slip into her dress, he was awakened by the rustling of the clothes. She saw him stir, but with her dress halfway to her knees, what could she do but continue, as he looked at her, smiling.

She hurried in pulling the dress up to an acceptable level as she said, 'I'm sorry. I thought I could slip this dress on before you woke, but, then, I'm sure you enjoyed the sight of me in bra and panties.'

He smiled at her. 'I enjoyed every square centimetre of it.'

As she completed buttoning up the back of the dress, she replied, 'Well, don't get worked up. Simply because fate has ordained that we share the same room does not change a thing. Understand?'

He had had just about enough of her egotistical belief that no man could resist her considerable charms. He could take no more and, with the increased size of the space allotted to them, he felt he did not have to take it.

He gave her a cool look as she started back into the bathroom, and exclaimed not too softly, 'You know, Amanda, I hate to pop your bubble but you do nothing for me. I am not attracted to you one iota. As a matter of fact, I could lie next to you in this bed, tonight, and not have one lustful desire. How does that grab you?'

He had made the exclamation in haste, without really thinking it out. He was not sure he could resist her charms in such close proximity.

She stopped in her return to the bathroom, and she gave him a contemptuous glare as she retorted, 'You're lying! You wouldn't last ten minutes before you'd be all over me. I know men!'

He remained cool, for he could smell victory, or, at least, a chance of a real interesting battle, as he replied, 'Would you like to put me to the test?'

'Oh, sure! Do you think I'm stupid? If I lose . . . you win! Nice try, Charlie, but, no thanks.'

'Then, how can we know for sure that you can produce an uncontrollable urge in me unless we put the thing to the test? I think you're afraid to test me. You're all talk, Amanda. You suffer from delusions of grandeur. When all the hype and the pizzaz are gone, you have the same equipment as any other woman.'

She was now getting upset with him, to the point that she had now lost sight of his game plan. She didn't care. She had to prove that she had it. She still suffered from an inferiority complex over the breakup of her marriage. And, it ate at her. This was her problem. She had not even begun to regain her self esteem, and now she was being challenged again . . . by another man.

She could take no more as she went to the side of the bed, replying, 'You are on, buster! Tonight, you can have one side of the bed, and I will take the other, but you have got to make me one solemn promise'

He asked, extremely interested, 'And what is that?'

She looked at him with cold eyes. 'When I call it off, it is off . . . do you know what I mean,' and she got even cooler, as she continued, 'No matter what is going on at the time. Think you can handle it, lover-boy?' and she smiled.

Now he had been challenged. He didn't give it enough thought, as he responded, 'You're damn right I can.'

She was not finished as she pointed her finger at him. 'And if you don't cease and desist, instantaneously, I will charge you with assault to the Mexican police, and from what I've heard of Mexican jails you just might lose your virginity in there. Do we understand each other . . . perfectly?'

He had no idea what he had gotten himself into, but he knew one thing for sure, he had crossed the line of no return, as he nodded, 'It's a deal.'

She smiled, sure of victory, as she went into the bathroom, saying, 'I'll be out in a minute, then, it's all yours, Charlie-boy.'

When he came out she was completely dressed and she looked fabulous. She had done her hair, her nails, and any other accessories that could enhance her beauty, and it was all justifiable.

He looked at her as she was just admiring herself in the full length mirror, and he acknowledged to her, 'You look great, Amanda . . . no kidding.'

She was pleased with the compliment, and in complete agreement, as she warmly responded, 'Thank you, Charlie, I'll be down in the bar having a drink,' and she cooed, 'waiting for you.'

He smiled in return . . . nodding.

It was a different looking bunch who assembled in the bar of the hotel from the scruffy looking crew who had disembarked from the *Polaris* earlier that day. Each gave an admiring glance to all the others, saying, 'Gee, do you guys look great.'

Of course, it was to Amanda to whom the most accolades were cast, for she was indeed the most beautiful woman in the bar at that time, and probably in the whole hotel.

She was wearing a slinky, low-cut dress, and the men in the bar stared without shame as she walked by.

The women's glances were more hostile, of course. As she sat at the bar, Amanda crossed her legs and with a slit three-quarters up her thigh, it was a sight to behold. She had patted the bar stool next to her as Charlie walked up, motioning for him to sit next to her.

She saw him admire the beautiful long leg mostly exposed, and she thought, 'I'll have him panting within an hour.'

As he admired the leg, he thought, 'This is going to be a rough night,' and he remembered her threat.

He, too, had been warned about Mexican jails by a friend before he embarked.

As they sipped their drinks and chatted, she lost no opportunity to make skin contact with him. Mostly by placing her hand on his, and once she patted him on the cheek, lightly. There was no doubt in his mind that she intended to make him suffer. She would lead him to the edge of the abyss, to the threshold of ecstasy, only to deny him at the moment of intended rapture.

He thought of Meagan, and his conscience hurt him. Was he being untrue to her? Not yet, he rationalized, and he was sure he would not . . . not of his own volition, anyway. But, when a man is pushed to the limit . . . and beyond . . . who can say with certainty?

All during dinner she was solicitous of him, smiling a warm smile, touching his hand.

'Damn, but she is good,' he thought.

Peg noticed it, too, and she smiled. She thought, 'Perhaps, my wild gamble is paying off, or, maybe, Amanda has got that most dreaded of diseases . . . hotel fever, for which there is only one cure.'

Peg touched her husband's hand under the table, nodding towards Amanda and Charlie. Arnie smiled . . . knowingly.

The engaged couple took little notice, being totally absorbed in each other.

As the meal was winding down, the roving Maharachi band, ubiquitous at all Mexican night spots, gave way to a real dance band which played a combination of Latin and American dance music, trying to please everyone of their world clientele.

When a slow, dreamy, dance tune began, Amanda placed her hand on his, asking, softly and sweetly, 'Dance with me, Charlie?'

He nodded and rose, pulling her chair back for her to rise. She smiled at him as she placed her arm on his to walk to the dance floor. As they embraced, at first, she did not hold him too close, but as the dance progressed, he could feel her body move in closer and her hand rested on the back of his neck. Once, she moved her head back and smiled at him . . . a warm smile . . . and then, she moved back in and held him closer than previously.

Then the men performed that required social gesture when several women are at the same table . . . they danced with all of them. Peg held Charlie close, not with any special intent – that was the way she danced with all men . . . even strangers. It was her style. The young engaged girl, Kate, afraid to send the wrong signals to any man but her Bill, stayed a respectable distance from the other men, reminding Charlie of his first date in high school.

The dancing party went on to the wee hours of the morning, and the consumption of Tequila accompanied the dancing.

The orchestra leader, in fractured English, announced that the next dance would be the last, and all the women grabbed their men by the hand, cooing, 'Oh, let's dance the last one.'

Amanda was no exception. She smiled at Charlie and, without even asking, took his hand and rose.

Charlie went along like a lamb being led to slaughter with a sprig of green grass as bait. In Amanda's case the bait was more of the prurient genre. She had just returned from the ladies room, and the wear and tear of the evening had all been repaired. The makeup was all freshly in place, the perfume had been reinforced . . . not that it had to be, for poor Charlie's nostrils had ingested it all evening.

He had tapered off his drinking some time earlier, for he knew he was headed for trouble and he needed a clear head.

They all entered the elevator together. Peg nestled her head in Arnie's shoulder, saying, 'I'm sleepyeeee.' Arnie grunted, replying, 'You'd better take a no-doze, baby.'

Kate snuggled her head in Bill's shoulder, not saying anything.

Amanda smiled at Charlie, leaning against him. He smelled the perfume behind her ears. He smelled the freshly-washed hair, and he felt the closeness of her body. It would be an untruth to say he was not aroused.

The elevator came to a stop and they each entered their own room. Amanda waited for Charlie to open their door and she smiled as she entered. She went to the closet area and began to remove her dress, making no attempt to hide herself or cover her body.

She lowered the dress and stepped out of it, standing in her bra and panties. She turned around to him, asking, 'Do you want the bathroom first?'

He looked at her for a moment, taking in that superb body and beautiful face, as she stood there, unashamed, allowing him his look.

He shook his head, saying, 'No, you go ahead.'

She spent some time in the bathroom, and he could hear her humming some tune he could not make out.

He was deep in thought as he pondered his next move. Could he do it? Could he resist her charms, with her lying there next to him in that bed. Was she still insistent on keeping the bet, or was she really in the mood as she had indicated all night in her every word and every gesture? He didn't know, and the only way he could find out was to expose himself to intolerable temptations.

He thought of Meagan. Once more, he had not called her. What could he do? He was being driven by circumstances beyond his control. He should never have come on this trip. Something told him it was a potential disaster.

Did he not ask Peg, 'Why do I feel like this is going to be a disaster?'

When she came out of the bathroom she was wearing a teddie, as usual, but this was not the same teddy . . . no . . this was a black lace one, and it shimmied as she walked.

She went to the bed, pulled the sheet back, eased herself in, and said softly, 'I'll be waiting, Charlie . . . don't be too long.'

He made no reply as he went into the bathroom. He leaned against the wall, thinking, 'What the hell can I do? If I back out, she'll say I'm a wimp, and she'll make damn sure the others on the boat know about it, too. If I ravish her which is what I want to do . . . what will she do? Will she go along with it, or is this still a game with her? Would she really file charges against me?'

He didn't know, as he began to undress.

He entered the bedroom in only pyjama tops. That was a decision he had to make. 'How shall I go in there? If I go in with all my pyjamas on, it will look kinda wimpy. If I go in naked . . . that will look tacky. After all, she did not come in naked.'

She was sitting up in bed when he returned.

She motioned to the bed, saying, 'Sit for a while, Charlie, we need to talk.'

Her demeanour was so different from what it had been on the cruise. Hell, he could have liked this woman under different conditions, and then, he thought of Meagan. There is nothing more awesome on this earth than an active conscience . . . one that will not play dead when the situation calls for it.

He sat where directed. She took one of his hands in hers, as she spoke, softly. 'I guess you know I've acted like a real bitch on this cruise . . . I know it, Charlie, and I'm sorry. It was due to several things, none of which make much sense at this moment, but they did then. I was appalled when Peg first informed me that I would have to share a room with a strange man . . . '

He smiled. 'You find me strange?'

She smiled. 'You know what I mean,' as she continued, 'and that, coupled with a traumatic bust up of my marriage . . . well, I felt the only way I could survive this trip with you in that small stateroom was to be obnoxious as hell.'

He shrugged. 'It worked too . . . I disliked you intensely.'

She brought his hand up to her lips . . . kissing it, saying. 'I'm so sorry. you're a nice guy, Charlie, which brings me to the real subject matter at hand,' and she looked embarrassed as she continued. 'We made a bet tonight.' He nodded. 'And at the time I made it, I was angry with you. You had challenged my womanhood . . . my sensuality, and I was already gun shy in that respect, so I made up my mind to drive you crazy, if I could,' and she looked sheepishly at him.

'You did a damn good job of it, too.' He shook his head.

She nodded, smiling, 'Well, I wanted to tell you that the bet is off . . . the feelings I have now are real. I want you, Charlie, and this is no game,' and she drew him to her, kissing him passionately.

He offered no resistance. She pulled him to her and he went, reluctantly, but without protest. They lay together for some time, kissing, caressing, and then, he pulled away from her.

She looked startled, as she asked, 'Is something wrong?'

He shook his head. 'Not with you, Amanda . . . '

'Jesus! Don't tell me I've got another one! Where do you guys come from. What's happening to American manhood!'

He looked embarrassed as he replied. 'No, no . . . it's not that! There is nothing wrong with me in that respect and there is damn sure nothing wrong with you either . . . '

She began to sob. 'Would you please tell me what the hell is going on? I can't believe my luck in men . . . '

And so he told her everything! And when he had finished, she said, 'I can't believe this . . . a faithful man!'

He smiled. 'Don't pin any medals on me, Amanda, if you knew how much I want you right now . . . '

She smiled. 'It's no sin to want, is it?'

'If it is, I'm guilty as hell, because I want you, now.'

She got up and paced the floor, wistfully. 'It wouldn't be any good, Charlie. One of us would be sorry in the morning, maybe both.' She laughed. 'You've really poured cold water on this thing,' and she laughed, went over to the bed where he was sitting and kissed him on the cheek, saying, 'I guess you'd better get out of my bed . . . '

'Your bed?' as he got up and went over to the other side of the room, taking some covers with him, but smiling at her.

As he tried to get comfortable on the floor he could hear very subdued sobbing coming from her. He said nothing for quite some time, not sure of what to say, or do.

Finally . . . 'Amanda? Are you alright?'

She replied, hardly audible, 'No Charlie . . . I'm not alright.'

He rose and walked over to the bed and sat next to her, taking her hand. 'What's wrong?'

She began to cry. 'Oh, Charlie, I need some cuddling. Please . . . can't we just cuddle for a while? I feel so all alone and neglected . . . I'm miserable.'

All the resentment and antagonism of the past few weeks had melted away and she was like a little girl as he held her while she cried.

She held him close as he stroked her hair, and between sobs, she uttered, 'I'm so sorry to be acting like this. I hate myself when I break down like this. I didn't want you to see me this way!'

'I know . . . I know, but it's alright.' He smiled at her. 'What's a good cry between friends?'

'Oh, Charlie . . . can we be friends? I don't want to fight with you, anymore . . . '

He continued to stroke her hair, kissing her cheeks. 'Of course we can be friends . . . good friends, too.'

Without saying anything she moved over in the bed and he slipped in next to her. She nestled her head on his chest and placed her arm around his body, nestling close to him.

For a long time no one said anything . . . they just lay there, holding each other, and finally, she broke the silence as she asked, 'Can't we just stay like this for a while until I go to sleep?'

He was torn with conflicting emotions. Desire was strong in him as it would have been in any man, but loyalty to Meagan also had some influence on him, but . . . Meagan was in Colorado, and Amanda was here next to him.

He replied, softly, 'I'm not sure you can trust me here next to you. I can't promise you that I can restrain myself.'

She raised her head to look at him. 'I'm not worried about that . . . '

'What makes you so sure?'

'If you put your hands any place they have no business, I swear to you that I will prefer charges against you in the morning,' and she laughed.

He laughed as he cuddled her again. She snuggled close to him, saying nothing more until he could detect the regular, deep breathing of sleep. He smiled as he lay on his back, looking at the ceiling.

He was lying next to one of the most beautiful and desirable women he had ever known in his life, and . . . he was thinking of another . . . Meagan. He was sure! He was in love. In time he also surrendered to slumber.

She was still asleep when he awoke in the morning. They had not drawn the drapes and the morning sun streamed through the east windows facing the ocean.

He eased out of bed and went to the windows to correct the situation, and as he did, she stirred, moaning, 'Good morning' and as her mind reviewed the events of the night before, she purred, 'I'm so proud of you, Charlie! You were a good boy last night.'

He stood next to the bed looking down at her, and he was still filled with desires for her, but he turned away, replying, 'I'm proud of myself . . . it was not an easy thing to do, I must admit, and if you don't get out of that bed, soon, my promise of chastity will be broken, I swear . . . no matter how many charges you file, I'll be all over you like flies on a manure pile.'

She laughed, jumping out of bed. 'I'm going . . . I'm going! I have to tinkle anyway,' as she disappeared in the bathroom.

He sat on a chair, thinking, 'Damn! Women! I hate them.'

After they had both dressed and were ready to go down to breakfast, he caught her arm, saying, 'Look, Amanda, all the things I told you last night about Meagan and me . . . well, could we keep that between us? Peg and Arnie know nothing about her and I'm not ready to break the news. OK?'

She smiled, kissing him on the cheek. 'It's our secret, Charlie . . . I swear to it.'

'Thank you. I appreciate it. Oh! One more thing before we go down to the lobby. You remember we can get our original room reservations for tonight. What do you want to do? Do you want to keep this one, or . . . ?'

She looked at him, smiling. 'Charlie, you were lucky to escape with your chastity intact, last night. Don't push your luck. If you and I share a room tonight, I promise you, you will be ravished by one horny blonde, so you make the decision for both of us.'

He smiled. 'I swear . . . it's tempting, but . . . I guess I owe Meagan that consideration . . . and loyalty. Two rooms.'

'You're a good man, Charlie! Meagan is a lucky woman, but you are simply awful for a woman's self-image as a killer type, which I foolishly believe I am,' and she giggled.

13

The group were talkative at breakfast as all the pent-up emotions of the week-long congestion on the boat gave way to loquaciousness, and euphoria.

Curiosity also entered the discussion, too, as the irrepressible Peg began to probe. She was of course aware that Charlie and Amanda were forced to share a one-bed room, but she did not know what the sleeping arrangements were between the two antagonists and it burned in her. Based on their stormy relationship on the boat, it was inconceivable to her that they could have shared the same room, much less the same bed, but she had to know, or, she thought she had to know. She watched the interplay between Charlie and Amanda during breakfast, and it was different. She knew that Amanda had been working Charlie over the night before during the meal and dancing, but she had done that from meanness . . . hadn't she? Every time Amanda had made some intimate gesture towards Charlie, had she not winked at Peg . . . the time accepted symbol for collusion? But, Peg felt there was no reason to continue the charade this morning . . . unless . . . and with a practiced eye . . . she watched and studied them.

Her eyebrows went up as Amanda asked, 'Charlie, dear, may I have some coffee? Thank you, love,' and he was rewarded with a dazzling smile. Are these not terms of endearment?

Peg asked neither party in particular, 'How did you two sleep last night in that cramped room with just one bed? Someone obviously had to sleep on the floor?'

Amanda gave her a mischievous smile, and she gave Charlie one, also, replying, 'Oh . . . not necessarily?

Really, Peg, do you think it is impossible for two people who have a deep-seated dislike for one another to share the same bed? After all, it was a king-sized bed.'

Charlie just smiled. He didn't give a damn if Amanda was having some fun with Peg. After all, as far as Peg knew, he was merely a disgruntled divorced man who was free to play the field, and Amanda was the field.

Peg received Amanda's reply with, 'Oh . . . really? Well, I guess it is possible in this permissive society of ours,' and she grinned, adding, 'I'm not sure I could do it, but, then, I don't hate men as you do, Amanda.'

Kate and Bill, the divorced couple, merely smiled at each other.

As breakfast ended, Charlie pulled Amanda aside. 'I want to go up to the room to make a phone call to Colorado. We'll settle the bill later . . . OK?'

She gave him a knowing smile. 'Go on and call Meagan, Charlie. Try to explain to her about last night . . . I dare you. We'll find out how much she loves you.'

'Are you crazy? I'll see you in a few minutes.'

'OK, lover . . . ' and she smiled at him.

As he entered the room he went over the time differences. It was Sunday morning in both places, and it was nine thirty in Colorado. Was she working today? He was not sure, but he dialled her number.

A sleepy . . . 'Hello?'

'Meagan, honey, it's me . . . Charlie.'

'Oh, Charleeee . . . where have you been? I've been crazy worrying about you. You promised me you would call from the boat, but, you didn't . . . oh, Charlie . . . I miss you.

'Meagan, you sound great! You don't sound the same, but, I miss you anyway.'

'I miss you, too. Why didn't you call? Oh, before you answer, guess who is here with me now?'

He joked, 'Not a man, huh?'

'Be serious, Charlie. Erin is home . . . isn't that wonderful?'

'Oh, yes . . . I'm sure you're happy about that.'

'Here she is, Charlie . . . she wants to talk to you . . . here she is, honey.'

'Charlie? . . . this is Erin.'

'Erin, I'm so glad to be able to finally talk to you. I'm so happy you're home, and I know Meagan is, too.'

'And, I have you to thank for it, Charlie! You and that wonderful Miss de la Rosa. I owe my life to you two.'

He was embarrassed at her lavish praise. 'I didn't do anything but strike the match. It was Monica de la Rosa who built the fire.'

'Well, anyway, I'm grateful to you both. I'd like to talk to you some more, but my mama is over here tugging at the phone, so . . . goodbye, Charlie . . . '

'It's me, again. Oh, Charlie, why didn't you call me? You said the boat had a phone.'

'It did, Meagan, but when I listened to the others use it, I realized we would have no privacy. I wouldn't be able to express myself like I wanted to . . . you know . . . tell you sweet nothings like people in love do . . . '

'Are you in love, Charlie? Really in love?'

'Yes, I'm really in love. (His brain was thinking . . . if you only knew what I went through last night . . . for you . . . you would never doubt me, again) Yes, Meagan,' he continued . . . 'I really love you . . . I do.'

'Charlie, I hate this long distance loving . . . I can't stand it much longer. When are you coming back to see me . . . and Erin?'

'The cruise will only last two more weeks.'

'Two more weeks? Oh, God, Charlie! I don't know if I can stand it.'

'Me, too, but after that . . . '

She caught the words. 'After that', as she asked . . . 'after that, Charlie . . . what happens to us?'

'Well, I'm not sure. Do we have to decide that, now? Over the phone?'

She replied, softly, 'No!' And then . . . 'Charlie, have you told the other people on the boat about me?'

He answered, sombrely, 'No . . . I haven't'

'Oh.'

'Does that matter to you?'

'Well, no! I was just wondering. How do you like your roommate? I hope he was not hard to get along with. I know that can ruin a trip.'

He thought fast. How could he tell her the truth? His brain raced for an innocuous answer, as he replied, 'Well, I did have trouble getting along with my roommate at first, but things have improved to a great extent, now.'

'I'm glad,' she replied with all sincerity.

They had run out of things to say, so he asked, 'How's school coming along?'

She became animated, again. 'Great! You notice how I talk? My teacher, the one who instructs me at night . . . well, she is tough, Charlie. She won't tolerate any bad grammar. You like the way I talk now?'

He laughed at her simplicity, and he loved it. 'Yes, Meagan, I love the way you talk, now, but, you see, I love all of you.'

'That's sweet. I love you, too.'

Erin had heard that and she grabbed the mouthpiece from her mother. 'I love you, too, Charlie . . . '

'Oh, Erin, you keep out of this . . . this man is mine! You find one of yurn,' and she had lapsed into her dialect.

She continued, 'Poor child. She's been away from men for so long, I can't let her out of my sight, Charlie . . . '

Erin yelled from across the room, 'That's not true, Charlie!'

He laughed. 'I guess we'll have to find her a man, Meagan.'

'I'm not too anxious to do that . . . unless she could find a man like you. You have any brothers, Charlie?'

'No. I'm an only child.'

She was serious as she replied, 'That's too bad. When God makes men like you, he ought to make a matching pair.'

'Why?'

'Well, when a girl wears one of them out, there'd be a spare,' and she giggled.

'I can see where your mind is.'

'Uh huh, it sure is. So, what are you going to do about it?'

'Just as soon as I can I will go to Colorado and cure your problem . . . '

'Supposing I can't wait that long?' she cooed.

'Supposing I can't either,' he retorted, realistically.

'I see what you mean, Charlie, honey . . . I'll wait if you will.'

He laughed. 'It's a deal. I have to go, now.'

'OK, aaaa . . . if you have to. I love you, honey.'

Erin yelled out, 'I love you, too, Charlie.'

He grinned. 'I love both you girls . . . bye.'

As Amanda entered the room he was just completing the phone call. She said, 'Oh, I'm sorry, I came back too soon and interrupted your call . . . '

'No! I was finished.'

Amanda gave him a mischievous look. 'Did you tell her you spent last night in the same bed with a gorgeous woman?'

'Don't be ridiculous!'

'Well, that is one way to find out how much she loves you.'

'If you were in her place, would you understand it, or, tolerate it?'

'Hell, no!'

'I didn't think so.'

She came over and sat by him on the bed, looking in his eyes, as she picked up one of his hands. 'I have to tell you something, and I hope you won't be offended by it.'

'I promise to remain calm.'

She nodded. 'I did a lot of thinking about you last night as I lay there in your arms. You thought I was sleeping, but I wasn't . . . I thought about you and me. I am deeply attracted to you, Charlie, and if you didn't have another woman in your life, I'd go after you . . . I swear it.'

He was surprised at her declaration, but he felt he should give it the respect it deserved as he replied, 'But, how can that be? Just a few days ago, we were at each other's throats, or so it seemed . . . '

'I know, but it was all an act on my part . . . a defensive mechanism. I wanted to hate all men for the time being.'

He laughed. 'I wasn't acting. I really learned to dislike you rather intensely for a while.'

'And, now . . . what of now, Charlie?'

He squeezed her hand, saying, 'I don't dislike you half as much as I did a few day's ago.'

She got up quickly and walked away. 'I've got to get out of this room. If I stay here much longer, I swear something will happen, Charlie . . . I can't hold out much longer. I'm going down to the lobby to see about my own room,' and she hurried out.

He watched her leave, as he pondered her remarks.

'How can that be? She is not really falling for me . . . she can't be. It's the proximity that does it . . . and the tropical climate. That's it! 'Oh, Meagan, if it were not for you, this could be one hell of a trip . . . but . . . '

The two men, Charlie and Arnie, having worked all day, were truly tired as the sun lowered itself over the western hills, and as each went to his room, each lowered himself onto the bed, groaning, 'Oh, my aching back . . . I'm tired.' And they dozed off, but when the women arrived . . . Peg and Amanda . . . fresh and rejuvenated from a day of leisure, they wanted to partake of the pleasures of Cancun . . . the food . . . the music . . . the nightlife. They wanted to see and be seen.

Peg had the wifely prerogative of saying to her husband, 'Get your buns off that bed . . . take a bath . . . and let's go.'

But, poor Amanda, she had no such proprietary rights with Charlie. she looked at herself in the full length mirror in her suite, turning one way and another, thinking, 'Damn, I look great!' And as she gave it one more turn, she continued to herself . . . 'and I have no date for the evening. I guess I've scared poor Charlie off with my threats against his chastity . . . oh, hell . . . what to do?'

She thought about it for at least thirty seconds and then she acted. She left her room and went to Charlie's across the hall, and knocked softly. No reply. She knocked again . . . louder this time, and in a moment, the door opened and a sleepy Charlie stood there, saying, 'Amanda . . . I didn't expect you . . . '

She brushed past him. 'Charlie, honey, I have to talk to you.'

He nodded, turning around as she passed him, sleepily responding, 'OK' and he returned and flopped on the bed.

As he went down he gave her a discerning look, saying, Damn, you look great, Amanda.' She did, too. She had on a pale blue dress which matched the colour of her eyes. It was tight fitting, with a long skirt and a short bodice. Her blonde hair was up and held at the back with a ribbon the colour of her dress.

She replied to his comment as she sat on the bed next to him. 'I know! I look like a million bucks and have no one to go out with. I need a date, Charlie! Now, you have two choices.' At the sound of the mild threat, he came more awake, as she continued, 'You have two choices . . . either you take me out, or, I will go down to the bar, sit at the stool, look seductive as hell, and play the field. The first good looking Latin stud that makes a play for me, and believe me, Charlie, they will come in droves, and I am the least bit attracted to him, I will allow myself to be picked up, and so help me, God, I will reward him with a night of passion he will never forget.'

She sat up, proudly, as she concluded, 'Those are your choices, Charlie. Either you can be a gentleman and save me from a night of debauchery, or you will have me on your conscience the rest of your life, for I am sure I will have emotional scars from this.' and she giggled, 'Probably some physical ones, too. What's your answer, Charlie, love?'

He smiled. 'Those are my only two choices?'

She squared her shoulders. 'Yes . . . just those two'

'And suppose I am overcome with uncontrollable desire? Will I be rewarded with a night of passion, too?'

She smiled. 'You might well be, Charlie, and there will be nothing either of us can do about it, either.'

He sat up. 'Well, you see, Amanda, I had a proper upbringing, as you well know. My mother, who is a stickler for these sorts of things, instilled in me a strong sense of knightly honour where damsels in distress are concerned, and I am imbued with an insoluble compulsion to aid any female in need, no matter the odds or consequences . . . '

'What the hell does all that mean, Charlie? Is it you or the Latin stud?'

He laughed. 'I believe in keeping it American.'

She leaned over him, kissing him on the cheek. 'Oh, Charlie, thanks . . . I owe you.' She arose, poking him in the ribs. 'Get up and take a bath . . . you smell a little . . . I'll be waiting in the bar,' and with a toss of her beautiful head, 'fighting off Latin studs, so don't be long . . . my resistance is low,' and pursing her lips . . . 'real low,' as she went through the door.

Just as sure as bees flock to honey, Amanda was surrounded by three or four men as Charlie entered the bar. It was obvious she was having fun, as he glimpsed her beautiful head between the heads of the hopeful swains as they jockeyed for position around her. She played them like puppets on a string, enjoying every minute of the game at which she was a master. She had fought men off all her life, beginning in high school, honing her talents in college, and becoming a master in the pre-marriage game of life. She enjoyed it, and it showed, but as Charlie walked up, she saw him, and stood up, making her goodbyes to the protests of all over-optimistic and over-stimulated males around her, patting this one on the cheek, that one on the arm, and to profuse looks of regret and despair, pointed to Charlie and walked away.

As she got near him, she cooed, as she took his arm, 'Whew . . . you got here just in time . . . my, but those guys are persistent,' and she whispered in his ear . . . 'quite persuasive, too. I just didn't know how much longer I could have held out, but, my hero is here, now . . . I'm safe. I'm also hungry. All that jousting works up an appetite, doesn't it?'

He smiled at her. 'I wouldn't know. I don't joust much, nowadays.'

She gave him a wicked smile. 'The day isn't over yet,

love. Oh, look, there are the rest of the gang . . . let's join them.'

As the night progressed the crew of the *Polaris* became more congenial in proportion to the amount of Tequila consumed, as is usually the case. As each male danced with each female in the party the difference from the night before was quite noticeable, even in the fanatically monogamous, Kate, the young engaged girl.

She allowed herself to be held closer, giggling, 'Gee, I love that Latin music . . . it does something to me,' which for her was a bold statement, accompanied by an embarrassed look.

But, to Amanda, this was a night made for love, and she felt it to the very soul of her being. She held Charlie exceptionally close in their dances, playing with his neck, whispering in his ear, kissing his cheek, looking longingly in his eyes, but she made no obvious comment, allowing instead for human emotions and longing to play out their role. She was certainly privy to the information of his last contact with Meagan, and with the practiced eye of her kind, she felt the time was ripe. After all, he was a healthy thirty-six year old male animal, and time took its toll on them . . . she knew that. She looked in his eyes often, and he looked in hers, saying nothing, for words were not necessary.

It was the wee hours of the morning when Arnie, the captain of the crew, announced with authority diluted by drink, 'I think we should all turn in. We shove off tomorrow at high noon.

'This brought groans from all present. 'Oh, no! That's too early!'

He was adamant. 'Anyone not on that boat at noon can swim to Belize!'

'Ohooooo . . . Arnie!'

Charlie looked at Amanda, saying, 'I guess we'd better turn in . . . that means us, too.'

She nodded. 'Just one more dance, huh?' And to the strains of, Good Night Sweetheart, she held him close and hummed in his ear, and lightly brushed his lips with hers as she looked deeply in his eyes. She knew what she was doing, and he knew what she was doing to him.

He asked, 'Are you trying to drive me crazy, Amanda?'

'If I thought It would help, Charlie, I would have no compunction about doing it.'

'What about Meagan?'

'Who?' she teased.

'You know, Meagan, the woman I love.'

She gave him a look of complete assurance, as she replied, 'Meagan is in Colorado, Charlie . . . Amanda is here.'

He nodded. 'I know. I think we had better go.'

She offered no protest as she released him, and taking his arm, they walked to the elevators, saying nothing at all. They were alone when the elevator doors closed, and she went to him, holding him close, her arms around his neck. He offered no resistance or protest.

She looked in his eyes, smiling, saying softly, 'Tell ya what, Charlie, let's see just how good a man you really are. I challenge you to a duel.'

'A duel? I don't feel like duelling, Amanda.'

'Come on . . . let's have some fun, Charlie. We'll be on that damn boat for another week, beginning tomorrow . . . come on.'

'What do you want me to do?'

'I want to renew our bet of last night. I'll bet you can't spend another night in bed with me, without ravishing me,' and she kissed him passionately, as if to illustrate the challenge.

He knew what she was up to. She had no intention of even giving him a chance to save himself, but he had lost a great deal of his resistance several hours and as many drinks ago.

He didn't reply, so she prodded him. 'Come on, Charlie, let's see how strong you really are.'

As the elevator door opened she took him by the hand and led him to her suite, handing him the key to her door. She smiled at him, seductively, as she brushed past him and went into the room.

He still said nothing as he closed the door behind himself. He was curious where she was going with this. He thought he and she had reached an understanding last night. He had told her he loved Meagan, and could not bring himself to deceiving her . . . he had told her . . .

She turned to him 'This suite has two baths, so you can take that one and I will take this one,' and she disappeared into the bathroom, smiling back at him as she did.

He didn't know what to do. He looked at the suite. It was a nice one. He smiled as he thought. 'Her husband must have been loaded and she must have made a healthy settlement.'

There were two queen size beds in the one bedroom suite, with a small living area and two baths . . . obviously designed to accommodate a family of four if they all piled into two beds.

He felt he should get up and walk out, now, while she was in the bath. He would call her on the phone and explain that he accepted defeat . . . he could not remain in the room without compromising his loyalties to Meagan. He had just about made up his mind to leave when she emerged from the bathroom. She was wearing a smile and not much more. She had on only a very sheer peignoir dressing gown, obviously purchased that day and for this purpose, for she had nothing on under it, and the full loveliness of her perfect body was quite apparent. He swallowed hard as he stared at her. She made no attempt to keep the peignoir closed, and it flared as she walked. She smiled at him, saying, 'Well, I thought you'd be ready for bed by now, Charlie . . . not interested in our little bet?'

'Your little bet, Amanda, I didn't agree to it.'

She was standing directly in front of him, and he stared, and she watched him stare, as she continued, 'I don't see the problem of two friends sharing a bedroom . . . especially when there are two beds in the room,' and she turned, pointing to the two beds, as she continued, 'You take that one and I will take this one. All I'm asking for is a night of friendship, Charlie . . . I'm lonesome . . . I think you owe me that much. Come on,' and she took him by the hand.

'But,' he protested, 'I have to go and get my pyjamas in my room . . . '

'Oh, Charlie . . . you don't need pyjamas! Haven't you ever slept in the buff . . . besides,' she cooed, 'do you realize that I have never seen you in the buff . . . come on, be a sport,' and she began to help him undress.

He was becoming angry. Men were supposed to be the aggressors, and she was breaking all the rules of engagement, so he protested, shoving her hands away, 'Oh, all right, Amanda . . . just to humour you. I'll sleep in that damn bed, but you stay in yours and I'll stay in mine, OK?'

She smiled, knowingly. 'Sure, Charlie, love, if that is the way you want it,' and she turned to go to her bed, and as she reached it, she removed the peignoir completely, faced him momentarily, and then, turning around and smiling but saying nothing, she pulled back the sheets and got in. She watched as he stripped to his shorts, only, and she giggled as he got into bed wearing them, but keeping his back to her. She smiled knowingly, once again.

He reached over to turn out his light, and she did the same with hers, saying, 'See how simple that was, Charlie? Goodnight, love.'

He said without enthusiasm, 'Goodnight, Amanda.'

The room was quiet for a while, and then, 'Charlie?'

'What?'

'Do you hear a mosquito buzzing in the room? I can never sleep with a mosquito buzzing around'

'Kill it then.'

'I can't do that. I hate bugs! Charlie?'

'Yes, Amanda?'

'Would you be so kind as to get me a glass of water?'

'Get it, yourself . . . you're not cripple.'

'I can't find my slippers and I can't stand to walk on a tile floor, it gives me the creeps . . . please.'

'Oh, alright, I'll get it.'

'Will you bring it to me . . . I'll turn the light on so you can see . . . '

He swallowed hard, thinking, 'I don't want to see.'

She sat up in bed as he handed her the glass, smiling at him as she took it. 'Gee, thanks.'

Even in her sitting position her lovely and perfect body was quite visible to him . . . all of it.

She smiled as she watched his eyes going over her, purring, 'While you're here, Charlie, I think that mosquito bit me on the back. Would you take a look. I obviously can't see my own back, or I would do it myself. Would you put some antiseptic on it? I have some on the bathroom counter . . . '

When he returned with the antiseptic she had conveniently turned over on her stomach, exposing her back. He, once again, swallowed hard, shaking his head as he applied the medicine to her back, with her saying, 'Not too much! I don't want to smell like antiseptic all night.'

As he rubbed on the medicine, she cooed, 'Oooh, that feels so good, Charlie . . . gee, thanks . . . Charlie?'

'Yes, Amanda?' with exasperation.

She turned over on her back. 'You feel like cuddling for just a little while? Just cuddling?'

He shook his head, smiling. 'Just cuddling? You promise?'

She smiled seductively. 'Uh huh, I promise,' and she moved over as he slipped in beside her, turning the light out as he did.

She smiled as he pulled the sheet over her nude body, and then she aided him, affecting modesty, by pulling it even higher, smiling at him as she did. She snuggled her head in his neck with her left arm thrown over his body. She attempted to throw her left leg over his but he moved his leg out of the way. She said nothing . . . just smiled as she cuddled closer. She began to play with the hair on his chest, making small circles with her finger. He looked down at her. He smiled.

She smiled, as she held him closer, whispering in his ear 'Oh, Charlie.'

He murmured. 'I thought we were going to try to go to sleep.'

She sighed. "I'm trying, Charlie . . . I really am, but, I'm uptight. I need to relax before I can go to sleep.'

He inquired. 'Is there anything I can do to help you to relax?'

'Uh huh.'

'What?'

'A massage would really help.'

'I don't think I know how to give a massage.'
'Want me to show you?'
'Uh huh.'

14

The prow of the *Polaris* headed southeast into the warm waters of the Caribbean Sea as she headed for Ambergris Cay. The day was sunny and warm and since the wind was out of the east the yacht was sailing close hauled, making a respectable eight knots across the water. The crew had regained their exuberance after their sojourn in Cancun.

This first day out everyone was on deck, enjoying the sights of the sea. Man-o-war birds, those great black kites of the sky, had followed them out for quite some time and the crew marvelled at their flying abilities as they swooped and climbed, apparently without reason, for just the sheer joy of being able to do it. Arnie was at the helm, smiling proudly, as his heavily mortgaged craft sliced through the blue waters.

Amanda, applying sun screen on that soft and lovely fair skin, smiled at all around her. She was now a contented woman, at least more so than when they had first embarked from Corpus Christi. She thought she was falling in love with her former antagonist, but it was not a truly happy kind of love, for he belonged to another . . . but unrequited love is still better than no love at all. This was what she thought, anyway, as she reserved her warmest smiles for him.

Peg, the observant one, noticed the new accommodation between the two, and she was happy. She rationalized that her foolish and chancy gamble had paid off. They had achieved compatibility after all, and that gave her some degree of satisfaction. The young engaged couple sat on the bow, looking off into the future, both theirs and the boat's. They had decided after two nights in the hotel at Cancun that, perhaps, a few days of abstinence and salt air would be beneficial to both their bodies and their minds, so they sat merely holding hands and smiling into each other's eyes, marvelling at the greatness of life.

As the day came to a close and the evening meal was just a memory the couples all congregated on the deck, each to their own space, and looked off into the darkening sea, each with his or her own thoughts. There was little talking for it was sacrilege to break the spell of moments such as these. Amanda and Charlie, not wishing to give the wrong impression to the others, merely sat close, not touching, but glances between Peg and Arnie, perceived more than that. Peg gave her husband an all-knowing smile as she bent her head towards them, and Arnie acknowledged the implication with a grin.

They sat there, all of them, until the fading light of day was replaced by the obscurity of night, except for that remarkable display of heavenly bodies so noticeable on a boat where the lights of civilization do not obscure the vision by competing with the stars.

Now that it was dark, Amanda took Charlie's hand. He offered no resistance although his thoughts during the long silence were of Meagan, he felt it was his humanitarian duty to be nice to Amanda. After all, she had made expiation for her former antagonism, and she had shown him that she could be a warm and tender human being . . . one who was badly in need of affection from the male of the species, and he squeezed her hand in return.

She brought his hand up to her lips, kissing it gently, smiling at him, saying, softly, 'It's beautiful out here on the ocean, isn't it?'

He nodded, although it was too dark for her to see it, so she prodded him, 'Isn't it?' as she poked him in the ribs, and then, chastising him, softly, 'Charlie, I realize you love another woman, but while we're here together . . . couldn't you just share yourself with me . . . for just this short while? It'll all be over in a couple of weeks and she can have you for the rest of your life . . . but, for now . . . '

He squeezed her hand, smiling at her. 'I'm sorry. You're right, of course. I promise you my undivided attention for the rest of the cruise . . . would that make you happy?'

'It would make me very happy, Charlie . . . it really would.'

'Amanda . . . what are you going to do with your life when we get back? Do you know?'

She sighed. 'No . . . I don't, and I don't even want to think about it. I may do nothing for a while. I think I'll go home to my mom and dad's place to get my life together. I don't think I told you but my folks are well off. We own a ranch in west Texas, a huge place, twenty-seven thousand acres . . . '

Charlie whistled. 'Whew . . . that's big! Do you have cattle on it?'

'Uh huh. But, it's hard to make money with cattle these days. My daddy says the only way to make money with cattle is to have some oil under them.'

And do you have some oil under them?'

'Uh huh . . . we have twenty or thirty wells last time I heard. I've been gone for five or six years, so I'm not hep to what goes on. I just keep getting those royalty cheques each and every month,' and she smiled.

Charlie grunted. 'So that's where you get your money. I thought you had soaked your husband in the settlement . . . '

She laughed. 'I did! I soaked him good . . . just for meaness! The queer bastard!'

'How was he able to fool you for so long?'

She smiled a vicious smile. 'The same way Adelle was able to fool you for so long.'

'Your point is well taken. I will drop the subject if you will,' he laughed.

She held him close. 'Yes, let's not think about our deviant spouses, Charlie . . . let's think about us two normal and lascivious people,' and she kissed him, feeling confident that the darkness of the night obscured their actions, but the ever observant Peg called out, 'OK, you two . . . try to be more discreet! I can see what is going on,' and she giggled, 'and I like it almost as much as you do. Gives me ideas . . . come here, Arnie, my love.'

Amanda giggled too, but Charlie was not happy about that. He still had Meagan on his mind and he felt guilty, but what could he do? He knew he had to fight the consequences of the close proximity of Amanda for two more weeks, and it was brought home to him as she whispered, 'It's late, I'm going to bed. Are you coming, now?'

He felt discretion dictated that he should not leave with her. After all, it looked so obvious to the others, so he said, louder than he had to, 'No! You go ahead and go to sleep. I'll try not to wake you when I go into the room.' He was proud of himself that he had sent the right message to the others.

He waited almost another hour before he allowed himself the luxury of going to bed. He had hoped, in his mind, that Amanda had gone to sleep, so the potential threat of infidelity would be minimized, at least.

He slipped into the room as quietly as he could, but on stumping his toe on the entrance door as he closed it, he uttered, 'Damn!' under his breath, but she heard it, for she was not asleep.

She said, softly, 'It's OK, I'm not asleep. I've been waiting for you.'

'Why? I thought you wanted to go to sleep.'

'I can't sleep. I have too much on my mind.'

'What is keeping you awake? I thought sure that night sea air would tranquilize you . . . it did me.'

'I need to talk to you . . . can we talk for awhile . . . just a few minutes . . . ' she pleaded.

He went to her bunk, the lower one, and sat on it, as she moved over, and then she sat up, arranging her pillow against the cabin wall. He waited as she collected her thoughts. She looked more serious than he had ever seen her.

She took his hand in hers. 'Charlie, I think I'm in love with you. I say, I think, because my emotions are so mixed up these days that I don't know what I'm doing in that department.'

He started to make a reply, but she placed her fingers

on his lips. 'No . . . please let me finish before you say anything. I know you are in love with another woman, and I am trying to respect that. I have my faults, I know, but I don't want to be a man stealer . . . not another woman's man . . . especially a woman who is not here to fight for her man. I want to be fair to her . . . to you . . . and me, Charlie. All I want to know is . . . is there a chance for me with you . . . even a little one? All I ask is that you tell me the unvarnished truth, and I will accept it, no matter how painful it is.'

He tried to form his words carefully, as he turned them over in his mind. She was a wounded animal . . . he knew that. She was hurting, badly. He could see no reason to hurt her, yet he owed his allegiance and his love to Meagan. Of that, he was sure, as he held her hands.

'Amanda . . . if there was not a Meagan in my life, I could very easily get into a serious situation with you. You are one of the most beautiful and desirable women I have ever met, and this week with you has been pure hell on my morals and my resistance. I've wanted you since the first time you smiled that beautiful smile at me . . . any man would, believe me, but, I don't know if you can understand this . . . my love and devotion to Meagan has always been there, staring me in the face, not letting me return your affection. I'm not sure you're in love with me, just as I was not sure I was in love with Meagan for a while. I find it hard to believe that a person can change his or her affections as fast as you and I have in the past few weeks. If anything happened between me and Meagan, which I hope will not, and I do not think it will, well . . . I'll come looking for you . . . believe me.'

She smiled. 'At least, you've been honest with me, Charlie. I'm a big girl. I'll survive this.' She giggled. 'At least, I have my money to console me. Think of all the poor girls who get rejected all the time and have no money to console them,' and she sobbed, softly, as she continued. 'Damn tears! Why do we women have to resort to crying all the time? Do you know that women have more tear ducts than men, Charlie? Why?' she sobbed.

He held her close. 'God made it that way so men could be brought to their knees by the sight and sound of a crying woman, and he becomes putty in their hands . . . that's why.'

'Oh, that's beautiful, Charlie! Charlie . . . do you think we could cuddle for a little while . . . I can't believe Meagan would begrudge me a little cuddling . . . do you?'

He smiled. 'No . . . she's a very generous woman.'

Amanda sobbed, 'Damn lucky one, too.' They held each other until he could hear her deep breathing and he released her and climbed into the top bunk.

* * *

The morning of the second day found them well into the Yucatan Channel which forms the separation between the Yucatan Peninsula and the island of Cuba. It is a bottleneck of sorts, and all the ocean traffic between the Gulf of Mexico and the Central and South American countries flow through the relatively narrow constriction, barely a hundred miles wide at its narrowest.

A cool front had come through during the night and the day was unusually bright and clear. Weather was CAVU . . . Ceiling and Visibility Unlimited as the pilots say.

Charlie was out on deck practising his celestial navigation, and as usual, Arnie was chiding him, teasing, 'Are we where we're supposed to be, Charlie, baby?'

He accepted the chide in good humour, replying, 'I know what you are doing, Arnie! You are going to run down the 86th line of longitude until you intersect the 18th parallel of latitude and ride that into Ambergris Cay . . . right?'

'That's exactly right, and if the trusty SAT–NAV doesn't go out, it will be a cinch.' And, he added, 'If the SAT–NAV goes out, we will depend on good ole Charlie Forester.'

Charlie laughed. 'And what if ole Charlie goes out?'

'Then, baby, we're in deep yogurt! But, I know that land is to the west and I'll do what Christopher did . . . head west without really knowing where I'm going.'

The women were in the galley, cooking. In a moment of generosity they had decided to prepare a sumptuous evening meal for their men, and each was at her own speciality, whatever it was, and the males had been ordered to stay out of the galley, an order they had no difficulty in following. They remained on deck, busy with the chores of sailing. Since the wind had changed to the north after the passage of the cool front, the craft was going in a following sea with the wind at her back – ideal sailing conditions and she was making a good ten knots as she headed south along the 86th west longitude line.

Arnie was at the helm and Charlie was at his side as he noticed a spot of white on the horizon to the east, coming from the direction of Cuba.

He pointed to the spot, saying to Charlie, 'Somebody is really busting water over there. I've been watching for quite some time and she is closing on us fast . . . real fast. Hand me those binoculars, Charlie, so's I can have a better look.'

As he looked and squinted into the sunshine, he handed the glasses to Charlie. 'Here, you take a look. What do you think it is?'

He watched for a minute or so, replying, 'It looks like one of those high performance boats the filthy rich buy as a play toy . . . you know the kind I mean. I think they go by the name of Cigarette . . . or . . . Magnum . . . or . . . something like that.'

'Uh huh . . . I've seen them in the boating magazines. Expensive bastards, too.'

'Yeah,' Charlie replied, 'They have something like a thousand horses in them, and they can go fifty or sixty knots if you push them . . . '

'Yeah. Can you imagine the fuel they consume?'

Charlie laughed. 'That's why I don't own one!'

'Are they headed this way . . . towards us?'

'Well, it seems that way, but they could be some rich guys and gals on their way to Cancun.'

'Could be,'

Within ten or fifteen minutes, with their fast rate of closure, it was obvious that the high performance boat was, indeed, heading for them, as Arnie asked, 'What the hell do they want with us?'

'Probably the Mexican Border Patrol, or, the US's looking for drug runners . . . '

'Yea . . . could be.'

As the boat drew within a hundred yards or so, they could see five men standing on deck, seemingly holding rifles in their hands. They were motioning the *Polaris* to stop by the use of their hands, palms down, and a downward motion.

Arnie shrugged. 'I guess there's nothing to do but come about and see what they want. Do you see any kind of insignia on the boat? Any markings of identification?'

'No. I can't make out a thing.'

'Don't all official boats of a country have proper markings?'

'I don't know for sure, but I think so . . . they should have!'

The boat continued heading directly toward the sailboat, but at a much slower rate. They could see the bow head down as the throttle was cut back. A man stood on the bow, holding on to the railing, as he fired a shot across the bow of the sailboat. The shot rang out across the open water, and the sound could be heard in the galley.

Peg came up the stairs, sticking her head out of the cabin, asking, 'What the hell are you guys doing? I told you I don't like guns, Arnie . . . '

Arnie turned to his wife, yelling, 'Get back in that cabin, Peg . . . keep all the girls down there! Don't come back on deck until I tell you to.'

The urgency of his voice so impressed Peg that, for once, she did not argue, and went back down the stairs, closing the louvered doors behind her.

The speedboat had come within ten feet of the sailboat, and the men on the *Polaris* were concerned. They didn't like what they were seeing. The men on the deck of the speedboat were all waving their rifles in the air like revolutionists and hollering in Spanish. Arnie, Charlie and Bill had all congregated in the cockpit of the sailboat, apprehensive as to what was happening.

Arnie, in his perogative as owner and captain, asked, 'What can we do for you . . . what do you want?'

'We want to come aboard, amigo. We just want to talk to you,' he said with a decided Hispanic accent, but using good English.

'We can talk without you coming on board,' replied Arnie.

'Now, amigo, that is not friendly. We just want to be friends with you . . . to talk to you.'

Arnie was now convinced they had no such friendly intentions, as he tried to invoke the rules of the sea, which dictated that permission must be granted before boarding a vessel not of your own, so he yelled out, 'You do not have permission to board this boat . . . stand off!'

The man fired a shot over the heads of the three men, much to the laughter and shouts of the others on his boat, and he yelled back, 'Thees gun ees my invitation, amigo!'

Charlie tugged at Arnie's sleeve. 'Maybe, we'd better humour them. They've got us outmanned and outgunned.'

Arnie asked again, 'What do you want with us?'

The speedboat was now as close as the two boats could be on the rolling sea without risking damage to either or both crafts.

The man, who was apparently the leader of a rather motly crew, now that close scrutiny was possible, asked, '"How many people on board?'

Arnie replied, 'Just us . . . just us three men.'

'And where are you headed, amigo?' The man continued to present a friendly demeanor.

'We're headed for Belize . . . on a fishing trip,' Arnie replied.

'Fishing . . . huh? How come I do not believe you, amigo?'

'I don't give a damn what you believe . . . amigo,' replied an indignant Arnie, while Charlie tugged on his sleeve, whispering, 'Stay cool, buddy! We're not in the driver's seat . . . they are.'

The sailboat had come about, heading directly into

the wind, and the three sails were flapping in the breeze, making noises as the nylon sails slapped against the wind, making conversation difficult to hear.

The three women down in the galley, looking through the galley windows and seeing the scruffy crew on the speedboat holding their assault rifles and automatic pistols, waving them and yelling, were in a state of panic. They sensed trouble . . . big trouble, and they held each other, afraid to talk, except to whisper 'Oh, my God!'

The leader on the speedboat motioned to the man at the controls of the speedboat, and in Spanish, ordered, 'Take her in closer . . . we will board.'

As the larger speedboat came close enough the five men all jumped on the sailboat at various places on its starboard side which they had parallelled for the boarding.

The three men on the sailboat watched in horror. They said nothing and did nothing, for they now sensed the best defence was to go along with them for the time being. They had weighed the odds, and they were not in their favour. All five of the men were now on the sailboat, leaving one man at the controls of the speedboat, which after the discharge of the men, moved off some ten yards or so, standing by.

The five men positioned themselves at various places on the deck and cabin of the sailboat, with the leader stepping down into the cockpit with the three men of the *Polaris* crew huddled together in a group. The leader was much cleaner in appearance than the others. He was typically Hispanic, as they all were, but of neater appearance and cleaner features. Some women, under different circumstances, might have considered him handsome in a Latin way. He was a little under six feet in height, of slim build, with hair as black as coal, and a full mustache, but a clean shaven face. The others, more scruffy looking, all had full beards and long unkempt hair, and looked as if they needed a bath.

The leader looked around the cockpit, and seeing a colourful silk scarf which could only belong to a woman, he placed his assault rifle under it and lifted it.

The hearts of the three crewmen sank as they fully realized the import of his discovery.

The leader turned back to the men. 'How many women do you have on board?', he demanded.

'I told you we are alone,' from a worried and lying Arnie.

The leader poked his rifle in Arnie's stomach, and to a groan from the poor fellow, the leader said, vehemently, 'Don't take me for a fool, amigo. I am not in the class with these pigs you see with me. I graduated from the University of Miami with a degree in sociology, so let's try one more time . . . how many women do you have on board?'

Before Arnie could answer the leader issued orders in Spanish, and two men jumped down into the cockpit and went down the stairs to the cabin.

The men of the *Polaris* in time honoured fashion, moved forward to protect their women, but the leader raised his rifle in the air and fired, saying, 'Don't be fools!'

The commotion down in the galley could be heard on deck . . . the screaming of the three women . . . their anguished cries of protestation as they were dragged and pushed up the stairs to the cockpit. Seeing their men still standing there, each woman ran to her man, holding him close as they recoiled in terror. Each man placed his arm around his woman, for assurance and protection. Amanda looked up at Charlie, with terror stricken eyes, eyes that pleaded for help.

It was Charlie who now spoke. 'Look, if it's money you want, we are willing to give you all we have. It won't be all that much because most of us have travellers cheques, but you can have all we have in cash . . . '

He was not allowed to finish as the leader laughed him down, saying, 'You Yankee bastards! You believe your money will buy anything, including my country. I don't need your money, amigo! I could light my cigars with hundred dollar bills, if I were so foolish. You see, I don't fool with sociology anymore!' and he laughed, 'I have found a much more lucrative trade. Where do you think we got this beautiful boat? We stole it from rich

Yankees,' and he smiled, showing a set of white, even teeth.

Charlie countered with, 'If you're not interested in money, then what are you interested in?'

The leader walked over to the women, and stopping in front of Amanda, he put his fingers in her hair. As she recoiled from his touch, he answered, 'We want your women!' At the sound of these words, spoken in accented perfect English, the three women gasped in horror, holding their men closer. Bill Morton, the young engaged man, foolishly young and foolishly brave, made an offensive threat at the leader.

Before anyone knew what had happened, a shot rang out and the young suitor fell in a heap on the deck. Kate, his fiancee, screamed in horror, as she fell over his body, yelling, 'Oh, no . . . my God . . . they've shot him . . . somebody, please do something!'

As the other two men moved forward, they were restrained by the beligerent motions of the bandits, for it can now be concluded that they were that, indeed, or much worse. Five guns were now aimed at them. Peg and Amanda clutched their men, shaking with fear they had never known in their lives.

The leader, still smiling, said, 'I hope that will convince you we are not playing . . . don't be foolish! All we want is your women, and then,we will leave you in peace.'

Arnie moved forward. 'You'll have to kill me too before you take these women.' Charlie nodded in agreement. The leader remained amazingly calm, as he responded, 'If that is what you want,' and he raised his gun.

It was the two women, Peg and Amanda, who protested to their men, 'No!', shaking their heads to dissuade them from any overt action on their behalf, as Peg, turned to her husband. 'Arnie . . . don't try to be a hero . . . what good will that do if they kill you?' Amanda nodded in agreement as she pulled Charlie back.

The leader laughed. 'See, hombres . . . your women have more sense than you do. They know we will not harm them. All we want, my men and me, is a little romance from these Yankee women. One thing I do have a fondness for, and that is blonde Yankee women,' as he once again touched Amanda's hair.

She recoiled, once more, but made no offensive gesture, not wanting to antagonize these men, who now held her fate in their hands. She merely held Charlie closer to her, as his arms went around her for whatever protection that afforded her.

It was Peg, pragmatic Peg, who volunteered, 'Look, Arnie and Charlie,' for the young girl, Kate, was still prostrate over her fallen love, who was apparently dead . . . 'If all this guy wants is sex and he's going to get it come hell or high water, why don't I just take him below and service him, so we can be on our way before someone else gets killed.'

Amanda looked at Peg with a look of incredulity, crying out, 'Peg!'

Before Peg could reply, the leader responded. 'That is generous of you, Senora, but eet ees not that simple. You see all these men up there,' and he pointed to the motly crew, 'They all need servicing, too, and,' he smiled . . . 'we don't have time for that, now. No . . . you will all come with us, pronto.' And he issued orders in Spanish as the men came down into the cockpit.

The leader motioned for the driver of the boat to come along side and to the screaming of the women and the fruitless protestations of their men, they were carried, kicking and crying on the shoulders of the scruffy bandits, and transferred to the speedboat.

Even poor little Kate, still sobbing over the loss of her loved one, was not spared, for she, too, was part of the booty they claimed, and she had to be dragged from the body of her fiancé. The women looked back, helplessly, as they were half carried, half dragged aboard the speedboat.

The transfer now completed, the leader issued more orders in Spanish and one of the bandits went down into the cabin. There was heard, the sounds of shots ringing out, the crashing of equipment being destroyed, as he systematically put out of commission all of the radios and navigational devices on board.

Arnies's heart sank even further, if that were possible, as he realized what they were doing, but his thoughts went back to the women, as he ran up to the leader, 'What will happen to them? How do we get them back?'

The leader smirked. 'I didn't say you would get them back! They will bring a good price in my country, where their services are valued highly, after some training by us,' and he laughed as he swung on board the speed-boat, giving orders to the helmsmen, and the powerful boat roared off, and the three women with it.

As they watched the boat become smaller and smaller in the distance, the two survivors, too stunned to speak, just sat there for a few minutes, trying to arrange their thoughts. Arnie bent down to place his finger on Bill Morton's neck.

'Is he dead?' asked Charlie. Arnie nodded.

'Jesus, Arnie, I can't believe this has happened. We've got to try to get these girls back . . . '

Arnie shrugged, as he asked, 'How do you propose to do that?'

Charlie spoke up. 'I'm going to see how much damage they've done to the radios . . . that is our only hope to get any quick action at all.'

Arnie accompanied him, and in despair, they viewed the damage . . . the total damage, for they had spared nothing. Arnie, in disgust, threw a book at the broken radio, as he went back topside, followed by Charlie.

They both looked at the body of Bill Morton, with Charlie asking, 'What'll we do with Bill? He'll smell in this hot sun before long.'

'Are you suggesting we throw him overboard?'

'No! I couldn't do that! But maybe we ought to cover him . . . to get him out of the sun, at least. It seems like the decent thing to do. Oh, God Arnie, we are in trouble,' and his thoughts went out to Meagan, and then, to Amanda, and his mind rebelled at the thoughts going through it.

The sailboat had remained in the same position during the boarding and kidnapping episode, and the sails were still flapping in the breeze as the two men sat there, mesmerized at their predicament. They looked at each other, and then at Bill, their fallen comrade. They both realized that if they had persisted in their overt moves to protect the women, they, too, would be lying there . . . dead.

Charlie suggested, 'Why don't we move him down into the cabin. We won't have to look at him, and he will be in a cooler place. We can't just sit here, doing nothing, Arnie . . . we've got to do something.'

Arnie was in a daze as he responded without emotion, 'Do you realize that only thirty minutes ago, I had a wife here, and, now . . . she's gone!' and he began to sob.

Charlie felt he had to say something. 'I know . . . I know! Don't worry . . . we'll get them back . . . somehow.'

'Sure, it's easy for you to say! You weren't married to Amanda, but . . . Peg is my wife . . . goddamit!'

'Amanda is still a human being, Arnie. You think I care any less for her welfare than you do for Peg's? and Kate's?

Arnie patted his shoulder. 'No, buddy! I was out of line. I'm sorry. Let's get Bill down below, and then decide what we're going to do.'

Amidst grunts and groans, they carried the lifeless body of their friend down the narrow stairs and placed him on the couch in the lounge area. They put a sheet over him, forming a shroud of sorts.

Finished with that grisly task, they returned topside. Charlie looked down at the spot where Bill had lain, and seeing a profusion of blood there, he picked a bucket from out of the locker under the seat, filled it with ocean water and commenced to wash the spot with a sponge.

Arnie had brought the boat about and she was once again under sail. Charlie joined him near the helm, asking, 'Where're you headed?'

Arnie shrugged. 'Cancun, I guess. That is the nearest place where we can report the kidnapping and get some official action.'

Charlie nodded. 'I agree. That's our best bet.'

Arnie said, sheepishly, 'I guess you'd better break out your sextant and nautical almanac to give me a course . . . I need you, buddy!'

Charlie nodded, but responded, 'We've been a day and a half getting here, so we damn sure won't be back before then . . . '

Arnie nodded, solemnly. 'Do you realize what those bastards can do to those girls by the time we can get some action . . . '

'Yeah! I try not to think of it, though.'

Arnie replied, 'I can't help but think of it. Geez, Charlie, did you hear what Peg volunteered to do? She was trying to save the other two girls by offering herself to that bastard. Is that a woman, or what?' he asked proudly.

'Yeah . . . Peg's a hell of a woman, Arnie.'

Arnie nodded, saying nothing, fighting back tears.

They sailed in silence for hours . . . each man deep in thoughts of his woman, and with Charlie, he had two women to worry about.

'How,' he thought to himself, 'will I ever explain this to Meagan? She is no fool! When I mention all the six people on the boat, she will ask . . . 'who is the other woman, Charlie? You never told me your roommate was a woman. You have lied to me, Charlie . . . something I thought you'd never do. I asked you to be honest with me . . . that's all Charlie, and you have lied.' Is incomplete information a lie? he thought.

As the sun set on this unforgettable and traumatic day, the men were gloomier than ever, for the night, when faced alone, is the loneliest time of the twenty-four hours to any human being. Do not worries have a way of magnifying themselves at night until returned to their realistic size with the light of dawn?

The two men did not sleep. They remained on deck, with each giving counsel to the other, 'Why don't you go below and catch a few winks? I'll handle the sails for a few hours . . . '

They each shook their head. 'No . . . Bill is down there! I don't believe I could sleep.'

It was a long night as each man's imagination went wild with thoughts of the women they had lost to the bandits . . . the modern day buccaneers. Each mentally visualized acts of debauchery too horrible to discuss with the other out of respect for the other's sensitivities, for these were civilized men, and the ones who had kidnapped the women obviously were not. They were animals in human form . . . depraved . . . degenerate! They could only shake their heads in despair.

15

As it will do without question, day began to break as the eastern sky gave way to the gray light of dawn. The wind had died down during the cool of the night and the sailboat was in a calm sea, not moving, much to the consternation of the two anxious men.

'Dammit,' lamented Arnie . . . 'not enough wind to fill the damn sails . . . dammit!'

Charlie nodded, saying nothing, for he had nothing of a positive nature to add, as he looked up at the sails.

As the morning grew on the heat of the sun brought a slight breeze out of the east, bringing forth from Arnie, 'Oh, baby, come on . . . blow . . . fill my sails . . . please!'

The morning lapsed into afternoon and they sailed on. As they took turns at the helm the off man would inevitably go to the head of the stairs going to the lounge . . . look inside at Bill Morton, as if to confirm . . . yes, he's still there. He would turn away, shaking his head in despair and return to the cockpit, saying nothing about the corpse.

Charlie stood up, looking at the sails, scanning the skies, and all he saw was blue skies and a deeper hue of blue water.

'Damn ships,' he lamented. 'When you don't need them, you have to worry about running into them all night long, and now, when we need one . . . nothing in sight.'

He did notice something, though, and he strained his ears to make sure before he called Arnie's attention to it, but Arnie had heard, too, as he yelled out, 'I hear an airplane!'

'Hell,' replied Charlie, 'That's not unusual! We're on

the line of traffic between Houston, New Orleans, and the South and Central American countries. Probably some damn airliner thirty-five thousand feet up. We'll be just another sailboat to them,' he lamented.

'No,' cautioned Arnie. 'He's not that high. Look, he is coming towards us,' and as the plane came closer, Charlie exclaimed, 'It's a business jet. What the hell is he doing at this low altitude?'

Arnie's face lit up. 'It's a Citation jet. The Coast Guard bought a bunch of them for drug surveillance. Look, he's coming right towards us!' The Citation, with a US Coast Guard crew at the controls, had descended to 500 feet above the water and as they passed over the sailboat, the roar of the twin jet engines was deafening, but to the ears of the men on the boat it was sheer music.

The two men were waving frantically as the jet passed over and to one side of the sailboat so the crew could give them a good fly-by look.

They watched helplessly, as the jet passed over, with Arnie asking, 'What good will that do us? They'll think we are just a couple of guys on a cruise with everything honky-dory,' he lamented.

'Look,' cried out Charlie, 'they're coming back for another pass,' and he tore his shirt off his back, and taking a fishing rod from the rack, made a white flag of sorts, and as the jet came screaming by again at a slower speed (the pilot had cut back to 250 knots, this time, instead of the cruising speed of nearly five hundred knots) the two men on the boat could see the pilot looking at them out of the side window of the cockpit . . . he waved as he went by.

'Well, big deal,' complained Arnie, 'so they know we're here . . . what good will that do?'

'Look, he's turning around again,' cried out Charlie, as he began to wave his flag, again. As the jet passed over, they saw a streak of flame shoot out of the bottom of the plane and the streak enlarged into a flare . . . half smoke . . . half fire, as Arnie cried out, 'It's a flare. I don't know what they are trying to tell us but a flare is the international distress symbol. They're trying to tell us something!'

The men watched as the jet began to climb and in a few minutes, disappeared to the north. As they lost sight of the plane, they once more became sombre. As far as they knew, nothing had been accomplished by the fly over, except, the US COAST GUARD knew where they were for they had clearly seen the insignia on the sides of the plane as it flew by.

With despondency once again setting in, they continued their path to Cancun, with a slight breeze driving them on. It was about mid-afternoon that Charlie, while playing with his sextant, scanned the horizon and as he panned through a point, he back tracked, seeing a protrusion on the horizon. He put his sextant down and picked up the binoculars which had a seven power magnification.

He returned to the spot on the horizon, yelling, 'Arnie! There's a boat coming towards us!'

'Can you tell if it's those same bastards bringing our women back now that they're finished with them?' He added, 'I'll kill them! I swear I will.'

'I doubt they'd be so thoughtful . . . no, it's a larger boat, and he's not busting water the way they did. No,' continued Charlie, as he continued to scan, 'he's bigger and slower.'

They waited for what seemed like an eternity as the US Coast Guard cutter, *Padre Island,* sliced its way through the water at twenty-five knots, heading straight for them. Their spirits were raised as they could make out the distinctive Coast Guard markings on the sides of the craft.

As the cutter came within sounding distance a sailor came out on the bridge, speaking into the hand loudhailer, 'Ahoy, *Polaris,* are you Mr Broadhurst?'

Arnie exclaimed, 'Hell, they know me!'

He yelled back, 'Yes! I'm Broadhurst! We have to talk to you! Our women have been kidnapped! We need help!'

The commanding officer of the cutter had come out on the bridge, and taking the loudhailer from the sailor, said, 'Calm yourselves, gentlemen . . . the women are safe in a hospital in Cancun.'

Arnie nearly collapsed at the news. He looked at Charlie. 'Did you hear that, Charlie? They're safe!' and turning to the officer once again, he asked, 'What happened?'

The officer replied, 'I can't explain it over this damn thing, sir . . . requesting permission to come aboard your vessel.'

Arnie smiled. 'Permission granted.' And turning to Charlie, he asked, 'How the hell is he going to do that? I can't believe they're going to bring that big baby close enough for him to jump?'

'No,' replied Charlie, 'look . . . they're lowering a boat.'

In short time, the officer had climbed over the gunwhales of the sailboat, telling the sailors to stand by. He gave them a big smile, saying, as he extended his hand, 'I'm Lieutenant Senior Grade, Harold Scoggins, the C.O. of that proud craft . . . '

Arnie took his hand, not letting him finish, 'The women, you say they're safe in Cancun . . . how do you know that?'

He smiled proudly. 'Good communications. The Citation crew spotted that Magnum boat early this morning. We've been looking for those birds for weeks. They're drug runners. They stole that Magnum boat about six months ago, and they have used it for running drugs from Colombia to Cuba. The Citation radioed a DEA interdiction boat,' and he grinned, 'we got boats just as fast as they do, but they don't know that. We commandeer those boats from the drug runners when we catch them.'

Arnie was impatient. 'But, the women . . . how are they . . . what kind of shape are they in?'

'I don't know that, sir, except they walked into the hospital on their own two feet . . . I know that.'

'Who took them to Cancun?'

'Well . . . let's see how it happened. The DEA boat is a fairly large boat, big enough to have a helipad on the stern, and they keep a chopper on board. Well, after the women were rescued from the Magnum, they were put on the chopper and flown to Cancun, and from what I understand, that is where they are now.'

But, how did you know about us?' asked Arnie.

'From the women . . . they told us everything about what happened on the boat. Those bastards will be charged with rape and murder. They're in big trouble, believe me, sir.'

'The bandits? Did they put up much of a fight when they were captured?' asked Charlie.

'No, sir! Those types are bullies. When they lose the advantage, they revert to what they really are . . . cowards.'

'The women?' inquired Arnie. 'Did they say what had happened to them . . . you know what I mean . . . what did the men do to them?'

The young officer looked embarrassed, responding, 'I couldn't say, sir . . . I'm not sure.'

'We've got to get to Cancun . . . I want to see my wife.'

'I can understand that, sir. We have orders to take you under tow. If you will lower your sails and stow everything loose, we'll hook a line to your bow cleat and get underway. We're not exactly a racehorse as fast boats go, but we are faster than you are under sail.'

The two survivors of the *Polaris* crew looked at each other, and smiled, saying, 'Let's go!'

* * *

As they entered the small hospital that served the area, the men looked anxiously in all directions, but they were soon collared by many official looking types, both Mexican and American, and taken to a room off the lobby. They were told by the officials that the women were undergoing examination and treatment and would be indisposed for some time.

Arnie interrupted, 'Treatment? Are they injured?'

The officials looked at each other, with one responding, 'They're not severly injured, Mr Broadhurst, but,' and he hesitated, 'They've been banged around quite a bit. The young woman, Miss Russell, I believe is her name,' as he consulted his note pad, 'she is in bad shape. Not physically, you understand, but emotionally. She is hysterical and cannot be calmed down. She has been sedated, I've been told. The doctors would not allow us to question her.'

Arnie whispered through his teeth, 'The bastards.'

The interrogation went on for nearly an hour as the two very nervous men made known their anxiety at seeing the women, and finally, they were released, and taken to the control desk of the hospital. The nurse in charge, a Hispanic woman, sympathetically gave them the room numbers of the three women, cautioning that Miss Russell could not be seen for the time being.

Arnie asked, 'You going to see Amanda? Give her my love. Tell her as soon as I see Peg I'll come to see her.'

Charlie nodded. 'Tell Peg the same thing.'

When he arrived at the room which Amanda was in, he paused at the door. A nurse, a nun, was coming out. The hospital was run by a religious order of nuns, both Hispanic and American comingled in an ecumenical endeavor of service to humanity.

She caught his sleeve, cautioning, 'Senor . . . not too long, por favor . . . la senorita es muy fatiga . . . she ees tired.'

He nodded, saying nothing. As he entered the semi-darkened room slowly, he could see the lonely figure lying on the bed, not moving.

He noiselessly made his way to the bed, and as he approached, she stirred and turned, and upon seeing who it was, she gasped, and turned her head to the wall, crying, 'Oh, Charlie, please don't look at me . . . please!' and she kept her head turned.

He noticed the hand mirror lying on the bed. She had been examining her face, he reasoned. He stood at her side, not responding to her comment, and even in the semi-darkness of the draped-closed room he could see the blue marks on her cheek, and the bruise on her forehead.

Anger welled up in him . . . extreme anger, and he fought to hold it back, as he touched her shoulder, saying, softly, 'Amanda, please look at me. I don't care what you look like at this moment . . . I just want to comfort you . . . to tell you I care . . . '

At the sound of these words, she turned to him, crying out, 'Oh, Charlie!' and her arms went around his neck as she began to sob, uncontrollably.

In the brief second he had to look as she buried her face in his, he could see the damage. Her lips were swollen . . . her cheeks were puffed . . . her brow had a huge bruise.

'Beautiful, beautiful, Amanda,' he thought to himself, 'What have they done to you?'

She cried for a long time, holding him close, not letting him see her, and finally her tears slowed and she released him, allowing him to look. Tears were streaming down her face as she looked at him, shaking her head in despair.

Several times she attempted to speak but the words ended up merely choking in her throat, as he touched her cheeks, and cautioned, 'hush . . . don't talk . . . you don't need to.'

He noticed she instinctively recoiled at his touch, so wounded was she by the touch of a man . . . any man. It was she who finally said, surprisingly, 'Why don't you pull up a chair, Charlie . . . you'll get tired bending over the bed that way.'

He complied with her request, drawing the only chair in the room next to the bed, and sitting, he could now look at her at the same eye level.

She asked, 'Did you see the other girls, yet?'

'No,' he answered, softly, 'I came straight to you. Arnie said to tell you he will be in later . . . '

She nodded, attempting a smile. He took her hand, and at first she tried to take it away, and getting hold of herself, she allowed it to be taken, then, she smiled, saying, 'I know I look like hell. I don't think I will ever look beautiful, again, Charlie.'

He smiled at her vanity. 'Sure you will, Amanda. In a few days, you will look like the same old gorgeous Amanda . . . '

'You don't understand . . . I feel ugly down deep inside . . . ' and she began to sob, again, continuing, 'do you have any idea what they did to us?'

He felt it was all coming out now . . . she had to talk. He shook his head. 'I can only imagine.'

She closed her eyes, trying to cast out the memory of it, as she continued, 'They did things to us that I thought no human being would do to another . . . things too horrible for me to tell you, as close as I've been to you the past week. We were prodded and abused in ways that nature never intended. They took their turns with each of us, passing us from one to the other, and each practised his imagination and fantasies on us . . . everything their demented minds could conjure up. And,' she sobbed, 'we were all in the same room. We were not even allowed the dignity of being abused in private. We were made to watch each other,' and she gasped and looked away, as she continued, 'And now I feel so dirty deep down inside that I want to die.'

'Oh, no, Amanda . . . this will pass in time . . . time heals all things,' he said without true conviction.

She shook her head. 'Time will not heal this. It's too deep, Charlie. I feel so dirty inside of me that if it were medically possible to have all my insides removed and replaced with new tissue, I would have it done. That is the only way I will ever feel clean, again. I want all the tissue that they touched removed from my body, no matter where it is, and I know that can never be done, so I am cursed. I've read about this, and I've heard about this, but I never in my wildest dreams imagined the horror of it all. Why, Charlie? Why do men have to do this to women?'

He sighed. 'I wish I knew the answer. I guess the only conclusion is that man is not truly civilized, yet . . . we only call ourselves that. If man were truly civilized, he would not rape or kill or make war, or any of those inhuman things we do to one another.'

She lamented, 'No man will ever want me again . . . I am soiled merchandise . . . soiled beyond repair.'

'Oh, no, Amanda . . . that is not true. Someday you will meet a man who will love you for you. This will mean nothing to him, if he truly loves you.'

She shook her head. 'No, Charlie, men like their women to be virginal. They might accept the lack of it in body, but not in spirit. My spirit is no longer virginal.' She sobbed, turning away from him, again . . . thinking.

The same nun came back into the room. 'You must leave, now, Senor . . . por favor.'

He nodded and arose, but Amanda turned to him, sobbing, 'You'll come back, won't you? . . . please!'

He took her hand. 'I have to check into a hotel and get cleaned up. Arnie and I never slept last night, and I just remembered I haven't eaten since yesterday. I'll be back after I get cleaned up . . . '

She smiled. 'I didn't want to say anything, but you could use a bath, Charlie,' and she managed a weak smile.

He patted her shoulder. 'You're going to be all right, Amanda, no doubt about it,' and he left. She smiled.

After, they had checked into the hotel rooms which the two men were able to procure only after official intervention by the Mexican Border patrol and the US Consul in Cancun. He did take a much needed shower and he smiled as he did, remembering Amanda's chiding on the subject, and then his thoughts went to Meagan. How would he ever explain this to her? Yet, he had to.

He rehearsed it in his mind, and then he dialled her number. For reasons of brevity and to avoid redundancy, only Meagan's half of the conversation will be reported here, and after the half hour explanation of what happened had been completed, we can report questions and exclamations such as:

'Oh, my God, Charlie . . . are you all right?'

'Geez!'

'Oh! Those poor girls!'

'Those bastards!'

'Erin, you won't believe this.'

'When will I see you?'

'Oh . . . not till then?'

'I love you, Charlie!'

'Please be careful!'

'I love you.'

As he returned to the hospital after giving a sanitized report to his mother and father, he first went to see Peg.

She smiled a weak smile as he walked in. Arnie was seated by the bed, holding her hand. She gave him a wave . . . indomitable Peg.

He went up to her and looked at her face. She was not as badly beaten as Amanda, at least, not visibly. He could only assume that Amanda was abused more because she was more beautiful, or she resisted more. He wondered.

Peg accepted his hand and his condolences, gracefully, as she asked, 'I guess Amanda has told you of our trials and tribulations at the hands of those animals,' she sobbed.

He nodded. 'Yes, please don't go through it, again,' and turning to Arnie, asked, 'How is Kate? Have you seen her, yet?'

'No, they won't let me in. She is in bad shape. She will need counselling for a long time . . . '

Peg interrupted, 'Poor kid, she is not as tough as Amanda and I are, and . . . she witnessed the murder of the man she loved. She's been through hell.'

Charlie responded, 'I hate to bring this up, now, but I guess we have to talk about it. We have to get Bill's body home . . . and we all have to get home, too.'

Arnie nodded. 'I called Bill's parents to give them the bad news . . . that was tough, believe me, but I had to get instructions on the body. They want me to arrange for shipment back to the States as soon as the authorities release it. It's sort of complicated, politically . . . he was killed in international waters.'

Charlie nodded. 'I thought about that. What are you going to do about the boat?'

'I've already made arrangement for a professional crew to take it back to the States.' He smiled. 'I've had enough sailing for a while.'

Charlie nodded. 'Yeah . . . me too. Well, I guess I'll go back to see Amanda . . . I promised her I would. I have to see what she wants to do about going home.'

Peg touched his arm. 'Charlie, I hope this will not affect your relationship with Amanda . . . you know what I mean . . . '

He shook his head. 'No, Peg, I'm not sure just what

you mean. Amanda and I are friends . . . good friends now, but that is all.'

She responded, 'Oh, I see,' and there was a touch of regret in her reply.

He made his way across the corridor to Amanda's room, knocking softly on the door. Once, again, the same nun came out, gave him a nod, and went out without saying anything. She was sitting up drinking some liquid as he went in.

She smiled, waving him in, saying. 'I'm so glad you came back. I was getting lonesome for you.'

Once again he pulled the chair up to her bed. It was now night time and the wall light was on. The visibility was much better than when he had seen her earlier in the semi-darkness, and the extent of her facial bruises angered him all over again, but he tried not to let it show, as he took her hand, asking, 'Amanda, we have got to talk about getting you home. Have you made any plans at all?'

She nodded. 'Yes. I've called my mom and dad and given them the bad news,' and she sobbed a little as she added, 'without the graphic details, for my father's sake. They will meet me at Houston International at seven tomorrow night. They have already made airline reservations for me. Poor Daddy, he wanted to charter a private jet to take me home, but I told him I wanted to go home with all of you.'

She sobbed again. 'We left together, and I think we should all return together . . . don't you?' she asked in little girl fashion.

He replied, 'Yes, I do.'

'I need you to pick up my airline tickets for me. The hotel concierge has them . . . will you do that for me?'

'You know I will.'

She brought his hand up to her swollen lips, kissing it, and then regretting the action, she put it down, again, saying, 'Sweet, dependable Charlie . . . what will I ever do without you?'

He smiled. 'Oh, beautiful, gorgeous, Amanda will do all right without me . . . I'm sure.'

She looked away. 'I'm not too sure, Charlie,' and as

she turned again to look at him, asked, 'Will I ever see you again after tomorrow?'

He smiled replying, 'Oh, I'm sure we will run into each other, again, someday. After all, we both live in Texas, and Texas is not all that big,' he joked.

She was not in the mood for joking. 'That's not what I mean. Will I ever see you, again? Really see you?'

'I don't think so. It's got to end someday, Amanda . . . you know that.'

She turned away again. 'I know it, but it will hurt, Charlie, and I don't need anymore hurt.'

'I know, but there is nothing I can do about it. I only wish I could . . . but I can't'

She nodded, saying nothing for a while, and then she asked, 'What of Bill? He is dead, is he not?'

'Yes, he is. Arnie has called his parents and gotten their instructions as to . . . '

'Oh, God! What a mess, Charlie! What did we do to deserve this?'

'We haven't done anything to deserve this. That's not the way life works. It's just like . . . well . . . like the bumper sticker says . . . LIFE IS A BITCH! AND THEN YOU DIE!'

She laughed. 'Tell me about it.' Then, 'Charlie?'

He could not help but laugh at that. It brought back pleasant memories to him . . . of happier times, as he responded, 'Yes, Amanda?'

'Since this will be our last night together . . . would you spend it with me? Platonically . . . I assure you.'

He laughed. 'You're a patient in a hospital bed. How the hell can I spend the night with you?'

'Well, it is a bed, isn't it?' she joked.

'Yes, but a hospital bed. There are nuns running all over the place.'

'I don't care! I want to cuddle. I need cuddling. I need someone to hold me close, to tell me I'm beautiful and desirable . . . and whisper sweet things to me. That's all I want . . . just until I go to sleep. Is that too much to ask of you? Warm friends like we've been,' she teased.

'No. That's the least a friend can do for a friend. Am I

supposed to climb in bed with you?'

'No, silly! I don't think I'm up to that. What would the good nuns say? No . . . just sit by me like you're doing now, but, closer, and hold me as best you can . . . you know how we used to do . . . '

He pulled his chair closer. She slid down in the bed until her head was level with his, and she placed her head close to his as he placed his head on the bed. She placed her arm around his head as best she could. As she snuggled her face in his hair, she began to cry, softly, running her fingers through his hair, occasionally drying her tears, unashamedly, in his hair. He said nothing. She really did not expect to hear anything, as she held him close, knowing that this would be the last time she would hold him for the rest of her life.

Much later, thinking he was asleep. she whispered the words, 'I love you, Charlie,' but he wasn't asleep. He heard the words. He made no reply, and it pained him not to.

The nun, making her routine inspection, quietly opened the door to the room and seeing them in that embrace, grinned, made the sign of the cross, looked towards heaven, and closed the door, smiling an angelic smile.

In time Amanda dozed off, and he slowly extricated himself from her grasp, and standing there for a moment looking at her bruised face, he bent over and kissed her on the cheek and tiptoed out of the room. As he passed the nurses' station, the three nuns present all smiled, knowingly, as they nodded to each other.

It was a sombre group who met at Cancun International Airport the next day for the return flight which would bring their odyssey to an end. Not much was said on the plane either, with each deep in his or her own thoughts. It had been a momentous and traumatic two weeks, and their lives would never be the same.

Walter and Marcia Winters, looking every inch the prosperous parents that they were, waited impatiently at the gate for their daughter, smiling bravely, as she walked into the terminal, with Charlie on her arm. She leaned on him . . whether through necessity or desire, we shall never know.

As she embraced her parents, accompanied by a great deal of crying between the mother and daughter, she took a waiting Charlie by the hand, bringing him forward for introductions.

'Mom . . . Dad . . . I'd like you to meet my very good friend, Charles Alexander Forester . . . my very good friend, without whom I don't know what I would have done.'

Greetings were exchanged by all, with the father saying, 'Are you the son of Alex Forester?' If so, I know your father . . . fine man . . . fine man!'

The time came to say goodbye. Amanda forced a smile, but this was not a happy moment for her. She knew this was the end of her relationship with Charlie and she was distraught though she tried to be brave. She excused herself from her parents and led Charlie around the corner to achieve some degree of privacy. She smiled at him through bluish, bruised lips saying, 'I know I don't look very sexy just now, and I can't kiss you goodbye because my lips are bruised, so what are you going to do about it, Charlie?'

'Well, we could cuddle for a while.' She smiled as she went into his arms, holding him close, not releasing him for a long time, and then she broke off and left hurriedly, without even looking back. Charlie smiled to himself, thinking, 'What a woman! I wish I could have met her at a different time . . . a different place . . . different circumstances . . . who knows? And his thoughts went out to the other woman in his life . . . the one foremost in his heart . . . Meagan!

16

His mother and father met him at the airport. This was unusual for Agatha and Alex Forester. Under normal circumstances they would never have done it, but these were not normal circumstances. Agatha rushed into his arms. 'Oh, my darling, Charles! How horribly your cruise turned out . . . these things seldom work out as we plan them, I've found but . . . '

The father worked his way into the pair . . . 'Charlie . . . I'm happy to see you hale and hearty, son,' and he embraced him.

The mother had now removed a tissue from her handbag and was drying her eyes, continuing to mumble about the dark side of life if one ventured too far from home and hearth, for to her home was a fortress, a bulwark against the foibles of the world. To her it had always been so.

After the tearful reunion, mother took son in arm, saying, 'But, you are now home, Charles, and everything will be all right. We will see to it, won't we Alex?'

The father, always having to bring his proud and pretentious wife back to reality, offered, 'But, Agatha . . . Charlie may have plans of his own. We can't plan his life for him, because . . . '

'Nonsense, Alex! Lives need planning as you well know, and Charlie's in particular, especially after Adelle . . . '

Charlie smiled at her. He understood her, even though he paid no mind to what she had to say half the time, as he countered, 'We'll talk about that later, Mother. For the time being I just want to forget the horror of the cruise, especially, the horror those poor women went through.'

As they walked to their car, the mother persisted. 'Charles, I certainly hope those men will be brought to justice on those assault charges (she could not bring herself to mention the word 'rape'). Those animals deserve to be summarily executed!'

'I'm sure they will be in big trouble, Mother, the least of which will be the rape charges. They will all be charged with murder and assault, from what we've been told, not to mention drug running. I feel it will be a long time before they are free men . . . if ever.'

'I should think so!' she replied, testily.

Having completed their return to the house and gotten ready for the evening meal, they were gathered in the library, as usual. It was a beautiful room, panelled in Honduras mahogany in a relief panel motif. It had a twelve foot ceiling as did all the first floor rooms in the two-and-a-half-storey house. The floors were of wood parquet, covered with an area rug of Persian make. The walls were lined with shelves loaded with books that had not been read in years. His father had bought the library estate of a former college Professor of Literature to fill the empty shelves after moving in. All attempts by his mother to have Charlie consume the Great Books were in vain. It was not his bent.

The room was warm and beautiful, and in the cool months, when the fireplace was fired, it was indeed charming, and Charlie had spent many an hour in it in his formative years reading the adventure novels he favoured, much to his mother's displeasure.

The father hesitated.

'Charles, I think you should take a few more days off . . . to recuperate, as it were . . . then, we should talk about the business. You know I'm not getting any younger, and, well, it is a family business, with all the company stock belonging to me, your mother and you. The business will be yours someday . . . I'm sure you realize that.'

He nodded. 'I do, Dad, and I want to do what is right by you and the business, but . . . '

The father, concerned 'You have reservations about all this?'

'No, sir . . . not about the business. Just my life . . . '

The father gave his son a quisical look. 'Your life? I'm afraid I don't follow you. I know you have had some drama in your life, lately, but, to use the trite old cliche, "life goes on" and it does . . . '

His mother, sitting there quietly listening to the conversation between father and son, finally spoke up. 'Charles, don't you think it is time we spoke of Meagan?' and as she looked at her husband, 'All of us?'

The father was truly perplexed. 'Meagan? Meagan? Who the hell is Meagan? Was she on the cruise?'

The mother looked at the son. The son looked at the mother. No words were exchanged . . . just looks. But he could read his mother's mind.

He knew he had arrived at the moment of truth as far as Meagan and his parents were concerned, so he replied, 'Dad, I've got to tell you something . . . about Meagan . . . who she is and,' he raised his hand in a gesture of futility, 'everything.'

The father nodded in his quiet fashion. 'I think that would be a good idea, since your mother is apparently already privy to this matter of . . . Meagan.'

So, he told his father the entire story just as he had to his mother some weeks earlier.

The father listened quietly, not even interrupting him for questions . . . just getting up now and then for a glass of sherry, his favourite pre-dinner drink, as long as it was dry sherry.

As the son finished his narrative of love discovered on the first leg of his odyssey, (he had neither the nerve nor incentive to mention his near involvement with the beautiful Amanda, not wanting to further confuse a murky situation) the father sat in contemplation, twirling his glass in his hand, thinking, and then. 'Charlie, I am trying to form a reply that will not be offensive to you, but, really, are you sure that your emotions are under control just now? I fully realize that Adelle's deception could have taken its toll on you, but you left this town implying that you hated all females,' and he smiled at his wife, 'with the exception of your mother, of course, and now, if I understand you, correctly, you fell in love with this . . . Meagan . . . just two weeks later . . . '

'Not at first,' he protested. 'I'm just beginning to be sure about her.'

The shrewd father pressed on. 'and just what happened to make you so sure, now? Did you receive confirmation from on high?'

Charlie knew his father was somewhat displeased with his declaration of newfound love. 'Thank God,' he thought to himself, 'I did not bring up the subject of Amanda. He would surely think I had lost my senses.'

He replied to his father, 'Dad, I know it looks foolish. I've told myself the same thing, but Meagan was so different from anyone I've ever met . . . so . . . so . . . '

The father shrugged. 'If variety is what you want, then, perhaps you should visit Mazie's for a few nights . . . '

'Alex!' protested the mother. 'Do you have to resort to using a house of ill repute to make a point? Really!'

'I'm sorry, Agatha, if I have ruffled your over active sense of morality, but I am serious. I don't think our son knows what he is doing these days. I've been patient with you, Charlie, but my patience is wearing thin. We still have a business to run . . . a multi-million dollar business, I might add. A business which will be yours when I go, and I think it is high time you paid some serious attention to it.'

Charlie was crushed by his father's onslaught. They didn't come often, but when they did, he got to the point in a hurry.

He gave his father a sheepish look as he replied. 'Dad, I have no argument with anything you've said. I just don't know what to do about it. 'Are you asking me to give up Meagan . . . to forget her?'

The father had now calmed down a bit. He had always been the warmth in the relationship between parents and son, while the mother had provided the chill. The father went to his son, putting his hand on his shoulder, replying with compassion, 'No son. I cannot dissolve feelings of love by a wave of the hand any more than I can of hate, and I've tried that several times in my business career. No! What I'm saying is . . . you've got to find out where you're going with this. What do you intend to do about Meagan? Do you intend to marry her?'

At the sound of these words the mother gasped but said nothing. Agatha always knew when she was in over her head. Trading gossip with the girls at the bridge club and passing summary judgement on those innocuous matters were fairly harmless and amusing, but . . . this involved her son . . . her only son, and she knew her business savvy husband was the superior negotiator, so she merely looked at her son and anxiously waited for his reply.

Charlie shook his head. 'I don't know if I am ready for marriage, yet.'

This was time for the mother to step in, she felt, as she inquired in a sanctimonious tone, 'Then what do you intend to do with her . . . live with her? . . . as these young people do nowadays?'

He thought about her question. What did he intend to do with Meagan? Had he thought of it? Meagan had. She had asked him once . . 'What's gonna happen to me?'

He replied to his mother. 'I don't think so, Mother . . . not unless we are married. She has already told me she would not be a kept woman . . . '

The mother was astonished. 'Oh? Good for her. Perhaps Meagan has more sense than I thought,' pleased with her observation.

He said, seriously, 'You'd be surprised how much sense Meagan has, Mother . . . and her morals. . . . I would compare with any woman I've ever met. She is highly moral, I assure you.'

The mother took on a proprietary look as she responded, 'Perhaps, Charles, you should bring Meagan home for a visit. That way, your father and I would get to meet her, and . . . '

'She wouldn't come, Mother.'

'And, why not? May I ask.'

He sighed. 'I asked her to come on the cruise with me, and she refused.'

'But, why?'

'I think she was ashamed of the way she talks. She is not a fool. She knows her shortcomings. She is not well educated, or . . . sophisticated, and she does not use the best of grammar, but she is going to night school to try to correct those shortcomings, and that is commendable, I think.'

The mother's hands went to her throat. 'Oh, Charles, darling, are you sure you want to continue with this relationship? Could she ever fit into our world?'

He could not help saying. 'You realize, Mother, you said "our" world . . . "your" world is what you really mean.'

The mother sat up in her chair, looking imperious, as she always did when attempting to assert her perceived superiority on the rest of humanity. 'Well, "my" world should be considered, Charles. We have our friends, your father and I, and well, she would be our daughter-in-law . . . really, Charles . . . that must be considered. We are substantial people in this town . . . very substantial, I might add . . . '

His mother's words fell on him like a thunderclap. He looked to his father for rebuttle, but none was forthcoming. Based on his past experience with his parents, that amounted to tacit approval from his father of his mother's comments, and it proved to him the hopelessness of his situation with Meagan. They would never accept her into their world, and she would not want to venture a try, so he was perplexed.

He could see that they had run out of conversation, and had accomplished nothing but identifying the problem, as if he were not aware of it. He expected more understanding . . . more compassion. After all, these were his parents . . . the two people who had given him life. If they did not accept the situation, why should the rest of the town?

He thought of Arnie and Peg and the rest of his friends. How would they feel about Meagan if he brought her back here to live. Knowing Meagan as he did, it would be a constant fight for acceptance and she would not take it lying down, and fighter that she was, it would be a constant battle which would eventually destroy their marriage . . . if they married!

He was a troubled man, as he thought of the situation. What could he do? Abandon her, simply because she didn't fit into his world? How could he do that if he really loved her.

The father arose, and he knew the discussion was at an end, with the father asking. 'Have we resolved anything, Charlie? Have you made up your mind as to what you intend to do with this girl?'

He shook his head. 'No, sir, I haven't I want to sleep on it tonight. I'll let you know in the morning.'

'That is fair enough . . . coming my dear? Goodnight, Charlie.'

Sleep did not come easy to Charlie Forester that night. His brain swirled with confusion, as he relived the past month or so in his life. How could things have gotten so screwed up? Damn that Adelle! It was all her fault. She started it all. If she had remained married to him, even while living a lie, he would still be married. He would never have gone on the odyssey to Colorado, and he would never have met sweet, simple, loyal, pure of heart, Meagan. Damn Adelle. Then he thought of Amanda . . . beautiful, gorgeous, desirable, tormented Amanda. Could she ever find contentment again after what she had gone through? Could she ever have a real relationship with any man again?

And his mind returned to Meagan once again. What did he owe her? What are the obligations of love? Trust? Fidelity? Consideration? Loyalty? Consideration? Love? Consideration? Caring? Consideration? Why did he keep coming back to 'Consideration' he wondered. There can be no love without consideration! They go hand in hand. The dividing line between lust and love is formed by consideration. Consideration, he thought to himself is what it is all about. When someone is offended by another, they ask, invariably. 'Didn't you consider me before you did that?'

When a child is bad, does not the mother say, 'If you had any consideration for me, you would not act that way.'

Consideration is caring! Charlie mused, if you really

loved someone, you will not hurt them. If I really love Meagan, I will do what is best for her . . . not for me! If you truly love someone, you put them first! If she will not fit into my world, then, I will enter hers and with that, he went to sleep.

At breakfast the next morning, his father and mother both continued to look at him, questioningly. They wanted answers to the questions of the night before, but said nothing . . . just looked at him.

Finally: 'Mother . . . Dad . . . I made a decision last night, as I promised you I would. At least, part of a decision.'

Both parents looked, expectantly, saying nothing, as he continued. 'I gave this matter a lot of thought, last night, for several hours, and I feel I cannot abandon Meagan simply because you feel you cannot accept . . .'

'Oh, Charles,' protested the mother, 'I did not say that!'

The father raised his hands. 'Please, Agatha, let him finish before you rebut.'

She pouted, lifting her coffee cup to her mouth, looking at them both in turn . . . hurt in her eyes.

'I don't mean to imply, mother, that you would never accept her. Meagan has a great deal of, how shall I say it . . . native charm . . . which I think you would enjoy. She is warm and . . . affectionate,' and at the mention of that word, the mother's eyebrows went up, but without comment, as her son continued, 'I feel I owe it to her to give this thing a chance to grow . . . if it is going to go anywhere . . . '

'And how do you propose to do that while trying to run a real estate company? Long-distance loving is not very successful, Charlie. It puts too much strain on the relationship,' asked the father.

He nodded. 'I know. That is why I am asking for an extended leave of absence from the company. You can terminate my salary if you want to. I will still have the proceeds of the stock dividends coming in, so I'll make out for a while.'

The father took the news with calm, but the mother's hands went to her throat, but she remained quiet, leaving the arrangements to her husband, for she was of the old school, when men used to be the head of the family, or, so they perceived. The father asked, 'And, how long do you think this leave of absence will require?'

'I'm not sure . . . two or three months, I will either ask Meagan to marry me, or I will break it off. I'm not even sure she wants to marry me.'

The mother could take it no longer. 'Why, that is absurd, Charles! That woman should break her neck to have you.'

He was offended by her remark. 'Mother, I would appreciate it if you would not refer to Meagan as "that woman" as if she came from some third world country. She bleeds just like us. Only the polish is missing. She would have been like your great grandmother was, you know the one whose pictures you hid from the family scrapbook, the one who gave birth out on the Texas plains while your great grandfather was stealing land and rustling cattle to found the family fortune you so sanctimoniously enjoy to this day.'

She gasped. Her hands went to her throat. 'Oh, Charles . . . Alex . . . did you hear that?'

The father laughed, interrupting, 'I don't think your correct and perceptive account of your mother's forbears is relevant at this time, Charlie. We're speaking of your young lady. I will promise to keep an open mind on Meagan. I don't believe in pre-judging people I have not met, for I have often been wrong with first or incomplete impressions, but, if you feel that is what you have to do, I have no big problem with it. And as for the salary, I think the Forester Company can afford to pay its vice-president during a three month leave of absence. Let's call it an educational sabbatical, for, truly, Charlie, I hope this will be educational for you, regardless of how it turns out,' and he gave his son a warm smile.

The mother, never to leave a good subject die a natural death, replied, 'If that is what your father wants, Charles, I will, of course, support him, as a proper wife should.' She emphasized the words 'proper wife', and it was not lost on the son.

He thanked his parents for their understanding,

announcing he would leave the next morning, after he had spent some time at the office during the day, today. He made arrangements for the trip, the usual things, clothing, money, transportation. Once again, he decided to take the Jeep . . . probably sentiment had some influence on his decision.

He had not called Meagan the previous night. He was too upset as the result of the conversation with his parents, while he was in the throes of indecision. Now, his mind was made up, and he could tell her of his plans. He dialled her number.

'Oh, Charlie! Where have you been? I've been so worried about you!' (he marvelled at how well her grammar and pronunciation lessons were coming)

'Well, my life has been a little hectic, lately, as you well know . . . '

'Oh, I know it! That horrible cruise . . . and those horrible men . . and those poor women . . . how are they?'

'The women are having a hard time just now. Two in particular, I'm sure will need counselling. Peg . . . the boat owner's wife is tough. She'll make it, but the other two . . . '

'Poor souls. You know, Erin and I can relate to them! We've been through the same thing. 'Course, we killed the bastard. It helps if you kill them . . . makes you feel better.'

He could not argue with her logic, but, instead, he asked, 'Guess what, Meagan?'

'Oh, Charlie, when will I see you?' she interjected.

'But, that is what I'm trying to tell you! I'm leaving tomorrow morning. I'm coming to see you.'

'Oh, Charleee. That's great. Oh, God, I'm so happy about that! When will you get here? Erin! Erin! Come quick! Charlie is coming. Ain't that great, honey?' Come here, talk to him . . . say hello to Charlie.'

'Hi, Charlie . . . I can't wait to see you. When will you get here? Oh! Not til then? She is pushing me out of the way, Charlie . . . bye . . . see you in a day or so!'

'Guess what, Charlie! Erin has a job. Where? Why at the cafe where I work . . . '

'Meagan, I want to talk to you and Erin about that when I get there . . . '

'What about that?'

'Can't you wait until I get there to discuss it?'

'Well, I guess so, if you hurry. Oh, Charlie, honey, you really didn't forget me did you? You're coming to see me.'

He laughed. 'Did you think I'd forget you?'

'I know how men are! Once they've gotten what they want, well, it's a new ball game for most men . . . you know that! Men are rotten people . . . not you, honey, but most of them.'

He laughed. 'I'm glad to know I don't fall in that category with most of them.'

'No . . . you're different. That's why I fell for you as fast as I did, and, as hard . . . Compared to the cruds I run into in that cafe . . . you're an angel, Charlie. You really are. Any woman in her right mind would fall for you . . . I bet you been beating women off all your life, but them days are gone, Charlie. I will fight like a tigress to keep you. You'd better realize that . . . no, Erin, you keep out of this conversation . . . this is between me and Charlie, honey. She always wants to butt in when I'm talking to you. She's got a crush on you and she ain't even met you . . . see how women are around you, sweetie . . . Charlie, do you realize you didn't even give me a picture of you to remember you by! I had to describe you to Erin . . . ought to be ashamed of yourself.'

He smiled at her verbosity. 'Look, I've got to go to bed . . . have to get up early tomorrow morning, so I'll say goodnight . . . '

'Oh, do you have to? Erin, honey, close your ears for a minute while I tell Charlie goodnight. She's giggling, Charlie, but she covered her ears, so . . . goodnight, sweetheart! I wish I had you in my bed, tonight, but it won't be long. Don't get lost on your way up here. Goodnight, honey.'

'Oh, Meagan, before I say goodnight, will you call Elmo and Blanche tomorrow and reserve a room for me for a week or so?'

There was silence at the other end, then, finally, 'I thought you would stay here. What's the matter?'

'Well, Meagan . . . Erin is home with you now, and she wasn't before . . . that is what is the matter. I didn't want to embarrass you before your daughter by assuming we would . . . '

'Oh, Charlie, Erin is twenty years old, now. She knows about how I feel about you . . . oh, honey . . . don't do this to me . . . '

He relented. 'Anything you say, Meagan. If that is the way you want it, it's OK with me . . . '

'That's the way I want it. I'll handle Erin.'

'OKaaaa! Goodnight. I love you.'

'Goodnight, sweetheart . . . I love you, too.'

He hung up, shaking his head. The thing about the sleeping arrangements was a spontaneous reaction. He had not given much previous thought about the situation, what with all the other trauma he had to worry about. He assumed that any mother would have chosen to exercise some discretion, even rudimentary discretion, as he mulled it over on his way to the shower. Erin was no kid anymore, though. She had been in a women's prison for a couple of years, or more. She had probably seen and heard things that would embarrass Attilla the Hun. He thought of Erin. What did she look like? She sounded nice over the phone. Her grammar was good and she spoke in polished terms. She had a high school education, like her mother, but more recent, in a bigger school, he assumed, since they had moved to the 'city' from Meagan's meagre beginnings out on that little ranch, or so he had been told.

Most of his time was spent in thinking . . . thinking . . . thinking, for his mind was still troubled. He didn't have it all worked out . . . not yet. And what of Erin? She was living with her mother at this time, for obvious reasons. She had nothing when she left. She was barely an adult, and after several years in prison, she certainly had nothing, now. What would happen to her? Would Meagan abandon her to the outside world this soon? Not hardly, he felt. She had pined for her too long to let her slip away this soon. Could she make out on her own? She was only a waitress. Could she live on that meagre salary in that small cafe.

That was what he wanted to talk to Meagan about. Their futures . . . plural . . . with an 's' on the end. His, Meagan's and Erin's.

* * *

'My God,' he exclaimed to himself as he crossed over the border to Colorado, 'If I do marry Meagan, Erin will be my step-daughter! I'll be a step-father!'

And the thought, at first, was chilling to him, and then, he smiled. 'I'm thirty-six years old and I have no children, and now I will have a twenty-year-old step-daughter. Soon, she will marry some man and have children of her own, and then, I'll be a grandfather. Geez . . . I don't want to be a grandfather at thirty-six, or, thirty-seven, or, whatever . . . not yet. I'm too young!' and his mind continued fantasizing until he saw the foothills of the mighty Rockies staring at him through the windshield. He smiled as he entered the township of Mountain View.

17

He had given them a running account of his progress on the car phone so Meagan and Erin were waiting for him as he entered the small village in which his life and fate had taken such a turn. Meagan and Erin had both taken the day off from waitressing in order to minister to each other those things that females do to make themselves more presentable to the male. It was difficult to gauge which of the two females was the more excited, for both, for different reasons, were in a state of high excitement and great expectation.

With Meagan, it was the anticipation of love renewed, seeing once again the man to whom she felt she would now dedicate her life. For Erin, it was the anticipation of meeting a man to whom she felt she owed her life, even if not in actuality. She was well aware that if fate had not intervened in the person of Charlie Forester, she could well have spent several more years in prison, a form of living death to a young twenty-year-old woman. To further add to her excited anticipation, she had never seen her benefactor . . . not even a photograph of him, and as does a young girl on a blind date, she had conjured up in her mind all sorts of descriptions of him, and now she would see him in the flesh.

He climbed the steps to the top landing, but before he could knock to announce his arrival the door swung open and a smiling Meagan flew into his arms, smothering him with kisses, murmuring the usual forms of missed love talk: 'Oh, Charlie! . . . it's so good to see you, again . . . oh, I missed you . . . oh, Charlie!'

He returned the tender expressions as best he could, trying to come up for air now and then, and finally, looking around, asked, 'Where's Erin?'

Meagan took him by the hand, leading him into the apartment, responding, 'She's here . . . inside. She wanted us to have a few moments to ourselves, first. Here she is!'

He looked around Meagan's head to see a lovely girl standing there, smiling at him.

Then, as her mother said, 'Erin, honey, this is Charlie,' she came forward and embraced him, warmly, kissing him on the cheeks, hugging him, saying softly, 'I'm so happy to meet you at last. You'll never know how much I owe you . . . so much,' and she hugged him again, as her mother stood by, smiling, and then they all hugged together, with Meagan saying, 'I've got all the people I love in my arms right now . . . how lucky can a person get.'

Charlie broke loose from the two women, and holding Erin at arm's length, finally got a good look at her. He was seeing a tall and slim young woman with long straw-coloured hair. She had the blue eyes of her mother's Irish ancestors. She resembled her mother to some extent, but was far prettier with features more refined than her mother's, probably due to the fact that the face had twenty years less wear and tear. She was taller than Meagan by some two inches. He estimated her height to be five feet eight . . . maybe nine. As he took in her loveliness, he could not help remarking to Meagan, 'You've got a lovely daughter . . . really lovely, Meagan.'

Meagan smiled in agreement, saying, 'Ain't she pretty, though,' and pulled the daughter to her, hugging her. Erin was blushing through her tears as Meagan was smiling through hers.

It was a highly emotional moment for all, and then pragmatic Meagan broke loose, saying, 'Erin, honey, let poor Charlie come up for air. We been smothering him with kisses so he can hardly breathe . . . '

He laughed. 'I'm not complaining! I love having two beautiful women hugging and kissing me. It's what every man dreams of . . . '

'See what I told you, Erin honey . . . don't he talk

sweet?' and turning to Charlie, 'You're in store for a lot of loving from two women in the next few days,' and laughing, added,'Course, Erin's loving will be a little different from mine . . . better be,' and she poked her daughter in the ribs.

Erin said, kidding, 'I don't know, Mama, now that I've seen Charlie, I'm not sure I can keep my hands off him, 'specially in my condition . . . '

'You will, honey . . . I promise, you,' the mother retorted, and taking Charlie by the hand, 'Come on, Charlie, sit down and tell us everything you've been up to . . . 'specially the cruise. Tell us everything, just like it happened. Erin, honey, get the coffee and cake, will ya?'

He was forced to relate the whole story to them and they sat in awe as they listened to the traumatic chain of events, with the usual, 'Oh, my God . . . oh, how awful . . . poor girls!'

It was Meagan who recapitulated the crew membership as she mulled it over in her mind. 'Let's see, there was Peg and Arnie, they owned the boat, and then, there was Kate and Bill . . . he was the one killed, and then, there was you and . . . Amanda . . . '

Charlie read the questioning look in her eyes, and Erin had the same kind of look, but nothing further was asked.

Meagan smiled, asking, 'You want some more cake, Charlie? Erin, honey, get some more cake will you . . . for Charlie?'

He was glad to get off the subject, so he asked, 'How would you two ladies like to go out to dinner this evening?'

Meagan smiled. 'You talking about supper? Where? At the cafe?'

Charlie replied, sheepishly, 'I guess it'll have to be the cafe for tonight, but not tomorrow night. We're going to Vail for a few days . . . how would you and Erin like that?'

Erin looked surprised. 'Oh, Charlie . . . not me too. You two need to be alone. You don't want me along . . '

Meagan looked at Charlie, not sure what to say, then, finally, 'Did you mean the three of us?'

'Well, sure, we're not going to leave Erin here by herself, are we?'

Erin protested. 'I don't mind, really. You two go on without me. Sounds like fun, Ma. Go ahead. I'll be alright.'

Meagan was at a loss. She wasn't sure what to say. She wanted to be alone with Charlie, but . . .

It was Charlie who spoke to break the impasse. 'Look, Meagan . . . Erin . . . we're a family, now, and families stay together. I called ahead for a two bedroom suite in Vail. It has a small living area, a small kitchen, two bedrooms, and two baths. It will be no different from staying here as far as privacy is concerned, and we will all be together to have some fun. Why, Erin, as pretty as she is, will have those college boys knocking on the door as soon as we hit town.'

Erin's eyes lit up at the sound of that and she smiled at her mother, expectantly, as the mother replied, 'If that is what you want, Charlie. I'm sure Erin will appreciate it. Poor child . . . she ain't had . . . oh, excuse me . . . she hasn't had much fun since she's been out.' And with a look of practicality about her, Meagan asked, 'But, Charlie, that will cost a lot of money. Vail is an expensive place. That's why I always used to drive through the town without even stopping for coffee. Why, do you know what a cup of coffee costs in that town?'

He laughed. 'No, and I don't care about that just now. Are we in agreement? All three of us are going . . . right?'

Erin sat there wringing her hands, but with a look of great expectation on her face, as she looked at her mother for confirmation, with Meagan saying as she looked at her daughter, 'I guess so, if that is what you want, Charlie. You're the man in this family.' Charlie was surprised at her declaration, but he said nothing. 'Then, it is agreed, we leave for Vail in the morning . . . the three of us.'

Erin could not contain her enthusiasm, as she exclaimed, 'Oh, boy! Oh, I've got to get ready. I've got to rinse a few things out before I can leave. You two will have to excuse me,' and she dashed off.

Charlie took Meagan's hands in his, and watching Erin disappear into the bedroom, he turned to Meagan. 'She really is a lovely girl . . . very pretty.'

Meagan laughed. 'What did you expect, with a mama like me? But, she continued, 'I was so happy to see that she didn't come out of that place a bitter woman . . . you know . . . mad at the world.' She shrugged her shoulders and said . . . 'what the hell! It's over with and I want to get on with my life.'

'That's good.' Charlie, beginning to get hungry, asked, 'You about ready to eat?'

She laughed. 'I don't ever get excited about eating where I work.'

'Would you prefer going some place else?'

She laughed. 'You know me, Charlie, I'm loyal. I feel I owe it to my boss to patronize his place. After all, he feeds me, and now he feeds my daughter,' and then she asked, 'You like the way I talk, now. People in the cafe say that I'm putting on airs since I met you, but I don't care what they think. I'm trying to improve myself . . . for you, Charlie. I want you to be proud of me. The money you send me, it all goes on improvement. Night school, grammar books. I feel like you are making an investment in me, Charlie . . . is it wrong to feel that way?'

He smiled at her candour. 'No . . . it's all right, but I meant for you to spend the money on things you want . . . extra things.'

'There is only one thing in this world that I want that I don't have, and it's sitting right here in front of me.'

He smiled, leaning over kissing her, but saying nothing more on that subject, until she said, 'Charlie, we have to talk about something, but now is not the time. I don't want anything to ruin our night together . . . nothing!'

'Is it something serious!'

'It could be, depending on how you answer my questions.'

'What? You've got me curious, now.'

'No . . . not now,' and turning towards the bedroom,

'Erin, we're going out to eat. Are you coming with us?'

She appeared at the door to the bedroom. 'No, Mama, you and Charlie go without me. I'm trying to decide what I will wear on the trip to Vail, not that I have much choice,' she joked, as she went back into the bedroom.

'OK, honey, if that is what you want,' and then to Charlie, 'Poor child, she doesn't have much clothes to decide on. There is not much you can buy on a waitress's salary in this little town, but Charlie,' she exclaimed, 'I don't want you going out and doing anything about that . . . I know how you are.'

'I can if I want to,' he teased.

'No, you can't. She's my daughter, and I will make the final decisions where she is concerned,' and she laughed. 'Come on, let's go before we get into a fight over this,' and she kissed him lightly.

The night was very chilly and she cuddled next to him as they walked to the cafe, not saying too much, just enjoying the warmth of each other.

They had the special which the waitress recited, ending with, 'six ninety-five.'

Charlie laughed. 'Nothing's changed on that score.' The talk at the meal consisted of small talk, mostly reminiscing about their last time together . . . the idyllic trip to Denver.

Supper over, and having nothing more to do in the small town, the couple began their walk back to the apartment. They were each nervous to some extent as they thought of the evening ahead of them, the one they had each anticipated since their last union.

It was Meagan who danced around the issue for a while, and then, 'Charlie, do you feel like it's going to be awkward tonight with Erin in the apartment? You know what I mean. I want you so much. I've thought about nothing but that for the past few days, but, I don't want you to feel embarrassed. I had a long talk with Erin about this. She knows it is no cheap deal. She knows we love each other, and that makes a difference, you know, and she said. ''Mama, I'm no kid! I know how the cookie crumbles. I know how men and women are, especially when they're in love,'' and then you know what, Charlie, she offered to go and spend the night with a girlfriend of hers, another waitress from the cafe, but I didn't think that was right. This is her home, Charlie.'

Her put his arm around her shoulder, pulling her close, as he replied, 'You were absolutely right. She should not leave her home . . . just for that.'

She returned the hug. 'I'm glad you feel that way. It makes it easier, but,' she giggled, 'I hope it won't affect your performance tonight . . . you know what I mean.'

He laughed. 'I know what you mean. I promise to do my best.'

When they got back into the apartment, Erin was not in sight, So Meagan tiptoed to her room, gently opening the door and peering in, went back to the couch, saying. 'She's asleep. Poor darling, she never goes to sleep this early. She's just trying to get out of our way . . . isn't that cute. She wants her mama to have her romance without interference. That's sweet. I've already bathed, Charlie, so you can have the bathroom as soon as I brush my teeth, and, Charlie . . . don't take too long.'

When he returned to the bedroom, she was sitting up in bed waiting for him. She turned the covers back, moving over to make room for him.

He turned out the light and slid in next to her, and turning to take her in his arms, but she held him off, saying, 'Charlie, we need to talk before we get started. I really didn't want to bring this up, tonight, but I have to, or it might affect my performance, if you know what I mean. I hate to, but I have to . . . it's bothering me like a boil that needs popping . . . '

He felt sure he knew what she was leading up to, and he hated to see her bring it up at a time like this, but, like she said, she had to.

He responded. 'Can't it wait until morning?'

'No, Charlie, it can't. I'm sorry, honey, but it's burning in me.'

He sat up, his mounting passion now on the decline, as he replied. 'OK, go ahead. I'll try to answer your questions as accurately as I can . . . '

She replied, softly. 'I'm more concerned with the truth than accuracy right now. I've been going over the names of the crew on that cruise and I have something bothering me real bad.'

He knew what was coming, but he replied. 'What is that?'

'Well, how many bedrooms did that boat have?'

'They are called staterooms, and it had three.'

'And, if I have this straight, the owners, Peg and Arnie, slept in one, and the engaged couple, Kate and Bill, I am sure slept in one, and that leaves two people with one stateroom, you and Amanda. Did you share a bedroom with her, Charlie'

He sighed a deep sigh, and then he related the story, the true story of how he and Amanda became roommates, and ended with. 'Yes, we shared a room, but not a bed. She had the lower bunk and I had the upper one, so help me God . . . that is the truth.'

She responded, quietly, 'I hope it is the truth, Charlie, because our whole future depends on it, so help me God. I just have one more question to ask you, and please tell me the truth, no matter what it is. Did you make love to that woman on that boat?'

He looked into her eyes, replying, 'I swear to you before God in heaven, I did not make love to her on that boat.' (If the reader will check back, he or she will find that this is an honest statement. Her question was . . . 'did you make love to that woman on that boat?' You will also remember that the possible affair in the hotel in Cancun was never verified.)

She looked deeply into his eyes, and satisfied that he had, indeed, told her the truth, she pulled him to her, whispering, 'That's all I need to know. We will never speak of this matter, again . . . ever. Come here, Charlie, I've heard all I need to hear. I'm not interested in any more talking . . . just action.'

Erin was as excited as a teenager the next morning as she prepared for the trip. She was up first and she smiled as she crept past their bedroom door, and her mother, who had been awake for some time, came out, putting her fingers to his lips, saying.'Shush . . . he's still asleep.'

The daughter whispered, 'You guys couldn't have had much fun last night . . . I didn't hear a sound.'

The mother looked embarrassed. 'You weren't supposed to. Now, put the coffee on while I get into the bathroom.'

Erin giggled. 'OK.'

As he entered the kitchen area later on, Charlie gave Erin an embarrassed smile, saying 'Good morning, Erin.'

She returned the smile, asking, coquetishly, 'Did you sleep well?'

He gave her a knowing smile in return. 'Not bad.'

'While Mama is in the bedroom getting dressed, what can I fix you for breakfast?'

'Oh, I don't want you going to any trouble for me. Can't we go to the greasy spoon for breakfast before we leave for Vail?'

She laughed. 'Are you making fun of the place where we work?'

'No! Just a statement of fact, Erin, but while we are on that subject, do you intend to continue to work there, or do you have something else in mind for the future.'

She sighed. 'Oh, I don't know. Ma and I have talked about it. She doesn't want me to be a waitress all my life. She says I deserve better than that, but, when I ask her, what?, she says . . . "I don't know . . . We'll have to see about that."'

'How do you feel about it? Do you want to be a waitress all your life?'

She shook her head. 'No! I want more, but,' and she hesitated, 'it's hard to break out. You know why there are so many poor people, Charlie, 'cause it's hard to break out. It takes money to get out of poverty, as foolish as that may sound, but it does.'

He nodded, surprised at her profound statement. 'I know what you mean, but if someone were to help you break out . . . '

She smiled at him, a beautiful warm smile. 'Are you

making me an offer, Charlie? Don't you have enough worries with my Mama? You don't need another generation to worry about.'

He mulled his reply, for, not quite yet willing to make a firm commitment to her or the mother, he said, 'If I did help you, and as of now I have no idea what that would be, I view it as helping your mother. You see, I'm very fond of Meagan, and her happiness is my happiness.'

She smiled. 'That's nice, Charlie. Speaking of Mama, what do you have in mind for her? Are your intentions strictly honourable towards her?' and she laughed, 'Or, is it too late to ask that?'

He laughed, too. 'It's too late to ask . . . I'm sure you know that.'

'Oh, well, my question is still relevant. are you going to bring her happiness or just more sadness . . . that's all I want to know . . . ' and before he could answer, Meagan made an appearance, fully dressed, smiling and asking, 'All right you two . . . I see you with your heads together . . . talking about me, I bet.'

'Uh huh, Mama, we were.'

'Anything you'd want to tell me?'

'Well, I was just asking Charlie what he intended to do with you?'

'And what did he say?' she asked, kissing Charlie lightly on the lips, saying, 'Good morning.'

Erin gave him a mischievous look, replying, 'He said he hasn't made up his mind about you.'

Meagan looked Charlie in the eye. 'Oh?'

Charlie poked her in the ribs. 'I didn't say that. She is baiting me . . . asking me if my intentions are honourable towards you.'

As Meagan picked up her coffee cup, she asked, 'And what did you say to that?'

'I told her it was too late for that.'

Meagan giggled. 'Erin, honey, I'm afraid he is right about that . . . it's too late.'

With Meagan and Charlie in the front seat of the Jeep, and Erin in the back seat, they started out on the country feeder road which would take them to

Interstate 70 and Vail. Erin was like a schoolgirl as she pointed out that mountain peak, that beautiful valley, that quaint little mining town as they climbed towards the Eisenhower Tunnel.

It was late summer and the weather was chilly at the higher elevations. No snow, as yet, but the trees were coming into their glorious colours, as nature picked up her brush and palette and began to paint. Spirits were high with the women doing most of the talking and Charlie grunting and smiling on cue, as they asked,'Huh,Charlie? . . . don't you think so? Oh, Charlie, you spoilsport!'

After checking in at the plush resort hotel in the middle of Vail Valley they took the elevator to their suite. Erin was goggle-eyed. To say that Erin was green as the spring grass was a truism, and she lacked her mother's street knowledge, not having been exposed to as many pick-up attempts due to her years of incarceration.

As Meagan had described it to Charlie in one of her more profound and tender moments, 'Charlie, Ah don heard every lie that a lying man can dream up to get a woman in the sack . . . Ah could write a book on it. Please . . . don't give me any 'o yurn.' That was long before the commencement of night school, of course.

As they entered the two-hundred-and-fifty- dollars-a-day suite, (off season) Erin walked around in a daze, exclaiming, 'Geez, Mama, this is beautiful,' and like a little girl, asked, 'which is my bedroom?' to which Charlie replied, 'Take any one you want,' and looking at Meagan, added, 'We'll make do with whatever is left.'

Meagan protested. 'Charlie, I wish you'd quit spoiling that girl. I'm the one you have to keep happy, if you want to be kept happy . . . '

Erin laughed. 'Mama's right, Charlie . . . don't look to me for comfort on a cold night,' and she added mischievously, 'not that I'd mind . . . '

Meagan slapped her on the butt, saying, 'That'll be enough of that, young lady! You'd better get out and find yourself a man before you explode.'

'I intend to start just as soon as you and Charlie point me in the right direction and turn me loose . . . whoeeee!'

Meagan shook her head. 'I just don't know about her, Charlie! You'd better keep her straight.'

'Why me? You're her mother!'

She gave him an all-knowing look. 'You know ah ain't used to city folks and city ways, Charlie, I'd be lost without you, honey,' and she kissed him.

He grunted. 'Uh huh, you're dumb like a fox, Meagan.'

She poked him in the ribs. 'And don't you ever fergit it, little chicken. Charlie, I'm hungry . . . must be this mountain air. Let's go eat. Come on Erin, honey.'

'Oh, Mama . . . no! I have got to bathe and do my hair first. I want to look good . . . you know . . . just in case someone comes up and . . . '

Her mother did not let her finish. 'Well, we'll wait for you downstairs in the lobby . . . huh, Charlie. You don't want to sit up here and watch her dress . . . '

Charlie gave them both a mischievous grin. 'Oh, I don't know about that.'

Erin giggled. 'Oh, Charlie . . . you naughty man,' But Meagan intervened. 'I'll decide for you, Charlie, honey. Let's go. We'll be in the lobby, Erin . . . I want to look around for a while.'

Charlie added, 'If we're not in the lobby, we'll be in the bar.'

'I'll find you guys . . . '

'Erin! Remember, you don't talk to any strange man . . . you understand me? Remember what I told you!'

'Yes, Mama . . . I remember.'

As they went out into the corridor, Charlie turned to Meagan, saying.'You shouldn't treat her like a child, Meagan. She is a twenty-year-old woman, and a pretty one, too.'

She turned to him. 'Charlie . . . Erin is my daughter . . . not yours! Please let me handle her . . . please, honey! I know what I'm doing. She is green, and she is horny. That is a dangerous combination, believe me.'

He nodded. 'I'm sorry. I didn't mean to interfere.'

'And I'm sorry I snapped at you. She is all I've got to show for thirty-six years of living in this miserable world, and I want her to be happy.'

'Then, let's seek her happiness, together, shall we?'
They had reached the elevator. 'OK! It's a deal.'
Charlie catered to Meagan's wishes as she toured the beautiful lobby with its huge exposed timbers and rustic decor. He had not the heart to tell her he had stayed in the place on many occasions on their skiing trips during the winters he and Adelle had come to Vail along with their friends.

As she pointed out this thing and that thing, he nodded and grunted as required, and then, finally, 'Let's go and have a drink. I'm thirsty.'

'OK, if that is what you want, sweetie. Charlie, speaking of sweetie, what would you prefer that I call you? You know . . . the lovey names. Do you have a favourite?'

'Just don't call me what Adelle called me, and there will be no trouble.'

'Well, what did she call you?'

He hesitated. 'Pumpkin,' he whispered

"Oh, geez, Charlie . . . I promise.'

They were sitting in the middle of the bar which was unusually crowded for the off season. Some of the college crowd were here on a last fling before the return to the campus. They could easily be identified by their loud talking and their glasses raised on high, as if they were badges of honour for all to see. Meagan's back was to the door, with Charlie facing it.

He heard the college kids at the next table get quiet all of a sudden, and then he heard murmurs and could see heads nodding towards the door. He looked up, and there she was. He saw Erin standing there, tall and stately. Her hair had been put up and her long neck formed a perfect pedestal for that beautiful face.

She stood in the doorway, statuesque as only a tall and thin woman can be, and still look lovely. She wore a nice dress – not expensive, but stylish . . . he could see that. She smiled as she looked around the room. He could hear the college boys at the next table sucking wind through their lips as they made comments as only they can.

He placed his hand on Meagan's saying, softly, 'I

think you'd better turn around and look at the door. There is a gorgeous woman standing there, looking this way, and I would not want you to miss her.'

She turned, complaining, 'Charlie, I'm not interested in looking at another woman,' and then she saw her daughter. She could not help but stare at her own child.

She placed her hand on Charlie's arm. 'Oh, Charlie, look at Erin. She is beautiful, isn't she?' and then she turned to look at the college boys at the next table, smiling as she remarked, 'And they know it, too. Look at them stare at her . . . oh, Charlie!'

He smiled in return, nodding his agreement, and feeling Erin had had enough time to bask in the limelight, he patted Meagan's hand, saying, 'She is beautiful.' As he rose to greet her, he repeated, 'Yes, she is really a beauty.'

Erin strode across the room with a practised gait, like a show horse which knows it is the object of all attention. She was smiling a gracious and confident smile as she looked first left, then right, and then straight ahead. The college boys' emotions had been stirred, for their threshold of excitability is very low, and they were quite voluble about it, not knowing or realizing the mother of the beautiful creature was sitting next to them, but as Erin approached they became quieter, foolishly believing she might be headed for their table.

But, they were soon brought to reality as she came to the correct table, and seeing Charlie standing to greet her, she coyly kissed him on the cheek, and to her mother, a gracious. 'Mother, it is so good to see you.'

Of course it was an act, but, admittedly, a good one at which even the most greenish of women are masters of the art.

Meagan whispered in her daughter's ear, 'You look gorgeous, honey. Now, sit down 'fore I kick your butt.' Erin giggled as she took the chair offered her by an admiring Charlie.

As she lowered herself into her chair Erin gave a quick glance at the covey of college boys at the next table who were ogling her without shame, nudging each other, whispering comments to each other, obviously of a pruient nature.

Charlie looked at her with nothing less than male admiration as he asked, 'What did you do to yourself? You look great!'

She smiled, demurely. 'Why, I just put my hair up and put on this ole dress . . . that's all, but I'm glad you approve, Charlie . . . '

Her mother grunted, putting her hand on Charlie's chin, turning it to her, replying, 'He's approving it too much. Over here, boy, I'm the girl you came in with . . . remember.'

He gave her a smile 'I remember! I was just admiring your beautiful daughter.'

Meagan replied, 'Can't say I blame you,' and she whispered to Erin. 'Did you notice those college boys at the next table, drooling all over themselves when they saw you?'

Erin gave her mother a mother-daughter look as she replied, 'Uh huh, I saw them . . . they're gorgeous.'

'Well, don't get too excited, honey, we came in to eat.'

'I know, but I can look at 'em, can't I,' she replied, giving them sideways glances.

The mother replied, 'Uh huh, but don't let them see you looking at 'em . . . gives them the wrong signals,' as she gave Charlie a motherly smile.

A waiter came up to the table, a male waiter . . . another college boy, no doubt, trying to combine the two great worlds of skiing and academics. He offered menus all around, asking for drink orders.

Charlie looked at Meagan, asking, 'Wine or liquor.' She replied, 'Wine for me.' And turning to Erin for her choice, Meagan replied, 'She'll have tea.'

'Oh, Ma! Let me have some wine. We're on a fun trip. Let me have some fun . . . '

She smiled at her daughter. 'I want you to have some fun, honey. I just don't want you to have too much . . . too soon,' and she looked at the table of college boys.

Before she could reply, a handsome young college boy was standing at their table, looking sheepish. He was over six feet tall, well built, with black hair, swarthy complexion, and he exuded confidence. If he had any complexes, they were not of the inferiority type. He stood there with his hands together before him, trying to look bashful, and as Charlie looked up at him, questioningly, he offered, 'Scuse me, Ma'am . . . Sir . . . but we were wondering . . . my buddies and I . . . if your daughter would like to have dinner with us. You see, we're all college boys . . . lonesome college boys, I must admit, and, well, if we could be blessed with her company during the meal, well, it would make going back to college less painful.'

While Charlie, remembering his own college day pitches, was thinking, 'Damn . . . he's good!' Meagan was thinking to herself, 'What B.S., but he is some cute.'

Erin was enthralled, even libidinously excited, if the truth were known, but she merely looked towards her mother for guidance.

Charlie rose to look the young man in the eye, but smilingly replied. 'You're a bit overbearing, don't you think! We don't know you. Why should we allow our young lady to join your group?' and he added, 'even if you are college boys.'

The handsome young man seemed contrite, as he replied, cooly, 'I realize that I have been forward, sir, and I apologize for my bad manners,' and extending his hand, he continued, 'Please allow me to introduce myself. My name is Braxton Miles the Third, and I come from a little town in Montana named Braxton.'

Charlie smiled, asking, 'Were you named after the town, or vice versa?'

The youth smiled. 'Well, sir, I guess the town was named after my grandfather . . . he named it . . . he owned it.'

'I see . . . '

The youth continued. 'I know we are acting rashly, sir, but you see . . . this is our last night in town, and, well, we don't have time to observe all the social graces which would normally govern our actions . . . if we had time. We just want her to sit and eat with us . . . right here next to your table. You could keep an eye on us the whole time. We're all nice boys, I assure you, sir.'

Charlie looked at the two women for instructions.

Erin's eyes were wide open with expectation and her mother's were wide open with apprehension, as the two women looked at Charlie for guidance.

Charlie smiled at the student, shaking his hand, replying, 'If it's all right with her mother, I see no harm in that, but you will stay right at this table, do you understand that . . . no going anywhere else with her . . . understand?'

'Oh, yes, sir . . . we understand.'

To Meagan's extreme discomfort, he asked Erin if she would like to have supper with them, and with eyes widened with excitement, which she could hardly suppress, she nodded, adding, demurely. 'If you think it is all right,' and she looked at her mother for confirmation.

Meagan replied, very softly, 'If you want to, honey.'

So Erin rose, smiling, while introductions were made between the young people at both tables, and the exchange was completed with a euphoria typical among the very young.

When the young had retreated to their table, Meagan grabbed Charlie's hand, asking, 'Are you sure this is OK? We don't even know these boys. And,Charlie, did you see how excited Erin was? She is so vulnerable just now. Did you notice that her eyes were wide and her nostrils were flaring? Oh, Charlie!'

He laughed. 'The same expression I've seen on you on some occasions . . . '

She kicked him under the table, smilingly replying, 'And you know what that expression does to me and for you!'

He nodded. 'Don't worry about Erin. She is right next to us . . . what can happen? She deserves some happiness, doesn't she?'

The mother looked at her happy and smiling daughter at the next table, and fighting back a tear, merely nodded, squeezing Charlie's hand in reply, and picked up her menu, asking, 'I wonder what their special is?'

After dinner had been served, Meagan, between bites, monitored the conversation and laughter going on next to them. She watched her daughter in her movements and body language . . . laughing at this one . . . pursing her lips in a pout at that one, and she thought to herself. 'Hell, she knows what she is doing . . . comes natural to all females, I guess,' and she turned her attention to the man she loved.

She smiled. She was happy. She fantasized how they were a family . . . she, Charlie, and Erin, and, suddenly it hit her, as it has hit women for millions of years. She wanted a baby! As she looked at Charlie, then across the way at Erin, she decided she wanted to give Charlie Forester a baby of his own . . . their own, and the idea began to burn in her as the evening went on. The more she thought of it, the more she wanted it to happen, and it gave her a warm maternal feeling just thinking of it. She reached for Charlie's hand, squeezing it, as she nodded towards Erin. Charlie squeezed back, smiling and nodding.

The meal was drawing to a close and the laughter and conversation at the next table had not subsided one bit as the vibrancy of youth drove it on.

Erin rose, coming over to her mother's side, wringing her hands, she bent over and whispered in her ear, 'Mama, they want to go over to the lounge side, where there is a little combo band. They want to dance. Oh, Mama, I want to go . . . can I?'

Meagan"s eyebrows went up. 'Dance? Where? Oh, Erin, I don't know,' and pulling Charlie towards her, repeated the words, asking, 'What do you think?'

Charlie smiled, replying, 'As long as we are in the lounge with them, I see no problem.'

But when this solution was offered, Erin pouted, 'Do you have to? It'll look like I'm a little girl who can't be trusted alone with men,' she whispered to her mother, to which the mother whispered back, 'You can't! That's why Charlie and I have to be there with you, honey. It's either that way, or . . . '

She pouted. 'Oh, OK!' and then, she proudly went back to her suitors to announce the decision.

There were yells from all. The other boys had now induced some college girls to join them and they now had the makings of a good party as they made their way towards the lounge, with Charlie and Meagan bringing up the rear . . . Charlie smiling . . . Meagan filled with maternal apprehension.

The band was of the ski crowd type, playing the kind of music which induced dancing of the variety where the two participants were several feet apart, never touching each other's bodies, with each gyrating in his or her own fashion. It required no skill, just body movement, so Erin was at no disadvantage whatsoever. It's the kind of dancing one can learn in a minute or two, and if one is not too adept at it, no one will ever know for it was not required that one partner need follow the other.

Meagan watched the young people gyrating for a while, commenting. 'I don't call that dancing, Charlie. They don't even touch each other,' and she smiled as she added, 'They don't know what they're missing, huh? And to think I was terrified when Erin said those boys wanted to dance. I could just picture them holding my baby so tight she could hardly breathe, just grinding away at her, but heck Charlie, that is harmless dancing if I've ever seen it.'

He smiled, nodding. 'Harmless, indeed, but you have to understand, Meagan, these young people are so accustomed to it,' and he hesitated, for he knew she hated the explicit word, as he continued, 'You know what I mean. Body contact in public means nothing to them anymore.'

She became worried as she digested his words, replying, 'I wish you hadn't reminded me of that,' and turning to him, taking his hand, implored, 'What's going to happen to her, Charlie? I want her to have more than I did, but . . . ' and her words trailed off, as she continued to watch her daughter having fun.

She continued, 'Look at her, honey, she is so happy. That's the way I want her to be . . . smiling and happy,' and then she became pensive as she asked, 'What's going to happen to all of us, Charlie? Our lives, Erin's and mine, are wrapped around you. What are you going to do with us, honey? We're your women, whether you know it or not. 'Course, you can get up and walk out of our lives. There's nothing stopping you . . .'

'Yes, there is.'

She asked in all seriousness. 'What?'

'I love you . . . I love you both. That's why I can't go anywhere, now.' He teased her with, 'My goose is cooked.'

At this moment she was filled with love in overflowing torrents but, being in a public place, she merely leaned over and kissed him, gently, with propriety, as she replied, 'And we love you, too. Erin's crazy about you . . . she told me. Poor child, she's never had a father, you know. She wants a father so bad, Charlie.'

'I'll be her father if you let me,' he half whispered.

'Oh, Charlie, you're so good to me . . . to us. What did I ever do to deserve you?'

He smiled . . . shrugged . . . saying nothing, turning to look at Erin having fun.

Meagan saw him look at his watch, and now having arrived at the stage of shared wavelengths that enamored couples seem to achieve, she offered, 'I know. It's getting late. Don't you think it's time we got Cinderella back to her room before the fireworks get started. You know how young people are when the last dance is played.'

The young couples had begun dancing closer as the night wore on, and they danced with both arms around the neck of the other. Meagan had just noticed that change in the arrangements, and as she saw her daughter dancing, she exclaimed, 'It's time to go, Charlie. Would you go out on the dance floor and get your daughter?' she smiled at him.

He shrugged, nodding. 'I think you're right, Mama, it's time we put our daughter to bed'

She knew the words were said in jest, but the sound of them thrilled her as she repeated them in her mind, 'Our daughter.'

The intrusion by Charlie was not appreciated by either of the dancers as Erin implored, 'Do we really have to go?'

He smiled. 'We really do. We have a hard day ahead

of us, tomorrow, and I'm sure these young men do too,' as he took her hand,but she pulled back, saying, 'Come on, Charlie, dance with me . . . just a while,' and she placed her arms around his neck.

He could smell wine on her breath, but he said nothing as he extricated himself from her embrace, saying, 'Come on, Cinderella. Say goodnight to these gentlemen.'

'Goodnight, fellas . . . it was fun.'

The eager suitor pressed on. 'But, sir, wait a minute! We're leaving in the morning. We're all meeting in the coffee shop at eight . . . for breakfast. Can Erin meet us then? Just for breakfast?'

She looked at Charlie with imploring eyes. 'Please, Charlie. It's just for breakfast . . . in the coffee shop?'

He smiled at her eager face, eyes bright with happiness, as he replied, 'I guess it's OK! Just for breakfast.'

She turned to her now perceived date, saying softly, 'goodnight, Brax . . . I had a great time.'

'Me, too! See you in the morning. Goodnight, sir.'

Having collected the mother, the trio made their way towards the elevator. As they entered, Erin leaned against the wall, looking off into space, murmuring softly, 'That is the best time I've ever had in my whole life. I think I'm in love.'

Her mother grunted a maternal response. 'You're in love with love, honey. You ain't seen enough of it to recognize it when you see it. Take a cold shower when you get to the room, and go to bed. You'll be back to normal in the morning.'

She shook her head 'I don't even intend to wash my hands before I go to sleep. I'll wash off his touch if I do.'

The mother looked at her lover, 'I think I'm going to be sick if I hear any more of this,' as she patted her daughter on the derriére, holding her close.

Contrary to her previous exclamations of intent, Erin was not long in falling asleep. She was a tired but very happy young woman. As she lay in bed, she relived every exciting moment of the evening for, poor child, she had had so few in her lifetime. She wondered 'Is this the way it is supposed to be . . . happiness and contentment. Is this the way it can be?'

Her self-imposed question was not answered, for she succumbed to slumber.

But, not so the older couple in the next bedroom. Sleep was delayed for an hour or so while they shared with each other the depth and fervor of their mutual love. Those passions now spent, they engaged in pillow talk, touching on the events of the evening.

Meagan observed, 'Did you see how happy she was, honey? I've never seen her laugh and joke so much. That's the way people should be, Charlie . . . happy and smiling. We don't need to hurt each other in this world. Why do we do it?'

He rubbed her hand with his fingers, lifting it to his lips, kissing it gently, 'I don't know, Meagan. I don't feel very profound just now, but I admit Erin was one happy young woman this evening.'

'Charlie? Tell me what you think.'

'About what?'

'Erin. Could any man really regard her as an acceptable wife if they knew she had served time for murder?'

He sat up, perturbed, as he looked at her. 'Damn it, Meagan, Erin did not serve time for murder. She did not commit murder! She acted in self defence. If she hadn't killed the bastard, he would have shoved that butcher knife in you, wouldn't he?'

'That's for sure!'

'Then, she is not a murderer. If she had had decent representation by a good lawyer, she would never have even been charged with it. It was a miscarriage of justice . . . that is what it was, and I don't want to ever hear you mention murder, again, where she is concerned.'

The vehemence of his reply pleased her, and she asked, again, 'Regardless of what you call it, will any young man like she met tonight ever accept her as a wife . . . a real wife?'

'Well, you saw the reception she had tonight from those college boys, didn't you? How can you ask that?'

She sat up in bed, indignantly. 'Oh, hell, Charlie, they weren't looking for a wife tonight. They were looking for a bedmate. They reminded me of a bunch of bulls looking at a pasture full of young heifers. You could read it in their eyes . . . '

'I didn't read that. I only saw a bunch of college kids trying to have a good time . . . '

She shook her head. 'You're a man, Charlie! You're made of the same material they are. Women can tell the difference, even if you men can't. What I want to know is . . . would one of those high-class boys who have towns named after their granddaddys ever ask my daughter to be their wife if they knew she had killed a man by shoving a pair of scissors in his back?'

He searched for the right words, 'If he loved her enough.'

She shrugged her shoulders. 'I wonder,' and she snuggled in his neck.

She had intended to talk to him about their having a baby, but she decided this was not an appropriate time, so she yawned, signalling to him that the night was over. He smiled, and held her close.

18

Erin was up early the next morning, still excited about the night before and further excited in anticipation of meeting the college group again that morning for breakfast.

When she saw Meagan and Charlie making an appearance in the suite just before she was ready to leave, she exclaimed, 'Geez, I hope you two aren't coming down to breakfast just now. The gang will believe for sure that I can't be out of your sight for one minute. Can't you guys find another place to eat?'

Meagan and Charlie exchanged glances, with the mother asking, 'Do you feel as unneeded as I do 'bout now? The kid has no further use for us,' she kidded.

'And it happened so early in our lives, too,' Charlie added. 'I thought this happened in later years, when your kids shunted you aside.'

'Oh, come on, you two! Gimme a break, huh! You know I love you, but give me some space, will ya?'

Meagan looked at Charlie, smiling. 'I guess the kid is right! How much trouble can you get into at breakfast? Go on, honey. Charlie and I will make other arrangements for breakfast, but, Erin . . . do not leave the coffee shop! Do you understand?'

As she exited the suite, 'Oh, OK.'

Meagan looked at her lover 'What'll we do for breakfast, now?'

He thought for a while, and with a gleam in his eye, replied, 'We can go back to bed.'

She took him by the hand. 'Uh huh! . . . in private, too.'

After . . . having coffee and Danish pastries sent up to

the room, they sat on the couch, talking small talk, mostly of Erin. Meagan sensed this might be the time, so she purred,'Charlie, do you like kids?'

And as he opened his mouth to reply, she cut him off with, 'The reason I asked is . . . well . . . you and Adelle were married for four years, and,' she shrugged, 'you never had any. 'Course, people don't have to have kids these days because there's so many ways of preventing. Did you and Adelle prevent . . . you know what I mean . . .'

Her question struck him in the heart. He had taken Adelle at her word when she told him she was trying to get pregnant. Of course, that was in their earlier and happier days, and over the years when he issued even a casual remark about their having children, and their apparent inability to do so, she would become defensive, with, 'I'm trying, Charlie. What more can I do? It takes two you know!' and she would pout for a while.

He thought of it all, and seeing that Meagan was expecting an answer to her question, he replied, meekly, 'I thought we were trying, but, now . . . I just don't know. She could have deceived me about that, too.'

He did not have the heart to tell her of the two abortions Adelle had confessed to. He couldn't

'Oh, honey . . . I can't believe she would have lied about that . . . something so sacred as a child.'

He grunted. 'Marriage is sacred, too, and she deceived me in that.'

She took a deep breath. 'Well, anyhow . . . did you want a baby?'

'Sure! Most men do. I did. I can remember how bad my parents wanted a grandchild, too. They would ask me, often . . . 'When are you and Adelle going to decide to have a baby?'

She felt she was on the right track as she pursued it further, 'Then, you really wanted a baby, huh?'

'Well, sure, but why are you on this subject?'

She took his hands in hers, looking deep in his eyes, and with all the conviction she could muster, 'Charlie, honey . . . I want a baby . . . your baby,' and before he could open his mouth to reply, she placed her fingers on his lips . . . 'no, please let me finish. This is no hair-brained idea of mine. I've thought about it until I am blue in the face, and, honey, I want to give you a baby . . . our baby.'

He started to respond, but she continued. 'I'm thirty-six. I don't have many years left to try. The older a woman is, the more risks there are . . . you know that,' and her voice broke under the weight of her words, 'but, oh, Charlie, I want one bad . . . I really do.'

He hesitated as he tried to speak, after having been cut off two previous times, but she eagerly awaited his words, with mixed emotions, though, for she had no idea what he would say.

'Meagan, I must admit I would love to have a child with you, but we are not married . . . '

She gasped in horror at his words. 'Do you think I want to have an illegitimate baby with you? Oh, Charlie! What do you think I am. Please . . . have more respect for me than that, and for the baby,' she pleaded, pulling away.

He realized he had hurt her. He took her in his arms, saying, 'No . . . no . . . I was not even implying that . . . I was just pointing out that we were not married, now, so we could not . . . should not . . . have a baby, now. That's all I meant.'

She had quit her sobbing at these words and looked at him, sadly. 'Charlie, tell me the truth. Do you ever want me to be your wife, or am I just a plaything to you? Do your really want a hick waitress working in a hick cafe in a hick town in a hick county of Colorado to be the wife of Charles Alexander Forester, of the Texas Foresters, All I want is the truth, Charlie! No bullshit, please!'

'Meagan . . . I'm not playing games with you! How can you think that? If I wanted to play games, I could have played with Amanda, believe me. She begged me to.'

He had not wanted to get into that, but his anger forced him to. He regretted it, and after her eyebrows went up at the mention of Amanda's name, he truly regretted it even more,but she replied, 'I promised you we would never speak of her, again, and I mean what I say, Charlie. I'm waiting for an answer to my question.'

He took a deep breath. 'I can best answer your question by telling you my father asked me the same question when I left home a week ago'

'And, what did you tell your father? I presume you told him the truth . . . as you know it.'

'I told him that I wanted to come to see you for a period not to exceed three months, and at the end of that time I would either ask you to marry me . . . or, break it off.'

She shuddered at the words, 'Break it off,' but she tried not to show it. She had never thought of 'breaking it off', and it scared her.

She moved back from him, saying, softly, 'Then, I am on probation for the next few weeks. If I fail to please you . . . I'm out! Oh, God, Charlie, do you realize what you are putting me through? Every time we make love, I will ask myself, 'am I pleasing enough? Every time I cook you a meal . . . is it good enough to please you. Do you like my hair . . . my laugh . . . the clothes I wear . . . do I snore in my sleep . . . Oh, my God, Charlie,' and she began to cry in earnest.

He realized it had not gone well, and he was as hurt as she was. He tried to take her in his arms, but she moved away, saying, 'No . . . not now. I've go to do some thinking about us . . . real thinking.'

She could hear the door being opened, and knowing full well that her daughter had returned, she got up quickly and headed for the bathroom, pausing only long enough to say, 'Tell Erin I am not feeling well. Take her out! Anywhere . . . go shopping . . . just be gone for a couple of hours. Please!'

Erin, effervescent as a fawn on a spring day, full of life, entered the suite, smiling, asking, 'Where's Mama, Charlie?'

He looked sheepish as he replied, 'She became ill all of a sudden. I guess it was something she ate last night. She wants to be alone for a couple of hours, she told me . . . '

'Oh, my God! I'd better go in to see her . . . ' and she started towards the bedroom, but he caught her arm. 'Not, now, Erin . . . trust me, please.'

She was confused, but, she relented. 'Well, OK, if you think that is best,' and then, 'Charlie, did you and Mama have an argument? Please tell me.'

'No! Not an argument, but, yes . . . a disagreement on something we discussed . . . something rather important.'

She shook her head. 'Important enough to make her sick?'

'Apparently so,' he replied, 'but, I promise you, it will be all right in an hour or so.'

'I hope so! I was having so much fun!'

He felt sorry for her. Why should she suffer for the sins of her elders? He took her hand, leading her out of the suite, and into the corridor.

She followed without objection, but as they entered the elevator, she asked, 'Where are we going?'

'We'll go down to the coffee shop, have a cup of coffee and decide what to do for a couple of hours.'

They looked at the other passengers in the elevator, and the stares were easily readable. 'What is that young girl doing with that older man?'

Erin smiled at him, and he smiled at her as she took hold of his hand, kissing him on the cheek, then she smiled at the older couple watching them. Charlie smiled at them, too.

As they sat at the table, waiting for the coffee to be served, she waited for him to say something about the quarrel with Meagan, and seeing he would not volunteer anything, she asked, with youthful simplicity, 'Charlie, what were you and Mama fighting about?'

He shrugged. 'I'm not sure she would want me to tell you.'

'Look, I don't have secrets with my mama, and I was hoping I wouldn't have any with you, so, please . . . '

'He sighed, looking off into space. 'She wants a baby.'

'Her hands went to her throat. 'Ohooo . . . that's great! So, what's the problem, Charlie? Impregnate the woman! Don't you men enjoy that little task?' she kidded.

'We're not married. That's the problem. Neither of us wants a baby out of wedlock.'

She nodded her young head, knowingly. 'Oh, so that is the problem, huh? We get back to the real trouble between you and my mama, huh, Charlie. Marriage! What are you going to do about it? You don't want to marry her, do you?'

'That is not true!'

As the waiter arrived with the coffee, she withheld her response until he had left, and looking at him over the brim of the cup as she sipped it, replied, 'Well, it sure as hell doesn't look like it if you're fighting over it.'

He hesitated. 'You know I love your mother, but, I just got out of a disaster, and I don't need another one, and . . . '

She smiled. 'There's more, huh? Why don't you just look me in the eye, Charlie, and tell me the truth even if you can't say it to her. No . . . wait! Let me guess, first. I don't know much about you . . . only what Mama has told me, but, I feel sure you come from a snotty rich family, and . . . you're not sure my Mama is good enough for you, or, more importantly, your family. Charlie . . . look me in the eye . . . tell me that is not so, if it isn't.'

He swallowed hard. He knew this street smart girl had hit the nail on the head.

He looked her in the eye, shaking his head, admitting, 'That's part of the problem, Erin, but, that knowledge would kill your mother if she even suspected it.'

She snickered. 'Do you blame her, Charlie? You men are really something! She is good enough for you to sleep with, but not to marry, huh! I thought you were different, Charlie, and I know my mama thinks you're different, but you're not.'

He was genuinely hurt, as he answered her, 'That's not true, Erin. I would marry your mother, tomorrow. It's not my family I am worried about . . . it's Meagan. I don't want her torn up in my world, and that is what will happen if she comes back to Texas as my wife. I care for her too much to allow her to be hurt by rejection . . . if it happens, and I believe it will.'

She placed her hand on his, looking at him with some sympathy. 'If that is the real reason, I owe you an apology, then. Just tell me one thing and we'll drop the subject. Do you love my mama enough to marry her regardless of what others think? That is the only kind of love we understand . . . Mama and me. You see, we're simple girls. We don't understand complicated love . . . conditional love . . . just plain old-fashioned love. Do you, Charlie?'

He looked deep in her eyes. 'Yes, I do.'

She leaned over the table, kissing him lightly on the lips, giggling. 'I've been wanting to do that since I first saw you, and since you're gonna be my step-daddy . . . well . . . '

He smiled. 'Be careful, young lady, I'm not your step-daddy, yet.'

She patted his hand, smiling. 'As bad as I want a man, Charlie, it won't be you as long as my Mama loves you.'

He sighed in disappointment. 'Oh, life is so cruel.'

She took a last sip of the cold coffee, then asked, 'What are we going to do for another hour or so? I don't want to go back to that suite until she's had time to cool off, believe me. When that woman is upset, she is hell on wheels.'

'Tell me about it!' and as he looked at her for a moment, he finally said, 'What do you say we have a great dinner party tonight . . . the three of us. We'll find the swankiest place in Vail, and we'll go there dressed to kill. What do you say?'

She was not too excited as she responded, 'I could get really excited over that if I had a date. I want a date, Charlie. I want to meet a man.'

He laughed. 'I thought you were in love with Braxton Miles the third . . . '

'Who?' She smiled. 'I was when he was in town, but,' and she raised her hands, 'he's gone! He can't do me any good. I want one in the flesh, if you know what I mean,' she giggled. 'Charlie, find me a date for tonight, and I will love you forever!'

'Suppose I agreed to find you a date for tonight,

would you try to help me get your Mama to forgive me for whatever I've done to make her mad?'

She smiled. 'If you get me a date with a gorgeous hunk, I'll take care of my mama, I promise you. And, Charlie, he doesn't even have to have money! Just be gorgeous, and alive, if you know what I mean.'

'Your mama is right. You are horny!'

She became serious as she pondered his comment, and then, 'Let me tell you what my love life has been like, Charlie. I was a virgin when I was raped at sixteen. I killed a man when I was sixteen. I went to prison when I was barely seventeen – a woman's prison, with no men, if you know what I mean. Oh, sure, some of us girls would fool around to keep from going crazy, but they were girls, Charlie! I like men! Do you blame me for being horny? I've never known love in my life. I've never had a man hold me in his arms, telling me sweet and tender things. Even if they're lies, Charlie, I yearn to hear them. Any woman would. I'm twenty years old, and no one has ever loved me,' and she looked around the coffee shop, embarrassed, as she suppressed tears.

He took hold of her hands, saying nothing for a while, then, 'No . . . I don't blame you one damn bit! Erin, I promise you that you will have a date, tonight, and with a real live hunk too.'

She smiled, dabbing her eyes with the napkin, and as she patted his hand, 'I'm going to like having you for a step-daddy, Charlie,' and she nodded at him, 'and, believe me, you will end up my step-daddy. You might be able to evade my mama, but you will never evade the two of us together. Your fate is sealed.'

He smiled at her. 'I think you're right, and now I wish you would let your step-daddy do something for you.'

She dried her tears. 'What?'

'Well, I would like to take you out and buy you a gorgeous outfit to wear tonight, and then a trip to the beauty parlour. I want you to be a knockout.'

At first she was excited, with her eyes widening, her mouth open, then, she shook her head. 'No, I can't let you do that for me. It's OK for my Mama, because she repays you in kind,' she giggled, 'I can't do that, so . . . no, thanks.'

He persisted. 'But, Erin, honey, it's for tonight. Don't you want to dazzle this man I'm going to get for you.'

Her eyes widened, and this time they remained wide, as she exclaimed, 'Let's go. It's a deal, but that man had better be gorgeous. Do I get to pass judgement on him first. I have never had a blind date and I don't think I would like one, either. I like to see merchandise before I buy it.'

'Let me see what I can work out, but first I want to take you to a dress shop . . . '

'Are you going to pick it out?'

'No, the final choice is yours. I just want to give you the male viewpoint . . . '

She became animated. 'Something sexy, huh?'

He nodded, as they rose to leave. 'Very sexy.'

After having purchased a very sexy and very expensive dress at one of Vail's most chic stores, he left a happy and ecstatic young woman at one of the town's chic beauty shops, which also abound in profusion, with the instructions to the owner-operator: 'make her look like Grace Kelly in her heyday, and you will be amply rewarded.'

As he bade her goodbye, Erin asked, 'Where will you be?'

'I'm going back to the hotel to face the music.'

'Sure you don't want me to be with you . . . to protect you,' she teased.

'No, thank you. You just look beautiful for tonight, and I will suffer whatever I have to suffer with your Mama.'

'OKaaa . . . bye, Charlie.' He blew her a kiss.

He was not very anxious to face Meagan just now, but he knew it had to be done sooner or later, and as he inserted the key in the door, he opened it slowly, hoping she might be asleep, but she was sitting on the couch in the living area of the suite. She had a nail file in her hand, and she was filing her nails without serious intent.

She smiled as she saw him, saying, 'Well, Charlie . . .

my master has returned. Where have you been and where is my daughter?' as she continued to play with the nail file, faking nonchalance.

He could see that she had been fooling with some numbers, seeing figures on the hotel stationery at her side. He told her of the plans for the evening, of his purchase of the dress for Erin, the promise of a date for her, and Meagan took it all in with self imposed poise and equanimity as she continued to file her nails, saying softly, 'Well, I'm glad to see that you two have been busy spending your money. How will she repay you for your generosity, Charlie? . . . the same way I do? It's expensive for a man to have two women to keep, but I suppose a man of your wealth can afford it, but I do wish you had picked someone other than my own daughter. That will be awkward, don't you think?'

'Are you trying to pick a real fight, Meagan? Erin doesn't deserve that! Maybe I do, but she doesn't!'

'Oh, you know I'm kidding about Erin's part in it, but, speaking of money, Charlie . . . honey . . . I hope you have a lot of it on you.'

He looked surprised. 'Well, I had some cash on me, but I spent it in the dress shop, and I gave Erin some to pay the beautician, and . . . why do you ask?'

She attempted a sly look, which was not easy for her, for guile was not her forte, as she replied, nonchalantly, 'I've been thinking about our relationship . . . a lot . . . and I think we ought to put it on a business basis, since being a kept woman, on approval, I might add, is a cold blooded business.'

So, that is it, he thought. Well, I'll let this run its course, so she can get it out of her system, so he said, 'OK, what do you have in mind?'

'Well, let's see! I figure you owe me about sixteen hundred dollars for services rendered. Now, that comes to a measley hundred dollars a night. That's not a bad price, Charlie, honey, 'cause the girls from Denver charge much more than that and they don't put real sentiment in it like I did,' and she could not suppress a slight sob as she mentioned the sentiment.

She continued, 'And then I'm not charging you for

the meals I cooked and the clothes I washed. I think that's reasonable, don't you?' and the tears came no matter how she tried to keep them back. She turned her head away from him.

He knew he was dealing with a wounded woman . . . a truly and deeply hurt one, and he knew he had to be careful, or it might be all over.

As he sat next to her, moving from the chair he had occupied opposite her, he took his book of traveller's cheques from his pocket and extracted his pen, saying, 'If you feel that is what I owe you, I will be happy to pay you, but I feel I must tell you that you are being cheated.'

She looked up, surprised. 'How? I thought I was being fair to us both. I really don't know the going price, not being in the business, but if you feel I am overcharging you . . . '

He attempted to take her hand, but she pulled it away, as he continued in spite of her rebuff, 'No, I meant you were cheating yourself, not me, for you see, the treasures you gave me are without price. What value can one put on a heart and soul? I believe you loved me,' and he smiled, 'each time, with all your heart and soul, and that is priceless.'

'Damn you,' she sniffed, 'don't try to sweet talk your way out of this . . . just pay the sixteen hundred! I'll be satisfied with that,' and she could not suppress a smile.

He took her hand which she now allowed, and bringing her fingers to his lips, he continued, 'Well, I still think you are undercharging me, and being a fair man, I want to add something to the sixteen hundred . . . '

She pulled her hands away. 'Charlie Forester, you know where you can stick your money, don't you . . . '

He smiled at her. He knew she was cooling off from her anger. He could read it in her eyes, as he teased, 'Now you're being crude! You always told me you didn't like dirty talk, and now, you're talking dirty yourself.'

You bring out the worst in me,' she replied.

'I'm sorry! But, to continue with the subject matter at hand, I think we ought to bring the account up to date,' and as he reached in his shirt pocket, he extracted a small dark blue jewellery box and he placed it in her hand, saying, 'I hope this brings my account into balance with yours . . . '

Her eyes widened as she took the box. No one in her entire life had ever presented her with a box from a jewellery store, and especially one with the title of Saks – Fifth Avenue on the small, discreet tag on the back of it.

Her hands trembled as she opened it, trying to look at the contents and him as the same time. She finally decided to concentrate her attention on the contents.

Her eyes widened and her mouth opened as she gazed on a blue-white diamond of obscene size. Her gaze went from the ring to his eyes, and then, back to the ring.

She extracted it from its holding tabs and held it up to the light, saying, softly, 'This looks like an engagement ring . . . '

He smiled. 'Yes, I think that is what they call them.'

She looked bewildered as her mind tried to absorb it all, and she asked, 'Is this an engagement ring, Charlie?'

'Well, if you'd prefer to call it a friendship ring, that is OK with me, but it is a little ostentatious for a friendship ring, don't you think? . . . '

'Charlie . . . are we engaged? Really engaged?'

'If you will have me, Meagan, I want to marry you . . . when I am free . . . '

Her bewildered mind asked, 'When you are free?'

He nodded. "I don't even know if my divorce from Adelle is final. You wouldn't want to marry a bigamist, would you?'

'Right now, Charlie, I wouldn't care what you are,' and she threw herself in his arms, kissing him, hugging him, smothering him with exclamations, some of which bear repeating and some of which were lost in the magic of the moment.

She sat up, then looking seriously, asked, 'What made you change your mind? Only a few hours ago, you said . . . '

'Do you have to have an explanation?'

'Yes . . . I want one! I need one, Charlie.'

He smiled. 'To tell you the truth, I can't afford to pay for your services, Meagan . . . '

She laughed as she rose, taking him by the hand, dragging him towards the bedroom,but he held back, asking, 'Wait a minute! What is this going to cost me? I'm about out of cash. Do you take plastic?'

She smiled at him. 'This one is on the house, honey.'

When Erin returned two hours later, beautifully coiffed, she inserted her key in the door, opening it gently to determine if the fight was still in progress. Hearing no loud sounds, she entered the suite quietly, looking around and seeing no one in sight, peeked into the bathroom, which was open. No one there, either, she mused; they must have gone out. Then she heard muffled sounds coming from the bedroom shared by mother and Charlie. She tiptoed to the door, leaning her head to get a better hearing.

She once again could hear the muffled sounds and she smiled, shaking her head, saying to herself, 'I think they made up.'

It was a blushing couple who finally left the bedroom, and seeing Erin sitting there watching TV and realizing she had been there for quite some time, they were visibly embarrassed as they heard her say, 'I guess you two have made up, huh?'

It was Meagan who moved first, walking towards her daughter with left hand extended, third finger displayed prominently.

The daughter stared, and then screamed in delight as she jumped up, embracing her mother and prospective stepfather, exclaiming, 'Gee, I expected you guys to be at each other's throats, but . . . this . . . an engagement ring . . . that is an engagement ring, isn't it? My God!'

The mother looked at the daughter, smiling, and then at her intended, asking, as if in confirmation, 'This is an engagement ring, isn't it, Charlie?'

He smiled. 'I told you it was, didn't I?'

'I know,' she replied, coyly. 'I just wanted Erin to hear it, in case I ever needed a witness,' she joked.

And then the mother, previously blinded by love noticed her radiant daughter. 'Oh, Erin, honey, you look gorgeous. Which beauty parlour did you go to?'

'The same one you're going to, if Charlie has any money left! Charlie, did you tell Mama about the party, tonight?'

'What party?' from the surprised Meagan.

'Our engagement party,' from a proud and smiling Charlie.

Erin's hands went to her throat. 'Charlie . . . did you get my date yet? I want to see him.'

Charlie shook his head. 'No! I was busy getting engaged. I'll do that while you take your mother out to buy a new dress and get her hair done . . . the works.'

Meagan looked worried. 'Charlie, honey . . . do you have enough money to do all this?'

He poked her in the ribs. 'I do if I don't owe you the sixteen hundred . . . '

'What sixteen hundred?' asked a confused Erin.

Meagan gave him a knowing smile. 'Your debt is cancelled.'

Erin, still confused, grabbed her mother by the hand, saying, 'Come on, we don't have much time and, Charlie, you don't either! Go get me a date . . . with a hunk . . . don't forget.'

With the women gone, he sauntered down into the lounge to see if any unattached men were congregated there. He went to the bar, ordered a beer and looked around. There were a dozen or so men there, but all with women hanging on their arms, claiming territorial rights. He finished his beer and went out into the bright sunshine. It was a little after noon, and he realized that with all the trauma of the morning he had not eaten breakfast or lunch. He was hungry. He decided to walk a few blocks to a small deli he and Adelle had gone to a few times on their skiing trips.

Damn Adelle, he thought, as he made his way through the winding narrow streets. The summer sights were so different from the snow-clad streets of winter, he noticed, as he admired the profusion of flowerpots in all directions.

As he approached the deli which was on one of the few streets which allowed vehicular traffic, he noticed the Jaguar pulling up and he could not help but notice the fine specimen of manhood which emerged from it. He was blond and athletic looking, tall and trim. Worked out, no doubt. He had on designer jeans, designer shirt, and his left arm proudly displayed a solid gold Rolex.

The stranger, seeing him headed for the deli, asked, 'Pardon me, but have you eaten here, before? Is it any good? A friend told me about it,' he added, showing a set of even white teeth. He spoke with a cultured, assured delivery, as if he often spoke in public.

Charlie replied, 'I've eaten here several times on past skiing trips. We always enjoyed it.' And as an afterthought, he added, 'I'm alone if you care to join me . . . be happy to have the company.'

The man flashed a brilliant smile, extending his hand to Charlie. 'Thanks for the invitation. My name is Howard Compton . . . but my friends call me Bud.'

He seemed to be about thirty. He was no kid, Charlie thought. He's educated and sophisticated! And looking at the new maroon Jaguar, 'he ain't poor, either.'

Charlie, extending his hand, asked, 'How do you get Bud out of Howard?'

He smiled. 'My dad gave it to me. My mother named me after her father, and my Dad did not care much for his father-in-law.'

Charlie smiled in return. 'Can't think of a better reason.'

The two men ate while engaging in small talk, the usual when men get together.

It appeared that Bud Compton was an attorney, just five years out of Columbia Law School. He had been working in the family law firm in Denver since graduation, but he was becoming disenchanted with the type of practice his father's firm specialized in.

'And what is that?' asked Charlie.

'Mostly real estate transfers and limited partnerships.'

Charlie smiled. 'That's my racket too.'

Bud looked surprised. 'Did you say you were an attorney, too?'

Charlie shook his head. 'No! I meant I was in real estate.'

The attorney rubbed his chin. 'Forester . . . Forester . . . are you connected with the Forester Company in Corpus Christi?'

'The same! That's us.'

'Well, what do'ya know? Small world. I did a limited partnership with your people a couple of years ago,' and he smiled, 'when limited partnerships were still popular . . . '

Charlie nodded. 'Before the S & L debacle, you mean?'

'Yeah . . . did you guys get hurt much?'

'No, we didn't fool with junk bonds. We do not leverage our deals too heavily. My dad likes no more than fifty percent leveraged . . . '

'Whew!' he whistled, 'you guys must have a private bank.'

'We sort of have. My mother's family owns the bank.'

The attorney shook his head. 'Charlie, you've got it made.'

'Oh, you know the old saying, the grass is always greener . . . '

'Yeah, I know. That's why I'm on my way to Salt Lake City, now. I want to talk to some of my Columbia classmates who are starting a new firm. Hell, if I put in a little start-up capital, I can be a founding father, which means I'll be a partner from the start.'

'Not bad,' replied Charlie, 'But you didn't stop in Vail just to have lunch, did you?'

'No, I have an old buddy here from Denver. We grew up together. He's married, now, and lives here with his wife. They're doing quite well. I'm going to spend a few days with them. His wife is trying to fix me up with a date for tonight, but I hate blind dates . . . don't usually end up too well.'

Charlie swallowed hard at that, but this was too good an opportunity to pass up, and besides he was running out of time. He was not sure Erin could handle this erudite and sophisticated man, but, what the hell, it was only for a supper party for one night, so he cleared his throat, and began, 'You know, Bud, this is a hell of a coincidence that you should mention a blind date. Let me tell you my problem . . . '

The young attorney listened impassively as Charlie told him of his dilemma concerning Erin's lack of a date for the evening.

He finally, with an air of sympathy mixed with apprehension, asked, 'Charlie, you wouldn't put me on a dog, would you? I know we just met, and I like you, but that is the best way to end this friendship,' and he laughed.

'I promise you she is no dog! She is as sceptical of this thing as you are. Tell you what. The girls are at the beauty parlour now, and should be out in an hour or so. Supposing I could arrange it so you could see Erin, without her knowing who you are . . . what of that?'

He sighed. 'That would sure help. You know, if I had not heard of your company, and if it were not your engagement party, I wouldn't touch this with a ten-foot pole.'

Charlie smiled. 'I wouldn't either, I swear.'

'OK, I'll agree, at this time, only to take a look at her, nothing more. If I am not interested in what I see, I will walk on by your table, scratch my chin as I go by, and walk out of your life,' he laughed. 'Where shall we do this?'

'It would be easy if we did it in the lounge of my hotel. I would just have to invite the girls down for an afternoon drink. They wouldn't be suspicious of that.'

'Where are you staying?' asked the young attorney.

'At the Summit . . . how about you?'

'Well, I haven't checked into any place, yet. At this time of the year, rooms are not hard to get. Besides, my buddy works with the tourist bureau. I'll just check into the same hotel. If we cut a deal it will save a lot of travelling for me.'

Charlie rose to go, extending his hand. 'Shall we say three o'clock, in the Summit's lounge.

The attorney nodded. 'Three o'clock . . . in the lounge.'

Charlie caught his arm. 'Bud, if this goes off, I owe you one.'

He grunted.'You damn sure do, and I will not let you forget, either. See you at three.'

Charlie was excited as he returned to the suite. The girls were not back, yet, but as he looked at his watch, he remarked, 'Only two thirty-five. Hope they're not too late. This fish is too good to lose, and I don't have much time to do any more fishing either.'

No sooner had he completed these thoughts than he heard the animated conversation in the hall of the two excited women, one excited over having just gotten engaged and the other, younger one, in an advanced state of anticipation over the prospect of meeting a man. She had faith in Charlie. He would not let her down . . she felt.

They entered the suite to find him nervously pacing the floor, as he asked. 'Where have you been? I've been waiting for you! We have to go.'

Meagan ignored his impatience. A woman in love, especially one who was recently engaged, has a singleness of purpose.

She went up to him, embraced him, saying, 'Kiss me, man!' and then, 'What are you nervous about?'

He kissed her. Then, taking another look at her and then at a smiling Erin, replied, 'Damn, you two look great. Oh, this is going to work out fine. Thank God you're not in jeans . . . '

Meagan took his arm. 'Charlie, what are you talking about?'

'Yeah, Charlie,' added Erin, winking, 'are you making any progress?'

Meagan, really confused, 'What's going on?'

'Well,' retorted Charlie, 'You already know about the supper tonight, and, well . . . Erin wants me to get her a date . . . '

Meagan assumed a motherly mode, as she indignantly replied to him, 'I don't want you hustling a date for my daughter with some stranger we don't know anything about. It's dangerous in this day and time, with all the kooks on the loose . . . '

'Mama!' replied an indignant daughter, 'Let Charlie handle this! He knows what he is doing . . . huh, Charlie?'

'I'm not sure,' he laughed, 'But, I promise, Meagan, to check him out first.'

'How can you do that?' she demanded, as he ushered them through the door into the corridor.

'We have our ways in the business world. There are no secrets, anymore, in this country of ours. Computers know it all,' he teased.

'Oh, hell, Charlie . . . do you mean I'll have a computer date?' asked a perturbed Erin. 'I can go down to the lobby for an hour and do better than that.'

As they entered the elevator, Meagan gave him a worried look, saying,'I don't like this. Where are we going, Charlie?'

'I just want to go to the lounge for a drink to celebrate our engagement . . . that's all. I don't like hotel rooms.'

She cozied up to him, replying, 'That's not true all the time . . . '

'All right, Mama . . . not in the elevator before your minor child,' teased Erin. 'Cool it for a while. It's my turn to get emotional for a change. You need a rest. Huh, Charlie?'

'Don't drag me into a family fight between you two over whose libido needs resting and whose needs action,' he smiled.

Meagan snorted. 'I don't think there is any doubt about that.'

19

As they entered the lounge the place was just beginning to get crowded. The happy-hour crowd was beginning to get an early start in that resort town where happy hour is anytime two or more people get together. They were escorted to a table against the wall, away from the entrance door and in the semi-dark room, visibility was not good. Charlie squinted to see if Bud had come in.

Erin squinted to check the crowd for eligible males, commenting, 'Geez, every man in the damn place has a woman hanging all over him. I don't stand a chance of getting a date in this town, Charlie.'

'Thank God for small favours,' grunted the mother, almost under her breath, but her daughter heard her.

'Sure, that is fine for you to say . . . you've got yours!'

'And, you will get yours too, if you're patient,' she responded, philosphically . . .

'OK, you two, as the titular head of the family, I say let's quit arguing about that and have a drink . . . waiter!'

As the young off season ski instructor took their orders, Erin gave him a sideways glance, and upon his leaving she pinched Charlie's arm, saying. 'He'll do, Charlie. Grab him.'

Charlie watched the youth depart, shaking his head. 'No, he's just a kid, Erin. I'm going to find you a grown man.'

'Hell, beggars can't be choosey. I'll take the kid.'

Her mother gave her a dirty look, as she sipped her drink, shaking her head, saying, 'I don't know what I'm going to do with you Erin . . . '

Erin smiled and winked at Charlie. Charlie was returning the wink when he saw Bud Compton walk in the door. He stood there for a moment, looking the place over, with complete assurance. Several of the women, already in possession of a man, but always looking for greener pastures,nodded to each other in a feminine gesture, complete with raised eyebrows, pursed lips, and a nod of the head in Bud's direction.

He spied the table of Charlie's and made his way in that direction. As he neared it, a table or two away, the couple sitting at one of the tables rose to leave and he moved to capture it before someone else did, to the protests of the waiter, who complained, 'Sir, I can get you a clean table over on the other side, if you will follow me,' which brought an immediate response of, 'No, this will do just fine. Just wipe it off, if you will, and bring me vodka on the rocks.'

Charlie was seated so he was facing Bud Compton, with Erin on one side and Meagan on the other. Bud, upon seeing Charlie, nodded in recognition. He had just come in from the outside and his eyes were not accustomed to the dark room as yet. Erin, whose eyes were accustomed to the dark, continued to view the possibilities.

As her eyes scanned across the countenance of Bud Compton, sitting there alone, with no woman in sight, her heart skipped a beat. She looked at him without shame, for she was a woman enthralled. She saw him looking at her, and he smiled and nodded, as if he were of a mind to flirt.

Her mouth became dry as she nudged Charlie's foot under the table, and as he looked at her, she said, softly, 'Oh, my God, Charlie, do you see what is over there, and he just smiled at me. Oh, Charlie, I want him . . . he's the one I want! If you really love me, Charlie, you will get him for me.'

Meagan heard all this muttering. She had been looking in another direction, and now, seeing her daughter in the throes of desire, she asked, 'What's going on with you two?'

Erin placed her hand on her mother's arm. 'Mama,

don't let him see you, but look over to your right. There's a man sitting alone at the table. He's gorgeous. I want him for my date.'

As Meagan took a quick glance at Bud, she patted her daughter on the arm, 'Sure, honey, and people in hell want ice water. You don't think something like that is running around loose, do you? Be reasonable, honey. Don't let yourself in for a big disappointment.'

Charlie heard this exchange between the two women, and he was having fun just hearing it. It gave him a feeling of power, as though he could arrange people's lives, granting a maiden her wish.

He looked over at Bud, who was now sipping his vodka, and Bud gave him a quizzical look, as if to ask . . . which one?

Charlie understood the look, and as unobtrusively as humanly possible, he nodded to Erin. Bud smiled, nodding his head and waving his glass in agreement. Charlie smiled, too. The deal was cut.

The agreement was reached, but Charlie decided to have some fun with it, as he touched Erin's hand. 'Erin, honey, is that the man you want for tonight? Would that make you happy?'

Meagan, hearing what was going on, interrupted with, 'Charlie, I don't want my daughter hurt. Don't start something you can't finish . . . please. It will just make the poor child more miserable than she is.'

Erin pouted, 'But, Mama, maybe he's willing, After all, I'm no dog, Am I Charlie? I think I'm damn pretty! 'Specially today, after all the money Charlie spent on me.'

He patted her hand, again. 'Erin, honey, if that is the man you want for tonight, that is the man you will have. Excuse me, please,' and he rose to leave. Meagan grabbed his arm. 'Charlie, please don't do this. You'll make a fool of yourself, and us too. We have our pride. I'm not begging any man for anything!'

He patted her shoulder. 'Now, now, honey, I know what I'm doing,' and he walked off with Erin's whisper in his ears . . . 'Oh, Charleeeee!'

The two women watched in astonishment as they

saw Bud stand as Charlie approached his table, smile, and extend his hand. The women were flabbergasted as the two men engaged in conversation, looking now and then at the table of the two women, who knew they were being discussed, especially as Charlie pointed to one, then the other, with Bud nodding his head. It would be fair to observe that the two women were uneasy, with one on the verge of embarrassment and the other, the younger one, in the throes of ecstasy; and as she saw the two men head for their table, came very close to wetting her pants in sheer excitement, as she whispered to her mother, 'Mama, he is coming to our table . . . oh, God, how do I look, Mama? Do I look all right?' but, before the mother could reply, they were there.

The two women looked up, the older with disbelief – the younger, mesmerized, but trying to look dignified . . . and desirable.

Charlie brought Bud Compton forward, saying, 'Meagan and Erin Mahoney, I would like you to meet an acquaintance of mine, Bud Compton, who hails from Denver.'

Meagan offered her hand, which the poised and polished attorney took, raising it to his lips, kissing it gently, saying, 'I understand you are the mother. I took you for sisters.'

Meagan smiled, and was his for the asking. He had won her over, and having done that, turned his attention to the daughter who was squirming in her chair, and taking her hand in his, he raised it to his lips, kissing it gently, as he said, softly, 'And this is Erin, a flower of the Emerald Isle, if ever there was one.'

It was Charlie who broke the magic spell, telling the women, 'Bud has graciously consented to join us for a drink or two. By sheer coincidence, he is staying in this same hotel . . . would you believe that?'

And, having brought his drink with him, he took the empty chair next to Erin. Her heart was in her throat. She was not sure she could respond if he spoke to her, but she swallowed hard, determined to do her best.

She was glad her mother asked, 'So, Mr Compton,

you're from Denver. We live not too far from Denver . . . in Mountain View.'

Charlie was amused at her measured speech pattern. She was determined that she put her best foot forward . . . for her daughter's sake. He made some reply to Meagan, and then he turned to Erin. She, for the first time, saw his light blue eyes looking at her, and no one but her. She quietly asked her God for strength, for she felt her legs getting weak.

He asked, 'And what do you do, Erin, besides adding to the beauty of the environment?'

Damn, thought Charlie . . . he is good! Maybe, too good for Erin's sake, and he felt sorry for her. What would she answer to the inevitable question, 'What do you do?'

Erin looked him in the eye, smiling. 'I'm a waitress in a cafe this summer.'

Meagan was heard to suck wind. Charlie smiled at her complete honesty, as he waited for Bud's reply.

The attorney nodded. 'A summer job as a waitress. I think that is a good idea for any young woman. My sister and a friend of hers did it one summer while on vacation from school. It's good training, I think.'

Erin smiled. Meagan smiled. Charlie smiled. Bud smiled, as he noticed Erin's drink empty. 'Please, may I get you another one? What are you drinking, Erin? Meagan? Charlie? My round.'

And so the ice was broken. Erin gradually settled down. As time went on she began to ask questions . . . make comments . . . giving coy answers to his questions, and as time was drawing to a close, with Charlie saying, 'Folks, it's time we got ready for supper,' which he felt was cue enough for Bud to make his move if he intended to, and he did.

Turning to Erin, he said, 'It is my understanding that you have no escort for this evening, as hard as it is for me to believe that is possible but, if you will be so kind as to allow me, I will be most happy to be your escort for this engagement supper.'

His words held her heart as in a vice. He had waited until the last minute to ask. She had felt sure he was not interested in her, and now . . .

She replied, softly, giving him a grateful and gracious smile. 'I'd like that, if you're sure you want to.'

He smiled, taking her hand in his, once again lifting it to his lips. 'I can assure you it will be my pleasure,' and turning to Charlie, 'Where shall I meet you, and at what time?'

'We're in suite 1409. Why don't you meet us there. Six thirtyish, shall we say. We'll have drinks and hors d'eouvres before we leave for the supper place.'

There, thought Charlie, that will show him that Erin comes from a proper home, even if it is a hotel suite . . . the pompous bastard!

'Fine, see you then! Meeting you folks was my pleasure, and I am looking forward to a great evening with two lovely ladies,' and, bowing, he walked off.

Erin was heard to groan. 'Oh, my God, I'm in love.'

The mother grunted. 'Oh, come on, Erin, you were in love last night with what's his name . . Brax. Tomorrow, it will be the next one . . . '

'No, Mama, I am really in love this time.'

'Uh huh, well come on. Let's go.'

She shook her head, replying, 'I can't walk. I'm too weak in the knees. Help me up, Charlie.'

Charlie laughed as he helped the young woman to her feet, saying, 'Come on, lover, you have a busy night before you so you'd better get some rest before dressing.'

She kissed him on the cheek as she rose, replying, 'I will be indebted to you until my dying day . . but, how did you do it? Why is something like him running around loose. Oh, God, I hope nothing is wrong with him, Charlie. You know what I mean.'

He smiled. 'Yes, I know what you mean. I'm sure there isn't. In fact, Erin, I'm not sure you can handle him. He is thirty years old, and you're only twenty. He has ten years experience on you. Ten years of very sophisticated experience.'

She giggled. 'At least I won't have to teach him anything, will I?'

The mother listening to this exchange, merely rolled her eyes, shook her head, and groaned, 'Oh, God!'

As they entered the hotel suite Meagan looked around the room then at Charlie, exclaiming, 'Oh, Charlie, why did you invite Bud up here tonight? This place is a mess. I will have to clean the bathrooms in case he has to go, and I have to make the beds . . . oh, Erin, come on, honey . . . you have to help me! We don't have much time, and, Charlie, you had better run to the supermarket for some food. Keep it simple. Get some cold cuts and some fancy bread . . . and, a few bottles of beer . . . '

Erin replied, 'I'll help you, Mama . . . let's go!'

Charlie could not help laughing as he took Meagan by the hand, and then Erin by the other, pulling them towards the telephone, as he said, 'You two, listen and watch! Consider this a form of continuing education for you both, now that we are all family . . . listen!' as he picked up the phone, looking at the various numbers for hotel services. 'Hello . . . yes, housekeeping, this is Mr Forester in Suite 1409. We are expecting guests this evening and we would like the suite freshened up before six o'clock. Yes, that will be fine. You can work while we are getting dressed. We'll use one bath at the time if we need to . . . fine . . . thank you.'

The two women smiled at each other and then at him as he dialled another number. 'Give me the hotel caterer, please . . . thank you . . . Yes, we are expecting guests this evening and we would like some light refreshments. Yes . . . all cold . . . nothing heated. Oh, a couple of bottles of Chablis will do . . . yes, chilled slightly, and for food, we'd like some medium-boiled shrimp . . . fixed on an attractive platter, with some dip. I'm sure you know what I mean, and, perhaps some caviar . . . preferably Beluga, with assorted crackers, etc. etc. That would be fine. No, thank you, we will not require any servers. Just arrange it all on the coffee table. Thank you. Yes, suite 1409.'

Meagan smiled at Erin. 'See, honey, how easy that was.'

Erin took his hand. 'Oh, Charlie, you're doing all this for me so I can impress Bud, aren't you! You're so sweet.'

He pulled her to him, replying. 'We're going to show that pompous attorney that the two Mahoney women are not to be trifled with, and now I suggest we start getting ready so we can get out of the bathrooms so housekeeping can clean them,' and he added, grinning, 'in case Mr Wonderful has to pee.'

The two women giggled and they all hugged. They were happy.

The two women, bathed, coiffed, dressed in new outfits, and the older one sporting a new diamond, stood admiring each other in the living room as Charlie finally laid claim to one of the bathrooms. Meagan stood next to her daughter as they both looked in the full length mirror.

She took her hand smiling, saying, 'Damn, but we look good, honey. You'd never know you were looking at two waitresses from the greasy spoon, would you,' she giggled.

Erin smiled, wistfully, 'I wish we were something else, Mama, but that is all we are. All this is just a dream, thanks to Charlie. But, when it is all over, we will be back to waitressing at the greasy spoon won't we?'

She looked at her daughter with compassion. 'I'm trying to get you out, honey, and I want out, too, but it all depends on what happens between me and Charlie. I can't do it without him.'

Erin nodded, squeezing her mother's hand. 'I know. Oh, Mama, I nearly died when Bud asked me what I did. I figured I'd tell the truth and let the chips fall where they might, but . . . he took it in the wrong way. He thinks I'm a college girl on a summer lark.' She sighed. 'What'll I do when he finds out the truth?' You think a man like him will want anything to do with a waitress in a cafe in a small town?'

'I don't know, honey. This is only a date for one evening. I don't think it will matter tonight . . . '

'But, oh Mama, I want more than one night with him,' she replied, plaintively.

The mother faced her daughter, taking both her hands, looking in her eyes. 'Erin, honey, take this thing one minute at a time. Don't go overboard over this man. You'll just be heading for a heartbreak. You're Cinderella, honey . . . not a princess!'

She squared her shoulders, poked her chin out, returning her mother's look. 'No, Mama, tonight, I'm a princess. Tomorrow, I'll scrub the floors and wash the clothes but, tonight, I'm going to be every inch a princess!'

The mother embraced her daughter. 'You're my princess every day, honey.'

'And, you're my queen, Mama.' And as Charlie entered the room, fully dressed, he caught the last of the conversation, smilingly added. 'And here is the king!'

The two women curtsied to him in loyalty, and they all embraced, with the women protesting. 'Don't wrinkle my dress . . . don't mess my hair!'

At the appointed time there was a knock at the door. Erin looked at Charlie, whispering, 'You let him in. I'll be in the bedroom making like I'm not ready.' Charlie smiled, motioned Meagan to a seat in a chair, and slowly moved to the door, opening it to a well dressed and smiling Howard Compton, attorney at law.

The attorney entered the suite, looked around, admiringly, saying, 'Nice . . . very nice,' and seeing Meagan smiling at him, went to her, again kissing her hand, saying, 'Meagan, you look even lovelier than you did this afternoon, and I really thought that was not possible.'

Meagan smiled, royally, as she countered, 'Are you sure you're not from the Emerald Isle, yourself, with all that blarney in you?'

He laughed, 'Well, I did spend a summer there, once, and I guess some of it rubbed off. Do you mind?'

'Oh, not in the least! I love it,' she giggled.

And then all heads turned towards the bedroom as Erin entered the room. Meagan watched Bud for his reaction. He was impressed and he showed it. His mouth opened a little and his eyes widened, and he smiled as he moved forward to greet her.

She moved like a princess. Her long blonde hair had been put up by her mother, and she wore a string of pearls around her long and slender neck. It was costume jewellry, of course, but on her it could be considered real for, like most beautiful women, anything looks good on them. Her dress, of the cocktail party variety, was cut above the knees, showing a pair of lovely, long and shapely legs. The dress was low-cut, revealing an ample breast on a woman so thin, lacking in what is vulgarly referred to as 'body fat'.

Meagan noticed the look in Bud's eyes, and she was undecided whether it was admiration or lust.

Bud, with practiced polish, moved forward to take her hand, which she extended, once again, with royal demeanour and he said, 'You look very lovely, Erin. I will be proud to be seen with you this evening,' and as an afterthought, 'or, any evening, for that matter.'

She rewarded him with a gracious smile. 'How sweet of you to say that.'

'Well,' volunteered the host, 'Now, that we have acknowledged the beauty of our women, can I interest you in a snack. Don't eat too heavily, folks, we have a big night ahead of us.'

The eating place which Charlie had selected was the closest thing to a supper club to be found in the swinging resort frequented mostly by the young crowd. It had the tables arranged around a small dance floor, and the band played mostly contemporary music but to placate the geriatric crowd, the only ones who could really afford the prices at Vail, they played, every now and then, a slow piece. It was to these slow pieces that Charlie and Meagan danced.

Bud and Erin, being younger and 'hip', danced in the disjointed fashion . . . except the slow ones. They, too, succumbed to the socially accepted practice of holding the other so close that to do so in like fashion any place other than the dance floor would be considered obscene and exposed to official rebuke.

Meagan and Charlie were sitting such a slow one out when Meagan, observing her daughter and her date languidly moving in unison to the beat of the music, grabbed her betrothed by the arm. 'Charlie, look at Erin and Bud! Look at how he is holding her, and look, how she is holding him. Why, they couldn't be any closer if they were . . . you know what I mean.'

He laughed. 'I know exactly what you mean. but you must remember, my dear, that is perfectly acceptable on a dance floor. It is one of society's foibles. It is a means by which couples can enjoy the warmth and tenderness of each other without . . . you know what I mean, and it is clean, too. No one has ever caught anything on a dance floor to be the best of my knowledge . . . '

She hit him on the arm. 'You're teasing me!'

He smiled, sympathetically, at her. 'I know how you feel, honey. I guess all mothers feel that way, but she is twenty years old. Do you expect her to die a virgin? You didn't wait until you were twenty, did you?'

'You know I didn't, but I was too young, and she is too.'

She is not too young! She is a grown woman! She and I had a long talk about that this morning . . . '

'You did? When? Where was I?'

'You were up in the room figuring out how much money I owed you for previous services rendered.'

She looked embarrassed. 'I'm sorry about that! But, what did you and Erin talk about? I want to know! I'm her mother.'

He became serious. 'She told me she had never known love in her entire life.'

'Oh, that is not true! I love my daughter very much . . . you know that!'

He nodded. 'Yes, I'm sure, but that is not what she means, Meagan. She means man–woman love.' He went on, 'Do you realize that she has never lain with a man, never been caressed, never listened to soft and tender words from the lips of a man, especially a man she cares for . . . and wants. She has lived the life of a celibate. Oh, she admitted that she and some of the girls fooled around in prison . . . to keep from going crazy, as she put it, but . . . real love . . . she has had none, and now if she has the chance to find some, do you deny her that right? Every living creature needs love of some kind . . . '

'But, illicit love?'

He smiled at her. 'And what would you call ours? It has not been sanctioned by the laws of man or God . . . only the natural laws of desire.'

She nodded, saying nothing at first, then, softly, 'I guess you're right, honey . . . her time has come, but . . . '

He smiled. 'No buts.'

She smiled back, shaking her head. 'No buts.'

As the evening came to a close and Erin and Bud were having their last dance, Meagan and Charlie gave each other a knowing look which meant.'It's time to go,' but the couple were still on the floor . . . dancing . . . whispering . . . holding.

Meagan said to her betrothed. 'I guess you'll have to go and break them up. She has to go when we do,' and after a stern look from her betrothed, she added, 'It's only the first date, Charlie. Never on the first date! It's cheap!'

He shrugged, and with Meagan in tow he went out on the dance floor, taking Erin by the arm, saying, 'Come on you two, it's time to call it a night.'

Surprisingly enough, they broke willingly, and the four proceeded to the exit and their cars. Bud had insisted on taking the Jag; whether he sensed opportunity or wanted to impress Erin we can only guess, but she was impressed as she sank into its lovely leather seats which still had that new smell.

However, they all showed up at the hotel together. Charlie was surprised, but he made no comment to the mother, who had expected it as right and proper. They all joked and laughed all the way up to the suite, and as Erin leaned against the wall at the doorway, Meagan started to engage Bud in conversation, until Charlie took her arm, saying. 'Goodnight, Bud, and I guess this is goodbye, too. I appreciate your staying over in Vail for this evening . . . '

Bud interrupted him with . . . 'Erin has talked me into staying over for a couple of days, so I guess I'll be seeing you tomorrow.'

Erin gave Charlie a knowing look . . . a pleading look, which he interpreted correctly, saying, 'Well, in that case, it's only goodnight. Come on, Meagan, dear, let's go in,' to Erin's subtle and thankful grin, as she added, 'Goodnight, Mama.'

They had hardly been in the room a few minutes when Erin came in looking like the proverbial Cheshire Cat. She said nothing as she lowered herself onto the couch, with her head on the backrest, smiling into space, groaning, 'Oh, I'm in love . . . I'm in love . . . I'm in love . . . '

Meagan taunted her. 'I thought sure Mr Charming would charm you right into his bed, tonight.'

She came alive. 'Oh, he asked me, but I told him no!' she pouted, adding, 'I said . . . what kind of a girl do you think I am? He said he was sorry. Then, he said most girls today are willing on the first date and I said, well, I am not one of those girls, and, besides, I said, you will get into that Jaguar tomorrow and I will never see you again, so do you really think I would go to bed with you and never see you again. Only animals do that! I want more out of life, and then he changed his attitude, and he said . . . look, I want to see you again. If I stay in Vail a few more days, will you go out with me, and I said . . . sure . . . and he said, well, how about tomorrow? . . . Will you spend the day with me? and I said . . . doing what? and he said anything you want, and I said I want to go to the top of the ski lift in a gondola and have lunch on top of the mountain, and he said if that is what your little heart desires, well, that's the way it's gonna be, so that is how it is. I knew you'd want a report, so, goodnight Mama . . . goodnight Charlie,' and she went smiling into her bedroom.

Meagan and Charlie stared at each other with Charlie speaking, 'I think our little girl can handle herself Meagan, honey,' with the mother smiling, adding, 'I think so, too. Now, it's time for me to take care of my man, now that my daughter is in tow, and she grabbed her betrothed by the hand, but he pulled back, protesting, 'I'm kind of worn out, honey, can't we just cuddle tonight?'

She smiled. 'Oh, I'm glad to hear you say that. It's been a hard day . . . Ah'm plumb wore out.'

As they lay in bed, cuddling, his thoughts went out to Amanda, for the cuddling reminded him of her. She always needed cuddling. Poor creature. How is she? Had she recovered from her trauma? He wondered. And then he turned his attention to the creature at hand as he whispered to her, 'I forgot to do something before we go to sleep . . . '

'Oh, Charleeee, you said you were too tired . . . '

'No! Not that! I am too tired . . . '

'What then? I want to go to sleep . . . '

'I forgot to tell you I love you.'

'Oh, Charleee, I love you, too.'

20

Meagan stirred in her bed, rubbing her sleepy eyes and seeing that her betrothed was still sound asleep, she eased herself out of bed, stood, stretched, yawned and scratched as she made her way to the bathroom to empty her bladder. She could hear noise coming from the other bedroom and, surprised that her daughter was up so soon after such a big night, she quietly went over to the door. She could hear her humming a cheerful tune.

She knocked lightly, and hearing, 'Come in, Mama,' she pushed the bedroom door open. Upon seeing her daughter completely dressed in white shorts, light blue blouse with the top button left undone, her hair done in a ponytail, secured with a light blue ribbon, the mother went to her as she stood at the bedroom mirror applying makeup, kissing the back of her neck. 'Good morning, honey.'

The girl half turned, smiled, 'Morn'in Mama.'

'My, my, but you're up early.'

She responded, 'Uh huh. Remember I told you Bud and I were going to the top of the mountain today.'

'Uh huh, I remember. I see you have your working clothes on. Trying to get that man real excited, huh?'

'Oh, Mama! I think this outfit is real cute. Charlie picked it out for me yesterday. You know he has real good taste in clothes . . . for a man.'

She laughed. 'He ought to. He's had enough practice.'

'Don't you like it?' she asked in all innocence.

'Oh, I love it. It's a bit revealing, though.'

The daughter laughed. 'You mean the shorts are too short, or the blouse is too low?'

'Both! Honey, don't give him the impression that you are too easy . . . not if you're really interested in this man . . . '

The daughter turned around, looking her mother in the eye, replying, 'Mama, I'm not stupid. Do you really believe that a man like Bud is going to get serious with me in a day or two. No, Mama, I know he's just playing with me, but, then, I'm playing with him, too.'

She turned back to the mirror. 'Sure, I'd like to have him for keeps, but, I know better . . . '

The mother hesitated 'Are you going to sleep with him?'

'Uh huh, if I get half a chance, and I'm pretty sure I'll have more than half a chance,' she giggled.

'You're sure you're ready for this, huh?'

She looked at her mother in the mirror, as she continued her preparations. 'When you met Charlie, were you ready?'

'I fell in love with Charlie! If I hadn't loved him he'd still be panting on the steps of our little apartment in Mountain View, like a young buck in rut.'

'That's the difference between you and me, Mama, I can do it without love . . . real love. Infatuation is enough,' she smiled. 'Besides, I owe myself this. I need it. If it wasn't Bud, it would have been someone else; you know that,' and with a final look in the mirror, she turned around, kissed her mother on the cheek, saying,'I got to go. Bud will be waiting for me in the coffee shop . . . '

Meagan grabbed her arm. 'Honey . . . are you going to do it, today?'

The daughter laughed. 'Mama! On a mountain top? I'm anxious, but not that anxious. No. I want to keep him panting a little longer. Men love the chase more than the act. I promise when you see me later today, I will still be virginal,' and she giggled, 'unless he just won't be denied.'

And she patted her cheek and left, pausing at the door to blow a kiss.

Meagan watched her disappear . . . smiled, and went in to see her lover, who was murmuring, 'Meagan, honey . . . bring me some coffee, please . . . '

As they sat drinking their coffee, Charlie watched Meagan play with her Danish pastry, barely nibbling as she brought it to her mouth.

He smiled. 'All right, what's on your mind? I know you well enough to know that you have a problem. Tell me,' and he leaned over to kiss her lightly, 'and I will make it go away.'

She returned his smile. 'You promise?'

'I promise. Tell me.'

'It's Erin.'

'Oh hell, Meagan, are you still determined to see that no man ever violates her sanctity . . . '

'No! I'm resigned to that. She's already told me she intends to sleep with Bud.'

'Well, hallelujah! And, you've resigned yourself to it, so what's the problem?'

She sighed. 'I guess it's my fault but, well, we've never had a mother–daughter talk. I don't know how much she knows about . . . you know . . how to protect herself . . . '

He laughed. 'So, that's it! You're afraid your little girl is going to get pregnant on her first outing.'

She shrugged. 'I did!'

He sat up straight in his chair. He could see what was bothering her and he had to agree with her. That would be a disaster, he thought. He knew that to a man like Bud, this was a game. Erin would be just another notch on his belt, of which he probably had many.

He placed his hand on Meagan's, as he replied, 'I see what you mean. I think you need to talk to your daughter if it is not too late. I'm sure you realize it could happen today . . . '

Her eyes widened. 'No! She promised me it wouldn't.'

He could not help laughing. 'She promised you it would't! How can she be so sure?'

Meagan laughed, too, replying. 'She said she never does it on top of a mountain in broad daylight. No, I think it will be tonight.'

'Well then Mama, you have time to educate her before the drama takes place.'

She now placed her hand on his, shaking her head. 'I can't do it, Charlie! That's why it was never done. I can't do it. You do it for me, huh?'

He exclaimed, louder than he intended, 'You want me to tell your twenty-year-old daughter about the birds and bees?'

'Uh huh! Please, Charlie! You can explain those things better than I can. You could use medical terms. I would have to use dirty words, and you know I can't abide dirty words.'

He looked to see if she was laughing. She wasn't. She took hold of both of his hands, pleading, 'Please, Charlie.'

He had to shake his head as he replied to her pleadings, 'Meagan, that is the strangest request I've ever had in my entire life.'

'Please do it . . . for me . . . and Erin.'

He swallowed. 'OK, honey, I'll do it, if she lets me. She may not want me to.'

'She'll let you. She loves you, Charlie. . . . like the father she's never had.'

He sighed, looking at this beautifully simple woman he loved. He took her hands in his, and rising, issued forth this profound statement. 'After that shock, I need some eggs and bacon. Let's go and eat.'

She pulled him back, and smiling seductively, 'Can't it wait a few minutes more?'

He smiled. 'Uh huh!'

As the afternoon shadows grew long and the happy hour began in the hotel, the betrothed couple returned from a day of sightseeing, walking, shopping. It was necessary for Charlie Forester to utilize the Cirrus mode of the ATM at The Bank of Vail, for his funds were running low.

Meagan watched, fascinated, as he inserted his card punched in the PIN numbers and lo and behold, the machine spat out dollars . . . lots of dollars. She felt she had a right to ask; after all, they were engaged . . . the prelude to marriage.

She cozied up to him, asking, 'How does that work, honey? Will that thing give you all the money you want? How do you pay it back? I know you have to pay it back, someday. I want a machine like that, Charlie. Will you give me one for Christmas?' she joked.

So he explained to her the intricacies of credit card living, asking, 'Haven't you ever had a credit card?'

'No! I don't believe in them. You don't get nuth'in in this world for nuth'in,' said she, lapsing into her native dialect as she pounded the point home. 'It makes people spend money they don't have, and I don't believe in doing that. You know,Charlie, I'm stingy. I've always had to watch my money . . . all my life. I know I sound like a hypocrite 'cause I've helped you spend all this money on me . . . and my daughter, but I know you . . . you had to do it, and I enjoyed it, but, when we get married,' and she looked at him . . . 'if we get married, you're gonna have to change your ways, Charlie. I'm gonna crack down on your spending. We have to save for our old age,' and she added, meekly, 'That is, if you marry me.'

He kissed her on the cheek, smiling, asking, 'Do you still doubt that I will marry you?'

'Well, let's put it this way. I'll feel more sure of it when I hear the preacher say the magic words,' and a tint of blush appeared on her cheeks. He smiled at her, thinking, 'Damn, but I love that woman.'

Meagan was nervous. It was six o'clock, and Erin had not returned home as yet. She pondered . . . maybe she did decide to do it on top of the mountain, after all, but before her mind could conjure up the image of it, she heard the key in the door. Erin, smiling, entered followed by Bud, also smiling. Meagan gave her daughter a quick once over to detect any signs of unusual flushness in her cheeks. Her blonde face showed evidence of sun and wind, but that had a different tone from a libidinous blush. Her blouse was not wrinkled.

She seemed normal, and Meagan breathed a sigh of relief as Erin, effervescent as ever, exclaimed, 'Oh, we had a good time, didn't we Bud.'

He nodded as he flopped on the couch, protesting, 'This woman wore me out,' and looking at Charlie, added, 'I don't know how you take both of them,

Charlie. It must be a fight just keeping up with them.'

Charlie nodded. 'It sure is!' Meagan gave him a knowing look, and she blushed lightly as she turned away.

Bud rose. 'Well, if we are going to make a night of it, Erin, I guess I'll go and bathe. What time shall I call for you?'

At the sound of the words, 'Make a night of it', Meagan's heart skipped a beat, but she girded herself as Erin replied 'Give me a couple of hours to repair the damage. I'll be ready at eight . . . no! Make it seven thirty . . . time is too valuable to waste, isn't it.'

He smiled as he made his way to the door, replying, 'Sure is. See you at seven-thirty.'

Meagan immediately turned to her daughter, asking, 'What did you do today, sweetie?'

Erin rose, smiling, 'What you meant to say, Mama, was, 'did you do it today, sweetie?' No, Mama, not yet,' and she went into her bedroom, but not before turning to smile at her mother.

No sooner had the daughter disappeared than the mother grabbed Charlie by the arm, imploring, 'Remember, you promised me you would talk to her before she went out tonight . . . you promised!'

'OK . . . OK, I promised and I'll do it, but, I have to think about what I will say, so . . . I need to think . . . '

She rose to leave, replying, 'And don't leave anything out, Charlie. Tell her all about it!'

He shrugged. 'All about it?'

As she disappeared in the bedroom, 'Yes! All of it.'

He sat and stared out the window. He got up and stared out the window. He returned to his chair. He took one hand in the other, and he stared out the window. He could hear the shower running in Erin's bath, so he breathed easier. He would wait until she got out of the shower, then he would do it. But in the meantime, he pondered his words, and he rehearsed the terms, especially the medical ones.

He waited a respectable length of time, allowing her to finish her shower and put some clothes on. He looked at his watch. He was running out of time.

He saw Meagan come to the door looking out and, seeing him there, she motioned to Erin's door, whispering, 'Go on!'

He shrugged, got up and walked to Erin's door, knocking softly. He heard her say, 'Come in, Mama.'

He put his head to the door. 'It's Charlie, Erin, I have to talk to you.'

'Can't it wait, Charlie, I'm dressing . . . '

'No! It can't wait.'

'Oh, OK, let me put a robe on . . . ' then, 'OK, come in.'

He entered and closed the door. As soon as the door closed, Meagan came tip-toeing out of her room, placed her head against Erin's door, straining to hear.

She heard parts of Charlie's preamble, and then she heard her daughter exclaim, 'What? I can't believe this!' and then raucous laughter from Erin, and then from Charlie.

She strained further, even arresting her own breathing to minimize audio interference, and then, Erin saying, 'I would like to know . . . ' but then she lost the rest of it, and Charlie had lowered his voice for she could not hear the reply, either.

She heard Erin exclaim, 'Really?. . . . geeze!. . . . I didn't know that!' and Charlie, responded, 'Sometimes, more!' to which Erin responded, 'Geez!'

We shall intrude only on the last part of the exchange as Erin said to Charlie, 'I appreciate the information, Charlie, but you see we had lectures in prison from gynaecologists and sociologists, and God knows who else. I could lecture on the subject if I had a mind to, but there is one thing those women teachers could not tell us girls. It can only come from a man.'

'What is that?'

'A girl has a difficult time judging a man's real intentions, Charlie. You men lie so much. You'd tell us anything to get us in bed . . . true?' she pleaded.

He nodded. 'True as gospel. We leave no stone unturned to accomplish that goal . . . why?'

She shrugged.'Bud has told me he could really fall for me if he let himself. Is he lying to me'

'Probably! He hasn't gotten you in to bed, yet. The chase is still on. That's a standard line. I've used it too.'

'How can I know if he is sincere? I don't want to lose him if I can hold on to him.'

'You can't know for sure until the dance is over.'

'What should I do, Charlie? I want him as bad as he wants me. We both know it.'

'Based on my vast experience in this field,' and he smiled at that, 'a woman has two choices. She can deny him his prize to gauge his real intent, or she can submit, hoping that he will stick around for dessert.'

'And if I deny him his prize, and he cranks up that Jaguar and disappears down Interstate 70 on his way to Salt Lake City, what then?'

'Then, you have solved half of the puzzle. You know what he wanted . . . nothing more.'

'And if I submit, and he stays around for a few more days, and then leaves . . . what have I gained?'

He smiled at her. 'I'd say you will have had a lot of fun, if he is any good at all.'

She smiled, nodding in agreement. 'OK, Charlie, you've helped me. I guess it's up to me, huh?'

'Those are the rules of the game. The woman dictates the time and the place and the frequency.'

She kissed him on the cheek. 'Thanks for trying, anyway.' She smiled 'Now, get out of here and let me dress, and for God's sake, get that woman away from my door before she gets calouses on her ear.'

He tip-toed to the door and opened it swiftly.

Meagan fell into the room, exclaiming, 'I lost an earring and I was looking for it. I thought it rolled over here . . . '

Charlie turned to Erin. She winked at him. He returned the wink, and taking his betrothed by the hand, closed the door and led her to their bedroom.

She could hardly wait to inquire, taking his hand, demanding, 'How did it go? Did you tell her everything?'

He calmed her down with. 'She told me things I didn't know, that's for sure . . . '

'Oh, Charlie, don't joke with me. Does she know

enough to protect herself? What was she asking you about men? I couldn't hear it through that thick door.'

He was playing with her. 'Well, let's see. She did have some questions about men . . . you know . . . not having had any actual experience with any . . . '

'What?'

'She seemed to be curious about quantity and quality and frequency more than anything else . . . '

'I don't understand . . . '

'Neither did I . . . '

'Oh, Charleee . . . tell me!'

'No, it is better if I show you.'

'Oh, Charleee . . . no! I'm not in the mood! I'm too worried about Erin tonight. Is she coming back to the room, or,' and the words pained her visibly, 'is she going to stay out all night?'

'I don't know, Meagan! The poor girl doesn't have a blueprint of the evening. You play these things by ear. As a woman you should know that.'

'Not me, Charlie! When I made up my mind about you, my plans were all made.'

'Are you telling me I had nothing to say about this?'

She gave him a demure look. 'Nothing much once I had my hooks in you.'

'But, suppose I hadn't come back to you after the cruise . . . then what, smart ass?'

She smiled, confidentially. 'But, you came back, didn't you?' as she kissed his ear.

He pondered her remark, saying,'I damn sure did.'

'Well?'

'I see your point. Since you're not in the mood, are we going to go out to eat, or shall we stay in and order?'

'I can't eat. I don't think I'll be able to sleep a wink tonight . . . worrying about my daughter.'

He groaned in despair. 'I can't believe this!' and as he pondered his predicament, he said, 'You know, Meagan, if you and I do have a baby, I hope it is not a girl. I want a boy.'

'Why do you say that, honey? I don't care what it is, as long as it looks like you. Why did you say that?'

'Well, assuming we have a baby in a year or so, and

she is a girl, when she is twenty I will be more than fifty-six years old, and I will be too damn old to have you keeping me up all night, worrying, every time she is out with a man. That's why!'

'You won't worry if he is a boy?'

'No, I'll let some other parent do the worrying, especially the mother of the girl he is out with . . .'

She sat up in bed, highly perturbed. 'That's a horrible attitude. Don't you hold your son responsible for what he is doing?'

'Sure!'

'Well?' she protested.

'Well, what?'

'Well . . . I'm not sure I want to have children with you, Charlie! You have a bad attitude!'

She saw him smiling at her. She snuggled against him, saying, softly, 'You were baiting me, huh?'

He returned the snuggle. 'Uh huh, I was baiting you.'

'That's better! I thought I knew you better than that!'

'Now, are you willing to have a baby with me?'

'Uh huh! Soon as we are married we can start on it.'

'Can we practice tonight?'

'No! I told you I was too upset over Erin, Charlie.'

'Hell, suppose Bud decides to stay in town for a week or so? Will you stay upset for a week?'

She didn't answer for a while, then, 'Oh, I don't know about that. A week is a long time.'

There was a soft knock on their bedroom door. 'Mama, I'm leaving now. Bye . . . bye, Charlie . . . '

The mother, wrapping her robe around her, rushed to the door, and seeing her beautiful daughter standing there, realized she would leave a girl but return a woman.

She lamented, 'Oh, honey . . . '

The young woman was sympathetic. 'What Mama?'

'Nothing . . . have a good time.'

She could not suppress a giggle. 'I intend to.'

They kissed. The mother watched as her daughter went to the door, and seeing Bud standing there, she thought she detected a leering expression in his face as he waved to her, but she decided it was her imagination, and she quietly closed the door and returned to her betrothed.

She said nothing, as she sat on the bed, looking off into space.

Charlie asked, 'Are you alright, honey?'

'She's gone, Charlie,' she lamented.

He pulled her to him. 'I know . . . I know. She is going out to do what women have done for hundreds of years, with or without the knowledge of their mothers. It's unfortunate you had to be in on the planning. It's better if mothers know nothing about it, don't you think?'

She nodded. 'Much better.'

He stood up. 'It's almost eight o'clock. If we're going to eat, we should get ready and go.'

She lay back on the bed, saying, 'You go, honey. I'm not hungry tonight. I want to be alone for a while.'

After he had gone, she lay in her bed staring at the ceiling trying to create a mental picture of what she thought was going on between Erin and Bud at that particular moment and she grimaced from time to time. She turned over in an attempt to go to sleep, hoping sleep would block out the images, but sleep eluded her and as her betrothed returned, seeing her staring at the ceiling, asked, 'Are you sure you're alright?'

She turned away from him. 'Yes, I'm alright. Don't worry about me. Did you eat?'

'Uh huh, but I didn't enjoy it.'

She murmured, not really interested, 'Food bad, or the service?'

'Neither. I don't like to eat alone . . . I missed you,' as he sat on the bed next to her, taking her in his arms. She responded with, 'I told you I was not in the mood . . . '

He smiled. 'I know. I just wanted to hold you,' and as he got up, smiled again, added, 'I bet about now, you hate all men, don't you?'

She turned to him, smiling, holding her arms out. 'Yes, you're all no good bastards.'

She had dozed off, sleeping fitfully, awakening from time to time, thinking she heard the door open, and then she did. She was both relieved and surprised. She didn't expect to see her daughter again that night. She shoved the covers aside, and giving her man a quick glance to assure herself that he was asleep, she left the bed. She looked at the clock which hotels install bolted to the night table . . . 2:35. She tip-toed to the door of the bedroom, cracking it lightly.

She saw Erin in the doorway to the suite, embracing Bud, and before she could withdraw and close the door she heard Bud whisper, 'I'll call you in the morning.'

Erin replied as she left him, holding his hand till that last moment, 'Not too early.'

Meagan quietly closed her door and returned to bed. She managed to fall asleep at last.

Charlie woke early, and having told Meagan he wanted to get a haircut, he went down to the coffee shop alone for a quick breakfast. She lay in bed longer than her early rising habits had usually allowed, and as she heard Erin in the bathroom, she let herself out of bed, and putting on a bathrobe, went out of her room. She didn't know how she would react when she saw Erin . . . what to say . . . what to ask . . . what not to ask.

Erin solved the problem by cheerily saying, 'Morning, Mama! Did you sleep well?'

'Morning honey, tolerable . . . not good, but tolerable.' She went to her daughter, looking her over. She walked around her slowly, with Erin turning her head as her mother circled her.

Erin laughed. 'Looking for combat scars, Mama?'

'Er . . . no, honey . . . don't be silly. I'm just half asleep, and I'm not too steady, yet,' she lied. She was looking for combat scars.

Erin took her hands, looking in her eyes with amusement, saying, 'Look,, Mama, look at me! I'm the same precious child you had yesterday. Nothing is different on the outside,' and she giggled, as she added, 'Only on the inside. I've lost my virginity, and I feel ten pounds lighter. It weighed heavily on me, Mama . . . '

Meagan turned away. 'Don't be tacky, Erin! That's not funny.'

She watched her mother walk away. 'Oh, Mama,

please face the facts of life. It had to happen some day.'

The mother sighed. 'I know. Thank God it's over. ' And then, she smiled at her daughter as she inquired, 'Did you enjoy it?'

'Uh huh, Mama, I did . . . very much. He knows what he is doing, believe me. He's no amateur.'

The mother looked surprised. 'How would you know?'

She smiled. 'I've heard the big girls talk in prison. Mama, I've heard of things your delicate mind couldn't handle.'

She turned away. 'And I don't want to hear them, either.'

She responded, cheerfully, 'OK . . . where's Charlie?'

'He went out to get a haircut. I'm to meet him in the coffee shop at ten.'

'What are you guys going to do today?'

She sighed. 'I told Charlie I didn't want to do anything today, but rest,' and she flopped in a chair.

The daughter, knowing her mother well, looked at her, finally a good hard look.

She moved closer, looking in her eyes, and sat next to her, taking her hand. 'Mama, you don't look well. Do you feel alright?'

The mother turned away for a moment, and then turned to look at her daughter, again. 'No, honey, I don't. I'm worried, Erin.'

'Why, Mama?'

'I've been bleeding, lately . . . from the bottom.'

'Is it just your period?'

'Oh, Erin, at my age you think I don't know the difference. No . . . this is real blood.'

Concerned, Erin asked, 'How long has this been going on, Mama?'

She looked away. 'For a while,' she said softly.

'Have you told Charlie?'

'No, poor darling. Lately, I've been putting him off, telling him I'm not in the mood.'

'Why haven't you told him? Are you afraid to tell him?'

She nodded. 'Erin, I just got engaged to the man. Do

you really believe I want to tell him, now, that he might have a sick woman on his hands?'

Erin looked at her. 'He would understand, Mama. I know Charlie that well.'

When Meagan didn't answer, Erin said, 'Mama, you've got to go to a doctor! How long has it been since you've been to a gynaecologist?'

She smiled. 'No doctor has seen my bottom since you were born.'

Erin's hands went to her throat. 'Oh, my God, Mama . . . twenty years. That's too long! You've got to go to a doctor,' and she added seeing her mother shaking her head, 'If not for your own sake, think of Charlie. You're going to be married before too long. Do you think you're being fair to the marriage?'

Meagan looked at her daughter, thinking how much she had matured in the past few months, and she could not help adding, since last night.

She responded. 'I don't know what to do, honey. This is supposed to be a vacation for us all, and now . . . '

'You think Charlie will mind you going to a doctor? For God's sake if he knew you were bleeding, he would insist on it. You know that!'

At those words, Meagan grabbed her daughter's hands. 'No, honey. Please don't tell Charlie about the bleeding . . . please.'

'All right, Mama, but you are going to a doctor, and today!'

She sighed, 'Maybe you're right. I should go but . . . how can I keep it from Charlie? You know how he is. He'll want to be there looking at my bottom along with the doctor,' she smiled, faintly.

'Don't worry about Charlie. I can handle him. I'll think of something. Did you say you were going to meet him in the coffee shop at ten? I'm going with you. We'll make some lame excuse about going shopping for some female things. Men never want to shop with women, especially for female things . . . '

'But,' protested the mother, 'how about you and Bud . . . '

She smiled. 'I'll call him and make some excuse. He'll have to live on his memories today, and believe me, I gave him enough to last him through the day. Come on, Mama, it's time to go.'

'Shopping? For female things? What kind of female things? We went shopping for those things two days ago . . . '

Erin gave him an exasperated look. 'No, Charlie, I meant really female. In case you don't know it, you're in the company of two women who still bleed every month, if you know what I mean . . . '

The mother protested. 'Oh, Erin . . . please!'

The daughter would not be deterred. 'Now, Mama, Charlie's a big boy. He was married to a woman for four years . . . he should know about these things, don't you Charlie?'

He nodded, offended that she should ask. 'Of course, I do.' And he sighed. 'OK, if that is what you want. I guess I'll have to find something else to do. I'll have to have the Cherokee serviced. That should be exciting.'

Erin nodded. 'See, I knew you wouldn't mind. And . . . Charlie, we need some money.'

He nodded, knowingly. 'I tried to give your mother a few hundred when we got here . . . for spending money, but you know how she is . . . with all that pride . . . '

Erin nodded, as she replied with her hand extended, 'I don't have that problem, Charlie, honey. I'll take anything I can get from a man,' and then she giggled, "ceptin a disease, of course!' Her mother, giving her a disgusted look, exclaimed, 'Erin!'

Charlie extracted two crisp, just out of the Cirrus machine, hundred dollar bills, and handed them to Meagan, but Erin intercepted them, saying, I'll take care of the money.'

She smiled at Charlie, kissing him on the cheek. 'I'm the one who hustled it, ain't I?'

Charlie kissed Meagan on the cheeks and she returned it with a weak smile, saying, 'Bye, honey . . . I love you.'

He nodded, perplexed . . . 'I love you, too. Have fun.'

Meagan nodded meekly, and they left.

Charlie watched them go, and having nothing to do at the moment, signalled the waiter for more coffee. He sat, trying to figure out what was going on.

21

The medical offices of Drs James and Ethel Herrington were located high on the slopes of the foothills above Vail Valley, much to the consternation of the older of the two women, bringing from her, 'They sure don't make it easy for you to see them, do they.'

The daughter shrugged. 'I guess they figure if you want to see them, you'll come, no matter.'

'How much did that taxi cost?'

'Don't worry about that, Mama.'

As they entered the beautifully decorated lobby, they looked around. Flowers were everywhere, thriving profusely in the ample sunlight streaming in through a solarium type roof on three sides of the lobby. A smiling woman in a white medical blouse watched them approach. She could detect extreme nervousness in both women, but especially in the older one. She admired the long slender legs of both, since she belonged to the genre of wide bottoms and thick legs.

'May I help you, ladies?' she asked pleasantly.

It was Erin who ventured forth, replying, 'Yes, I hope so. My mother needs to see a doctor . . . a gynaecologist, I guess.'

The woman smiled. 'That's the only kind we have. Do you have an appointment?'

Erin shook her head. 'No! We're just visiting in Vail for a few days, but,' and she lowered her head, looking around, and then realizing there were no others but women in the place, 'you see, my mother has started bleeding . . . from the bottom.'

The woman nodded. 'I see. Then, you really need to be seen on an emergency basis . . . '

'Uh huh, it's an emergency.'

'Would you prefer to see Dr James Herrington, or Dr Ethel Herrington?'

Meagan inquired. 'What's the difference between them?'

The woman smiled, patiently. 'One is a man and one is a woman, but in addition to that, Dr James is a surgeon, and his wife is not. But, some women feel more comfortable with another woman . . . '

'Oh, yes,' exclaimed the prudish Meagan, 'I would prefer a woman doctor. You see, it's kind 'o personal.'

The woman smiled, with amused understanding. 'I understand. Then you need to see Dr Ethel. Please have a seat over there, and fill out this form. What kind of insurance do you have?'

Meagan looked at Erin and Erin looked at her mother, shrugging, but replying, 'We don't have any insurance, but we have cash.'

The woman's eyebrows went up. 'I see. Just leave the insurance questions blank, then.'

The two nervous and inexperienced women selected two chairs near a huge salt water aquarium, teeming with fish removed from their native habitat in the tropics and relocated in a cold and hostile environment in the mountains.

As they sat, Meagan inquired, 'I wonder how much this will cost. I don't want to spend too much money, Erin. I hope we can give some of the two hundred back to Charlie.'

'Mama, I don't care how much it costs, and I'm sure Charlie doesn't either,' she protested. 'Now, let's fill out this form,' and as she began to ask her mother the usual questions, Meagan pouted, 'Why do they have to know all those personal things?'

Erin smiled. She had filled out such forms several times when seeing the prison doctor on routine medical check-ups given the women each year.

She turned, patting her mother on the hand. 'Because they need to know your medical history, Mama.'

After nearly an hour of waiting, during which Meagan complained . . . 'you could bleed to death waiting to find out why you're bleeding in the first place . . . '

'Be calm, Mama. Look, she is waving for us to come. Come on, let's go,' as she helped up an unwilling patient. The nurse who had come out to see them, asked, 'Meagan Lewis'

'Uh huh, I'm Meagan.'

'Come with me, please,' and to the daughter, 'I'll take good care of her. Please wait here. We'll keep you informed as to what is going on,' she smiled.

A hesitant Erin, responded, 'Oh, OK. I'll wait right here. I'll be right here, Mama.'

A scared Meagan allowed herself to be led into the pristine white halls of the busy clinic, turned, smiled weakly at her daughter and disappeared. Erin returned to her seat, and seeing a coffee counter, arose and poured herself a cup of the warm brew. She picked up a copy of Redbook and returned to her seat . . . to wait.

Charlie, on his fourth cup of coffee, sat munching on a roll, still wondering at the turn in events. He saw Bud enter the coffee shop and hailed to him, beckoning him to join him.

Bud, smiling, and extending his hand as if he had not seen Charlie in months, said, 'Well, ole buddy, I see you've been deserted, too. Erin called me, cancelling out for the day. What's going on?'

Charlie nibbled on his roll. 'Want some breakfast?,' and not waiting for a reply, 'I don't know what they're up to.'

Bud hailed a waiter, 'Coffee and two biscuits, please.' Turning back to Charlie, 'How long will they be gone? Erin and I were going to drive to Breckenridge for the day . . . just to look around.'

Charlie shrugged. 'I don't know . . . '

Bud, in a confidential tone, 'So you and Meagan are going to get married, huh?' Charlie nodded, saying nothing, as Bud continued, 'Say, tell me all about these Mahoney women, will you?'

Charlie, giving him a suspicious look. 'What do you want to know?'

He smiled his infectious smile, usually reserved for women he was trying to charm, 'Everything about them. How did you run across them? What do they do for a living? What is their background? Stuff like that.'

Charlie gave him a knowing smile in return, asking, 'Is this a Grand Jury hearing, counsellor?'

Embarrassed now, and knowing he was not overly discreet in his questioning, Bud meekly replied, 'Sorry, I didn't mean to get personal. No offence intended,' he smiled.

'And, none taken,' replied Charlie, using the worn out old cliche.

Bud persisted. 'It's just that I am intrigued by Erin. She is one hell of a woman, Charlie, but I guess you know that. It seems to run in the family, huh?'

Charlie was becoming annoyed with him. 'What runs in the family?'

'Well, you know . . . that animal quality about them. Whew, that Erin is something in bed . . . '

Charlie turned on him, viciously. 'Listen, Casanova, I am not interested in hearing the lurid details of your trysts with Erin. Keep them to yourself. She will soon be my step-daughter . . . family! Do you understand that?'

He replied, contritely. 'I'm sorry. I didn't mean to . . . '

Charlie shook his head. 'I'm sorry I jumped down your throat, but you struck a nerve. Erin's been through a lot lately. You took advantage of a very vulnerable young woman.'

He protested, 'I can assure you I did not take advantage of her . . . it was quite mutual, believe me.'

Charlie nodded. 'I'm sure it was. I didn't mean to accuse you of anything, Bud. I'm upset right now. I think something is wrong with one of those two women, and I can't figure out what it is.'

The attorney was contrite. 'Is there anything I can do before I leave . . . '

Charlie looked surprised. 'Are you leaving . . . you mean . . . Vail?'

He nodded. 'Yes, I've decided to go on to Utah.'

'Does Erin know you're leaving today?'

'No,' he replied. 'I'll leave her a note. Well, I guess this is goodbye, Charlie. It's been fun. Give Meagan my love. I hope everything is all right with them.'

Charlie didn't even look up. 'Yeah . . . see ya around, Bud.'

A very nervous and impatient Erin paced the floor. Her mother had been gone for two hours and no one had come out to tell her anything . . . no one! She walked up to the desk.

The woman with the broad bottom and thick legs smiled, asking, 'May I help you?'

Erin nodded. 'Yeah, I would like to know what is going on with my Mama. Could you find out?'

The woman was sympathetic. She was accustomed to handling inquiries from nervous relatives.

She said, 'Wait here, and I'll see if I can get you a report,' and she went into the labyrinth of hallways.

In a few minutes she returned with a woman in tow, a woman all dressed in white; an attractive woman, probably fifty, but neat and trim . . . quite attractive for her age.

The woman smiled, extending her hand, saying, 'Miss Mahoney?' to which Erin nodded. She continued, taking Erin by the arm, leading her into an office, 'I am Dr Herrington . . . Dr Ethel Herrington, not to be confused with my husband,' she smiled.

Motioning Erin to a chair, she leaned against the desk. 'We have to run some more lab tests on your mother, to be sure of our diagnosis before . . . '

Erin's throat went dry. 'Lab tests? What is wrong with my mother?'

The doctor gave her a reassuring pat on the hand. 'We're not sure, yet, as to the extent of our preliminary findings, but your mother,' and she hesitated, 'may have some problems.'

Erin was now horrified, but she tried not to show it. She knew she had to be brave. 'Problems? What kind of problems? My mother is healthy as a horse . . . '

The doctor nodded, knowingly, thinking to herself, 'They always are,' as she replied, 'We have detected some foreign tissue on her cervix. We have to do a biopsy to determine if it is malignant or not . . . '

At the sound of the word, malignant, Erin's hands

went to her throat. Tears filled her eyes as she repeated the doctor's words, 'Malignant . . . biopsy?'

The doctor tried to reassure her. 'Now, please don't imagine the worst, It might be just a simple matter of snipping the tip of the cervix off . . . lots of women have that done without further damage . . . '

She knew her words were empty and she said them only to reassure the young woman 'and', she continued, 'it could be something more serious. That is why we have to run some tests . . . to confirm . . . '

She rose. 'I have to go now. Are you and your mother alone in Vail? Is there someone else you can call . . . for support? Your mother tells me she is recently engaged . . . the man . . . is he here in Vail?'

Erin nodded 'He's at the hotel, or, somewhere . . . '

As the doctor went through the door, 'Perhaps, dear, you might want to call him . . . for support. Your mother will be undergoing tests for a while. Sorry, we have no cafeteria in the clinic. I'll keep you informed.'

And she left a shattered and distraught daughter, who returning to her chair, looked at the floor, whispering, 'Oh, my God. Mama!'

She sat for a moment or two, wondering what to do, then she thought of Charlie. 'Charlie! I've got to call Charlie,' and she raced to the phone and dialled the suite. No answer.

She dialled the desk. 'Yes, we have seen Mr. Forester this morning . . . yes, he went out.' She dialled Bud's room. No answer. She dialled the desk, again. 'Yes, Mr Compton was seen but he was out too.' She felt so alone, so all alone as she returned to her seat.

Then, she rose, returned to the phone and called the hotel desk, again. "'Please have Mr Forester call me at,' and she looked at the pay phone number, reciting it to the desk clerk, 'Please have Mr Forester call me, immediately. Thank you.'

And as she returned to her chair, to herself, 'Please, Charlie . . . call, I need you.'

The phone rang thirty minutes later. She rushed to answer it, but, no, she was not Mabel Carter, and she returned to her seat.

Over a nervous hour later, the phone rang again, and she heard a familiar voice. 'Charlie? Oh, Charlie, I need you,' and she gave him the address and how to get there, and to his insistent inquiries of,'What's going on, honey? You sound so distraught,' she replied, 'I can't tell you now, Charlie, just come, please.'

He was pulled over by a City of Vail policeman only three blocks after he had left the parking garage, and as he explained the reason for his law breaking driving, the policeman replied, 'Follow me! I know a short cut to the clinic. My wife goes to Dr Herrington!'

As he rushed from the parking lot to the front of the clinic he could see Erin pacing the sidewalk. She ran to him, crying, as she grabbed him, holding him close, she began to relate, between sobs, the situation as she knew it. There were gaps in her delivery due to near hysteria and lack of understanding, but Charlie quickly pieced it together, and in a nutshell . . . his betrothed had big problems.

He took the sobbing young woman by the hand, imploring, 'Erin, honey, pull yourself together . . . she needs you. I need you. We'll whip this problem, no matter what it is . . . '

She held his hand, sobbing. 'I know . . . I know.'

By the time the sun went into hiding behind the tall mountains to the west, the drama had unfolded and the problem had been identified.

'If only she had gone for periodic checkups,' the doctor lamented, 'It could have been caught in the early stages. So many women go through this,' Ethel Herrington lamented. 'I did, too. Doctors are not immune to it,' she smiled at Charlie, as she gave him a completed run down.

He nodded. 'What is the worst case scenario, doctor?'

The doctor replied. 'We won't even discuss the worst case scenario, for it may never come to that. Many women have had a hysterectomy and never experienced any more symptoms or problems.'

'Hysterectomy?' asked Charlie and Erin, almost in unison, as they looked at each other.

The doctor nodded. 'It is my understanding in talking to Mrs Lewis (she had given them her married name of Lewis) that you intend to marry soon. I hope you understand that if Mrs Lewis has a hysterectomy, she will have her uterus removed. She will be unable to bear children.'

At the sound of these words Charlie's mouth went dry as he remembered her words, spoken so passionately, 'I want to give you a baby, Charlie,' and he nodded to the doctor's declaration, replying, softly, 'I understand, doctor,' and he smiled, weakly, as he responded, bravely, 'It's not the end of the world, is it?'

He felt Erin's hand slip into his. 'When may I see Meagan?'

The doctor replied, 'She's had a rough day, poor thing. She told me, in a moment of jest, that she felt like a heifer at a bull convention. She has quite a sense of humour doesn't she?'

He smiled and nodded. 'She's quite a woman.'

Hours later Charlie and Erin escorted a pale and weak Meagan to the Cherokee out in the parking lot. She smiled, trying to be brave. She had insisted on the doctor giving her all the options available to her and she insisted that it be done in the presence of her betrothed.

The doctor, sensing her worries about her impending marriage, her desire to bear a child for this man, made an eloquent presentation, having suffered the same fate, herself . . . after she had been married and had two children.

Meagan leaned heavily on Charlie, not through necessity, but through desire to let him know she needed him more than ever, but she was troubled. She knew she was not the same woman she was only a few days ago. Like her daughter, something deep inside her had changed . . . for good.

It was only at Charlie and Erin's insistence that she agreed to eat anything that evening, and only in the suite.

'I don't feel like being around people, tonight. You and Erin go down and eat . . . I'll be all right, honey. Go on.'

They both protested in unison. 'No! We'll stay with you. We'll eat here in the room.'

'My God, what do you think I am? A cripple? I can still walk,' and she added, smiling, 'even if I have been violated ten or twelve times, today.'

'Are you sore, Mama?'

'Uh huh, I sure am, honey.'

Charlie kidded, 'Does this mean we're not going to make mad passionate love tonight, Meagan, honey?'

She was repulsed at the thought of it. 'Oh . . . Charleee.'

Erin rose, shaking her head. 'You two . . . just like high school kids.'

Meagan shook her head. 'Not any more, honey! Not for a while!

Erin rose, looking around the suite, saying, 'Well, if you two are not going to eat, I guess I'll call Bud and explain about today . . . '

Charlie took her hand as she went by. She stopped, looked at him, and sensing he knew something she didn't, asked, 'Something wrong with that too, Charlie?'

He nodded, unable to look her in the eye, replying, 'I don't think he's there, Erin, but you can try.'

She made her way to the phone, and before she could pick up the receiver to call, there was a knock on the door. Her eyes brightened. She felt sure it was Bud, coming to see about her.

She rushed to the door, and upon seeing a bell hop standing there, her jaw dropped in disappointment, as he asked, 'Miss Mahoney? . . . Erin Mahoney?' and he thrust a long box into her hands, adding, 'I've been trying to deliver these all afternoon, but I guess you were out . . . '

She took the box, looking at it with mixed emotions, saying 'Thank you.' and to a look of extreme disappointment on his face, offered him no tip.

Her mother and Charlie watched as she opened the box and extracted one dozen long-stem roses from it, and with eyes wide with excitement, exclaimed, 'Oh, long stem roses! Aren't they gorgeous? Bud is so sweet,' and then she removed an envelope from the box. They watched as her expression changed from delight to distress as she read. She said nothing as she placed the card on the couch, got up, picked up the roses, walked to the waste basket, and dropped them in and walked to her bedroom, closing the door behind her. The beginning of a sob was heard just as the door closed. Charlie picked up the card. He felt he knew what it said, but, for Meagan's benefit, he read out loud. . . .

My dear Erin,

By the time you read this, I'll be gone – on my way to Utah.

Meeting you was wonderful! You're wonderful!

But, I have to confess to you – I'm married. We were separated, but last night we talked on the phone, for hours. We're going to try again.

I wish it could have been!

Thanks for the memories.

Bud.

As he finished, he looked at Meagan. She was crying, softly, murmuring, 'Oh, my poor baby.' She began to rise, adding, 'I've got to go to her . . . '

He grabbed her arm, detaining her. 'No, Meagan, let me go. You've had a hard day. You don't need this. Believe it or not, she needs advice from a man, now . . . not her mother.'

She sat back down, tired. 'All right, honey, but be gentle with her . . . she's in pain, too.'

He made his way to her door, listening. He could hear her sobbing. He knocked, gently. 'Erin, honey, it's Charlie. Let me in. I want to talk to you about this . . . '

'Go away, Charlie . . . I'll be alright.'

He persisted. 'Erin, honey, if you love me, you'll let me in for a minute.'

She opened the door, saying nothing, and as he entered she returned and flopped on the bed in a foetal position, sobbing. He sat next to her, placing his hand on her shoulder, comforting her, saying nothing for a while.

Finally, she turned to him, whispering, 'Why, Charlie? Why did he lie to me? Why do men do it? I trusted him, too. He deceived me. He used me. I feel like a whore,' and she added, sobbing, 'who didn't even get paid . . why, Charlie?'

He continued to rub her shoulders, not knowing what else to do, and he was forming the words in his mind. She allowed herself to be turned to face him, and then she sat up in bed, and then, went into his arms, sobbing. 'I hate men, Charlie! You're the only one I love . . . and trust.'

He held her close. 'I know . . . I know.' He let her cry until she had no more tears left.

He smiled at her. 'Now, can we talk?'

She shrugged. 'What's there to talk about? He's gone. He left me, the bastard. If I had known he was married he would never have so much as held my hand, much less . . . ' and she let it die a natural death.

He took her hands. 'Erin, honey, this was something that had to happen, sooner or later, and it is well that it happened at this stage in your life.'

'What do you mean? You act like it is a good thing,' she sobbed.

'In a way, it is.'

She was perturbed. 'How can you say that?'

'A wise man once said that you're not really a man until you've had your heart broken, at least once,' and, he smiled, 'I'm sure the same rule applies to women.'

'That's not funny, Charlie . . . it hurts.'

'Sure it does. That's what the saying means. This is a tough world out there. You should know that better than most girls your age. You've spent a few years in prison for something you should have been given a medal for. That wasn't right. Those poor women on the boat with us were raped and abused. That wasn't right either. Every day people are subjected to unfair things thrown in their way by fate, and some of them pay horrible prices because of them. Consider yourself lucky. The only damage is to your pride . . . your ego, and some bruised feelings. The only permanent damage is the loss of your virginity, and you must admit you were just dying to lose that, anyway. He just happened to be the one . . . '

She smiled. 'But, if he had been honest with me. He lied.'

'I know! Adelle's whole four years as my wife were lies. You remember you asked me if I thought he was lying to you, and I said . . . probably. A man will lie, cheat, and steal to get a woman in bed, once he's made up his mind to do so, and she gives him the slightest encouragement, and you did, Erin.'

'I hate men. Believe me, the next one is going to have a hell of a fight on his hands.'

'That's what I mean. You won't be so easy, or so trusting next time.'

'Oh, Charlie, men are no-good bastards.'

He smiled. 'Only where women are concerned.'

She embraced him, saying. 'OK, I'm alright, now. Go back and see about my mama,' and as he rose to go, she smiled, 'It's been a hell of a day, huh, Charlie?'

'Uh huh, and sometimes they come in bunches, like bananas.'

She got out of bed, embracing him, whispering, 'Thanks, Charlie.'

He tried to hold her close, but she backed away, smiling. 'Don't hold me too close, you male bastard.'

He laughed. 'You're gonna be OK, honey.'

As he returned to a nervous Meagan, she was curious. 'How did it go?'

'She'll be all right. I convinced her it's the best thing that could have happened to her at this stage in her life.'

Meagan snorted. 'And she believed that?'

He smiled. 'I think so, but she hates all men . . 'ceptin me.'

Meagan nodded. 'That's good. For the time being. Is she going out to eat?'

'No, I don't think so. I think she wants to sleep,' and as he said that, Erin came to the door, looking at the betrothed couple sitting there. She gave a weak smile, 'Are you all right, Mama?'

Meagan returned the smile. 'I'm fine, honey.'

'OK, I'm going to sleep. I don't intend to wake up before tomorrow. If any man calls for me, I'm not in,' she joked, as she closed the door.

Meagan turned to Charlie. 'Poor darling. Heartbreak is so painful.'

'How do you know? Has yours ever been broken?'

'No, and it never will. I'll never let any man break my heart, Charlie . . . not even you. It might break, but no one will ever know it, believe me!'

'You're a hard woman, Meagan.'

'It's a hard world, Charlie. And speaking of that, we have to talk, honey.'

'Tonight? Its been a hard day for you, and all of us . . . '

She took his hands. 'I know, but, we have to. It's about us.' And as he gave her a perplexed and questioning look, she continued, as she removed the ring from her finger and placed it in his hand, saying, softly, 'I'm letting you off the hook, Charlie. We're not engaged any longer.'

Her words reminded him of Adelle's sudden and unexpected declaration on that fateful day, and the memory burned in him as he asked, 'What are you talking about?'

She shook her head, with difficulty, replying, 'I think it's the only fair and honourable thing I can do for you. In the very near future something is going to have to happen to me, according to what that doctor told us today. That's why I wanted you there when she said it. I won't be able to give you a child, and I know how much this means to you, so . . . you are free to go and find yourself some young and healthy woman who can do that for you,' and her last words were lost in sobs.

He smiled at her, taking her hands in his. 'So that is what this is all about. A baby? A baby, Meagan?'

She nodded, looking away, blinking away her tears.

He took the engagement ring from the palm of his hand, and he took her left hand. She tried, meekly, to protest, but he was not to be deterred, as he went down on his knee, placing the ring on her third finger, saying, 'Meagan Mahoney, Charles Alexander Forester requests the honour of your hand in the holy state of matrimony . . . the sooner the better, Madam, and he would appreciate a prompt reply, without conditions or qualifications of any kind. What is your answer, Madam?'

She could not answer, for the words would not come, but she blinked away a tear or two and she nodded, smiling.

The bedroom door, which was slightly opened, emitted a passionate, 'Oh, Mama . . . oh, Charlie, I'm so happy,' and she raced to embrace them.

They held each other for a long time, until Charlie pulled back, saying, 'Whew, this has been some day!'

'It sure has,' echoed Meagan, managing a weak smile, as they all continued to hold each other in a warm embrace.

Meagan broke off first, asking her daughter, 'I thought you were asleep. Were you eavesdropping all that time?'

She replied, not embarrassed in the least, 'Yes, but now that I know you're OK, I am going to bed for real.'

Megan took her hand. 'How are you, honey? Are you all right?'

Erin managed a weak smile. 'Me? Sure! I'm OK. Night.'

They watched her leave. 'Her heart's broken, you know,' Meagan murmured to him.

He nodded. 'Better now than later, when it is more serious.'

'Uh huh,' she replied as she led him to the bedroom, and giving him a mischievous smile, continued, 'You know, engaged couples at our age usually celebrate their engagement in bed, but . . . I'm sorry, honey . . . I don't feel up to it.'

'I know. We'll celebrate later. You need to get some rest. We're pulling out in the morning.'

She grunted. 'Back to Mountain View! I guess my holiday is over and I'll get back to the cafe. I hope I still have a job . . . '

He looked at her in surprise. 'You don't think you're going back to work, do you?'

She looked at him with pleading. 'I don't know what I'm going to do, Charlie. I don't know what your plans are . . . our plans . . . ' as she added, 'your plans for me.'

He took her hand and led her to the bed, motioning for her to sit, as he took his place beside her. He took hold of her hand. He could tell the day had been hard on her. She looked tired . . . and worried. He wanted to comfort her.

'Meagan, you're going to be my wife. I don't want you working in that cafe any more. I want to take care of you . . . and Erin.'

She nestled her head in his neck. 'Oh, honey, I'm so afraid of the future. Without you, I don't know what I'd do. I'm worried about Erin's future. She has no training at anything. All she can do is hurry and marry some man who will take care of her. I hope she gets a good man . . . one like you, Charlie.'

'Don't you want more for her than to jump into a quick marriage to some man . . . just to have some security?'

'Well . . . sure . . . but . . . '

He held her close. 'Meagan, I've been doing some thinking about us . . . all of us. Heavy thinking. I have made some decisions I want to discuss with you. Do you feel like talking now?'

She put a pillow upright and leaned against it, replying, 'I'm a little tired, but, go ahead, honey . . . we need to talk.'

He moved to the other side of the bed and climbed in next to her, with his pillow upright also.

He placed his arm around her and drew her close as he continued. 'Well, as I said, I've been doing some heavy thinking, and here is what I think we should do. As soon as I can find out if my divorce is final, I want to get married right away, if that is all right with you. I want Erin to live with us . . . for a while. I've got ideas for her future, too . . . '

'What ideas?'

'I don't know for sure, yet, but I think she should go to college. Erin has too much potential to waste in being a brood mare for some cowboy hillbilly . . . '

'Oh, Charlie, I think so, too, but . . . '

'We don't have to decide on the details tonight, Meagan . . . '

She snuggled closer. 'OK honey . . . whatever you say.'

He sat up, excited. 'And for us, here is what I'd like to do . . . if it is alright with you . . . '

'Oh, Charleeee, anything you decide is alright with me, honey. What about us?'

'I want to open a real estate business in Colorado. I want us to live here . . . in the mountains . . . '

'Oh, Charlie . . . are you sure this is what you want? What about your family? Your business is in Texas . . . '

'No, Meagan, my father's business is in Texas. Mine will be in Colorado, after I open it here.'

'But, what will you do here?'

'We'll open a real estate office. We'll buy and sell, and in time, we'll do some developing . . . condos . . . malls . . . '

She sat up. 'You keep saying . . . 'we' . . . '

'Yes, Meagan . . . "we" . . . you and me . . . and Erin. You two will be on the payroll, but,' he remarked, sternly, 'you'll have to work. We will be the whole office force,' he laughed.

'But honey, I can't even type,' and her face lit up, 'but, Erin can! She took typing in high school. She can still type.'

He smiled. 'See! This will work out if I can swing it.'

She looked serious. 'But don't you need a real estate license to act as a real estate broker . . . I think?'

He nodded. 'Uh huh, and I don't have time to go through that, either . . . '

'Then, what will you do about that?'

He smiled . . 'Simple! I'll buy an existing agency, and the broker will have to work for me for five years. It'll be part of the sales agreement . . . '

She interrupted. 'But, honey, that will take a lot of money. Can you do it? You know what I mean? Do you have that much money?'

He looked serious. 'No, not now, but, if I cashed in my chips with Forester Companies, I would have . . . '

'Oh, honey, are you sure you want to do that? What will your daddy say . . . and your mama?'

'I don't know what my father will say, but I know for sure what my mother will say,' he smiled.

'Oh, Charlie, I just don't know about all this. I'm worried. You will be splitting from your family, and I'm the cause of it all,' she lamented.

He tried to soothe her. 'No . . . no! That is not true. I've been wanting to make a change in my life. I haven't been contended for a long time. You were just the excuse I needed to do this . . . She laughed. 'What a sorry excuse, huh?'

He squeezed her hand. 'Now, sorry excuse, let's go to sleep.

She slid down in the bed, cuddling him. 'OK'

Several times during the night the daughter would get out of her bed, tiptoe to the door of her room, and hearing nothing in the way of sound in the living area, would tiptoe to the door of the bedroom of the betrothed couple. With her head against the door, listening intently, and hearing no noise, would return to her room, feeling that her mother was asleep. She was happy. In her mind, no noise was good news. She felt sure, knowing her mother as she did, the sound of talking would indicate a lack of sleep on the part of the betrothed. Since romance was unlikely, she reasoned, talking could only mean troubled discussion.

She tossed and turned the entire night, for she was a worried woman. What of her mother's future? What of her's? If something happened to her mother, how would she fit into the life of Charles Alexander Forester? Did he want her to fit into his life? No! He would probably say goodbye to her and return to his family in Texas.

She could not suppress her tears. 'Damn . . . what a day this had been!' She hated men . . . all except Charlie.

22

It was a wistful bunch who left Vail Valley the next morning. It had been several days of fun, laughter, carefree times and of discovery for the participants. Erin had discovered that real love did not come cheap, or easily. Meagan, who had always considered herself as sturdy as a farm mule discovered she was not. Charlie had discovered that his fiancee had an apparent malignancy and his future step-daughter had a broken heart; one was curable and the other . . .

But, the indomitable human spirit being what it is, they smiled, ready to go on with their lives. As the Jeep Cherokee headed east on Interstate 70, Charlie and Meagan related to Erin the decisions of the night before. She sat wide-eyed as he told her of his plans for them. She had moved to the edge of the seat, her elbows on the back of the front seat, as she exclaimed at each new declaration . . . 'geez!'

And as he unfolded his plan for her to go to college, she asked with wild excitement. 'Where?'

He swallowed hard. He had not thought of the details, as he asked in return, 'Where would you like to go?'

He silently prayed that she would not mention a private university, and he breathed an audible sigh of relief as she exclaimed, 'The University of Colorado . . . at Boulder. I've always dreamed of going there.' And as she warmed to the subject, 'You know, Charlie, I've got a high school equivalency diploma . . . I got it in prison. I made good use of my time there. I spent a lot of time in the library, too,' she said, proudly.

He nodded. 'I'm glad to hear that. You're a Colorado native, so getting you into Boulder should not be too hard.'

'Oh God, Mama, I always wanted to be a coed. I want to be a cheer leader, too. Do you think I can be one? Am I pretty enough?'

Her mother looked back at her. 'You can be anything you want, honey, if you put your mind to it.'

She nodded. 'That's true, Mama.'

As the Jeep neared the town of Frisco, Charlie slowed down to exit the Interstate, with Meagan asking, 'Are you stopping, honey? I need a tinkle if you are . . . '

Erin piped up. 'Me, too! I got to go real bad, Charlie.'

He shook his head. 'Women . . . you have got to have inferior plumbing to the male animal . . . '

The two women began to chastise him at once, with Meagan getting in the best punch. 'Funny thing . . . you men are mighty interested in our plumbing systems . . . '

He knew he was outnumbered and out-manoeuvred, as he pulled into a Holiday Inn, telling the women. 'Let's go in for coffee and a pit stop for you girls, and I want to get an area map so I can get around . . . '

Meagan looked surprised. 'Why do you want a map to get around here?'

'I think this would be a good area to settle in. The economy is good in summer and winter, so I'm sure the real estate business is good. Think you girls will like it?'

'Oh, I do,' replied an excited Erin. 'I'll learn to ski, and . . . '

'Hold on, girl,' her mother admonished, 'don't get your butt in high gear, yet. Charlie said we're just looking, huh, Charlie?'

'Sure, but when we decide, it will be a family decision. We'll all vote on it . . . '

'See, Mama,' she teased as they headed for the rest rooms.

When they returned from the ladies' room, Charlie was waiting, impatiently, taking both by the arms, leading them to the door, with Erin asking, 'Where are we going? I thought we were going to have coffee . . . '

'No,' he replied as he led them out, 'coffee will just make you tinkle more. Besides, we'll have coffee in Breckenridge.'

'Breckenridge?' they asked in unison.

'Uh huh, this town is too small. We have to go where there is more action. I've skied there many times. It's a nice town, with a nice shopping area and all. I think you'll like it.'

Meagan announced, proudly, 'I was in Breckenridge, once, myself. 'Course, we didn't stay long. That's an expensive town on my budget,' she laughed.

Charlie smiled. 'It's an expensive town on anybody's budget. Skiing is not a poor man's sport.'

'Uh, uh!' lamented Erin.

They spent most of the day in the beautifully restored town, and then made their way back to the interstate and went on to the Dillon/Silverhorne area. Charlie went to a real estate office and got the ubiquitous maps the agents in the valley proudly passed out, and what the agents didn't have the tourist bureau did. With an armful of maps and brochures, and a head full of ideas the trio, tired but satisfied, headed back to Mountain View, high in the hills west of Denver.

As they pulled up to the second storey apartment over the garage, Meagan laughed. 'I guess this is what they mean by coming back to reality, huh, Charlie? A week of living in the lap of luxury, and now this,' as she waved to the apartment.

Charlie and Erin shared her laugh, with Erin pontificating, 'We were happy with it before Charlie came along and spoiled us, Mama,' and turning to him, she continued, 'You ought to be ashamed of yourself, Charlie. Fooling around with two country girls like us . . . turning our heads with luxury things . . . ought to be ashamed . . '

'I didn't hear you complain in Vail,' he retorted. 'You seem to enjoy being spoiled.'

She put her arm in his. 'You bet! And, any time you want to do it, again, I'm your girl!'

'Back off, Erin, 'fore I tear your hair out. He's mine,' she joked.

'Oh, I know, Mama, but I want a Charlie of my own.'

He smiled at them as they climbed the stairs to the

apartment, with Erin getting in the last lick, with, 'You love having two gorgeous and desirable women fighting over you, don't you, Charlie?'

'Uh huh! Ah shur do,' he teased.

When he broke the news to her, Meagan began to cry. 'But, Charlie, we just got engaged and you're leaving me?' she lamented. 'I haven't even had time to get tired of you,' she teased.

'I know, honey, but I've got to go home and present my plan to my Dad. I won't enjoy this job, I assure you, especially having to listen to my mother's opinion of my plan. She will have a fit! Are you sure you and Erin don't want to come with me? I think this is a good time to meet my folks; after all, we're engaged.'

Meagan sighed. 'I'm not up to it, honey . . . I'm really not, and I have to go to Denver for more tests. It just wouldn't work out . . . '

He nodded. 'As usual, you're right. I'm sorry I won't be here with you when you go for the tests . . . '

'I'll be OK. Erin will be with me.'

'I'll leave you enough money to take care of you and Erin until I get back, and I will leave you my Mastercard also. Don't be shy about using it. We'll be married, soon. I hope you realize that.'

She nodded, smiling weakly. 'I know. I can hardly wait. I'll try not to spend too much of your money while you're gone.'

Erin heard that, replying, 'I'll take care of that end, Charlie . . . don't worry,' she teased.

'No she won't, Charlie, don't worry about that wild animal spending your money. I'll take care of that.'

Erin teased, 'You sure you don't want me to go with you Charlie. Maybe we can find a rich Texan for me while we're there. I hear Texas is loaded with rich boys just looking for a good time girl like me . . . '

Charlie shrugged. 'I would think you'd had enough of playboys for a while, after Bud . . . '

'Who!' she smiled. 'Bud? Who's Bud?'

'I'm glad to see you have a convenient memory . . . it helps!' and turning to Meagan, he took her in his arms, telling Erin, 'Turn your head, child, I want to tell your Mama goodbye.'

* * *

Agatha Forester sat up in her chair looking imperious, as she listened to her son present his plan for his future life. She listened, impassively, only lifting her eyebrow now and then; whether to express pleasure or outrage was difficult to discern. It was easy to interpret the expression on the face of his father; he was greatly distressed as he listened, but he made no interruptions. His demeanour could best be described as stoical and resigned. When his son had finished, he leaned back in his chair, crossing his long legs in the opposite direction, shifting his body to ease his arthritic hip. Then he rose, walking to the fireplace.

The weather had turned cold and a warm fire crackled in the huge opening. He turned to look at his son. Charlie smiled inwardly. His father had always used that pose when making profound observations, and he felt sure one was forthcoming, and it was.

'I guess you've thought this thing through very carefully, Charlie. I can tell. What can I say?' and looking at his wife, he added, 'What can we say? You're thirty-seven years old. You're a grown man, capable of making your own decisions, but I hope you realize what you're getting into.' (He had not told them of Meagan's apparent malignancy. He felt sure they would think he was out of his mind . . . especially his mother).

The father continued. 'We, your mother and I, felt sure this Meagan thing would go away, but apparently, it has not, and will not.'

Charlie bridled at the reference to the word 'thing', in describing her, but he said nothing.

The father continued. 'You know what a man works for all his life, Charlie? He works for his family. He wants to provide food and shelter for them and in some cases, as in ours, he builds a business hoping the son will take over and add on to what he has built.'

The father smiled. 'Come to think of it, that is a monstrous assumption, isn't it? How presumptuous of us fathers to feel that our sons will be happy to have us arrange their lives for them!'

The mother felt she had to protest. 'But Alex . . . '

He raised his hand and she stopped in mid-word, lowering her head to elicit sympathy from any, or both.

The father continued. 'I guess if I had given enough consideration to you, I could have asked you . . . do you want this?'

Charlie felt guilty now. His father had said this without bravado, which was generally his style. He looked old, Charlie thought . . . older than he remembered, and he had only been gone a few weeks. Perhaps, he thought, we don't spend enough time looking at each other, or talking to each other. Seeing the father had nothing more to add, Charlie rose, going to stand in front of his father.

'I guess I've been a disappointment to you, Dad, and I'm sorry . . . '

'No . . . No!' the father protested. 'I hope I didn't give you that impression, son. No, the point I'm trying to make is that if a mistake was made, it is mine. I should have asked you if you really wanted to be in this business.'

'But, Dad, I like the real estate business. I'm not leaving it. I'm just transferring my end of it to Colorado, to be near my wife . . . '

Agatha Forester could sit still no longer, as she exclaimed, 'It is a wife's duty to follow her husband, no matter where it is. It has always been that way!'

He looked at his mother with sympathy, and yet, he questioned her words. 'Would you, Mother, have followed Dad to Timbuktu to be his wife . . . away from your family's banking fortune? Would you have done it, Mother?' he demanded.

She looked at her husband for support, which was not forthcoming, for the husband knew very well she would not have, as she countered, 'I think you will admit, Charles, that the circumstances are not the same. My family had a sizeable banking fortune here. It would have been insane for your father and me to have forsaken that. After all,' she sniffed, looking at the husband, 'it was my family's money that made it possible for your father to . . . '

The husband interrupted. 'Agatha, my dear, all present are aware of those facts and they are not the issue at hand. The issue at hand is Charlie's decision to leave his family and the family business and relocate in Colorado, while, at the same time, taking of himself, a wife and a twenty-year-old step-daughter . . . that is the issue at hand,' and turning to the son, he said, meekly. 'if that is your decision, Charlie, so be it. I'll agree to your selling out your company stock, if that is what you want, but . . . '

Charlie looked up. 'But, what?'

'Are you open to a counter offer?'

Charlie smiled. There was the old horse trader coming out. He could trade with the best of them, and he enjoyed it too.

The son replied, 'I never turn down a good counter offer, Dad. You taught me that.'

The mother sat up, interested. She was always fascinated by her husband's business acumen. She had often said he was second only to her father, the old reprobate who had taken advantage of half the people in Texas in his prime, and enjoyed doing it too. She stared at her husband, waiting his words, with the deference of a proper wife.

Warming to the occasion, the father's eyes lit up. 'If you are hell-bent on moving to Colorado, why don't we do it the right way? Why don't we open a branch office in Denver? We are involved, already, in several limited partnerships in that area. We know some substantial people there. You could head the office. What do you think of that?'

Charlie was half excited at his father's offer, for it was more than generous and he knew it. It was a loving father's attempt to keep his son in the fold, so to speak, and they both knew it, but he had a problem.

'Well, that is a very generous offer, Dad, but . . . '

'But, what?' asked the father.

'I don't want to live in Denver. It's too big. Meagan and Erin are small town girls. they would not fit in with

Denver society anymore than they would here . . . '

The mother emitted a huff and a sort of snort, but she said nothing, with the father, feeling he was near to cutting a deal, replying, 'Hell, son, I don't care where you live if the deal will work for us both. You mentioned Breckenridge. That's fine with me. I've been there many times . . . good town . . . good economy, too.'

'Yes,' the son responded, 'I was very impressed with it during the day we spent there, but, gee, Dad . . . you've made a very generous offer and I'm interested. I don't deny that I'd prefer to have the Forester Company umbrella over me if I start this venture.'

And, looking at his mother, 'I'm sure mother is not interested in the nitty-gritty details of this thing. Why don't we continue these talks at the office.'

Looking to the mother for concurrence, the father responded, 'Good idea . . . the more I play with it in my mind, the more I like it.'

The mother was not to be denied, though. 'Charles, you are quite correct! I am not interested in the business details, but I am interested in the woman you intend to marry. Don't you think it is time that we met . . . Meagan and I?'

He looked sheepish as he replied, 'I tried to bring her down this trip, but she had some medical tests to run . . . '

He caught himself, but not in time to avoid raised eyebrows from an interested mother: 'Medical tests? May I ask what kind of tests, or am I being too personal?'

He fudged his answer, not wanting to tell the whole truth. 'I'm not sure, Mother, but I think it is some kind of female trouble. It is not serious, as far as I know,' he lied.

The mother nodded. 'I see. I hope it is nothing serious.'

He gave her a weak smile. 'I hope not, too,' and turning to the father, 'I'm ready to go when you are, Dad.'

The agreement concluded with his father was far more generous than he had ever hoped. He had wondered how he could swing the deal financially on his comparatively limited resources, but now he had the backing of a multi-million dollar corporation behind him.

His father had suggested that he immediately buy a condo complex near Breckenridge as a base of operations and to provide a source of ready cash flow to better afford the salaries of the two newest employees of the Forester Companies . . . Meagan and Erin Mahoney. Erin could be the office secretary and Meagan would be the office manager and administrator of the condos. Who better to handle the myriad assortment of humanity that rented the units on a weekly basis. But, putting Meagan to work was not Charlie's real concern. It was only a ruse to have her on the company payroll so she could be included in the company's very liberal health plan. Charlie, without elaborating to his father, knew he might need that very much, and soon.

When his father moved, he moved fast, as was his style. A draft for a substantial amount of money had been forwarded to a Denver bank with a branch in Breckenridge to enable Charlie to purchase the condo complex, buy himself a home and open an office, and pay his employees and himself.

The father asked, 'Do you really believe you can handle the office with only Meagan and the daughter, Erin is her name, I believe?'

He laughed. 'Dad, if you knew those two women, you wouldn't ask.'

'Well, ' grunted the father, 'I'll leave that to your good judgement. When will you be returning and, more importantly, when do you intend to marry that young woman? If I'm ever to have any grandchildren you had better get busy.'

Charlie swallowed hard at the words. He felt sorry for his father now, for in all probability, he would never have any grandchildren . . . not from Meagan, anyway, but he merely smiled, joking, 'You're right . . . I am running out of time.' And in an attempt to change the subject, he added, 'I'll be flying back as soon as I can get reservations,'

'What about your car? Don't you think you should drive your Mercedes back so you can use the Jeep for the office crew to show customers properties from time to time.'

He patted his father on the back. 'You're right, as usual. I guess I should drive my car back but, damn, I hate that long drive to Colorado, but I guess the battery in that Mercedes does need charging by now,' he laughed.

The father smiled. 'We've been letting my secretary drive it to keep it charged. She wants you to give it to her, I think.'

He gave his father a knowing look. 'Keeping Betty happy is your job dad, not mine.'

The father nodded, looking embarrassed, as he replied to the son. 'You've always known, haven't you . . . about Betty and me?'

He nodded. 'For quite some time, and believe me Dad, I don't blame you one damn bit.'

The father seemed contrite, like a small boy who had been caught doing something he had no business doing.

He patted his son on the shoulder, 'I'm glad you understand. It helps,' and as he began to turn away, he exclaimed, 'I almost forgot to tell you, Peg Broadhurst called several times . . . said she had to talk to you in the worst way . . . better call her before you leave.'

'Peg? Wonder what she wants. I'll give her a call, now,' and he left to go to his room. He was embarrassed that he had to look up her number; a number he had kept in his head for years. She answered on the second ring . . .

'Hello . . . '

'Hi, Peg. It's me . . . Charlie Forester.'

'Oh, Charlie, I'm so glad to hear from you.'

'Yeah . . . me too. It's been a long time. How're you doing? How's that reprobate husband of yours?'

She avoided the question. 'I'm fine. Look, Charlie, I need to talk to you. Can we have lunch, tomorrow?'

'Well, sure. I guess I can break free. I am trying to get back to Colorado . . . '

'I'll only keep you a short while . . . please.'

'Sure, Peg. Where? The yacht club?'

'No. Any place but there. Too many unpleasant memories. How about Carlo's? Remember it?'

'Sure. Twelve noon?'

'Uh huh . . . see you then. Nite Charlie.'

'Goodnight, Peg.'

He hung up, thinking, 'She sounds funny . . . different. Oh, well, I guess I'll find out soon enough.' As he dialled Meagan's apartment later that night, she seemed cheerful until he told her he was driving back, instead of flying.

'But, Charlie, honey, that'll take two more days. I miss you, sweetheart.'

'I miss you, too, but remember . . . they say that absence makes the heart grow fonder.'

She teased, 'They also say, out of sight, out of mind.'

'Tell me about your tests. What did they say?'

She hesitated for a moment. 'Can't we talk about that when you get back?'

'Well, sure, if that is what you want . . . '

'That is what I want. Oh, Erin, go away! Charlie doesn't want to talk to you, do you, Charlie?'

He teased, 'Sure I do. Put her on.'

'Charleee . . . we miss you! Come home, quick, before I fall in love with someone else. Why, I met the cutest truckdriver today over at the cafe . . . '

'I thought I told you I didn't want you working at that cafe, anymore . . . '

'I wasn't working, Charlie. I was a customer. Can't I even go for a piece of pie and a glass of milk? Geez!'

'If you keep eating all that pie and milk, you will get a big butt like most of those waitresses at that cafe.'

'Oh, I don't know. I kinda think my butt would look better with a pound or two on it . . . '

And she had the receiver grabbed out of her hand by an impatient mother, who exclaimed, 'Give me that phone if all you and Charlie are going to talk about is your butt. Charlie, when can I expect you? I want to see you so bad?'

'Well, I'm leaving here first thing the day after tomorrow, and if I drive like mad, I should get there the following night, maybe late, but wait up for me, or,' he teased, 'I'll have to wake you up.'

She smiled to herself. 'You won't have to wake me up, I promise you, honey.'

'But,' he hesitated, 'are you all right? You know what I mean?'

'Yes, sweetheart, I know what you mean, and, yes, I'm all right. It's nothing you have to worry about,' and she added, significantly, 'for now.'

'Then, I guess I'll say goodnight. I love you, Meagan.'

'I love you too, Charlie.'

'Oh, Meagan . . . '

'Yes, Charlie?'

'Let me talk to Erin for just a minute . . . please.'

She seemed puzzled as she responded, 'Well, OK. Erin, Charlie wants to talk to you . . . bye, Charlie.'

'Hi, Charlie . . . it's me . . . the woman you really love. Oh, Mama, quit pinching me! I'm just kidd'in.'

'Erin . . . get serious for a minute,' from Charlie.

'OK, Charlie . . . what?'

'How is she really doing?'

She hesitated, making sure her mother had left. 'She's OK, Charlie, she really is. Don't worry. Just come home to us . . . please!'

23

When he walked into Carlo's the next day at eleven-fifty, he thought he would have to wait for Peg for at least a half hour. She was never on time, but as he entered the Hispanic eatery and looked around, he spied her already seated with a drink in her hand. She saw him and waved. As he neared the table she rose to greet him. She held him in a close embrace as they hugged, and then, she stepped back, pursing her lips for a lip to lip kiss, lightly, as kissing kin do.

'Oh, Charlie, it's so good to see you,' and tears came to her eyes. She blinked them back continuing to smile.

He teased, 'I wanted you to miss me, Peg, but not to tears.'

She nodded, hugging him, again, 'I've got so much to tell you.'

He looked around. 'Where's Arnie? I thought sure he'd be here with you. Doesn't he love me, anymore?'

She gave him an embarrassed look. 'Arnie and I have split, Charlie. That's one of the things I wanted to tell you.'

He was dumb-founded. 'Aw, no, Peg! Not you and Arnie! You two were meant for each other . . . '

She hailed the waiter, ignoring the comment for a moment. 'What'll you have to drink, Charlie . . . my treat.'

He mumbled something about a drink, still shocked by her announcement, then, 'What happened, Peg?'

She shrugged. 'You men have strange ideas about your women, especially when it comes to our purity.'

'I don't understand . . . '

She took a deep breath. 'It was a great marriage until

the . . . ' and she paused . . tears in her eyes, 'until the rape on the cruise. After that,' and she once more blinked back her tears, 'he could not accept me anymore, if you know what I mean. I was soiled merchandise as far as the bedroom was concerned.'

He was incredulous. He couldn't believe what he was hearing.

'Oh, no, Peg . . . I can't believe he blamed you for that rape . . . '

She shook her head. 'No! He didn't blame me. He just couldn't accept me anymore . . . that's all. You men like your women to be virginally pure even though you move heaven and earth to soil every woman you can get your hands on,' she said with bitterness.

She sighed, shrugged her shoulders, and went on, as if to convince herself, 'I was a hell of a wife to him, Charlie . . . you know that! I never was unfaithful to him. Not one damn time, and I could have . . . believe me. Oh, I admit I flirted a lot, even with you,' she smiled, 'but it never went any further. I helped him build that business to the point that he could buy that damn boat.' She shook her head as if in disbelief. 'That damn boat!'

He shook his head, as if in protest, but she continued, 'But, I didn't ask you here today to talk about Arnie and me. I still think we'll work it out. It'll take time, but he's not seeing anyone else, and,' she paused for emphasis, 'God knows that the last thing I want now is another man. In time, he'll realize what he's losing. I've been a good wife to him, Charlie . . . he knows it,' she insisted.

Charlie nodded, asking, 'Have any papers been served?'

She shook her head. 'Oh, no, it hasn't come to that, and I don't think it will. He didn't even want to move out, but I asked him to when . . . when . . . ' and she sobbed, 'when he rejected me. I have my pride, Charlie. Any woman would have resented that. You know that!'

He nodded. 'He'll come around, Peg. I'm sure,' and as the waitress brought his drink, he took a sip and then, looking at her, asked, 'How are you doing since then . . . personally? And, Amanda? Do you ever see her? And, Kate? How is she doing?'

Peg took another sip, sniffed, wiped her eyes with a tissue, and sniffed again. 'That's what I wanted to talk to you about, Charlie. I thought you'd want to know . . .'

'Sure, I want to know,' he replied, not sure what she wanted him to know.

'To start off with Kate,' and she began to cry again, quietly, trying to suppress her tears. 'she is in a mental institution. Poor kid. She cracked up, Charlie. Her mind just couldn't take it. She was soft. It is not good to be soft in this world, Charlie, especially for a woman. It's better to be a mean bitch.'

He nodded. 'It helps. I'm so sorry to hear about Kate, even though I hardly knew her, she seemed to be a sweet kid,' and he could not wait any longer: 'And, Amanda? Do you ever see her any more?'

Peg looked at him, her eyes flooded with tears. 'Amanda is dead, Charlie . . . '

'Oh, no . . . ' and as he took her hand in his, 'What happened?'

Peg regained her composure, removing her hand from his to blow into a fresh tissue. She took a deep breath, and she reached for her purse. She extracted several pieces of paper, newspaper clippings it seemed, and she handed them to him. His eyes widened as he read the headings:

SOCIALITE/BEAUTY QUEEN TAKES OWN LIFE

and another one:

FORMER BEAUTY QUEEN KILLS SELF

He had read enough. He looked at Peg, wide-mouthed, asking, 'For God's sake, Peg . . . what happened to her. Why would she do something like that. She had so much to live for. She had it all . . beauty . . . brains . . money . . . my God! What would make her do a thing like that? Have you seen her since the cruise?'

She nodded. 'She came to see me some time after we

got back from the cruise. She was very distraught. She told me she was pregnant, and she was sure it was a result of the rape. She didn't know what to do about the baby. She told me she could not bring it to term. She said she would not want to have the baby of a man she detested, and to make matters worse, she had no idea whose baby it was. They all took turns with us, you know,' and she once more began to sob.

Charlie moved over to her side of the booth and took her in his arms. She went willingly, burying her head in his neck, remaining there until she had composed herself.

She drew back, looking around the room, embarrassed. 'I'm sorry! I'm OK, now,' but he remained on her side of the booth.

She sighed, then continued, 'We talked about an abortion for her. I told her I would stay with her during the whole thing after she told me her parents did not know about the pregnancy. She said it would kill her father to know of it. Poor soul, I wonder if she thought about the alternative she took . . . whether her father would have preferred that.'

He hated to ask. 'How did she do it?'

'Didn't you read the articles? She blew her brains out!'

He shuddered. He recoiled. Beautiful, gorgeous Amanda! He could not help but form a mental image of that beautiful head being destroyed . . . then, he was forced to put it out of his mind.

Peg studied his reactions, adding, 'She left a very peculiar suicide note . . . quite strange, although quite appropriate, for her, I would imagine.'

He seemed interested. 'What did it say?'

'It didn't say very much. She scrawled in large letters, 'LIFE IS A BITCH – THEN YOU DIE!' Does it mean anything to you?'

He nodded. 'I've heard it before.'

He sat there, quietly, for a long time, with Peg watching him.

She placed her hand on his. 'I'm sorry I had to tell you this, but I felt you had to know.' She paused.

'Charlie, is there any possibility that the baby was yours?'

So that was it. That is what this is all about, he thought? He looked at her, quietly asking, 'Did Amanda give you the impression that it could have been mine?'

'No! It was of my own doing, Charlie. I know you and Amanda got real thick at the end,' and she smiled, 'after you made peace with one another. I just wondered,' she murmured.

He looked her in the eye. 'I can assure you, Peg, the child could not have been mine.'

She repeated. 'I just could not help wondering. I didn't think it was. She would have kept it if it had been yours, I'm sure. She was in love with you, Charlie . . . did you know that? She told me so. She told me you were in love with another woman . . . in Colorado? Is that true, or did you just tell her that to hold her off?' She smiled. 'I know how rotten men can be.'

'No, it's true. We're to be married when I get back.'

'Oh, I see. Well, I wish you all the happiness in the world. You're a nice guy, Charlie, even if you are a man,' she teased, 'and, now, I guess we should order lunch, huh?'

'I'm not hungry, Peg. I can't get Amanda out of my mind.'

'I know what you mean. Poor girl. What a life! Fate played a dirty trick on her . . gave her everything a woman could ask for. What happens to people, Charlie? Are some of us truly marked for destruction from the start?'

He smiled. 'If I knew that, I could make a lot of money advising people on what to do and not to do.'

She smiled. 'Knowing the human race as I do, do you think anyone would listen?'

'Probably not! Peg,' changing the subject abruptly, 'would you like me to talk to Arnie? Perhaps, I could do some good about getting you two back together . . . maybe . . . '

She became pensive. 'No, thank you. He'll come back when he finds out how wrong he's been. It's all in his head, Charlie. I'm the same woman he married all those years ago. That rape might have changed my mind and my soul, but the body is still the same. All it takes is a good shower and a douche to correct that. He'll realize that in time.'

Her earthy remark shocked him, but that was Peg . . . earthy and honest to a fault.

He replied, 'OK, if you're sure.' He rose to go, smiling at her as he helped her out of the booth, joking, 'If you get any more good news, give me a call.'

She smiled bringing him close to her. 'I will. Charlie, I wish you and your girl all the happiness in the world. I really do, love,' and she kissed him on the lips, softly, as they always did. She smiled and walked off, turning at the door to blow him a kiss.

He thought, 'Damn fool, Arnie.'

24

Meagan stood looking at the house, nestled against the hill which nestled against the higher hills, which nestled against the mountains, the great Rockies. It was a chalet type of design, covered with Western red cedar. It had high-peak roofs, and several balconies from the upper floor bedrooms. It sat on ten acres, more or less, and a stream ran across the front yard, if five acres could be called a yard. A picturesque laminated-wood bridge spanned the stream, and if one looked carefully, every now and then a rainbow trout could be seen scooting by on its way to the White River.

Charlie placed his arm around her, and with Erin on his other arm, asked, 'Well, ladies, how do you like it?'

'Oh, Charlie, it's gorgeous, but, why did you bring us all the way out here to see it? Are we going to broker this for a client?' She was proud that she had learned some real estate jargon, already.

'Uh huh,' he replied. 'I can buy it cheap on a distress sale, so I thought the firm should pick it up while we had the chance. How do you like it?'

She purred. 'Oh, I love it. What a beautiful house? Huh, Erin?'

Erin replied. 'I love it, too. I wonder what it's like to call something like that, home.'

Meagan looked pensive. 'I wonder . . . '

'Well, girls, you will have the chance to find out, because, if you like it enough Meagan, honey, it will be your house,' and he added as he looked at Erin, too, 'our home.'

Meagan's jaw dropped. Her eyes widened. She looked at Charlie, then at Erin, then at Charlie, and all she could say was, 'Oh, Charlie, don't play games with me, honey. You trying to break my poor ole country girl heart?'

He placed his arm around her waist, smiling down at her. 'This is no game, honey! If you like it . . it's yours. I'll buy it for the company, regardless, so you don't have to take it, if you don't like it. I have the key if you'd like to take a look at it.'

Tears were streaming down her cheeks as she looked at him, shaking her head in disbelief.

He motioned to the car, saying, 'If you ladies will get in, we'll drive up to the house . . . '

'No,' she protested, 'let's walk, so I can savour every step as we get closer to it.'

'If that is what you want,' and taking the two women by the hand, said, 'come on, girls, let's take a look at our home.'

As they walked to the front door, she paused, then looking at him, said softly, 'Please, Charlie, carry me over the threshold, just like they do in the movies . . . . like Scarlett and Rhett . . . please,' and she raised her arms in anticipation.

He smiled, handing the key to Erin, saying to her, 'If you will be so kind as to open the door, I'll carry Scarlett in, but damn it, Meagan, I am not carrying you up the stairs to the bedroom . . . '

She laughed. 'I'll bet you wouldn't say that if Erin wasn't here . . . '

Erin laughed. 'I'll wait in the car if you two want to consummate this house deal right now.'

Charlie picked up his betrothed, laughing. 'It'll wait.'

As they entered the split-level foyer, he placed Scarlett on her feet and she gazed inward and upward. The stairs led to the lower level with a huge living area. It had an exposed beam ceiling and the feature wall boasted a stone fireplace capable of taking six-foot logs. There were book shelves on either side of the fireplace, all done in cedar.

She stood with mouth open, and then, looking around she descended the stairs and sat in the nearest chair, exclaiming, 'I have to sit down, honey, I feel weak . . . this is too much for me,' and then she noticed . . . the house was completely furnished.

'Charlie. All the furniture is in place. Did you have it furnished?' she asked in panted breath.

'No,' he replied, proudly. 'It came furnished. The woman who owned it was a decorator, but she and her builder husband split a few months ago and, well, she wanted nothing to remind her of him, so she sold it all. Nice, huh?'

Erin had walked off on her own, taking a tour, and she could be heard from room to room to exclaim, 'Geez . . . will you look at this! Geez! Oh, Mama! Oh, Charlie! Geez.'

Meagan rose to her feet, taking Charlie's hand, saying, 'I have my strength back. I want to see it all, but, mainly, the kitchen and the bedroom,' as she smiled, 'The two rooms that keep a man happy.'

He took her hand, replying, 'I can't argue with that.'

As the tour ended, he asked 'Well, do you like it? Shall I buy it for you?'

She embraced him. 'Do you have to ask? Charlie, I've never owned anything in my life, not even an outhouse, and now. . . . '

'Meagan, your old life is finished . . . for good. You're going to embark on a new life . . . a new odyssey . . . with me.'

'Oh, honey, you've made me so happy,' and seeing Erin coming down the stairs from the bedroom area, asked, 'Erin, honey, how do you like it?'

'Geez, I love it. Can I have my choice of bedrooms, Mama?'

'No you can't, honey, but you can have second choice, huh Charlie,' as she hugged him, again.

The two women hugged him simultaneously, with Meagan looking into his eyes, saying, 'Oh, Charlie, God blessed me the day you walked into that little cafe and I asked . . . 'What'll you have, cowboy?' Did you ever dream it would end this way?'

Erin joked, 'I damn sure didn't Mama . . . '

'Hush, Erin, or I'll send you to your room,' the mother teased.

Erin replied, laughing, 'I don't mind in the least.'

'Come on you two, if you like the house, then it is all settled. Let's go eat. I'm hungry.'

'Oh, Charlie, let's eat here, in our home . . . please. I'll cook something, won't we Erin?'

Erin grinned. 'Uh huh, Mama. We will.'

Charlie laughed. 'We have no food in this place, as yet.'

'Do you have any money left to buy some?' Meagan joked.

He pulled out both pockets, shaking his head. 'No!'

Meagan replied, 'Then I guess we'll have to live on love.'

Erin exclaimed, 'Sure, that's fine for you and Charlie! What do you expect me to do . . . starve?'

Meagan and Charlie pulled her close. Meagan said, 'No, honey, we have enough love for you, too.'

Charlie broke loose, and going to the door, 'I suggest we find a restaurant and express our love over a good meal.'

Erin countered with, 'I'm with you, Charlie.'

Meagan shrugged her shoulders. 'So much for romance, I guess. Let's go. I'm hungry too.'

As they returned later that night after a drive from Summit County where the house was located, they climbed the steps to the little apartment.

Huffing as she reached the top, she turned to her betrothed, asking, 'Charlie, honey, tell me . . . is it really true that I won't have to climb these miserable steps any more? I can't believe it.'

'It's true, my love . . . for sure. If it's alright with you let's move tomorrow,' and as they entered the drab apartment, he asked, 'How much of this stuff do you want to take with you? I need to know so I can rent a truck large enough to carry your furniture . . . '

She grabbed his arm. 'Charlie, honey, did you notice that the whole house was furnished? With nice furniture?'

'Uh huh, I sure did.'

'And did I understand you to say it went with the house. In other words, we own it?'

'Uh huh.'

She looked around, pointing to her worn out, frazzled furniture; smiling, saying, 'Why on earth would I want to take this miserable stuff with me?'

He smiled back. 'I agree, but I just wanted to make sure. I thought you might have some sentimental value on it.'

She held him close, purring, 'Didn't you tell me that I was beginning a new life from here on out?'

'I sure did.'

'Then, Charlie honey, when I walk out of this apartment tomorrow, I want nothing but the clothes you've bought me, and as far as I'm concerned they can burn the damn place down. I have some unpleasant memories of this place. You know it was where Erin got raped by that no-good husband of mine. I think of it every time I look at that spot where she killed him.'

She shook her head, adding, 'I will never miss this place as long as I live. The only pleasant memory I have is that night I brought you home to sleep,' and she teased, 'That night you were one of the homeless.'

'See what happens when you bring strays home.'

She held him close, nuzzling his neck, whispering, 'Uh huh.'

He inquired, 'How long do you think Erin will be at the cafe?'

She broke away. 'Not long enough for what you have in mind, I'm sure . . . later, sweetheart . . . I promise.'

He looked concerned. 'Meagan . . . are you sure you're able to do it . . . you know what I mean,' he teased.

'My God, honey, are we going to go through this every time you get in the mood, or I get in the mood. Let me worry about it. If I can't I'll let you know . . . OK?'

He said, contritely, 'I didn't mean to harp on it. I just want to be sure you're all right, that's all . . '

'I'm all right for now . . . OK?' and as she heard Erin come through the door, she poked him in the ribs. 'See what I mean. Oh, Erin, honey, did you tell the gang at the cafe goodbye for me?'

She shook her head. 'No, Mama, I think you should

go and tell them goodbye, yourself. They all asked about you, and when I told them we were moving, tomorrow, they all said, ''Isn't Meagan coming to say goodbye?'' I think you ought to, Mama. It's only right, huh, Charlie?'

Not wanting to get into the argument, he merely said, 'If she wants to . . . it's up to her, Erin.'

'Oh, I guess Erin is right.' She chuckled. 'I was glad to have that miserable job when I needed it. I'll go and tell them goodbye, tomorrow, I guess, but for now I'm tired. I'm going to bed now. Are you coming, Charlie . . . honey? Sweetheart?' she teased.

Erin grinned. 'I think you ought to go, Charlie. Something tells me you might be missing out on a hell of a lot of fun.'

'Oh, Erin, you're so tacky some times,' the mother scolded, smiling.

'I know, Mama, but I'm honest as hell too. Have fun!'

As they climbed into bed later, Meagan began her slide over to his side, but Charlie pushed her away, saying, 'No, not tonight, Meagan.'

Hurt, she inquired, 'Do you have a headache, sweetie?'

'No, I feel fine.'

'Well, what's the problem?' she laughed. 'Can't cut it anymore, huh?'

'Don't taunt me, woman. I want to wait until tomorrow night, that's why.'

'What is so sacred about tomorrow night, may I ask?'

He drew her close to him. 'Because, Meagan, my love, tomorrow night we will be in our new home . . that's why!'

'Oh, I see! Well, haven't you ever done it two nights in a row, Charlie, or are you getting too old?'

He thought about it for a while, replying, softly, 'I see your point. Come here, woman. I guess we do owe one to the old place, don't we?'

She slid over. 'Uh huh!'

25

To celebrate their leaving Mountain View and the cafe, Erin suggested they all go out for one last breakfast at the place. 'Slumming,' as she put it, to which Charlie replied, 'I'll be burping that breakfast all day, Erin,' to which Meagan, offended waitress that she was, retorted, 'Oh, Charlie, you have a nerve! You were happy to eat there when you came to town.'

'Uh huh, but not when I leave it.'

She took his hand. 'Come on, it'll be fun, especially when I tell them where to shove this job . . . '

'Meagan!' he shouted. 'You're being very tacky now.'

'I know it honey, but there are times in this world when you just gotta.'

They loaded nothing but their personal belongings in the U-Haul trailer Charlie had hooked up to the Jeep and, as they took a backwards glance at the little village which had been their home for several years, Erin and Meagan waved through the rear window like silly schoolgirls on an outing. Why? Because they were happy. They were doing what thousands . . . maybe, millions of people have wanted to do in their lives. They have left it behind and started a new one, believing down deep in their hearts, that the new would be an improvement over the old.

It was a hectic day of packing and unpacking, loading and unloading, rushing into town for groceries and a myriad of other things they had forgotten from time to time. When time came to start supper, Meagan looked at Charlie, with begging eyes, and Erin looked at him with begging eyes. He was no fool. He was tired, too, and he knew he had two tired women on his hands, so he did the only thing any decent man could do. He took them by the hands and said, 'Let's go find a good restaurant.'

There were no words of protest from either female as they compliantly allowed themselves to be led to the Mercedes for a trip to town.

Charlie observed as they started down the entrance drive to the front gate, 'You sure you want to live way out here in the country? You have to drive miles just to get a loaf of bread and a quart of milk?'

Meagan looked back at the house . . . her house. There was a full moon shining and the moon beams played hide-and-seek with the fascade as the scud clouds moved over it in a gentle breeze.

Her eyes became moist as she murmured, 'Uh huh, I'm sure,' as she turned to him.

He saw the moonlight reflect from her moist eyes and he thought, 'God, I love that woman.'

This was to be their first night in their own home. Meagan and Erin had never lived in such a place. They had never known any degree of privacy in the small apartment and Erin in prison, had certainly not experienced any, where even going to the bathroom is a spectator sport. They were amazed at the room each had . . . their space.

Erin teased, 'I'll be lonesome, Mama! Why I won't even be able to listen to you and Charlie in the bedroom anymore. What'll I do for entertainment.'

Without shame, Meagan replied, 'Watch TV.'

Charlie had that expectant look that men get at times like this, for he had been promised a night of pure rapture on this, their first night in their own home, but he was worried as he watched his betrothed later that evening. She seemed listless as they dressed for bed, and when she announced that she was going to take a shower, after having showered just before going to eat, he was concerned. He took her hand, bringing it up to his lips, asking, 'What's the matter, honey? Is something wrong? You look pale . . . '

She smiled a weak smile, kissing his fingertips too, as she responded, 'It's a good thing you ravished me last night honey, because I'm afraid tonight is out. I'm bleeding, again, and it is not my period time, so I guess I still have problems. I'm sorry.'

He held her close. 'Oh, Meagan, honey, I don't care about that. I'm only worried about you. You have to go back to the doctor, again. We have to find out what is going on . . . '

She turned away from him. 'I already know what is going on, Charlie. I have cancer.'

He had never heard the dreaded word before from her or the doctors, and he was shocked. He shouldn't have been. He had felt it all along, but he felt sure they could whip it . . . the two of them, and as he held her close he whispered., 'We'll beat it, honey . . . you and me, together . . . we'll beat it. You'll see.'

She nodded, looking at him, trying to smile 'Sure. It will take more than that to get Meagan Mahoney down,' At the mention of her last name, she looked at him. 'Charlie, you didn't mention it, yet. Did you find out if your divorce was final or not?'

'Oh, I'm sorry honey. In the excitement of the house and all, I forgot to tell you. Yes, I'm a free man.'

She walked to the bed, still holding his hand and, as they both sat, she began to sob softly.

She looked at him, shaking her head. 'Charlie, I'm giving you one more chance to leave me now with no hard feelings and find yourself a healthy young thing. I don't feel I have the right to hang you with this. If you leave me now, I swear to you I will never hold it against you . . . ever. I think you're a fool if you don't,' and she could not suppress the tears.

He took her to him, holding her close, as he responded, holding her chin in his hands, looking deep into her eyes, 'Not only am I not leaving you, Meagan, but I want us to be married as soon as possible.'

She returned his deep look, with tears filling her eyes. 'I hope you realize that you will be a widower before too long a time . . . '

He said, 'Hush . . . don't talk like that. You don't know that for sure . . . '

She nodded. 'I know . . . believe me, I know.'

'Even if that is true, and I don't believe it is, we will live it to the fullest.

'I can take it, you know . . . I really can. I will have only one regret when I go . . . only one.'

'What regret?'

She sighed. 'I wanted to give you a baby so bad, honey. That will be my only regret. I can't give you a baby now. It's too late, Charlie. I didn't tell you, but the doctor said I need a hysterectomy and in a hurry. They wanted to do it while you were gone, but I wouldn't let them. I wanted to be married first. I want you to marry a whole woman.'

'But that is not the end of the world, Meagan. Thousands of women have hysterectomies every year and live to ripe old age. You will too, I promise you.'

'Don't make promises you can't keep, Charlie. It is not in your hands, honey. I wish it was. Can we be married soon?'

'We'll be married as soon as I can make arrangements. I'm sure we'll have to have a blood test, don't you think?'

'I'm sure we will.'

'I'll have to call my parents to see if they will fly out for the wedding. I am sure my mother would want to give us a big blast in Texas, but that is out of the question now. We'll have to settle for a small wedding out here. Do you mind?"

'It's the only kind I feel up to. Will your parents come out for it, do you think?'

He shrugged. 'I don't know why they wouldn't. How about you? Do you have relatives you'd want to invite for the ceremony?'

'No. I have aunts and cousins spread around, but we're not close. If they got an invitation from me they would think I just wanted presents, so . . . no. I just want Erin as my bridesmaid, that's all. How about you?'

He thought about it for a while, replying, 'No, I will

ask my Father to be my best man. That's all,' and in a moment of excitement, he asked,'Where would you like to go on your honeymoon?'

She considered for a moment. 'Nowhere. I want my honeymoon to be in this house . . . our home. I want to spend as much time as I can in it, before . . . ' and she didn't finish it, as she gave him a weak smile.

'Well, if that is what you want for now we can always go on a honeymoon later.'

She shrugged her shoulders in despair. 'Sure . . . later.'

He rose and went to the phone. 'I'll call my parents right now. It's not too late. I hope they are still up,' as he dialled his father's house number. The phone rang several times before he answered.

'Dad. It's Charlie. I hope I'm not calling too late, but I have great news for you and mother. Meagan and I are getting married! When? As soon as we can. Yes, we are in a hurry. No, Dad,' he chuckled, 'she is not pregnant.' (Meagan winced at these words) 'Do you think you and Mother can fly out for the ceremony? Oh, she is asleep. Well, you two talk it over in the morning and call me as soon as you can. Yes, Betty has the number. I called her this morning. OK Dad, yes, everything is fine . . . going OK. Yes, I'll give her your love. Goodnight, Dad.'

Meagan sat up in bed. 'What did he say?'

Charlie smiled. 'He said wild horses could not keep him away.'

'And your mother? What about her?'

'Well, she was asleep, but I feel sure she will come if he does.'

'Oh I see. I hope so. When did you tell them it would be? I don't know when I'm getting married,' she teased.

'If you feel up to it in the morning, we'll get all the legal work done, and then we can plan a wedding . . . OK?'

'OK,' she smiled, 'but, Charlie, keep it simple, huh, I know how you are.'

He pulled her to him, holding her close. 'How am I?'

'You're the sweetest, most lovable, most generous, most adorable man in the whole world and I love you so much it is a sin.'

'I'll forgive you if God does,' he teased.

She snuggled into his neck, whispering, 'See what I mean, Charlie, You're a saint.'

He smiled, holding her close.

She was up early the next morning. He could hear her downstairs, humming and singing, sometimes to herself and other times quite audibly. He had no trouble making out the words to Pasty Cline's great hit song . . . *Crazy*. He smiled as he heard her accent the words. "Ca–raazy . . . Ca––raazy for loving you . . . "

He went to the edge of the balcony which formed the hallway to the bedroom area and he could see her with a feather duster in her hand, busily dusting the furniture which had all been spotlessly cleaned prior to their moving in.

He chided her. 'Why are you cleaning furniture that was cleaned just two days ago . . . may I ask?'

She looked up at him, smiling. 'Good morning to you too, honey. Oh people don't know how to clean anymore, Charlie. If we're gong to have a wedding soon, I've got to get this house in order.'

He was delighted that she felt that well this morning so he laughed it off, replying, 'Go ahead if that makes you happy, but don't get too involved with what you're doing. Remember, we have to go and get all the papers and the blood tests, and . . . '

She gasped. 'Oh, my God! I forgot. I'm coming . . . '

A voice came from another bedroom door as a sleepy Erin, eyes half opened, cried out, 'Geez, can't you guys be quiet? You never made that much noise in that little apartment . . . geez!'

Meagan winked at her betrothed. 'I'm going up to get dressed.'

He teased,'Aren't you going to fix my breakfast, first?'

She pondered that. 'Oh, honey, please fix your own. I've got to get dressed.'

He shook his head. 'I thought you said only two days ago that the two rooms to keep a man happy in were the kitchen and the bedroom . . .

She stuck her head out the bedroom door, yelling back at him, 'Well, you didn't have much fun in the bedroom, last night, so there is no reason to break that trend in the kitchen this morning.'

As he stuck his head in the refrigerator for the juice, he murmured to himself. 'Makes sense to me!'

She, once again, stuck her head out the bedroom door. 'Charleeee, you never tell me what we're going to do. Where are we going and when are we coming back?"

He raised his head. 'Oh, I forgot to tell you. We're going to Denver for a couple of days . . . '

She was adamant. 'See what I mean, Charlie! If I hadn't asked you, you wouldn't have said a thing until I climbed into that car,' and she added,'without any clothes . . . or nothing!'

He was truly contrite. 'I'm sorry. I forgot to mention it.'

She stuck her head out the door, again. 'See what I mean? I promise you, Charlie, I'm cracking down on you after the wedding,' and she giggled. She felt good today.

Erin took her usual position in the back seat of the Mercedes, sitting on the edge with her arms on the back of the front seat.

'Mama, what colour dress are you getting for the wedding? I hope it's a colour I like . . . '

She grinned at her daughter. 'I thought I was getting married.'

'Well, you are, but I want my dress to match yours, and I only look good in a few colours.'

The mother turned around, asking, 'Who told you you were getting a new dress for the wedding?'

She smiled demurely. 'Charlie.'

She poked him in the ribs. 'Anything else I should know about my wedding, Charlie . . . honey?'

'Uh uh . . . nothing I can think of,' he teased.

She leaned back. 'Oh, I'm so glad you and Erin have everything under control.' and then, sitting up, hurriedly, 'don't you think I should see my doctor before the wedding,' and, with a side ways glance at her daughter, 'You know what I mean.'

The daughter interrupted. 'I know what you mean, Mama. I think it would be a good idea, too.'

The mother shook her head in resignation. 'Oh my God, don't we have any secrets from this girl?'

The daughter grinned. 'Not too many Mama. Remember, we're a family.'

Charlie became serious. 'Yes Meagan, I think you should see a Denver doctor for a second opinion.'

'Oh God, Charlie, will they want to run more tests?'

'Yes I'm sure they will, and I think you should want them to. You don't want them to form an opinion based on the same tests from Vail do you?'

'Sure, that's easy for you to say, It's not your body that's being violated every hour or so.'

He became sympathetic. 'I know, honey, but I think it's best for you to know the truth, don't you.'

She became pensive. 'Sometimes, I think it's best not to know the truth. The truth hurts you know.'

Erin became sad. She sat back in her seat, saying nothing for a change. She had nothing to say.

They rode in silence for quite some time. Finally Meagan sat up, excited once again, 'You know what I'd really like to do, if we have time in Denver . . . '

'What?'

'Remember that beauty parlour you talked me into going to when I didn't want to . . . remember:'

He smiled. 'I remember. They made you into the ravishing beauty I see before me now.'

She smiled in agreement. 'Uh huh, they did too. Can we go back there?'

'You can do anything you want sweetheart! You're going to be a bride. No man can refuse his bride anything. You know that.'

She grinned. 'If men could keep that attitude, Charlie, do you know there would be no such thing as divorce.'

He smiled, looking at her. 'I know that.'

26

It was a cold, miserable day in Denver as the trio made their way to Stapleton Airport. It was the kind of day when people in the high Rockies wished they were on the gulf coast of Texas and the people from the gulf coast of Texas wished they had remained there. It looked like snow. The ski bums would be happy, but they were the only ones.

Meagan was scared as the Mercedes veered around the icy roads.

She scolded the driver. 'Honey, please slow down. You're driving too fast. . . .'

He was already irritated from the adverse driving conditions. 'Dammit, Meagan, you sound like a wife.'

'Well, I'm trying to live long enough to become one,' and realizing she had said the wrong words, she became quiet and contrite. 'I'm sorry, honey. I just don't want us to wreck before we pick your daddy up at the airport. Is he flying commercial?'

He shook his head. 'No, he and some other men have a Lear jet they own together . . . sort of a time share plane. The Lear is too expensive to justify any of them to operate separately, so they bought it together. Works out fine if there is no conflict of scheduling.'

Erin, innocent thing that she was, inquired, 'How fast does it go Charlie?'

He shrugged. 'Depends on the winds but, with no wind to count on, she'll do an easy four hundred knots at altitude.'

'Geez!' came from the back seat.

Meagan had been reluctant to ask, for she knew it was a touchy subject with him, but she wanted to know. 'You still don't know if your mother is coming or not . . . '

He was embarrassed to reply. 'I only know what Dad has told me. She has a bad cold, and when he called last night and asked about the weather, he told me she might not come because she felt like she was getting the flu. My mother is very susceptible to the flu, it seems. He did say she was quite upset, or would be, if she could not come for the wedding.'

Meagan turned to look out the window, replying. 'I see.'

They had parked in the general aviation parking area and, bundled against the cold and rain, they made their way to the waiting room. Charlie inquired at operations if the Lear had come in and was informed that it was entering the traffic pattern at the moment.

Meagan was excited as she prepared herself to meet her future father-in-law. She had already girded herself for the event of the mother's no-show.

She squared her shoulders and stuck out her jaw, thinking to herself, 'It's her loss, not mine!'

She felt if she were to ever have any kind of relationship with the parents, it would be through the father. She had written the mother off as a lost cause, but she had given no inkling of that to her husband. On the contrary, she had feigned real regret at her possibly not showing up.

The two women stood close to Charlie in the waiting room as the sleek little jet came to a stop on the ramp. The flagman crossed his arms to signal a cut off of the twin jets. They watched with great anticipation as the door slowly opened and a man emerged, alone. It was the pilot opening the door and checking to see that the ladder leading to the tarmac had dug in properly. He descended, and as good corporate pilots are trained to do, he reached into the plane for a golfing umbrella for his passenger.

Charlie moved forward as he saw the familiar figure of his father emerge from the plane. He wore his leather cap, his trademark on cold days. Charlie knew that if his mother were on board, the father would open the umbrella, take her hand and bring her close to him to share the umbrella but, as the father stood talking to the pilot, obviously giving him instructions as to the plane's return schedule, there was another person appearing in the doorway, and Charlie's and Meagan's heart gave a leap, but it was only the co-pilot coming out to stretch his legs before the return flight.

They waited, but no one else could be seen, and the reality of the situation had set in. The mother had not come to her son's wedding.

Charlie forced a smile, and turning to the two women, he asked, 'Please wait here in the lounge. The weather is too bad. I'll go out and meet him, and bring him in. That'll give you ladies time to primp,' he smiled.

Meagan returned a smile, at least, a brave attempt. She was hurt . . . very hurt, for she interpreted the mother's refusal to come as a rejection of her. She could see it no other way. She fought back tears as she watched her betrothed go out into the weather.

Erin could read her thoughts, and she placed her arm around her mother's waist, and whispered. 'What the hell, Mama! We'll do it without her.'

Meagan smiled weakly, as she watched Charlie rush out to meet his father. Alexander Forester looked very much like what he was . . . a rich and successful man. He wore a full length leather coat of matching leather to his cap. They could see, through the mist and rain, his grey hair below the line of the cap. He was smiling as he saw his son, and a fine set of almost white teeth showed, crowned with a well trimmed moustache the same colour of grey as his hair.

The two men embraced each other, and the women could see the father bring the son under the umbrella as they walked. They made a few steps, and then they stopped to engage in conversation. It seemed animated at times, with one gesturing with his hand, and then the other. They would walk a few steps more, and repeat the process.

Meagan began to get nervous. Her hands were sweating and she scolded herself for being nervous. Erin could feel her hand tightening her grip on hers, and she squeezed back, chiding, 'Relax, Mama, he is only the second most important man in your life. Why should you be nervous?'

The mother looked up smiling, replying, 'I've got a feeling that this man is going to be very important in my life. He may hold the key to my future with his son,' she replied, nervously.

Before she could complete the sentence, the doors to the foyer opened and Alexander Forester saw her standing there. He flashed his grin for which he was so famous in the business circles of South Texas. Many a Texas matron had been charmed by it, as well as their spouses, for he always concluded a business deal with a warm handshake and an even warmer grin.

He didn't wait for introductions. He walked up to the two women – stopped – smiled – turned to his son, saying, 'Charlie, tell me which is the mother and which is the daughter. I can't tell.'

It was at that instant that Meagan Mahoney fell in love with her future father-in-law, and it would last as long as she did.

He dropped all pretences as he took her in his arms, saying, 'Meagan, my dear, I'm so happy that we finally meet.'

He held her at arms length, looking at her deeply. She was surprised. She was not intimidated one bit, as she felt sure she would be. He was as warm as she expected the mother to be cold. Then they embraced again.

He broke off, and looking at the expectant young woman standing nervously by he exclaimed, 'And this must be Erin. What a lovely creature! Charlie I don't know how you can stand it. No man deserves having two beauties like this around him.'

Charlie grinned. 'How true.'

Since no mention was made by either side of the mother, it was Meagan who broke the ice. 'I'm so sorry Mrs Forester could not make it . . . '

Charlie's eyes widened. 'Oh, in the excitement of it all, I haven't had time to tell you, but she is in the hospital.

She's really got the flu, and . . . and . . . well, she insisted on Dad's coming to the wedding . . . and she sends her deepest regrets to you, Meagan . . . she is so sorry.'

The father reinforced the son's argument. 'She is really sick, poor thing. I had almost decided not to come, myself, but she would not hear of it. She insisted that I came, so we figured the best thing to do was to put her in a hospital where I would not have to worry about her,' and he corrected it to, 'Anymore than I would have to.'

Meagan felt better about the mother's absence. It was apparently true. She was ill. She couldn't believe they would lie about that . . . either of them, as she responded, 'I'm so sorry to hear that she is ill. I hope she will be better real soon.'

The father smiled. 'I'm sure she will, my dear. Now, let's try not to let her illness and her absence cast a cloud over this great occasion,' as he nodded to the outside, adding, 'In spite of the weather. My God do people really enjoy living in this stuff?' I guess so, or the ski resorts would dry up. Come to think of it, we're getting ready to invest a lot of money in these parts, so I'd better get used to it myself, although it will take some doing.'

Charlie smiled at all. 'Shall we start back?'

The father watched as the pilots carried his luggage into the waiting room, and he turned to his son. 'What's the game plan, Charlie?'

Charlie and the two women watched as the pilots carried two pieces of matching leather luggage and four cardboard boxes and placed them on the floor.

The father raised his hands, waving the pilots off with, "Don't worry about the luggage, fellows. You had better get into the air before they close the airport . . . '

The chief pilot shook his head. 'It's too late, Mr Forester. They've already closed it. The ceiling is down to the ground. It looks like we're here for the night.'

Erin, being twenty years old and in unbelievably good health, heard these words like a clarion call to action. With practised eye, she now paid attention to the two pilots, which she had not wasted her time in doing before. A quick glance told her the older one, about forty, was obviously married because he looked like it, and upon closer scrutiny,confirmed it with a glance at his wedding ring.

But, the other, who had already stolen a few discreet glances, was not. He had that unmarried look. They smiled at each other, but the pilots knew their place. They were hired help until the boss told them otherwise.

Alexander Forester took command, for it was his style. He turned to his son, saying, 'I don't want to try to run this show, son, but don't you think it is foolish to head for the high country in this kind of weather. It is getting late and I've driven on those mountain roads often enough in my long life to know better . . '

'I guess you're right, Dad, but the only alternative is to bunk down in Denver for the night. We have no reservations at any of the hotels, but I guess we could get some.' He looked at the women. 'Do you girls have enough clothes for a one-night stop over?'

With eyes widened in anticipation, Erin nodded without looking at her mother, and then, the mother sensing her daughter was on a hunting expedition with the young pilot, smiled and nodded.

Charlie shrugged. 'I guess we need to get some hotel rooms, Dad. They're liable to get scarce if they shut Stapleton down for the night. That big terminal will empty fast for those who can get rooms.'

'You're right, ' answered the father, and being accustomed to these schedule changes, he turned to the pilots. 'Eric, you and Darren get to the phones and get us four or five rooms.'

Erin's heart jumped. His name was Darren. She loved the name, she felt.

'Any place in particular, chief?'

Alexander Forester looked at his son, gesturing. 'Any preference, folks?'

Charlie replied. 'I don't think we can be choosy. The airport Stouffer is real nice, isn't it, honey?'

Meagan's heart felt a tug. It was there they had first . . . you know! She smiled in reply, with Charlie nodding to the pilots.

It was the chief pilot who told his assistant, 'I'll take care of the hotels. You get on one of the other horns and call Corpus. Tell them what the deal is on the weather,' and turning to Alexander Forester, he added, 'We were supposed to take Mr and Mrs Clayton to the Bahamas in the morning . . . '

Alexander Forester shrugged. 'He'll either have to go commercial or postpone his trip but, I'm sure with two hundred fifty million in the bank, he can solve his problems.'

Erin looked at her mother, and they both swallowed hard.

The head pilot returned, smiling, 'I had to take three suites, Mr Forster. The single rooms were all gone.'

'That's fine, Eric. We'll make out if one suite has two bedrooms . . . '

'It has, sir. I put the rooms on my corporate card so we could confirm. That's the only way they'd take it.'

The older man nodded. 'That's fine. Just handle it like you usually do, with the corporation billing the Forester Company.'

'Yes, sir. As soon as Darren gets back, we are ready to go if you are. I've got the Lear in a hanger. Cost some bucks, believe me, but I know that is what the partners like.'

He nodded. 'That's right.'

As the young co-pilot returned, Erin had the first opportunity to give him a real once over. He was of medium height, slim build, with dark hair combed back without a parting. His complexion looked like his mother had succeeded in making him eat all his veggies, every day. She felt warm about a man for the first time since her Vail excursion into the world of never-never. Her libido was aroused, and as her mother looked at her, she tried very hard to keep her nostrils from flaring . . . a dead give away to her knowing mother. She did not see the mother's smile.

As they approached the hotel desk Meagan began to twitch nervously and she pulled her betrothed off to one side with a whispered, 'I have to talk to you, Charlie.'

He allowed himself to be guided behind a lobby

column, replying, 'Sure, honey, what is it?'

'The rooms,' she responded. 'I don't want you and me to share a room . . '

'But, why? We've been doing that for months,' he interjected.

'I know, but your father was not there. I can't, Charlie. It will look so cheap . . . like I'm your mistress instead of your intended.'

He looked to see if she was serious. She was. He understood her feelings and he respected them, foolish and unnecessary as they were.

He smiled. 'OK, honey, if that is what you want.'

He returned to the group as his father signed in for all in the party.

He pulled his father aside, and in a whisper, asked. 'Do you mind if you and I share a suite, Dad. I'll explain later.'

The father looked at the son, then at Meagan, and he nodded. 'Fine with me,' with a puzzled look. The father looked at the group. 'Let's see then, the room arrangements are Meagan and Erin in one suite. Charlie, you and I in one, and the two fly boys in the other.' He smiled. 'Is that OK with everyone?'

As Meagan shook her head in assent, Erin gave her a quizzical look, but said nothing.

The bellhop who had been standing nearby, nodded, picked up the keys, and said, 'Follow me, please,' and headed for the elevators, followed by all.

After removing his leather coat and hat in the room, the father went to the telephone. 'I've got to call your mother. Do you want to talk to her, Charlie?'

'Well, I guess I should inquire about her health,' he replied, smiling at his father who was dialling the number.

The phone call to the mother over, the father sat on the bed watching his son open his luggage.

He watched him for a while, then, 'Charlie, I don't mean to pry, or be presumptuous, but I assumed you and Meagan would share a room. Correct me if I am wrong, but haven't you two been cohabiting for the past few months?'

He looked embarrassed. 'Sure, we've been living together for several months but . . . she has this old fashioned idea of morality, especially around you, that we should maintain our decorum until after the ceremony.' He shrugged. 'I know it is silly, but you don't know Meagan . . . '

The father laughed. 'I'm beginning to know her, and I must say, son, she is a charming girl. I can see what attracted you to her. She is different, isn't she, but quite charming. And, that Erin . . . what a beauty. I just can't believe that girl was ever in prison . . . '

'I know. That is a wild story . . . like something from a soap opera, but it is true.' and looking at the father, asked, 'Are you hungry? I'll call the girls and see if they're ready to eat.'

The father hesitated, then, 'Let's make a big night of it. The weather is too bad to leave the hotel, but I can have the caterer set up an engagement supper in one of the private rooms which most convention hotels have, and . . . '

The son looked at the father with some resignation as he responded, 'Let me see if Meagan is up to it. She's been ill, lately, and . . . '

The father looked up. 'Oh? I'm sorry to hear that. Getting ill just before the wedding is not too good. I hope it is not anything serious.'

'I'll explain it to you later tonight . . . when we come back from eating. I'll call the girls, now.'

Meagan seemed to be in a good mood during the supper. The father gave her a scrutinizing glance from time to time to detect what her illness was. He had assumed it was a cold but, he concluded, that was not it. She sat at his right throughout the evening, and she was surprised to see how warm he was. She had assumed he was as cold as the mother appeared to be. Didn't he have to be to live with her? But, he was not. He was warm and attentive, with a ready wit and laugh to go with it. She liked this man . . . this father of the man she loved and would marry. She wished he lived closer. They could be real friends, she was sure.

Alexander Forester touched her hand, motioning his head towards Erin and the young pilot, smiling, 'I think we have a budding romance going on there between Erin and Darren.'

Meagan smiled. 'At that age, Mr Forester, it doesn't take much, does it?'

'No,' he replied, 'not as I can recall those years in my life, and,' he continued, 'Meagan, I wish you would call me Alex, if you can bring yourself to do it. Mr Forester is so formal and stiff. It makes me feel old . . older than I am, and that is old enough. Can you do that?'

She gave him a warm smile. 'It won't be easy, but I'll try, if you'll bear with me when I forget.'

He nodded. 'Do the best you can. I want us to be good friends as well as married kin. I'm really a country boy at heart, you know, from the hills of west Texas . . . a Texas hillbilly, my wife calls me,' and he added, 'when she is angry with me.'

She smiled. 'And, I'm a Colorado hillbilly.' She laughed. 'I guess we're both a pair of hillbillys,' and she felt compelled to lean over and kiss him on the cheek.

He smiled, saying softly, 'Thank you, my dear. I appreciate that. I wish my wife had come, Meagan. She doesn't know what she is missing in not meeting you and Erin.'

'Well, perhaps, in time . . . '

'Hey, hey . . . you two!' from Charlie. 'What is all that kissing going on between my betrothed and my father? I knew, Meagan, honey, that once you met the father the son would be on the way out.'

She laughed. 'Oh, I wouldn't say that, now, but, if I had met him first . . . well . . . '

27

There was a pianist just off the postage-stamp dance floor, and he began to play the nostalgic music of his trade. Erin had that hungry, 'gee, I wish he'd ask me to dance' look on her face, so the young pilot, who could read facial expressions as well as the next, asked, 'Would you like to dance, Erin?'

She smiled, nodding yes 'But, I don't dance very well.'

He smiled back. 'Neither do I, but I'm willing to try if you are. When music is that slow, you can usually fake your way through it.'

'Uh huh . . . I hope so.'

They held each other close . . . real close, saying nothing, just swaying to the slow music. Her hatred of men had lasted only a few weeks, for she did not hate this man one iota, as she nestled her head in his neck. He swallowed often as they moved.

He mentally played with the idea of applying for a job in the Denver area. He wondered if Breckenridge had an airport. Emotions and desires would run high that night with the young couple, only to end in frustration for both, for they were too heavily chaperoned for anything to happen, and then, there was a mental block also. Erin had vowed never to do it on the first three dates . . . with anyone! Not after Bud and Vail!

It was an awkward moment as the party approached their rooms, for all three suites were contiguous, and they had to say goodnights in public, so to speak.

Erin and Darren had wanted to linger longer on the dance floor, but her mother squashed that with a whispered,'It will look cheap, Erin! What will Mr Forester think of you? You just met Darren.'

Even Meagan had a problem of propriety and decorum. She wanted to tell her man goodnight. She wanted to be warm, but platonic, for the sake of appearances. Charlie wanted to be warm, not platonic, and he didn't give a damn about appearances, but all he got was a kiss on the cheek.

He nodded . . . confused and frustrated, as he left her and went into the suite with the father. He sat in a chair in the living area, brooding and moody.

The father was amused as he watched him, making the observation, 'Women are strange creatures, son.' He laughed. 'Every time I think I have them figured out, they fool me again.'

Charlie looked up.'You mean you don't have mother figured out, yet?'

The father smiled. 'No, your mother has no more surprises left in her. I always know what she will do or say. No, it's Betty I'm referring to. I guess you're old enough to know we've had a relationship for over ten years.'

The son nodded. 'I know about it. Do you love her?'

'Charlie, the longer I live the less I am able to define the emotion . . . love. I guess the reason is it means different things to different people. You take that young couple, Erin and Darren, tonight. You could feel the hormones flowing in the interaction between them. It couldn't possibly be love, since they had only just met, but what else would you call it but passion? What Betty and I have, I can only characterise as companionship on a very warm scale. We each needed something from the other, and we each give the other what we need. Does that make sense to you?'

He nodded. 'I understand that very well. I've tried to understand my love for Meagan. At first, it defied conventional wisdom. Amanda would have been more my type had I met her at the right time, but,' and he paused for just a moment in memory of that tormented creature, upon whom life had bestowed all blessings but one . . . contentment.

The father observed, profoundly, 'Love makes us do strange things, Charlie. Take your mother for instance.

She is a fine woman, a lovely woman, but completely lacking in human warmth and compassion. Ours was not a match made in heaven, I guess you know, but I love her in my way,' and he smiled as he added, 'I guess I should say . . . her way.'

'Does she know about Betty?'

'Oh, sure! Your mother is no fool. She figured that out a long time ago.' He sighed.'She told me . . . "if that is what you want, Alex, so be it, but you will have only her, not me. You can't have it both ways. All I ask of you is that you be discreet and never embarrass me in public or private. I will continue to be your wife for the sake of appearances, only."'

He smiled, adding, 'Needless to say, your mother and I have a very platonic relationship, but it has worked for us. And now, I don't want to press you, Charlie, but I think there was something you promised to tell me. If you still want to, and since we are getting profound, I guess this is a good time.'

The son nodded, swallowing hard, looking at the floor, but the telephone rang. He gestured.'I bet that is Meagan.'

He picked up the receiver. 'Hello . . . '

'Oh, Charlie, honey, I hated saying goodnight to you that way. You know that this is not the way I wanted it, but I just don't feel right about sharing a room with you with your daddy next door. He would think we were doing it . . . you know what I mean . . . '

He could not help but smile. 'Yes, Meagan, honey, I know what you mean. It's OK . . . don't worry about it.'

He wanted to say, 'This is the way it has been ever since we have become engaged, thanks to your outmoded, countrified, unrealistic sense of morality, ' but he didn't because his father would have heard him.

Instead, he tried to soothe her with, 'Have a good nights' sleep,' but she would not be deterred. She felt she was missing something and besides she was tired listening to Erin mooning over the young pilot . . . her latest love.

'What are you and your daddy doing, Charlie?'

'We're talking about you, Meagan . . . '

'Oh, Charleeee . . . can I come over?'

'No . . . it's too late. Go to sleep, Meagan.'

'I don't want to! I'm not sleepy.'

'Go to sleep, Meagan. Goodnight.'

'Goodnight, Charlie. Charleeee?'

'What, Meagan?'

'You didn't say "I love you, Meagan",' she teased.

'Consider it said. Now, go to sleep.'

He shook his head as he put the phone down, with his father laughing. 'Meagan, no doubt! You were saying?'

He became solemn as he sat down in the chair. 'You remember I told you earlier that Meagan was ill and you hoped it was not serious . . . well, Dad, it is serious,' and he shook his head as he added, 'about as serious as it can get.'

The father looked astonished at these words. He took the chair next to the son, replying, 'Perhaps, you had better tell me everything, no matter what.'

Charlie had a very difficult time relating the entire episode in what he hoped was the correct chronological order, going all the way to the genesis of their relationship in that dingy cafe in Mountain View. He would rise, every now and then, walk to the window, looking out at what was now a full-fledged snow storm. The blowing snow swirled in circles as the wind played games with the geometry of the building.

The father from time to time would say, 'Oh, my God,' and when he felt his son was finished, he attempted a brave smile, adding, 'But Charlie, it can't be as helpless as you make it out to be. Thousands of women have hysterectomies every year and they live out a long and normal life,' he said with much conviction.

Charlie nodded. 'That's what I know, but, you haven't heard the worst, yet.'

The father looked surprised. 'How can it get much worse?'

He sighed. 'I went back to talk to the doctors, without Meagan being with me. You know how you always taught me to go to the source when you wanted the true story.' The father nodded.

The father girded himself for what was coming. He felt it would be traumatic, as the son continued, 'They told me the cancer had spread to the lymph glands. She is terminal.'

The dreaded words shook Alexander Forester to every fibre of his being. All he could think of asking was, 'Are they sure? Have you had a second opinion?'

He nodded, solemnly. 'They're sure. When they tell you something that serious . . . they're damned sure, believe me.'

'Does Meagan know that she is terminal?'

He shook his head. 'No! All they've told her is that she has uterine cancer and that she needs a hysterectomy, but she gives me the impression that she either knows, or feels it is worse. She is no fool.'

And he then placed his hand on his father's arm, asking, 'And please, Dad, never give her any indication of this. Don't exhibit any form of pity. Don't be deferential to her in this matter. Treat her as you would if you really didn't know. You don't know, Meagan like I do. It would wound her to be treated with pity . . . as if she were going to die right away.'

'How much time does she have?' the father asked, solicitously.

'They're not sure. With luck, she could last a year.'

'Does Erin know?'

He shook his head. 'No, I don't want to tell her, now.'

The father shook his head in despair. 'And, we're still going to have a wedding, aren't we? I admire you, son, for what you're doing. It takes a hell of a man to do this in light of the reality of the situation.'

'Please, Dad. Don't make a hero out of me. She is the hero. She is the one with guts . . . not me.'

'No matter what you say, Charlie, it takes guts to do this. Many men would have cut and run at this news but, at least, you have the decency to stay with her until the end. That takes character. I'm proud of you.'

'She offered me a chance to get out . . . twice.' And he had to suppress a sob. He did not want his father to see him cry if he could help it.

The father placed his hand on the son's shoulder. 'I know money can't solve this problem in the long run but, Charlie, there is so much that can be done, nowadays. We can take her down to Houston, to the M.D. Anderson Cancer Centre. They do marvellous things down there. They could prolong it. I'll provide all the money you need . . . '

He shook his head . . . 'I appreciate it, Dad, but she will not agree to it. I know. She has told me she will never agree to radiation treatment of any kind. She means it too.'

'I can understand her position, although I don't agree with it. When I get sick I want every ounce of modern technology to be tried on me.'

Charlie nodded. 'Well, now I guess you know as much as I do about it. How do you think mother will take this news?'

'I would prefer that we not tell her at this time.'

He nodded. 'She will find out in time, believe me.'

The father replied in agreement, 'But not until the wedding is over. Let's get you two married, first. I know your mother well. She is not known for her compassion. He smiled, adding, 'only for her practicality.'

The son inquired 'Do you think she can ever accept Meagan as her daughter-in-law?'

The father looked embarrassed. 'In outward appearances, yes, for to do otherwise would be a bad reflection on her, but true acceptance comes from the heart, Charlie,' and he raised his hands in despair, adding, 'that, I really can't say. Your mother has two sides to her psyche . . . both pronounced. One side enables her to see the world as it is. The other side forces her to see it as she perceives it should be. Does that make sense to you?'

He smiled. 'Dad, I've tried all my life to understand my mother. I've never succeeded, yet.'

The father placed his hand on the son's shoulder. 'Don't feel alone, son. Now, let's get some sleep.'

28

The front which had produced all the snow the previous night had passed through and the day broke cold and clear. The group, still tired from a combination of travelling and partying slept late that morning in the airport Stouffer. They had agreed to meet in the restaurant at nine for breakfast. The two pilots had left at daybreak, for duty called them out to the airport.

The co-pilot, as they taxied out for takeoff back to Texas, called ground control. 'Take off ground . . . Lear, niner, niner, seven, requesting taxi instructions for your active,' and as he waited for a reply, shut the mike off, smiling at the pilot. 'I think I'm in love, Eric!'

Before the pilot could respond, ground control came back with, 'Lear, niner, niner, seven, taxi out to runway 8L and hold.'

'Roger, Lear niner, niner, seven to 8L . . . thank you.' The pilot was now free to ask,'How many times have you fallen in love this week?' The co-pilot blushed. 'Three times, but this time is for real, Eric.'

'Uh huh, I've heard that, before, too.'

The radio crackled. 'Lear, niner, niner, seven, switch to 128.05 for departure . . . Lear, niner, niner, seven . . . Roger. Stapleton, niner, niner, seven now holding in number one on 8L. Clear to go, niner, niner, seven'

And they spooled the twin jets and roared down the runway, back to Texas.

The father and son were down in the coffee shop at least an hour before the two women showed up, due to an inability to sleep late. The father, who normally did not sleep well anyway, had a fitful night. The story of Meagan's problems burned in him all night as his mind played with various scenarios of his son's future life with the dying woman. What future life? He concluded, but he said nothing to the son as he played with his coffee.

The son, nervous as any bridegroom should be, toyed with his cup, looking nervously at the entrance door, as he sipped his coffee without interest, then he saw them enter, smiling. Each had on a new outfit, a result of some pre-wedding shopping, and each looked great. Meagan looked rested, he thought. She first went up to Charlie, surprisingly, kissed him on the lips, and then to her future father-in-law, a kiss on the cheek,

He rose to greet her, for he was of the old school, responding with, 'Good morning, my dear, you look lovely, as usual,' and to Erin, who also gave him a kiss on the cheek, 'You look especially lovely, this morning, Erin.'

Erin smiled a warm smile. She had fallen in love twice in the past twenty four hours, once with Alex Forester, and once with Darren. This is not difficult for a girl of twenty since their capacity for love and to love is so great.

She looked around for the two pilots, and not seeing either, asked, 'Where are the fly boys?'

Alex Forester, sensing her loss, replied, 'Probably half way back to Texas by now, I regret to say, Erin.'

She looked sad, 'Oh, I see. Did he leave a message?'

Alex smiled, as he lied, 'Darren said to be sure to tell you, goodbye, and that he enjoyed the evening tremendously.'

She smiled. 'Oh, that was nice of him.'

Charlie smiled at the two women, asking,'Are you ready to order?'

Meagan patted her stomach. 'Oh, honey, I ate enough last night to last me a week. I'll just have coffee, please.'

He nodded to Erin, who replied, 'Not me, I'm hungry.'

The two men laughed at the marvellous resiliency of

youth, as Charlie patted the hand of his betrothed, asking, 'Well, Meagan, my dear, are you ready to travel back home to get married?'

She held his hand tight for a moment. She smiled at him, then at the father. 'Uh huh, I shur am.'

The father turned over the events of last night in his mind. He smiled at her too, saying, 'I can hardly wait for it,' and then his face lit up. He turned to her.'I almost forgot to tell you, Meagan, dear, that my wife and I have given you and Charlie a complete service for twelve of china and silver. We hope you like it, since we had no inkling of your choice of pattern, but, Agatha made me be sure to tell you that if you don't like it, we'll take it back and exchange if for one you like. She said to be sure to tell you that we won't mind the exchange one bit.'

Meagan's eyes lit up. She had discounted any wedding gifts at all, since there was so little family, no friends, and no invitations to anyone. She had resigned herself to it, and now, a complete service for twelve!

She was speechless for a while as she thought about it. She had always fantasized in years past of presiding at a formal dinner in a formal dining room, with servants to do her bidding as the lady of the manor, and as she had looked around her dingy apartment over that garage, she would shrug, thinking . . . fat chance! And now, she had it all . . . formal dining room in a lovely home, beautiful service for twelve, and she would be the lady of the manor.

She had it all, thanks to the two men before her, and she smiled, regally, as she thought of it all, saying, 'I can't wait until we get back to our home, Charlie. I'm ready to travel when you are,' and she smiled at Alex, too, adding, 'and I'm ready to get married, too.'

The father gave her a warm smile. 'And we are ready to welcome you into the family, my dear, with open arms, I can assure you,' and looking at Erin, 'and your lovely daughter, too. We have never had a daughter, as you know, and we will consider you our daughter and Erin to be our granddaughter, and if you and she will permit us, we would be honoured.'

Erin beamed. She had always wanted a father, and she considered Charlie almost to be a brother rather than a step-father, because of the age differences, but, Alexander Forester, now, that was different. She had always wanted a rich father, and since that was impossible, she would gladly accept a rich grandfather. She beamed, rewarding all with a warm smile.

Charlie rose, and looking at the group for concurrence, asked, 'Shall we hit the road for the high country?'

It was crowded in the Mercedes when all four occupants and their luggage were piled in. The father inquired, 'Why didn't you take the Jeep Cherokee for this trip. Would it not have been more practical in this weather, and we would have had more room?'

'Yes, Dad, It would have made more sense,' he smiled, winking at Meagan who shared the front seat with him. Erin was delighted to share the rear seat with her prospective grandfather and she smiled at him often as they headed out of Denver on I-70 West. The snow ploughs had worked through the night and the interstate was fairly free of the dangerous white stuff. Meagan was nervous. She started to criticize Charlie's driving on several occasions, but a stern look from her betrothed changed her mind, and instead, she smiled at him, warmly, making small talk.

The father was quiet for a while, thinking, wondering, then, 'I've been meaning to ask. Where are you two going on your honeymoon?'

Meagan welcomed the opportunity to speak as she volunteered, 'Charlie asked me the same question, and I said I didn't want to go anywhere . . . that I wanted to honeymoon in our home . . . didn't I, sweetheart?'

He nodded. 'Uh huh, you sure did.'

The father replied, 'Well, I can understand your feelings, my dear, but I was prepared to offer to send you and Charlie to Hawaii for two weeks or so . . . '

'Oh, that is very generous of you, Alex,' retorted Meagan, 'but, I want to spend some time in our home.'

She laughed, 'I still haven't gotten used to it, yet. Wait until you see it . . . it's beautiful.'

He nodded. 'Yes, I'm sure it is, my dear. I'm glad you like it so much,' and he silently thought,'You are quite right! You had better enjoy it while you can.'

He had promised his son that he would not dwell on the impending fatal illness of his prospective daughter-in-law but, in truth, he could not get it out of his mind. Everytime she spoke, especially of anything that would take place in the future, he weighed it against the clock and calendar to see if she had time. He shook his head as he looked out the window.

He was glad when Erin attempted to engage him in conversation, asking, 'Mr Forester, do you ski?'

He chuckled. 'Many years ago . . . yes I did, but, when you reach my age, abstinence is the better part of valour as the saying goes. Do you ski, my dear?'

She sighed. 'No. I never had the chance to learn, but, I'd like to. I'm going to, too. Charlie said he'd teach me, huh, Charlie.'

'Ah shur did, honey,' he mocked her.

As they drove up the entrance drive to the house, Meagan shouted, 'Stop the car, Charlie!'

He came to a screeching halt. 'What the hell is wrong with you, Meagan?'

She pointed to the house, glistening in the bright sunshine, with it's new coating of snow clinging to the roof and any other nearly horizontal surface it could get a grip on.

She sighed. 'Oh, look at it, Alex, isn't it beautiful?'

He was amused, as he replied, 'Yes, my dear, it is picture postcard beautiful. I am impressed. I wish Agatha could be here with us now to enjoy it, too.'

She turned to him smiling coyly . . . 'Did Charlie tell you he carried me over the threshold when we first went in. It was so romantic . . . '

The father smiled. 'That is lovely, Charlie. I never knew you were so romantic, son.'

He knew he was being teased as he replied, 'I wasn't until I met this woman,' and he smiled at her.

The father leaned back in the seat . . . pleased. Whatever reservations he had conjured up in his mind about this country bumpkin of a girl, he now put out of his mind. She was warm, charming, simple, uncomplicated, and, unfortunately . . . she was dying.

29

The wedding of Meagan Mahoney and Charles Forester could not be construed to be the social event of the decade, or even the week in that picturesque town of Breckenridge, Colorado. Since neither of them was overly religious by nature, they opted for a ceremony presided over by a Justice of the Peace, in his chambers over the drug store.

Alexander Forester, the best man, smiled to himself, thinking, 'Sometimes, things happen for the best. I can see my wife at this ceremony, trying to look imperious,' and he could not help but add, 'And who would give a damn.'

Meagan could not have been more thrilled had the ceremony taken place in the Canterbury Cathedral with the Archbishop of Canterbury presiding. She was now married! She was now Mrs Charles Alexander Forester. She loved her new name . . . had a nice ring to it, she thought.

As the JP pronounced the magic words to Charlie, 'You may now kiss the bride,' she turned to him with tears in her eyes, and one small one running down her cheek. It ran over her lips and she rewarded her husband with a warm, soft, and slightly salty kiss, but he didn't care. He was in love.

He held her close for a moment, whispering something in her ear, which the best man and the bridesmaid did not hear, but they laughed, too, as Meagan giggled, looking sheepishly at her husband.

Erin, not knowing what protocol demanded, never having been through this before, turned to the best man, her new self proclaimed grandfather, put her arms around him and kissed him on the cheek. He smiled. He was pleased . . . and thrilled.

The JP's wife, as she usually did, threw rice at the honorees as they exited the room, followed by the rest of the wedding party. It was a simple ceremony by many standards, but, like the proverbial cliche says, beauty is in the eyes of the beholder, and the beholders thought it was very beautiful.

Alexander Forester asked that he be allowed to host a fabulous wedding party at the most exclusive lodge in town, of which there were many, but, 'No, thank you,' responded the bride. 'I want the wedding supper to be in our home . . . '

'But,' asked the groom, 'How can you swing that, sweetheart? You can't get married and cook a meal at the same time . . . can you?' he teased, smiling.

'No, my darling! I'm good, but not that good. I thought my father-in-law could solve that problem for us. It's cheaper than a trip to Hawaii, isn't it,' she smiled at him.

The father-in-law laughed. 'It sure is, my dear. I'll take care of everything if I may borrow your car for a few hours. I need to go into town to see a caterer . . . '

'Oh, please, Alex,' protested Meagan, 'nothing too elaborate! I know how you Foresters are,' she quipped.

'No, Meagan. It will just be a simple dinner for four.'

As he parked the Mercedes in front of the caterer's office, the proprietress was standing at the window overlooking the street. She smiled, admiringly, as she saw the distinguished looking gentleman alight from it. She saw the full length leather coat with matching cap. She watched as he looked up and down the street, and then her heart gave an encouraging beat as she watched him walk up to her door. She pretended to be busy as he walked in, and as the receptionist pointed her out to him, it was only then that she strode forward, smiling her warmest smile, and offering her hand.

He returned her warm handshake, saying, 'I need a caterer for a small wedding party. Can you help me?'

She was a woman who loved weddings, as long as they were not hers, and she knew what it took to throw a good wedding party.

She smiled, replying, 'You have come to the right place,' and as they talked she asked the mandatory question, 'How much do I have to spend?' but she asked it with such charm, that he didn't mind a bit.

He smiled. 'Whatever it takes to have a party for four. How bad can it get?'

She gave him an impish look. 'Depends on whether you want a memorable party or not. Are you the groom, sir?' she inquired with interest.

He laughed. 'Not hardly. I'm the father of the groom.'

Relieved, she replied, 'I see. Let me propose these things for your consideration, sir, and we can build on it, or,' and she felt she was insulting him, 'we can cut down to fit your budget. Do you require a private room somewhere?'

'No. The bride and groom have just bought a very nice large house and the bride wants the wedding supper to be in her dining room.'

'How charming! Then, the house has all required china and silver, I would imagine?'

He answered proudly, 'Yes . . . all brand new.'

'Well, then, let us see . . . '

The house was garlanded with flowers, and in Colorado in the middle of winter, that does not come cheap. A string quartet was brought in to provide music. Meagan's new, and quite impressive, service for twelve was taken out of wrappings, run through the wash, and laid out. Impressive candelabra with long tapered candles were placed at each end of a magnificent floral centre piece on the large dining room table in the formal dining room.

Meagan sat at one end and her husband at the other. She seemed regal as she sat there, Charlie thought. She smiled often at the twelve people seated at her table. Twelve people, did you say? The cateress, a lovely divorced woman of some fifty years, as mentioned, knew how to throw a party. When she found out the party would consist of only four people, she was disappointed, even horrified.

She placed her hand on his, for emphasis, asking, 'May I be candid with you, Alex?' (It had taken her only thirty minutes to get on a first name basis. She had an infallible nose for money – especially big money). 'We can't have a proper wedding party with only four people . . . that's absurd!'

'But,' he stammered. 'We don't know any other people here. What can we do?'

'Alex, dear,' she purred, warming to the subject, 'let me handle this, will you? If you will permit me, I will find eight lovely people to round out the party and fill up the table. Is that all right with you? Why, you don't even have a partner for the evening . . . a handsome man like you,' she pouted. 'That is sacrilege,' she exclaimed, demurely.

He, being an old hand at this, now knew where she was going with it, as he asked, 'But where could I possibly find a dinner companion at this late hour?'

She placed her arm in his, smiling at him. 'Won't I do?'

His moustache bristled. 'Of course, my dear, you're a very lovely woman. I would be proud to have you as my companion, but . . . Erin? What of her? She will have no escort . . . '

'Alex, my dear, I have a son at home who will be perfect for Erin . . . let's let the children be to themselves, shall we, while the adults have some fun.'

His moustache quivered even more, and his emotions came to life. He had envisioned this as a dull evening, the kind that one suffers through for family, but, now he could foresee great expectations later on. He quickly thanked fate for arranging his wife to get the flu at a most propitious time.

But he still had some questions. 'But, the other six people . . . where will they come from?'

'Alex, my dear, Breckenridge is full of all kinds of people at this time of year . . . from tacky to terrific, but I would not bring total strangers into your son's home.

No, these will be substantial people. How about some professional people who love a good party? I know many of them.'

'Well, you seem to have the situation well in hand. I think I should talk to my son and daughter-in-law about this. After all, it is their wedding . . . '

'Oh, I agree.'

Charlie and Meagan said, 'What the hell!'

Erin, when told that Grace's son, for that was her name, was a ski instructor, smiled profusely, and her nostrils were seen to flare a little at the mere mention of a new man for her to consider.

What had started out as a potentially very dull party turned out to be one hell of a good party. Grace was a pro, no doubt about it. She had been divorced for two years after her third marriage, and vowed she would never marry again. She had learned one thing in the game of life, the boy-girl game. It was give and take, with take the more desirable of the two.

If the events of that wedding are chronicled, it will be difficult to decide who had the most fun . . . Charlie and Meagan . . . Alex and Grace, or Erin and Todd. Alex, being the courtly southern gentleman that he was, refused to allow Grace to drive home alone that night at so late an hour, so he took her home in Charlie's Mercedes. That impressed Grace so much that she invited him in for a nightcap. One thing led to another, and . . . !

Alex later considered coming often to Breckenridge to check on the new operation he and Charlie had started.

Erin, hindered by her sacred vow not to indulge on the first three dates, pointed out to an insistent ski instructor that three dates only required three days, mathematically. He offered to teach her to ski . . . free! She accepted.

And what of the newly-married couple? As they climbed into bed that night, Charlie smiled.'Whew, that turned out to be one hell of a wedding party, didn't it honey?'

'Uh huh,' she replied as she slid over to him, 'but, you ain't seen nothing, yet.'

* * *

A happy and satisfied Alexander Forester left Breckenridge in a rental car. He refused their offer to drive him to Denver to meet the Lear for the return trip to Texas, with Erin almost insisting that she drive him.

She had asked, 'Will Darren be there?'

The mother inquired, 'I thought you had a new love, Erin, honey?'

She smiled. 'You can't have too many, Mama. There are dropouts, you know!'

As the Lear climbed up to altitude Alex took out his briefcase and went over the bills for the wedding party. Grace, being the efficient businesswoman that she was, rewarded him with the bills the very next day.

'Since you will be leaving town, soon,' she quipped, adding, 'of course, I could mail them to you, or,' and she got a mischievous look in her eye, 'we could meet in Denver in a week or so and I could deliver them in person.'

He patted her hand. 'That would be nice for the future, but for now, I'll take them in person. I'll give you a cheque before I leave.'

He took out his pocket calculator and added up the total tab, which was considerable.

'Whew,' he exclaimed to himself, 'Hawaii would have been a lot cheaper.'

As he looked out of the small circular windows of the Lear, seeing the morning sun glistening off the high range of the Rockies, he leaned back in the seat, smiling. 'It was worth every penny of it. That was a hell of a party,' and thinking of Grace, he smiled.

30

Agatha Forester sat before the huge fireplace in the library of their home, a wool Afghan covering her legs. She had only returned home from the hospital that morning after a stay of nearly a week. She was miserable in her huge house, alone except for the servants who waited on her.

Her stay in the hospital had given her much time for reflection . . . on her life . . . her marriage . . . her son . . . her son's marriage. In spite of her haughty and imperious manner, a manner born of heredity and developed and enhanced over the years, she was an intelligent woman with a keen and perceptive mind.

Her reflections had brought her no comfort. She was not a happy woman, she concluded after much soul searching. Her husband was a husband in name only, and finding no warmth and tenderness in their relationship, had sought comfort and warmth elsewhere. What really irritated her was that he had found it and was apparently happy and content with the arrangement. Oh, yes she knew of Betty and of her relationship with her husband. It was all that she, Agatha, could do to be civil to her at office functions, the few that she attended. And, since Betty had been divorced from her husband for some ten years, and obviously had no intention of finding another one, she was apparently happy with the arrangement.

Why shouldn't she be, she asked herself on many occasions. Alexander Forester was wealthy, healthy, and handsome, and he was her boss. Could it get any better for an executive secretary who didn't want another go at marriage in this liberated society.

No, the only loser in this entire scenario was she . . . Agatha Forester.

She tossed off the Afghan and walked to the foyer where a mirror was mounted above the mail table, a mirror placed there many years earlier to enable their female guests to have one last look at themselves before making their grand entrance. She shrugged at herself as she looked in the mirror. She saw a woman of nearly sixty years, a face so lovely so many years ago, and now, a face showing the effect of years of gravitational pull on its cheeks and eyes. Her hair, dark in her youth, had now been allowed to seek its own hue, which was totally grey. Her figure was still lean, thanks to her lineage. No woman in her family had ever had a waist or weight problem.

She continued to look at herself, thinking, what have you got to show for sixty years of living? A son who had moved away and married a woman who . . . And she thought of Meagan . . . a woman who was a waitress in a truck stop, or worse, and with a daughter who had already, at age twenty, served time in prison for killing a man who had raped her. My God, what kind of people are these, she wondered, as she pulled the Afghan around her and returned to the library. What had her son gotten himself into? And her husband had the audacity to attend the wedding, just as if everything had been proper and acceptable.

She was glad, in retrospect, that she had got the flu. If the flu had not struck she would have come up with some other excuse not to attend the wedding. Why should she, the mother of the foolish groom, by her presence, sanction such a union – one doomed to failure as sure as the sun sets in the west.

She was now in a much better position to say, when her son would return from a broken marriage, 'Charles, dear, I tried to tell you . . . '

Returning to her chair, she rang for the maid to bring her a fresh cup of hot tea. She heard a car coming up the gravel drive. As the Hispanic maid came in with the steaming cup, she asked, 'Rosita, did I hear a car driving up?'

'Si, Senora, eet ees Señor Forester. He ees back.'

She was happy to hear that. She had been lonesome for him. In spite of their platonic relationship they held each other in high esteem . . . they respected each other. She started to rise to go to the door to greet him, but, as she reclined in her chair, she felt she would make a more convincing picture as a convalescent if she remained seated, so she did.

She could, however, manage a smile, which she did as he entered the room, smiling his infectious smile, as he went to her. 'Agatha, my dear, I am so glad to see you home from the hospital.'

She managed a weak smile. offering her cheek. 'Don't kiss me on the mouth, Alex, I might still have the bug.'

He laughed. 'All right, I must confess I don't want to catch the flu,' and he added, in an attempt to be charming, 'not even from you, my dear.'

She rewarded him with a smile. 'Please sit and tell me all about the wedding.' And, to the maid who was still standing there, anticipating some instruction. 'Rosita, please bring Mr Forester some hot tea. Is tea all right, Alex?'

'Tea will be fine, dear,' as he removed the overcoat, handing it to the maid.

He sat in a chair opposite her, giving her a close scrutiny. 'You still look a little peaked, my dear. Are you sure you should have come home so soon?'

She sighed. 'Oh, Alex, I had to! I was so tired of lying in a hospital room. I wanted to be home when you arrived too,' she said with conviction, giving him a smile.

'That's very thoughtful of you, Agatha . . . I appreciate it.'

'Now,' she said, as she sipped her tea, 'please tell me all about the wedding.'

He accepted the tea from the maid, and looking into his wife's eyes, he replied, 'I wish you could have been there. It was a lovely affair. Very small . . . very personal, but,' and he smiled . . . 'very nice.'

As he sipped some tea, he warmed to the occasion.

'Agatha, I wish you could meet Meagan and Erin. They are really two charming women. I can easily see how Charlie was captivated by Meagan. She is . . . how shall I describe her . . . really different from any woman he has known, I'm sure. She is a country girl, simple and pragmatic, but, warm and loving. She is the kind of person who picks up strays and brings them home to feed and care for them,' and he added, 'out of compassion. But, she can be as tough as she is soft.'

Agatha sighed. 'I hope, Alex, your analogy about strays does not apply to our son. How's Charles? Is he happy?'

The father nodded. 'I think he's very happy, except for one thing,' and he became sombre.

She looked concerned. 'What do you mean?'

He could not keep it from her any longer, he felt. She would have to know sometime, and the sooner the better to face it. He took a deep sip of tea and placed the cup on the coffee table.

He gave a shrug of the shoulders as he looked at his wife.

'Agatha, I have to give you some disturbing news about all this, and I hope you are well enough to accept it.'

Her eyes widened. She sat up in her chair. She, too, placed her cup on the coffee table, as she placed her hands on her breasts, expecting the worst as she noticed the sombre look on her husband's face.

'What is it, Alex? I can handle it, if it concerns our son. I want to know . . . please don't spare me the details.'

He tried to reassure her. 'It's not Charlie, dear, it's Meagan,' and as his wife's eyes widened with fear mixed with curiosity, she asked, 'Meagan? What is wrong with her? Oh, Alex, I knew this would happen . . . '

He was curt with her. 'Oh, Agatha, please don't be judgmental before you have all the facts. This has nothing to do with your prejudiced opinion of the girl,' and he girded himself to say the fateful words . . . 'She has cancer. She is dying, Agatha. She will not last a year.'

The mother's mouth opened. Her eyes widened. Her hands went to her cheeks. 'Oh, my God, Alex! I can't believe what I am hearing. I feel weak,' and she fell back in her chair.

He rushed to her, taking her hand. 'Forgive me, my dear, if I have shocked you so badly. I could not think of an easier way to say it,' and he shook his head, 'Unfortunately, there is no easy way to say that, is there?'

She tried to compose herself, still in a state of shock, as she sat in the chair, moving her head from side to side, asking, 'Did he know when he met her, or is this a recent development?'

'No, he had no knowledge of it when they met, but he did find out after they had agreed to marry. I don't know exactly when they found out . . . in Vail, I think, when they were celebrating their engagement, from what I understand.'

The mother began to compose herself. Her demeanour was returning to normal as she asked, 'Did Meagan know she had cancer when she agreed to marry our son?'

He shook his head. 'No, not at first, from what Charlie has told me . . . '

She interrupted him. 'Cancer of what, Alex? You didn't say, did you?'

'No, I don't think I did. It is cancer of the uterus.'

The wife gave him a knowing look. 'I'm no authority on cancer, Alex, but cancer of the uterus is usually solved rather easily by removing the uterus in a hysterectomy. I have several friends who have had that done and they seem perfectly healthy to me,' she said with conviction.

'That's true, dear. I'm aware of that, but, I haven't given you the whole story, as yet.'

She stiffened. 'Please do, then.'

'Her cancer has spread to her lymph glands. It is spreading to all her body. That is what the doctors base their terminal predictions on,' he said, sombrely, as he looked down at the floor.

The air went out of her lungs. Her hands went to her

lap. She asked, 'How is Charles taking all this?'

The father's face lit up as he replied, 'He is taking it like a saint, Agatha. I am so proud of him. It takes a hell of a man to accept that kind of news, especially after she has offered him, twice,' he emphasized with two fingers, 'to let him out of the engagement.'

She looked interested. 'He told you that?'

'Yes, he did, and I am proud he decided not to go. He has character, Agatha! A lot of men would have cut and run, if given the chance, but our son did not. He's acting like a man should,' he said, proudly.

She raised her head, replying, softly, 'I can't decide if he is a saint or a fool, Alex.'

He went to her, taking her hand. 'No, Agatha, don't talk that way! If only you had met her . . . '

Her concern increased . . . 'Does Meagan know?'

He was not quite sure of her meaning . . 'Does she know she has cancer, or, does she know she is terminal?' She sighed, 'Both, I guess,' she shrugged.

'I know she is aware of her malignancy, but as to the terminal part, I must say that I don't know how much they have told her.'

Agatha Forester shuddered, answering, 'It must be awful to know you are dying . . . that there is no hope,' and for the first time, she felt compassion for her new daughter-in-law.

She looked at her husband, with new understanding in her heart as to the reality of the situation, as she admitted with some degree of contrition, 'I guess, Alex, I have not handled this very well, have I?'

He released her hand, shaking his head.' I guess, Agatha, my dear, you sometimes let your head rule instead of your heart. I must confess to you that I, too, had great reservations about this whole affair when Charlie first explained it to me, but, oh, Agatha, if only you could have met Meagan, you would have loved her too . . . I'm sure. She had a very captivating manner, and that Erin,' he smiled, 'she is a heart breaker, too.'

She shuddered, again, as she scolded him. 'Oh, Alex, please don't use the past tense when you speak of her . . . it is so depressing even in the present tense.'

'Forgive me, dear, I know what you mean.'

She was thoughtful for a moment, then, 'Are they so sure that something can't be done for her?' and her eyes brightened as she continued, 'We could bring her down to M.D. Anderson in Houston . . . remember what they did for my Aunt Harriet . . . '

'No. What?'

'Well, I'm sure they prolonged her life for several years . . . '

'Sure, and they bombarded the poor woman with enough radiation to build several nuclear bombs, and her hair fell out and she holed herself up in a room for all that time, not wanting anyone to see her in that condition.'

'But,' she protested, 'she was alive.'

He stood, ready to terminate the conversation. 'I don't know about you, Agatha, but life . . that kind of life . . is not that precious to me. Is it to you? If so, you had better give me detailed instructions as to what you would like me to do for you if the situation warrants it in your own case.'

'Please don't go, yet, Alex. I've been alone for almost a week. I want some company. I'm sick of this house. I want to get out, and, besides, you didn't tell me how you enjoyed the trip except for the bad news concerning Meagan. Was the wedding party nice? You told me when you called me at the hospital that you had someone plan a wedding supper for you. Was it nice? Did Meagan like the china and silver? Did you use if for the supper?'

At the mention of the supper, his mind went back to the night with Grace, the cateress, and he smiled. 'Why, yes, it was a delightful evening. Everyone had a lovely time.'

She seemed sincere when she stated, 'I wish I could have been there.'

He looked at her sympathetically. 'I wish you could have, too, my dear. Now, if you will excuse me, I think I'll go up and unpack. I need to go to the office to see how things have gone in my absence.'

She smiled at him, saying nothing . . . just nodding.

His arrival at the office was met with more visible enthusiasm than he had received at home, for as soon as he entered his private office, Betty had followed him in, closing the door. He turned to her with arms opened and she readily went to him, holding him in close embrace, raising her face to his. He kissed her, tenderly. 'Oh, Alex, dear, it is so good to have you back home. I missed you. Did you miss me?' she asked, coyly.

He held her hands. 'Of course, I missed you. I always do.'

She looked at him, mischievously. 'And did you behave yourself?'

He smiled the smile she loved so much, replying, 'As well as could be expected with my son and his bride present.'

'How are the newlyweds?'

He started to tell her the whole story, but having just gone through that with his wife, he decided to tell her later, answering, 'They're just fine.'

'Where did they go on their honeymoon?'

He shrugged. 'Nowhere! I offered to send them to Hawaii, but the bride said no. They have just bought a lovely new house, and she said she preferred to spend it there.'

'How practical can you get? Do you like her?'

He became serious. 'Yes, I like Meagan very much, Betty. I hope you get to meet her, someday,' and after reflecting, added, 'soon.'

She smiled. 'She'll have to come here to meet me, I'm sure.'

31

The Breckenridge branch office of the Forester Company real estate division was now opened for business. Charlie had located a small local real estate office which had been in business for the past thirty-five years. It had been headed by Orville Chapton, a World War II veteran who was now nearing retirement age, and then some. He listened, intently, as the younger man put forth his proposition.

'Now, Mr Chapton . . . '

'Please call me Orville,' he protested as he puffed on his pipe.

'Very well . . . Orville. Incidentally, were you named after Orville Wright, by any chance?'

'Yup . . . sure was. My dad was an old WW I pilot . . . flew with Rickenbacker, he did, and my dad thought so much of the Wright brothers that he named me after Orville Wright.'

He smiled. 'Would you believe I have a brother named Wilbur?'

'I believe it,' Charlie responded, smiling, anxious to get on with it, 'But, back to business . . . I know that you are anxious to retire, Orville, and I want to help you do it. You and your wife . . . Myrtle . . . is it not,' and he smiled at the woman sitting there, 'have worked hard all these years and you deserve to take a rest, but you see what I have to offer you is a chance for you two to have your cake and eat it too, as the saying goes.'

'How so?' he asked, with years of rural pragmatism making him suspicious of any deal too good to be true.

'By that I mean, you and Myrtle can come and go as you please, but you will be a silent partner in the

Forester Company operation. Quite frankly, we need you only for your broker's license until we can procure one of our own.'

He gave Charlie a sly look. 'I knew that was what you wanted all along, young man,' and he took a deep puff on his pipe. It had gone out, so he took out a box of wooden matches, struck it on the bottom of his shoe, sucked in, and watched the smoke rise.

He smiled, satisfied at his success. 'You say me and Mrytle can come and go as we please. You mean I don't have to punch the clock if I don't want to?'

'That's right. If you feel like sleeping late one morning and coming in at ten . . . that's your privilege, Orville. Just be available to help us with appraisals . . . introduce us to the locals . . . advise us on good deals . . . steer us away from potentially bad deals . . . that's all.'

'I didn't hear you mention any pay.'

'Well, of course, there is the original purchase price for your agency, which I might point out is very generous, and you will receive the usual brokerage commission on the deals you close, as well as your wife, who I understand is also licensed as a broker.'

'She is,' he nodded, blowing out more smoke in Charlie's direction, causing him to cough.

Charlie added, 'Of course, we would like to retain your name for five years . . . to give the firm the local touch.'

'How would that work? I can't believe a big company like Forester would be willing to hide under my name.'

'No . . . not forever, but for the first five years we would be willing to call the firm Chapton/Forester & Associates. After your five-year buy-out period is over, you would have nothing to do with the firm anymore, and we would change the name to the Forester Company.'

He puffed once more. 'Let me get this straight. The purchase price would be fifty percent down and the remaining fifty percent spread out over the five year period . . . that right?'

He nodded. 'That is the essence of it in general form.

The attorneys can hammer out the details.'

Myrtle Chapton, who had been in the room the whole time, saying nothing, but listening intently, looked at her husband.

He smiled. 'What do you say, Mama? It is as much your business as mine,' as he patted her hand.

She gave him a warm smile, nodding. 'I'm willing if you are, Papa. Now, maybe we'll have some time to spend with the grandchildren,' and looking at Charlie, 'he seems like a nice young man, Orville.'

Orville put his pipe on the desk. He rose, extending his hand. 'Looks like you got yourself a deal, young fella.'

Charlie smiled. 'Looks like it, Orville,' and reached for the older man's hand.

'I guess you'll want me to move out of this big office and take one of the salesmen's offices, huh?'

Charlie nodded. 'Uh huh, but no hurry, Orville.'

Orville smiled. 'One more thing, boss. Can Myrtle and me have a vacation before we report for work?'

Charlie laughed at the man's sense of humour. 'Sure Orville, but a vacation without pay.'

'Fair 'nough! Come on, Mama, let's go see the grandkids.'

With the papers signed and proprietorship firmly established, Charlie called in the painters and decorators. This resulted in his first post-marital fight with his wife and step-daughter; over colours, fabrics, furniture, and accessories . . . even the type of coffee pot and cups.

Charlie wanted china cups, 'Because they are classy and paper cups are tacky, that's why, Meagan,' he shouted, exasperated, as she retorted, 'Who's gonna wash them cups, Charlie . . . not me! I'm an executive, you told me.'

'And not me,' echoed Erin, 'I only know how to type. These hands were not meant for dishwater.'

He stood his ground. 'You hillbillys are something. One day in the office and you're trying to tell me how to run the business,' and he gave his beloved wife a mischievous smile.

She went up to him, holding him close. 'You ain't seen nothing, yet, Charlie.'

'No,' chimed in Erin. 'You ain't seen nothing yet! When do I get my coffee breaks, Charlie?'

He laughed. 'You haven't hit a lick of work, yet!'

'I showed up, didn't I? That's something! What do you want me to do except sit in that front office and look beautiful?'

'I want you to review all of Orville's files.'

'Why?'

'Why? Why? When I give you instructions, Erin, you don't ask why . . . you do it! I'm the boss, Erin, that's why!'

She purred. 'That's not what Mama says . . . '

He slapped her on the butt. 'Git!'

'OK . . . I'm going.'

Meagan became serious. 'I hope this is not a typical workday, honey. If it is, we won't last a month. How many of those salesmen of Orville's did you keep?'

'I kept them all . . for the time being. We'll ask some of them to leave in a month or so. We need them now.'

'Uh huh, that's for sure. I'm going to work with Erin on all those files. If I don't hold her nose to the grindstone, she won't do a thing. You've ruined that girl, Charlie. It's your fault she's worthless now.'

'And how is that so?' he demanded, smiling.

'You've got her believing she is a rich gal and doesn't have to work for a living. That's what I mean.'

'I never told her that.'

'You didn't have to. Ever since your daddy said he wanted her to be his granddaughter she thinks her you-know-what doesn't stink.'

'Meagan . . . that's tacky!'

'I can't help it, Charlie. I'm cracking down on her, starting now, and I'm cracking down on you, too,' she smiled.

'How're you gonna do that?' he asked.

In spite of its tumultuous beginning the office of Chapton/Forester and Associates gradually took on some semblance of order. Erin had been put in place by her mother. She had now resigned herself to the fact that she had to work if she expected a weekly cheque. She would have preferred working in an office with dozens of eligible young men, but she concluded . . . 'life is cruel,' and she had to content herself with skiing lessons several times a week from Todd, the ski instructor, 'the boyfriend of the month.'

Meagan, the office manager and shack bully, peeked into the office of the executive vice-president, Charles Forester, asking, 'Busy?'

He smile as he looked up. 'Never too busy for you, my love.'

She walked in and plopped in a chair.

He thought she looked tired, and said so. 'Do you feel all right, honey?'

She shook her head. 'I'm always tired, Charlie. I don't have any energy.' She shook her head. 'It's a good thing I'm not still waitressing in that cafe. . . . I couldn't do it,' and smiling at him added, 'it's a good thing you came along and rescued me, honey.'

He pulled up a chair next to hers.'Don't you think it's time you made a decision on the surgery, Meagan. You said you wanted to put it off so I could marry a whole woman. Well, I have, and now it is time we face the truth. I think you should go through with the hysterectomy, honey.'

She looked at him straight in the eye. 'It's my body, Charlie, and although you act like you own it, you don't . . . it's mine, and I'll decide when and where . . . '

'My, my . . . aren't we testy this morning . . . '

She looked contrite. 'I'm sorry, honey! I don't mean that the way it sounded, but . . . '

'I know. I took no offence at it . . . '

She sighed. 'I guess I should go back to Denver for a new check-up to see if it is worse.'

He was greatly pained by her lack of knowledge. He thought to himself, 'Poor thing. If you only knew.'

He replied to her, placing his hand on hers, 'I think that would be a good idea. Let's go for a couple of days. Orville and Myrtle will be in town to watch the office while we're away. What do you say?'

She nodded. 'I guess so, I'll go and call for an

appointment, now. Will you come with me?'

'Of course I will . . . you know that.'

She returned to his office a few minutes later. 'They can see me Thursday and Friday. They said the testing would take two days at least. Can you get away?'

'We were going to close the condo deal on Friday, but that can wait until Monday. I'll call the attorneys.'

'Oh, honey . . . '

'Now, Meagan, don't fret about that. That deal can wait.'

She smiled. 'So can I.'

He longed to tell her. 'No, you can't . . . don't you understand that?'

When Erin heard the news of the Denver trip, her eyes widened with excitement. 'Oh, boy . . . a trip to Denver!'

'You're not going, Erin, honey,' from the mother.

'But, why? I always go to Denver with you and Charlie.'

'You used to, but not anymore. You're a working girl!'

'Then,' she pouted, 'I want to retire . . . now!'

The mother replied, 'Let's see . . . you're almost twenty-one, so you only have forty-four more years to go before you reach sixty-five. Isn't that wonderful? Time flies by so fast when you're having fun.'

She pouted, again. 'Oh hell! Go without me. You'll miss me, you'll see . . . 'specially Charlie.'

Meagan acted braver than she felt as she replied, 'I'll see to it that he doesn't miss you one bit, Erin, honey.'

She was introspective as they drove east on I-70, looking out the window, not saying much. Charlie would glance at her from time to time. He knew she was deep in thought, but he was not sure what she was thinking.

He poked her in the ribs. 'A penny for your thoughts, honey.'

She turned to him, half smiling. 'I can't sell them for that price . . . I'd lose money,' and she became serious as she continued. 'Charlie, you know I'm dying, don't you?'

He swallowed hard as the words hit him. 'Oh, honey, don't talk like that. You don't know that.' He wanted to say more, but he couldn't think of anything that would encourage her without being a lie. He felt awful.

She nodded, as she continued. 'I know, Charlie. I feel it in my bones. I feel like the life is draining out of my body, even now.'

'Are you in pain?' he asked, solicitously.

'No, not yet, but it's coming. I hope I can be brave when the time comes. I'm not afraid of dying, Charlie. I believe I'm going to heaven to be with God, even though I can't say He and I have been close friends of late. I sorta lost my religion after Erin's rape. I didn't think God would allow something like that to happen to a good girl like her.'

He wanted to stop her from saying any more, but he felt she had much more to say, and she did. 'You know, honey, the thing that I hate most . . . well, two things, really. I hate leaving you so soon after our marriage, and,' she suppressed a sob, 'I hate leaving you without a part of me to remind you of me . . . a baby.'

Oh, God, he thought! Please don't do this, but she continued: 'If only I could have lived long enough, and been healthy enough . . . to give you a baby . . . I'd die happy. 'Course, I wouldn't like leaving my baby behind, but I know you'd take good care of it. Erin could help you raise it, though I guess in time she'll have some of her own to worry about.'

He nearly screamed out . . . Oh, God, please make her quit this.

'But,' she continued, 'I guess it wasn't meant to be,' and she sighed, 'But, I want you to know, honey, that you have made me one happy woman . . . in spite of . . . '

'Oh, Meagan, honey, don't do this to yourself . . . '

She ignored him. 'Charlie?'

'Yes, hun?'

'I've been thinking of something. When they take a woman's uterus out, do they take away all the egg producing stuff, too?'

He looked hopeless. 'Oh, Meagan, I don't know about that. You'll have to ask the doctor about those things. Why?'

She became pensive. '"I was just thinking about something.'

'What?'

She sighed, turning back to the window. 'I don't want to talk about it now. Maybe later.'

32

The doctors, two of them, came out to the waiting room to talk to him. They ushered him into a small conference room just off the lobby to the OB/GYN section of the large hospital. One doctor motioned him to a chair. The other sat down, indicating that the older man would speak. He stood across the small conference table from Charlie. He became grave and very professional as he cleared his throat.

'Mr Forester, I am sure you will want to have all the facts concerning your wife's condition. Incidentally, congratulations. I understand you and Meagan have gotten married since I last saw you.' The other doctor, who had been looking at the floor, looked up, surprised.

The older man continued. 'I wish I could report to you that things have improved, but in truth they have not. I told you, previously, that it had spread to the lymph glands and it is now well established there. This means, of course, that it now has access to all parts of her body, or will, in due time. We recommend that she have her hysterectomy, immediately. I can't promise you that it will go into remission after that but, with radiation treatment, perhaps, and I repeat – perhaps, we can prolong the inevitable.'

Charlie raised his hands in a futile gesture. 'I am sure you know already that she has told me she will not agree to any kind of chemotherapy.'

The doctor sighed. 'I know that is her position, and that is most unfortunate. It might help . . . some,' he said, without much conviction.

'We'll see,' Charlie replied, 'Perhaps, she'll change

her mind,' and as he rose to leave, remembered to ask, 'Did she ask you any questions about eggs and fertilization and what have you?' he asked, embarrassed to broach the subject.

The doctor stopped. 'As a matter of fact she did. She had quite a few questions about invitro fertilization. Have you and she discussed this matter? I'm sure you and your wife realize that her getting pregnant is out of the question. You'd be courting disaster there, I assure you, and we have made our views known to her in that regard.'

He replied, weakly, 'We've discussed it only briefly.'

The doctor added, 'I told her there were doctors who specialized in that. It is not one of my specialities, though, but I can recommend one if you folks are interested.'

'I'm not sure what she has in mind just now. I'll have to wait and see. I will not recommend anything to her, though. She will have to make her own decisions. Thank you for your time, doctor. Is my wife ready to leave, now?'

'I think so, but I will check to find out. Goodbye,' and as he extended his hand, added, 'Good luck.'

She was unusually quiet on the return trip to Breckenridge, content to merely look out the window, and, from time to time: 'Did the doctor tell you about the test results? Did he discuss the treatment options with you? What do you think I should do?' After giving the best answers he could to the difficult questions, she would, once again, look out the window, saying nothing, just thinking.

Then, 'Charlie, I guess we had better go ahead and schedule the hysterectomy as soon as possible.' She managed a weak smile. 'I don't guess we'll have much use for that old thing anyway, since he told me I can't get pregnant, or,' and she shrugged, 'at least, I shouldn't.'

'I agree you should have the operation as soon as possible, but I will leave the actual date setting to you, but I don't think you should put it off any longer.'

She nodded. 'I know . . . Charlie?'

He smiled at her. 'Yes, hun.'

'I've been reading a lot lately about test tube babies and surrogate mothers and that sort of thing. How do you feel about that?'

'About what . . . specifically?'

'You know, having some other woman carry the baby to term with a fertilized egg from the real parents being planted in her. You've read about that, haven't you?'

'Sure, and I've seen the cases on the six o'clock news where it has not worked out too well.'

'What do you mean? Is it dangerous?'

'Well, no! That is not what I mean. Oh, I guess there is some risk involved, but that is not what I'm referring to.'

'Then, what are you referring to?' she insisted.

'Well, there have been many cases in which the surrogate mother has changed her mind about giving up the baby . . . '

She sat up, perturbed. 'Well, there is nothing she can do about it, legally, if she got paid and signed papers and all . . . is there?'

'I won't argue the legality of it, but she can raise such a stink . . . and get a lawyer and sue for custody.'

She gave him a shrewd look, replying, 'Supposing the surrogate mother is your kin? Like, for instance,' and she lowered her voice almost to a whisper . . . 'Suppose the surrogate mother was Erin . . . ' Her voice trailed off as she waited for his reaction.

He pulled the car off the interstate and took her hand in his, trying to remain calm, as he inquired, 'Is that what has been going through your mind all this time? You want to have Erin carry a baby for you?' and he added, 'and for me, too?'

She swallowed hard, nodding. 'Uh huh. Don't you see, honey, it is the only way we can have a baby of our own. Do you mind? Would you agree to that?' she pleaded.

He tried to be compassionate. 'Meagan, honey, you're asking me if I mind? You're asking the one person who has the easiest job in this whole venture. All I have to do is provide the seed,' and he smiled, 'a usually easy and pleasant task.'

She shook her head, looking him in the eye. 'No, Charlie, honey, your job is much more complicated than that. If you agree, and if it is successful, I will be leaving you with a child to raise on your own, unless,' and she suppressed a sob, 'unless you marry again and find some woman to help raise it, but,' and she began to cry in earnest, 'I don't want just any woman to raise my baby, Charlie . . . you know how particular I am.'

Before he could answer her a Colorado state trooper's car pulled in behind the Mercedes. Charlie cursed the bad luck, saying to himself, 'He picked a hell of a time to do this.'

He rolled the window down on the driver's side. The trooper looked in and saw Meagan crying. He asked, 'Are you all right, Ma'am?' and addressing Charlie, 'Is something wrong, sir?'

Charlie sighed. 'No officer. My wife just came back from having some medical tests run in Denver, and she is not feeling well. I just pulled off the interstate to let her compose herself . . . that's all.'

He looked at Meagan with suspicion. 'Is that right, Ma'am?'

She wiped her eyes with a tissue, nodding. 'Yes, Officer, that is right. I had a weak spell, but I'm all right now. Can we go, now? I'd like to get home before dark.'

The trooper tipped the brim of his hat. 'Of course, Ma'am. I just wanted to be sure you folks were OK . . . that's all,' and he looked around the car's interior with professional suspicion.

Feeling sure she had told the truth, and seeing nothing of a suspicious nature, he smiled, tipping his hat once more, saying as he walked off, 'Have a good day, folks, and drive carefully.'

As Charlie merged with the interstate traffic he looked at his wife. She seemed composed, so he asked, 'Do you want to discuss this some more now, or do you prefer we wait until tonight?'

'No! Not tonight, honey. I want to talk about it, now.

I don't want to use pillow talk to discuss this.'

She smiled a warm smile, adding, 'You men will agree to just about anything in bed . . . you know that.'

He grunted. 'Not this man!'

She shrugged and grunted back, poking him in the ribs. 'Yes, this man, too.'

He returned to the subject. 'We haven't talked about the really important person in all this . . . Erin! Have you discussed this with her, yet?'

She sighed. 'No, I haven't. Do you think she'd do it for me . . . for us? she inquired, giving him a quizzical look.

'I have no idea Meagan, but I think you had better discuss this with her before you do much more thinking about it, unless you're willing to have some other woman do it if Erin won't agree to it.'

She sat up. 'NO! If Erin won't do it, then,' and she lowered her voice, 'I don't want anyone else.'

He nodded. 'I understand but, you know, I'm sure this is a big thing to ask of her at this time in her life. She is excited about going to college, as you well know, and this means a whole year out before she can go, unless,' he laughed 'she is willing to be a pregnant coed.'

She answered, seriously. 'I know. I've thought about what a sacrifice she'd be making, but,' and turning to look him in the eye, 'don't you think I've sacrificed for her in my lifetime?'

He nodded. 'Of course you have, and I'm sure she is aware of that. I personally think she'll agree to it, but the only way to find out is to ask her.'

She nodded, not replying, returning to looking out the window.

He drove on for a few miles, mulling the matter over in his mind, and then. 'Meagan, honey, you know you should talk this over with a doctor, soon, so you'll have all the facts in hand before you make the final decision.'

'I know, Charlie, but I had to start with you. You're my husband. 'Course, if you don't want to do it, I can always find me a stud who will,' she smiled.

33

Meagan was nervous as she rehearsed in her mind the way she would present the idea to Erin.

She shook her head in resignation as she exclaimed to herself, 'I can't believe I'm nervous about talking to my own daughter, but . . . this is so important to me . . . and so demanding on her. She is so young and carefree. She's not ready for a baby. But it is not really her baby. She's just an incubator, but . . . it is her body that has to feed and nourish it and she is the one who has to go through the misery of delivery. Do I really have the right to ask her to do this. If she were a stranger, it could be a cold-blooded business deal. We'd pay her so much money for a job . . . like any other job, but this is my daughter. I would never offer her money, and she'd never take it. but, if she doesn't do it, then it won't get done and I'll never give Charlie a baby of his own . . . of our own.

'Erin, honey, I'd like to talk to you . . . in private,' as the supper dishes were being put away and she had sent Charlie out for ice cream . . . or something.

'Oh, Mama, I can tell when you have something serious on your mind. I want to go to bed. I'm sleepy. Can't it wait until later?'

'No, Erin. I'd like to discuss it with you, now.'

'Oh, OK, if you insist. What did I do wrong, now?'

She put her arm around her daughter's waist, smiling, as they walked to the living room couch.

'You didn't do anything wrong, honey . . . not that I know of anyway,' and motioning to a seat, she added, 'I just want to discuss an idea with you. I need your help if it's going to work . . . that's all.'

'You know, Mama, I will do anything in the world for you . . . you know that.'

She smiled at her daughter. 'We'll see, Erin honey,' as they took their seats. 'You know I want to give Charlie a baby more than anything in the world, but the doctors tell me I can't even think about it,' and she said solemnly, 'I guess they're right.'

Erin's eyes became filled with apprehension as she weighed her mother's words, thinking, 'How do I fit into this?'

The mother took her hand, and with tears beginning to flow, 'I want you to have a baby for me and Charlie, if you will do it . . . '

Erin's eyes widened. 'Oh, Mama, I like Charlie, but I could never do it with him . . . even if you asked me to. I love Charlie, but not that way. I just couldn't,' and now, tears filled her eyes as she pulled her hands away from her mother's.

Meagan smiled, proud of her daughter's declaration of morality, even if misguided and mistaken. She shook her head.

'No, honey, I could never ask you to do that . . . especially with Charlie. He's my man alone. No, you wouldn't have to do it with anybody, if you know what I mean. I'm sure you've heard of artificial insemination, haven't you??'

'Well, sure . . . I know about it, but that is mostly for cows and bulls, isn't it?'

She smiled at her daughter. She felt sure Erin was having fun with her. She knew her worldly daughter knew better than that. She continued, patiently, wanting to get done with it before Charlie returned. This was woman talk and not suitable for the male ears, and besides, he might come up with some creative ideas of his own for sperm transfer.

'No, honey, I'm sure you are aware that it is done on people, too. I'm not even sure I can do what I have in mind. I don't know if my eggs are healthy or not. I just am not sure of anything, just now, except I want to give Charlie a baby of our own.'

'You mean, Mama, they would plant one of your eggs in me and I would carry the baby for you?' she asked with great apprehension, knowing full well that this was what her mother meant.

The mother placed her hand on her daughter's, again, replying, 'Uh huh, that is what I am asking you to do for me, but before you answer, I want to tell you what you're getting into, honey.'

The daughter nodded, attempting a faint smile.

'For all practical purposes, you will be just as pregnant as if you had done it on your own . . .'

'But, without the fun of having done it,' she quipped.

'That's true,' the mother responded, trying to humour her, as she continued, 'you will go through all the things any other woman goes through when she is pregnant. You will get morning sickness.

'You will get to feel you are carrying a watermelon in your belly as you get bigger. You will have stretchmarks on your beautiful belly that will stay there for the rest of your life unless you have them removed, and, worst of all, in nine months you will have to deliver the child. As you know, it hurts like hell,' and she felt she should mention, 'why, I can still remember my labour pains for you,' and she sighed, letting that sink in for effect.

Erin nodded, sympathetically, patting her mother's hand.

'And then,' said Meagan, 'even after you go through all that, the baby won't even be yours. You'll be the sister as well as the surrogate mother,' she laughed.

Erin remained deep in thought for a long time; her young mind mulling over all the ramifications.

Her eyes widened as she asked, 'How do they get that thing in my belly?'

'The doctor inserts it in you.'

'How? Does he have to make a hole?'

Meagan smiled. 'No honey, you already have one provided by nature. They'll use that one.'

'Oh . . . I see.'

The mother pressed on. 'You know you had made up your mind to start college in the fall. I hope you realize that will have to be put off a year if you agree to this.'

The daughter nodded, saying nothing.

'Oh, honey, I know I am asking you to do something I shouldn't be asking you to do, but if you don't, then I can't leave part of me behind for Charlie,' and she smiled at her daughter, 'You will be all I have to show for a lifetime, and I will have to be content with it, and I will be. You're a beautiful girl, honey, and I am proud to be your mother. I wish your real daddy would have thought enough of me to have married me. Then, maybe, a lot of things that happened to us would never have happened, but he was young, and . . ' and her voice trailed off.

'Mama, how do they get one of your eggs out of you? Will they have to cut you to do that?'

She smiled a smile of resignation, as she shook her head. 'Honey, they're gonna cut me regardless. I'm just hoping they can do all this with one cut,' and the tears began to flow.

'Oh, Mama, please don't cry. It just tears me up,' and taking her mother's hands in hers, she said, proudly, 'If you want me to do this for you . . . well, by God, I'll do it.'

They hugged and cried, and then Erin pulled back, asking, 'Do I have to nurse that brat, too? I don't know if I want a baby pulling on my boobs. They'll never be the same, again.'

'We'll settle that later . . . OK?' the mother replied.

Erin smiled. 'Poor Charlie, he'll be ticked off when he finds out he won't enjoy this as much as most fathers get to do.'

Meagan laughed. 'Don't worry, he's already been advised of that in no uncertain terms.'

Erin asked, 'Is he agreeable to all this?'

'Uh huh, he wants a baby, too, and so does Alex. He wants a grandchild real bad.'

Erin smiled. 'I bet that baby won't ever be poor,' and she giggled. 'will it?'

Meagan shook her head. 'I hope not! I didn't enjoy it too much in my life,' and then looking into her daughter's eyes, asked, 'Do we have a deal, honey?'

Erin hugged her mother. 'Uh huh, Mama, we have a

deal. Now, I'm going to bed to get my rest. If I'm gonna get pregnant soon, I need to get in shape.'

Meagan watched her daughter go up the stairs, and she blinked back a tear as she looked upward, which she had not done in quite some time. 'Thank you, Lord, for sending me that child.'

Charlie walked in about that time, exclaiming, 'I couldn't find Tutti-fruiti, hun, but I bought you three other kinds to make a choice on,' and he looked at his wife, suddenly becoming sombre as he observed, 'You look like you've been crying, Meagan. Is something wrong? Do you feel OK?'

She blinked back the latest tears. 'It's nothing to worry about, honey . . . they're tears of happiness. I talked to Erin about the baby, and guess what Charlie . . . she agreed to do it.'

'Oh, I felt sure she would,' and he sat next to her.

'But, she feels sorry for you! She said you'd miss out on a lot of fun this way. She is so tacky, at times.'

He nodded. 'And so right at times, too.'

Meagan held him close.'That's tough, Charlie.'

'Uh huh . . . I can see you're really concerned for my comfort and emotional well being, Meagan, honey,' he kidded.

She nuzzled him. 'I didn't know you were suffering. You should have said something.'

He went along with it. 'Well, I am, and right now, too.'

She giggled. 'Do I have time to eat my ice cream, first?'

'No, ice cream gives you cold lips. It can wait, can't it?'

'OK, put it in the freezer, Charlie, but I want to be carried up the stairs,' she laughed, 'to conserve my energy.'

He held out his arms. 'Climb up, Scarlett.'

There was pillow talk later that night. Lots of pillow talk, for there were plans to be discussed in detail. Questions were asked for which neither participant had the answers. There were even questions which were not asked which should have been asked, but, due to lack of knowledge, were not.

'When the details had run into the so called brick wall, Charlie astutely observed, 'Meagan, honey, we have to see the doctor . . . soon.'

The fear of the anticipated surgery wiped out all the evening's earlier pleasures as she responded, sombrely, 'I know honey, I guess it's time to face the music, huh?'

He wished he had some inspiring words of wisdom and encouragement to give her, but all that emerged from his lips was 'I think so, Meagan,' and they held each other close until slumber replaced apprehension.

But in Erin's case, slumber eluded her altogether. She was a worried woman; her mind played with different scenarios as she tossed and turned the night away. Her imagination went wild as she pictured herself dying in childbirth, bleeding to death as the doctors frantically tried to stem the flow of blood, and having that scene played out, she pictured herself on the University of Colorado campus at Boulder, waddling across the quadrangle in her grossly pregnant condition, trying to get to the next class on time, and not being able to, and being continually gigged for tardiness.

But even worse than that; and even worse than bleeding to death, how could any boy look at her in that horrible condition, with extended belly and consider any romance with her. She would be worse off than a cloistered nun as far as romance was concerned. And, horrors, what if she met a boy and fell in love. Could he return her love? Not hardly, she felt.

What man would accept that corny explanation for her pregnancy: 'I'm having a baby for my mother!' That would be more difficult a selling job than Mary had in explaining to Joseph about her predicament, and she felt sure that she, Erin, would not have Divine help in selling her story.

As she lay awake, staring at the ceiling, the reality of what she had promised her mother came home to roost. This was not child's play. This was real.

Her contribution was to be much larger than she had originally envisioned, but, as she turned over to attempt sleep, she murmured, 'You're a big girl, Erin honey, and you're playing for keeps. This is not child's play, anymore.'

At breakfast the next morning the group was quiet as

each pondered the events and decisions of the night before. Erin munched on a slice of toast without enthusiasm, watching her mother and Charlie exchange glances. Charlie broke the silence and the tension with, 'Erin, honey, your mother tells me that you've agreed to have the baby for us. I want you to know we both appreciate it very much.'

She managed a weak smile. 'It's the least I can do for two people I love so much. Besides, it will give me something to do until school starts in the fall,' she grinned.

The mother turned to her. 'Erin, honey, I know you probably did a lot of thinking about this last night . . . I know I did. Do you have any reservations about it? It's not too late to change your mind, you know.'

'You're right,Mama. I did a lot of thinking about it and, no, I don't want to change my mind. I want to do it for you. God knows you've sacrificed enough for me in my lifetime . . . '

The mother interjected. 'Erin, I don't want you to do this because you think you owe me something.'

'Why else would I do it, Mama? Do you believe I'm doing this to satisfy some maternal instinct? I don't have maternal instincts . . . not yet, anyway. I'm doing it because I love you, Mama. You do things for people you love . . . that's why!'

Meagan felt she had been put in her place, as she responded, 'Oh, I see. I guess you're right, honey, but I want you to know Charlie and I are really grateful.'

She smiled at both and resumed munching on her now cold toast.

She put it down, saying, 'When is this going to happen? If I'm gonna be a mama soon, I need to make arrangements with my social life,' she kidded.

Meagan looked at Charlie for confirmation, replying, 'It will happen as soon as we can make arrangements. 'I'll call my doctor this morning when we get to the office . . . '

Charlie rose. 'Speaking of the office, it's time to go. Ready, girls?'

Erin smiled. 'We have to talk about maternity leave for me, Charlie.'

He smiled at Meagan. 'She has a point, you know.'

'Uh huh, but let's get her pregnant first.'

Erin said as they went out to the car, 'I saw some of the cutest maternity clothes the other day at the mall . . . simply precious, Mama. I can hardly wait to get pregnant,' she laughed.

Meagan took hold of her husband's arm, responding, 'Charlie, honey, this could be more expensive than you thought it would.'

He shrugged. 'Isn't it always the father who pays? But, they usually have more fun than I will have doing this.'

Meagan kidded, 'Poor darling! Maybe we can come up with something creative to help you enjoy it more.'

He smiled, 'You promise?'

She replied, 'I promise,' and then she became solemn, again, as they drove off. She dreaded the next few weeks as she had never dreaded anything in her entire life.

34

As they were wheeled out of their joint room in the Woman's Hospital in Denver, where they had spent the preceding night being prepared for their surgery, the mother and daughter were nervous and scared . . . for two diametrically opposed reasons.

They kissed and held each other's hands as they were placed on their respective stretchers to be delivered to their respective operating rooms where two teams of surgeons would perform on each the required surgical procedures to remove from Meagan her uterus and some of her eggs; for Erin, the procedure was more simple but no less important, for into her body the fertilized egg was to be deposited in her womb and there, hopefully, it would grow on the warmth and nourishment of her own body.

With gynaecological surgeons in one operating room and fertility specialists in the other, each performing the tasks of their particular disciplines, the deeds were done without complications, as the surgeons explained the outcome.

The mother had been given a general anaesthetic while the daughter had not.

As Erin, in good spirits, was returned to her room, she seemed ebullient as she saw Charlie, asking, 'Where's Mama? How is she? How did it go?'

He bent to kiss her on the cheek 'Your mother came through fine . . . just fine. She is in recovery and will be for sometime. How are you, honey?'

She gave him a warm smile. She was glad it was all over.

'I feel fine, Charlie. Didn't hurt a bit,' and she could

not help attempting some levity. 'The least they could have done was let you watch, Charlie. I've never in my life had so many strangers looking at my bottom. It's humiliating,' she pouted in her excited and exhilarated state.

Then, seriously, 'Do they think they got it all, Charlie? With Mama? You know what I mean,' avoiding the dreadful word.

He shrugged.'I don't know, honey. They tell me they have removed the source of the cancer, but,' and he could not tell her of the spreading of the disease to the lymph glands. He just couldn't do it. Both women were kept in the dark as to the extent of the problem. It was a judgement decision he had made after consultations with the doctors. He had wanted from the doctors some note of acquiescence, but all they gave him was, 'You will have to make that decision, Mr Forester . . . we can't make it for you.' And, he had. He hoped he had made the right one, but he was not sure. He would never be sure for the rest of his life! He had made it by putting himself in her shoes.'Is it not better,' he had asked himself, 'to enjoy the remaining days without the spectre of certain death staring at you every minute of every hour of every day? Would every chance of happiness be dampened by that dark cloud of the mind, shutting out any chance of sunshine.

Every look . . . every glance . . . every emotion would be dampened by,'I'm dying! Why should I laugh when I am dying? How can I be happy when I am dying?' Every grasp at happiness would be tainted by the ever-present underlying but overriding thought, 'I'm dying.'

And, he continued in his mind . . . would her knowing really change anything? No! Not one iota, but her knowledge of it could change everything, for it would preclude all hope.

He knew her well enough to know she was the type who would say, 'Tell me the truth, honey. I want to know the truth,' but, she never did ask it. He justified his deception on the basis that she never asked, and he never volunteered. He felt she really didn't want to know the truth. No! He decided . . . it is best to believe there is a chance, and if I am wrong in deceiving her, he concluded, may she forgive me.

And he continued his examination of conscience with regard to Erin. If the mother didn't know, then Erin could not know either, for the young, emotional and volatile young woman could not have handled it. She would have betrayed the secret with her compassion for her mother. It would have to come out in some form or other, he concluded with self justification.

He felt vindicated as he drove the two women home after their release from hospital, for they were in a jovial mood as they talked incessantly to each other and Charlie. Meagan looked more rested than she had in quite some time, thanks to periodic pills to ensure she did rest. The surgery had gone well. She pouted as she showed her husband the stomach scar in one of their private moments in the hospital, while Erin had gone to the coffee shop accompanied by two resident doctors.

'Yes,' she had promised them, 'if I ever need a doctor, I'll call on you fellas.'

As Meagan exposed the scar she said, 'Look what they did to me, honey, and to think we paid them good money to desecrate my belly like that,' she laughed. 'Good thing you saw it in its prime, or you never would have married me now.'

'Oh, I don't know. Sorta gives your stomach some character.'

She pouted.'Are you telling me my stomach didn't have any character before.'

'Oh, no! I would never say that. As a matter of fact, I have always told the boys at the pool hall that your stomach had more character than any stomach I've ever seen.'

She covered her stomach with her hospital gown. 'You're teasing me, Charlie. You might just never get to see this stomach again, ever,' she pouted.

'Aw . . . you know I'm kidding, honey. Look what I've brought you to cheer you up,' and he handed her a jewellery box. Her eyes widened as she opened it, exposing a pair of diamond earrings.

'Oh, honey, they're beautiful. thank you so much,

but you shouldn't have, after all the money we'll have to pay for this surgery.'

He nodded. 'Thank God for the Forester Company medical plan.'

"'Oh,' she responded. 'I forgot about that. In that case,' as she removed the earrings from the box, 'I'll keep them.'

The banter continued all the way back to Breckenridge and home. The late winter snow was still on the ground but spring was not too far off, and with spring – renewed hope for mother and her husband.

For the daughter, who felt she had life in her, although it was only a few days old, spring was a time of renewal and how better to renew than with a new life. She was sure she was pregnant. She had no evidence, but an inner feeling, and she often placed her hand on her belly as if to confirm the fact. Her mother saw her do it, and she smiled, too. They were happier than they had been for a long time.

The firm of Chapton/Forester was now in full operation, and the entire office force was now back at work. The secretary, Erin, had missed her last period, and under a different set of circumstances this omission would have struck terror in the heart of an unmarried woman, but not this time. The mother of the secretary had monitored the situation on a daily basis as the appointed day came and went, with, 'Anything yet, honey?'

'No, Mama! You will be the second person to know.'

'Oh, Erin, I'm so excited, honey. I just feel it in my bones. I know you're pregnant.'

Erin laughed. 'All my life, Mama, you've told me to try not to get pregnant before I got married, to keep my legs crossed around men, and now you're trying to make me get pregnant. Shame on you, Mama!'

'I know, honey, but this is different . . . special.'

They hugged, with Erin responding, 'I know, Mama. I'm doing the best I can,' and she patted her belly.

Meagan suppressed a tear, then, 'Erin, please don't tell Charlie you missed your period. It might be a false alarm. I don't want him to be disappointed. Wait until you miss the second one.'

'He won't be put off that long, Mama. He's been asking me every day.' She laughed. 'You'd think he was my unmarried boyfriend and he was sweating it out.'

'I know he's nervous, but, let's wait, honey . . . please.'

35

The calendar indicated that spring had come to the high country, but the weatherman had apparently not seen the calendar as a late winter snow storm dumped a foot of new snow on the mountains. This brought happiness to the ski buffs, but despair to those longing for warm summer breezes.

Erin sat at the kitchen table, pencil in hand as she counted the days on the calendar.

To herself, 'Let's see. I was due on this day, and I didn't, so, if I count twenty-eight days from that date, it brings me to this one, and . . . oh, hell, I don't know how to do this. All I know is . . . so far . . . nothing for two months.'

Before she could enjoy the prospect that she was pregnant, she felt a spasm of nausea in her stomach. She barely made it to the bathroom in time to discharge her breakfast into the toilet bowl. Kneeling, with one hand on the lavatory cabinet and the other on the wall, she gasped for air. Getting to her feet, she staggered to the lavatory, reaching for a wash cloth and wetting it, applied it to her cheeks. the cool water felt good on her flushed cheeks. She looked at herself in the mirror.

She gasped. 'My God! I'm pregnant!'

She ran out of the bathroom, ran up the steps to the bedroom where Charlie and Meagan were sleeping late this Saturday morning. She gave a quick knock on the door and without waiting for a word of any kind, threw the door open, and to the two astonished faces peering at her out of the semi-darkness, screamed, 'I'm pregnant!'

Meagan sat up in bed, half asleep, half awake, as the

words sank into her brain. 'Oh, Erin, are you sure?'

'I'm sure, Mama. I just vomited my breakfast! I feel pregnant.'

Meagan held out her arms to the daughter, beckoning her to come to them.

'Oh, honey . . . thank God. It's happened. Oh Charlie, did you hear that? We're gonna have a baby of our own. Come here honey, get into bed with us so we can hold the baby, too. Move over Charlie.'

Charlie, just coming awake, moved over as if in a trance. Erin climbed in over him and snuggled next to her mother. They hugged, and then Erin hugged Charlie, and then all three snuggled together or, would it be more appropriate to say . . . all four snuggled together.

Charlie hugged Erin, exclaiming, 'You did it, Erin. I'm so proud of you, honey!'

Meagan sat up, offended. 'Hey . . . wait a minute! She didn't do this alone you know,' and once again filled with motherly love and satisfaction, she held her daughter close to her again.

They lay there for some time in close embrace, until Erin, now that the euphoria had past, sat up saying, 'Geez, guys, I'm sorry I broke in on you like this, but . . . I was excited. I hope I didn't interrupt anything.' she giggled.

'With good news like that, you can interrupt us anytime,' responded Charlie.

Erin now felt embarrassed wedged in between Charlie and Meagan, saying, 'Well, I guess now that the news has been broken, I'd better get out of your bed, huh?'

'Not if you don't want to,' Meagan replied, 'Huh, Charlie?'

'No. I've always dreamed of being in bed with two good looking women, and now I have,' he teased.

'I'll bet you didn't want one of them to be pregnant, though,' Erin giggled, as she climbed out over him, saying, 'Try not to get too excited when I climb over you, Charlie, 'cause nothings gonna happen . . . huh, Mama?'

'You can bet your life on that, honey,' Meagan said.

Erin stood by the side of the bed, looking at the two, asking, 'Well,what do we do, now? What's next?'

Meagan got out of bed, reaching for a bathrobe on the foot of the bed. 'You go to the doctor . . . that is what is next, honey. We want everything to go right with this. It is our only shot. We don't want any mistakes. You've got to make contact with an obstetrician who will take care of you until you deliver, and Erin, honey, you will follow his every instruction, do you hear me?'

As she neared the door, she turned.'All right, Mama. I'll be a good girl, but . . . can I keep skiing?'

'Only if your doctor says so,' screamed Meagan to an empty doorway and then, turning to her husband. 'I'm gonna have to watch her like a hawk, Charlie, and I expect your help in controlling her.'

He arose, yawning. 'Anything you say, honey,' as he made his way to the bathroom.

Meagan's heart was filled with joy as she sat on the edge of the bed. She felt euphoric . . . until the pain hit her. She lay back on the bed, her hands on her mouth to suppress the scream she felt was coming. She breathed heavily.

'Oh, God. Why? At a time like this. Why?'

She lay there in a foetal position until her husband came out of the bathroom. He looked at her lying there with her eyes closed, and he felt a warm glow come over him.

He went to her, putting his hand on her shoulder, asking, 'You've decided to go back to sleep? Why don't you. It's Saturday and we really have nothing to do and,' looking out the window at the falling snow, 'there is nothing much we can do outside today, anyway.'

She sat up, now that the pain had subsided. She took his hand in hers, and motioning to the bed, said, softly, 'Please sit down a minute honey, I want to talk to you.'

He noticed that her happiness had been replaced by gloom, and he felt sure he knew why, as he responded, 'Sure, honey, what's up?'

She searched for words. 'Charlie, I've changed my mind about the chemotherapy treatments. I've decided to take them. Is that all right with you?'

He took her hand. 'Why, of course, if that is your decision, Meagan. I'll do anything you want to do, honey. What made you change your mind?'

'The baby. I want to live long enough to see my baby,' and she began to sob. He hated moments like this. He held her close, replying. 'Why, you will live long enough to see our baby have babies, and then some,' he lied.

She shook her head, smiling at him. 'Sure, honey, if you say so,' and she rose to go to the bathroom. Looking back, adding, 'would you make the arrangements for me to start treatments as soon as you can?'

He nodded. 'I'll take care of everything.'

As she entered the kitchen some time later her mood had swung the other way. She was now cheerful and happy, kidding Erin from time to time about her impending loss of figure as the baby grew larger and larger.

Erin nodded, giggling. 'I know, Mama. That's the only thing I really regret about this whole thing, and that is the loss of my figure. It is sinful to ruin a figure like mine . . . huh, Charlie?'

'It sure is, doll, but it is only temporary. Why, when this is all over you will look better than ever. You will have the bloom of full womanhood on your face. The glow of motherhood will shine like a beacon on a dark night,' he teased.

'What bullshit,' Erin responded.'Why don't you have the baby so you can have the glow on your face, Charlie?'

He smiled. 'I'm not built for it, honey. You know that.'

'Uh huh! I know. I wish men were, though.'

Meagan interrupted. 'OK, you two. You're not going to change anything with wishing for it, believe me. Erin, why don't you get dressed and we'll go to town and see if we can find an obstetrician for you, and Charlie, why don't you talk to my doctor in Denver and see what he says about the . . . ' She caught herself, and giving Erin a sheepish look . . . 'about the treatments.'

'What treatments, Mama?' from a surprised Erin.

She gave her daughter an embarrassed look. 'I've decided to begin chemotherapy treatments, honey.'

'Oh, Mama, I'm so glad you've decided to do it,' and she went to her mother, hugging her.'What made you change your mind?'

Meagan put her hand on Erin's belly. 'This made me change my mind.'

Erin placed her hand over her mother's, and with a wicked gleam in her eye, asked, 'Charlie, would you like to put your hand on the baby, too?'

Meagan removed her hand, waving Charlie off, smiling 'That won't be necessary, Erin. He might make a habit of it.'

Charlie merely smiled, replying, 'It would only be a manifestation of my impending fatherhood.'

'Bullshit, Charlie,' Erin grinned, 'It would be a manifestation of your impending manhood.' Charlie merely smiled.

* * *

As winter surrendered to spring, the life in the womb grew stronger while the other grew weaker. Erin had begun to show as the old expression goes, and except for a new maternity wardrobe to show for her trouble she was not happy with her protruding stomach. She was self conscious wherever she went now that she had lost her svelte figure. She felt that everyone, men and women alike, took notice of her. As for the eligible young men who used to oggle her . . . well . . . 'They don't even look at me anymore, Mama . . . it's awful. I hate being this big in the belly.'

Meagan laughed. 'You ain't seen nothing yet, honey, you're only four months. Just wait!'

'Oh, Mama!'

Meagan, although unknown to her, was not responding to the chemotherapy. Charlie had asked the doctors to be evasive when answering her questions concerning the progress, unless the news was favourable. They had to be evasive. Her hair began to fall out, much to her distress. She hated that. What woman wouldn't? As her appearance deteriorated, her desire to correct it became obsessive. She refused to let even Charlie see her without a hat on or a kerchief around her head, even in bed.

'But, that is foolish Meagan,' he pleaded. 'Do you think it makes any difference to me?'

'Yes, Charlie, it makes a difference to you . . . and to me.'

'Well, why don't you take it off after we put the lights out? At least, you wouldn't have to sleep with it on,' he argued.

'You will see me in the middle of the night, if you wake up,' she pouted.

'I promise not to look at you . . . OK?'

'I don't know if I can trust you, honey,' she teased back. 'I look like a freak and I know it. Do you really think that it is doing me any good – what I'm going through?'

He couldn't tell her the truth, so he replied, 'It certainly is not doing you any harm, Meagan.'

'That's not true, Charlie. Look at me! I look like hell.'

'I love you no matter what you look like.'

She patted his hand. 'Thank you, honey. And while we're on the subject of love . . . I know you haven't been getting your share of that either, and I'm sorry, I really am, but I just don't feel like it, and I don't think I should, anyway, but, oh honey, I'm so sorry. I've let you down in everything, Charlie . . . I'm so sorry . . . '

He held her close. He started to stroke her hair, out of habit, until he remembered she had none. He stroked her neck, her shoulders, her breasts, until she placed her hand on his, saying, 'No, honey, you'll just get excited for nothing.'

He felt foolish as he replied, 'I'm sorry. I forgot.'

She began to cry, softly. 'I'm sorry, too,' and she added after some time, 'Charlie, if you want to go and find some other woman . . . for affection . . . I don't mind. I really don't, as long as you come home to me . . . after . . . '

'You know you don't mean that, Meagan.'

'No I don't, either, but I thought I owed you that.'

He kissed her tenderly. He felt and tasted salty tears on her cheeks, as he responded, 'Thank you anyway, but we'll share this difficult period in our lives . . . together,' and he held her close.

She snuggled, sighing. 'I love you, Charlie.'

'I love you, too, Meagan.'

'Charlie?'

'Yes?'

'Do you want a boy or a girl,'

'As much trouble as we've gone through to have this baby, I'll settle for anything with one head, two arms and two legs,' he teased.

'Me, too, but I'd like to give you a little boy.'

'Why, a boy?'

'So you can take him fishing and hunting . . . and play baseball and football with him, and do all the things daddies do with their sons.'

'Well, if we had a girl, you could do all the things mothers do with little girls . . . '

'Oh, Charlie, let's be practical about this. I'll never see that child grow up. I'm just praying to see it born.'

'Meagan . . . please don't talk like that. You don't know.'

She sighed. 'Yes, honey, I know.'

He said nothing, having nothing to say that would be honest and encouraging to her.

She felt like talking, evidently, as she continued, 'I wish I could have met your mother, Charlie, before . . . ' and she let it die.

He was curious. 'Before what?'

'Well, I would have liked to meet her when I still looked like a normal human being, but now . . . no.'

He sat up. 'Are you saying you don't want to meet her, now.'

She shuddered. 'No, not now, honey. Not the way I look.'

'But,' he protested, 'I talked to Dad last night, and he said mother is talking about coming to see us.'

She sat up in bed. The kerchief fell off her head, but in her excitement she ignored that too, exclaiming, 'No!

No! You've got to call them and tell them I can't see them . . . not now!' she implored.

'But, what shall I tell them? What excuse will I give them? For God's sake, Meagan, I can't tell my parents they're not welcome here.'

She looked at him with determination, her eyes on fire. 'I don't care what you tell them, Charlie. I will not let your mother see me looking like this! Promise me, please!'

He shook his head. 'All right honey, I promise, although at this moment, I don't know what I'll say to them.'

36

As the winter relaxed its grip on the high country, the snow pockets tucked into the crevices of the mountains, hidden from the sun, were all that could be seen of the winter's legacy from Dillon valley far below. The population of the resorts changed too. As the snow birds, the ski bums, left and returned to their routine lives, attempting to make and save enough money to return next year to repeat the process all over again, the summer tourists began to make their appearance.

They were a different breed, the summer tourists. The sleek and young blonde gods and goddesses of the slopes gave way to a more portly aggregation of the 'mom and pop' crowd, accompanied by the children. But to the merchants of the area, money was money, no matter whether it came from fur-lined ski suits or wildly coloured Bermuda shorts.

The real estate agencies were busy unloading the condos bought in haste by a ski crowd and selling them to time share companies which peddled them as a summer retreat for a week or two of family pleasure. Whatever the reason, Charlie's real estate business was booming. As Orville Chapton and his wife loosened their hold on the business they had founded after World War Two, the increased work load fell on the newly formed Forster organisation.

Erin, now heavily pregnant, had no heart for the office job, and she made it perfectly clear to her boss, step-father, and biological father of the baby growing in her womb. 'You know, Charlie, I can't be a brood mare and a secretary at the same time and do a good job of each. I'm good but not that good!'

He nodded with understanding. 'I know, Erin. If you want to stay home and spend the days with your mother, I'll be happy to get a replacement for you here at the office.'

'Well,' she complained, 'I really want to do my share, and I hate to lose my salary. You pay good,' she joked.

He replied, patronizingly. 'I will continue to pay you while you are on maternity leave. You know that.'

She sighed, 'Since Mama quit working here at the office, it's just not fun like it used to be when she was here.'

He gave her a serious look. 'Well, she just didn't feel like doing it anymore. She said she is not up to it.'

'I know. She's getting weaker every day, Charlie . . . I can see it.'

He looked away, not wanting her to see the tears in his eyes, replying. 'Yeah, I can, too. I feel so sorry for her.'

'Oh, God, Charlie, don't let her hear you say that. She doesn't want any sympathy . . . you know that.'

'Yes, I know.'

'I hate to see her sit there in that lounge chair, looking out of those big windows, just staring out into space. What do you think she is thinking about?'

He breathed a deep sigh. 'I guess she is thinking about dying, Erin. Most people in her situation do, I guess.'

Erin began to sob, reaching in the purse under her desk for a tissue. 'Oh, Charlie, please don't say that. I can't stand to think of it. It makes me so sad. I'm afraid it will affect the baby if I get despondent too much.'

'I'm sorry, honey. I guess we shouldn't dwell on it as much as we do, but I can't stop thinking about it, either.'

She became pensive as she continued to wipe her eyes, sobbing softly.'You know what she makes me do, Charlie?' He shook his head.

She continued, 'She makes me sit next to her on the couch so she can put her hand on my belly, feeling the baby,' and then she sobbed. 'She asks . . . do you feel him kicking, Erin? Please let me know when he kicks you . . . I want to feel it, too,' and rising abruptly, she headed for the rest room sobbing,

'Excuse me, Charlie, I have to tinkle. That little devil presses on my bladder something terrible,' she smiled.

While she was gone, several prospects came through the door, and he had to turn his attention to them.

He smiled, saying in best salesman fashion, hand extended, 'Hi, I'm Charlie Forester . . . may I help you?'

Meagan sighed heavily as she let herself down onto the couch facing the television set. She flicked the remote button, and after running through the soap operas and CNN, she flicked it off with a snap of her wrist. She put her head back on the couch cushion, looking out the window at the mountains which formed a backdrop for her home.

Tears came to her eyes as they did most days. She tried to get all her crying done when she was alone in the house so that Erin and Charlie would not see it. Her day time nurse, Helen, came in from the kitchen, and seeing her eyes wet, gently scolded her. 'Now, Meagan, you promised me you wouldn't shed any more tears, and here you are . . . '

Meagan turned to her, smiling weakly. 'I lied to you, Helen. I cry all the time when you're out of the room. I'm beginning to enjoy it. It's my time to feel sorry for myself when my husband and daughter are not here to see it.'

The nurse took her hand, pressing it tightly. 'I know, dear, but you should look on the bright side, if you can.'

Meagan snorted. 'What bright side? Describe it to me so I can recognize it when I see it.'

Helen was nearly sixty years old and had been nursing for nearly forty of those sixty years. She had seen it all, but she felt she had seen enough and decided on retirement, but, fate intervened. Her husband, who had decided on retirement to coincide with hers, died of a heart attack on the first week away from their jobs.

With the pragmatism of her mountain-folk background, Helen had shrugged her shoulders, 'I guess that

God didn't mean for me to retire,' so when the phone call came from Charlie, accompanied by heartfelt pleading and the promise of a hefty pay cheque she agreed to take on Meagan as a private, daytime only, case.

Helen tried to respond to her cynical comment philosophically, but, instead,'Meagan, honey, I can feel what you are going through. I've seen it so many times, I can feel it, too.'

Meagan looked at her, eyes blurred. 'Can you?' and as she once again looked out the window, continued, 'You know what makes it so hard, Helen?'

'What, honey?' as she held her hand.

Meagan shook her head. 'It happened so fast.'

'You mean the cancer?'

'No! I mean I had no time to enjoy the happiness I took nearly forty years to find. That is what's so unfair. I had a poor and hard childhood. Then, I got pregnant in high school.' She sighed. 'I know I have no one but myself to blame for that, but I thought I was in love . . . you know how it is at that age . . . '

Helen nodded, too, the womanly understanding, patting Meagan's hand. 'I know how it is, honey.'

She continued, 'Then, I had to raise Erin all by myself. That was hard to do on a high school education in a modern world. What could I do but work like a mule? And men – I fought them off when I had desires as strong as they did, but I had fear and regrets to go with them, too. I didn't need another child, and men,' she repeated, 'You know how rotten they are. They don't give a damn about you as long as they get what they want.'

Helen nodded sympathetically, 'Amen to that.'

Meagan would not be denied. she had told Helen all this the first week she was hired, but, it had come out again, feeling if she recited it enough times, perhaps she could find some justification for it all. 'And then, I made another mistake, marrying that no-good bastard who raped my precious little virgin. Then, she went to serve time for something she was not to blame for. I only lived for one thing, then, and that was to get her out.'

She sighed.'But what can a poor, half educated waitress do in fighting the system?'

She turned away from the nurse to look out the window again, then her face turned into a smile.

Turning back to the nurse, she grinned,'And then he came into my life . . . Charlie.' She was quiet for a moment, obviously enjoying her reverie.

She turned to Helen, half giggling. 'Do you know I took him home with me the first night? Oh, nothing happened, mind you! I'm not an easy woman,' and she shook her head. 'No he had no place to sleep that night.'

She smiled . . . 'Filthy rich, and he told me he had no place to sleep that night! Can you imagine that? You know what?' she mused . . . 'I think he was pulling my leg, Helen. I think he thought he had an easy lay,' but she giggled, 'I told him the only warm thing he would get that night was a warm bed,' and she announced proudly, 'that's all he got, too.'

She became pensive. 'You know, Helen, a girl has to be so careful. I'm sure as we are sitting here talking that if I had let him in my bed that night . . . well, he'd gone and walked out on me the next morning, smiling and satisfied. You agree?'

Helen smiled. 'I sure do, honey, men are no damn good.'

Meagan grabbed her stomach as the pain hit her. She placed her hands on her belly, as if to support the pain as it raced through her.

The nurse rose, putting her hands on her shoulders exclaiming, 'Meagan . . . maybe, you need to rest for a while. You've been doing some emotional talking, and . . . '

She shook her head. 'No! I want to say it all. I want to tell you how I feel. I can't tell Charlie or Erin all this, and you're all I've got, Helen,' she said, pleadingly.

The nurse still looked concerned. 'Do you want another pill, now? It's time, you know,' as she looked at the grandfather clock against the wall.

Meagan shook her head. 'No. Not until I finish. They make me groggy. I want to talk for a while . . . please.'

The nurse nodded, 'Sure, honey . . . you talk all you want to.'

Meagan managed a smile as she looked out the window. A bird was pecking on the window frame, trying to capture an insect for a meal.

She continued.'And then, when he came back the next night . . . you see he couldn't get the part for his Jeep, so he had to stay in town for another night.'

She giggled . . . 'You know, Helen, I finally got Charlie because there is no Jeep dealer in Mountain View.' And she became pensive as she added, 'When he was satisfied to spend another night in my apartment without tearing my door down,' and she giggled again, 'Not that I'm much of a prize, but I'm not bad when I'm fixed up. You should have seen me when I came out of that beauty parlour in Denver after Charlie told them to fix me up, but,' she mused, 'anyway, when he didn't try to knock my door down, I knew he was the man for me. I fell for him like a ton of bricks but I didn't tell him at first. You know,' she said, proudly, 'a girl can't play her hand too soon.'

'How true,' Helen observed, as she could tell Meagan was now exhausted, but she felt she could not make her stop.

Meagan sighed deeply. 'Then, it happened in that hotel in Denver. Oh Helen, have you ever experienced ecstasy?'

The nurse giggled.'Yes, but I married someone more dependable.'

Meagan laughed, holding her stomach. 'Oh, Helen, that is a good one.'

Then she became sombre again. 'Then, just when everything is falling into place and I can see happiness staring me in the face for the first time in my life,' and she turned away, asking, 'Why, Helen, why?'

'Honey, if I knew the answer to that one, I could unlock the secrets of life itself!'

Meagan became pensive. 'Do you think I'm being punished for past sins?'

'Oh, Meagan . . . NO! Based on what I now know about you, you've been a good Christian woman. You don't deserve this because of past sins!'

She seemed mollified if not satisfied. 'That's what I think too, but why?'

The nurse shook her head. 'I don't know, honey. I wish I did. Why did my Rupert die the week he retired?'

Meagan seemed interested in the question. 'How did he die?'

She smiled a weak smile to make a point. 'He had a heart attack,' she replied with outstretched hands.

Meagan became pensive. 'I see,' and as another severe pain racked her body, she cried in suppressed sob, saying, 'I'm ready for that pill now,' and looking at the clock, added, 'Charlie and Erin will be home soon. I hope I'm still awake to put my hand on Erin's belly and feel my baby kicking. I enjoy that so much, Helen. Did you enjoy that when you were pregnant?'

Helen, who had given birth to seven children, four boys and three girls, replied, smiling, 'Uh huh, but only during the day . . . not the night.'

Meagan became pensive. 'I wish I could feel it any-time.'

As the nurse returned from the kitchen with a pain killer and a glass of water, a car could be heard coming up the gravel drive.

As she hurriedly swallowed the pill, and consumed a half glass of water, Meagan smiled, handing the glass back to the nurse. 'Thank you. I hear Erin and Charlie coming home. I'm taking the pill at the right time. I hope I won't feel any pain while I talk to them about the day.'

The nurse smiled, knowingly. 'I guess since the next shift is coming on duty,' she joked, 'I'll go to the super-market and see what I can scrounge for my supper. I've got some of my grandkids coming to eat with me, tonight. Good night, Meagan.'

She held her hand for a long time, saying, 'Good night, Helen. I hope I didn't bend your ear too much, but I wanted to talk.'

'I know. It helps,' and turning to Charlie and Erin as they came through the door, 'The patient is all yours, second shift'

Erin, at the same time as she told the nurse good-night, went to her mother. 'How're you doing, mama?' as she bent over to kiss her.

Charlie and the nurse exchanged a few words at the door. Meagan gave them a curious look, replying to Erin, 'I'm doing just fine, honey . . . how is the little mama doing? Come here . . . let me feel him for a while.'

As Erin sat next to her mother and placed her hand on the now kicking infant, she inquired, 'You always refer to it as a ''him'', Mama, how are you so sure it's a boy?'

Meagan giggled. 'He has an extra bump right here . . . feel it?'

She shoved her hand away. 'Oh, Mama, you're terrible,' as they both giggled, looking at Charlie as he came over to kiss Meagan.

'Hi, hun, how's it going, and what are you two giggling over?'

Meagan gave him her cheek, replying, 'Girl-talk, Charlie, and how are you doing, sweetheart? What's new at the office? What's going on in the outside world?'

He sank into a chair, loosening his tie, sighing. 'Well, business is booming, and the secretary gave me notice today that she is going on maternity leave, effective immediately,' he smiled.

Meagan started to cry out in pain at the latest spasm. She could feel the pain killer working at last, and she was grateful, as she responded, 'I thought you'd work until you were seven months at least, Erin. Are you getting tired already?'

Erin lowered herself into a chair. 'Uh huh, I'm losing my zip, Mama. I get tired a lot sooner than I used to, and then, being at the front desk, I have to put on a happy face when sometimes I don't feel like it,' she pouted.

Meagan turned to Charlie. 'How do you feel about that, honey? Can you do without her?'

He smiled. 'It will be tough, but we'll manage.'

Erin gave him a coy look. 'Don't you get sarcastic, Charlie! I've carried my load lately, if you will excuse the pun.'

Charlie laughed, nodding, 'You sure have, honey, and

the pun is acknowledged. It was a good one, too. I'm glad to see that you haven't lost your sense of humour,' and turning back to his wife, 'Well, how are you and Helen getting on? OK?'

'Uh huh, I like her very much. She is good company, and she is a good listener too, when I get to talking about the past . . . '

Charlie gave her a discerning look. 'Why have you been talking about the past?'

She smiled in resignation: 'Because the past is all I have, Charlie. I don't have a future.'

She was sorry it came out that way. She had promised herself to try to be cheerful around Erin and Charlie. She had promised, but . . .

He didn't know what to respond to her. He hated it too, when she made statements of desperation like that but, he concluded to himself. 'Who can blame her?'

Erin, sensing the tension, rose, smiling. 'What would you like for supper, tonight, Mama? I'll fix you anything you want that can be made in a microwave in ten minutes or less,' she joked.

'I'm not hungry, honey. Just fix Charlie something . . . if you feel like it.' She giggled. 'If you don't feel like it, then, there is always the pizza man who delivers.'

Charlie decided that pizza was a good idea but, instead of calling the man who delivers he wanted to go out to get it, himself. He wanted time to think.

As he headed out the long drive to the main road leading into town he mulled over his situation . . . his and his family. He had been married hardly a year and his wife was dying. His step-daughter was pregnant with a seed not of her own, nor of a man with whom she was in love . . . not boy-girl love.

Soon, he reasoned, he would have a dead wife and a new baby. He shook his head in disbelief. How had his life taken such a turn in so short a time? Damn Adelle! It was all her fault!

As he turned on to the state road he narrowly missed hitting an oncoming car, so deep was he in meditation. He shook his head. That was all they needed, Meagan and Erin, for him to get himself killed at this stage of the game. The thought of such a disaster caused chills to go down his spine. Meagan would soon die, he reasoned, with or without him . . . but Erin . . . ? What would happen to her . . . and the baby? Of course his father would see to it that they were taken care of . . . but his father was not a young man. What if he died soon after Charlie did? Could he count on his mother to raise his child and care for Erin? He owed Erin some security for what she was doing.

He decided he had to talk to a financial adviser and an attorney . . . and soon. 'I could leave this earth with a hell of a mess on somebody's hands.'

37

The chemotherapy treatments had been difficult for Meagan. She dreaded them, especially so because she had such little faith in their outcome. She held a hand mirror in her shaking hand, turning it to get the right light from the sun streaming through her bedroom windows. As she viewed herself, she merely shook her head. Tears came as shaking her head, she saw her skin hanging loose on its frame.

'You have to eat, Meagan,' cautioned Helen.

'I'm not hungry. Don't you understand that?'

She viewed the sunken eyes, now framed with black pouches. Their sky blue colour had now changed to bluish black, and they seemed to have sunken deeper in her skull with each passing day.

She heard the bedroom door opening, and as Charlie and Erin came in she quietly placed the mirror under the covers.

She attempted a smile as she reached for her head, making sure her turban was adjusted, asking, 'And where are you two off to now?'

Erin came in first, taking her hand, replying, 'Don't you remember, Mama, Charlie and I are going to Lamaze class. We're late too, so we can stay only for a minute. I didn't know you were back from your treatment so soon. (Erin could not make herself say the word – chemotherapy).

Meagan sighed. 'Helen and I just got back. Hello Charlie, my darling,' she added, weakly.

He attempted a brave smile as he bent to kiss her. She offered her cheek. Her cheek was all she had offered him for the past few months, refusing her lips, with, 'I know my breath must smell bad, Charlie.'

He brushed the offered cheek. He regretted their loss

of intimacy, but he smiled at her. 'How're you doing?'

She managed a brave smile. 'I'm doing just fine, honey. How're you doing in Lamaze class? Are you learning anything?'

Her voice was raspy, so much so that she hated the sound of it and did no more talking than she had to.

'I'm learning that breathing is the whole secret. If you breathe properly, having a baby is quite simple, huh, Erin?'

'Bullshit, Charlie!' Erin replied, taking his hand. 'Come on, we have to go. Bye, Mama.'

'Bye, honey. Be careful.'

Erin, holding her stomach to support her sagging belly, said, 'Come on, Charlie . . . let's get this over with,' and as she waddled through the door, she could be heard to say, 'God, I hate men!'

Meagan watched them go, and as they disappeared through the door Helen came in with a syringe in her hand, a syringe loaded with morphine.

Meagan swallowed hard, saying, 'Thank God you're here with my dope. I need it. I could hardly stand the pain when they were talking to me,' she rasped.

Helen made her way to the bed and reaching for the skinny figure lying there, helped her turn on her side to have access to her equally skinny bottom. She grimaced as she noticed how prominently Meagan's hip bones protruded. As she inserted the needle she heard a groan from her patient.

Meagan asked, 'Is that the new dose?'

'Yes, honey, the doctor increased it like you asked, but that is it until you see him, again. You'll have to make do with this potency, I'm afraid.'

Meagan nodded as she rolled over on her back. Groaning, she replied, 'I'll try to make do with it.'

'That's a good girl. Want to watch some TV?'

Closing her eyes, she replied, 'No, I want to sleep. I want to go to sleep and never wake up, again.'

Helen had gotten pragmatic with her, replying, 'Now, Meagan, you know you don't want to do that before you see that baby of yours . . . do you?'

She rasped. 'No, that's true. I want to see my baby.'

The nurse went to the windows, pulling the drapes shut, darkening the room. As she turned back to look at her patient, Meagan was snoring with her mouth open, making a horrible rasping sound.

Helen repressed a tear, shaking her head, saying to herself, but almost audibly. 'Why do I take these jobs? Oh, God, it is so hard to watch someone die like this,' and wiping her eyes on her sleeve, she tiptoed out of the room, turning to take one last look, shaking her head once again.

* * *

Charlie paced the corridor of the delivery suite, as nervous as any expectant father could be. He should have been at Erin's side, helping her through the delivery as any Lamaze trained father should be, but, at the last moment she changed her mind.

'No Charlie, it's not like you're my real husband who has been looking at my bottom for months or years. You've never seen it, and I don't want you to see it now.'

'But that's ridiculous, Erin. What good did it do for me to go to those classes with you if I'm not going to assist in the delivery?'

She giggled. 'You're not going to assist, anyway. I will be doing all the work. You just want to watch . . . that's all, and I don't want you to, so that's it. Get out of here.' She moaned and groaned in response to a new contraction, repeating, 'Get out, Charlie, please!'

The doctor came out into the waiting room, beckoning to him to come forward. He was smiling, so Charlie assumed the news had to be good.

The doctor extended his hand, saying, 'Congratulations, Mr Forester, your wife has just delivered a healthy and beautiful seven pound, six ounce baby boy.'

Charlie ignored the mistaken reference not wanting to take time to explain the whole thing, but he smiled a wide smile, returning the handshake, asking, 'And, Erin, how is she?'

'Oh, she is fine . . . just tired. She is a narrow-beamed woman, as you know, and sometimes they have trouble in delivering, but she did a good job . . . a real trouper, I would say. You can go in to see her in a minute or two. She is putting on some makeup.'

He grinned, 'You know how these beautiful women are.'

'I'll be in in a few minutes. First I've got to make a phone call. Excuse me, please!' he said, excitedly.

'Yes, Meagan honey, we have a son . . . a healthy boy! How much? Let's see, he said seven pounds, six ounces. Erin? Oh, yes, she's fine . . . just tired, but fine. No, I've not seen her yet. I will in a minute. I wanted to call you first. Yes I know, honey, I want you to see him, too. It will only be a day or so, from what they tell me. Yes, I know it's snowing outside. Yes Meagan, we will keep his head covered. Yes honey, I love you, too.'

He went to the room where they had taken Erin, and he knocked on the door softly.

A voice answered . . . not Erin's – 'Come in.'

As he turned the knob a nurse was coming out. She smiled, saying, 'Come in, Mr Forester, your wife is expecting you, and she is all prettied up, too, and look at what she has in her arms.'

Charlie made no reply to the nurse, concentrating on the two people in the bed. He saw a smiling Erin holding a blanket-covered bundle of humanity.

She waved him in. The nurse left, smiling discretely, closing the door behind her. He walked cautiously to the bed as if he were walking on eggshells.

Erin had a dazzling smile on her face as she cooed, 'Look, Charlie, isn't he beautiful?' She uncovered the small pink face within the blankets. 'Isn't he the most beautiful baby you've ever seen in your whole life?'

Charlie peeked, smiling at the miracle grimacing before him. The baby grunted and snorted, irritated at being disturbed from his slumber.

Charlie smiled. 'Oh Erin, honey, you did a good job, and we're so grateful to you . . .'

'Oh,' she exclaimed, 'did you call Mama?'

'Uh huh, she is ready to jump out of that bed and come here to see him.'

Erin believed him. 'She'd better not! He'll keep,' and then, demurely, 'Don't you think you ought to kiss me, Charlie? A father usually kisses the mother, doesn't he?' she asked in all seriousness, turning her lips up to him.

She added, 'I just brushed my teeth and used mouth-wash, so I know I smell good.'

She offered him her mouth, not her cheek, and he kissed her softly on the lips, adding, 'You did a good job, little mama. Big mama and I are proud of you.'

She smiled a satisfied smile. 'I did, didn't I?' as she looked down at the bundle of joy resting in her arms.

He stood to go. 'I guess you want to rest, now. I'd better go so you can sleep . . . '

'Oh no,' she exclaimed, 'I'm too excited to sleep. Besides,they tell me I have to try to get some food into this little rascal and she raised the baby to her breast which she was uncovering, a breast swollen with milk.

He felt embarrassed and he turned away, saying, 'I guess I'd better let you have some privacy . . . '

'No, you'd better stay Charlie, and get used to the sight of this. I'm not going to do a hiding routine every time I want to feed this baby . . . now, you sit and watch.'

She smiled that precocious smile of hers, adding, 'I know you're real horny, these days, but try to control yourself.'

And so saying, she inserted her nipple into a waiting and grasping little mouth, which needed no instructions on what to do . . . he did it.

Charlie was fascinated. He had never had a ringside seat at a sucking baby before, and he smiled as he pulled up a chair.

Erin leaned back on her pillow, smiling, saying softly as her glances went from Charlie to the baby, 'This has got to be one of the most satisfying feelings in the world, Charlie. It makes it all worth while.'

He nodded, smiling. 'I can only imagine, but, I would think it would be.

She smiled back. 'Oh, it is,' and with eyes wide.

'Charlie, did you call your folks?'

His hand went to his mouth. 'Oh God, I forgot in all the excitement. I'll be right back,' and in a moment of levity, added. 'Don't go away, Erin.'

She waved a hand at him. 'Go Charlie.'

Alexander Forester answered the wall phone in the breakfast room as he and his wife had their ritual morning coffee together.

Thinking it was a routine office call, he gave a disinterested, 'Hello. Charlie? How are you?'

'Fine, Dad . . . just fine. Guess what? You and mother are the proud grandparents of a fine seven pound, six ounce boy.'

The father gasped. He knew the baby was due, but to become a grandfather at his advanced age. 'Oh, Charlie, I am so happy to hear that! Seven pounds, you say?'

He replied, proudly. 'No, Dad, seven pounds, six ounces.'

Turning to his wife who, although sipping her coffee, had heard enough to know what had happened, he exclaimed, 'The baby is here, Agatha! A healthy boy. Isn't that wonderful?'

Tears came to Agatha Forrester's eyes. She slowly placed her cup on the table, reaching out for the telephone, which her husband handed her.

Her hand shook a little as she almost whispered, 'Charles? Oh, Charles, I am so happy for you and Meagan,' and looking at her beaming husband, 'and for us, too. How is Erin? Oh, that is good. I'll bet she is glad that is over. Poor child, and it was not really hers.'

Charlie thought he could detect genuine compassion in his mother's voice. He was not sure because he had not heard it too often.

She became more animated as she continued, 'Oh, I would love to see him, and,' as she smiled, 'hold him to my bosom,' and turning to her husband, while still speaking into the telephone, 'Alex, why can't we fly out there to see them?'

The husband smiled a reply, raising his hands, nodding, replying, 'Why not?'

Charlie heard these words and Meagan's admonition

burned in his brain. 'No, Charlie, I do not want them to see me like this!'

The mother asked, proudly, 'How do you feel about that, Charles. I know things will be a little confusing at your house for a few weeks, but we'd love to come if you could put us up. Of course,' she continued before he could reply, 'we could go to a hotel if it is not convenient for you and Meagan to . . . '

Oh God he thought, swiftly. What can I say that will not offend them? His brain raced for ideas, but none came . . . not acceptable ones.

He shook his head, grateful that his mother could not see his face as he responded, 'Mother, I really don't think this is a good time . . . not now, anyway. I hope you and Dad will understand. Please wait a while longer, if you don't mind.'

She heard these words and she was deeply offended. She felt she had made an magnanimous offer . . . a peace offering, as it were, and she had been rejected by her own son.

She was hurt, as she recovered, replying, 'Well, if you think that a delay is best at this time . . . well . . . of course, we'll abide by your wishes. Yes, I realize you have to get back. Yes, I'll say goodbye to your father. Yes, goodbye, Charles,' and as she handed the phone back to her curious husband who was trying to comprehend the hurt look on her face, she said, so softly he could hardly hear her, 'He doesn't want us to go out to see the baby . . . not now, anyway.'

'But surely, Agatha, there must be a good reason for that. Did he say why not?'

Still shocked, shaking her head, 'No, he merely told me that this would not be a good time. Oh, Alex . . . '

He truly felt sorry for her. She was badly hurt, he could see that, and he went to her, putting his arm around her, saying, 'Surely, there is some explanation for all this. I'll call him later when all the excitement has faded. I'll try to find out why, and until then, Agatha, please don't get yourself too worked up over this . . . '

She looked out the breakfast room windows, shaking

her head. 'Perhaps, the birds are merely coming home to roost, Alex.'

Since she had been looking out the window he assumed she was speaking literally, and he looked out the window to see what she had seen, but he soon realized there were no birds out there . . . not now, anyway. Her cliche was her way of expiation for deeds done, or, undone.

He said nothing more as he went to her, kissing her cheeks, saying, 'I'm off to the office. I'll let you know, dear, after I talk to him, again.'

She merely nodded, placing her hand on his cheek as he bussed her. He thought he felt moisture on her cheek, and as he tried to look for confirmation, she turned her head, again, looking out the window.

As he walked through the arched doorway leading to the kitchen area, he looked back at her. She was deep in thought. He felt sorry for her, as he shook his head, walking through the hallway on his way to the rear porte cochere and to his car.

Later that day, a troubled Alexander Forester tried to reach his son. He had left the hospital, he was told, and as he confirmed Erin's room number, he called to Betty, asking her to send an impressive floral bouquet to both mothers.

When he called the house and asked to speak to Meagan, Helen took the call and looking at Meagan shaking her head. 'No! I'm sorry, Mr Forester, but your daughter-in-law is sleeping, now. She is heavily sedated, you know. Yes, sir, I will certainly tell her you called. I know she will be sorry she missed you. Yes. Goodbye. What's that? Of course, I'll have your son call you as soon as he comes in. Goodbye.'

Charlie came in some time later and he virtually ran up to the bedroom where an excited Meagan awaited him. He rushed up to the bed where she had been since her last injection. She was drowsy, but her adrenaline began to flow. She tried to sit up, and with his help she did.

She grabbed his hands, shaking them with her own vibrations. 'Oh, honey, tell me about him . . . please. Who does he look like?'

He sat down calmly, hoping she would calm down, too. He began, smiling, 'Oh, Meagan you ought to see him . . . '

She smiled . . . she sobbed . . . her sunken eyes took on the first hint of interest he had detected in some time. She had come to life, again, and he went on in detail about the delivery.

After, she lay back on her pillow, exhausted. Her limited strength drained by the excitement of the baby had all but left her.

Helen had been there the whole time, sharing her joy at the description of the event, but her professional responsibilities took over as she said to him softly, 'She's tired, Charlie. I think you should let her rest. Having that baby has worn her out too,' she smiled.

Meagan had closed her eyes, but she was smiling.

Helen walked to the door with Charlie, taking his arm, saying, 'Your father wants you to call him. He is at the office, or so he said when he called.'

Charlie merely shook his head as he walked out, taking a last look at his wife, who still had a happy smile on her face. He smiled, too.

He gathered his thoughts as he went to the phone in the family room on the lower floor. He dialled the office number, the private one to Betty's office.

She said, 'Charlie? Congratulations, Daddy! How is everyone? Both mothers? Oh, that's just great. Yes, he's in . . . sure . . . hold on . . . talk to you later, Charlie . . . bye.'

'Charlie. . . . that you? I've had a hard time reaching you. Is everything OK over there?'

'Yes Dad, everything is fine . . . yes! Look, Dad I know what is on your mind and I'd like to explain about my request to you and mother not to come out now . . . '

'Well son, you don't really have to explain, you know . . . '

He persisted. 'Yes, Dad, I do. I owe you that, and,' he added, 'Mother, too.'

The father waited for him to continue, sensing that the explanation was difficult for his son.

'Dad, the reason I asked you and Mother not to come

out to see us now, is that Meagan . . . '

The father interjected. 'I guess Meagan is pissed off with your mother, huh? Can't say I blame her, either.'

The father could not see him shaking his head. 'No Dad, it has absolutely nothing to do with you or Mother. It is Meagan who is the problem, or so Meagan thinks.'

'I don't understand, son.'

He sighed into the phone, quite audibly. 'She doesn't want you to see her looking like this.'

'Does she look that bad, Charlie?'

'Oh yes, Dad. Poor thing, she looks awful and she knows it. She keeps a hand mirror in her bed with her, and she checks her appearance all day long.'

He paused,'You see, the problem is . . . Mother has never seen her at all, even when she looked good and healthy, so how she is now is all that Mother will have to remember her by. That's the problem.'

The father nodded, knowingly. 'I can understand that, but then, your mother will never get to see her alive . . . Oh, son, I'm sorry I said that . . . '

'It's OK Dad, we have to be realistic about this. You're right in what you said. Mother will never see Meagan alive, I feel sure.'

The father felt too dejected to continue. He sighed, replying, 'I guess I'll let you go now, Charlie. I know you have a lot to do, trying to run a business, going from the hospital to the office and your home . . . two women to look after . . Is there anything I can do for you?'

'Yes Dad, there is . . . '

'You name it son, and it will be done.'

'Please try to explain to mother about this. I hope, with all my heart, that she will understand this. I don't want her hurt any more.'

'Don't worry about your mother, Charlie. I'll handle her at this end. She must realize that this is of her doing. She had ample opportunity to meet Meagan before now,' and he added, 'The birds have come home to roost.'

Charlie joked 'Don't you mean the chickens have come home to roost?'

The father smiled. 'Whatever! Goodbye, Charlie. Give

Meagan and Erin my love.'

'Goodbye Dad. Good luck with Mother.'

The father laughed. 'Son, I've been making excuses to and for your mother for over forty years. I'm actually good at it.'

'Dad?'

'Yes, son?'

'I'd like you and Mother to come out as soon as practical, to see the baby.'

'We'd like that, Charlie. Just let us know when.'

38

Meagan was in a state of near apoplectic excitement as she awaited the arrival home of her baby, so much so that nurse Helen was concerned for her welfare.

'Now, Meagan, honey, I know you're excited about the baby coming home, but really, you should try to calm yourself . . . '

She gave a smile and a rasping reply. 'I don't want to calm down, Helen. This is one of the greatest days of my life. I want to enjoy every second of it,' and, attempting a brave attitude, 'I don't want you to give me my morphine shot now,' and she added, meekly, 'Not until I ask you for it . . . OK?'

'OK honey, if that is what you want, but don't try to be too brave.'

Meagan was looking in her mirror, turning it one way and another, trying to get the best angle as she applied some powder to her pale face, commenting, 'I want to look as good as I can when he sees me for the first time, you know.'

Helen smiled. 'Do you think he will remember that twenty years from now?'

'I guess not, but I need this for me too. What time is it?'

The nurse looked at her watch for the fifth time, replying, 'It's ten minutes later than it was when you asked me the time ten minutes ago . . . it's nine forty-five, Meagan,' and rushing to the window and looking out, she exclaimed, 'Here they are!'

Meagan groaned as she attempted to sit up in bed by herself, and seeing her predicament, the nurse came to her. 'Wait a minute honey, I'll help you. There . . . comfortable?' and as she heard the front door open, added,'Now, let's have a big smile for them when they come in, huh.'

Meagan smiled, nodding. Her breathing increased as her excitement grew. Her hands shook, and she rested them on her lap to steady them. She heard footsteps on the stairs and her heart beat faster.

Her eyes were rivetted on the door, and as Erin came through carrying the baby, smiling a radiant, proud smile, Meagan moaned, 'Oh, Erin, honey, bring him here,' and holding her arms out, added. 'Give him to me. I want to hold my baby.'

As Erin lowered him and softly placed the infant in her mother's waiting arms, she pulled the blanket back so that his face was exposed.

Meagan shook her head, smiling at Erin, and then looking back at the baby through watery eyes, said, 'Ohoooo . . . look at him.'

While all this was going on, a smiling and useless Charlie stood by next to Helen.

'Oh, Charlie,' as she motioned for him to come forward, 'look at our baby. Oh, isn't he beautiful. Oh, God, what a happy moment for us, huh, Charlie?' as she tried to cuddle the infant.

Her strength would not allow her to lift the infant up to her, so she let him go back on her lap again, satisfied to just gaze at him. The baby grimaced and it appeared that he smiled. 'Oh, he's smiling at his mother . . . little angel . . . '

Erin turned to wink at Helen, and Helen smiled, with Erin complaining, 'Mama, do you think you can break away from him long enough to say hello to your own daughter . . . remember me, Erin, the one who helped you with this thing. . . . '

Meagan turned to her daughter, offering her cheek, smiling replying, 'Hi, honey . . . I'm sorry if I neglected you, but . . . ' and she looked back at little Alex.

Erin bussed her on the cheek. 'It's OK Mama, I forgive you, considering the reason.' Then, 'I hope I can take him away from you for a few minutes. I want to change his diaper and then I have to feed him . . . '

Meagan looked up pleading. 'Feed him where I can watch, honey. I want to watch him suckle.'

Helen came forward, reaching for the baby, and lifting him and turning to Erin. 'You take your coat off, honey, while I change this little rascal's diaper. We have the nursery all ready for him, complete with a month's supply of diapers,'

Charlie came forward, bending down to kiss Meagan on the cheek. 'Do you have time for your husband now that you have seen what we have produced,' and turning to Erin, 'with the help of this little brood mare, here.'

Erin whacked him on the butt 'Gee, thanks, Charlie! Now that I have delivered the kid, you treat me like excess baggage, huh?'

He brought her forward to him, as he stood by the bed, replying, 'No honey, your mother and I will be eternally grateful to you for what you've done for us,' and turning to his wife, 'Huh Meagan?'

Meagan, breathing hard and fast, took Erin's hand, and with tears in her eyes, 'Oh, yes, Erin, without you . . . ' and she could not finish the words, just looking at her daughter and smiling, while squeezing her hand.

The door opened and a smiling Helen and a newly dried Alex returned to the group.

'OK, he's dry and hungry. He squirmed and complained the whole while, and I can confirm, Charlie, he is a boy.' She smiled. 'He has all the equipment to qualify,' and she handed the baby to a waiting Erin, who began to sit on the bed and expose her breast to the waiting infant.

Meagan's eyes widened, and waving to Charlie, said, 'Charlie, why don't you step out for a while so Erin can feed the baby in private . . . '

Erin continued to bare her breast and introducing the nipple into the baby's mouth shook her head, motioning Charlie to a chair with, 'No, Mama, I have already done this a dozen times in front of Charlie and this is the way I want it to be.'

She smiled at her mother,. resting her hand on

Meagan's adding, 'You're just old fashioned, Mama,' and as she smiled at the suckling infant . . . 'There is nothing more natural in this world than a mother feeding her baby and I want Charlie to watch so he can appreciate what we women go through, so pull up your chair, Charlie,' and she added mischievously . . . 'and get your thrill for the day.'

Meagan, too weak to protest, smiled as she watched the hungry infant suck voraciously at the swollen breast. She smiled as she took hold of Erin's hand with her left and, and then reached for her husband's with her right one.

Holding hands with one another, the trio smiled in unison, especially when they saw the trickle of excess milk easing its way down the fat little pink cheek moving up and down.

Erin smiled at her mother. 'Are you happy, Mama?'

Meagan looked at her daughter, then her husband, then at the sucking infant, as she replied, pensively, nodding, 'As happy as I've ever been in my whole life,' and her head went back on the pillow, exhausted by all the excitement.

Her eyes went to Helen standing nearby, and the look said it all to the discerning nurse, now accustomed to her patient's every look.

Helen, reluctant to break up this domestic scene of love and serenity, moved forward touching Charlie's arm, whispering, 'She is very tired. She really should rest, you know,' and lowering her voice even more, added, 'She needs a shot. She is in pain. I can tell.'

Charlie nodded, and taking Erin by the arm, signalled with his finger to his lips, 'Let's go so she can rest,' and he helped Erin to her feet as she continued to hold the nursing infant to her breast.

She smiled, knowingly, and followed Charlie out of the room.

The nurse went to the bedside table and withdrew the syringe from it's sterile container, and injecting it into the supply vessel, watched as the prescribed amount was sucked into the cylinder. Meagan, too, watched with eyes dimmed, but able to tell the nurse,

'Thank God you asked them to leave. I could hardly take the pain anymore . . . Oh, God,' as she shook her head, and groaned as the needle was inserted.

She remained on her side saying in a low and weak voice, 'He's a beautiful baby, ain't he, Helen,' returning to her former country dialect.

Helen bent over her, kissing her sunken cheek. 'He's as pretty a baby as I've ever seen. Now honey, try to get some rest. You've had a hard and exciting time.'

Meagan nodded, saying nothing more as the narcotic fluid eased its way through her body, bringing her temporary relief from her misery.

Helen watched her for a while as she always did after an injection to ensure she had no unusual reaction, and feeling she was all right, she began to tiptoe out of the room, but as she neared the door, she could hear the raspy voice saying, 'Thank you, God, for letting me live to see him . . . '

The nurse turned back to look at her. She had turned to face the windows, looking out at the sky and the mountains.

Helen watched her for a moment, musing to herself, 'I wonder what that poor tormented brain is thinking about,' and, shaking her head in despair, left the room.

As she continued nursing the baby in the kitchen, with Charlie making a pot of coffee, Erin said, 'Charlie, I feel so grateful that Mama got to see the baby before . . . before . . you know what I mean, huh?'

He came behind her, placing his hands on her shoulders, looking down on the sucking infant.

'Yes, Erin, I know what you mean, and I am grateful too. She wanted to see that baby so bad . . . ' and he walked away wiping his eyes so that Erin could not see him.

Erin watched him go, feeling sure he was crying. She began to cry, softly, too, but she wiped her eyes with the corner of the baby's blanket.

She sniffed, looking at Charlie, then, 'Charlie, come here, please. Sit with me a while. Now that this is all over I think I'm having post-partal withdrawals.'

He came over and sat down in a chair next to her, wiping his eyes unashamedly, asking, 'What do you mean, Erin?'

She looked down at the nursing infant, then, raising her head and looking into his eyes, said softly, 'I'm going to have a rough time with this thing, Charlie. After Mama goes, my world is going to fall apart. I'm afraid. While I was carrying the baby I felt I had something to contribute, but now, any lactating female could take over from here.'

She wiped a tear. 'What's going to happen to me, Charlie?'

He felt great compassion for the beautiful young woman before him. Life had not been kind to her so far. He thought of Amanda. She was beautiful too, and life certainly was not kind to her. He could not let that happen to Erin, he vowed. He took her hand, the one not pressed against the baby's cheek, and he looked into her longing glance, as he responded.

'Erin, honey, I swear before God in heaven that I will look after you all your life. I swear it. You know that I have legally adopted you. You're my legal heir . . . you and the baby. My father's estate will see to it that you never want for a thing.'

She shook her head. 'That's not what I mean, Charlie. I want a life of my own . . . a husband of my own . . . a baby of my own,' and looking down at the infant at her breast, 'I want something of my own to call my own. I gave birth to him and he's not even mine to keep. You know what I mean?'

He nodded. 'Yes I know what you mean, but can't we talk about this some other time? I can't handle it, now.'

She smiled, placing her hand on his. 'I know. I'm sorry for being a cry baby at a time like this but, as I said, I guess I'm having post-partal withdrawals, or something. Don't pay any attention to me,' and she shifted the still hungry infant to the other breast.

Charlie rose and went to the refrigerator, turning to ask, 'What do you want for lunch? I'll fix you something.'

She shook her head 'Uh uh, Charlie. Now that this thing is over and this little rascal is out of my system, I intend to get back to my fighting weight.' She sniffed. 'I want the boys, when they see me again, to know damn well what they have missed.'

He went to her, kissing her on the cheek, smiling. 'Now, that's the Erin I know and love. Give 'em hell, babe!'

She smiled. 'You can bet your sweet ass on that!'

39

Meagan's condition deteriorated to the point that she could no longer be cared for at home. In the two weeks since they had returned home with the baby she had over exerted herself in an attempt to spend some time with the infant, and the effort had taken its toll on her.

But she would not be denied. She was like a woman driven. She had to be moved to the intensive care unit of the hospital, a move which had more effect on Charlie and Erin than it did Meagan. She was hardly aware of it as she was taken to the hospital. Helen agreed to stay until the end which she felt would not be too long. The job had been especially hard on her for she had made the awful mistake of allowing herself to become emotionally involved with her patient. In private moments it was questionable who cried the most on the female side, she or Erin. Sometimes, in the privacy of the kitchen, they cried together.

She agreed to become an auxiliary nurse in the intensive care section. This was possible only because she had worked previously as an intensive care nurse, and was accustomed to the emotional drain of a lingering death watch.

Charlie and Erin spent as much time as they could, for each had different distractions which must be attended to. A house nanny had been hired for the baby at home, so that Erin could spend her available time with Meagan.

Charlie, poor Charlie, was a man in a daze as he divided his time between the office, the house, and the hospital. He, too, had dark circles under his eyes due to worry and a lack of sleep. He called his parents to advise them that the time was near.

The father took the news sombrely. 'Are you sure, son, that you don't want us to be with you at this difficult time? We'd be most willing to fly out today, if you want us to . . . '

Charlie pondered the question, knowing that Meagan would not know the difference. He replied, 'Yes, Dad, if you and Mother are willing . . . I'd like you to come out. I could use some support. Is Mother willing to come?'

'Don't worry, Charlie, she'll come.'

It was late at night, probably ten or so. Charlie was sitting with her. Helen had gone home after a long ten hour day. She was sure she would pass away on that shift and stayed to be there. She wanted to be there at the end. But that stout heart held out, reluctant to surrender her life to the unknown. She had been asleep, or was it a coma? Charlie could not tell the difference.

She stirred, groaning a little, and looking at him with half closed eyes, whispered, 'I love you, honey, just as plain as day.' He smiled, 'I love you too, Meagan.'

She tried to raise her head, but he patted her arm. 'No, be quiet, my dear . . . do you need something?'

She half nodded. 'I'm thirsty. Please get me some water.'

'Of course,' he said, and he reached for the pitcher sitting on the night table.

Her eyes followed his moves, and she grunted, 'No, fresh water. Get me some fresh water . . . '

He knew full well that the pitcher had been replaced only an hour before, but he shrugged, 'OK, I'll get some fresh water for you, honey,' and he picked up the pitcher and walked to the door.

He walked through the door without looking back. He went out to a water cooler in the corridor, filled the pitcher and started to return to the room.

A nurse stopped him in the hall near the entrance to the intensive care area, asking, 'How is your wife doing, Mr Forester?'

He smiled, not in a mood to talk to her. 'Just fine, thank you,' and he walked off, returning to the room.

As he entered the room he looked at her and he knew

. . . Her head had gone back and her mouth was open as were her eyes, staring at the ceiling, as if intent on something she was watching.

He walked to the bed, looking down at the woman he loved . . . for so short a time. He suppressed a sob as he reached to close her eyes. Strange, he thought, how quickly the body begins to cool off.

He picked up the intercom button and pushed it. The crisp voice of the desk nurse came on. 'Yes? May I help you?'

He had a difficult time in saying the words. 'I think you had better come in to see my wife.'

She asked,very professionally. 'Is it urgent sir?'

He shrugged, 'No . . . no hurry! She's dead.'

He went to the phone in the hall and called Erin first.

As she heard the dreaded, but expected words, she merely groaned, 'Oh, poor soul, Charlie, her misery is over, and now our's will begin. Do you want me to come to the hospital to be with you? The nanny can stay with the baby . . . '

'No, Erin,' he mumbled, 'there's no sense in your coming out in this weather. You can't do any more good, here. I'll make the arrangements to get her to a funeral home . . . '

At the sound of those words, Erin groaned. 'Oh, Charlie.'

'I know, honey . . . I'll be home as soon as I can.'

She nearly hollered into the phone. 'Charlie?'

'Yes?'

She suppressed a sob. 'Your father called. He and your mother are on the way first thing in the morning. They're coming in the Lear. They said they hoped they'd get here in time,' and her voice choked on the words.

'I guess they won't make it, huh? Bye Erin. I'll see you soon. Please wait up for me.'

'Oh I will . . . I promise. We need each other, Charlie,' and she repeated it. 'We need each other.'

'We sure do, honey.'

It was nearly two hours before he got home, and as he entered the house he could see Erin in the family room before a roaring fire. As he approached her, he could see the baby resting on her bosom, sound asleep.

He went to the front of her, and she put her finger to her lips. 'Shush . . . I just got him back to sleep. He's been very fussy,' and she sobbed, 'Do you think, maybe, he knows his real mama is dead.'

He nearly collapsed onto the couch next to her, replying, 'No, I don't think so . . . poor little fella.'

She looked at him with wet eyes. 'Wanta hold him for a while? I have to tinkle,' and she transferred the sleeping infant to his father.

He stirred but remained asleep. Charlie slid down on the couch making a bed for the baby on his chest, arranging his covers to ensure he was not cold. He looked reflectively at the fire, watching the flames leap into the air as if in a frenzy.

The spruce logs crackled a tune as the air bubbles exploded. The warmth of the fire and his weariness took a toll on him, for he soon fell asleep.

Erin came back and looked at the sleeping pair. She smiled. She quietly lowered her body next to Charlie's and snuggled her head into his shoulder. She reached over and placed her arm around him and the baby.

She thought of her mother, whispering to herself, 'I'll take care of them, Mama . . . I promise I will.'

NEPHILIM

the Fallen Ones

a novel by Walter Keith York

published by Green Shoelace Books

Contents

Illustrations

Hebrew Matrixes

Woe unto you that desire the day of the LORD! to what end is it for you? the day of the LORD is darkness, and not light. As if a man did flee from a lion, and a bear met him; or went into the house, and leaned his hand on the wall, and a serpent bit him. Shall not the day of the LORD be darkness, and not light? even very dark, and no brightness in it?

Book of Amos 5:18–20

JARVIS

1

We work, we plan – we struggle to organize our lives into a pattern. Our obsessions with our goals and plans for the future seem all encompassing as we journey through life. We want to believe that our circumstances are controlled by our actions and thoughts – that we are indeed in the driver's seat of life and can determine the course – if we but exercise our will. We ignore signals that life gives us – warning that a single unexpected event can alter our lives forever.

And so it was with Martin McDonald – a motivated man with a very successful software company. His company, *Threshold* – since beginning in 1983 – grew to be one of the most respected independently owned software companies in the world.

Threshold has been credited with ingenious innovations – giving Martin the option of "cherry picking," and only taking on work that challenges himself and his talented staff. In each employee's office – or cubical – is a plaque that states, "Outrageous rates must be matched by outrageous results."

All employees of *Threshold* earn top dollar – right down to the man who cleans the floors. Martin's brilliance is a given – which has garnished his employees' respect to an almost awesome degree.

Martin is the man. Martin is in total control.

That was the story of his life – a story that would be forever altered on a rainy Sunday afternoon.

Two government agents in a rented convertible rolled through the picturesque New England town of Brentwood and proceeded to the exclusive suburb of Brentwood Acres. They turned on to the street that led to Martin McDonald's house.

A balding, heavyset man on the passenger's side folded a map and laid it on the seat. His upper body was huge and muscular. He had almost a cartoon-like appearance – like Popeye's foe Bluto. He looked over at his partner:

"I think you'd better pull over."

The driver glided to a stop under the shelter of an oak, took off his baseball cap and stuffed it under the seat. He looked over at his partner,

William Jarvis:

"What's the trouble?"

The older man took a drag of his cigarette, and rubbed his chin in an anxious gesture:

"Holeman told us to approach him when his wife wasn't around."

The driver shrugged. "He also told us not to approach him at work."

His partner stared forward, his cigarette dangling in his mouth.

The driver – Agent Snider – was much younger, but had a more confident, self-assured demeanor. He began slowly as if to relax his older partner:

"McDonald is a workaholic – he's either at work, at home, or at the country club. His wife seldom leaves the house." He thought for a moment and continued in a quiet, concluding tone:

"Sunday is a low stress day for most people. He canceled a golf game because of the rain – so . . . as organized as this guy is, he's probably caught up with his paper work. He's probably bored. This guy is go go go." He made an offhand gesture:

"This might be the time."

The older man took a deep breath. "It's my call, Snider."

"Well," Snider began, "I understood that you made that call when he canceled his golf game."

The old man watched the rain pour down:

"I just told you to ride out towards his house."

After a few moments passed, the younger man turned and smiled at his partner. "It's your call, Jarvis."

Jarvis lit another cigarette. "The Bureau is hot for this guy; we spent more time briefing this one than the other three combined."

The car phone rang and the older man picked it up and nervously blinked as he listened. He glanced over at Snider and put his hand over the receiver of the phone and spoke in a low voice. "It's director Holeman; he wants to speak to both of us." He activated the speaker phone.

"Can you both hear me?"

They answered.

"Where are you now?"

"A block away from Golfer," the older man replied.

"OK . . . is it still raining?"

"Still raining hard," Jarvis answered.

"Golfer made a couple of calls to work, but didn't say that he was going in," the Director began. "His wife is still home." A few moments passed:

"Listen . . . we didn't get the Australian."

Jarvis sighed:

"I thought he was in the bag – a lay-down piece of cake."

The director spoke anxiously:

"This thing has a higher top than I thought . . . I'm getting some high level pressure that I wasn't expecting. We have to get Golfer."

"Do we approach now?" Snider asked. "What's the plan?"

The director continued:

"Since you men left we received some more information from the computer of that shrink that his wife goes to. From the doctor's files we learned that the wife's brother was killed in Nam while Golfer's family pulled some strings to keep him from serving. Work the points that we discussed, but go heavy with the patriotism angle – you know – Golfer's chance to do something altruistic for his country."

Jarvis spoke up:

"We play on his control obsession like we discussed?"

"Yes, but in combination with the patriotism angle. Forget our limit and take whatever he asks for. If it's outrageous, take it anyway. *And leave the suitcase with the money to cement the deal.* Golfer *will* work for us. Are you men ready?"

"So," Jarvis concluded, "you want us to approach now?"

Jarvis and Snider listened as the director cleared his throat:

"Don't be offended, Jarvis; but I want your partner to do the talking on this one. Are you listening, Snider?"

"Yes," replied the younger man.

"OK. Feel him out as you go. Remember – he responds well to flattery but don't be obvious by kissing up to him. Don't let him intimidate you – he hates weakness. Don't sugarcoat anything – especially if his wife isn't in the room. And listen, Jarvis . . ."

"I'm here," he dryly answered.

"Golfer is a drinker, so go ahead and take a few slugs. He won't care if he smells it on your breath. Golfer gets totally wrecked on scotch every Friday afternoon. His golf game was canceled; so it's my guess that he's having a few pops right now." Silence for a moment. "Listen, Jarvis . . . if you go in there and nervously flit about you'll blow this thing. Just sit back and enjoy the show. Now go get it done."

A few moments passed. Snider reluctantly began:

"Look, Jarvis, I . . ."

Jarvis cut him off in mid-sentence:

"Holeman has been a director for only two months; but he's still the boss. It's Holeman's call. You're good at thinking on your feet." He looked out the window and sighed – then back at Snider:

"I haven't really lost my nerve," he objected; "it's just that I've been doing this for twenty years – it can wear on you . . . and my wife's passing hasn't helped." He gave his partner a knowing smile:

"We'll see how you're doing eighteen years from now."

Snider thoughtfully rubbed his forehead and glanced over at his partner:

"So . . . you're cool with this?"

Jarvis reached under the seat and produced a pint of bourbon:

"Give me a few minutes and I will *get* cool." He took a gulp and glanced around at the opulent houses.

Snider felt awkward:

"Jarvis . . . I had dinner with Holeman; and he went on and on about the fine work that you've done for the Bureau over the years."

Jarvis made a sour face:

"Everything is all right," he said unconvincingly.

"No – I want you to hear me out. Holeman told me that the rookies have the balls but the older agents have better instincts. He said I needed to learn about that from you – and he told me a few of stories where your instincts had made all the difference." Snider paused and stared out into the pouring rain:

"I think I'm learning already."

Jarvis seemed more casual:

"How so?"

Snider enthusiastically began – gesturing all the while with his hands:

"If you hadn't told me to pull over we would have missed Holeman's call. We wouldn't have learned how important this man is. Maybe Holeman knew what he was doing when he put us together." He glanced over and smiled:

"Maybe we make a good team."

Jarvis winced in spite of not wanting to.

The younger man's brow knitted:

"Who is this Australian fellow?"

"Somebody the bureau wanted aboard. Actually, they wanted him more than McDonald."

Snider shrugged:

"That's the first I've heard of him." He then glanced around and drummed impatiently on the steering wheel.

After enjoying a final swig, Snider put the bottle back under the seat:

"Let's go see Golfer."

McDonald's driveway was wide enough for two cars and looped under a covered carport. The house was castle-like and made of blue granite. A granite stairway led to the double doors of the main entrance.

Jarvis marveled as he took it all in:

"What was the name of that old black and white movie?"

"Citizen Kane," his partner replied.

The old man grabbed the door handle and confidently looked over at his partner:

"Let's go see Citizen Kane."

After explaining to the maid that they we there to see Mr. McDonald about a business matter, they were led to a large room at the back of the house that opened to the patio and gardens. Everything was brand new and very opulent. The furniture looked as if nobody had ever sat on it.

The young, pretty woman politely asked:

"Is Mr. McDonald expecting you?"

"Please apologize for us that we didn't call first," Jarvis began; "but stress to him that it pertains to a very important matter."

Jarvis watched her intently as she walked out of the room:

"Something tells me that she wasn't hired for her brains."

Jarvis walked over to a window and looked out at the gardens. They were manicured to the point that they hardly looked real. The guesthouse was larger than Jarvis' house and had a large slate patio with round tables and umbrellas. Next to the guesthouse was a garage made to look like a stable. It was all blue granite.

"Well . . . what is this 'very important matter?'" Martin McDonald inquired as he marched into the room.

Everything about Martin's appearance said success. Tall, blonde, handsome, and fit – he cut a good figure in his golfing attire. He switched his glass to his left hand and graciously extended the right to the older man – as if sensing that he was in charge.

They shook hands.

"I'm Jarvis," he motioned; "this is Snider." He cut his eye at his partner and then back to McDonald. He then produced his identification, as did Snider.

McDonald seemed a bit taken back; but before he could speak, Jarvis continued in a quiet tone:

"The government wishes to hire you on a contract basis; but, for right now let's just keep everything between the three of us. Indeed, if we don't come to an agreement it would be better if no one knew that we came to see you."

He was visibly relieved:

"We're pretty busy; but we can take on more business – if the opportunity justifies it."

Smiling assuredly, Jarvis made an informal gesture and answered, "That's great."

McDonald motioned towards his glass:

"I don't usually imbibe this early; but my golf game was canceled. I guess it is a self-prescribed boredom inhibitor. Perhaps you gentlemen would like something – perhaps some tea or coffee."

"I'll have a scotch . . . if that's OK?" He pointed at Snider. "Nothing alcoholic for Snider."

McDonald looked puzzled. "I didn't think you people were allowed to drink on duty."

"We're not on duty – not officially." Jarvis said conclusively. He noticed an ashtray and pulled out his cigarettes:

"Do you mind?"

"Not at all," he said as he rang for the maid. When she appeared he glanced at Jarvis:

"What brand of scotch would you like?"

"Cordou, if you have it."

McDonald lifted his brow:

"That's my favorite single malt." He rubbed his chin and seemed to be studying Jarvis who had assumed a very non-aggressive, comfortable posture. "What is it that you like about Cordou?"

"I like all the things that you don't taste, and the subtleness of the things that you *do* taste."

McDonald seemed impressed:

"And how do you take it?"

"You might think that this is somewhat plebeian; but I keep the bottle in the fridge and drink it on the rocks in an insulated glass." Jarvis made an offhand gesture:

"I know, the high-brows will say to take it 'neat.'"

"I really don't like drinking out of plastic glasses," McDonald began; "but I like it out of insulated glasses made of glass."

Jarvis acted shocked. "You're kidding."

"Not at all. I keep Cordou chilled and take it as you do – but drink it out of insulated 'glass' glasses. Actually, I had them made for that very purpose."

He handed his glass to the maid:

"Pour this out and bring two of the usual – one for my friend Jarvis." He gestured inquisitively at Snider:

"Coffee is fine," Snider said. "Black."

McDonald noticed that Jarvis' eyes were glued to the maid as she left the room:

"Actually . . . I have two maids – one for lookin, and one for cookin."

Jarvis smiled smugly and looked around at the gracious setting:

"All it takes is money."

McDonald took on a cautious air:

"I would bet that there are a few people in your occupation that have made some *good* money."

Jarvis was pre-occupied with the room and didn't respond. The maid appeared with the drinks.

Making a ceremonious gesture, Jarvis sniffed the concoction and slowly took a drink – opening his mouth in an odd way as he savored it:

"Dew of the angels' wings," he boldly declared.

"Perhaps your partner would like to try a glass?" McDonald offered.

"No . . . he's driving," Jarvis dryly stated. Then, completely ignoring his partner's puzzled countenance, he walked over to a revolver that was mounted on the wall:

"That's in mint condition – very nice."

"You know about those?"

"It's a Colt Walker – I've never seen a finer one. More muzzle energy than most modern pistols. They're actually quite accurate – and devastating."

McDonald took the weapon down from the wall and handed it to Jarvis. The barrel was marked "U.S. 1847."

"I've done a bit of pistol shooting," McDonald began. "I can't imagine that this weapon is very accurate." He shrugged. "Those sights don't lend themselves to accurate firing."

Jarvis made a face:

"No way, McDonald! If you were galloping along on a horse chasing a Mexican bandit, do you think that you would use your sights?" He took the weapon with both hands and illustrated. "Like this . . . you come down – point." He looked over at McDonald:

"Loaded heavy she'll come up on her own. Then you come down again – boom!"

McDonald motioned to the door that led out to the gardens:

"Come out here with me."

It had stopped raining and the three of them stood by the railing of the patio.

"Do you see that statue with the red flowers around it?"

Jarvis pointed:

"The naked guy?"

McDonald laughed:

"My wife can't stand it when I walk around the bedroom naked. So what does she do?"

The old man slowly nodded:

"She buys a statue of a naked guy."

McDonald turned to the old man and made a face:

"Exactly. I can't stand the thing." With that he descended the stairs; and, beginning from the railing of the patio, began to pace off the distance to the statue. When he returned he did the same:

"Eighty yards," he announced.

"So . . . ?"

He pointed at the antique gun. "So, Mr. Jarvis, can you hit that statue at eighty yards with that Colt?"

"Six out of six – piece of cake."

He took the Colt from Jarvis and aimed it at the statue:

"If you hit it at all, it will be pure luck." He looked over at Jarvis. "Six times – no way!"

Jarvis took a sip of his drink:

"I guess we're lucky that all the Indian fighters weren't like you." He grunted. "We'd all still be living in New England."

They stared at each other for a few moments.

"OK – we'll see," McDonald said as he walked back into the house.

Jarvis and Snider followed along behind; but McDonald proceeded to another part of the house. Jarvis and Snider were left alone.

Snider stared motionless at Jarvis for a few moments. "I hope you know what you're doing."

Jarvis ignored him.

The maid brought some more drinks and freshened Snider's coffee. Then, an enthusiastic McDonald reappeared and handed Jarvis a box:

"I have ammo for all my weapons. Do you know how to load the Walker?"

"Do you want me to load it?" came his surprised response.

"Yes. Load it heavy – for actual combat." He smiled and wiggled his eyebrows. "I think it's time to deal with 'pencil dick.'"

Jarvis laughed and then noticed McDonald's expression. "You're serious. You want me to destroy your statue?"

"I'm inviting you to try. There isn't anything but woods behind it."

They stared at each other.

McDonald smiled:

"You won't hit it. Not once."

Jarvis opened the box and started rummaging. He opened a can of black powder and sniffed. "It's fresh." He kept rummaging. "Aha – this is the ticket." He held up a conical bullet. "It's a little different than the ones they used back then – it's made to closer tolerances."

McDonald watched intently as Jarvis loaded the huge revolver.

McDonald and Snider followed Jarvis out to the Patio. Jarvis stood at the railing:

"Chest!"

He leveled the weapon to the target and the Colt roared and belched smoke. The slug slammed into the statue with a commanding crack. Powder and large chucks flew. With both eyes opened, Jarvis didn't flinch as the pistol reared upwards and backwards. The monster settled back to its original holding position for two more successive shots – each followed by the resounding sound of impact and flying debris. By then the view of the statue was mostly obscured by smoke as the torso of the statue toppled with a thud. All that remained was a small part of the lower torso and the legs.

McDonald was dumbstruck as he stared through the smoke at the carnage that the old Colt had reaped. "That's incredible!"

"A nine inch, seven groove, precision barrel," Jarvis began. "For all intents and purposes, it was, in its time, more like a hand held repeating carbine in the hands of the right person."

"But unwieldy," McDonald pointed out.

"You can swing a carbine faster," Jarvis agreed. "The weapon needs to be understood in the context of the era in which it was introduced, and the competing weapons of that time." He looked up at the house:

"I figured that this would draw out your wife."

"She left just a moment before you arrived."

"When is she due back?"

McDonald shrugged. "Around six."

"When does the maid leave?"

"At five – as soon as the cook arrives."

"Why don't you give her the afternoon off – that way we can talk better." Jarvis glanced around the estate:

"I think we should go back inside."

"Let me finish the last three rounds," McDonald said as he took the Colt from Jarvis.

Jarvis stood back and looked over at his partner who threw up his hands in disbelief.

The first shot was way low and dug through the wet lawn.

"You're anticipating the recoil," Jarvis told him. "Hold it firmly but don't fight it. Let it ride back with you – the weight will absorb the recoil."

There was no telling where his next two shots landed as they were heard crashing through the woods.

"Are you sure there's nothing back there to hit?" Jarvis asked.

"No, there aren't even any footpaths through those woods. There probably isn't another house for a quarter of a mile."

Returning inside, the three settled once again in the back room. The maid was dismissed.

McDonald and Jarvis went back and forth about firearms, and both agents presented their personal arms and back-ups for McDonald's perusal. Jarvis preferred revolvers and carried a .357 Magnum. Snider carried a 10 mm semi-auto.

Their host motioned towards Jarvis' empty glass. "Would you care for a little dividend?" he offered.

"Yes, thanks."

As soon as he was out of the room Jarvis looked over to his partner:

"Listen Snider," he began in a low tone, "when McDonald returns I want you to excuse yourself – say that you had a phone call."

His partner stared in disbelief.

"I think it would be better if I talked to him alone," Jarvis advised him.

Snider rolled his eyes. "If you screw up, it's your butt." He took a deep breath and considered the situation for a moment. "Well . . . you two seem to be hitting it off."

As if he was reading Snider's mind, Jarvis concluded in a self-assured tone. "Don't worry about Director Holeman."

"Well . . . he *is* our boss; and *I* was supposed to handle this one." He glanced over and managed a feeble smile. "Good luck with him, Jarvis."

After McDonald returned, Snider excused himself as planned and the conversation turned to skeet shooting.

Jarvis glanced at his watch and then to McDonald. "As far as you know, is our conversation being monitored?"

"I'm quite sure that it isn't. This house, and *Threshold*, are systematically checked."

“What do you know about the Bible codes?” Jarvis asked.

He settled back in his chair holding his drink. “Just recently a fellow approached us with a software idea related to the Bible codes – something about displaying the results in three dimensions. He had a proposed model for the software. The idea was that we would not get paid up front – but through a royalty arraignment. He was going to market it.”

“And . . .?”

“We sent him walking. There just wasn’t enough potential revenue to be worth the time involved.” He gave Jarvis a curious look:

“Where are we going with this?”

Jarvis considered it a while and then began:

“About six months before the 9-11 mess, the government funded a small research project to investigate the phenomena of whether or not there are secret messages encoded in the Bible. This was sparked, to some degree, by the claims of some researchers that the Bible codes could be used to predict future events.” He scratched his chin for a moment:

“The first phase was to determine whether there was even enough evidence to merit a continuation of the project. This was the information gathering phase.” He ducked his cigarette and looked up at McDonald:

“I understand that you know Ed Roth?”

He nodded. “I know him very well – we went to school together. He comes into town once in a while and we golf. He used to have his own company, but now spends all of his time with government projects. And I understand that his old team – most of them – are still with him.” He sipped his drink:

“Electronic surveillance and counter-surveillance.”

“That’s right,” Jarvis began. “It was Ed’s job to design the facility and equipment for a team of eight. The idea was to snoop the Internet, read e-mails and copy the data banks in the computers of people who worked with the codes.”

“That’s easy to do,” McDonald concluded. “It’s pretty easy to get past conventional fire-walls.”

Jarvis gestured to emphasize his next point. “From the very beginning, Roth could tell that every move of the team was being monitored – but he couldn’t tell who was doing it. So . . . Roth and his team dropped their other work and devoted their efforts full time – until they could determine exactly what was transpiring.”

“And?”

“They never figured it out – so Roth redesigned the facility into two parts. The first facility – the one that was known to be monitored –

essentially stayed the same. This was connected to the Internet, and its role was still information gathering. The second facility was created to analyze the information – I guess that you might say it was like a nuclear submarine on land."

McDonald broke in. "With an internal power source and internal life support – connected in no way from the outside after securing, and, most likely, covered by a shell made of specific sound-absorbing and electromagnetic shielding materials."

"You got it."

"And how is that idea working?"

"Not so well. The people that were recruited for the second phase were all identified – most likely by the same outfit that was monitoring phase one. They couldn't stay in the sub forever; and most of them had families. These people were subjected to every kind of electronic harassment imaginable – both they and their families were harassed. There was no stopping it; and Roth couldn't figure out who was behind it."

McDonald seemed perplexed. "What's the status of the project now?"

"The project is shut down. None of the original recruits show up there any more. The 'Sub' is used for a variety of other purposes. You know – high level conferencing and the like. And, for the people that were recruited for the project, the harassment has stopped."

McDonald slowly shook his head:

"I don't get it . . . I don't get it at all."

The agent's face seemed drawn as he continued:

"Neither Snider nor I had anything to do with the project. There is only one man that we report to, and *he* had nothing to do with the project. That's one of the reasons that we were assigned to contact you."

There was silence for a few moments as they both stared at each other.

"I'm listening," McDonald softly stated.

"Have you ever heard of an outfit that the Israelis call 'Niyaq?'"

"No."

Jarvis rubbed his forehead. "Well . . . they're some kind of secret organization, with apparently unlimited resources and technology. Nobody seems to know what they're up to. They haven't been implicated directly in any terrorist activities, but are suspected of eliminating certain targeted individuals and leaving an invisible trail to follow." They made eye contact:

"Roth believes that Niyaq wrecked the project and that they are keeping their eyes peeled for a startup elsewhere."

McDonald gestured. "Does the Bureau think that Niyaq is tied to bin Laden and Al Qaeda?"

“They did at first; but the investigations following 9-11 haven’t turned up any links?”

“This Niyaq group sounds pretty trick.” His countenance dropped:

“Hey, what were we doing shooting that Colt outside? Who’s to say that Niyaq isn’t shadowing you?”

Jarvis seemed self-assured:

“I can’t imagine that even Niyaq has the manpower to shadow every government agent and every person that is involved with computers in the entire U.S. If they do, then we have lost already.

Having said that – if they are shadowing Threshold and you personally, then our display in back of the house should convince them that nothing clandestine is taking place. If they really *are* targeting you, then they will know that you like to golf, you drink a bit, you shoot a lot of skeet, and that one of your hobbies is firearms. If they were watching us, then they saw two clowns with drinks in their hands shooting at a statue with an antique weapon. If they witnessed that, then there would be no reason to further investigate Snider and I.” He continued:

“If they are listening to us now then the game is over. But this is a safer bet than if you flew to Washington – or if we talked by phone.

This project would have probably died out by itself if not for all the sophisticated interference. This is what is so hard to understand. From what I have learned, the Bureau didn’t really find out anything about the Bible codes that would have merited a heavily financed effort to stop the project.”

“Yeah,” McDonald broke in, “but there is somebody out there that is willing to spend a bundle just to shut you down.” He slowly shook his head:

“It’s a puzzler.”

Jarvis rested his chin on his fist and stared off at nothing. The rain had started again and the wind was blowing it against the back of the house. After a few moments he began:

“The idea now is to start independent research outside of Washington in a number of places which are autonomous to each other.”

McDonald’s lips twisted. “And you want to employ *Threshold* to conduct research on the Bible codes?”

“Well, not exactly. The government wants *you* to conduct this research. The idea is that you do it at home.”

McDonald thoughtfully sipped his drink. He looked over to Jarvis and smiled:

“Are you sure you have the right man? I don’t know any Hebrew; and I know nothing about Bible codes – nor do I have any interest in the subject.”

Jarvis ducked out his cigarette. “Your job wouldn’t be to find hidden messages in the Torah. What we want you to do is to develop a new kind of Bible coding software."

"I wouldn't know where to start; it's all just too foreign to me." He smiled courteously:

"I'm going to have to politely decline."

Jarvis gestured to make a point. "I need to explain that we have a fellow that is going to work with you . . . a fellow named Michael. He has a vision for a new type of Bible coding software, but needs a good software man to implement it. So . . . if you come aboard, you and Michael will be a team."

"This guy is just going to come over to my house and tell me what he wants me to do?"

"Well . . . our thinking is that Michael will replace your handyman – the old guy that lives in the guesthouse."

His host made a face:

"Replace Vincent? I don't know . . . he's been with us a long time . . . and he is very good – and trustworthy."

Jarvis gave McDonald a most curious look:

"Oh . . . you'll like Michael – *everybody* likes Michael."

"Nah . . . my wife will never go for it. She thinks the world of Vincent."

"The plan is that Vincent quits, Michael shows up at the door, and your wife hires him on the spot." Jarvis threw up his hands:

"Everybody loves Michael."

McDonald squinted. "And what happens to our good friend Vincent?"

"Vincent gets an offer that he can't refuse."

McDonald wasn't convinced:

"I won't have to do anything? I come home one day and this Michael character is living in the guesthouse – after being hired by my wife?"

"You got it. Everybody loves Michael."

"So . . . if I come aboard, Michael will be my boss?"

"Yes."

"Is Michael your boss?"

He hesitated a few moments. "Yes . . . I suppose that you could say that."

"Does he work for the Bureau?"

"Michael doesn't have anything to do directly with the government or with the Bureau."

"I'm confused. Who selected this Michael character for the project?"

Jarvis squirmed in his seat:

"I'm really not authorized to tell you that, Mr. McDonald. But I will say that this project has a higher top than you would imagine."

McDonald lifted his brow:

"I have a pretty good imagination."

"Well . . . you'd need a *hell* of an imagination to figure this one out."

McDonald considered it for a moment:

"How long do you think this little project will take?"

"I really can't answer that; but this is a win-win deal for you. You can bow out any time you want. Just give me the word and Michael is gone. You can go about your business as usual." Jarvis gave him a curious look:

"I can say that because I know it won't happen."

McDonald laughed. "Because everybody loves Michael?"

"You got it!"

"And what if I tell you that this is all nonsense; and I just don't have the time to fool with it?"

Jarvis shrugged it off. "Then I'll be on my way." He thought for a moment:

"You're in business to make money – right?"

He lifted his brow. "So . . . what's your deal, Jarvis?"

"No paper trail, no checks . . . just cash – all clean money in small bills, twenties and fifties."

McDonald made a sour face. "Money is not the issue . . . I'm not going to put my family at risk for money. I have lots of money."

Jarvis was nonchalant. "Well . . . here's a chance to do something altruistic for your country."

"Is that what this is? Is that what this is all about?" Martin asked as he looked over at Jarvis.

Jarvis studied McDonald's face for a reaction:

"This is your country asking for help. Sometimes folks have to take a risk when they serve their country."

McDonald grimaced. "I was never in the service. You might say that some strings were pulled." He shrugged. "You know . . . Vietnam." His countenance dropped as he mused for a moment. "It was a bad war – nothing good came of it." He looked intently at Jarvis:

"Is this a good war? Is this a cause worth dying for?"

Jarvis began:

"The first World War was called, 'The World War – the War to End All Wars.' Of course, after WWII, it was viewed as what it was – a senseless trench war that slaughtered millions.

In the Bible, there is also a 'War to End All Wars;' but I am betting that this one *really will end all wars*." He shrugged. "At least for a season."

He smiled:

"A very *long* season."

McDonald seemed a bit taken back. "Are you a student of the Bible, Mr. Jarvis?"

"I am."

"That surprises me. Actually, this whole thing surprises me. I must confess that I really don't know *what* to make of it."

Jarvis laughed. "That makes two of us." He looked over at McDonald and grew serious:

"On the one hand I am full of wonder at what may come. On the other hand I am filled with trepidation, and yes, a bit of doubt and disbelief." He nodded knowingly:

"But this is normal. As long as I *keep plugging* I will be OK. It's normal to have doubts once in a while. Strength comes when you overcome your doubts, fears, and disbelief."

There was a long silence.

Seeming more relaxed, McDonald began – his tone more casual and off-hand:

"I must confess that this Michael character sounds somewhat interesting. What does he do for a living?"

"I really don't know what he does. I've only met him few times – and he spooked the hell out of me."

Taken back, McDonald inquired. "Just how do you mean?"

Jarvis took a deep breath. "Do you know what an aura is?"

"Yeah."

"It's weird . . . I swear that there was like an aura around this guy. I really can't describe it." He stared into his drink for a few moments and then up at McDonald:

"You'll find out for yourself."

McDonald was vexed. "Maybe I'll come on board and maybe I won't." He looked intently at Jarvis:

"The first thing that you will have to do is talk to me. Tell me what this is really about." He motioned with his hand:

"No BS, just tell me what you know."

"Mr. McDonald, the best that I can do is guess."

"Then guess," McDonald concluded.

"The most obvious scenario is that there might be something encoded in the Torah that has to do with the end-times. Niyaq represents the end-times bad guys and the USA represents the end-times good guys." He shrugged:

"Perhaps the Limeys, Israel, and a few other countries are in on this too. I really don't know."

McDonald set his drink down and caught Jarvis' eye. "So . . . this might have something to do with the rapture . . . or, say for example, the dead in Christ?"

"There is no telling."

"OK – I'll do it." He laughed heartily. "I don't know why I'm doing it; but I'll do it!"

"Great. The next step is to build you a little office in the basement."

McDonald twisted his lips. "I would think that the next step would be to sign a contract."

The old man shook his head. "No contracts. I'll bring you say a hundred grand in cash when Michael arrives. We'll see how it goes after that."

McDonald groaned:

"I'm a businessman, Jarvis – a successful one I might add. I didn't get here taking deals like this. Hell, I don't really know if you two are FBI. You have IDs – big deal. Give me a break – you pull up dressed like soccer fans driving a Mustang convertible." He rolled his eyes:

"I'm going to have to make a few calls to make sure that you are who you say you are."

"*No calls*," Jarvis stated emphatically. "I'll have Michael bring you the money when he comes. After a week or two if things are going OK, then we can renegotiate."

McDonald leaned forward in an aggressive posture. Before he could speak, Jarvis continued:

"If you are going to work for Uncle Sam, then you will follow orders."

"You're pretty clever, Jarvis," McDonald began in a sniping tone. "If I don't serve my country, it will be because of my unwillingness to step in line and march with the boys . . ."

"Just like you did before," Jarvis cut in. "You can color your butt any way you want to – it's your butt. Marching with the boys is how stuff gets done. If you are still the same spoiled brat that you were in the 60s, then I have wasted my time."

McDonald scooped up his drink and angrily strutted over to the sliding doors that led to the patio. After a few moments he turned to face Jarvis. He had calmed down and his countenance was non-threatening. "Did you serve?"

"Yeah."

"Vietnam?"

"Yeah, I retired as a Colonel."

"Well . . . it is actually quite logical to follow your orders under the circumstances. There is risk involved." He pictured in his mind the devastation of the statue:

"My family might need your skills."

Jarvis was expressionless as he took a healthy sip of his drink.

"We have a deal, Mr. Jarvis – no calls, no contracts," Martin declared. "We will see where we are in a week or two – no guarantees. And I can bow out any time I want." He returned to his seat and looked over at Jarvis:

"And *you* are the boss."

"What about Michael?" Jarvis asked him.

McDonald threw up his hands in a conciliatory gesture. "He's the boss too." He smiled good-naturedly:

"Do we have a deal?"

Jarvis extended his hand and smiled broadly as they shook. "We have a deal.

Under no circumstances will you contact the Bureau except if something goes amiss. And listen, if somebody from the Bureau contacts you about working Phase Three, then you are to tell them that you are not interested." He stared at McDonald. "Do you understand?"

"Yes."

"If that happens I want you to let me know. OK?"

He nodded.

Jarvis reached into his pocket and produced something that looked like a cell phone with no keyboard:

"This device has two switches. This one will call out – there will be someone on the other end to help you if you need it. If you can't talk, then this switch activates a homing signal. Enable the switch and help is on the way. You can tell which is which, because the beacon switch has this little ridge on it. That way you can reach into your pocket and flip it on if need be. Do you follow what I am saying?"

Concern showed on his face. "Yes, I do."

He passed the device to McDonald:

"Go ahead and try it. Tell whoever responds that 'this is a test;' and pass it over to me."

McDonald inspected the device for a moment:

"Did Eddie design this?"

"Yeah, he did . . . go ahead and try it."

McDonald hit the "call out" switch and held the phone to his ear.

"Yes sir?"

"Ah . . . this is a test. Here is Jarvis."

"Affirmative."

Jarvis took the device. "I'm going to switch on the beacon – check the coordinates."

"Affirmative."

Jarvis flips the "beacon" on.

"Good signal – I have you."

"I copy that. Over and out."

"Over and out."

Jarvis reached into his pocket:

"This is the charger. The battery will run the beacon for about a day. You check the battery like this. See? Check it once in a while – keep it charged up."

"Can my wife and daughters get these?"

"Your wife and daughters will know nothing of this." He looked very intently at McDonald:

"This is very important – you must tell no one about the project. *No one*. If you go out of town, call your itinerary in – we need to know where you are at all times."

"Should I carry a gun?"

"The reason that I am furnishing the device is to make you feel safe – not paranoid."

"I understand that; and I think it's a good idea. After I hit the beacon, how long before the cavalry arrives?"

"At most 40 minutes – maybe less." Jarvis noticed McDonald's concern:

"Everything has been done to guarantee the integrity of this project. I'm not expecting any problems."

McDonald looked sour:

"As far as the integrity of the project is concerned . . . don't you think that my family will wonder what I'm doing in the basement with the handyman?"

"Didn't Vincent have meals in the house frequently? Wasn't he almost like one of the family?"

"Well . . . yeah," he stammered, "how'd you know that?"

"I was briefed. So . . . Michael will get to be like that . . . sort of one of the family. Nobody will think twice about you spending time with him as they will probably spend some time with him as well."

McDonald laughed. "Oh. Because everybody loves Michael?"

"That's right," Jarvis replied with a repressed smile. "Now we fix up your room in the basement."

"Like a sub?"

"Yes. The plan is that you remodel the basement, and put in the office at the same time. It will be more clandestine that way."

McDonald nodded knowingly. "And your people will do that, of course."

"Yes. A home remodeling company will call on you at *Threshold*. The name of the company will be . . ." He looked inquisitively at McDonald.

"How bout, 'Acme Home Improvement.'"

The old man took out a small notebook and began to write:

"That's got a ring – albeit a trite one. And the man who will call on you will be . . ."

"Jeremiah," McDonald volunteered.

Jarvis writes it down and puts the notebook away.

McDonald gestured:

"After Acme finishes then Michael comes?"

"Yeah." Jarvis struggled to organize his thoughts:

"Listen, McDonald . . . there are a few things that I need to tell you about Michael." He took a deep breath:

"He seems to have an instinct for knowing things."

"Knowing things? How do you mean?"

"Well, for example, let's suppose that Michael says, 'I have a feeling that so and so will happen.' How you should read that is that this thing *will actually happen* – even if there is no logical way that Michael would have foreknowledge of it. Do you follow me?"

"No."

Jarvis looked frustrated. "I really don't know how else to put it. Look, McDonald, just take what he says seriously. Believe him." He threw up his hands:

"OK? Can you remember that?"

McDonald was puzzled. "Yes, I can remember that."

"Good – cause I'm not going to be around. I'd like to be; but it is a security risk." He caught McDonald's eye and looked resolute:

"You will have Michael to talk to. You can trust him as you could your own father. Trust no one else. *No one*."

"I'll remember. Tell no one – trust Michael."

"Good."

They stared at each other for a moment as McDonald tried to digest what Jarvis was telling him. When he began again his tone was more off-hand and casual:

"My wife will hire him?"

"Yes."

McDonald stood up and strode around the room in a nonchalant fashion:

"He is just your average handyman who will give me a hundred K in clean cash – twenties and fifties."

"Yes."

"And then Jesus comes and we all live happily-ever-after."

Jarvis cracked a wide smile. "That's how the story goes."

Jarvis watched as the rented convertible pulled up. He detected Snider's concern when he caught his partner's eye behind the rapidly flipping wipers.

When he climbed in Snider stared at him intently as if trying to read his face:

"How'd it go?"

Jarvis lit a cigarette and glanced about. "Not so good."

His partner banged his hand against the steering wheel. "Damn!"

The old man slowly cut his eyes toward his protégé:

"Take it easy," he said in a low tone.

Seeming desperate, Snider clenched his teeth and moved his head from side to side. "*I* was supposed to handle it. So . . . you screw up and *I* take the fall. Now *I* have to explain why *I* am coming back with a hundred thousand in cash and no deal." He glared at Jarvis:

"Holeman told you to take *any* deal to get this guy. How could you lose him with that kind of carte blanc?"

"I'll explain the whole thing to Holeman." He looked disgusted. "Don't worry about it."

"How can you be so damned off-hand about this thing?"

Jarvis took a deep breath, turned to his partner and manage a forced smile:

"I told you I would cover it. You will come out smelling like a rose."

His partner clenched the wheel as he drove along:

"While you are at it – tell Holeman that I want a different partner. Better yet, I'll tell him myself. I tell him you got bombed and discharged a weapon on McDonald's estate.

You're done, Jarvis. You're a hazard to work with. I should have never agreed to work with you!"

Jarvis was unaffected. "Hey, pull in up here at Wendy's."

"What the hell for?"

"I'm hungry."

"You got to be shittin me!"

"You really need to watch your language, Snider; you sound like a drunken sailor."

Snider did not slow the car. Jarvis nudged him hard:

"I said to pull in."

Snider looked over at Jarvis and his expression raised the hairs on the back of his neck. He braked and pulled into Wendy's.

Jarvis sat down and began eating. He could see Snider frantically waving his arms and talking into the cell phone. Everything was going as planned.

ED ROTH'S DUMP

2

It was Friday morning and Martin McDonald had taken the day off. A couple of weeks had passed since the Bureau contacted him. The remodelers were scheduled to finish up that morning and Martin had set a golf game with his friend Ed Roth for that afternoon. It was sunny and cool – a perfect day for golf.

McDonald was having coffee in the kitchen when one of the workers approached him:

"We're finished. Are you ready for a tour?"

He set the newspaper down, looked up and smiled. "Lead the way."

Proceeding to the basement, the man pointed to an area to the right of the door to the Sub:

"Put your right hand here. After you hear the sound you can open the door. If this spot gets soiled, just clean it off from time to time." He motioned:

"Go ahead."

He followed instructions and opened the door. The lights were on and there was a faint sound of moving air.

"When you open the door the lights and the air purification system come on," the man told him.

McDonald looked around the room. It was ten by twelve with two computers, comfortable office chairs, and empty bookcases. There were no windows or decorative enhancements.

The man began again. "It doesn't look very homey. Be sure that you don't use any nails or screws. If you want, you can stick some things to the walls." He motioned:

"There are two programs that I need to show you on the blue computer." He took two little cards from his pocket and placed them next to the keyboard.

Martin glanced at the first little card: It had two programs and passwords printed on it. There was another password on the second little card – it just read "Password," with a long series of number and letters.

"What does 'Password' have to do with?" Martin asked.

"You need to read program one *very carefully. Don't do anything before you have studied program one completely. I cannot over-emphasize this point. Don't lift either of the computer towers. Do you understand?"*

"Yes."

The man started the blue computer, opened "Program 1" and carefully keyed in the password:

"This program tells how the office systems work," the man began. "Everything is automatic." He thought for a moment:

"The batteries will need replacing in a year or so; but the system should run flawlessly until then. All systems have been checked and double checked. When you are familiar with this program, uninstall and delete it. The other program opens your research data banks. I'm to instruct you to commit these passwords to memory and then destroy this first little card. *Be careful to never put an incorrect password into the computer.* You need to read 'Program 1' *very carefully*. The second card you are to keep under the keyboard so that it is just barely visible. Do you understand?"

"Yes."

The man reached out and shook Martin's hand:

"I'm finished, sir."

"Wait a minute," Martin began, "I need to ask you . . ."

"I'm finished sir – I have completed my assignment. I'm not authorized to involve myself further."

"The second computer," Martin insisted, "you didn't say anything about that."

"The white one is for the other person. Does that copy, sir?"

"Uh huh, I mean, that's affirmative."

They stared at each other for a moment. The man's face was like stone.

Martin escorted him to the door, receiving polite smiles but no rhetoric.

"But what do I do if I have problems with the systems?" he asked the man as he was leaving.

The man stopped and thought for a moment:

"I wasn't instructed to brief you on that, sir."

The man and his two associates climbed into the old truck and drove away. Even the painted sign on the cab looked old and faded, to the extent that the phone number was no longer legible.

"I wonder how they did that," he said to himself.

He clopped down the basement steps and entered the Sub again. He started the blue computer, opened "Program 1" and keyed in the password. As he read, he marveled at the sophistication of the systems.

"Ed Roth must have spec'ed this out."

The batteries would only charge if everything else was off. Oxygen, temperature and humidity were monitored and controlled. The only thing that wasn't automatic was the removal of water accumulated by the dehumidifier. For anyone requesting entry to the sub whiled occupied, a special knocker was on the door. There was also a manually activated viewing port to identify anyone requesting entry. There were no outside monitors.

Martin was curious about the third password. He skimmed down until he found the reference:

"Application of the third password (the separate card) will detonate explosive devices that have been installed in the computer towers. The devices are also set to detonate if either tower is lifted from the table. The charge of these devices will terminate personal that occupy the room without endangering the structural integrity of the parent structure. Keep this card under the keyboard positioned so that it is partially visible."

Martin shut down the computer. He thought back to the day that agents Jarvis and Snider had visited him. He could hear Jarvis' words:

If you are still the same spoiled brat that you were in the 60s, then I have wasted my time. He took a deep breath and thought to himself:

"If I hadn't been drinking I would have probably turned the old man down." More of Jarvis' words came to mind:

Well . . . here's a chance to do something altruistic for your country.

Martin felt manipulated. He had underestimated the old man who had covered up his cleverness by his off-hand manner. A Marine Colonel with decades of service to the FBI – Martin was a pup compared to this man; and he felt like one. He was not trained to take risks – not this type of risk. He needed someone to talk to.

"This is nuts," he said out loud.

Thoughts raced through his mind. Was Ed Roth's visit happenstance or was there something else to it? Was it coincidence that he would show up the very day that his systems were put in place?

This is very important – you must tell no one about the project. No one echoed the old man's voice in his ears.

But he could trust Ed – he had known him for years. Then he remembered his own words that day:

Well . . . it is actually quite logical to follow your orders under the circumstances. There is risk involved. My family might need your skills.

No . . . he would have to follow Jarvis' mandates to the letter. He understood that he would have to, in Jarvis' words, *follow orders . . . if you are going to work for Uncle Sam . . . .*

Jarvis also told him that he had entered into a "win-win" deal; and that he could "bow out" any time he wanted to:

"I have to be alive to 'bow out,'" he said to himself.

Ed Roth seemed moody on the front nine. Martin tried to loosen him up; but his responses were short and measured. Ed surprised him by suggesting that they call it quits after nine holes.

The country club had remained virtually unchanged for fifty years. Any attempt to remodel or modernize anything was always voted down. People who objected to the old fashioned clay tennis courts, or to the small swimming pool, were simply advised to join another club that had better facilities. Membership was fixed and could only be sold with approval.

Martin turned to his friend as they entered the club lounge:

"Do you want the bar or a table?"

Ed seemed to be looking at something outside. "Can we go back to the house?"

Martin shrugged. "That's fine. I'll meet you back there."

Back at Martin's estate, the two settled into the back room. The maid appeared.

"Hi, Angie," Martin began. "Bring me a Paw . . . and a Stoley Gibson on the rocks for Eddie."

"Hold the Vermouth?" the maid asked.

Ed nodded and smiled.

When the maid brought the drinks, Ed was surprised to see that his host was drinking a can of beer:

"What happened to the scotch?" Ed inquired.

"I'm getting out of the habit of it. I don't know – it just doesn't seem to hit the spot anymore."

"I never thought I would hear you say that. Is your doctor bugging you about it?"

Martin shrugged. "No more than usual."

"Well . . ." Ed lifted his glass to his old friend. "It's good to see ya, Martin."

He saluted back. "You too, pal."

A few moments passed. Ed had gone through half of his drink and one onion.

"You were pretty quiet today. You OK, Eddie?"

Ed looked a bit sour. "Been working pretty hard."

"How many times have we golfed at the club?" Martin asked.

"Couldn't tell ya – forty . . . fifty, maybe more." He looked over:

"What's your point?"

"When we were in the lounge, you were looking at something outside when you suggested that we come home. What were you looking at?"

"Woods . . . it would be cake to train a laser on that window pane from those woods and listen to every word that we said."

"That never bothered you before?" McDonald leaned forward:

"What's going on; and why are you carrying a concealed weapon?"

Ed was uneasy:

"Where's your maid?"

Martin made a face:

"Are you paranoid, Ed?"

Ed became agitated:

"Oh, lucky me if I were. Then I could take medication and perhaps the delusions would subside. Unfortunately, my state was brought about by real circumstances."

Martin rang for the maid. He remembered when Jarvis had suggested dismissing her.

"Another round?" Angie inquired.

"Why don't you take the rest of the day off?" Martin suggested.

Angie looked uncomfortable. "But . . . your wife isn't feeling good today."

"I'll check in on her."

"Very good," she said as she turned and left the room.

"How's Rachael doing?" Ed asked.

Martin moaned:

"About the same. It's getting harder to include her on things. She usually backs out at the last minute."

"I'm sorry to hear that. Is she still going to that shrink?"

"She's got a different one. I made her switch. That other guy bilked me for a small fortune – he would have kept her coming forever. Anyway . . . she's got a female shrink this time. We'll see if anything comes of it." A few moments passed:

"Tell me about the gun, Eddie."

He looked at his empty drink. "Do you still keep my Stoley in the freezer?"

Martin grinned. "It's in the same place as always."

Ed's expression became gentle:

"You're a good man, Marty. You've been a good friend . . . all these years."

Caught off guard by his uncharacteristic show of emotion, Martin stammered as he spoke:

"Well, ah . . . you're a good friend too, Eddie."

"Come on and have a drink with me, Marty. I'll make em."

"That's fine. The Stoley's in the freezer to the left, the Cordou's in the fridge to the right."

Ed laughed. "Some things never change."

Martin called out to him as he headed towards the kitchen. "And lot's of ice, Fast Eddie."

When Ed returned, they entered into quiet conversation and savored their drinks. Ed wasn't himself – he looked tired and worn.

"Are you lubricated enough to tell me what's wrong?" Martin asked him.

Ed gathered his thoughts for a moment and then began:

"I never speak about what I do. Yeah . . . you know what I do in general terms – but I never speak of it and you don't inquire. In my line of work Congress is simply left out of the loop. We have zero leak tolerance. We can't have people talking at cocktail parties and then have a herd of Betty Ford Clinic flunkies blabbing all over Washington. One of the reasons that I have made a niche for myself is that I keep my mouth shut. Sometimes I hear sensitive information; but I keep my mouth shut."

"Well, Ed, you're also good at what you do," Martin added.

His friend's brow lifted:

"Notwithstanding, one slip of the tongue and I am out of the loop – no second chances."

"OK . . . so where are we going with this, Eddie?"

"Well . . . now there's something that I *can* talk to you about . . . because you already *know* about it." He caught Martin's eye:

"If you leak, you didn't get it from me because you were approached by the Bureau. Get it?"

Martin's heart raced; but he tried to look casual:

"I'm not with you."

"Oh." Ed looked somewhat disgruntled. "Well . . . we can talk about something else."

Some awkward time passed where neither man spoke. Finally Martin spoke up:

"What's with the gun, Ed?"

"Yeah . . . you're into guns. What do you think of this one?" he said as he drew the weapon from his shoulder holster and handed it over to Martin.

"It looks just like . . ."

"Aha! It's just like *Jarvis' gun*. I know he was here. What's the big deal?"

Martin recoiled:

"Jarvis told me to tell *no one*. So you show up and seem to know all about it." Martin acted very anxious. "I'm very confused."

"Jarvis told you about the first two Bible codes projects, right?"

"Yeah, he did," Martin confessed.

"Well, the project that Jarvis tried to recruit you for was called 'Phase Three.' The idea was that if *some* of the researchers were identified and harassed, then at least *some* of them might go undetected and be allowed to operate."

Ed made an exaggerated gesture:

"Well, hell – *everyone* was identified – all of them! You're lucky you turned Jarvis' proposition down."

Martin's heart pounded. He struggled to act nonchalant:

"I didn't know that the project had been shut down."

"Well . . . it has. I busted my buns on Phase Three. I designed a miniature version of the Big Sub. You know, for these 'autonomous researchers' to use. Eight of these units were installed – usually in the man's home."

Martin took a drink and noticed that his hand was shaking a bit. "And . . .?"

"Like I said, they were identified – all of them."

"But . . ." Martin stammered, "how do you *know* that they were identified?"

"Well . . . they were all directly contacted. Some received phone calls, some got e-mails, one guy was electronically robbed." He paused for a moment, looked downward and rubbed his forehead:

"One man's child was kidnapped. The ransom letter simply read, 'Shut it down!'"

Martin felt nauseated. "And. . ."

"The Bureau scrambled. They didn't even worry about being clandestine – they simply went and retrieved all the equipment."

"What about the kidnapped child?" Martin urged.

"He showed up unharmed. They treated him like a prince. He watched TV and played video games . . . ate like a king."

"Any leads?"

"I have no idea – but I would doubt if they have any." Ed noticed his friend's countenance:

"Take it easy, Marty. You look like you've seen a ghost."

"I live a quiet life. I'm not used to all this gun-toting and . . . and bizarreness."

"Well . . . just chill-out for a while. I didn't mean to upset you. Jesus, I didn't think you were so sensitive."

Martin's eyes widened:

"Sensitive! Hell, Eddie – you've got kids. Shit . . . I have two daughters. They could have been kidnapped . . . killed, or God knows what!"

"But you were smart, Marty – you turned the Bureau down."

Martin looked intently at his friend:

"I don't get it. If this project was such a big secret, then how can you know so much about it?"

"I know about it now that it's terminated. But initially, all I did was build and test the prototype Mini-Sub. I didn't know the names of any of the people that were approached for the project."

"How'd you learn that I was approached?" Martin asked him.

"Agent Snider was bitching to me about Jarvis. Snider has a big mouth – he's on suspension."

"You know Jarvis?"

"I've worked with him for years. He's tested a lot of my equipment. He is one of the guys that I get feedback from."

"Humph, small world," Martin noted.

"You told Jarvis that you knew me?" Ed asked.

"Actually, he asked me about it." Martin squirmed in his seat. "Do you know how many people were approached for Phase Three?"

"Jarvis told me. Something likes twenty-five."

"The people that were approached, but declined . . . were any of them harassed?

"No."

"None of them?"

"None of them. . . . least ways, none that the Bureau knows about." Ed considered it:

"There was *definitely* an internal security problem. The people in the Bureau that were in the loop on Phase Three are being formally held or are on suspended duty being investigated."

"What about Jarvis?" Martin asked.

"Jarvis is off-duty. I'm sure he could care less – he's due to retire this year."

"When was Phase Three shut down?"

"It all happened on a Friday. Let's see . . . it would be three weeks ago today."

Martin's attention turned to the revolver on the table. "Tell me about the weapon that you and Jarvis are carrying."

"It's a seven-shot .357 Magnum . . . Tritium sights and a trigger job. Other than that it's just a factory steel .357 with a 6" barrel. Jarvis has a guy that builds guns for him. He put this package together for me."

McDonald sipped his drink:

"I'd like to get good with a hand gun. I've seen what Jarvis can do with a revolver – I've seen him shoot."

Ed was surprised. "When was this?"

"Follow me; I want to show you something."

With that Martin led the way to the back window and pointed towards the statue:

"See there?"

"Jesus . . . what happened?"

"Jarvis knocked it down with three shots from my Colt Walker."

"I thought the Walker had never been fired."

"Well – it has now. Three times by Jarvis and three times by me. I couldn't hit anything with it."

"Do you mean to tell me that Jarvis did this the day that he came to try to recruit you for Phase Three?"

Martin nodded. "That's right."

Ed marveled:

"I hadn't heard that story. Whew, Jarvis is gone for good now." He slowly shook his head:

"Things won't be the same without Jarvis. Damn . . . we had a lot of fun together." He looked over at his friend:

"He taught me to shoot pistol. He would test new ammo – and stuff like full autos and compact grenade launchers."

"That's good, Eddie – maybe you can teach me to shoot a hand gun."

Ed gave Martin a curious look.

"What?" Martin asked, "What is it?"

"Is there something that you're not telling me?" Ed asked.

"No," Martin said unconvincingly.

Ed studied Martin's face intently:

"Do you swear on God?"

Martin look annoyed:

"Damn it – if there was something that I wanted to tell you then I would *tell* you!"

"Look, Marty, if you are in any kind of trouble . . ."

"I'm OK," Martin interjected. He avoided Ed's inquisitive stare and looked off.

"I need to use the bathroom," Ed announced.

"You know where it is."

Ed got up and began walking towards the kitchen.

"Why don't you use the bathroom back here?" Martin asked.

He turned around and managed a smile:

"I missed my morning regular. I'd rather use the one by the kitchen . . . you know."

"Suit yourself."

Ed surprised Martin when he brought him another drink:

"I might be a while – thought you might need another."

"Thanks, Eddie."

Ed took his time in the bathroom. After a while, Martin heard Ed yell out from the kitchen:

"Are you ready for a refill?"

Martin wandered back to the kitchen and handed Ed his glass:

"Jeez, Eddie, I thought you'd fallen in."

"Some things you just can't rush," he said with a chuckle.

"I need to take a leak," Martin said as he headed to the bathroom:

The light and the exhaust motor were on. He noticed one of his wife's cigarette butts floating in the commode. *Sometimes they don't wash down*, he thought to himself.

When he finished his business, he flushed and watched the butt disappear. He then joined his friend in the back of the house:

"What can you tell me tell me about Jarvis?" Martin asked as he sat down.

"He was a Captain in Nam and retired as a Marine Colonel. He's been with the Bureau about twenty years. His wife died suddenly about a year ago. I guess there was some guilt – you know, he was gone a lot in the service . . . and then all those years with the Bureau. He got pretty squirrelly after her death. He always liked his cocktails; but after his wife died he started binge drinking. He got into a few scrapes."

"What does Jarvis drink?" Martin asked.

"Bourbon."

Martin rolled his eyes. "What kind?"

"He doesn't seem to care – whatever is in the well." Ed noticed Martin's expression:

"Why are ya smirking, Marty?"

Martin slowly nodded as he spoke. "Jarvis is pretty clever."

"You ever see that show, Columbo?" Ed asked.

Martin laughed:

"That's exactly what I was thinking." His expression changed:

"Ed . . . why did they assign Jarvis to the Phase Three project? You know, as sensitive as that project was, and with Jarvis' drinking."

"I've wondered about that." Ed shrugged:

"I really don't know; but there seems to be a tie-in with Jarvis and the project."

"How so?" Martin asked him.

"We went to one of Jarvis' watering holes one day after shooting and he got on this 'end days' stuff. I'm tellin ya . . . his ideology is way out there – *way out there*."

"And you figure that is tied into the Bible codes project somehow?"

"Jarvis knows the Bible like the back of his hand. He's really into it." He thought for a moment:

"Ironically, he has killed more people in the line of duty than any other agent alive."

"It just doesn't fit, does it?" Martin offered.

"Yeah . . . but see . . . he gets those types of assignments. Cause . . . he's a soldier . . . and he likes to fight it out with the bad guys. His nickname is 'Dirty Harry.' Some agents have refused to work with him."

"Because of the associated risk?"

"I would think so."

"Well," Martin began, "I would think that he would be a good one to have around when the shit hits the fan."

Ed nodded. "He's the best."

"Even now?"

"Well . . . probably not *now*." Ed noticed Martin's countenance:

"What's the matter?"

"Nothing. Tell me what you know about Niyaq."

Ed's eyes widened:

"Where did you hear about Niyaq?"

"From Jarvis."

Ed stared off into space. "Jarvis has to go. That is a breach – big time!"

"So?"

Ed grew concerned:

"I'm doing some running off at the mouth. This can't go any farther."

"Come on, Fast Eddie . . . if the two of us can't talk . . . ."

Ed took a healthy slug of vodka and gathered his thoughts:

"Right now there is a person missing from the FBI, two people missing from the CIA, and three soldiers missing."

"Soldiers?"

"Yeah . . . high ranking soldiers who were exposed to sensitive information."

"Niyaq?"

"Whenever something happens that can't be explained, it is always Niyaq. You know – it's like saying that the devil did it and there is no remedy. Who is the devil . . . and what do you do to stop him?"

Martin watched as Ed drove off. He dumped his drink and made his way upstairs to check on Rachael. Her bedroom door was locked.

"Rachael . . . are you all right? Raech!"

"Just a minute, Marty."

As was often the case, Rachael had gotten up, showered and put on make-up – only to go back to bed again. When the door opened she was standing in her robe. The room was dark and the TV was going. She was still holding on to the doorknob.

Still an attractive, statuesque woman – she was slim and nicely built; but the crows feet had started to appear around the eyes; and her countenance was melancholy.

"It's like a cave in here, Rachael. Why don't you open the blinds?"

"What do you want, Marty?" she asked in an impatient tone.

"I'm just checking on you, hon." They stared at each other for a moment. "Well . . . can I come in and talk to you for a minute?"

"Sure," she said unenthusiastically. She turned and got back into bed:

"How's Fast Eddie?" she asked.

Martin sat down in the chair next to her. "He's fine."

"God . . . you reek of booze. Why do you have to get bombed whenever Eddie comes by."

"Well . . . oh, I don't know, Rachael." He looked around the room; his expression was drawn:

"How can you stand to stay in here all day?"

Her expression became ugly:

"Did you come in here to lecture me?"

"No."

"To argue?"

"No. I came to see how you were, Rachael."

"Well . . . now you've seen." She reached for a pill container on the night stand:

"Would you go and fill this for me?"

Martin read the instructions on the label. "It says here that you are supposed to take one every six hours."

"So?"

He held up the bottle. "So . . . I've seen you take three of these at once."

She looked up at the ceiling and huffed. "I always take three. One of them doesn't do anything. Well . . . not anymore." She glared at Martin:

"Did you and Fast Eddie have just *one* drink?"

"I've been doing better with the scotch." He shrugged. "And Eddie is an old friend."

She softened. "Yes, you *have* been doing better."

A few moments passed and Martin spoke up. His tone was soft and non-confrontational:

"Rachael, when we first went to see that new shrink of yours, the first thing that she said was that you needed to get off of some of the medication."

She became defensive. "Yeah . . . and I *have* gotten off some of it."

"Like what?"

"Like the Methedrine."

"Yeah . . . that was the stuff you used to take before we went out. That helped a lot . . . then you would drink too much and not eat anything."

"True. But at least I would go – now I don't go anymore."

They stared at each other.

"Why didn't you come down and say hi to Fast Eddie? That was a bit rude. He's your friend too; and he thinks the world of you."

She was hurt. "I didn't want him to see me like this. I'll see him next time."

Martin slowly shook his head:

"That's what you always say – and 'next time' never comes."

Her eyes watered:

"I wish that you could climb inside of me and see how *I* feel. Maybe then you would understand and have some compassion. A tear rolled down her face as she glared viciously at Martin:

"You can go now. Thanks for checking to see how I was."

Martin stood up.

"Aren't you forgetting something?" She threw the empty pill bottle at him:

"Have Vincent pick it up – you don't need to get pulled over with booze on your breath. Call it in."

As usual, Vincent greeted him at the guesthouse door with a good-natured smile:

"Hello, Mr. McDonald."

Vincent was wiry and in his late sixties. When Martin went out of town he would always stay in the main house. It made Rachael feel safe. Martin thought the world of him.

"Hi, Vincent. Rachael needs to have this filled."

He looked at it. "I just had this filled!"

"When?"

"Let's see . . . Tuesday."

"Great," Martin said in disgust.

Concern showed on Vincent's weather-worn face:

"How's she doing?"

"She's getting worse."

"When Holly went off to school she took a nosedive," Vincent noted.

"What am I going to *do* with her, Vincent?" Martin lamented.

Vincent shook his head:

"I don't have any answers. Just don't blame yourself – it isn't your fault."

"Then whose fault is it?" Martin came back.

Vincent looked sympathetic:

"Why does it have to be anybody's *fault*?"

"Well . . . I hope she feels better by Sunday – the girls will be home."

"Don't worry," Vincent said, "she always puts on a good show for the girls."

Martin got up to leave. "Thanks, and good night, Vincent."

Martin made some coffee and settled into the sub. He took the little card from his wallet and carefully opened his research data banks.

"All I would have to do is plug in this little password . . . and boom!"

He started to read but his heart wasn't in it. Indeed, Martin just wanted the whole thing to go away.

He shut everything down and went upstairs to the den and unlocked the drawer where he kept his Colt Python revolver. It was fully engraved and had never been shot. He loaded it with hollow-point bullets:

"I don't even have a holster for this gun," he muttered to himself.

He tucked it into his belt, made sure that he had the beacon phone with him, and climbed the stairs to bed.

MICHAEL

3

Saturday morning found Martin – coffee cup in hand and dressed for golf – casually meandering around the grounds. When Vincent approached him he noticed something odd in his demeanor:

"Good morning, Vincent."

Vincent put his hands in his pockets and looked about anxiously:

"I'm afraid that I won't be able to work for you anymore."

Martin was startled. "Why?"

He smiled broadly. "My son called late last night. He's purchased a ranch in Montana."

Martin couldn't hide his surprise. "A ranch? I thought that you and your son gave up on that idea years ago."

Vincent marveled. "It's very strange. When my son was eight years old he saved a little girl from drowning. Well, the father of that girl died in his sleep – he left my son a heap of money."

"When did this man die?" Martin asked.

Vincent supplied the date and Martin realized that it was soon after Jarvis' visit.

Vincent looked pleadingly at Martin:

"I promised my son that I would help him if he ever got his ranch."

Martin felt a bit shaky. "Yes, I know that, Vincent; and . . . and I fully expect that you should keep your word." He considered it a moment:

"I'm surprised that the estate could be settled that fast."

"I'll stay until you find someone to replace me," Vincent volunteered.

"No . . . get your stuff boxed up today. I'll have it shipped to you. You can pack some clothes and fly out in the morning."

Vincent looked pleased. "Are you sure?"

"Yes." Martin smiled:

"And . . . and I'd like to give you say . . . ten thousand as a bonus."

Vincent solemnly shook his head. "I can't accept that. Plus, we have money now."

"Yes, but that is really your son's money. They looked at each other.

"Hey, you could surprise your son's boy with a horse." Martin suggested.

Vincent looked elated. "I'll just hand him the reins. And . . . when he looks at me funny I'll simply say, 'Don't you want to ride your horse,

Billy?'"

"It's a deal then?"

Vincent nodded enthusiastically. "Yes, it's a deal."

Martin became somber:

"Don't say anything to Rachael – I'll handle that. I don't want her to get freaked just before the girls arrive."

"No goodbyes?"

"We'll come to visit. Heck, I'll shoot some coyotes and prairie dogs for you."

Vincent beamed:

"Well sure, we'll still see each other. I'll bet that Rachael and Holly would like to come as well."

"I'm sure that they would."

Vincent was overjoyed:

"I'm sure it will all work out for the best."

Martin had just arrived at the club when his cell phone rang:

"Hello?"

"Martin," his wife began, "has Vincent quit?"

He was lost for words. "Ah . . . well . . . ."

Her voice was insistent. "Just tell me, Martin – yes or no?"

Martin collected his thoughts. "I didn't want to tell you just yet – with the girls coming and all." His heart pounded:

"How did you find out?"

"This man in my kitchen told me. He wants Vincent's job."

"A man? What man?"

A few moments passed as he listened in the background as his wife and the man exchanged dialogue.

"His name is Michael – what should I do?"

Martin's knees felt weak as he leaned against his car:

"Well . . . hire him if you want. You know how much we paid Vincent; but I wouldn't offer him that much to start."

Her voice was emphatic. "I want you to come home and talk with him. Your golf game isn't that important."

"This one is, hon; I'm trying to get a contract with his company."

She hung up in his ear.

Fear gripped Rachael – like the talons of a hawk gripping her heart.

She found it hard to breathe. She pictured her bedroom – safe and secure. "Run!" a voice from within her cried. Her pills . . . her vodka . . . if she could just get back there and lock the door. She could dial Martin – or 911.

She felt the stranger's hand on her shoulder.

"No, stay here with us!" the voice in her head cried out.

She heard a sound like the cry of a multitude of anguished souls. As the stranger wrapped his arms around her the noise in her head abated. She felt something rushing into her soul – something wonderful.

Martin gripped the steering wheel tightly. It was after five and he knew that Rachael would be upset with him for staying at the club so late. He dreaded the idea of the scene that could unfold with the girls both home from school.

But, for some reason, he felt relieved. Perhaps it was because now he would either have someone to talk to concerning his predicament – so naively volunteered – or the problem would be gone for good. It all depended on whether or not Rachael would hire Michael.

Rachael was not the type to make that kind of decision on her own; but Jarvis had stated that she would indeed do just that. Martin felt a strange calm come upon him. He relaxed and loosened his grip on the wheel.

The front door was unlocked and Martin could hear laughter coming from the kitchen. After receiving hugs from the girls, he turned to Rachael and the other man – who was wearing a long apron. Rachael seemed to be beaming with enthusiasm. She smiled broadly and motioned to the man:

"This is our new handyman – Michael."

Martin extended his hand. He felt something tingly – the sensation was warm and loving and ran all through him. He didn't want to let go of his hand as he stared into eyes that had a special sparkle.

Michael was younger than he had suspected – maybe in his twenties or early thirties. He was slight of build with fine, handsome features. His thick black hair showed no distinguishable part and hung way past his shoulders. His dark beard contrasted his light complexion. But what was the most striking were his eyes which showed a deep, perhaps even mystical, contentment.

His daughter Holly gave him a curious look:

"You can let go of his hand now, dad."

"Oh . . . well . . . welcome aboard, Michael."

"We're fixing supper, dad," his other daughter declared.

He loosed himself from Michael eyes and glanced at his wife:

"Well, Rachael . . . you've changed your mind about eating out?"

"Michael knows a lot about French cooking . . . and wine too. He lived there for quite a while."

Martin's brow lifted. "That's interesting; perhaps we'll go down and select a bottle for dinner. I have a bit of wine in the basement. Pretty good conditions for it down there." He thought for a moment:

"Your accent – is that French?"

Michael laughed. "I have an accent in French as well."

"What is you first language?" Holly asked

"Hebrew, and I probably have an accent there too."

"Oh . . . as I live and breathe, we have a multi-lingual handyman," Martin said tongue in cheek. "Has Rachael told you what your duties will be?"

Rachael turned to Michael:

"My husband is very business oriented – business, business, business." Then to her husband:

"Come taste this sauce."

He sampled it and declared: "That's quite extraordinary – what is it?"

"Sea urchin sauce," Rachael said, "made with reduced Cognac and thickened with . . ."

"Arrow root," Michael chimed in.

"Excellent," Martin applauded. "And what does this go with?"

"A seafood Pâté."

"And the entrée?"

"Medallions of Pork Sauce Robert."

Martin enthusiastically rubbed his hands together:

"Look, Michael; the girls both like wine . . . this looks like we're going to need two bottles. How bout a Chardonnay for the appetizer?"

Michael didn't like the idea:

"They finish too strong. How about a Brut Champagne? An American natural would be good as well."

"Fine. And a dry red for the entrée?"

Michael nodded. "Yes, you can surprise me."

Martin was getting into it. "Excellent. I'll chill the champagne and about an hour before dinner put some ouillage to a dusty Bordeaux." He walked over to the stove:

"And this is the Sauce Robert?"

"Try it," Michael suggested.

He tasted it and lifted his brow. "Wow, I've never had anything quite like it."

"It took us all day to make it; but next time will be much easier," his wife informed him. "Now we have brown roux, blonde roux, and demi-glace all ready to use. She smiled at Michael: "So . . . next time it will be a snap."

Martin looked around. "Well . . . this is fun. Perhaps someone would like a little cocktail? He turned to his new handyman:

"Michael, how about a little taste before dinner?"

"Some wine would be good. Anything that you have opened."

"Well . . . I'll open some – you name it."

"I have some wine opened," Michael told him. "It will be my treat."

Martin watched as Michael headed towards the back of the house:

"Where's he going?"

"Probably to the guesthouse. He's all moved in," his wife announced.

Still wearing his impish smile, Michael reappeared with a pitcher of red wine:

"I think it would best if we all helped ourselves."

Martin shot his wife an odd look when Michael began filling water glasses with ice and passing them around.

"What should we say for a French *salut*?" Martin's daughter Holly asked.

Michael lifted his glass. "Romanee Conti."

"Romanee Conti," they all repeated

"This is good – real fruity," Molly noted.

Martin obligingly sipped his wine. He then went and got a wine glass, poured some more, and began sniffing and swirling the wine in the glass – tasting it as he did so. He had a curious look on his face.

"Is there something wrong?" Rachael asked.

"No . . . it's just that . . ."

"What."

He looked very perplexed. "Nothing . . . forget it"

"Um, it *is* good," Holly noted. "What is it?"

"It's Romanee Conti," Martin broke in. He looked at Michael:

"It's Romanee Conti, right Michael?"

Michael smiled. "Well . . . it *does taste* like it."

At dinner Michael seemed to focus on the girls – asking them questions about their school curriculum and hobbies.

"Holly has this idea of getting married," Rachael broke in. "She's only a sophomore."

Holly frowned. "Do we have to get into that?"

"Well, dear, I thought we could get Michael's opinion on the matter. Michael?"

Michael looked across the table at Holly:

"Tell me about him, Miss McDonald."

She smiled. "We're deeply in love."

"But why are you getting married now?" Michael politely asked.

"I would die if I lost him – just die."

"Well," Michael began, "I suspect that he feels the same about you."

"Yes, I'm sure that he does."

Michael thought for a moment:

"Sometimes the passion of wanting exceeds the passion of having. Right now you want a husband; but do you need one at this time? Be wise – don't tarnish what you have. Nurture it and let it grow . . . get married in due time – when you get out of school. Then you will both want *and* need the things that marriage offers.

Right now you will both have to give up a lot if you get married. You will sacrifice your sorority life and a myriad of other things that are unique to college life."

Holly became anxious. "But what if he decides to date other girls?"

"What would be wrong with that?" Rachael broke in. "You two dated all through high school."

"I think that you should date other men," Molly said smugly; "then you could find out how truly boring Bobby is."

Molly and Holly were different in every way.

Holly was dark-haired, tall and statuesque with beautiful skin and lovely tapered hands. Everything about Holly was beautiful.

Molly was short with big hips, shorter legs and blonde hair; and she was crude of manner despite her mother's tutelage.

Martin ignored Molly's snide comment:

"Michael has a good point. Getting married now could actually harm your relationship. Have the two of you considered that possibility?"

"Don't tarnish what you have," Holly said to herself. "Maybe you're right, Michael; things are good now."

"Are the two of you engaged?" Michael asked.

"Yes," she sheepishly replied.

"You are?" Rachael sputtered, "Where's your ring?"

Holly avoided her mother's eyes:

"I left it at school. I didn't want you and dad to see it."

"Have you set a date?" Michael calmly asked.

"No."

Michael smiled generously:

"Fine. Talk to him about setting the date after college. I think that he might be relieved."

Martin was enthusiastic. "I think that they *both* might be relieved. Right Holly?"

Holly looked away.

"Well," Martin gently began, "won't you even consider *talking* with him about it?"

"Actually . . . I think I *would* rather wait . . . like Michael says," Holly announced.

Martin sighed with relief and gazed over at Rachael.

"What about dating other boys?" Rachael asked.

"I'm not going to tarnish what I have. Things are good now; I'll just have faith that things will be just as good when we get out of school."

Martin looked approvingly to his daughter. "That was well put."

"And very wise," Michael added.

"Tell us something about yourself," Molly insisted. "Your first language is Hebrew; are you Jewish?"

"Yes I am."

"What are you doing eating pork?" Molly asked.

"I'm not orthodox."

"Are you a messianic Jew?"

"Yes. The Christians would call me that; but the orthodox Jewry would simply call me 'Hashmootz.'"

"Hashmootz? What does that mean?" Rachael asked.

"The traitor."

"You don't look Jewish," Molly blurted.

"Jews today do not look like the Jews of old. They look more like their captives than the Jews of say, king David's time." He looked back and forth from Molly to Holly:

"In other words, you can not always tell *what* a person is simply by looking at him."

"I don't get it. Why are you just a handyman?" Molly asked.

"I believe that I just answered that question."

Rachael looked embarrassed:

"Forgive my daughter, Michael; I didn't raise her up to be so forward – especially with people that she just met."

Molly turned to her mother. "Can I ask him what his last name is?"

"No, Molly. This is a social dinner – not an interrogation."

Molly was taken back by her mother's uncharacteristic assertiveness:

"Well . . . I'm not a Christian. Christianity is a dying religion."

Michael smiled nonchalantly:

"Yes, Molly, you're quite right on two counts. Martyrdom is a primary precept of the faith; and the faith in general is dying.

The Christians nations have stopped making babies and the non-Christian nations are having many babies. The non-Christian nations are taking over the Christian nations from within – through immigration and by using democratic systems to promote their ideologies while debasing Christian precepts. It is the revelation of prophecy." Michael smiled at Molly:

"Yes, Molly, Christianity is a dying religion."

Molly made an ugly face. "I never heard anything like that."

"You are young; you may be a witness of it." Michael's demeanor was sad:

"Would you be a witness for good?"

Molly looked around the table, and then back to Michael:

"You mean . . . like good and evil . . . the devil and all that."

"Yes."

"I don't believe in that," Molly emphatically declared.

Michael nodded knowingly:

"Just the same, your vote has been cast."

Molly glared hatefully at Michael:

"What's that supposed to mean?"

Rachel looked uneasy:

"She was brought up going to church. It seems like ever since she went off to college . . ."

"Our great liberal institutions," Martin added.

Molly became indignant. "I have a mind of my own, thank you. When a Christian nation fights a war, they label themselves good and they label their opponents bad. That doesn't make them good any more than it makes those who they oppress bad."

Rachael's jaw tightened. "That's enough, Molly." She looked around the table and forced a smile:

"This is all so delicious."

Molly was quiet for the rest of the meal; but an awkwardness lingered. She had done it once again.

Martin was getting ready for bed when he heard a gentle knock. The door opened and Rachael entered wearing a robe. He couldn't remember the last time that she had been in his bedroom:

"What is it, Rachael?"

Rachael smiled self-consciously:

"I thought that you might want to come in with me."

Although surprised, he acted nonchalant. "Yeah . . . that's fine."

They settled into bed and Rachel turned off the light and gently held Martin's hand.

"We used to always talk with the lights out before we went to sleep. Remember?"

"Uh-huh." He also remembered something else – but he didn't say it.

Martin was at a loss. Had Rachael finally flipped completely? He didn't know what to expect.

"We had our own little cozy, secret place that we would go to," she softly told him. "But . . . I always felt that, at certain times, there was someone listening. Sometimes there was a faint roar – like distant wind. Remember?"

Martin pondered. "Yes, – I do remember that. We would say that the angels were listening."

"Those were good times."

They laid together quietly for a few moments. The wind was moving the branches of a large oak; and the shadows moved over the bed.

"I'm glad you're feeling better, Rachael; I really need you right now. I'm very confused."

"Are you waiting for an invitation, Martin?"

He laughed. "Do I need one?"

Rachael did something that she hadn't done for a long time. Then they luridly made love – intense and satisfying. They laid in each other's arms – each with their own thoughts. Peace was all around them.

"Everything is going to be all right," Rachael declared.

"Well . . . right now that's the way I *feel.* But . . . Rachael . . . what made you say it . . . with such conviction? I mean . . . how do you *know* that everything will be all right?"

"Martin, you don't have to know *all* of the details; *all* you *have* to *have* is *faith.*"

"God . . . you sound like . . ."

"Like I used to sound – way back when?"

"Yeah." Martin considered it for a moment. He sat up in bed and looked down at his wife's contented face:

"What . . . what's happened to you, Rachael? Tell me."

"I really haven't had much time to think about it. What was very strange was that when I opened the door and looked at Michael I knew in my heart that I knew him – but I couldn't place the face."

"Knew him? From where?"

She shook her head:

"I don't know. It was spooky – I can tell you that much.

Martin, I think Michael performed an exorcism on me."

"An exorcism – like casting out demons?"

"Yes – I heard them in my head – just like you and I are talking now. They were afraid – they were desperate – as if they knew what was about to happen to them."

"Is that what has been troubling you – all this time?"

"Yes . . . I think so."

"And now you're OK?"

"Yes. It happened so fast – but so thoroughly."

Martin let out a deep sigh and his eyes watered. "It all started when we began to drift apart. I . . . I think I could have prevented it if I had just been more attentive and caring."

She gently took his hand:

"Don't be so hard on yourself; I could have prevented it also."

"What do you mean, Rachael?"

"It doesn't matter now, Martin – it's behind us. The best thing that we can do now is look back and learn from it."

Martin wiped a tear from his eye. "Still . . . I need to apologize . . . apologize for being so cold towards you."

She looked up and saw a tear run down his face. She gave his hand a gentle squeeze:

"It's all right, Martin – everything is all right."

Martin felt like confessing; but Rachael had mercifully let him off the hook.

There was silence for a few moments and then Rachael spoke up:

"Molly didn't like Michael. Not at all."

"Did you catch what Michael said to her?" Martin asked. "He said, 'Would you be a witness for good?' Not, 'I hope that you will be a witness for good.' And then he told her, 'Just the same, your vote *has been cast.*' That sounds like some kind of doom."

"Molly is different," Rachael admonished.

"Yes," Martin agreed, "in a bad way. She is pretty on the outside – ugly on the inside. She's never really been a part of the family. Always to herself – always separate. It's almost like she hates us."

"She seems to especially loathe Holly," Rachael admitted.

Martin nodded:

"I know it. Holly seems to be her opposite in every way."

Martin sat up in bed and looked over at his wife. "Tell me what went on with you and Michael."

"Michael at first put his hand on my shoulder; and then he put his arms around me.

I woke up on the floor. Michael was sitting at the kitchen table. I asked him what had happened? He simply answered, 'You are free, Rachael.'"

"Then what?"

"He asked me if I wanted him to stay and I told him 'Yes.'"

"And?"

"Well . . . the girls came in and . . . we decided to cook dinner."

"When did Michael move his stuff into the guesthouse?"

Rachael's lips twisted. "I guess it was while I was sleeping on the floor. It's all a bit . . . strange. Don't you think so?"

A BAD SIGN

4

Martin always arrived at work at 7:00 AM sharp. His secretary was also in the habit of showing up at that time – even though Martin had made it clear that it wasn't necessary for her to do so.

Usually Martin would seclude himself in his office. But oftentimes he would spend a few moments with his secretary – just chatting over coffee and doughnuts.

She had been with him almost from the beginning and was considered by Martin to be indispensable to the operation of the company – so much so that at a Christmas party she was given a plaque that read "The Boss." That way, when Martin instructed someone, such as a new employee, to "go ask the Boss," that person knew exactly where to go.

Sheila was an articulate brunette with pleasant features and a figure that even the most modest clothing couldn't hide. She had a sardonic wit that was a match for Martin's. Rachael was, at first, taken back that Martin had hired her. Sheila sensed this, and went out of her way to develop a personal relationship with her. After a time Rachael waxed trusting. She had one son by a failed marriage, and after that ended, remained single.

Sheila looked up when Martin entered:

"Eddie called just after you left yesterday."

"He probably wants to play golf – I'll call him." He looked down at Sheila:

"Sheils . . . you're looking great – as usual," Martin jibed, "and the paragon of efficiency – aptly attired and well-rested. I'll lavish some more compliments on ya after some coffee." With that he strutted into his office. Leaving the door opened behind him; he peeked around the corner and added, "I'll take it without."

Monday mornings usually found Martin in low spirits. This was usually from too much scotch, too much Rachael, or a combination of both. Sheila was, therefore, a bit surprised to receive such a cheery greeting. On Monday mornings, "take it without," meant "hold the rum."

Sheila fixed his coffee and brought it to him. She studied his expression as she sat it down:

"Aren't we the perky one. I guess that things went well with the girls' visit."

He sipped his coffee, looked up at her and smiled. "Couldn't have gone better."

"How's Rachael doing?"

"Fantastic."

Sheila couldn't hide her surprise. "Gosh . . . I've heard that her new shrink was good . . ."

"It didn't have anything to do with the shrink. She had an exorcism on Sunday."

Her jaw dropped. "You're joking."

"No . . . I'm perfectly serious."

Sheila was totally aghast. "I didn't know that you believed in such things."

He gave her a curious smile. "Well . . . it's quite scriptural . . . you didn't know that?"

Sheila slowly shook her head in disbelief. "You're killing me, Marty. Exorcisms . . . scriptural . . . what gives?"

"There's a lot more to this Christianity deal than most folks imagine. There's power, there's peace, there's promise, there's prophecy."

Her eyes narrowed. "Are you foolin with me, Marty?"

He pointed at himself and smiled as the innocent accused:

"Do I look like I'm fooling with you, Sheils?"

She stood up and paced back and forth in front of his desk:

"You look like you've flipped!"

Martin casually shrugged. "OK, spiritual discernment isn't one of your biggies. Well, you are still efficient . . . and, if I dare be so bold, pretty foxy."

She stared off and sighed. "Foxy," she said to herself, "for all the good *that* does me."

"Well . . . I thought that you and Mark . . ."

"Mark has been dismissed; we're no longer together. I don't want to talk about Mark." She paced around the room for a few moments and then looked back at Martin:

"My sex life is beyond hope. How many women do you know whose favorite TV star is the Energizer Bunny?"

Martin roared with laughter; but Sheila remained sullen:

"Maybe I should try that shrink of Rachael's; or maybe I should just quit waiting for you."

She hung her head:

"Whew . . . I wish I hadn't said that."

Martin was quick to respond. "If it makes you feel any better, I'll bet I've fantasized about you a thousand times."

She smiled. "You're dammed right it makes me feel better. Can I tell you something awful?"

"Go ahead."

"I guess . . . I always thought that . . . you know . . . if . . . if Rachael got really bad . . ."

"Can I tell you something awful?" Martin asked.

She took a deep breath. "Go ahead."

"Whenever you find some new guy to date . . . I secretly hope that things won't work out." He avoided her eyes:

"When you go out with people I feel jealous . . . you have always been my forbidden fruit."

Sheila also turned away:

"And you mine," she concluded.

There was an awkward silence. Sheila forced a casual tone:

"I always believed that you, in a lot of ways, blamed yourself . . . you know, for Rachael's condition."

He made a face:

"Well . . . I don't anymore. Yeah, I think that I might have aggravated it a bit – but I don't blame myself . . . not like I used to."

"Aggravated it? How?"

"Her condition didn't change overnight. It was a long process – a long, slow deterioration. She was becoming withdrawn; and at the same time I was becoming totally consumed with *Threshold*." He thought for a moment:

"I had plenty to do; and she would always play the perfect role when I needed her." He looked over at Sheila and sighed:

"I was a bit selfish. I didn't really make any attempt to help until her lack of function became apparent to others – until it became an embarrassment to *me*."

"Oh . . . cut it out, Marty – don't be so hard on yourself. You're a good man. Heck, if you weren't, you'd have jumped my bones long ago." She blankly stared off:

"I don't think that I could have turned you down."

"It wouldn't have been good," he dryly stated.

"The sex?" she pleaded.

He shook his head:

"No . . . the aftermath."

"I know it. And also, if we had started in on it, I would have suspected that you could cheat on me as well. Heck, you never even give me a hug at our drunken Christmas parties. Everyone else does."

Martin gazed at her curiously over his glasses. "Yeah, that's why we always had such a good turn out." He made a face:

"Hey – what got us on this?"

"I don't know," she said somewhat disgusted.

After a long silence Sheila spoke up:

"Tell me what happened to Rachael. I mean – did she change (she snapped her finger), like that?"

Martin leaned back in his chair and considered it. "Yeah, she did."

"Well come on," she continued impatiently, "tell me what's going on. I mean, did you get a priest to come over? What's the deal?" She rolled her eyes:

"God, this is like pulling teeth."

Martin marveled. "Sheila . . . "

"What? What is it?"

He slowly shook his head and stared off at nothing:

"It's weird . . . ah . . . you think that you know what's going on in life . . . you think that you've really got a handle on things . . . and then something happens to let you know that you are really in the dark . . . that you really don't see the big – the true – picture." Martin suddenly winced as he recalled Jarvis' words: *Tell no one.*

"And?"

He took a deep breath:

"OK . . . Rachael had a chance encounter with a total stranger – someone that neither of us had met. Well . . . apparently this fellow sensed Rachael's distress and puts his arms around her. The next thing that Rachael remembers is waking up and having the stranger tell her that she is free."

She curled up her nose:

"Free? Like from demons?"

"Yeah, like from demons." He threw up his hands:

"She's a totally different person – like she was when things were good for us."

"Even as far as . . ." She wiggled her eyebrows.

He wiggled back. "Yep."

"Wow, do I ever need a hug from *this* guy! Can you arrange it for me?"

"Well I . . . I don't know . . ."

Her countenance sank. "Oh . . . you're not telling me everything. What – do you think I will gossip? Don't you know me better than that?"

"Sheils," he protested, "I wasn't even there at the time. A hug . . . some sleep . . . and presto – she's free! That's the whole story."

"Well," she calmly began, "I don't ask you for much. I wanna meet this guy. I . . . I've been thinking of visiting Audrey."

"Rachael's shrink?"

She lowered her eyes. "I'm depressed. It's like a profound emptiness . . . gloom . . . pessimism. And . . . I don't really have anyone to talk to about it."

Martin shrugged it off:

"Oh . . . you've been down before – you'll snap out of it."

She looked pleadingly at Martin: "I don't ask you for much. I want to meet this guy." She searched his face:

"I believe in God. Perhaps my problem is spiritual – like Raech's was. Perhaps I need spiritual help."

"Well . . . Maybe."

"Martin . . . promise me that you will at least *try* to get me some help – some spiritual help."

"Well . . . ?"

"Do you know where this Michael character is?"

"Yeah . . . yeah, I do."

Her voice choked with emotion:

"Promise me – pleeease?"

He nodded and managed a faint smile. "OK . . . OK."

"Oh . . . you'll forget," she sighed.

"No . . . I won't forget. I . . . I'll see what I can do."

She perked up. "Promise?"

"Yeah . . . I promise."

(Later that day) Sheila looked up at Martin: "Are you going somewhere?"

"Home."

She glanced at the clock. "Home?"

"Yep."

"It's a bit early to go home."

Martin gave her a curious look and turned the plaque on her desk around so it faced her.

"The Boss," she read in a dry tone.

"Yes," he said with a twisted smile. "It's meant to be funny. You know . . . like 'ha ha.'"

"Ha ha," she mimicked. She considered him for a moment:

"You're like a kid with a new toy."

He pointed his finger up as if to correct. "No, I'm like a kid who has found an *old* toy. One that he liked to play with a lot."

She let out a long groan, betraying her disappointment.

"Can I stop and get you anything tomorrow?"

"Yeah, some fresh batteries."

"Rachael. Rachael . . . I'm home. Raech?"

She came out of the kitchen:

"What are you doing home so early?"

"Are you glad to see me?"

"Well . . . yeah."

"Then I am right on time," he said while giving her a knowing look.

"OK. Just go a little easy. You know . . . I need to get used to it again."

He bowed subserviently:

"One gentle poon-tang coming up. Will there be anything else madam?" he asked as he motioned towards the stairs.

Her eyes narrowed a bit:

"Should I be worried about you? Is their any reason that I should be worried about you?"

Rachael felt herself drifting off to sleep.

"What's Michael been up to today?" Martin asked her.

"Well . . . I spoke with him about nine o-clock. He asked me something about the lawnmower. I told him to wait and talk to you about it."

"What's wrong with the mower?"

"He wanted to know how to start it."

"Which one?"

"The little one."

Martin laughed:

"Well heck – you just pull the cord. He didn't know to do that?"

She became impatient. "I don't know. Why don't you just go and talk with him?" She looked at the clock on the night table:

"I need to start dinner."

"What happened to the cook?"

"I fired her," Rachael confessed.

"Why?"

"She got all bent out of shape about Sunday. I had told her that we were going out to eat and we ate here."

"So . . . what's the big deal?"

Rachael made a face as if smelling dirty feet:

"Well . . . you know how she is; she likes to control everything. Apparently she was offended somehow and snidely mentioned that the Henderson's had approached her about cooking for them."

"Hmm . . . and what did you tell her?"

"I told her not to let the door hit her in the butt on the way out."

Martin chuckled. "Good for you. The trouble with old corset buns was that she was so damned efficient, trustworthy and dependable, that I couldn't come up with any reason to fire her."

Rachael belly laughed. "Yeah . . . what do you say, 'gee, I'm sorry to fire you Mrs. Sauerbraten; but Martin and I just can't stand you. Nothin personal.'"

Martin slowly nodded. "Good for you, Raech – well done." He got out of bed and started to dress:

"So . . . where's Michael now?"

"He was gone for a long time. And . . . when he came back, I saw him in the backyard talking to someone."

Martin perked up:

"What'd he look like?"

She threw up her hands:

"A man."

"Well . . . was he heavy set?"

"Yeah."

"An old guy?"

"Yeah."

"Tough lookin?"

She bent around and looked at him:

"Yeah."

"Real thick neck?"

"Uh-huh."

"Had a big banana nose?"

"Yes."

"Curly grey on the sides, but bald on top?"

"That's right."

"His torso doesn't seem to match his legs."

"Yeah. His legs look too small for his torso," Rachael agreed.

Martin nodded enthusiastically. "He's bowlegged and when he walks he looks like . . ."

"A bulldog!" Rachael exclaimed.

Martin buttoned the top of his shirt, put his hands on his hips, and looked down at Rachael.

"A bulldog?" Rachael asked.

"Yep."

Rachael became impatient. "Well . . . who is it?"

Martin feigned a sour look:

"I don't know, Raech. You were here; why didn't you get his name?"

Rachael casually sat back and folded her hands in front of her:

"When you were in college you just didn't know when to quit being funny. Are you experiencing some kind of mid-life regression? Should I be worried about you, Marty?"

He bent down and gave her a gentle little kiss. "Don't you worry your pretty little head." With that he headed towards the door.

She called out after him. "Marty? Do I need to worry about you? Marty?"

Next to the guesthouse was a patio with a table and umbrella. Martin found Michael there. He had in front of him what looked like a Mason jar filled with grape juice and a big, insulated, plastic coffee mug. He was reading a newspaper.

"Hello, Michael."

Michael politely stood. "Mr. McDonald, it is very good to see you."

Martin smiled and shook the young man's hand. "It's turned into a beautiful day." He looked down to see that Michael's mug was filled with ice:

"What are you having?"

"Some wine. Please . . . join me," he said as he motioned to a chair. "I'll get you a glass."

A smile stretched across Martin's face. "That's fine, Michael."

Michael quickly returned with a large mug similar to his – also filled with ice. He poured some wine for Martin and set it in front of him.

"My wife said that you asked about the mower?"

Michael's brow knitted:

"Yes. I could not make it to go."

"The little mower? The one that you push?"

He nodded. "Yes. I found the starter button; but I am thinking that the battery does not work. Also, there is a handle on the top of it that appears to be broken. It is very loose."

"The little button is soft and made of rubber?

"Yes."

Martin sipped his wine and chuckled to himself.

"I have amused you?"

Martin tried to compose himself. "Well . . . the little button primes the motor. The loose handle is supposed to be loose. It's attached to a rope. You pull it to start the motor."

Michael smiled:

"I see. And you are amused because the most un-handy of men would know that."

It was hard for Martin not to laugh:

"Yes."

Michael seemed concerned. "Is this going to be a problem?"

Martin lifted his hands apologetically:

"No . . . we just need to get our stories straight. Folks are going to notice that Vincent is gone and . . . and that you're here. So . . . we say that the young man with the beard and long hair is Michael – our . . .?"

He nodded. "Yes, of course."

Martin thought a moment. "Vincent used to drive around a lot. Your know, fun little errands."

"I do not have a driver's license. I am from New York City."

Martin became a bit serious. "I suppose that it's not a good idea for you to drive, or to get a license to drive."

"That is correct," Michael agreed.

Martin changed the subject. "I don't drink a lot of it; but this tastes like Beaujolais."

"Do you like it?"

"Actually . . . it's just perfect for a warm afternoon. Very good indeed." He holds up the Mason jar to the sunlight:

"It's almost too dark for a Beaujolais."

"I like them young, big, and fruity."

"So . . . it *is* Beaujolais. How old would be *too* old for you?"

"No more than two years. The vintage is like an expiration date for me. In the Beaujolais, I would rather have a mediocre new wine than a good vintage that is four or five years old."

"Well . . . the ice is a good idea. The wine is big enough to hold it. And it is very refreshing."

"Then . . . you are pleased?"

"Very much so."

"Then," Michael raised his mug, "that pleases me."

Martin scratched his head and gazed about:

"Do you know how to fix stuff?"

"Stuff?"

"Yeah. Like, for example . . . a door."

Michael made a face. "Do they come with manuals?"

Martin rolled his eyes and exhaled. "Listen, Michael. If anybody asks . . . you are our new cook to replace Mrs. Rhedenbacker. OK?"

He nodded. "Yes, very good."

Martin got an idea:

"If it's OK with you, Michael, we might want you to actually cook for a party sometime . . . OK?"

"Yes . . . that would be good."

"I mean, you could eat with us and all. We could get someone else to serve. You'd be the chef."

"You could introduce me as Chef Boy-Ar-Dee-A-Yid," Michael told him tongue in cheek.

Martin lifted his glass. "Done."

Michael sipped his wine and leaned back in his chair. Seemingly content with the world, he glanced around the grounds:

"This is a lovely setting – very peaceful."

Martin reflected for a moment. "Well . . . it's become peaceful since you arrived." He looked over at his new friend and became serious:

"Michael . . . you helped Rachael yesterday – I want to thank you for that."

"You are very welcomed, Mr. McDonald."

"Please, call me Marty."

He nodded. "Very well."

Martin mused a few moments:

"Well . . . I guess . . . ah . . . I guess that you performed an exorcism on my wife." He studied his face. "Do I have that right?"

"Your wife experienced what is frequently called – by the Christians – a baptism of the Holy Spirit."

"Well . . . it worked – whatever it was." Martin smiled and glanced around at the grounds: "I think that I have a few angels spinning around me. I feel pretty good."

Michael nodded. "Yes, I can tell."

"I understand that Jarvis was here today, Michael. What was that all about?"

"He brought me a disc and a suitcase to give to you. He said that you knew about the suitcase."

"Yes, I know about the suitcase."

"If I might ask . . . what is in the suitcase?" Michael asked.

"A payment."

"Money?"

"Yes."

Michael looked concerned:

"For what?"

"Well . . ." Martin began, suddenly caught off guard, "it's a payment for working on the software project. That *is* what this is all about, isn't it?"

Michael's countenance dropped. "Oh . . . that is not good."

"Huh?"

"Well . . . I had no idea that you were a mercenary. I thought you were volunteering your services for the sake of a greater cause."

Martin felt shamed. "Well . . . that was part of the deal that I struck with the Bureau."

Michael looked surprised. "The FBI?"

"Well . . . yeah," Martin stammered, "the FBI."

Michael was distraught:

"Has the FBI contacted you since Mr. Jarvis was here?"

Martin became erect:

"No. Well . . . I had a golf game with Ed Roth."

"That name sounds familiar," Michael puzzled.

"It should – he does a lot of contract work for the government. He designed that quiet room in the basement."

Michael's expression pained. "What did you tell this Ed Roth?"

"Nothing."

"I need to know what was said."

Martin's eyes darted about as he gathered his thoughts. "It was very confusing. I . . . I didn't know what to make of it. You see . . . Roth knew that I had been approached by the FBI; but he also believed that I had turned the Bureau *down*."

"What did you tell him?" Michael asked anxiously.

"Jarvis said to tell no one about the project – not even Rachael. So . . . I just went along with what Roth believed happened between myself and the Bureau."

Michael sighed with relief. "That is good. Oh . . . that is very good."

Immediately Martin stood to his feet and began to pace around nervously – his hands in his pockets. He stopped and addressed Michael:

"It's time that you told me what the heck is going on. I am endangering my family and deserve to know what gives."

"You need some things clarified," Michael added.

"Well . . . yeah, I do!"

"Mr. McDonald . . . Mr. Jarvis led me to believe that you would be in my service to attempt to create a new software program."

"Well . . . that *is* correct. I agreed that you would be the boss and that I would be working for you."

"Ah, but that is not the case. You are working for yourself. You are a mercenary."

"I'm confused. Where are you going with this? What does all of this mean?"

"It means that we will not be working together. You need not worry about the security of your family. I will be gone in a few hours."

Martin was visibly stunned. His first thought was not the project, nor the money, nor the safety of his family – his first thought was of Rachael. What would become of her if Michael would leave today? He couldn't let that happen. Fear gripped him.

Michael was taken back by the severity of Martin's reaction:

"Sit down and enjoy your wine, Marty. It is still a beautiful day. There is no crisis here, just a minor misunderstanding."

He sat down again – his mind raced for a solution to his new dilemma. He forced himself to look casual and sipped his wine:

"I just can't get over this wine. I have never drank it like this."

There was an awkward silence. Occasionally Martin would look over in Michael's direction.

"I am *not* a mercenary," Martin emphatically stated.

Michael's brow lifted. "No?"

"No," he firmly reiterated. "I didn't take on this assignment for money; and, so far, I have accepted none. I took it because I wanted to do something for my country. Heck, the only deal that I was offered was one where payment was involved. Jarvis used money as an inducement. I naturally assumed that the other people that were recruited for the Phase Three Project would be compensated as well. If you are the person to negotiate with, then, rightly, you should have conducted the negotiation yourself. If there was ambiguity, then who is to blame? Certainly not I."

They stared at each other for a moment. Martin could detect the beginning of a smile on Michael's face:

"Mr. McDonald. Would you agree to embark on a software project under my instruction?"

"Yes."

"Bear in mind, there will be no monetary compensation. You will be expected to donate your time."

"I agree."

"Well, then it is done," Michael exclaimed with considerable enthusiasm.

Martin breathed a sign of relief and looked over to his friend:

"Tell me, Michael – does Niyaq have a counterpart. Jarvis insinuated that. I mean, ya can't have bad guys without good guys."

Niyaq's counter-organization is called Lebeh. However, this Lebeh is not as large, as well-organized, or as well-financed as Niyaq. And Lebeh does not have the solidarity of purpose that Niyaq has."

"How many people does Lebeh have?"

"This I do not know. To a large degree they function in cell groups."

Martin was surprised. "Cells?"

"Yes. Usually, the only members that a cell will know about are the other members of their particular cell. They are compartmentalized. I am sure that you can see the wisdom of that."

He nodded. "Sure, if someone is fingered, then he can do limited whistle-blowing." He thought for a moment:

"Actually, the only person that I could finger would be Jarvis. I don't know your last name. Heck – I'm not really certain about your *first* name."

"So . . . you are assuming that I am a part of Lebeh?"

Martin shrugged. "Well . . . aren't you?"

"No."

Martin was taken back:

"Then . . . how do you know so much about them?"

"From Mr. Jarvis."

"Then . . . Jarvis is Lebeh?"

"Yes . . . good old Dirty Harry," Michael began. "He has exposed himself a lot. If someone gets hit it will most likely be him. He would die before he exposed anyone. Soldiers like him are hard to find."

"He is clever like a fox."

"Very much so . . . and with excellent instincts."

Martin sipped his wine and then caught Michael's eye. "I'm still a little fuzzy about something."

"Go ahead."

"Who am I working for? You, the Bureau, or Lebeh?"

He considered it for a moment.

"You are working for me. I chose you for the software project; but my people found out that you were on the FBI's list for the Phase Three Project. That's when I contacted Mr. Jarvis.

Mr. Jarvis is with Lebeh – they have a lot of people in the Bureau and they pulled some strings to set up Jarvis as the one who was to contact you for the Phase Three Project. Jarvis was to squash the deal between you and the Bureau so that I could work with you. At the last minute, this fellow Holeman directed another agent to go with Jarvis."

"Wow," Martin marveled. "Jarvis pulled it off. He recruited me for you, while working as a government agent."

Michael nodded. "Yes. And with another government agent watching the show."

"So . . ." Martin began, "had I not been on the government's list of recruitees, then *you* would have contacted me?"

"That is correct. I would have been the one to pay you a visit. I was the one that chose you."

Martin was taken back. "Huh . . . how about that." Something occurred to him:

"Wait a minute – who brought in the mini-Sub? I thought those guys were FBI."

He shook his head vigorously. "Lebeh wanted the mini-Sub to test – but I wanted nothing of it.

The mini-Sub idea for the FBI Phase Three Project was stupid. The American government cannot do anything without spending a fortune. All the mini-Sub idea did was to tip off Niyaq as to the location of these supposedly 'autonomous researchers.'"

"I'm confused. Where did the Sub come from?"

"The first Sub – that was dismantled when Phase Three crumbled – was hijacked."

Martin's jaw dropped. "Hijacked?"

"Yes. Lebeh has made it a habit to borrow Ed's new gadgets. Of course, the government blames Niyaq."

"Ah . . . so that's why poor Eddie was so paranoid." His eyes narrowed:

"Wait a minute. Lebeh is using *my* house to test and spec out one of Ed's silent rooms?"

"I did not want that; but it ended up that way.

Somehow we got stuck with that Sub in your basement. It is not a good thing."

"So . . . did Jarvis foul things up?"

Michael's lips twisted:

"Yes. Perhaps . . . perhaps he had too much to drink that day. But . . . well . . . Mr. Jarvis had three itineraries – one from the Bureau, one from Lebeh, and one from me."

"Humph – it sounds like he forgot about *your* itinerary. I mean, where is Jarvis' *first* allegiance?"

"His first allegiance is to me. Jarvis doesn't drink anymore. I told him to quit; and that I couldn't trust him if he continued drinking."

"Well . . . I wouldn't think that it would be easy for him to quit – he was really pounding them down when he was here." He curiously eyed Michael:

"You helped him quit – didn't you? You gave him a little zap."

"Yes. But when we are done here, I think he will start again. He misses it."

"I still don't get it. What does Lebeh expect from us?"

"From us? Well . . . they don't know anything about *me*. But there is a disc that they want examined. And, they wanted to test the Sub."

"What kind of disc?"

"Everything in due time will be explained."

"What about Ed Roth? I mean – shouldn't we be worried about him?"

"Well . . . did you act suspiciously? Was their anything unusual about the two of you playing golf together?"

"Ed was wearing a sweater. Even when it got warm he didn't take it off. I noticed when he took a swing that he was wearing a gun. A big gun."

"Well, that is not a bad sign. Maybe he is worried about Niyaq."

"Yeah . . . he told me that he was; but why is that a good sign?"

Michael's brow lifted. "It may be a sign that he hasn't made a deal with Niyaq."

Martin nodded. "Yeah . . . I suppose that's true."

"Do not get paranoid, Martin. People make mistakes when they are afraid. You must be at peace and have faith."

"Yes, you're quite right, my friend."

Michael smiled. "So . . . are you all set to go ahead with this?"

"There is still a lot that I don't understand. This business with Niyaq perplexes me."

"Be patient," Michael interjected. "There is much to learn to fully understand Niyaq and their business. And, as far as the silent room in the basement . . . well, we can't do anything about it now."

Martin took a deep breath:

"Michael . . . I'm just a bit overwhelmed by all of this."

"That is fine – and it is to be expected. Just relax and do your best. Come on – do not sink on me – have faith. You are not in this alone."

He perked up. "Yeah – that's right. We're in this together – you, me, and Jarvis."

Michael grew serious. "Martin . . . you have to do as I tell you to do –

even if it sounds all wrong." He studied Martin's face:

"Do you understand what I am telling you?"

"Yes . . . and . . . and I want it that way, too."

"That's the spirit."

Martin looked on curiously as Michael motioned at the guesthouse. He glanced around to see Jarvis approaching with a large envelope under his arm:

"Hello fellows," Jarvis casually said. He looked at Michael:

"So, you've made up your mind about this character?"

Michael cut his eyes to Martin. "Yes, I have. It is time for us to begin."

"OK," he dropped the envelope on the table, "that's it for me."

Martin watched as Jarvis walked away:

"Not much of a talker." He picked up the envelope and then looked at Michael:

"Didn't you forget to tell Jarvis something?"

"For instance?"

"Well . . . for instance to take back the suitcase."

He chucked. "I told him that already. Do nct worry, Mr. McDonald, the money will be donated to a good cause."

They stared at each other.

"What does "bamboozled" mean?" Michael asked.

Martin sighed. "Oh great . . . you can read minds."

"Just sometimes."

Martin began somewhat reluctantly. "When a person is bamboozled, he is . . . he is beguiled into doing something."

Michael nodded:

"Then be of good cheer, Martin – the Lord bamboozles people all the time. He has to do that to get people to work for him."

"Good. I feel *much* better now." His eyes narrowed suspiciously:

"You're not going to do that a lot – are you?"

"Read your mind? I do not do it on purpose." He pointed to the envelope:

"Those are the instructions to create the software. When you are finished I will test it to make sure that it functions properly. Keep it nearby – that is the original and there are no copies. I want you to sleep with it at night."

Martin sat the envelope down and sipped his wine.

"Also," Michael began, "from now on no more wine – or any other alcohol. We must be clear-headed – always." He looked down at his mug:

"Perhaps I have been imbibing a bit too much. I have been taking advantage of my little respite."

Martin gave Michael a curious look:

"Imbibing too much? What are you talking about? I couldn't even get a buzz from what you put down."

He made a face. "There is an old joke – where a man is about to be shot by a firing squad. The man is offered a cigarette and he says, 'no thanks – I'm trying to quit.'"

"So?"

"So . . . I am that man."

Martin felt his heart sink.

"Marty?"

He looked up from his papers. "Hi, hon."

"It's late. Come to bed. You can bring that stuff with you."

He looked at his watch. "Yeah . . . OK."

Martin crawled into bed beside Rachael and carefully slid a revolver under his pillow without her noticing. He was wearing his glasses and had the envelope with him.

Rachael turned over to face him:

"Marty . . . I think that you are trying to protect me. You know . . . by not telling me things."

"Uh . . ."

"It's all right. All I know is that things are a lot better now. That is enough for me."

She stared at him and tried to read his expression.

Martin managed a thin smile. "Rachael . . . if anyone asks about Michael, just tell them that he is our new cook. He came to the door looking for work and one thing led to another." He looked at her knowingly:

"Don't say anything about that other stuff. OK?"

"OK."

FAR OUT

5

Martin glanced out the back window to see Michael sitting on his patio – sipping coffee and reading a newspaper. He glanced at his watch – 6:30 AM.

"Good morning, Marty," Michael said as he approached.

"Another great day."

"Yes," Michael replied.

"What's on your docket today?" Martin asked as he sat down.

"I would like to use the computer."

"OK, I'll open the Sub for you."

"Let me finish the paper. Just leave the door ajar."

Martin made a face. "Ajar?"

"They can not steal anything from us from us now – except that envelope."

"Oh . . . well . . . I'll leave it that way for you. When you leave just remember to turn off the lights – that'll allow the batteries to charge.

I assume that you know how to operate the computers?"

"Yes."

Martin studied Michael's face:

"You know that you don't want to lift either of the computers?"

Michael nodded.

"You know about the password under my keyboard?"

"Yes."

Martin took a sip of his coffee and looked around:

"I need to go to the shop and order some things for the project."

"It is supposed to be quite simple," Michael told him.

Martin's expression turned sour:

"It makes absolutely no sense. I really can't imagine that this contraption will serve any function."

"I was told that you would say that. All you have to do is build it. I will test it when you are finished. OK?"

Martin rolled his eyes. "OK, but I want to go on record as saying that I don't see how this software – if you want to call it that – will do anything."

Concern swept across Michael's face. "Well . . . is it that you do not understand the instructions?"

"No, I *do* understand the instructions. Software is my business – this just doesn't look like anything that will *do anything*. Plus, it is written by someone whose grammar is awful and doesn't appear to know *anything* about software. The only disc included was 'The Torah.'"

"So . . . what is the problem?"

"Well, the Hebrew letters are written with the beginning connected to the end; and then I have to refer to these . . ."

"Just do it, Marty," Michael interjected. "It will work."

"Good morning, Sheils."

She looked up to see Martin standing in front of her studying a sheet of paper. "Hi." She studied his expression:

"What's up?"

"I need to order some things," he said, still studying the paper. He put the paper down in front of her and moved around to her side of the desk. He pointed:

"These three items here – you might have to call around to find them. Get started on it right away."

"Are you forgetting that I have to . . ."

"I'm not forgetting anything. Do this first."

She looked up at him sheepishly. "OK."

Martin turned and headed toward his office.

"Marty?"

"Yeah?"

"I need a project number. You know, to take the guess work out of knowing who to give this stuff too."

"Oh. Charge each item to a different project; but remember to give it all to me when it comes in. OK?"

"Huh?"

"Just do it that way, OK?

'But . . ."

He turned around to address her:

"This is important, Sheils. Don't work on anything else until you get it done."

She nodded. "OK. Ah . . . you have a stack of stuff to go through."

"Stuff?"

"Yes, the stuff that you didn't go through yesterday."

"What do I have this afternoon?"

“You’re meeting with a client at three.”

“Oh. That’s Donovan’s project – he can handle it. I’ll be gone by then.”

“Did you remember to call Eddie?”

“Ah . . . call Ed and tell him that I’ll get up with him when things slow down a bit.”

“Rachael. I’m home . . . Raech?”

She came from the back of the house. “Hi hon. I was just about to go to the store – anything you want?”

“No.”

“You’re out of beer.”

“That’s good. Have you seen Michael?”

“I haven’t seen him all day.”

When Martin opened the door of the Sub he startled Michael.

“You frightened me, Marty. Next time give me three knocks and allow me to look through the peephole.”

“Fine. From now on it will be three knocks. That can work for both of us.” He had a number of books under his arm, and the envelope. After arranging them at his work station, he sat down and turned to Michael:

“I see that you’ve also brought some books,” Martin noted.

“Did you get everything ordered that you need?” Michael asked.

“Yes. Everything will be here tomorrow. I’ve got plenty to do in the meantime.”

“Good,” Michael said as he turned his attention back to the computer screen.

“What’s that you’re doing?”

“I am looking at the disc that Mr. Jarvis brought.”

“Oh . . . the disc from Lebeh. What’s the deal with that?”

“Well . . . it is very interesting. Many insights concerning the theology of Niyaq.”

Martin scooted his chair over. “Tell me more about it.”

His friend leaned back and gathered his thoughts:

“Lebeh was tailing someone that they were pretty sure was connected.” He looked at Martin:

“When I say ‘connected,’ it means . . .”

“Connected with Niyaq,” Martin surmised.

“Exactly. So . . . apparently this fellow suspected that he was being followed and tried to get away. When they cornered him, he poisoned himself and attempted to smash the disc with his feet."

"The disc is OK?"

"The disc is OK. So . . . Lebeh looked at the disc; and there were all these Bible code results on it.

Lebeh men went back to that person's previous rendezvous and found two computers. One that was connected to the Web, and another that was powered by a battery and an inverter – like we have here. The tower to the inverter-powered computer was gone – the rest of it was still there. The man never came back."

"Wow. How'd that person know that someone could hack into his computer through the power lines?"

"You've got the idea."

"Was the guy that Lebeh caught an Arab?"

"Yes."

"What about the fellow with the computers?"

"He was an American – a white Christian college professor. Apparently, he had rented a small apartment off-campus where he conducted this research."

Martin was taken back. "What did he teach?"

"Biblical Hebrew."

"Wow," Martin said as he slowly shook his head. He suddenly winced:

"I suppose this man is now missing?"

Michael avoided Martin's eyes. "Yes, he is. He has a family. There has been quite a stir about it."

Neither man spoke for a few moments. Martin's lips were tight – he squirmed in his seat and glanced around the spartan interior of the Sub:

"So," Martin began, "what's your take on all this?"

"Take? Well . . . it looks like Niyaq paid this man to do some research – quite a lot of research. There are a lot of abbreviations used that refer to things that are not explained on the disc; but I think that I can discern their meaning."

"So . . . what's the story?"

"The story is that Niyaq – assuming that they are behind this – is interested to find out if the precepts of the New Testament Book of The Revelation are encoded in the Torah."

"Why?"

"I think I know – just from looking thus far. But . . . it is not so easy to explain."

Martin made a face. "Well . . . explain something – I'm part of the team now."

"Yes, of course you are." He scrolled around for few moments. "Here – read this."

Martin began to read aloud:

"The above seems to indicate the validity of much of the last disc concerning Satan's role – plus The Revelation Precept 2, with the association of the Enoch precept 4. And, assuming that the search area is the text size limited to just that part of Genesis that refers to Cain, the probability of this association (shared letter OTA term) is very remote (see notes.)" He looked at Michael:

"I have no idea what this means.

You need to have a bit of patience with me. Having said that, I do know the Bible pretty well – but in English."

Michael nodded. "All right. Going backwards (looking at the results), it seems that 'The Revelation Precept 2' refers to the idea that the anti-christ in The Revelation is indeed the resurrected Nero Caesar."

"I've read theories about that. Isn't it true that many peoples' names can be calculated to the same number 666? As I understand it, that number is attained by transliterating a name in Hebrew and adding up the numerical values of the letters."

"It is not that simple. The majority text of The Revelation is compiled from three ancient manuscript sources. Two sources number the Beast (anti-christ) at 666; and one of the sources numbers the Beast at 616."

"Why the difference?"

"One source excludes the silent Greek letter N."

"Ah . . . and the value of the silent N, in Hebrew, is 50?"

"Exactly."

"Wow – that's pretty scary." He considered it for a moment:

"So . . . how does Cain fit into the scenario?"

"The Book of Enoch has Cain and Abel battling it out in the latter days."

"Now, you've lost me."

"Well . . . if both are correct, then Cain and Nero are one and the same entity. I believe that this is what he was fishing for in this matrix. Plus, it appears that Niyaq believes that the anti-christ in The Revelation is also an embodiment of Satan himself."

"The Beast is Satan, Nero, and Cain?"

"That seems to be what they believe."

"What's a matrix?"

Michael pointed to the screen. "Everything inside of this box is the matrix. This matrix has 24 spaces between the rows. That is because the first term that was entered, 'Caesar (is a) lampstand,' has a skip of 24 spaces between each letter in the surface text (ELS, equal-distant letter sequencing); and, the first search term entered determines the matrix skip interval (the distance between the rows). The professor labels these as the 'ELS term.' Got it?"

"Yes – there are 24 spaces between each row."

"Right. And this particular matrix has 32 rows to form a box 24 by 32. See?"

"Yeah. And this square is a little chunk of the Bible?"

"Genesis," said Michael.

"Yeah. And when you fill a row with 24 letters, then you start all over on the left side."

"Yes, but you start all over on the right side. Hebrew reads right to left. So . . . in this particular matrix there are 24 columns and 32 rows."

"OK . . . I got ya. So . . . what purpose does the matrix serve?"

"Conventional thinking believes that the matrix is an ideal way to display terms graphically in a picture format, to show how terms are related to each other by proximity (closeness) and skip (ELS). Having said that, there are a few leading edge software outfits like CodeFinder that are experimenting with alternate ways of displaying results, as there are many limiting factors with the current system."

"Like what?"

"Well . . . if you are really interested, then you need to take the time to read what this fellow has to say about it." Michael smiled curiously:

"You do not have the time for it now; but you will later."

"So . . . what does this matrix mean to you?"

"Let us look at the matrix report:"

Caesar Menorah

The ELS reference is 24 characters between rows.
There are 10 displayed terms in the matrix.
The matrix starts at Gen. Ch 3 V 21 Letter 25 and ends at Gen. Ch 4 V 14 Letter 8.
The matrix spans 768 characters of the surface text.
The matrix has 32 rows, is 24 columns wide and contains a total of 768 characters.
RV computation, Genesis.

OPENED TEXT AGREEMENT.

1. ותהר ותלד את קינ

And she conceived and she bore Cain.

CAIN'S APPELLATIONS

2. קסר מנרה (ELS term)
Caesar (is a) lampstand.
'Caesar' shares a letter with 'Cain'.
Skip 24, RV 3.387.
Initial Entry Term. Odds of occurring in Genesis are 1 in 2438. Odds of occurring in the defined search area (4217-5402) are 1 in 561,000.

3. שטני קא לי
My adversary (Satan) (is) vomit to me.
Skip -76, RV, 3.816.

CAIN'S DAMNATION

4. קין שא בית אש
Cain, suffer to bear the house of fire!
Skip -45, RV 5.348.

5. שם הדלק ים אש
Kindle there the lake of fire!
Skip 29, RV 5.851.

6. אבדו שוה מכבש
He brought forth his own destruction from the Lamb.
Skip 26, RV 6.799.

TRIBULATION TRAP

7. תוה לסאי השמיני
Mark for my measure of the eighth!
Skip 28, RV 8.781.

8. יהוה הפחם חש
Has YHVH made ready their trap?
Skip 77, RV 5.618.

9. קדח ירא בבנה בור הוא שאו
He kindled fear when building a pit that you shall suffer to bear.
Skip 23, RV 16.372.

Michael continued:

"It is the author's contention that this matrix represents very good evidence that it is encoded that Nero and Cain and Satan are one in the same person – the anti-christ from The Revelation.

What the author wanted to do was to enter a search term in the hopes that *it would share a letter with "Cain"* in the text – a term that would insinuate Nero and Satan (and also Cain with the shared letter), and be associated somehow with the book of The Revelation.

Well, his Initial Entry (IE) was **'Caesar (is a) lampstand'** and it shared a letter with Cain. It is also the author's contention that the surface text mention of Cain – that it shared a letter with – is the best possible match. Therefore, the ideal target area – in which to share a letter – is only three characters in length.

To get the probability that this ELS term would occur in his search area, he added 24 spaces ahead of the first biblical occurrence of Cain, and 24 spaces behind the last occurrence of Cain. He then supposed that this was his search area. That's how he came up with the probability of the Initial Entry, 'Nero menorah' (lampstand). He also noted that this probability did not reflect the actual occurrence of the ELS term as a shared letter with Cain, but only reflected the probability that the ELS would occur *at all* within the defined search area."

"Are his assumptions valid? I mean, do you suppose that his probability calculations are accurate?"

Michael shrugged. "I do not know about his assumptions; but the probability that this ELS term would occur – in what he claims to be his search area – is calculated by the software and is considered to be quite accurate.

In the matrix report he shows the probabilities for all the terms based on a search area of the book of Genesis; and then he has a special note for the probability that the Initial Entry term of 'Caesar menorah' would occur in the text where Cain's name is mentioned. The probability that he got from the software was 1 chance in 561,000. But, he is not a mathematician; and I am sure that he wanted to impress the people that he was doing the research for."

"What are these R-Values?"

"The software works this way. CodeFinder will give the user the probability of the Initial Entry in odds. See? You might expect 5,000 occurrences, or, you might expect less than one. But, in the report, R-Values are given, which, if the operator so chooses, can be converted to odds. Ideally there are two bell curves that can be used to determine odds;

but CodeFinder uses the one which is the most accurate with odds over one (the primary function); so . . . the less than one odds may be off a little, but not dramatically. See?"

"Well . . . not really. It's a bit complicated." He thought for a moment:

"That long term – '**He kindled fear when building a pit that you shall suffer to bear**,' convert that one to odds."

"Alright."

He made a few clicks:

"There you have it – the odds that this term would occur by chance coded in an ELS string in Genesis are about 1 in 23,500,000,000,000,000."

"Pretty slim odds."

"Yes. But those odds assume that the string is planned and not random – and that, my friend, is a big assumption; especially if the researcher cannot match up topically-related terms to show that the Bible codes are recognizing his strings and relating them to other strings."

"I'm not following you," Martin admitted.

"It seems to me that the probabilities are somewhat of a mute point. The professor only uses phrases and not single words pulled from a dictionary. Once a string of letters gets to a certain length, then it should not occur *anywhere* in the codes by chance. And . . . since long strings occur frequently in spite of chance, the larger issue then becomes – *how to relate these strings to one another*; and, *what protocols should be adopted to define the legitimacy of a string*." Michael slowly shook his head:

"It is somewhat complicated."

"Well," Martin began, "that *is* pretty trick software. I suppose the Israelis came up with it."

"You would think so; but an Australian actually wrote the software. I guess you could say that he teamed up with this American from Colorado. The American would come up with ideas and the Australian would implement them."

"Hmm, that's interesting. So . . . what does this matrix mean? Does it make sense to you? It doesn't to me."

"He found this matrix with the original entry of '**Caesar lampstand (menorah)**;' and Caesar shares a letter with Cain in the Bible text.

"I don't follow what '**Caesar (is a) lampstand**' is supposed to mean."

"Where is Satan's Throne in The Revelation?" Michael asked.

"In hell I suppose."

"Yes, it is in hell – but the souls of Pergamos dwell in hell – where Satan's Throne is (according to The Revelation). Pergamos is one of the *seven living congregations*; and these congregations are called – in The

Revelation – lampstands. Because Satan's throne is in one of these congregations (lampstands), it is the author's contention that Satan could be *referred* to as a lampstand. So . . . that ELS term would tie Cain (shared letter with Caesar), Caesar, and Satan to the book of The Revelation and to the anti-christ. Get it? Caesar, Satan, or Cain – (is a) lampstand."

Martin wasn't convinced:

"Yes, but that is a lot to assume just from the occurrence of one two letter term that shares a letter with "Cain" in the open text.

"True, but in this matrix the author has seven *other* ELS terms that concur with that assumption." He looked at Martin:

"See?"

"Ok, I'm with you."

Michael continued:

"You might call Pergamos the good guys of hell (Nod). They have behaved well in life, and are not restricted from the life experience as are the other spirits of hell."

Martin nodded. "You know . . . that Initial Entry *is* pretty clever." He thought about it for a moment:

"But it never occurred to me that Satan himself – the archenemy of God – would be alive as a human during the last days."

Michael turned back to the screen. "As far as I know, that's not something that is generally agreed upon by the people of Lebeh." He shrugged:

"I've never heard it preached from a Christian pulpit."

"Yeah – that's pretty far out." Martin reached for the Bible:

"But that contradicts The Revelation."

"Why does that contradict the text?" Michael asked.

"It's simple," Martin began; "if the Beast is destroyed in the Lake of Fire, then he would no longer exist to be shut up for a thousand years as The Revelation illustrates."

Michael considered it a few moments:

"Being cast into the Lake of Fire is the final abandonment of God. After that, a spirit is forever "outside" of the possibility of finding salvation and being a part of the Godly domains of heaven and Earth. Nowhere in The Revelation does it say that these spirits cease to exist. To the contrary, there is a passage in The Revelation that states that those thrown into the Lake of Fire after the final judgment *will still exist*; but will be *outside* of God's spiritual and material creations."

Michael opened the Bible:

"Start reading here – on the last page of the Bible – after the final judgment when all is brought to completion."

22:14 Blessed are they that do his commandments, that they may have right to the tree of life, and may enter in through the gates into the city.
22:15 For without ('outside' in most translations and in the Greek) are dogs, and sorcerers, and whoremongers, and murderers, and idolaters, and whosoever loveth and maketh a lie.

Martin nodded:

"I'm with you. One scriptural rendering is that the Beast and the False Prophet have already had – in effect – their final judgment of total abandonment and will be imprisoned with their lot for 1000 years. After the thousand years are finished, they will be able to deceive the nations from their operation in the spirit realm; but they can never see life again and will share the fate of those who do not pass the final test."

"Yes. That is the slant that Niyaq is taking here.

In The Revelation, it is the Dragon that is cast into the pit and imprisoned for a thousand years. The Dragon is *all* of the souls who take up Satan's cause. The men of Earth who side with the Beast during the coming woes will be numbered among Satan's Dragon.

We know that the rebellion had a specific leader – he is talked about in Ezekiel chapter 8 as being the Jealous One – who had a seat in the Temple of the Most High God. In Isaiah he is the fallen angel of light, Heylel . . . I guess you would know him as Lucifer. In the book of Job he is The Satan, or Adversary (attacker), and was the ultimate source of Job's woes.

The Revelation is a riddle. In verse 20:2, the *Dragon* – who is the serpent of old – the Devil and Satan – is locked up for a thousand years.

Ultimately, *all* leaders get their power from their followers. Listen to this:"

13:2 And the beast which I saw was like unto a leopard, and his feet were as the feet of a bear, and his mouth as the mouth of a lion: and the dragon gave him his power, and his seat, and great authority.

Michael continued. "In the twelfth chapter of The Revelation the war in heaven is illustrated. It was the *Dragon* that fought the angels of heaven. Satan alone could not have waged war against the Throne; just as Satan alone could not control the physical world."

Martin agreed. "I see. So, the Dragon stands for Satan's entire multitude; and it was that collective body that was prophesied to be imprisoned for a thousand years. And, Niyaq believes that their leader (SatanNeroCain – the anti-christ) will be imprisoned as well. But, will still guide and influence the world from the shadows when the thousand years are finished."

Michael nonchalantly shrugged. "Well . . . it seems obvious that this is what Niyaq *wants* to believe. They had this professor look for evidence of it in the Torah codes.

Having said that, Niyaq wants to *change*, times, laws and prophecies. Niyaq wants the Beast to have *victory* – not to end up in a jail fashioned by Yahweh."

"So you figure that Niyaq *wants* their leader to be Satan himself – the Top Dog – the Boss?"

Michael nodded. "It appears that way. There is no telling how much other data this professor has fed to Niyaq. Looking at this disc, I assume that this is a project in progress, as many of his matrixes are only partly developed."

"Show me how this software works; and let's examine the rest of this matrix."

"OK . . . look. We open CodeFinder program. Then, go to the file menu, and select Import Search Results. See? We just click on 'Caesar Menorah,' which is the title of the search list. Now hit the search button – there it is. Now (he points with his finger) there is "Cain" in the opened text."

"That's Cain?"

"Yes . . . in English it would be like QYN. It is pronounced Qayin (קין).

"Huh?"

Michael gave Martin a curious look. "If you read it left to right – like English – what do you suppose that it would say?"

"Wow – *Niyaq*."

Michael acknowledged him and continued:

"So . . . we just double click where Caesar shares a letter with Cain and the verse containing the ***Opened Text Agreement*** **(OTA)** comes up – in both Hebrew and English. It's a great system.

The OTA is important to the professor. His terms must share a letter with this passage of the Bible text; or, at least, be able to be extended to do so."

Martin read the verse in Genesis that CodeFinder found as the Opened Text Agreement:

"'**And the man knew Eve his wife; and she conceived and bore Cain, and said: 'I have gotten a man with the help of the LORD**.'

So?"

"If you look at the report, the author just shows, '**And she conceived and bore Cain**.'"

"So?"

"So . . . in The Revelation, the anti-christ is brought out of the pit and *conceived* as a man. In the pit you *do not* see life – at least not until it is appointed for you to do so."

"OK," Martin began, "now explain the rest of it."

"This fellow usually uses one band on his high skip matrixes; but with his low skip arrays he often uses several bands."

"Bands?"

"These are different skip ranges that are visible in a matrix. In this matrix, one band is around a skip of 25, the next one around 50, and the next one around 75." He thought for a moment:

"I find it very interesting that the professor has his terms grouped topically. He has three topics – two terms in **'Cain's Appellations' (descriptions)**, three terms in '**Cain's Damnation**,' and three terms in '**The Tribulation Trap**.'"

Michael pointed:

Under the topic **'Cain's Appellations (descriptions),**' '**Caesar (is a) lampstand**' is grouped with '**My adversary (Satan) (is) vomit to me**.'

The Hebrew word for adversary is 'satan.' So, we see here the descriptions for **Cain – 'Caesar,' 'lampstand,' 'Satan,' and 'vomit.'**

The word **'vomit'** is found a lot in the professor's results to describe the occupants of hell."

Michael pointed:

"The next topic is '**Cain's Damnation**.'

"Cain is commanded, '**Cain, suffer to bear the house of fire**.' See? In The Revelation there are only two souls who are completely banned from God's plan (the Beast and the False Prophet) – they are cast into the lake of fire. I like '**house of fire**,' as it insinuates that this will be Cain's abode."

He pointed again:

"'**Kindle there the lake of fire!**' See? **'Lake of fire,'** that is what it is called in The Revelation.

Do you see what he is doing? He is establishing that the subject of the array is one in the same with the entity that is cast into the lake of fire." He pointed again:

"This is the last one under that sub-title:

'**His destruction he has brought forth from the Lamb**.'

The idea here seems to be that Cain has caused his own destruction.

The verbal root used here (destruction) also means 'to wander away,' or 'lose oneself.'"

"I'm with you. Why is 'is' in parentheses?"

"The 'is' is assumed, as there is not an 'is' in the Hebrew language."

"Oh."

"He has three terms under his '**Tribulation Trap**' topic."

Michael pointed:

"'**Mark for my measure of the eighth!**' This is a good one – I like this one. It is the author's contention that NeroCain is commanding the False Prophet to require all the inhabitants of the Earth to worship and him take his mark. Here, it is Cain who sets the stage for the **'Tribulation Trap.'**

The matrix asks the question, '**Has YHVH made ready their trap?**' There is much in prophecy that illustrates the tribulation as being a trap for the wicked. This ELS string asks if Yahweh has set their trap. And indeed, the matrix answers the question:

'**He kindled fear when building a pit that you shall suffer to bear**.'

The idea here seems to be that the condemned spirits will know that a pit is being prepared for their dungeon and are fearful of it."

"YHVH means Yahweh?" Martin asked.

"Yes. To the Christians he is the Lord God; but in the text he is referred to by name."

"I didn't know that," Martin admitted.

"Orthodox Jews are not allowed to speak the name of God in any form," Michael pointed out.

"So . . . what do they call him?"

"Hashem – The Name."

Martin considered it. "I remember from reading the New Testament that the Jews were pretty big on laws."

"The orthodox Jews have 613 laws that they must follow; and modern Jews have more interpretations and caveats of these laws than their ancestors did."

"Well . . . let me ask you this, Michael. Are you telling me that this is a genuine coded message from God – one that has laid dormant all the centuries just waiting for the computer to be invented?"

"From what I know about the Bible codes, this fellow is making a good case for this particular matrix. It is not a pretty one to look at because it is very narrow and the terms do not display well. But, his terms are all good phrases; his skips are low; his matrix is small; and his search area is tiny." He thought for a moment:

"Let us try something. Let us see how many times '**Caesar Menorah**' shows up coded in Genesis." He clicked a few things and looked back to Martin:

"That's the only occurrence. Let's expand our search area to the Torah (the first five books)." He went through the same process:

"The next occurrence is at an ELS skip of 12,614 (12,614 spaces between the letters). According to this software, it has about an even chance of showing up at that skip."

"Michael, I really don't understand the term '**Mark for my measure of the eighth**.' What does 'the eighth' refer to?"

"In The Revelation, the Throne possesses the keys to death and hell. But, in the text, they only mention death – which is the seven living congregations. Most people miss this concept when they read The Revelation:

Death is simply where people go when they die – back to their spiritual abodes to await another life. Hell – or, as the professor codes it – Nod, is the place where souls are restrained from seeing life as a punishment. My point is that there are eight spiritual congregations alluded to in The Revelation – not just seven."

"Yes," Martin said, "but that is just an interpretation; and The Revelation is a riddle and can be interpreted a number of different ways."

"That is correct, Martin – but this precept is explained in The Revelation."

"Show me."

"All right, let's read a few verses." He opened The Revelation and turned to chapter 17. "Start reading here."

17:7 And the angel said unto me, Wherefore didst thou marvel? I will tell thee the mystery of the woman, and of the beast that carrieth her, which hath the seven heads and ten horns.
17:8 The beast that thou sawest was, and is not; and shall ascend out of the bottomless pit, and go into perdition: and they that dwell on the earth shall wonder, whose names were not written in the book of life from the foundation of the world, when they behold the beast that was, and is not, and yet is.
17:9 And here is the mind which hath wisdom. The seven heads are seven mountains, on which the woman sitteth.
17:10 And there are seven kings: five are fallen, and one is, and the other is not yet come; and when he cometh, he must continue a short space.
17:11 And the beast that was, and is not, even he is the eighth, and is of

the seven, and goeth into perdition.

"Do you understand?"

"No," Martin answered.

"In the Book of Enoch, the seven spiritual mountains (congregations) are mentioned in two separate places. It is also illustrated that there is a giant gulf established between them so that spirits cannot travel into or out of them. In other words – the heavens are all sovereign and cannot mix together. And, in Enoch, on one of these mountains there is the Tree of Life."

"Those are the heavens that were established after the great spiritual war in the heavens?"

"Yes, but the Bible says that Satan and his rebels were *cast out* of their graves (the seven nations of the heavens) and that no place in heaven was left for them.

Looking at these verses, there are two scenarios illustrated here – the seven kings and the seven mountains. But let's just consider the seven mountains (spirit nations) right now. Read verse 11 again."

17:11 And the beast that was, and is not, even he is the eighth, and is of the seven, and goeth into perdition.

Michael continued: "See? The Beast is of the seven because some of his spirits have graduated to a living church (Pergamos); but he is also the eight mountain (congregation) – hell, or the land of Nod (wandering)."

"That's interesting. But, it doesn't say "the eighth mountain" or 'the eighth congregation.'"

"That's true," Michael concurred. "But it tells the same story – as a riddle."

"Like The Revelation?"

"Exactly. The matrix is all about Cain. '**Mark (a masculine singular imperative [you mark!]) for my measure of the eighth**.'"

Martin lit up. "I get it. The people that receive the mark of the Beast will become a portion of the eighth congregation – which is hell, the pit, the land of Nod."

"Yes, now you have it. In The Revelation it is the task of the False Prophet to require the mark. So . . . I agree with the author that NeroCain is giving him his instructions – *You mark* for *my* measure of the eighth! See? That would make the Beast and the Satan *one and the same*.

Notwithstanding the professor's results, Martin, you need to bear in mind that a lot of the researcher's predispositions are reflected in his Bible coding results. And, also, mistakes can be made. Here, I'll show you.

The author tries "Nero(n)Cain" as a title for the Beast. Look at this string:"

נרונקין שנא נזנה. **Nero(n)Cain – to hate, he played the whore.**

"Oh, I'm with you," said Martin enthusiastically; "he is associated with the Great Whore of The Revelation."

Michael lifted his finger to make a point. "Ah, but not so fast. I looked it up and the author made a mistake. The Niphal stem is not used in the root zaneh (the last word). So, with his word spacing, it means, **NeroCain – to hate, we play the whore**."

"Oh, so they are separate entities?"

"Not so fast," Michael reiterated. "To make it say what we want it to we just change the word breaks. Look here:"

נרונקין שנאן זנה. **NeroCain, to hate (hating) them (plural fem.) he played the whore.**

"Spirits can be feminine. So, to hate them could mean . . ."

"Hating the entire company of Yahweh – His spiritual empire which is holy Jerusalem – the Throne," Martin volunteered.

"Exactly. So, now do you see how the code results can be manipulated by the researcher?"

"Yes. That term could mean 'we play the whore,' or 'he played the whore.'"

"That's right," Michael said.

"OK . . . but doesn't a matrix have a specific topical theme? Isn't the researcher stuck to that theme?"

"Yes. But he is also free to pick and choose what terms to include, and to manipulate those terms as we have illustrated here."

"I see. So . . . where does that leave us as concerning Bible coding results?" Martin asked.

"Apparently the author recognizes these problems as well. To minimize wiggle room he only allows terms in his matrixes that either share a letter with the same passage where the OTA is found, or can be extended to do so within close proximity. He marks the latter with 'NE.' I would guess that 'NE' means 'needs extension.' If you read his commentary, he lists the NE terms because they *might* be extendable; but he doesn't know how. And remember that 'OTA' means 'Opened Text Agreement.'"

"A term out of the Bible text that has to do with the theme of the matrix."

"That is correct. The professor only uses biblical Hebrew words and verb conjugations; and he restricts himself to attested verbal stems. He has very strict protocols. He makes the point that the Opened Text Agreement cannot be manipulated – where the terms at ELS can. This researcher always bases his results on Opened Text Agreement.

As for this particular matrix – I think that it speaks for itself. It is compact and the terms all tell the same story. But, if you didn't believe in these precepts, then you would not have *looked* for them. And, of course, neither would you have *found* them. See? Perhaps another researcher can find a better matrix that contradicts this one."

"What would the professor do if he needed to use a modern word – one that wasn't in the ancient vocabulary?"

"Bear in mind that there are no absolute rules to follow in Bible coding – at least not yet. Therefore, the professor developed his own rules because protocols *must* be established. He does make the point that his search was theologically based; and that there would be no need for modern words such as 'atomic' or 'UFO.'"

"I wonder what happened to the guy."

"There is no telling – Niyaq plays hardball."

Martin gazed about as if in contemplation. "So, how do you spell 'Abel' in Hebrew?"

Michael smiled. "It would be like this: הבל."

"So . . . how is that pronounced?"

"**Hebel**."

"That's interesting." *Lebeh*, Martin thought to himself. "But why do you suppose that Niyaq is so interested in the book of The Revelation?"

"It is their strategic manual. You see, Niyaq *does not* want things to come to pass the way that they are outlined in The Revelation. Niyaq intends to *change* times and laws."

Martin was hanging on every word. "Change times and laws? How?"

Michael turned around to face Martin:

"OK. Niyaq does not share their war plans with Lebeh; but it is obvious what they *need* to do to change times and laws."

"I'm listening."

"In a nutshell, Lebeh believes that Niyaq has a three-pronged strategy. First, to seek out and destroy the firstfruits. Second, to avoid nuclear holocaust. And third, to gain control of the Tree of Life."

"Yes . . . I understand about the firstfruits – they are Jews from the twelve tribes – sealed and kept from death during the tribulation. They are the remnant that remains after the tribulation, to be the firstfruits to God and to the Lamb. They are the ones that will begin the new world." He thought for a moment, and then addressed Michael:

"I suppose that Niyaq would like to avoid the nuclear holocaust because it is prophesied that the Beast will prevail against the forces of good on Earth. So, if the multitudes of the Beast *are destroyed*, it will be the nuclear winter scenario that destroys them, and *not* the multitudes of the living saints that will battle them on Earth. Do I have it right?"

"Yes."

"I'm a little fuzzy about the third point."

Michael began. "If the children of the Beast achieve a victory on Earth, then they will need to sustain their posterity. To do so they will have to seize control of the Tree of Life from holy Jerusalem." They looked at each other for a moment. "The Tree of Life is the portal that spirit takes to enter human life. To be born and re-born."

Martin nodded. "OK. That's why it is so unusual for Cain to be conceived; because he was banned from seeing life by holy Jerusalem until the Day of Judgment. To deny access first you must control the portal to life – the means of entrance – the Tree of Life."

Michael smiled approvingly. "You have it. It is good to see that you are not ignorant of these things."

"I would suppose that NeroCain is in the world now," Martin speculated.

"Yes."

"Does Lebeh know who he is or where he is?"

"I do not think so."

"Well, what about your people, Michael – do they know where he is?"

"No."

"Well . . . the Throne let him in – surely they must know."

Michael shrugged. "I cannot answer that. You see, I do not know everything – not by a long shot."

"Do you suppose that Niyaq has found the Beast?"

"I do not know."

"Well . . . there are many terrorist factions; are they all connected with Niyaq?"

"I do not know if *any* of them are. Most of these groups are too sloppy and disorganized to function the way that Niyaq does." Michael lifted his finger to make a point:

"The Beast will unite them *all* – they will recognize *his voice* and *all follow him*. This united force is the Dragon – the ultimate source of the Beast's power – as it is illustrated in The Revelation. In Genesis, these antediluvian people were called the Nephilim – *the fallen ones*."

Martin spoke up:

"Certainly, if the Beast is in the world, then so is his accomplice the False Prophet. And, with equal certainty, Elijah and Moses should be here too." He looked inquisitively at Michael:

"Well?"

"Certain things I can tell you and certain things I cannot. Do not ask me about Moshe and Eliyahu."

Martin looked sour. "Oh . . . in case I'm captured and tortured by Niyaq. That's a comforting thought."

Michael turned back to the computer.

"My wife and I believe in reincarnation," Martin began; "and a lot of our friends do too. I was wondering – do Jews believe in it?"

"There are all types of Jews."

"OK . . . what about orthodox Jews?"

Michael considered it. "Well . . . I haven't taken a survey; but I would say that most educated orthodox Jews believe in the precept of reincarnation.

Orthodox Jews are much more learned when it comes to their religion than Christians are. Just as there is support for reincarnation in the New Testament, there is support for it in the Old Testament as well. In modern Christianity you have an abandonment of the precept of reincarnation – but it was not that way when the faith first began."

"Well, let me ask you this . . ."

"Shouldn't you get back to work? You can look at these anytime – I showed you how to do it. Once you get the matrix on the screen, just 'view,' 'Matrix Report,' and you can read the definitions of the terms of the matrix. The definitions are all in English. Or, if you want, just right click on the term in the matrix and the translation will pop up."

"Are we in such a hurry?" Martin asked abruptly. "Are we pushed for time on this project?"

Michael closed the screen that he was viewing and turned to study Martin's expression:

"Are you worried about Rachael?"

"Darn it, Michael – are you reading my mind again?"

"Well . . . call it a hunch."

Martin seemed agitated and stood to his feet. He paced around the small room and then stood before Michael:

"Well . . . if you leave in a hurry then what is to become of Rachael? I don't want her to end up back where she was."

"That won't happen."

"How do you know that?" he asked pleadingly.

"I will see to it that it does not happen."

"You have the power to do that?"

"Yes." He looked at Martin. "All you need to do right now is *trust* me. And you need to exercise the faith that you *have*. Faith will cast out fear." He smiled:

"You still have many doubts, Martin. You need to calm down."

Martin sat down and nodded to himself. "Yes, you're right." He looked up:

"Let's get back to the nuclear holocaust. Niyaq wants to avoid it. Do I have that right?"

"Yes," Michael answered. "A nuclear holocaust is inevitable. Man will mean it for evil; but Yahweh will use it for good. Do you understand?"

"Yes, I think I can see where you're going. The occasion of the nuclear holocaust will eradicate mankind from the planet and allow Yahweh to start again with a clean slate. He will make sure that His chosen will be preserved to be the nucleus of this new beginning."

"Yes, Martin, that is the basic precept."

"OK," Martin began, "the Dragon (multitude) of the Beast – his seed – the Nephilim from Nod – will be brought out of the pit for the tribulation. The Beast will want to preserve his seed by avoiding the nuclear holocaust, and keep his seed flourishing by controlling the Tree of Life."

"That is all quite true, Martin; but there is another problem facing Nod:

On Earth you have Lebeh and Niyaq; in the spirit world you have the Throne, which is holy Jerusalem, and the domain of Nod. These are the two great contradicting spiritual empires." He lifted his brow. "OK?"

"I'm with you."

"All right, let us look at another scenario. A nuclear holocaust occurs; but Nod, somehow, wrenches away from the Throne the access to the Tree of Life. How does this profit Nod?"

"Well . . . if there is anybody left at all, why couldn't they use the Tree of Life to give birth to their own spirits – to start a new world of their own?"

Michael got to his feet and scratched his head. "There was something that was left out of Yochanan's book; and I really do not know why."

"Something missing from The Revelation?"

"Yes. You see, after a full-scale nuclear exchange, eventually all flesh would perish. This precept is found in the New Testament, and alluded to in the Old Testament. It is the Throne that will heal the poisoned planet and allow life to continue."

"Yes," Martin began, "'... except those days should be shortened, there should no flesh be saved.'"

"Very good. Open the Bible to Zachariah – the very end." He pointed with his finger. "OK. Start reading here."

14:6 And it shall come to pass in that day, that the light shall not be clear, nor dark:
14:7 But it shall be one day which shall be known to the LORD, not day, nor night: but it shall come to pass, that at evening time it shall be light.
14:8 And it shall be in that day, that living waters shall go out from Jerusalem; half of them toward the former sea, and half of them toward the hinder sea: in summer and in winter shall it be.

"You believe that the healing of the planet will be a physical miracle brought about by the Throne," Martin concluded. "When the light breaks and the clouds disappear, this will mark the end of the nuclear winter, the proclamation of the Kingdom, and the beginning of the millennial age of peace."

"Yes, this is what I believe the scriptures tell us.

Tell me, Martin, what do you think this means – *in summer and in winter shall it be*?"

"Well, I suppose that means it will happen to the whole world – where it is summer, and where it is also winter.

But . . . it doesn't actually say that the poisoned world is healed, Michael. Instead, it only insinuates the sky will clear at the time that the living waters flow. There are a bunch of assumptions here that the reader needs to make."

Michael took the Bible from Martin. "Are you familiar with the book of Ezekiel?"

"Yes."

"Yahweh himself treats Yechezqel to a number of visions. What did Yahweh call him, the prophet Ezekiel?"

"He called him, 'son of man.'"

Michael handed him the Bible. "Start right here. This is one of that prophet's visions."

47:8 Then said he unto me, These waters issue out toward the east country, and go down into the desert, and go into the sea: which being brought forth into the sea, the waters shall be healed.
47:9 And it shall come to pass, that every thing that liveth, which moveth, whithersoever the rivers shall come, shall live: and there shall be a very great multitude of fish, because these waters shall come thither: for they shall be healed; and every thing shall live whither the river cometh.

"See?" Michael began. "And there is a similar reference in the book of Enoch."

Martin nodded. "That is pretty clear as far as the Throne healing the world; but how does this relate to Nod and the Tree of Life?"

"Think about it, Martin." With that, Michael took the Bible from Martin, casually sat down and began thumbing through it.

After a few moments Martin spoke up:

"Oh . . . now I got ya. Perhaps Nod can't pull off that kind of miracle – to heal a poisoned planet. So . . . if there is a nuclear holocaust, possession of the Tree of Life will not profit Nod. *They will have a portal to nowhere!"*

"Bingo."

"So . . . controlling the destiny of the Earth has to be their prime directive. If they can do that, it could buy them time to fight the Throne and seize the portal to life."

Michael nodded. "Now you have it. Can we get back to work now?"

Martin was deep in thought. "But still . . ."

"What . . . what is it?" Michael impatiently moaned.

"Well . . . if this nuclear scenario is so important to the whole picture, then why isn't it accurately spelled out in The Revelation?"

"OK. Get yourself a piece of paper and make three columns. Start with the first seal, then the first trumpet, then the first bowl. Then do the rest. Do you understand? Three columns and seven rows. Write down what would be applicable to the nuclear winter scenario, and then read them in that order – left to right just like English (1,1,1 – 2,2,2, etc.). That will give you the scenario. There is one entry that appears to be out of place; but it does not have anything to do with the nuclear holocaust scenario. It is a riddle. The whole book is a riddle."

"Why? Why is it a riddle – something that important?"

Michael took a deep breath and looked up at the ceiling. He pointed to the papers at Martin's work station:

"Martin . . . I m ordering you to get to work."

Martin's brow lifted curiously. "Ordering?"

"Ordering."

"Well . . . what are you going to do, Michael – cast down fire from heaven – bring plagues down upon me – perhaps you're going to put a permanent part in my swimming pool?" He looked over at his friend who was rubbing his chin as if deep in thought.

"Well?" Martin implored.

Michael feigned a serious look. "I'm thinking," he solemnly uttered.

Martin chuckled and turned back to his work.

PANIC

6

Martin was suddenly startled by two raps on the door of the Sub. *Two raps*!

Terror seized him – it took his breath. His eyes darted around the surreal red-lit room and rested on the viewing portal of the door. What lay on the other side?

He imagined Rachael standing helplessly with a dark assailant holding a knife to her throat.

His mind raced. The beacon phone – he'd forgotten it. But wait – the beacon phone wouldn't work *inside* the Sub!

What a fool he was not to realize how *hopelessly* helpless he was. Everything that he loved would be taken away from him. And for what?

A gun – he didn't even have a gun. If he would *just* have a chance to kill *one* of them. If he *only* had *something* besides his *bare hands*. Indeed, they *all* would be *well* armed – and probably wearing body armor as well.

"Rap rap!"

He caught his breath with one giant gasp. Did they hear him?

Michael, he thought to himself, *where is Michael*?"

"Rap rap! Rap rap rap!"

He looked at his watch – 2:00 AM. This would be the perfect time for a surprise. Perhaps they already had Michael. His girls were gone – but what would become of them?

Never had he experienced such terror – the thought of seeing Rachael tortured before his eyes. Wait – he would tell them everything – he would help them – join them – whatever it took to save Rachael, *that* he would do. He swore that if she were to survive this, he would never again endanger his beloved Rachael.

"*Rap rap rap rap rap.*!"

When he stood to his feet his knees buckled beneath him. He tried to catch himself on the chair but toppled over and landed on his back. The air knocked out of him and he lay helplessly gasping for breath on the floor – staring up at the red light on the ceiling. His heart felt as if it would pound out of his body as he struggled to breathe with all the strength that he could muster.

Martin felt himself awakening. A hot pain shot through him. When he breathed it hurt worse. The hot searing pain was coming from his ribs. When he remember what had transpired, fear gripped him anew. He looked at his watch. It was 3:30 AM! Why hadn't they kicked in the door? It didn't make any sense!

"Wait a minute . . . it must have been Rachael," he concluded out loud.

Of course, he thought, *she must have awoken to find me gone and went looking for me.*

He held his side and gingerly ascended the stairs. Most of the lights downstairs were on. He went into the den and pulled his revolver from the drawer.

When he got to the top of the stairs he could see that the lights in their bedroom were on. When he appeared in the doorway, Rachael, who had been in bed reading, looked up in surprise:

"Marty!" she exclaimed as she leaped out of bed. She stopped short when she realized that Martin had a gun in his right hand. Her jaw dropped and she looked down at the weapon:

"Marty? What in heaven's name is going on? Where have you been!"

He hurriedly set the gun on the dresser and came to hug her. He let out a shriek as she hurt his ribs. She was dumbfounded:

"What in heaven's name . . ."

"I . . . I hurt my ribs. I . . . I need to sit down." He looked up at her from the chair next to the bed:

"Please, Rachael, bring me something to drink."

She put her hand on her hips defiantly:

"I'm not going to do *anything* until you agree to tell me what is going on." She clenched her teeth. "I've had it – you're making me crazy!"

Martin vigorously nodded and motioned with his hand. "OK – but go ahead, Rachael; I'm not up for walking the stairs right now."

Rachael soon returned with a tray with two glasses, an ice bucket, a small water picture and a bottle of scotch. He hastily poured and took a healthy slug. Rachael pulled up a chair beside him and plopped a couple of ice cubes into his glass. She poured some water for herself and leaned back in her chair. She considered her husband:

"You're white as a ghost. Do you want me to call Dr. Morris?"

He held up his hand as if to calm her:

"No, Rachael . . . just sit there . . . just sit there until I can get my act together."

Rachael could see his hand shaking as he sipped his drink. He let out a long sigh:

"Oh God, Rachael."

Rachael put her hand on Martin's shoulder to comfort him. "Whatever it is we can get through it together. I haven't been well for a long time; but I'm better now. I'm stronger . . . I can help you get through whatever this is."

Martin took a deep breath and began:

"I've gotten us into a big mess. A *big* mess! And I have endangered you and the girls." He looked over at her:

"I made a deal – but the deal was that I could bow out anytime." He faked a smile:

"See? I can just call it quits."

"Well . . . that doesn't sound so bad."

"Do you remember that Sunday you went to visit Martha?"

"Yes . . . that was a few weeks ago."

He nodded. "Yes . . . that was when it all began. Actually, I was sort of duped into this whole mess."

Martin recounted the entire story and left out no details. It took him three scotches to tell it.

Rachael considered what he had said and concluded:

"I don't think that you should quit."

He reached under the mattress and pulled out some papers from the envelope that Jarvis had given him:

"Here . . . listen to this: 'Important much that parallel. For not parallel not function.'"

"So?" Rachael asked.

He threw up his hands. "So . . . this guy is a freaking moron. And there is no way that this software will do *anything*."

"How do you know that?"

"Software is my business, Raech," he said in a disgusted tone. "Why should I endanger my family for nothing?"

"What did Michael say?"

"He said that if I built it then he would test it to make sure that it functioned properly."

She tightened her lips and nodded. "Then you should *do* it."

"But *I* don't have to do it," he protested. "Almost *anyone* could handle it – it's not that hard."

"But Michael chose *you*, Marty."

Martin marveled. "Aren't you the least bit *afraid*?"

She shrugged. "Well . . . you always said that the world will to be totally destroyed. If so, dying is a moot point. The only thing that is important is the chance to make a contribution." She looked over at him:

"You are *not* a coward. When you heard the knocks at the door you were worried about *me,* and not yourself." She studied his face:

"Well . . . am I right?"

"Yeah," he reluctantly replied. "But . . . but what's your point?"

"Loving your wife and wishing her safe doesn't make you a coward." She smiled:

"So . . . you're *not* a coward. And . . . well . . . I think you should help Michael."

He frowned and slowly shook his head. "I'm afraid that they'll get their hands on you." He looked up pleadingly:

"I can't stand the thought of it."

She shrugged. "Well . . . that is the risk that we have to take."

He lifted his finger to make a point. "Ah . . . but we don't *have* to let them take us. If we are armed then we can force them to shoot us – to kill us outright." He nodded vigorously. "That would be the ideal scenario."

"Whatever."

He forced a smile. "I'll tell the Bulldog to get us some pistols to carry – he'll know what to get. And some good rifles – all I have are bolt and lever guns."

"Whatever you think is best."

Something occurred to him:

"Michael will probably fire me. He told me not to drink – and he told me not to tell you *anything.* God . . . I even blabbed to Sheila that Michael had performed an exorcism on you." He groaned:

"See? I'm not being *cool.* I'm blowing this *whole deal*!"

"Well . . . I don't know Michael's last name; and you didn't tell me what the Bulldog's name was. Just see what Michael has to say about it and we'll take it from there. That's all that you can do."

"OK . . . I guess that is all I *can* do."

"So . . . were you working on the software last night? Is that what you were doing down there?"

He stood to his feet and motioned. "Come with me." He handed her the revolver. "You take this."

She hesitated.

"You'd better get used to it," Martin grunted.

On the way to the Sub Martin loaded a rifle and brought it with them.

"This should go through body armor – but it shoots slow."

They settled into the Sub and Martin started his computer:

"Remember when we used to study the book of The Revelation?

Well . . . we never made much sense of it." He pointed to the screen:

"Look at this. These are the seven Seals, Trumpets, and Bowls. Read the stuff that is in bold type. Read it from left to right. It perfectly illustrates the scenario of a world-wide nuclear winter."*

Rachael looked at the table:

"The aftermath of a full scale nuclear exchange."

He nodded. "Exactly."

Martin picked up the Bible and thumbed through The Revelation. "Look here. Read this."

15:3 "And they sing the song of Moses the servant of God, and the song of the Lamb . . ."

"So?"

"Don't you see? The Revelation is a riddle. Elijah and Moses are the two slain messiahs of The Revelation. So . . . why is this the Song of Moses and the Lamb?"

"Oh . . . what happened to Elijah?"

"Exactly – it's a riddle. It *could* mean that Elijah and Jesus are the same entity."

Her lip curled up. "Why couldn't it mean that Moses and the Lamb are the same entities? Plus . . . it says in the New Testament that John the Baptist is Elijah – not Jesus."

"True. It also says in the Book of Hebrews that '. . . it is appointed unto men once to die, but after this the judgment.' But The Revelation presupposes the precept of reincarnation and illustrates it over and over. Indeed, in The Revelation the very worst characters live again. Like Paul said – 'the resurrection of the just *and* the unjust.'"

"So, then . . . you're saying that Christ's last coming might be a Malachi fulfillment concerning Elijah; and that Elijah in The Revelation is illustrating Christ's prophesied return."

"Yes."

She shook her head. "That's a giant conclusion to reach from that one vague passage. Aren't you getting a bit carried away?"

He shrugged. "Well . . . maybe I am; but it *could* mean that Jesus is in the world today."

"And he will be martyred *again*?"

"Yes. One day we will be watching the news on TV and see the dead body of Christ lying in the streets of Jerusalem."

"Along with Moses."

He waved his hands wildly. "Yes. I mean, they probably won't have signs on them saying who they are; and they might be in with a pile of other folks. Heck, folks probably won't know *who* they are – at least not until they see them rise. That won't be on TV. Probably just a few people will see that. An underground movement will no doubt start from the seed of those who witnessed the dual resurrection – just like a movement started after the resurrection of Christ."

"Isn't the messiah suppose to rule? How can he rule if he is dead?"

"In Psalms 89 and in The Revelation it says that the ruling messiah will be the first born."

"That makes sense. First, you have to be *dead*, to be the *first* born in the Kingdom of Peace."

Martin's eyes squinted. "Are you poking fun at me?"

"Well . . . I will if you are going to tell me that Michael is Jesus Christ."

They stared at each other for a few moments.

"Marty . . . the garbage man told me that you were paying him twenty bucks a week to go through our garbage looking for wine bottles; and that you would give him ten for every bottle that he found."

He rolled his eyes. "Yeah . . . I saw the empty bottle of Thunderbird on the kitchen counter and assumed that Ralph had retrieved it. Well . . . it wasn't from *our* garbage – he just wanted the ten bucks." Martin thought for a few moments then continued:

"That night that you, Michael, and the girls cooked dinner – Michael was bringing in Romani Conti by the pitcher. I can't afford to buy that stuff! We must have had five grand worth of it." He marveled. "We were drinking it on the rocks in water glasses!" He wiggled his finger at Rachael:

"Where are the empty bottles, my dear?"

"Isn't there something like a 'Napoleonic Syndrome?'"

"No, sweet thing – to have that I would have to think that *I* was Jesus Christ."

She tried to conceal her smile:

"Oh . . . instead, our handyman is the Savior of the World. Yes . . . that is much better. Humph, and to think that I was worried."

"Don't be a wise guy, Raech."

"Come on, Marty."

"That one afternoon I bet we guzzled three or four of the best bottles of Beaujolais that I have *ever* tasted."

"We guzzled?" Rachael asked. "How much did Michael drink of it?"

"Michael never drinks very much. I couldn't even get a buzz from what he puts down. But that's not the point." He wiggled his finger at her again:

"The wine bottles, babe. You can't have wine without wine bottles."

"If you don't believe the New Testament, then why should you believe that Jesus could turn water into wine?"

"I didn't say that I didn't believe the New Testament; I just said that I didn't believe that it was perfect in every *detail.*"

"Maybe The Revelation isn't perfect in every detail – maybe it isn't true at all."

"You're not helping," he concluded in disgust. "You're not helping at all."

Rachael considered it for a moment:

"The last time that you got on one of these theological kicks you got us kicked out of church – do you remember that?"

He nodded. "Yeah – but I was right, damn it!"

"I'm trying to remember what that was all about," Rachael mused.

"It was all about reincarnation – about Paul and the Book of The Revelation. My point was that Paul had knowledge of the precepts of The Revelation and that The Revelation represented the essence of early Christianity – the essence of Christ's message concerning the essential precepts of salvation."

"Refresh me."

"OK. What did the Jews get really ticked off at Paul about?"

"I don't remember."

"It was his preaching that *all* would be resurrected – the just *and* the unjust."

"So?"

"So . . . that precept is *only* found in The Revelation which indicates that Paul, and other early Christians, were aware of The Revelation precepts way before The Revelation was supposedly visioned and written down. That, of course, would mean that at least some of The Revelation was taught by Christ."

She nodded in agreement:

"OK . . . I remember now . . . The Revelation contradicts much of Pauline doctrine, which points to the possibility that Pauline doctrine was interjected at a later time – probably after Constantine held that meeting."

"Yeah – that was the Council of Nicea." Martin lifted his finger to emphasize a point:

"Not only that, but when the New Testament was edited, they left in some parts where Paul contradicted himself by illustrating The Revelation's scenario of salvation."

"I don't remember that."

He picked up the Bible and pointed to a verse in I Corinthians, Chapter 15. "OK . . . start reading here:"

15:19 If in this life only we have hope in Christ, we are of all men most miserable.
15:20 But now is Christ risen from the dead, and become the firstfruits of them that slept.

15:21 For since by man came death, by man came also the resurrection of the dead.
15:22 For as in Adam all die, even so in Christ shall all be made alive.
15:23 But every man in his own order: Christ the firstfruits; afterward they that are Christ's at his coming.
15:24 Then cometh the end, when he shall have delivered up the kingdom to God, even the Father; when he shall have put down all rule and all authority and power.

"I remember now," Rachael began. "The Revelation scenario has Christ as the one who was martyred and saved and rejoined Yahweh from the very beginning. The next saved are the elect, which are called the chosen or the firstfruits. Next in line for salvation are the ones who find it at His next coming. And, after that, the ones who are saved at the final judgment, which is also referred to as the white throne judgment." She looked over at her husband:

"Do I have that right?"

"Bingo. My point – to the Righteous Reverend Fundamentalist Breath – was that Paul confirms The Revelation's scenario of salvation while the only hoopla that the modern church recognizes is the doctrine that states that a guy can just sit on his butt, and, just one time – in one life – confess his belief in Christ and everything will be done. If that were true, then there would be no *need* of a Second Coming *or* a Final Judgment."

"Yes, now I remember. And then you read to the preacher from that place in The Revelation that states that *everybody* will see life again."

"Yep . . . everybody except the Beast and his prophet." He turned the Bible back to The Revelation and began to read at Chapter 20 and verse 4:

20:4 And I saw thrones, and they sat upon them, and judgment was given unto them: and I saw the souls of them that were beheaded for the witness of Jesus, and for the word of God, and which had not worshipped the beast, neither his image, neither had received his mark upon their foreheads, or in their hands; and they lived and reigned with Christ a thousand years.
20:5 ***But the rest of the dead lived not again*** *until the thousand years were finished. This is the first resurrection.*

Rachael made a face. "Yes. The preacher and his wife came over to our house for a quiet dinner. After you read that passage they stormed out."

"Yes . . . but the dog got to eat their steaks."

Rachael laughed. "You're a sick puppy, Marty."

"Do you remember his sermon the next Sunday?"

She made a face and nodded. "How could I forget it? And he was glaring directly at *you* when he gave it. Can you remember the passage that he quoted?"

Martin searched around for a few minutes and then began reading from the Book of Romans:

16:17 Now I beseech you, brethren, mark them which cause divisions and offences contrary to the doctrine which ye have learned; and avoid them.
16:18 For they that are such serve not our Lord Jesus Christ, but their own belly; and by good words and fair speeches deceive the hearts of the simple.
16:19 For your obedience is come abroad unto all men. I am glad therefore on your behalf: but yet I would have you wise unto that which is good, and simple concerning evil.

Rachael looked disgusted and slowly shook her head. "How could I forget – you stormed out of the church right in the middle of his sermon, with me following behind you."

He shrugged. "Well . . . if I had it to do over, then I would do it differently."

"How so?"

"I would flip him the bird on the way out."

This time she didn't laugh. "Not one person in the church called us after that."

"Well . . . that was the idea – that was the whole point of the passages that he quoted."

Rachael's expression was sour. "At the time I considered you the spiritual head of the family. And I thought that you were right to challenge the preacher."

Martin cut his eyes suspiciously. "And?"

"Things got worse for us after that. We were going to find a new church to go to but never did. You should have kept your big mouth shut."

"Well honey, if you are going to parade yourself as a fundamentalist, then you should be able to defend scripture – not have a tantrum and run away."

She looked away. "Before that we were close to God. We were happy and didn't gulp down scotch. It all started to change after that. That was the turning point." She turned to him and searched his expression:

"You goofed. Admit it, Marty – you fouled us up."

He looked pained. "I need another drink."

"Marty, it's 4:30 in the morning!"

"All the more reason – this day is already shot." He perked up:

"Hey . . . let's get in the car and drive up to that little place in Maine. We could be there by this afternoon. Lobster and Chardonnay on the dock?"

"You can't run away from this, Marty."

"No . . . but I can have another drink. Come on, let's get out of this freaking box – it's giving me the creeps."

He shut down the Sub and went around the corner to the basement bar to fix another scotch. Rachael sat down next to him.

She gently put her hand on his arm.

"Am I losing it, babe?" he softly asked.

"You were OK until today."

He moaned. "Don't you get it? *Today can happen again*! I'm just not geared for this."

"Well who *is*?" she objected. "*All* heroes are afraid. A hero is one that does things that frighten him because these things *have* to be done."

He let out a long sigh. "I'm glad that I told you about it."

"Me too. I knew that something was up."

He looked over at her. "When did you first suspect something?"

"Marty . . . some of those *workers*, that – supposedly – were remodeling our basement . . . they were very articulate . . . some of them wouldn't know which end of a hammer to grab . . . dainty hands with no calluses."

"What about the statue?"

"I asked Vincent about it and he simply said, 'too much scotch.'"

Martin laughed. "That pretty much sums it up."

"I love to hear you laugh." She watched him as his countenance grew serious.

He took another drink.

"That's not helping."

"Before all of this happened, all I wanted to do was work hard, be organized, and grow the business."

"And now?"

"Well . . . Michael made a comment that seemed to mean that his future wasn't . . . wasn't very secure."

Her eyes widened. "Like he might get killed?"

"Yeah . . . that's how I took it. And then, today, I just wanted to rap with him. You know, just talk about different stuff." He lifted his brow. "He's a very interesting character."

"Yes, he is."

"Well . . . he indicated that we needed to hurry along with the software project."

"And?"

He looked distressed. "That's not good – that we need to hurry. That means that we're not safe. If we were safe then there would be no need to hurry.

I finish the software, Michael leaves, and then what? Will we be safe? Will we ever be safe again? Christ – the government has no defense against Niyaq – what hope do we have?"

"Marty . . . where are you going with all of this?"

He threw up his hands in desperation:

"I don't know! Don't you get it! *I don't know*!"

"You've always been in total control. Now you have *no* control; and you can't stand it."

He stared into his glass and slowly nodded.

She looked around helplessly. "Marty, I don't know how to help you."

"Honey, I've lost my nerve. How do I get back my *nerve*?"

Her eyes darted about as she gathered her thoughts. "Well . . . is that your *only* problem – your nerve?"

He looked over at her. He was tired, drawn looking, and very drunk:

"What are you talking about?"

"Do you believe that Michael and his people are of God? Do you truly believe that you are dealing with the good guys?"

He nodded. "Yeah, I do."

Her brow lifted. "Really?"

"Yeah!"

She stared intently into his eyes. "Then just go ahead with it and do your best." She looked around the room a moment and gathered her thoughts:

"At first you were excited about it – you were as happy as I have seen you in years."

"Yeah," he muttered to himself, "but then reality set in. Can't you understand? We're sitting ducks – the girls too. Do you know how easy it would be to kidnap the girls!"

"Niyaq can't learn anything from us. Heck, Marty, you have no idea what this software is suppose to do."

Martin's eyes raged:

"Don't be a damned idiot, Rachael! Torture is torture – do you think Niyaq is going to stop interrogating us just because we say we don't know anything? Folks disappear and are never heard from again – that's the way Niyaq plays! Jesus . . . can you imagine what would happen if Niyaq got their hands on you and the girls?"

She made a face. "I wish that you weren't so drunk. I wish that I could talk to you."

He looked totally disgusted. "Well . . . I'm not *so* drunk – not *so* drunk that I can't see what is going down here. Whew . . . it's like being cast in a horror movie." He threw up his hands in a helpless gesture:

"But guess what, love – this is real." He marveled:

"I never would have guessed that my life could get so *totally* screwed up!"

Martin slumped down and rested his head on his hands.

Something occurred to Rachael:

"Wait a minute, Marty – there is no way that Michael can be Jesus."

"Huh?"

"Well . . . if he is playing the role of Elijah in The Revelation, then he must be killed at the appointed time – half way through the last seven years of Daniel's seventy week scenario. And he will be killed in Jerusalem – not at our house."

He looked over at Rachael. "Well . . . yeah, that's right."

"The New Testament says that people will follow many false messiahs in the latter days. It is *imagined hysteria* like you are experiencing that will *fuel* these movements."

Martin looked about confused:

"Your point is well taken."

When Rachael began her tone was soft and comforting:

"Michael is a holy man; he proved that when he healed me of my spiritual sickness. That is all we need to know. Don't let your imagination get the best of you."

He gazed at her and managed a feeble smile. "Yes, you're right. I need to sober up and get it together."

"I'm going to put you to bed."

"I'll *never* fall asleep."

"I'll give you something to sleep – don't worry about that."

"What about Michael?"

"I'll talk to him."

"What about work?"

"I'll call Sheils and tell her that you'll be late."

She took his arm and lifted him from the stool.

"But . . ."

"Don't be dead weight."

"Watch out for my ribs!"

"Which side?"

"Left side."

She tucked him into bed and gave him three pills and a large glass of water.

"How long will these take to work?"

"Chew them up and drink lots of water." She handed him two more pills.

"What are these?"

"Vitamin B complex – take em."

As soon as she left the room he chambered a round into his Weatherby rifle and placed it next to him on the bed.

"Good Lord, I'll probably break my shoulder if I have to use this thing," he said out loud.

He went over to the dresser and retrieved the beacon that Jarvis had given him. He got back into bed and switched the "call out."

"Yes sir."

"Ah . . . I'd like to speak with Jarvis."

"Can you hold?"

"Yes."

"Affirmative."

After a few minutes Jarvis came on the line:

"McDonald?"

"I'm here."

"What gives?"

"I want you to bring me some guns?"

"What do you want?"

"Well . . . I want some pistols for concealed carry – complete with shoulder rigs – ones that can penetrate body armor."

After a short silence Jarvis spoke up:

"How many do you want?"

"Three – and I want three assault rifles that can pierce body armor."

"What caliber?"

"You decide."

"What kind of sights do you want?"

"You decide . . . and bring plenty of ammo."

"I'll have them there Tuesday after lunch – is that OK?"

"Well . . . what's wrong with having them here today?"

"Tuesday *is* today."

There was silence for a moment.

"McDonald – you sound like you're bombed," Jarvis barked

"I'm OK."

"Damn it, McDonald – we can't afford any screw ups! Don't screw around with me – I won't put up with it!"

"Oh? I was led to believe that Michael was running the show."

"I'm not going to have some drunken draft-dodger running rough-shod with military weapons. I'll check with Michael before I bring you *any* firearms."

"Up yours, Jarvis! I'm a damn sitting duck! I'll be here after 1:00 PM. No guns no software!"

"Damn you, McDonald! Get it together!"

He turned off the beacon phone and settled back into bed. He took a deep breath and slowly shook his head:

"I'm not geared for this."

Rachael couldn't sleep and positioned herself on the back patio and waited for Michael to appear. At 6:45 AM she noticed him coming out of the guesthouse with his coffee and paper in hand. She walked down to greet him:

"Good morning, Michael."

"Hello, Mrs. McDonald. You are looking a bit disheveled this morning. Did you have trouble sleeping?"

She sat down and wasted no time recounting the evening's activities. Michael seemed unaffected by it all.

"This gentleman that you call the Bulldog – the one that you saw me talking to – do you know what his real name is?"

"No."

"Well . . . Mr. Bulldog called me this morning and suggested that we get someone else for the software project. Apparently your husband woke him up and was very belligerent."

She winced. "And?"

"Well . . . I did not choose your husband because he was perfect. If that was my prerequisite, then I would have no candidates at all," he said tongue-in-cheek. He considered it for a moment:

"Mr. Bulldog does not seem to like your husband very much."

"Why is that?"

"He is a military man and was thoroughly briefed on your husband."

"Vietnam?"

"Yes."

"Well . . . if I might ask, why *did* you choose my husband?"

He gave her a curious look. "That is a long story – a *very* long story."

"So . . . that means that you aren't going to answer me. Marty said that you like to talk in riddles."

"Martin wants quick answers."

"And sometimes there are *not* any quick answers."

Michael nodded.

She looked fearful. "So . . . what now?"

"When he wakes up tell him to come see me. Nothing has changed. Tell him that Mr. Bulldog will bring him his guns."

She sighed with relief. "My husband has found himself in a situation that he can't control." Her lips twisted:

"He is having trouble with that. And . . . well . . ."

He raised his hand to stop her. "Just tell him to come see me and that everything is all right. And tell him to leave the door to the Sub ajar."

She smiled. "OK."

"But no more drinking," Michael insisted. "I promised Mr. Bulldog that I would bail out if that happened again. Keep an eye on him." He smiled comfortingly:

"Everything will work out. Trust me."

"I do," she insisted.

"Yes, and so does your husband – he just has breaches of faith from time to time. He will need to work on that."

She thought of something:

"Oh . . . I need some wine bottles to put some candles in; and I was wondering if you had any?"

"Wine bottles? No, I do not have any. Does your husband not have any?"

She felt her heart pound but acted nonchalant:

"Well . . . he didn't open any Sunday night. You supplied the wine. I just thought that I could use your empties."

"Sorry, Mrs. McDonald – I do not save them."

Early that afternoon the doorbell rang. Rachael opened the door, forced a smile, and politely gestured for Jarvis to enter:

"Please, come in."

He stood there awkwardly:

"Ma'am – I have quite a bit of stuff to bring in."

"Let me help you," she offered.

Some of the boxes were too heavy for Rachael but she helped with all that she could. When they finished there was an immense pile in the foyer. Jarvis wiped some sweat off his brow and handed Rachael an envelope:

"I went to the trouble of explaining everything in detail. Your husband knows about guns – I don't foresee any problems."

"Well . . . would you like to sit down for a minute? Perhaps you'd like something cold to drink?"

"No ma'am – I really must be going." He glanced around:

"Where are Michael and your husband?"

"Downstairs."

He grabbed the door knob. "Well then . . . I really must . . ."

"I need to talk to you," Rachael interjected. She studied his expression:

"It will only take a few minutes."

They settled at the kitchen table. Rachael avoided Jarvis' eyes and nervously began:

"I'm not sure that I know how to put this."

"Just say it," Jarvis responded somewhat curtly.

Rachael squared off:

"OK. I want you to lay off my husband. No more cracks about his past."

"Oh . . . the poor little boy . . ."

"That's the kind of stuff I'm talking about. Knock it off!"

Jarvis was taken back. Rachael continued:

"Just because my husband isn't some kind of Rambo hotshot doesn't mean that his services aren't essential to this project. Your judgmental crap is *way* out of line – it's your fault that we have Ed's abortion in our basement. If Niyaq is on to us, it'll probably be because of your freaking screw up!"

Jarvis jerked to his feet:

"I don't have to take *your* garbage any more than I have to take your husband's garbage! Your screw-up husband is dispensable as far as *I'm* concerned. He wasn't supposed to tell you *anything*!"

"Yeah? Well you ain't no General anymore; and you're not running the show – so why don't you just sit your butt down and get real!"

"Colonel."

"Whatever."

Jarvis sat back down and casually folded his hands in front of him. They glared at each other.

"You're a pistol," Jarvis concluded in a dry tone.

"I need to have one of those beacon things like Marty and Michael carry."

He remained silent and avoided her eyes.

"Answer me, Jarvis," Rachael insisted.

Jarvis looked disgusted. He finally spoke up:

"OK . . . anything else?"

"Roth must have had his head on backwards when he designed that Sub thing."

"I'm listening."

"What are Michael and Marty supposed to do if Niyaq comes to the door? They can't call out. What do they do – wait until the door comes crashing in and then lift up a computer tower and blow themselves to bits?"

"Mrs. McDonald, I didn't have anything to do with the design of the Sub. But I do know that the original idea was to just have the computer towers blow up if one of them was moved from the Sub, or if the phony password was entered.

At that time, neither Lebeh – nor the government for that matter, had apprehended a single person from Niyaq. So . . . it was decided to make the Sub a weapon; and make its user-friendly qualities a secondary concern. The Bureau was using civilians as . . . Niyaq bait.

The idea of the password is that if Niyaq enters the Sub, then they will blow themselves up when they find and enter it. If they try to move the towers they will blow themselves up. The bomb is strictly anti-personnel and won't really damage the house. The idea was that the perhaps the killed Niyaq members could be identified. This, of course, could result in more Niyaq members being apprehended."

"Will the bombs destroy the whole room – the discs and all of that?"

"No . . . I don't think so. They could only put so much explosives in a computer tower. If they made it too heavy it would be a tip-off when it was lifted."

She made a face:

"Oh . . . so then the other Niyaqers who are outside at the time of the explosion can come in and get whatever they want?"

"You have a point," he admitted. "But bear in mind, Mrs. McDonald, the Sub wasn't specifically designed by our government for Michael's project."

"Why can't you make the bomb hot enough to destroy everything in the room? I mean . . . at that point who cares if the house burns down. Keep the password thing; but get some devices that we can carry to blow up the Sub remotely. Do you get what I'm saying? And make it possible to call for help *inside* the sub."

"I see what you mean. The way it is now – Niyaq can just bust down the door, take what they want and split. Niyaq is probably too clever to fall for the phony password or lift up the towers. Heck, this booby trapping business is their forte."

They stared at each other a moment.

Rachael lifted her brow:

"So?"

"OK. So . . . you're not the dumb bimbo that I imagined you'd be."

Rachael managed a faint smile. "Then you'll do it?"

"I'll call Michael tonight . . . yeah, I'll do it."

"Wouldn't it be safer to talk to Michael now?"

"I'll talk to Michael *now*," he responded irately.

He looked off and slowly shook his head, and then back to Rachael:

"Anything else?" he sniped.

"Be nice to my husband. He respects you. He thinks you're hot stuff for some reason." She took a deep breath:

"Can't you *pretend* that you respect him . . . as a favor to me?"

He pointed at her. "OK – but as a *personal* favor – and you owe *me* one."

She smiled and gently nodded:

"Fair enough."

It was nearly eight PM when Martin returned from the sub. He made it through the day on coffee and pizza.

"I need something for my stomach," he complained as he entered the kitchen.

"How did it go?" Rachael asked.

"I worked my tail off. It's been the longest day of my life. I'm totally beat."

"Well . . . what did Michael do?"

"He sat there the whole time looking at that disc."

"I suppose that he wanted to keep an eye on you. You know – so you'd get on the ball and get some stuff done."

He gave her a curious smile. "Well, my dear, you suppose *wrong*."

"I'm listening."

"OK. I'm working away – but I position myself so that I can look over and see what Michael is doing on his computer."

She rolled her eyes and sighed.

He ignored her. "Anyway . . . he keeps coming back to the same terms.

On one of them, he got out some of his biblical Hebrew reference books. You know – to check the validity of the terms."

She shrugged. "So?"

"So . . . I got up one time and stood behind him and he instantly closed out the screen that he was viewing – but I made a mental note of it."

"So?"

"So . . . when Jarvis came to get Michael, I opened Michael's computer, found some of the stuff that he was looking at, and printed it out."

"And?"

He reached into his pocket, produced several papers, and waved them in her face:

"I've got some of it right here."

She became impatient. "Get to the point, Marty."

"Later that afternoon I left the sub and walked around a bit to get some air. Well . . . I forgot to knock when I returned and caught Michael in the act."

"The act?"

"Yeah. He was deleting entire sections from the computer so I couldn't view them."

She made a face. "How do you *know* that he was doing that?"

He threw up his hands. "I asked him. Well . . . he can't lie."

"Get to the point," she urged.

"I think Michael doesn't want me to view a lot of the stuff on the disc as it might give away the purpose of the software that we're trying to develop."

Rachael saddened. "Well . . . then why are you doing what he *doesn't* want you to do? Why do you have to be such a smart-ass all the time? Why can't you just do as you're told?"

"I guess I just can't help myself."

She sighed. "Go ahead with your story."

He showed her one of the papers:

"Here, look at this. This professor guy is fooling around with what they call gematria. Look – 12,000 . . . 144,000. What does that bring to mind?"

"The number of the firstfruits – the elect – the remnant of the Jews that will start the new world."

"Bingo. OK . . . look at this term:"

לוח בכורי אל ותאמנו אדמ Tablet of (writing of) firstborn (firstfruits) of God. And you have been established man."

“And the text that he matched it with says that Esau is trying to figure out how to kill you.”

“So?”

“So . . . don’t you see a connection? Man has been established in the tablet of the Firstborn. This can be a reference to the Torah – the five books of Moses. See? The firstfruits – which are the firstborn of the new world, are established in writing. Get it? According to this – the chosen of Israel are, somehow, listed in writing.

And you can draw a parallel between Jacob and Esau, and Cain and Abel. See? The evil brother is plotting to kill the firstfruits.” He studied her face and continued:

“Da-ah? According to Niyaq, the evil brother Cain is the anti-christ. So – the anti-christ wants to somehow stop the elect from receiving their prophesied inheritance.”

“Oh, so you think that the software has something to do with identifying *who* the firstfruits are; and that it is encoded in the Torah?”

“Yeah.”

Rachael was totally disgusted:

“So . . . now if Niyaq catches us we can give away the purpose of the project. Isn’t that what Michael was trying to avoid?”

“If Niyaq catches us we will just start blasting away. We have the firepower now. They will be forced to shoot us.”

“Great.”

“We can’t let them take us. Not under *any* circumstances. The first thing we need to do is stash pistols all around the house. Out of sight but not out of reach.” He went into the foyer and retrieved a box filled with small revolvers:

“See? You peel this off and stick it under the table. Then you put one of these little guns in it. Pretty clever, eh? We’ll stash them everywhere.” He went into the foyer again and came back with two assault rifles:

“Just keep one of these babies close at hand.” He handed her one:

“That one is yours. Just push this little thing like this. Now you’re ready to go. It holds 20 shots. Now – we’ll stash spare magazines everywhere.” He made another trip to the foyer:

“This is your rig,” he said as he handed her a revolver and shoulder harness:

“This gun can go through body armor and has sights that glow in the dark.” He handed her the revolver:

“Pretty light, eh? It’s made out of Titanium. Just point and squeeze just like you do with the snubbies – you don't have to worry about a safety like you do with the rifles."

She inspected the gun.

"You got it?" Martin asked.

Rachael was familiar with firearms. "Yeah . . . I got it."

They sat quietly and contemplated.

"What about the girls?" Rachael asked.

Martin pained. "I don't know *what* to do about the girls."

Fear showed in Rachael's eyes. "Should we talk to them? Warn them to be on the lookout? Will that keep them safe?"

He looked desperate. "I don't know what to do about the girls. Let's start stashing these things around the house."

"What about the cleaning lady?"

His lips twisted. "Yeah . . . ah . . . I guess you'll have to let her go."

"Oh . . . that's just great."

***Seals**	***Trumpets***	***Bowls***
1. Conqueror goes out and starts war.	**1. Vegetation struck. 1/3 of all the trees are burned up. All the grass is burned up.**	**1. Foul and loathsome radiation sores appear on men.**
2. Peace is taken from the Earth and people kill one another.	**2. Something like a great mountain burning with fire is thrown into the sea (nuclear explosion). The sea is poisoned. 1/3 of the fish in the sea die and 1/3 of the ships are destroyed.**	**2. The currents spread the radiation throughout the sea. All of the fish in the sea die.**
3. Food becomes scarce.	**3. 1/3 of all fresh water supplies become polluted from the nuclear fallout.**	**3. Air currents carry the radiation fallout. All fresh water supplies are polluted.**
4. War hunger and disease kill 1/4 of mankind.	**4. The affects of nuclear winter begin. Darkness covers 1/3 of the Earth.**	4. Men are scorched with great heat. They blaspheme God and do not repent.
5. The dead in Christ become impatient. They are told that they will have to wait just a little longer before their deaths will be revenged upon the wicked ones.	5. Five months before the Kingdom is proclaimed, demons rise from Nod with special powers to torment all of those living on the Earth except God's sealed elect.	**5. Wind currents carry the dark clouds. Darkness covers the whole Earth. Men gnaw their tongues because of the pain, but still they don't repent.**
6. There are great earthquakes. Mountains and islands are moved.	6. There is a great land war. Two hundred million soldiers are involved. 1/3 of mankind is killed. Those that remain do not repent.	6. Demonic powers influence the leaders of men to gather them together for the final battle of the Age.
7.There is silence in heaven for 1/2 hour as God listens to the prayers of the faithful who remain alive. *This is a prelude to the spiritual rapture of the living Saints.*	7. The kingdom is proclaimed. The kingdoms of this world have become the kingdoms of Yahweh and his Messiah.	7. There are great earthquakes such as have never been in the Earth before. Many traces of the old world vanish.

TOTALLY FAR OUT

7

A few days passed and Martin settled into a routine. In the morning he would go in to work early, and join Michael in the Sub after lunch. A man had come to rig a higher explosive device with a remote activator; an internal communicator was installed; and Rachael was given her own beacon phone. It was Friday; and Michael gave the customary three raps on the door of the Sub.

"Hello, Martin."

"Hi, Michael," Martin replied as he sat down.

Martin usually brought his assault rifle; but today it was conspicuously missing.

"Where is your big gun? Michael asked, "the one with the big book?"

He lifted his brow and looked over at his friend. "Book? Oh . . . magazine. Well . . . I guess I'm tired of toting it." He lifted his jacket:

"I've still got my pistol."

Michael smiled knowingly. "You have settled down. That is good." He twisted his lips:

"Your guns will not save you. You know that – yes?"

Martin turned around and started shuffling his papers. "Yeah – I guess I know that." He caught himself:

"Well . . . then . . . why did you have Jarvis bring em?"

"I was hoping that they would give you comfort until you settled down again," Michael replied.

"Well . . . I guess I've settled down. I've gotten a lot done the last few days. But . . . I'm starting to get burned out. What's the chance of taking a break?"

"OK. Maybe we should just take the afternoon off."

Martin lit up:

"Yeah – that's the ticket. We can sit on your patio and have some ice tea. Maybe order a Pizza. We'll bring a Bible and Raech can join us. OK?"

"Yes . . . OK."

They gathered at the table under the umbrella.

"Tell us about Lebeh?" Rachael asked Michael.

He thought for a moment:

"Actually, Mr. Jarvis knows more about them than I. According to him, there is not as much solidarity as one would expect. However, there *is* solidarity among Niyaq – they know who their enemies are and have a very exact strategy.

There are a variety of beliefs associated with Lebeh. That is one of the reasons that the organization must be fragmented into individual cells. If the cells were ever brought together for a meeting there would be – according to Mr. Jarvis – chaos."

"You've lost me," Martin interjected; "what binds Lebeh together?"

"Well . . . it has become obvious that the turmoil in the world does not have a diplomatic or political solution. The only solution would have to be theocratically based. This is one of the themes of The Revelation; and it is the prophecies of this book that holds Lebeh together. Many people in high places and vast influence are asking themselves, 'if the prophecies of The Revelation are indeed true; then *how* do we *deal* with it; and what – if anything – can *we do*?'"

He took a sip of his tea and continued:

"Mr. Jarvis tells me that right now it is mostly a spy game. Lebeh wants to know what Niyaq is doing and vice versa. The only project that I know about is the one that we are working on."

"I got the impression that Lebeh didn't *know* what we were doing," Martin pointed out.

"That is true."

Martin was frustrated:

"You've lost me again."

"Why is that?"

Martin sighed. "Michael, would you do me a favor? Would you just answer me in plain language that I can understand? I mean – half the time when you answer me, I still don't have a clue."

"Well . . . I am sorry, Martin – what is it that you want me to tell you?"

"Jarvis brings me a hundred grand . . ."

"He brought one hundred and fifty thousand. He said that the money was clean but I couldn't tell – it looked old and used.

One hundred thousand was meant for you and fifty was meant for your partner that would work with you to decipher the disc."

"Lebeh knew that I would need someone to help me?" Martin asked.

"Yes. You were to be the software expert and I was an individual well-versed in the Old Testament and biblical Hebrew

"OK . . . did Jarvis give the money back to Lebeh? I mean, it was their dough – right?"

"Yes – the money came from Lebeh; but Mr. Jarvis did not take it back to them. It was set aside to continue our project:

Everything takes money, Martin. When we are finished here, there are many that will pick up the banner and continue. This project will eventually spread all over the world." He nodded solemnly:

"Lebeh pledged to help bring the prophecies of The Revelation to fruition. I merely gave them the opportunity to keep their word. We need millions – not billions – but it has to come from somewhere."

"That's a fancy way of saying that Lebeh is paying for nothing. I mean, they got to fool with the Sub, but they could have taken that anywhere to test."

"Martin, I *really am* preparing a disc for Lebeh; and I am sure that they will find it informative."

"Oh . . . pertaining to the professor's work that he did for Niyaq?" Martin asked.

"Yes."

"OK . . . I got ya. You're doing something for Lebeh and I'm doing something for you."

"Yes. That is an adequate summary."

"Is Lebeh Jewish or Christian?" Rachael asked.

"Lebeh has both messianic Jews and Christians."

"What about the orthodox Jews?" Martin asked.

"By definition orthodox Jews accept the wisdom of the sages – the Talmud. That excludes the New Testament. When an orthodox Jew converts to Christianity he is ostracized by his orthodox brethren. He becomes Hashmootz."

"Hashmootz – the traitor," Martin concluded.

"Yes."

"I see," said Martin. "There is no middle ground."

"That is correct. Orthodox Jewry has a pronounced anti-Christian bias. Many of them see the fruits of Christ in the Crusades, in the inquisition, in pogroms, and in Nazi Germany. If one really considers their views objectively, it is quite easy to see where their position originates.

It says in The Revelation that '. . . the testimony of Jesus is the spirit of prophecy.' Yes . . . he prophesied the destruction of Jerusalem in 70 AD, and the holocaust to come. So . . . what's to be happy about?

Having said that, there *is* solidarity among the Christians and Messianics as far as recognizing the scenario of nuclear holocaust; and mutual agreement that genuine peace – as illustrated in The Revelation – will be a religious miracle that will – according to the prophecy – begin the last seven years of this age.

Many in Lebeh desire peace; but they do not want it with the Beast as a world leader. And many of them want the new age of peace to begin; but they do not want to see the entire world destroyed as its prelude."

"Michael," Martin began, "do you think anyone besides NeroCain can bring peace to the Middle East?"

He shook his head. "No – I do not believe that anyone else can do that."

"Well . . . do you think that a full-scale nuclear exchange can be avoided?"

He shook his head again. "No – I do not think that it can be avoided.

What makes The Revelation unique is that it is truly a prophecy for the nuclear age – for our times; and it is a prophecy that will affect everybody on the planet – not just the Middle East."

"And each passing day makes the prophecies seem more real – more believable," Martin added.

"Concerning The Revelation, do the Christian views differ from those of the messianic Jews?" Rachael asked.

"The Revelation is a riddle – but there are aspects of it that appeal to the Christians; and there are aspects of it that appeal to the messianic Jews. And indeed, there are those – according to Jarvis – that agree on many of the particulars of the book."

"So," Martin chimed in, "both the Christians and the messianic Jews can find what they're looking for."

"That is one way to put it. Moses and Elijah are the primary characters on the side of good. They witness against the Beast and the Messianics find that believable. They are martyred and translated to heaven – just like Enoch, Elijah and Yeshua were. Also, all who merit it come alive again in the next age – this is a solid rabbinical belief. Yeshua plays his part and 'the Lamb' is used as an appellation."

"What about the Nicean controversy concerning the identity of Christ?" Martin asked.

"The true identity of the Nazarene has always been a point of contention; and, as you stated, this was one of the main issues addressed when the council was convened at Nicea in the early 4th century A.D. Apparently, the same controversy still exists among the members of Lebeh.

Having said that, when the Council of Nicea voted that Christ was to be accepted as none other than Yahweh Himself, the religion became, by its own proclamation, primarily a gentile one. This precept was heresy to most Jews."

"Pre-existence and reincarnation were also voted down at Nicea," Martin added.

"Yes. But those issues aside, the primary message of The Revelation is simply that those alive on the Earth during the tribulation will miss the age of peace if they align with the Beast. That is the main issue of salvation that the book illustrates. These other issues are mere points of debate compared to the central theme of The Revelation."

"Weren't a lot of manuscripts burned after the Council of Nicea?" Martin asked. "Aren't we to thank Rome for many of the Christian practices that are contrary to the original teachings of Christ?"

"Yes. Those things are true as well; but, with those things in mind, can you actually say that the council killed the faith?"

Martin shook his head. "No, the council didn't kill the faith. The Holy Spirit has always been the center of the faith; and the council could not destroy that."

Michael considered it for a moment:

"Do you think then that if the council *had not* made the rulings that it did, that the Christian faith would have been the better for it? Do you believe that Yahweh was not aware of the happenings on Earth?"

Martin looked puzzled. "Where are you going with this?"

"Let's take a look at The Revelation," Michael proposed. "Read starting here."

6:9 And when he had opened the fifth seal, I saw under the altar the souls of them that were slain for the word of God, and for the testimony which they held:
6:10 And they cried with a loud voice, saying, How long, O Lord, holy and true, dost thou not judge and avenge our blood on them that dwell on the earth?
6:11 And white robes were given unto every one of them; and it was said unto them, that they should rest yet for a little season, until their fellow servants also and their brethren, that should be killed as they were, should be fulfilled.

"What do those passages refer to?" Michael asked.

"Well," Martin began, "they refer to the dead in Christ. These souls have martyred themselves for a higher cause and have been accounted worthy by the Throne to attain (be born into) the age of peace and the resurrection from the dead – you know, as the Master said in Luke (20:35). These are Jews and gentiles alike. They will not be alive to suffer through the tribulation, but have earned their white robes of martyrdom. They are accounted for salvation."

Michael nodded. "Yes, I agree with you.

When Constantine – the emperor of Rome – convened the Council of Nicea, Christ had been dead for three centuries. What was needed was a religion that could sustain the winds of time and produce the fruits of the age of peace.

How would your highbrow ideas of reincarnation have benefited this cause? Would it be a help or a hindrance? Would the number of the dead in Christ be greater if people believed that they would have many chances to please God and find their place in the next age? Can there be a religion that will exist in waiting for two millennium? I think not."

Martin considered it. "So . . . The final product of the council illustrated the apocalyptic doctrines alongside of a belief structure that would sustain a waiting church?"

"Yes," Michael answered. "And now, the apocalyptic doctrines that are pertinent to *this* time are coming into focus."

Martin was taken back. He looked knowingly at his wife:

"Well . . . I never looked at it in that vein. But . . . I can see Michael's point. To believe in the higher morality of Christ and the simple belief of reward after death is what sustained the faith and was the moral anchor of the western world. It worked. How can you fault something that worked so well?"

"You can't," answered Michael.

"What about the rapture?" Rachael asked.

"According to Mr. Jarvis, many of the contributors of Lebeh believe that they will be raptured and saved *before* the tribulation; and that Christ will appear on the physical Earth with an army and defeat the forces of the Beast."

"Tell me this," Martin began, "are the wealthy Christian contributors just trying to find out the date of their rapture so they will know when to spend all of their money?"

"Mr. Jarvis told me that some of them expect to be raptured with their *physical* bodies and then come back with Christ's army, and, in the *physical* world, defeat the Beast and his multitude. Many of Lebeh are hoping to *survive* the tribulation by the rapture." Michael shrugged:

"Perhaps they intend to keep their possessions intact." Michael's countenance grew dim:

"If things do not work out the way that they believe, many will lose faith – many will conclude that their faith is flawed and side with the Beast."

Rachael eyes widened. "Lebeh people will join up with the Beast?"

"Being a part of Lebeh does not guarantee salvation," Michael asserted.

Rachael spoke up. "Marty tells me that you've been studying that disc for a week and it is filled with coded messages referring to the book of The Revelation; and that Niyaq had this man search for these messages. So, in effect, these messages are a window to understanding the theology of Niyaq."

"Yes – you have it right. In my view, Niyaq's interpretation of The Revelation is very sophisticated – as good as any that I have seen or heard about."

Rachael was aghast. "What?"

"Why would you be so surprised?" Michael asked.

Martin interjected. "Niyaq is interested in God's plan because they want to *change* times and laws. It is important for them to understand God's latter days' plan."

Rachael looked back and forth from Michael to Martin:

"You two are telling me that evil understands Christianity better than Christians do?"

"Yes," Michael began, "in many cases this is true – at least at this level."

"Tell us about Niyaq's interpretation of The Revelation?" Rachael requested.

Michael began:

"The Revelation was one of the latter of the apocalyptic writings (the period from about 200 BC to about 100 AD), and is unique in that it is the only one to mention the name of Yeshua (Jesus). The infatuation that Niyaq has with this book also confirms their belief in the legitimacy of the Nazarene as a true messenger of Yahweh."

"Niyaq believes in Jesus?" Rachael asked.

"No," Michael answered. "Apparently, they believe that he is their prime foe in the physical world; and that his message was the true condemnation of Yahweh, and the final summation of the doctrines of salvation. They are *forced* to *believe* in their *own* power and ability to defeat the Throne."

She nodded. "I understand."

Michael continued:

"The apocalyptic writings are varied; but most share in common a lack of Jewish nationalism, and the idea that Jews and gentiles alike will have to vie for their salvation at some predestined time in the future.

I do not have all the answers; but apparently the Throne decided to put a summary of the essence of human spiritual metaphysics in the Bible – but, in the form of a riddle, as the naked truth would never be canonized. From what I have read on the disc, Niyaq has a good grasp of the inner meaning of The Revelation."

"So," Martin concluded, "Niyaq views The Revelation as a *true* revelation."

"Yes. Apocalyptic means to 'lower the veil,' to reveal the hidden truth."

"The bottom line?" Rachael asked.

"Yes – I guess you could call it 'the bottom line.'"

"Tell me, Michael," Martin began, "how does your bottom line differ from Niyaq's."

Michael considered it:

"You need to understand that Niyaq does not accept the biblical definition of evil. Putting that a different way – Niyaq does not agree with the apocalyptic writers' general precept that evil is a bad force that needs to be eliminated. They simply believe that evil is an alternative choice that each soul can freely take. From the very beginning, it has been evil's contention that if enough souls chose their camp, then good would simply be defeated. Indeed, the end result would be that the land of Nod would populated by Yahweh's cherubim."

Martin marveled. "That is *totally far out*.

So . . . having said all of that, Michael, how does your bottom line differ from Niyaq's; or, at least, how does it differ from the views expressed on the disc?"

"Again, Martin, I need to append some additional qualifications:

I take the view that evil's pathetic existence is due to that fact that they were at fault and were punished justly. They see their deplorable condition to be a result of oppression by the Throne. And, given that predisposition, they have a potential remedy for their condition. Their remedy is *not* for them to change their ways – but, to defeat the Throne to better their conditions via free access to life and a myriad of other grievances.

With those things in mind, my *interpretation* of history differs from Niyaq's; but the history that we both reference is the same. Same story with a different slant; and, with any good fortune, a different ending." He looked back and forth from Martin to Rachael:

"OK?"

Martin spoke up:

"So . . . in modern terms, you are apologizing for being politically incorrect from a spiritual perspective?"

"Well . . . from a *metaphysical* perspective."

"I see what you're saying," Martin agreed.

Michael continued:

"Also, my interpretation of history presupposes the precepts of pre-existence and reincarnation. As a result, it will differ dramatically from those who do not view those precepts as axiomatic."

Martin nodded. "I understand, Michael. So . . . give us a history lesson."

Michael began:

"After the Earth had matured to a certain state, it was decided that spiritual entities from heavenly Jerusalem (the Throne) would experience life in a material world. We are referencing a time prior to the great spiritual war. So . . . harmony did not exist in the heavens at this time. To avoid the disharmony of the heavens re-manifesting itself on Earth, the Throne decided to list those who would be accounted worthy of this life experience in a *book of life.* Those entities that were thought to cause problems in the arena of life were excluded from this *book of life.*

Many names from Yahweh's spiritual kingdom were listed in the *book of life;* and many from other gentile (foreign) spirit nations were listed as well."

"The idea was to avoid the disharmony that existed in the heavens by restricting those who would see life," Martin concluded.

Michael nodded. "Yes, that was the idea. But trouble started almost from the beginning when NeroCain rebelled and accused the Throne of many lies. Many spirits, who were not destined for life, joined this cause; and there were some who *were* destined for life who believed the propaganda and rebelled against the authority of the Throne.

Confusion reigned as those not destined for life (the Serpent – the Dragon) beguiled their way into the life experience under the pretense of an unjust ruling by the Throne. Yahweh's chosen king was also rejected by his own people as a result of the beguiling force of the Dragon – the multitude of the Beast that numbered as a third of all the heavens.

Man's sojourn on the Earth became chaotic; and finally Yahweh gave the rebels an ultimatum – 'butt out!' But the rebels *would not* back down. The rebels launched a pre-emptive strike; but Michael and his spiritual army were well prepared. The Throne won the war and regained control of the portal to life – which is the tree of life in Genesis. As it is stated in Genesis, 'So he (Yahweh) drove out the man; and he placed at the east of the garden of Eden Cherubim, and a flaming sword which turned every way, to keep (guard) the way of the tree of life.'

Therefore Cain and his followers were thrown out of the heavens and peace and harmony were established in those spiritual realms – the gentile nations and the Throne.

As I told Martin, in the *book of Enoch* seven mountains are illustrated.

On one mountain stands the tree of life; and a great gulf is set so that spirits cannot pass from one congregation to the other. In the Bible, 'mountains' often refer to nations or congregations. Nod is the eighth congregation and they are separated to wander. Nod means 'wandering' in Hebrew.

Michael leaned back and sipped his tea. Rachael and Martin stared at each other.

"That's it?" Rachael asked. "I don't get it. What's the big riddle?"

Martin raised his finger to make a point. "The riddle is – what do you do now?"

She made a face:

"Huh? The Throne won. What's to do?"

Martin marveled. "So . . . that's what all this crap is about."

"I don't get it," Rachael complained.

"Listen," Martin began. "Nazi Germany started with lies – propaganda. First Hitler accused and then he attacked. But are *all* Germans guilty? Should they *all* be banished – every one of them?

Propagandists know how easy it is to get people to believe lies. It's my view that *all* Germans *should not* be held responsible for the actions of the Third Reich. Indeed, many were helplessly swept along; and many were beguiled into believing the lies of the Nazi propaganda machine." He looked at Michael:

"That's it – isn't it? I mean, after the Throne won the great spiritual war, these were the questions that they were forced to address. How could they weed-out the bad from the good unless they gave them *all* a chance?"

"You have the precept," Michael agreed. "It was decided to give them *all* a chance on the level playing field of life, for the benefit of those who would prove themselves worthy of the experience. For the worthy ones, eternal life would be the reward – the opportunity to live over and over again for eternity.

It is hard to imagine what it is like in the separated heavens that were established after the great spiritual war – we have no remembrance of that other world. It is certainly abundant with peace, harmony and love; but still, there are qualities of life that *do not* exist in the spirit realm. In life you have the thrill of the perfect illusion of mortality and the depth of feelings and sensations that the life experience offers. It was this coveted life experience that initiated the great spiritual war."

"Who would get to play and who wouldn't," Martin concluded.

Michael nodded. "Yes, in essence that is what it is all about. That is *still* what it is all about. And, the coming events of the tribulation will seal the fates of many souls pertaining to their opportunities to experience life:

All who dwell on the Earth in those last days – save the chosen of Israel – will have a choice to make. Those that choose the good – even though it means death – will receive the reward of eternal life. They will not be affected by the second death which is the final judgment. The Beast and the False Prophet will be banished, and all who serve him cast into outer darkness. There will be new heavens and a new Earth. What this means is that both the heavens (the seven spiritual abodes of the righteous, and the land of the wandering exiles), and the physical Earth, will be rearranged as far as who will occupy them. Satan will lose many souls from Nod (the dead in Christ); but Satan will also gain his portion that chose to receive his mark in the land of the living. It is the hope of Satan that this process will *strengthen* his spiritual army in numbers, and give him an *advantage* when he goes up against the Throne in the spiritual war following the tribulation of Earth. *This is why it is so important to make the precepts of salvation known during these latter days.*

Many Jews will return to heavenly Jerusalem to stay. It will be their first time there since the fall of man. And it will be their first glimpse of the purified holy Jerusalem – the re-creation following the great spiritual war where the rebels were defeated.

The gentiles of the dead in Christ will visit the Throne for three and one half years; after that, they will return to their spiritual homes, with those who did not follow the Beast, and will enjoy the life opportunities of being born into the age of peace.

The followers of Cain will have to wait a long time to see life again. The new recruits of hell will find that their way back to their old spiritual abodes has been blocked – they will find themselves in the company of the Nephilim – cast into outer darkness – the land of Nod."

"So," Martin began, "for the saved Jews it will be a pilgrimage home; and for the saved gentiles it will be a visit and the marriage banquet of the Lamb?"

"Yes. Those of Nod who have found favor in regards to their works in life will not experience the tribulation, but will be a part of the congregation that the Christians call the dead in Christ. A spiritual army will be sent to fetch them up to the Throne. This is illustrated in The Revelation. These lost sheep are the living congregation of Pergamos. They are souls of Hell (Nod) who have found redemption by their works in life – specifically, by being martyred for a higher cause."

Rachael nodded. "So . . . the decision of the Throne after the great spiritual war was to allow *all* the rebels the opportunity to experience life for the benefit of the good ones – that will prove their works in the arena of life."

Michael smiled:

"Yes – now you have it. *That is the Curse of the World.* Under the new covenant that was made after Yahweh's forces defeated the rebels, all would live again and be judged on the level playing field of life. Those of Nod – who were judged worthy by the Throne (Pergamos) – will be granted access to the tree of life. But the rest will be restrained – as those in a pit who cannot escape – souls that cannot find their way back to the life experience. Some whose names were written into the original *book of life* will be blotted out. Some, whose names were not in the *book of life,* will be given a new name and find salvation. These events will transpire at the Messiah's next coming. This is the great lesson of the seven living congregations. Read it again with this in mind and you will find this precept very accurately illustrated."

"That's amazing," Rachael said. "No wonder there is so much evil in the world."

"Especially now," Michael added. "The gates of hell have been opened to life, and the Nephilim are pouring in. As it says in The Revelation:

13:8 And all that dwell upon the earth shall worship him, whose names are not written in the book of life of the Lamb slain from the foundation of the world.

"I understand," said Martin. "The ones *not* in the *book of life* who receive new names will not dwell on the Earth at that time."

"Exactly," Michael agreed. "Those of Nod who are called to see life during the tribulation are condemned already. The Revelation says that *all* of them will worship the Beast.

Yahweh knows these souls well. He knows from their history what they will do in the arena of life. This is the wisdom of Yahweh and the illustrated wisdom of his judgments."

Rachael chimed in. "But not *all* who dwell on the Earth whose names *are* in the *book of life* will worship the Beast?"

Michael nodded. "Yes, that is the message of salvation for those who dwell on the Earth. Only the chosen of Israel are exempt from this. In The Revelation they are the congregation of Philadelphia:

3:10 Because thou hast kept the word of my patience, I also will keep thee from the hour of temptation, which shall come upon ***all the world,*** *to try them* ***that dwell upon the earth****.*

Martin spoke up. "Michael, many Christians believe that verse is a promise of the rapture of the church."

Michael laughed. "Do not the Christians take *all* of our promises and apply them to themselves?"

"Yeah . . . they do," Martin admitted.

A disgusted look came over Michael:

"Well . . . perhaps the Christians should realize that if Yahweh will trade away his promises to the Jews, then the promises to the goyim are of little value."

Martin winced and looked over to his wife. Apparently they had hit a nerve.

After a few moments, Martin took the Bible from Michael and turned to the congregation of Pergamos:

"Look, Rachael, the promise given to Pergamos is different than the others." He read:

2:17 He that hath an ear, let him hear what the Spirit saith unto the churches; To him that overcometh will I give to eat of the hidden manna, and will give him a white stone, and in the stone a ***new name written****, which no man knoweth saving he that receiveth it.*

"There it is," said Rachael. She turned to Michael:

"Does it show in The Revelation when they get their new names?"

"Yes. The spiritual army of heaven makes two charges. One, to deliver the worthy ones from hell, the other to defeat the forces of evil." He read:

19:11 And I saw heaven opened, and behold a white horse; and he that sat upon him was called Faithful and True, and in righteousness he doth judge and make war.
19:12 His eyes were as a flame of fire, and on his head were many crowns; ***and he had a name written, that no man knew, but he himself.***
19:13 And he was clothed with a vesture dipped in blood: and his name is called The Word of God.
19:14 And the armies which were in heaven followed him upon white horses, clothed in fine linen, white and clean.

"For verse 12 the majority text substitutes *'names,'* for *'name.'*" Michael looked back and forth from Rachael to Martin:

"Yes, it is a riddle – but it is in there."

Rachael picked up the Bible. "There are some verses that never made sense to me before. This is to the congregation of Sardis." She read:

3:1 And unto the angel of the church in Sardis write; These things saith he that hath the seven Spirits of God, and the seven stars; I know thy works, that thou hast a name that thou livest, and art dead.
3:2 Be watchful, and strengthen the things which remain, that are ready to die: for I have not found thy works perfect before God.
3:3 Remember therefore how thou hast received and heard, and hold fast, and repent. If therefore thou shalt not watch, I will come on thee as a thief, and thou shalt not know what hour I will come upon thee.
3:4 Thou hast a few names even in Sardis which have not defiled their garments; and they shall walk with me in white: for they are worthy.
3:5 He that overcometh, the same shall be clothed in white raiment; and I will not blot out his name out of the book of life, but I will confess his name before my Father, and before his angels.
3:6 He that hath an ear, let him hear what the Spirit saith unto the churches.

She marveled. "Now I understand. Even though the souls of Sardis are written in the *book of life,* the tests of life have proved them unworthy and they are *not* accounted among the dead in Christ. If they fail the upcoming test, they will have their names blotted from the *book of life*."

"Yes," Michael said, "except for a very few of them as verse four states. In that verse it makes it clear that those who have earned their white robes of martyrdom, and not subsequently soiled them by bad works, will be included among the saved saints."

"The covenant following the fall of man seems to mostly benefit Nod," Martin volunteered.

"It depends on how you assess the situation," Michael began. "The Rebels meant it for evil; but Yahweh's ruling meant it for good – to cause many people to live."

"Didn't Joseph say something like that in Genesis?" Martin asked.

"Yes, he did. And, if we are to draw that parallel, then, in the final count, more will be taken from Nod than are added."

"And the final count will be those written in the *book of life* at the time of the final judgment?"

"Yes."

"I'd like to see some of these coded messages that the professor found for Niyaq." Rachael said.

They settle into the Sub and Michael started the computer.

"There is so much in here," Michael pointed out. "What would you like to look at?"

"I'd like to see something about the great spiritual war," Rachael replied.

Michael scrolled around:

"He has a good one on that subject.

The author claims that the Book of Genesis is a hotbed of low skip matrixes.

This one is he calls 'a single narrow-band, dual-cluster matrix:'

'Single, narrow band,' refers to the fact that there is only one ELS grouping presented and that it is narrow in width with only skips 58-60 being attested.

'Dual cluster' refers to the fact that two OTAs (Opened Text Agreements) are illustrated in close proximity with a shared topic."

Rachael made a face and looked at her husband.

Martin spoke up. "I'll explain all of that later, Rachael.

Go ahead, Michael."

"What is interesting is that commingled with the original text are hidden messages that elaborate on the text. Actually, in some cases, they do much more than that – they give an alternate rendering."

"Like a built-in kabbalah," Martin noted.

Michael continued:

"This matrix has 59 spaces between the lines. It is not as narrow as the last one that I showed Martin. Therefore, the ELS strings are more easily discerned visually. The message:

There was a particular entity called (anointed) by Yahweh to deal with the rebel threat. This occurred at the time of Noah in the Genesis time frame. This entity was given the task of driving out the rebels.

In the matrix, Nero is named as the leader who was inflamed when Yahweh made the declaration to cut off the posterity of the strong ones – the Nephilim – who had dominated the Earth during that ancient time.

An attack was launched against Yahweh, but the attackers were wholly consumed.

Let's bring up the matrix report and look at the cluster on the top left:"

War in Heaven

The ELS reference is 59 characters between rows.
There are 10 displayed terms in the matrix.
The matrix starts at Genesis 5:19 Letter 3, ends at Genesis 7:1 Letter 18.
The matrix spans 1749 characters of the surface text.
The matrix has 30 rows, is 38 columns wide and contains a total of 1140 characters. RV computation, Genesis.
Two clusters. Band width, 3.

<u>**OPENED TEXT AGREEMENT 1 and 1a**</u>

1. ויקרא את שמו נח

And he called his name Noah.

1a. הנפלים היו בארצ בימים ההמ

The Nephilim were in the earth in those days.

2. מובא משיח תנו לו וו (ELS term)
The entrance of messiah, give to him a hook!
Messiah shares a letter with **Noah.**
Skip -59, RV 10.006.

3. תם כחם שמשיח
That messiah will make an end to their strength.
Skip -60, RV 5.941.

OPENED TEXT AGREEMENT

4. ויאמר יהוה אמחה את האדם אשר בראתי מעל פני האדמה
And he said YHVH, I will bolt out the man which I created from on face of the ground (Earth).

5. הה נרו מה חמם בו
Woe to Nero! What aroused them against him?
Skip -58, RV 6.987.

6. מדר גוים נוא
Because posterity of Nations restrained.
Skip -60, RV 5.404.

7. עלת יהוה בהו נכי
A burnt offering of YHVH (as a wholly consumed obligation to God) (is) the desolation of my attackers.
Skip -58, RV 8.038.

8. לחמים ערו ילה (NE)
Destroy attackers! Let him waste away.
Skip -58, RV 5.811.

9. אם מות שם ארה
The mother of death is there gathering.
Skip 60, RV 4.254.

Michael continued. "The professor chose to list two Open Text Agreements which occur in close proximity in the cluster. In the first one, Noah is introduced, **'And he called his name Noah.'** In the story of the flood, Noah is chosen of Yahweh as the savior of His people. Indeed, the parallel to Christ Jesus could not be more obvious.

In the second Opened Text Agreement, the Nephilim *(Nephilim: the Fallen Ones)* are introduced, **'And the Nephilim were in the earth in**

those days.' The significance of this mention is underscored by the fact that the Nephilim are only mentioned two times in the entire Bible.

So . . . we have, as the Opened Text Agreement, the interaction of the Christ figure and the Nephilim that were causing the chaos on the Earth. To further underscore the Christ link to Noah, in the first ELS string, **'The entrance of messiah - give to him a hook,'** the word **messiah** shares a letter with **Noah.** This appears to be this messiah's entrance as a tool of Yahweh. He is given a hook. In the Bible there are a number of references to a hook being placed in the jaws of the wicked so that they will be taken back to where they came from. This is the Messiah's assignment.

The second ELS string of that cluster, **'That messiah will make an end to their strength,'** alludes to the strength of the Nephilim; and the fact that this messiah will prevail over them.

So . . . we have a very exact scenario described by four very concise terms in the tiniest conceivable proximity.

Let's look at the second cluster:

The OTA reads, **'And he said YHVH, I will blot out the man which I created from on the face of the ground (Earth).'** Yahweh's ultimatum, *My spirit shall not abide in man for ever, for that he also is flesh; therefore shall his days be a hundred and twenty years,* comes just before that but the author chose to use the later passage as his OTA.

He organizes his report in the order that he wishes it to be read:

'Woe to Nero! What aroused them against him?'

The question is answered:

'Because posterity of Nations you restrain!'

Nero didn't like the idea of Yahweh kicking him and his bunch out of the life experience. By this time the Nephilim were running the show. Here, Yahweh is saying that it is He who will control who experiences life.

'A burnt offering of YHVH (as a wholly consumed obligation to God) (is) the desolation of my attackers.'

Here the precept is introduced that implies that the rebels indeed attacked the Throne. This precept is emphasized again with a parallel string (same skip [ELS]) that runs along on the next line over:

'Destroy attackers! Let him waste away.'

One cannot help but to deduce that the one wasting way is indeed NeroCain.

The last ELS string is **'The mother of death is there gathering.'"**

Martin marveled:

"That's quite incredible. God, I wish I had known you in college – you would have been center stage when the doobies went around."

"Martin!" Rachael objected.

"Come on, Raech – can you imagine sitting around a hookah with this guy?"

She wasn't amused:

"Cut it out, Martin."

Michael looked puzzled:

"I do not understand this 'doobie and hookah.'"

"Martin's big claim to fame in college was that most all of his roommates flunked out of school because of 'doobie and hookah,'" Rachael volunteered.

"Well, Martin is wiser now – and will, I trust, stay away from doobie and hookah." He looked back and forth from Martin to Rachael:

"I have amused you?"

It took them a while to settle down.

"So," Martin began, "in Genesis you have these hidden messages connected to the text. The professor previously connected Satan to Cain, and as an incarnation that spearheads evil regimes (Nero and the Beast) throughout history – finally culminating in his final conflict where he attains world domination.

I take it that the story of the flood was a parable with a hidden meaning. That meaning, according to the professor's results, was that there was a spiritual war at that time in the history of man where Yahweh defeated the rebels and regained control of the tree of life.

Do I have it right?"

Michael answered:

"In the Bible text, evil is destroyed by a flood of water. In this matrix, evil is prevented from continuing its posterity by a flood of attacking angels – the spiritual army of Yahweh. Perhaps one should allow credence to both precepts.

There was indeed a great flood that was a part of legend when the Torah was written. The Torah would have been incomplete if it did not make a reference to it. But, you also need to understand that the Jews of old had certain beliefs that were not totally accurate."

"For example?" Rachael asked.

"Well . . . modern man looks up at the sky and knows that he is looking at vacant space. The Jews of old thought they were looking at water . . ."

"And, if Yahweh wanted to, he could just poke a hole in it and flood the world?" Martin surmised.

Michael nodded. "Yes. And people wondered why it was that journeyers from afar spoke with strange words."

"So . . . that riddle was solved with the Tower of Babel parable," Martin pointed out.

"Yes. But all of the parables of the Torah are true and parallels can be made that are of great significance. Do you understand, Martin?"

"Yeah . . . like when Joseph made the statement about God meaning it for good, to save many people alive."

"Yes," Michael agreed. "And Yeshua said that the latter days will be like the days of Noah."

"Bingo. The same evil souls are here now; and the same hooks are prepared to yank em back."

"Yes . . . that is a bingo, Martin."

"Please, Michael – don't start talking like my husband. In some ways he never made it out of the sixties."

Michael laughed. "You think then, Rachael, that Martin will be a bad influence? I assure you – many, much more powerful than he, have tried and failed."

"Who are you?" Rachael whispered.

Michael didn't answer.

"Come on, Michael," Martin pleaded, "say something like, 'who do the people say I am?' Let's have some fun with the old girl."

"What else would you like to look at?" Michael casually asked.

"Are there more Genesis low skippers?"

"Yes . . . they go on and on. What's your fancy?"

"What about that precept that you talked about where Yeshua goes into Nod and takes certain souls back to the Throne to wait for the kingdom to be proclaimed. Do you have anything on that?"

"Yes. But I think that preliminary remarks are in order:

The professor was able to find an abundance of low skippers tied to the Genesis text; but, when he attempted to find some of the other more abstract metaphysical mysteries of The Revelation, his low skip Genesis search became more difficult. Indeed, the presumption is that the book of The Revelation is *not* coded; and, the precepts that the professor was looking for did not have an obvious OTA to match with in the book of Genesis."

"So . . . what did he do?" Martin asked.

"He set CodeFinder at the maximum skip range and coded a wrapped Torah."

"Wrapped Torah?"

"Yes. He connecting the end of Deuteronomy with the beginning of Genesis and set his search range at plus or minus 152,402 skips.

He then began to see if obvious Initial Entries would occur and then looked for extensions of same. He then looked to see if an appropriate OTA could be found to match the terms that he discovered. Let's take a look at what he found out about the precept that you inquired about. Here is the report:

Nod and the Tree of Life

כלאשרבומומלאתקריבוכילארצוניהיהלכם
רכניעשהעלתורתנזרוידבריהוהאלמשהלאם
זרהכהנוהוציאאתהאלמחוצלמחנהושחטאתהל
יושמבעריהגלעדועבדיכיעברוכלחלוצבאל
חתהאבנימלוחתהבריתאשרכרתיהוהעמכםואש
כיינצואנשימיחדואישואחיווקרבהאשתהאח
ואתמתושלחשלשמאותשנהויולדבנימובנותו
מאתהלושמענינתתיכספהשדהקחממניואקברה
סכעליהנסכויצקעליהשמנויקראיעקבאתשמה
כמצרימהליהמאפרימומנשהכראובנושמעוני
הזההוציאיהוהאתבניישראלמארצמצרימעלצ
להחשנשתיטבעותזהבונתתאתשתיהטבעותעלש
תחימאתהראשואתהפדרעלהעצימאשרעלהאשאש
זביכבסבגדיוורחצבמימוטמאעדהערבוכייר
דתמלמשפחתמלביתאבתמפקדיובמספרשמותלג
הדנעמיאלבנגמלילמטהאשרסתורבנמיכאללמ
לישכממשפחתהשכמיושמידעמשפחתהשמידעי
צידנימיקראולחרמונשרינוהאמרייקראולו
העממשפטצדקלאתטהמשפטלאתכירפנימולאתק
עתיאתמריכואתערפכהקשההנבעודניחיעמכמ
כשגדולואתהתבואאלאביכבשלומתקברבשיב
לבנשתיבנותשמהגדלהלאהושמהקטנהרחלועי
רעבבארצכנענויוספהואהשליטעלהארצהואה
תיוכבדדתולולאשהותלדלואתאהרנואתמשה
כראישאתבתולאמהלאתצאכצאתהעבדימאמרעה

The ELS reference is 22604 characters between rows.
There are 3 displayed terms in the matrix.
Wrapped Torah, 1.8X.
The matrix has 25 rows, is 34 columns wide and contains a total of 850 characters.
RV computation, wrapped Torah.

אנה שהי תת עצ החיים נוד מי גנ בוא
Where is my Lamb to give the tree of life? Nod whose garden is to come.
Skip 22604, RV 20.948.

OPENED TEXT AGREEMENT

כל אשר בו מום לא תקריבו כי לא לרצון יהיה לכם

But whatsoever hath a blemish, that shall ye not bring; for it shall not be acceptable for you.

תת עצ החיים נוד

To give the tree of life to Nod.
Initial Entry Term.
Skip 22604, RV 5.329.
Probability of occurring by chance, 1 in 213,000.

'Wrapped Torah, 1.8X.' What the professor means by this is that the matrix takes 1.8 passes though the text of the wrapped (connected) Torah."

"It just keeps going around and around," Martin concluded.

Michael continued:

"The professor was quite pleased with this find as it was his first attempt with the wrapped Torah search. His Initial Entry bingoed (that is the term that he used); he then extended it (some people call this 'snooping a term'), and then found what was undoubtedly the best Opened Text Agreement in the entire Torah. All in all it took him only a few minutes to find this for Niyaq. The professor was quite pleased and said that the wrapped Torah was like 'finding gold.'"

"I'm not sure that I understand his ELS," Martin stated. **'Where is my Lamb to give the tree of life? Nod whose garden is to come.'** I don't get it."

"Read what the prophets said about 'the garden of God,' and 'the garden of Eden.,'" Michael suggested. "Indeed, for those accounted worthy of the next age, this earthly experience will be like the garden of Eden. Once again, Yahweh will choose who is to partake in it."

Martin marveled: "Just like the first time."

"Yes. Start reading here in Ezekiel."

36:33 Thus saith the Lord GOD; In the day that I shall have cleansed you from all your iniquities I will also cause you to dwell in the cities, and the wastes shall be builded.
36:34 And the desolate land shall be tilled, whereas it lay desolate in the sight of all that passed by.
36:35 And they shall say, This land that was desolate is become like the garden of Eden; and the waste and desolate and ruined cities are become fenced, and are inhabited.

“There are many more passages like this one,” Michael told him. “Use your concordance.”

“Show me another one.”

“OK . . . read Isaiah 51.”

51:1 Hearken to me, ye that follow after righteousness, ye that seek the LORD: look unto the rock whence ye are hewn, and to the hole of the pit whence ye are digged.
51:2 Look unto Abraham your father, and unto Sarah that bare you: for I called him alone, and blessed him, and increased him.
51:3 For the LORD shall comfort Zion: he will comfort all her waste places; and he will make her wilderness like Eden, and her desert like the garden of the LORD; joy and gladness shall be found therein, thanksgiving, and the voice of melody.

Martin looked at his wife:

“Wow . . . I guess you don’t have to fool with the codes to get spooked. That’s right out of The Revelation. The Jews are either looking at the pit or the garden of Eden.”

“As are the gentiles,” Rachael added.

“Now do you understand the matrix?” Michael asked.

“Yes. Anyone that the Lamb does not bring up from Nod will have his part in the pit prepared by Yahweh for the Beast and his followers. Those he takes up from Nod will be born into the next garden of Eden.”

“Now you have it.

The professor liked this one. It is purely a Revelation precept that is found nowhere else in the Bible.”

Martin twisted his lips curiously:

“Why does this guy make such a fuss about this Initial Entry business? Is a term somehow worth more if an ELS term is guessed than if it is simply read?”

“When things settle down you need to read some of this for yourself – it is very interesting.

To answer your question:

Operating this software is like playing a video game where ‘beat the odds’ is the name of the game. And the same game can be played *to find* a matrix; as the professor did with this one.

So . . . maybe when the professor hits a home run he likes to brag about it. I guess he is saying that he has figured out the game. Bear in mind, when you enter a term, CodeFinder tells you what your odds are of getting a random match.”

"Why do you suppose that there are only two terms in this matrix?" Martin asked.

"Perhaps it is because they so perfectly relayed the precept that Niyaq was looking for. I really don't know; but this same theme pops up over and over in the professor's results."

Rachael made a face.

"What is it?" Michael asked her.

"I just don't get it. Those odds must be wrong. That's like picking one man at random out of a crowd of 213,000 people. Martin and I were at Woodstock; and we know what a crowd of people that size looks like."

"Mrs. McDonald, you are *so* wrong," Michael began. "It is *not* random. It would only be random if the Torah *was not* coded." He studied her face:

"Do you understand?"

"No."

Michael began:

"With his low skip research, the professor proved to himself that certain precepts of The Revelation were coded in the Torah; and he learned that the Bible code recognizes 'Nod' as 'hell.' OK, Mrs. McDonald?"

"OK."

"According to the professor, one of the tricks is to code a term (in biblical Hebrew) with the least amount of letters. OK?"

"OK," Rachael answered.

"Having said that, let us look at the term again. The professor *originally* plugged in the phrase, *to give the tree of life to Nod.*

תת עצ החיים נוד.

תת This is the shortest conjugation of the verb 'to give.'

עצ החיים This is how 'the tree of life' is spelled in the text.

נוד This is the word (according to the professor) that the Bible code recognizes as meaning 'hell.' He left out the prefix ל (to) before נוד (Nod) which is commonly done in biblical Hebrew.

Martin spoke up. "So . . . you're saying that it is an educated guess, and not a random shot in the dark?"

"Exactly. And then the professor snooped fore and aft of that term."

אנה שהי תת עצ החיים נוד מי גנ בוא

אנה שהי Where (is) my Lamb?

תת עצ החיים נוד. To give the tree of life to Nod.

מי גנ בוא Whose garden (is) to come.

"As you can see, after the professor snooped the IE he re-voiced it. And then you have a perfect OTA – **But whatsoever hath a blemish, that shall ye not bring; for it shall not be acceptable for you. "**

Martin lifted his brow:

"So . . . do you think that this is a random occurrence; or do you think that this message was somehow coded into the Torah?"

"I think it was put there," Michael replied.

"Convert the RV of that one to odds."

"OK. But bear in mind that to the code skeptics this is a mute point."

"Why?"

"Because they will just say that it is random coincidence; or that the message is abstract and cannot be theologically substantiated.

From the beginning of Bible code research, there have been those who have investigated the codes in the hopes that they are real; and there have been those, who, from the beginning, have maintained that they are just randomness.

Indeed, evidence that the codes are real would be very disquieting to the theologies of many people; and, in the same vein, such evidence would be a delight to many others."

Rachael spoke up. "Are you saying that the code critics are atheists?"

"From what I have seen, the code critic camp appears to have more atheists per capita than does the other."

Michael made a few clicks:

"This RV of 20.948 converts to odds of 1 chance in 887,000,000,000,000,000,000."

"Maybe the professor's IE was 'the tree of life;' and he snooped that," Martin suggested.

Michael shook his head:

"You have not gotten the idea yet.

Look. Let's open CodeFinder to a wrapped Torah at max skip and plug in "the tree of life' as you propose.

See down in the corner? CodeFinder is telling me that it expects about 926 matches. We hit 'search' and 940 matches are found.

Do you have any idea how long it would take you to snoop 940 terms? Remember that the results are in script continua – there are no word breaks; and these phrases do not just pop out at you."

Martin nodded. "Yeah, I see what you mean.

I did read a little bit of the stuff that Jarvis brought from the Phase One Project. Apparently the Bible text critics think that it is folly to search the

Torah for coded messages because the original Torah is no longer extant."

"These are the arguments of fools," Michael asserted. "Are they Mikha'el – to know the ways of the High One?

After a certain point in history the letters of the Torah were preserved. Do these people think that Yahweh did not know of this?

I say that Yahweh has provided us with the proper Torah. Unlike these text critics, I do not claim to know how Yahweh works His wonders."

"Show us another wrapped matrix – one with more terms," Martin requested.

"All right, but a few preliminary remarks are in order:

The professor prefers results that are related to the text; but many code researchers do not share this preference. The display of a matrix has a certain number of skips between the rows, and will only display certain ELS strings that share a letter with the term that is selected for the Opened Text Agreement. Having said that, if one wanted to show all of the terms found that share a letter with the OTA, then a number of screens must be used in order for these ELS strings to be seen.

OK?"

"Yeah," Martin said. "A given screen will only show certain multiples of the ELS term. The ELS term being the first one entered."

"That is correct.

What the professor found was that ELS strings from different bands (ELS groupings) that intersected the OTA phrase, were topically related to each other; and, each ELS grouping was a sub-topic of the OTA's central term.

He also found that certain OTAs were 'sweet spots' that attracted terms that related to it. In other words, the ELS, if it was a good one, would find the 'sweet spot OTA,' and would be in a very narrow or parallel ELS band that would be sub-topical to the central topic of the OTA. Also, the professor found that these 'sweet spot OTAs' would oftentimes contain internal lateral low skip terms. It is really quite fascinating."

Martin slowly shook his head. "You've totally lost me."

"Well . . . let us look at one of these that the professor prepared for Niyaq.

Some preliminary remarks are in order:

As you know, the 69th week in Daniel's 70 week prophecy ended with the death of the messiah. The messiah died at Passover. So, the logical beginning of the last week (seven years) of the Christian age could possibly be at Passover. And, the logical ending of the last week (seven years) of this age could possibly be at Passover as well."

"Which would mark the beginning of the age of peace, the marriage supper of the Lamb, and the proclamation of the Kingdom," Martin realized.

"Yes. That being one possible scenario, and the fact that the professor was coding The Revelation precepts for Niyaq, the mention of the Passover in the Torah was a logical 'sweet spot' for these ELS terms to connect with. OK?"

"Yeah."

"And indeed, the professor found that to be the case:"

Passover to Yahweh

There are 11 ELS terms associated with the Opened Text Agreement.
1 ELS term is internal to the OTA.
There are 5 topics related by ELS bands. 4 are BW,1. 1 is BW,2.
Wrapped Torah.
RV computation, wrapped Torah.

<u>OPENED TEXT AGREEMENT WITH INTERNAL LATERAL TERM</u>

ויעשו בני ישראל את הפסח במועדו. בארבעה עשר יומ בחדש הזה
בינ הערבימ תעשו אתו במעדו ככל חקתיו וככל משפטיו תעשו אתו

Let the children of Israel keep the Passover in its appointed season. In the fourteenth day of this month, at dusk, ye shall keep it in its appointed season; according to all the statutes of it, and according to all the ordinances thereof, shall ye keep it. (90 Letters)

שמ רנ השביע (Lateral term)
There to sing, "he caused to swear an oath."
Skip -3, RV 4.689.

Passover to Yahweh

Who is Cain?

The ELS reference is 32583 characters between rows.
There are 4 displayed terms in the matrix.
Wrapped Torah, 3X.
The matrix has 29 rows, is 52 columns wide and contains a total of 1508 characters.
RV Computation, wrapped torah. Band width, 1.

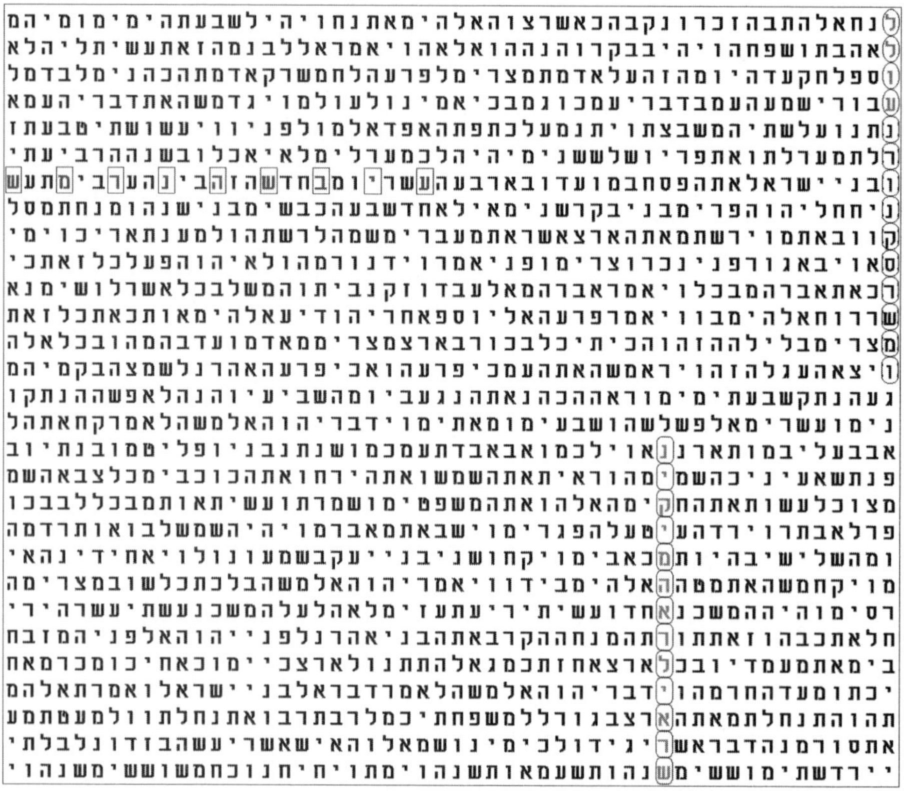

שמ רנ השביע **(Lateral term in OTA, Passover)**
There to sing, “he caused to swear an oath.”
Skip -3, RV 4.689.

שר איל ראה מי קינ
See who is Cain? A ruler of strength. **(NE)**
Skip -32583, RV 4.921

ללוע נרונ קסר שמו
Nero (n) Caesar is the name of the one who behaved wildly.
Skip 32583, RV 7.962.

נרונ קסר שמו
Nero (n) Caesar is his name.
Initial Entry Term.
Skip 32583, RV 3.229.
Odds of occurring by chance, 1 in 1,694.

Passover to Yahweh
The Fate of Nod

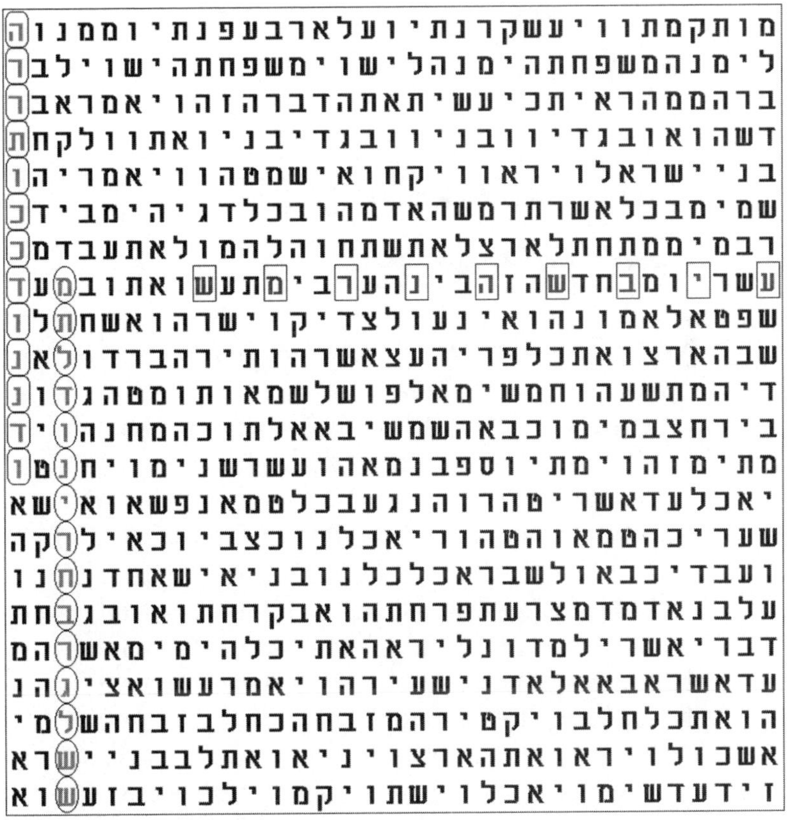

Terms are 96751 characters between rows.
There are 3 displayed terms in the matrix.
Wrapped Torah, 6.66X.
The matrix has 22 rows, is 33 columns wide and contains a total of 726 characters.
RV computation, wrapped Torah.
Band width, 1.

שמ רנ השביע (Lateral term in OTA, Passover)
There to sing, "he caused to swear an oath."
Skip -3, RV 4.689.

שש לגר בחרי נוד לתם
White linen for the stranger of Nod I chose for integrity.
Skip -96751, RV 8.891.

הרר תוכ כדונ נדו
The mountain (congregation) of your mark, as One judged they wandered.
Skip 96751, RV 5.699.

Passover to Yahweh
The Rescue of Hell (Nod)

דבראתכלאשראצוכואהרנאחיכיד
מואכלוחדשימימהצאנובקרישחט
תמלבבכעשיתזאתואחשכגמאנכיא
חהעלהואתכלדמהישפכאליסודהם
מנסעוהגדגדהומנהגדגדהיטבתה
תנלעבדיכולבנימאמרימלנועשו
בנלצבאתמועלצבאואליצורבנשד
בבעיניכמרקלאנשימהאלאלתעשו
תכלהחלבאשרעלהקרבואתשתיהכל
לרשתאתארצמכיברשעתהגוימהאל
יארוהיולדמביבשתויאמרמשהאל
עשריומבחדשהזהבינהערבימתעש
תחוארצהויאמראדניאמנאמצאתי
עלהזכרתמימיקריבנוושחטאתוע
הורישמלאתיראמהמזכרתזכראתא
ניתרוחתנוכהנמדינוינהגאתהצ
ילאחדכבשאחדבנשנתולעלהשעיר
עיניהישפטיהוהביניוביניכוי
שלחנוערכתאתערכווהבאתאתהמנ
כובשכבכובקומכוקשרתמלאותעל

The ELS reference is 121518 characters between rows.
There are 3 displayed terms in the matrix.
Wrapped Torah, 7.6X.
The matrix has 20 rows, is 25 columns wide and contains a total of 500

characters.
RV computation wrapped Torah.
Band width, 1.

שם רן השביע (Lateral term in OTA, Passover)
There to sing, “he caused to swear an oath.”
Skip -3, RV 4.689.

אברו שאולה ים קא
I fly him into hell, a sea of vomit.
Skip -121518, RV 4.140.

ימש מצא ראשיתו
Let him depart to find his beginning.
Skip 121518, RV 3.297.

Passover to Yahweh
Where is the Savior of the Waters?

תרצהוחגלהומלכהונעהבנותצלפ
ליהונתנהיהואלהיכבידכוהכי
קלוהמימעלהארצוייחלעודשבע
אהאמוותאמרחלאלאהתנינאלי
דומזקנלאיוכללראותויגשאתמא
ממנורבוגמהכהנימהנגשימאליה
יהוהאתמשהויעשואתהכתנתששמע
הולאתזנההארצומלאההארצזמהא
עשריומבחדשהזהבינהערבימתעש
אתאלהכאלהתעשוליומשבעתימימ
מכילאאתבניכמאשרלאידעוואשר
דינחנוואינעמואלנכרירכבהוע
יענובניחתאתאברהמלאמרלושמע
אליוספבחלמיהנניעמדעלשפתהי
לכמעליהשמרלכאלתספראותפניכ
וביומהשביעישבתוינפשויתנאל

The ELS reference is 32364 characters between rows.
There are 3 displayed terms in the matrix.

Wrapped Torah, 1.6X
The matrix has 16 rows, is 25 columns wide and contains a total of 400 characters.
RV computation, wrapped Torah.
Band width, 1.

שם רן השביע (Lateral term in OTA, Passover)
There to sing, "he caused to swear an oath."
Skip -3, RV 4.689.

איה מושיע המים
Where is the savior of the waters?
Skip -32364, RV 2.761.

עברני גן עדן
He crossed me over to the garden of Eden.
Skip -32364, RV 3.851.

Passover to Yahweh
My City Rejoiced

The ELS reference is 133609 characters between rows.
There are 3 displayed terms in the matrix.
Wrapped Torah, 7,45X.
The matrix has 18 rows, is 26 columns wide and contains a total of 468 characters.
RV computation wrapped Torah.
Band width, 2.

שם רן השביע (Lateral term In OTA, Passover)
There to sing, "he caused to swear an oath."
Skip -3, RV 4.689.

אנשי תבל מהל ששו עירי (ELS term)
The men of the world He mixed; My city rejoiced.
Skip 133609, RV 8.883.

בתם במוצ ההרים שבע
With integrity against the extortioner, the mountains to be satisfied.
Skip 133608, RV 8.507.

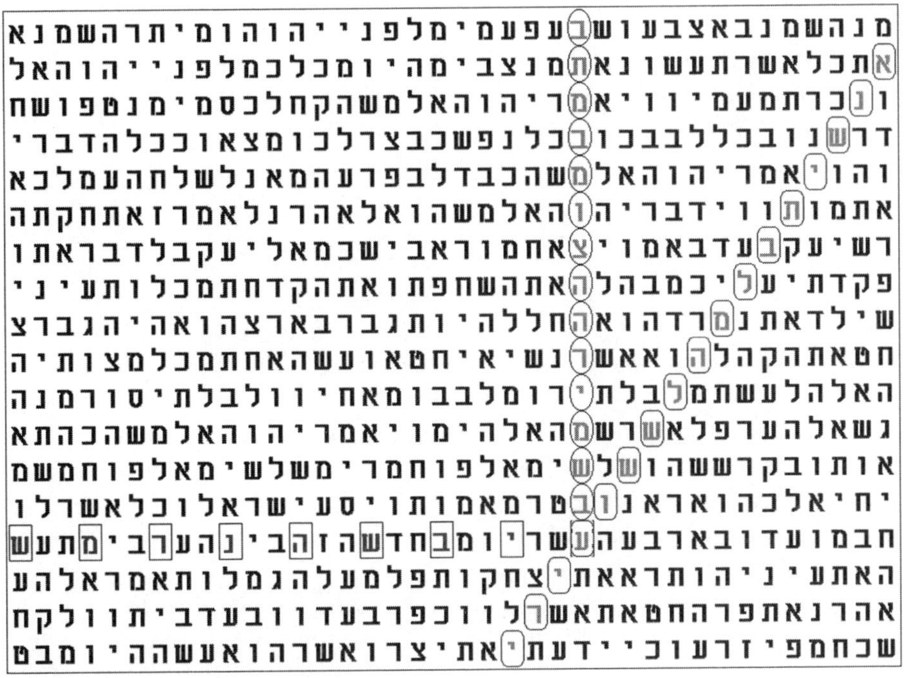

בתמ במוצ ההרימ שבע
With integrity against the extortioner, the mountains to be satisfied.
Skip 133608, RV 8.507.

Michael continued:

"The professor shows his OTA passage from the Torah that refers to the Passover. He shows his low skip lateral term, 'There to sing, "he caused to swear an oath."'

I think this is a good one:

The professor's assumption is that the proclamation of the kingdom will occur around Passover. At this time the saved ones are joyously singing.

As many of these souls had just found salvation because they swore an oath to Yahweh and not to the Beast, the logical presumption is that they were well pleased at this point to praise in song the one who *caused* them to swear this oath. This is the gospel message of salvation:

Matthew 10:38 And he that taketh not his cross, and followeth after me, is not worthy of me.
Matthew 10:39 He that findeth his life shall lose it: and he that loseth his life for my sake shall find it.

Michael continued:

"In The Revelation, a song of praise is lifted up to the Lamb. Perhaps this is part of the 'new song' that is sung in The Revelation.

In a world gone mad – with the Nephilim committing acts of unearthly cruelty – the act of martyrdom is the quintessential summary of a soul who needs to express to his God that His system of morality is the superior choice for the structure of civilized man. In this way a soul can vote his ballot in pure faith. Indeed, the act of martyrdom is the ultimate statement that all values and causes are *not* equal, and a divine precept of salvation that will determine the habitations of the new heavens and new Earth.

In the matrixes, the professor shows this low skip lateral term that runs through the passages referring to the Passover.

The first topic is **'Who is Cain?'**

There are 2 parallel terms in this one. The first one:

'Who is Cain? A ruler of strength.'

This next one I find interesting:

'Nero (n) Caesar is the name of the one who behaved wildly.'

The way Nero (n) Caesar is spelled here is the same from which the transliteration of the number 666 is derived. So, we find the answer to the number 666 riddle of The Revelation in the Bible codes.

This last term is there to illustrate that **'Nero (n) Caesar is his name'** was an Initial Entry. Once again the professor hit a home run with one of his plug-ins (Initial Entries). He hit this one at the odds of 1 in 1,694.

Indeed, the professor has a list of terms that should not appear once in the codes by chance, but show up 2 and 3 times. It is his contention that sooner or later two identical terms will be found of such a length as to quiet skeptics for good.

The second topic is **'The Fate of Nod.'** The two inevitable fates of those who dwell in Nod are, I believe, illustrated quite well:

'White linen for the stranger of Nod I chose for integrity.'

Indeed, all who attend the marriage supper of the Lamb will be given garments of white linen. There are many such references in The Revelation. So, the ones chosen of Nod to receive such are accounted worthy of the next age.

'The mountain (congregation) of your mark – as One judged, they wandered.'

On the other side of the fence – the fate of those who take the mark of the Beast is that they will be cast into outer darkness to wander. Nod means 'wandering' – the land of Wandering. 'Mountain' is a biblical synonym for 'congregation' or 'nation.'

Those who fail the judgment of the Righteous One, will not be able to return to their spiritual homes but will be cast out to wander.

This next one is interesting. In The Revelation there are many apocalyptic images presented. Some are explained and some are not. A great beast rises up from the sea, and the whore of Babylon is seen sitting on many waters. Both of these strange images have seven heads and ten horns. The angel with Yochanan explains that *The waters which thou sawest, where the whore sittith, are peoples, and multitudes, and nations, and tongues.*

If indeed this array is about The Revelation, then it should use The Revelation's imagery. Just like the above example of 'white linen' and the use of 'mountain' for 'congregation,' 'waters' can mean 'peoples' or 'congregations.'"

Martin nodded. "That makes sense."

Michael continued:

"With that in mind, the next topic is **'The Rescue of Hell (Nod).'**

'I fly him into hell – a sea of vomit.'

I like this little term. Here, it appears that Yahweh is giving the signal for the messiah and his army of angels to advance into hell. 'Sea' is a congregation in The Revelation terminology.

The word 'vomit' is often associated with the inhabitants of Nod in the professor's results.

'A sea of vomit' would be a congregation that Yahweh has vomited up as something foul and unpalatable (hell, Nod). Here, the first charge by the Lamb into hell (from The Revelation) is illustrated."

Martin smirked. "Niyaq must have *loved* that one."

Michael continued:

"'Let him depart to find his beginning.'

Indeed, the ones he brings back from hell will be – like all those who find salvation at the end of this age – the *beginning* of the age of peace. I like that matrix and the terms are parallel and only one space apart.

The next topic asks the question, **'Where is the Savior of the Waters (congregations).'**

The answer:

'He crossed me over to the garden of Eden (paradise, the age of peace).'

This next topic is good:

'My City Rejoiced.'

The first term:

'The men of the world He mixed; My city rejoiced.'

The ones who find salvation, and are rejoicing in holy Jerusalem at the marriage supper of the Lamb, will be a mixture from all nations, tongues, tribes, and peoples.

'With integrity against the extortioner, the mountains to be satisfied'

I like this one.

In The Revelation, the forces of the Beast prevail over the saints in the physical struggle. It is the *integrity* of the saints that *saves them*; and not their ability to defeat the Beast in the *physical* world. This same precept was also illustrated in **'The Fate of Nod**' matrix.

It is interesting for me that both of these terms share the same letter in the lateral term that means **'he caused to swear an oath.'**

And, indeed, 'extortioner' is an apt appellation for the Beast. Worship me or you cannot buy or sell! Worship me or your family will die! That is extortion at its highest extreme.

Truly, the congregations that attempt to overcome the extortioner (the Beast) with integrity alone, will rejoice in the city of God – dressed in white linen – singing 'he caused swear an oath' before the Throne of Yahweh. They will be from all the nations of the world – crossed over to the garden of Eden by their Savior to be the beginning of the age of peace.

But the report also warns of the return of Nero Caesar – Cain – the ruler of strength. Just as he confused many when he rebelled in the days of old, surely he will use the same beguiling tactics again. For great will be the deception in the latter days. And there will be great signs and wonders to reinforce these lies. So much so, that – if the chosen of God were not sealed from this deception – even some of them would be misled to follow the Beast and take his mark (Matthew 24:24).

Yahweh will show mercy for the ones of Nod who have shown themselves worthy for salvation and will arrange for their rescue. But, for those who take the mark of the Beast, there will be abandonment and wandering in the outer darkness of Nod."

Martin spoke up:

"The Muslim extremists are *already* acting on behalf of the Beast. They are *already* killing the Christians and the Jews who share a belief in the God Yahweh."

Michael considered it:

"Surely, the bad Muslims will find the bad Muslims; and the Beast will find them. Just as certainly, the Beast will find many to join him who are *not* Muslims. Read the news, Martin; it is not *only* Muslims who are acting out harshly against the Jews.

Not all Muslims will join the Beast. Indeed, there will be those accounted for salvation from *all* nations; and the Muslims are not excluded in that regard. So, it is a mistake to judge all Muslims as having one mind.

Having said all of that, Martin – when you meet the bad ones, you shall surely know it – for they shall be coming for you."

The hair on the back of Martin's head stood up. He looked at Rachael and after a few moments spoke up:

"Raech . . . do you see what I mean about this guy?"

HASHMOOTZ

8

Michael and Martin were working in the Sub when they heard three raps on the door.

"That's probably Rachael," Martin said as he went over and looked through the peephole:

"Yeah . . . it's her."

When she entered, both Michael and Martin were startled by her panicked expression.

"What is it, Rachael – what's the trouble?" Martin asked.

Her eyes shifted nervously back and forth from Martin to Michael. "I dozed off on the couch and had the worst dream."

Michael spoke up. "A dream? Tell us about it."

"Well . . . it didn't last very long; but it was very vivid. And it frightened me terribly. I . . . I saw Ed." She looked over at her husband. "You know – Fast Eddie. And . . . he had a demented expression . . . and . . . he had what looked like an old dagger clutched in his right hand. He was sneaking up on someone whose back was turned. As he raised the dagger over his head to strike, the man with his back tuned and looked back in horror."

"And?" Martin pleaded.

"Marty – you were that man!" she said frantically. "You were that man!"

Concern swept across Michael's face. "Fast Eddie? This is the man that you played golf with – your old friend – and the man who was responsible for building the small Subs?"

"Yes," Martin replied.

Michael groaned and slowly shook his head. "This is not good. This is not good at all."

"Well – it's just a dream," Martin emphasized.

"I do not think that it was *just* a dream," Michael asserted. "I think this is not good . . . not good at *all*."

"Michael," Rachael began, "do you think that Marty's old friend has betrayed him?"

Many minutes went by – Michael said nothing. He stared off into space as if in a trance. And then a serene smile spread across his face and he turned to address Martin and Rachael:

"I must admit that this has caught me by surprise. But be of good cheer. We will not lose – we control the heavens and the portal to life. We have many tricks to use against our foe – many more than they have. So . . . be of good cheer." He looked over at befuddled Martin:

"Tell me about the day that you played golf with Ed Roth? Can you think of anything peculiar about that day?"

Martin considered it for a moment. "Yes. He acted distant while we golfed . . . and . . . he wanted to quit after nine holes. He never did that before. And . . . then he wanted to come back to the house instead of having drinks in the lounge like we usually do. He acted very emotionally – recounting what good friends we had been for so many years."

"Guilt?" Michael speculated.

Martin tried to shrug it off:

"Perhaps. Well . . . certainly in the light of Rachael's dream . . . if we are to take it *that* seriously."

"Apparently, Marty, Michael thinks that it's important. I'm telling you that I have *never* had a dream like that before. Never!"

Michael raised his hands defensively. "OK, OK – just take it easy, Mrs. McDonald." He turned back to Martin:

"Did Mr. Roth go down to the basement while he was here?" Michael asked.

"No – I was with him the whole time."

"Are you positive?"

He anxiously rubbed his forehead. "Wait a minute . . ."

"Think Marty – think," Rachael pleaded. She looked over at Michael:

"They were both pretty blasted. I'm not sure how much my husband can remember."

"Cut it out, Rachael," he snapped back.

"I wish both of you would calm down. This is not helping," Michael scolded.

Martin lifted his finger to make a point. "Hey. Ed said that he wanted to use the bathroom but chose to use the one at the other end of the house."

"Where the stairway to the basement is," Rachael concluded.

Martin sneered. "Yeah . . . I didn't think about it at the time; but Ed made the point that he might have to sit on the John for a while. And . . . and I used that bathroom after he did. The exhaust fan was going but there was no stink – and one of Rachael's cigarette butts was floating in the toilet. But . . . but when *I* flushed, it went down." His eyes grew wide as he stared at Michael:

"But . . . it's just a dream . . . a silly dream!"

Rachael's jaw tightened: "Marty, you told me that all of those mini-Subs were the same. Eddie would be able to recognize one just by looking at the door. He wouldn't need to go inside."

Martin was obviously agitated. "OK, OK!"

"How long was Mr. Roth out of your sight, Martin?" Michael asked. "Was it five minutes?"

He shook his head. "Longer – maybe ten or fifteen."

"How could you be so stupid, Marty," Rachael accused. "He could have done *anything* in that length of time."

Martin ignored his wife and turned to Michael. "So . . . what do we do now?"

"Call Mr. Jarvis. He is not far away. Tell him to come. Don't sound panicked; just tell him that I want to see him."

"Now?"

"Yes."

Michael thought for a few moments:

"I think I will go sit under that big oak tree. I want to speak to Mr. Jarvis first, then to Rachael, and then to you, Martin." His smile was genuine:

"Do not be worried – it will all work out. I will come back here when I am ready. Give me a little time. And be careful what you say when you are outside the Sub. Assume that they are listening to us."

With that he rose to his feet and left.

Martin's conversation with Jarvis was very short. "He'll be here in fifteen minutes."

Rachael was distant, silent.

"I told you that I wasn't geared for this," Martin said in a whisper. "I've blown this whole thing – just like I told you I would." He wrung his hands:

"Oh . . . why did Michael choose me for this? I mean . . . if he is so damned wise . . . ."

Rachael's expression softened and she took her husband's hand:

"Michael said that it would be OK."

Martin tried to collect his thoughts:

"Michael used Jarvis' name in front of you. I told him that you didn't know his name." He looked disgusted and shook his head:

"Well . . . he ain't no Jesus. Jesus would have seen this coming."

Her brow lifted. "Would he?"

He sighed. "I don't know, Rachael. I don't know anything." His eyes blinked anxiously:

"When we get upstairs please be careful what you say. I think Michael is right – I think that they are on to us. I can feel it."

After Jarvis arrived, Martin hustled him down to the Sub without saying a word – Rachael followed behind. Once inside he nervously recounted Rachael's dream and Michael's reaction. They also recounted Roth's missing fifteen minutes the day he visited the house.

When Jarvis spoke he was concerned but calm and calculated:

"Where is Michael now?" He asked Martin.

"He's outside sitting under a tree. He's just sitting there on the ground. He wants to speak with us all separately. He told me that he would come in when he's ready."

Jarvis managed a comforting smile:

"So . . . how are you doing, Martin? You OK with the booze?"

He nodded and gave his wife a quick glance:

"I'm fine, Jarvis."

Jarvis searched his face:

"What about the software?"

"Things haven't changed since we talked to you on the beacon phone yesterday. I haven't got it working yet."

"Well . . . how much longer will it be?"

Martin's face twitched a bit. "Don't know. Maybe a day . . . two . . . three."

Jarvis turned to Rachael:

"When was the last time you spoke to the girls?"

Her stomach churned and her heart pounded:

"They're both away at summer school. I spoke with them a couple of days ago. They were fine."

"How far away are they?"

"About two hours."

"Do you ever go to visit them?"

"Yes . . . I mean . . . I visit my sister who lives about twenty minutes from campus. We usually take the girls shopping and then to lunch."

Martin spoke up:

"Probably the best thing to do is to take what I have done so far and have someone else finish it." He looked knowingly at Rachael and then back to Jarvis:

"Michael hasn't told me what the software is supposed to do."

"Well . . . we'll see what Michael says," Jarvis concluded.

"What do you suppose he's doing out there?" Rachael asked. "He just stares off into space."

"He's praying," Jarvis told her.

"Listen, Jarvis," Martin confidently began. "I'll stick it out if need be. Whatever Michael says I'll go along with. But we need to do something about Rachael and the girls." He studied Jarvis' face:

"Don't you agree?"

"Yes."

"So . . . what's your thinking?"

Jarvis considered it a moment:

"We can have our men start shadowing the girls immediately. Rachael . . . you go visit your sister. Run the beacon on the way and our men will shadow you. Once we get you, your sister and the girls all in one town together, perhaps then we can get you out by helicopter if need be."

Martin looked frightened:

"If Niyaq is tailing the girls then that will be a tip off – won't it? I mean . . . when we pull the girls out, Niyaq will know that we're on to them."

"Yes, but that is what we might do if something goes wrong *here*." Jarvis studied Martin's face. "Get it?"

"Yeah . . . it's a good plan. Better than what we have now." He turned to his wife:

"Just go visit your sister and do the things that you normally do." He looked over to Jarvis: "Right?"

"Yes. Our men will keep their eyes on you and the girls – we will get you out if need be. Call here and check on your husband – as you would usually. But be careful what you say. OK, Mrs. McDonald?"

"Yes."

Martin mused for a moment:

"What about putting some men around this house?"

"We've done that from the beginning."

Martin was surprised:

"Does Michael know that?"

"Yeah, he knows about it. I have eight men out there and a myriad of motion detectors and cameras. A mouse couldn't sneak up on us."

Martin was taken back:

"Why didn't you tell that to Rachael and me – maybe we wouldn't have been so damned paranoid."

"No offense, Martin – but you aren't always the cool cucumber," Jarvis calmly revealed. "The less you knew the better. That has been the policy from the start – Michael and I agreed on that."

Martin groaned:

"Well . . . your point is well taken.

Hey, perhaps Roth hasn't blown the whistle on us yet?"

Jarvis shrugged:

"We'll just see what Michael says about it.

Show me how to use this internal communicator. And then . . . ah . . . excuse me for a few minutes."

Martin did as Jarvis requested and he and his wife left the Sub. After only a minute, the door to the Sub opened:

"OK . . . come on back in, Martin," Jarvis said. "You wait outside for a few minutes, Mrs. McDonald."

Jarvis managed a faint smile and addressed Martin:

"You've sobered up nicely, McDonald."

"Thanks, Jarvis. This stuff still gets on my nerves; but I keep plugging."

"That's the spirit." He thought for a moment and continued:

"Lebeh has been tailing Roth for a long time – we never let him out of our sight. We were tailing him when the two of you played golf." He caught Martin's eye:

"We soon learned that we weren't the only ones tailing Roth."

"Niyaq?"

"Probably."

"Roth told me that he thought someone was after him," Martin informed him. "He was *very* paranoid."

"I don't doubt it." Jarvis' face grew tight:

"And there is something else. When our man came to set the higher explosive charge in the Sub he noticed that a wire was hanging off the device."

"The device wouldn't have fired?" Martin gasped.

"That's right. We didn't find Roth's prints on it but it looked like it was wiped. We couldn't really determine if it was an installation mistake or if it had been tampered with."

"Roth's prints might have been there from the start and he wiped it clean," Martin pointed out. "He had the time to disable the device when he was here at the house."

"Yes. I don't think our people would have been so careless with that essential part of the Sub."

The communicator buzzed and Jarvis picked it up but held it so that Martin could hear:

"This is Jarvis."

"It is done, sir."

"Affirmative," Jarvis said. He put the communicator down and glanced over at Martin who looked paled and shocked.

"You killed Eddie," Martin whispered.

Jarvis took a deep breath and avoided Martin's stare:

"How well did you know him?"

"We were roommates in college and have kept in touch ever since."

Jarvis looked away:

"I hope you understand that we probably saved the lives of his family. Niyaq won't have any business with them now that Ed is gone."

Martin stared off and looked numb:

"But . . . won't that be a tip off to Niyaq?"

"We figured that Niyaq was tailing him; so we had Arabs do the hit. A lot of his equipment is used to snoop the Arabs; so they would be a real threat to Roth. We have been planning the hit for sometime – they were just waiting for the go-ahead. If Niyaq didn't witness the shooting we made sure that there were other witnesses."

"You want Niyaq to think a radical Arab group did it?"

"Yes."

"You guys have Arabs working for you?"

"Yes, a few of them."

"That's clever."

Jarvis caught Martin's eye:

"Don't tell Michael or Rachael."

"OK." He intensely rubbed his forehead as he digested what had just transpired:

"Are you going to go ahead with the plan for Rachael and the girls?"

"Yeah."

Martin summoned up a feeble smile. "Thanks buddy."

"That's OK. I like your old lady – she's a pistol."

Martin nodded:

"Yeah – she is."

"Let me ask you, McDonald . . . were you, Michael, and Rachael down here in the Sub when you talked of Rachael's dream?"

"Yes."

"Good. Why don't you go talk to your wife and I'll set things up concerning her trip to visit her sister. From now on you'd better be careful about what you say when you're not in the sub – just make idle chit-chat. There's the chance that Roth bugged the house. No one would know better how to do it than he."

“Ever since Rachael’s bombshell we have been very careful about talking outside of the Sub.”

“That’s good, Martin.” He nodded and smiled approvingly. “Good thinking.” He looked at his watch:

“Give me ten minutes and then you and your wife can come back here and we’ll wait for Michael.”

The three of them waited an additional hour in the Sub before Michael showed up. When Michael arrived he instructed Martin and his wife:

“Go upstairs and do something that you would normally do. Have lunch; but be careful not to let fear show in your voices.”

The McDonald’s excused themselves and left Michael and Jarvis alone.

Michael looked intense:

“Niyaq knows everything,” he began. “They have listened to every communication on our beacon phones, and, most likely, every word spoken outside of this Sub. They know that we are close to finishing; they know that you put a bigger bomb in the basement; they even know the purpose of the software. The only transmission that they have not listened to is the Sub’s internal communicator; and they are working on that – we can’t trust it anymore.”

Jarvis was surprised. “McDonald told me that you hadn’t told him what the software was for.”

“Apparently, Martin figured it out and discussed it with his wife. The only good news is that they do not know that we are on to them. And they have not figured out a way to hear us talking in this Sub.”

Jarvis looked nervously about. “So . . . what’s the plan, Michael?”

“The Throne gave me a perfect plan to preserve the software. It is foolproof – there is no way that Niyaq can thwart it. But . . . we need to finish it first – we need a little more time.”

Jarvis leaned forward in anticipation. “All right. So . . . what’s my part?”

“I’m not sure that you *have* a part.”

Jarvis was taken back:

“Huh?”

“Lebeh has been rendered dysfunctional. They have been infiltrated and corrupted beyond repair. There is no one left that you can trust. Mr. Jarvis.”

“What about Ed Roth?” Jarvis asked.

“Out of fear for his family’s safety, he betrayed his friend.”

"We've been doomed from the beginning," Jarvis groaned.

Michael smiled. "Do not lose faith now, Mr. Jarvis; we are almost finished."

Jarvis gestured wildly. "That's one way to put it. We'll never make it out of here alive. Surely you must know that."

"Yes, I know that."

Jarvis was confused:

"But . . . you plan on finishing the project?"

"Yes, of course . . . we are almost there."

Jarvis lit up:

"I still have my Lebeh boys outside. Things can't be as bad as you say – they haven't seen anything suspicious. Heck, nothing can get close to this house without us knowing about it."

"Some of those people outside are Niyaq. You have been betrayed, Mr. Jarvis.

Everybody in Niyaq has our pictures now – you, me, and Martin's."

"We've had it, Michael!"

"No . . . the Throne has it figured. Their plan will work."

Jarvis shook his head. "I don't get it."

"You don't *have* to get it," Michael emphasized. "The Throne told me all that I need to know." He looked troubled:

"But . . . we still need some time. We need some time to finish the software. If Niyaq comes blasting in here before we have finished the project then . . . then the project will fail."

"Can you tell me the plan?" Jarvis pleaded. "Maybe I can figure out a way to buy us some time." He searched Michael's face:

"You know that you can trust me."

"Yes, I know that, Mr. Jarvis. And so can you trust me when I tell you that the project will succeed if we can just buy some time before Niyaq moves in on us.

Niyaq has put *all* of their physical resources against us. In the same way we will fortify where our strength is – in the spiritual realm.

Not by might, nor by power, but by my spirit, saith the Lord of hosts." He smiled confidently:

"And we will win, Mr. Jarvis. We will win!"

"You're confusing the heck out of me, Michael," Jarvis dryly concluded. "Is there nothing more I can do?"

"Yes, Mr. Jarvis. You can come up with a plan to stall Niyaq until we have the software project completed."

"You just want a little time to finish?"

"Yes."

"But . . . what about getting out? What about getting past Niyaq?"

"It is not possible for us to get out. Lebeh is no match for Niyaq. All I am worried about is that Niyaq will take us prisoners.

Mr. Jarvis, you must not let that happen. You must fight them. You must force them to kill us."

Jarvis was devastated:

"But . . . how will we get the software out?"

"Do not worry about that, Mr. Jarvis – I have already told you that the Throne will take care of that." Michael searched Jarvis' face:

"Can you buy us some time, Mr. Jarvis? Can you buy us enough time to get the software completed?"

Jarvis thought for a few moments:

"When I talk to the men in the woods will Niyaq will know every word that I say?" Jarvis asked him.

"Yes. Not all of them have betrayed you. But . . . I do not know how many are still loyal to Lebeh."

Jarvis looked disgusted. "I chose eight men that I was *sure* that I could trust."

"Who is running things out there?" Michael asked him.

"Wilcox – I served with him in Nam for Christ's sake."

"Think, Mr. Jarvis – think."

Jarvis snapped his finger:

"I got it. I'll go out and talk to Wilcox. I'll tell him that we are near to completing a software project for Lebeh. "I'll . . . I'll tell him that as soon as it's done I want it flown out safely to Lebeh. I'll tell him that when I give the signal, then he is to get a chopper in here to carry out a disc. I'll tell him that this disc is very important and that we're worried about Niyaq getting their hands on it."

"And then what?" Michael asked.

Jarvis smiled confidently:

"When the chopper comes I'll shoot the sucker down. That'll bring police and fire in here and force Niyaq's hand."

"You can do that? You can shoot a helicopter down?"

"Piece of cake. Lebeh doesn't have any military choppers. I won't have any problem downing a civilian chopper. See? Niyaq will be pretending to be Lebeh – they will have to use what looks like Lebeh gear."

"And then what?"

"If Niyaq takes over that position as you say that they can, then they will wipe us out. They have the firepower to do it; and we have the power to *force their hand.*"

Michael slowly nodded approvingly:

"Yes, I understand what you are saying. Mr. Jarvis. Thanks to Martin, we have our own means of defense. With fire and police on their way, they will be forced into a final confrontation." He reached over and put his hand on Jarvis huge shoulder:

"And none of us will not be taken prisoner by Niyaq," Michael concluded. He nodded approvingly at Jarvis:

"Your plan is a good one, my friend. We are in a position to control the timing. Niyaq will believe that they are simply waiting for us to complete the software and hand it over to them. That will buy us the time to complete it."

"I think it will work," Jarvis enthusiastically agreed.

Michael was very pleased. "Yes, Mr. Jarvis – that is an excellent plan." He gave a sigh of relief:

"Well . . . calling you in here may have saved the project."

"Yeah . . . I always wanted to go out with a bang." Jarvis grimaced.

"What is it, Mr. Jarvis?"

"It's my fault that things have to end this way." He looked pleadingly at Michael:

"Can you find it in your heart to forgive me?"

"Mr. Jarvis – I know that you meant well."

"Do . . . do you suppose that God will forgive me?"

"I would say *yes* to that, Mr. Jarvis; but . . . I am not God."

They fell silent for a few moments. Finally Jarvis spoke up:

"And . . . and Mrs. McDonald?"

"Yes . . . we need to talk about that."

Jarvis explained to Michael what he had planned concerning Rachael's trip to her sister's house.

Michael considered it for a few minutes:

"Well . . . go ahead with that."

"But . . . I told her to keep the beacon running – won't they will be able to track her if she has the beacon on?"

"They will track her anyway. Go ahead with your plan. If she has the beacon on Niyaq will think that we are confident. That is what we want them to think."

Jarvis groaned. "But what about her . . . what about Rachael?" he asked in a desperate tone. "They might think she has the software."

"We'll just have to risk that. Before she leaves, talk with your men concerning the airlift. Yes . . . Niyaq will follow her, and perhaps search her for the software."

"God . . . is there no other way? Michael – I think it would be better if she just stayed here."

"She will die if she stays here."

"Yes – but it will be an *easy* death. *I* will make sure of that."

"Let the angels look after her. Let her go to visit her sister as planned."

"Michael – that's a lousy idea," Jarvis rudely blurted. "We can't let Niyaq get their hands on Rachael. Do you have any idea what they will do to her?"

Michael calmly shook his head:

"No. There are things that you do not understand. We must let her leave."

"I told Mrs. McDonald to call here as she usually does," Jarvis informed him.

"That's good. Niyaq will expect her to do that." Michael smiled:

"Send in Mrs. McDonald."

Rachael sat down next to Michael and feigned a weak smile. "I need to tell you a story."

"Go ahead."

"After Martin and I got married, we started going to a little Pentecostal church. We were very happy then." She looked off as she recounted it:

"One night I dreamt that an angel had come to get me and we flew off into the sky. Below us was a beautiful house. My heart soared when I saw it; and the angel and I flew into one of the windows.

I said to the angel, 'whose house is this?' and she answered and said, 'it is yours.' And then I asked her what I had to do to own this fine mansion. She told me that I didn't have to do anything – it was mine already.

I felt such joy as I explored the house and savored the views from every window. I came across a room that had a big bow on it. When I asked the angel about it she said that it was Holly's room. In my excitement I searched for other rooms with bows. I was ecstatic when I saw another bow. Certain that I had discovered Marty's room, I inquired of the angel – but she told me that this room was mine.

'Are there no more bows?' I asked the angel.

'No,' she said, 'but there may be yet another one.'

I woke up feeling profoundly sad. Even though I didn't fully understand the dream, I wept for hours."

"And now . . . now you understand the dream?" Michael asked her.

"Yes. Holly has made her place in the next age. Martin's salvation still hangs in the balance. Martin has yet to die a martyr's death, and fulfill his mandate for salvation."

"Did you tell this dream to your husband?"

"Yes . . . well . . . years ago I told him."

Michael smiled:

"Good. Let us pray that, when the time comes, this dream will come to his remembrance."

"Should I remind him of the dream – explain it to him?" she anxiously inquired.

Michael shook his head assertively. "I do not think that would be wise. His decisions must be his own."

"Mr. Jarvis and Martin think that it is best that I go and look after the girls."

Michael tried to read her face:

"And . . . what do you think, Rachael?"

"I think that I need to stay here. I can encourage Martin – he will listen to me." Her eyes filled with tears:

"Michael . . . Martin still doesn't get it. He thinks that you came to save *me*."

"Martin will do better if he thinks that you are safe. Surely you must realize that. The last time he stumbled it was because he feared for *your* safety."

Her eyes widened:

"But . . . but that is deception. What can keep me safe; what can keep the girls safe?" she whimpered.

Michael gently took her hand:

"Please . . . listen to me, Mrs. McDonald. I do not know all of the particulars; but I can tell you that the Throne will have more for you to do."

She looked puzzled. "In this life?"

"Yes. And there will be a period of refreshment – a period of happiness, faith, and peace. This will occur *before* anything else is required of you. And Holly will be happy. She will find a new sweetheart before her engagement to Bobby is broken."

She looked down at the floor and slowly shook her head. "I won't be happy without Martin." Her face suddenly lit up:

"Aha! I interpreted the dream incorrectly – Martin will *not* have to be martyred."

"Your interpretation was true, Rachael. Just remember that when you leave here you will not be alone – a legion of angels will be under your charge. Trust your instincts and they will guide you. Do not count on Lebeh for any help."

"But . . . but Jarvis said . . ."

"Do not count on Lebeh," Michael reiterated. "Niyaq is going to move against them in a big way. Trust your instincts and have faith. If Niyaq gets their hands on you just tell them that we plan to put the software on a disc and have it lifted out by a Lebeh helicopter."

She looked at Michael and threw up her hands in desperation:

"That's it?"

Michael considered it for a few moments:

"It says in Proverbs that, *the king's heart is in the hand of the LORD, as the rivers of water: he turneth it whithersoever he will.*

Rachael, it doesn't say 'the *good* king's heart.' Just believe that which I have said concerning your future – let the Throne worry about the particulars."

She hesitantly nodded. "And what about Molly?"

"The angels didn't mention Molly." He gently took her hand:

"Remember that, after the coming woes, all but two will see life again. If she misses her chance for salvation there will be other opportunities. We serve a merciful God."

She hung her head down and groaned.

Michael patted her hand comfortingly:

"When you leave the Sub I want you to smile confidently. Can you manage that?"

"I'll have to trust my angels to help me with that one."

Martin was nervously pacing when Rachael opened the door of the Sub. He marveled when he saw her:

"She . . . she's just glowing," Martin reverently stated.

Rachael took Jarvis' hand as if he were a child and began to lead him away. "Come, Mr. Jarvis – let's go upstairs and have some tea."

Jarvis looked over his shoulder and smiled at Martin:

"She's a pistol."

Martin closed the door and addressed Michael:

"So . . . judging by the look on Rachael's face – we've got it made."

Michael beamed enthusiastically:

"We are going to hit them with everything we have. What is that word of yours? Bamboozle? We are going to bamboozle these Niyaq people."

Martin sat down next to Michael and put his feet up on the desk in a cocky gesture:

"Tell me the plan."

"Well, for starters, you were correct in your presumptions concerning the purpose of the software."

"Huh?"

"The Throne told me you figured it out. Martin – the Throne knows everything."

"Well . . . sure . . . ah . . . I would think that they would." He looked around somewhat dazed:

"I guess they mean for us to finish the project."

"They absolutely insist on it. Are you up for it?"

"Well . . . sure . . . of course." He marveled:

"I knew when I saw Rachael's expression that everything was going to work. I knew it!" He caught himself:

"Did they say anything about Rachael?"

"They told me that she will experience a period of refreshment – of peace, joy and happiness. And, after that, the Throne will have something for her to do."

"Fantastic! We serve a good God. Thank the Lord!"

"Indeed," Michael confirmed.

"I can't tell you how relieved I am. Michael – I was so worried about her. Is she to go to her sister's house?"

"Yes."

"Good. And we'll finish up here?"

"Yes. But we have to be very careful, Martin. Niyaq knows the purpose of the software; and every available resource that they have will be dedicated to getting it. We cannot count on Mr. Jarvis' people in the woods – Niyaq is among them and will seize the position."

Martin's countenanced dropped like a rock:

"Huh? Well . . . how can we leave?"

"We will not be able to leave."

Martin looked numb. Michael continued:

"The house was bugged and Niyaq has been listening in on our communications with Jarvis. But they don't know that we know that. So . . . we have the advantage."

"We do?"

"Yes. They know that we have not finished the software. So . . . they will wait until we complete the project before they make a move. Do you not understand? We are the ones in control but they believe that *they* are in control. Jarvis will give the people in the woods a signal and they will send in a helicopter for the purpose of safely flying the software to Lebeh."

"But . . . the chopper will have Niyaq in it – won't it?"

"Yes. Jarvis said that he will knock the helicopter down and then we will fight them."

"We're going to fight Niyaq?"

"Yes."

"But . . . but how can we win?"

"They will be forced to kill us; but that is much better than being taken prisoner. Do you not agree?"

Martin's expression pained.

"I did not say that it would be easy, Martin."

"But how do we get the software out?"

"That will be done by the Throne. All we have to do is finish it and be wise enough not to be captured by Niyaq."

Martin put his hand to his mouth.

"What is it?" Michael asked him.

He began in whispers as someone on his deathbed:

"It's Rachael's dream – the one that she had long ago." He looked stunned. "I finally get it." He marveled:

"Is . . . is her faith so strong that she could find such peace in the knowledge of my salvation. Is her faith so strong that she can welcome my untimely death? Where did she find such faith? Surely I shall die." He looked pathetically at Michael:

"You . . . you told all of this to Rachael . . . didn't you?"

"Yes."

Martin marveled:

"Where . . . where did she find such faith?" He stared at Michael like a zombie:

"You will die too, Michael. And Jarvis will die. But they will have no reason to kill Rachael." Fear seized him:

"They won't torture Rachael after the rest of us are gone. They will have no reason to do that. It would gain them nothing." Tears filled his eyes:

"Right?"

"I told you what the Throne relayed pertaining to your wife. You can trust that she will be all right. Now it is up to you, Jarvis, and me. Rachael will go to her sister's and will not come back. Jarvis will stay here with us."

Martin stared intensely at Michael. "You knew. You knew all along."

"Yes – I knew that your salvation was not assured."

"Well . . . is that fair. I mean . . . is this going to work? Will this do it?"

"During the coming woes many will know that their only choice is life or death. You still have choices that you can make. You could cut and run with Rachael and count on Lebeh to save you."

"That wouldn't buy me very much life – would it? And that would spell the end for Rachael."

"If that is how your faith interprets it, then from that you should base your actions," Michael advised him.

"If I left my post and died on the run, the Throne wouldn't count that as a martyr's death. It would just be a death."

"I do not make those decisions."

Martin was unraveling:

"I . . . I'll have to be careful when Rachael leaves. If they detect emotion in my voice that will tip them off."

"Yes, you must be on your guard. Spend some time with her in the Sub before she leaves."

"Yeah – that's the ticket."

"There is another matter," said Michael.

"What's that?"

"The Throne told me that you made a promise to someone. They expect you to keep that promise." He studied Martin:

"Do you understand that?"

He shook his head. "No . . . I'll have to think about that one."

Michael continued:

"The Throne has given me very exacting instructions. It is a foolproof plan. It will look like we have lost; but we shall be the winners."

"Like the saints in The Revelation," Martin said without sharing Michael's enthusiasm.

"Yes. All you have to do is follow my instructions. You must follow my instructions to the letter."

Martin sadly stared off. "OK, Michael."

Michael studied Martin's face:

"I have one more thing to tell you. This is very important."

"Go ahead."

"Have you ever awoken in a strange place . . . and you didn't recognize your surroundings?"

'Well . . . Yes."

"Then, you know how frightening that can be."

Martin nodded.

"If that happens then you must pretend that you can not remember anything . . . and . . . and that you have . . ."

"Amnesia?"

"Yes . . . amnesia. Stay where you are and wait for Zak."

"Zak?"

'Yes . . . Zak. Only *he* can help you – you must wait for *him.* This is very important. Can you remember that?"

"Yes. I'll say I can't remember and wait for Zak."

Michael nodded and smiled:

"Good. I'll send Rachael down to say goodbye."

Rachael and Martin wept together and hugged. After they composed themselves they sat for a long time holding hands. Neither seemed to know what to say. When Martin finally spoke up his voice was choked with emotion:

"It's all clear to me now. That dream . . . that dream you had long ago. In my heart I knew what it meant; but . . . I was in denial – I forced it out of my belief structure.

I *wanted* to get away from the church. Whenever I was there the dream would haunt me – convict me.

So . . . I poured myself into my work. If I didn't have God's approval, then I would seek the approval of men. That way I could prove myself – prove my worth.

So . . . I became as Citizen Kane. Your dream was my sled Rosebud – the little message from God that was worth more than all of my earthly accumulations. And, when my earthly possessions became of no consequence, I could do naught but to cling to your dream – the divine message that held the key to my future."

Tears streamed down Rachael's face as she considered her grieved husband:

"Martin . . . I . . . I asked Michael if I could stay. I'm ready to leave this cesspool of a planet. Michael is right; the Earth *is* being filled with the sea of the Lord's vomit."

"But . . . but Michael told me that you are to find happiness and serve the Lord again."

She shook her head. "I can't believe it."

"The part about serving the Lord?"

"No . . . the part about finding happiness. Plus . . . my trip to my sister's will only endanger the girls *more*."

"Yes – I thought of that. But . . . I guess Michael wants to get you out. Jarvis is going to stay."

"You will need Jarvis' strong shoulders," she pointed out.

"Yes, Rachael, I will need Jarvis' strong shoulders. I'm . . . I'm not feeling very strong. I can't honestly say that I feel up for this."

Rachael's smile was genuine:

"I know in my heart that when the time comes you *will* find the strength."

Martin wiped a tear:

"I'm weary – I just want it to end. It . . . It's just all too much for me, Raech."

"Ask God to help you rest tonight, Martin. Then you will feel stronger tomorrow."

"Yeah . . . OK." He shrugged. "It certainly won't hurt to ask Him." He gathered himself a little:

"Thanks, Raech, I'll remember to do that."

A few moments passed and Rachael spoke up:

"How does Michael plan to get the software passed Niyaq to his people?"

"He says that the Throne gave him a plan that is foolproof; but he didn't share it."

"Maybe . . . maybe he was afraid that you would tell me."

"Probably." Martin marveled:

"I wonder what it will be like to breathe air again – to be born again in the next age. I wonder what life will be like."

Her eyes sparkled:

"Do you suppose that we will be together again?"

He smiled. "Sure, why not? Maybe, if I don't totally screw this deal up, you and I can go to the head of the line of souls who are waiting to see life. Michael says this project is very important, and that the Throne is going to concentrate all of their power on it until it comes to fruition. It all has to do with gathering the elect – the chosen that will begin the new world."

"So . . . you called that one correctly – you figured it out."

"Yeah. The trouble is – now Niyaq knows it too. So . . . the powers of heaven and hell are going to collide – right here!" He stared off and slowly shook his head:

"Michael wants to put up a good fight and force Niyaq to kill us. He doesn't want to be captured."

She took her husband's hand. "I'm not up for goodbyes. Plus, I'll be calling and checking in with you – just like always."

A hint of courage showed in Martin's smile:

"That's the spirit, hon. This isn't goodbye – this is just a brief intermission."

"Can you hear the phone ring in the Sub?" Rachael asked.

"No. But Jarvis will be here."

"Yes. Or . . . you can call me."

Martin nodded:

"Be very careful what you say, Rachael – we must not let Niyaq know that we are on to them. We must have time to finish the software project."

"Michael explained all of that to me." She looked panicked in spite of trying not to:

"So . . . I'll talk to you tomorrow."

They looked at each other and the tears flowed. Martin drew her close:

"Rachael . . . did . . . did Michael tell you what to do if Niyaq gets you?"

"Yes . . . he said to tell them that we plan on getting the software out by helicopter."

"That's right," Martin began, "tell them everything you know. It doesn't matter – they know everything already. The only thing that they *don't* know is that we know that we are on to *them*.

"Michael says that I will be all right – I have to believe that."

"Yes . . . we both need to believe that," Martin agreed.

They gazed at each other one more time.

"Rachael . . . oh Rachael."

BAD BOYS BAD BOYS

9

It was 10:30 PM Sunday night. Michael and Martin had worked practically nonstop on the software since Rachael had departed the day before.

Jarvis had contacted the men in the woods and had given them instructions.

Earlier that afternoon their first disc functioned perfectly. Martin breathed a sigh of relief thinking that they had finished. But instead, Michael had Martin created disc after disc. Over and over, Martin would repeat the procedure for both creating the software and testing it. After they had a pile of three or four discs, Michael would melt them in a small toaster oven that they had brought into the Sub. Both Michael and Martin were weary.

"OK, Martin, we're going to do it one more time and then quit. We've finished the project."

Martin groaned:

"Thank God – I am *so* burned out."

"Tell me again the equipment that you need to create the disc."

Martin reiterated it again with Michael following along with his notes.

"Now, Martin . . . how do we create the disc?"

He went through the procedure flawlessly.

Michael smiled:

"And what do we need to operate the software?"

"Three things – a set of numbers, a pulse, and a birth date."

"How many pulses are there?"

"One hundred and forty-four."

"And how do you know which pulses to use? How do you order them?" Michael asked.

Martin looked disgusted:

"I've told you that ten times."

"Tell me again," Michael said patiently. He leaned back and looked at his notes again as Martin spoke:

"That's good, Martin. What is your first entry?"

"It goes pulse, numbers, birth date."

"What is another word for pulse?"

"Area."

Michael got up and stood behind Martin: "OK. Go slow so that I can watch you. The pulse is 32; the birth date is 7-9-85; and the numbers are 4, 9, 2." He watched as Martin made his entries:

"Good . . . now see if you can tune it."

Martin turned a knob first to the left, and then to the right:

"No good – it's a reject."

"Let's see if this last disc functions properly," Michael said. "How do we test to see if the disc is good?"

"I use a pulse of 12, Holly's birth date, and the numbers 11, 6, 3."

He made the entries, tuned it a bit, and the sequence came up on the screen. "There it is – that's a good one. This disc works."

Michael flopped down in his chair and clapped his hands:

"We have finished, my friend. Now . . . melt this last disc and take the Bunsen burner and destroy that equipment you bought. Melt it all beyond recognition. Then, burn these notes and all the instructions and we are finished."

It took Martin some time to destroy the equipment as he had to wait for the air system to clear the smoke. When he had finished burning the last bit of the notes, he turned to Michael:

"I really didn't believe that it would work."

"How *does* it work, Martin? I really do not understand the principles involved."

"It all has to do with frequency – harmonics. If a number of inputs perfectly harmonize, then the sequence shows up on the screen."

"I see."

Martin considered it for a moment:

Michael, where do the 'numbers' come from?"

"They come from God. They are received through the Spirit."

"Huh?"

"Actually, it is an old technique and thoroughly biblical."

"Like for instance?" Martin queried.

Michael picked up the Bible and thumbed through it for a few moments. He pointed to a passage in Judges:

"Start reading here."

7:4 And the LORD said unto Gideon, The people are yet too many; bring them down unto the water, and I will try them for thee there: and it shall be, that of whom I say unto thee, This shall go with thee, the same shall go with thee; and of whomsoever I say unto thee, This shall not go with thee, the same shall not go.
7:5 So he brought down the people unto the water: and the LORD said

unto Gideon, Every one that lappeth of the water with his tongue, as a dog lappeth, him shalt thou set by himself; likewise every one that boweth down upon his knees to drink.
7:6 And the number of them that lapped, putting their hand to their mouth, were three hundred men: but all the rest of the people bowed down upon their knees to drink water.
7:7 And the LORD said unto Gideon, By the three hundred men that lapped will I save you, and deliver the Midianites into thine hand: and let all the other people go every man unto his place.
7:8 So the people took victuals in their hand, and their trumpets: and he sent all the rest of Israel every man unto his tent, and retained those three hundred men: and the host of Midian was beneath him in the valley.

Martin nodded. "So . . . God selected the 300 – through the Spirit. In the same way the Spirit will give the numbers to those who the software will select. Those with valid numbers will be culled from among the wishful thinkers. "

"Yes."

Martin smiled. "So, Michael . . . what do we do now?"

Michael scratched his head:

"Well . . . what do you *want* to do? We have indeed finished the project."

"I'm so tired that I can't think anymore. I've had it big-time." He stared off and thought of Rachael. His eyes became wet and he turned so that Michael couldn't see.

"Why don't you go and call your wife?" Michael suggested.

He discretely wiped his eyes:

"Are you reading my mind again, Michael?"

"Well . . . that is what I would do if *I* were you."

Martin avoided Michael's eyes:

"So . . . are *you* going to call anybody?"

Michael looked melancholy:

"Oh . . . I would like this . . . I would like this very much – but it is not possible. Niyaq has my picture – but they have nothing to match it with. My people are safe . . . I will not endanger them."

Martin was taken back:

"You've never had your picture taken for an ID or a driver's license?"

"No. I have never had my picture taken. Well . . . once or twice by mistake – but those pictures were destroyed. My life was a preparation for this moment. It was prophesied."

"Prophesied? You mean in the Bible?"

"My parents received the prophecy when I was very young." Michael smiled wearily:

"That is all that you need to know, my friend. I grow weary talking – it is time for bed. Yes?"

"Yes."

"Tomorrow will be an exciting day. I need my rest; and I suggest, Martin, that you rest also."

Martin shook his head:

"I won't be able to sleep."

"Yes, you will, my friend. You *must* sleep – your head needs to be clear tomorrow – there are still a few things that you need to do."

"OK, Michael – I'll see you in the morning."

"Good night, my friend."

"You've got the disc?" Martin asked.

Michael lifted his brow. "The disc?" He looked perplexed for a moment and then caught himself:

"Oh . . . the disc . . . yes, that is all taken care of – do not worry."

Michael found Jarvis at the kitchen table re-assembling a .308 rifle. He looked tired and drawn as he meticulously inspected the parts with his rough, stubby fingers. He seemed older than his years; his countenance revealing the struggles and tribulations of his life. Martin sat down next to him:

"Will you clean a rifle for me as well, Mr. Jarvis?"

Jarvis took off his glasses, rubbed his eyes and turned to Martin:

"Yeah, I'll clean one for you. You feeling OK?"

"I wish I had never gotten involved with this. I don't want to leave my family. I don't want to call my wife and say goodbye. I'm . . . I'm just a frightened little boy."

"The first time I saw combat, I shit in my pants and hid," Jarvis dryly confessed.

"Is this your idea of a pep talk?" Martin sarcastically asked.

Jarvis considered it:

"I have killed people and not known in my heart if it was justified – not known for sure if God saw me as an avenger or as part of a greater problem. Nam was like that." He looked at Martin sympathetically:

"I know that I'm on the good side now. If you panic, if you lose it altogether, remember to call on God for help." He shrugged, put on his glasses, and turned his attention back to his rifle:

"That's my pep talk, Martin; that's the best I can do."

Martin rolled his eyes:

"Well . . . that's more than I expected. Do you have any other pre-battle advice to share?"

Jarvis viewed Martin over his glasses:

"Pray. That's what I always do."

It was all that he could do to make it upstairs to the bedroom. He slipped off his shoes, put on his pajamas, laid down, and dialed Rachael. Rachael's sister answered:

"Hello?"

"Hi. What are you guys doing up there?"

"Oh . . . hello, Martin. Well . . . we spent the day with Holly. Molly went to some kind of concert. You know Molly – she does what she wants to do."

"Yes . . . I know Molly."

"Rachael and Holly just got back – they just got back from Molly's apartment."

"Well . . . put Rachael on. Ah . . . good to hear from you, Agatha."

There was some conversation and then Martin heard his wife's voice:

"Martin?"

"Hello, Rachael."

"I've called several times. Mr. Jarvis didn't want to disturb you. Are . . . are you all right?"

"Tired. I can't remember when I was this tired."

"Well . . . a good night's sleep will fix that."

"Yes. I feel OK – I'm just whipped. So . . . tell me about your day, Rachael."

"Things have been a bit weird. There was some kind of bomb scare in town and the police searched my car when I arrived."

Martin's heart pounded:

"Did they search you?"

"Yeah . . . well . . . they had a lady cop do that."

"So . . . what else is going on?"

"I spent the day with Agatha and Holly. Holly is here – she is going to spend the night. Holly and I just got back from visiting with Molly."

"Agatha didn't go along?"

"No. Agatha and Molly don't get along – you know that."

"Yeah . . . well . . . is there anything new with Molly?"

"Molly said that two detectives came to her apartment and asked about Michael."

"Michael – the man we hired?"

"Yes. It was a bit vague; but apparently he is suspected of doing *something*. They wanted to know his last name."

"That makes absolutely no sense. I can't imagine Michael being wanted by the law. Did Molly's apartment have that funny smell?"

"Yes. Well . . . it smelled mostly like incense."

"Don't take anything Molly says too seriously," Martin advised her. "Sometimes that girl just doesn't have a clue."

"She'll grow out of it – right?"

"Whatever. Ah . . . how long are you going to stay with Agatha?"

Rachael looked around to see where Agatha was:

"Agatha is lonely. She wants me to stay a few more days."

"That's fine. I like Agatha – she's always welcomed here. Maybe you can bring her back with you."

"I'll suggest that."

They had so much to say – yet they could say nothing.

"Agatha coming might be good for you, Rachael. And . . . and I'm getting behind at work and need to catch up."

"That sounds good."

The seconds ticked away. Wasted seconds.

"Rachael?"

"Yeah?"

"Tell me more about your day."

"Oh . . . Holly found a lively Pentecostal church. It was great, mostly young people. You know – songs – praise and worship."

"That reminds me of that little place where we use to go."

"Yes. The same kind of service – very enthusiastic."

There was another awkward silence.

"It rained here this afternoon," Rachael began. "Did you have some rain?"

"Well . . ."

"It doesn't matter. Why don't you go to bed and call me in the morning?"

"OK . . . I'll give you a ring around eight," Martin told her.

"I love you."

"I love you, too."

"Goodbye."

"Goodbye, Martin."

Never before had Martin felt so totally alone. He felt empty – hollow. He thought of walking down to the guesthouse.

No. Was he such a child that he would need to lean on this young man?

There was nothing to do now except wait for tomorrow.

"Give me rest, Lord – give me rest."

"Martin?"

"Rachael . . . I can't see you. Who . . . who are you talking with."

"An angel. We've come to pay you a visit – you're sleeping."

"I am?"

"Yes."

"What's going on . . . I still can't see anything."

"The angel says that you shouldn't worry about me."

"What does the angel look like? I can't see him."

"She's behind me, Martin – I can't see her either."

"What's that I hear?"

"There's someone coming; the angel is calling for help; we've got to go."

"Rachael. Rachael? Rachael!"

Rachael was the first one up. She put on a simple white blouse and jeans. She hadn't worn the jeans for a few years and had to struggle to get them zipped. Most women her age wouldn't look good in that type of outfit – but she did.

"They will stretch a bit after I wear them," she thought.

She was in the kitchen having coffee and donuts when the doorbell rang. She looked up at the wall clock – it was 6:00 AM.

She looked through the peephole to see Molly with two tense looking men in suits behind her.

"Give me strength, dear Lord," she said to herself as she unlocked the door.

She recounted the angel's visit while she had slept, and also what Michael had told her the day before.

This was the moment of truth.

"They woke me up," Molly scowled as she pushed by. "I haven't even had my coffee."

"There is some made fresh in the kitchen."

Rachael studied her daughter's angered expression as she passed. Molly stopped short and turned to glare at the two men:

"Just leave me alone! My mother knows more about that Jew than I do."

The two men smiled as they entered the house; but their eyes didn't match their smiles.

We're from the FBI," the taller man said. "We just need to ask you some questions."

The taller man looked and talked like an American – he spoke perfect English and seemed articulate and polished. The shorter man looked Arabic.

"I'll need to see some IDs."

"Yes ma'am," the taller man said as he and his partner efficiently flashed them. He kept his phony smile and motioned to the darker looking man who disappeared after Molly.

Rachael took a deep breath:

"So?"

"We just need to ask you some questions," he reiterated. "I understand from Molly that your sister and daughter are here. We need to talk with them as well."

"They're sleeping," Rachael protested.

The man pretended to be sympathetic:

"I'm sorry, Mrs. McDonald; but this is very important – it can't wait."

She heard the other man speaking with Molly in the kitchen. "OK. I'll get them out of bed."

Rachael's first thought was to use the cell phone in her bedroom – but something warned her against that.

She gently woke up Holly and Agatha – simply saying that they needed to come down to the living room.

They met the American at the head of the stairs:

"I'm so sorry for this inconvenience," he said as he stepped aside.

At the bottom of the stairs they saw the other man standing over Molly. She looked dazed and was sitting on the floor. Her mouth was bleeding.

"What in heaven's name!" Agatha cried as she ran to comfort Molly.

"Get away from her!" the American bellowed.

The charade was over.

When they turned around, the American was holding a silenced pistol. He playfully wiggled his eyebrows and smiled. "It doesn't make much noise."

A bullet went through the mirror next to Holly. He was delighted with himself and laughed – if you could call it that. "See – very little noise."

The man sat down – still clutching the pistol.

He studied his captives; but his eyes seem to linger on Holly:

Holly was tall, long legged, and much more attractive than her sister with thick black hair, fine features, and perfect white skin that contrasted her dark eyes.

When the man slowly looked her up and down her expression was likened to a sacrificial virgin. Rachael felt sick when her precious Holly instinctively gathered the front of her thin summer robe as she looked at her pleadingly for help – her eyes wide with terror.

Indeed – this was Martin's nightmare come true. And he had been proven right – death would have been better. Rachael could have brought *everybody* a gun. Perhaps she could have used the cell phone. She could have at least insisted that Holly put on some clothes. Now it was too late to do *anything*.

"We don't have much time," the man with the pistol said.

He then looked down at Molly and motioned to the other man.

The shorter man grabbed Molly by the hair and pulled her screeching to her feet in one quick motion. With his left hand he held her head back as his right hand came across her face. I snapping noise was heard and then the man kneed her groin and expertly jabbed her in the kidney as she slumped over. She lay gasping in the fetal position – blood oozed from her nose and began to form a thick, dark, puddle.

Agatha began shrieking and the man took careful aim and put a bullet in her forehead. Her head jolted backwards and she collapsed wide-eyed in a heap like a stringed puppet.

Holly slumped to the floor – still clutching the top of her robe. Here eyes were fixed, her breathing short and shallow. She appeared to be in shock.

Rachael felt the coffee and donuts come up in her throat. She fell to her knees and vomited.

The American casually looked on – as if taking delight in her distress.

When she was finished she leaned up against the wall and attempted to catch her breath:

"You . . . you don't have to do this. I will tell you . . . I will tell you everything I know."

The man leered at her:

"Yes – I *know* you will." He motioned:

"Here – sit here next to me."

She wiped her chin with a shaky hand, smeared it on her jeans, and feebly rose to her feet.

She had to step over her sister whose hideous expression revealed the horror of her death.

When she sat down next to the man she caught Molly's eye. She seemed to be aware of what was happening, but laid very still – her eyes twitching, trance-like, grotesque.

"So," the man began in a casual, offhand fashion, "let's start with the envelope; the yellow one that the FBI man brought:"

He scratched his chin and looked up at the ceiling. "Let's see . . . I'm trying to remember his name."

Rachael stared down at the floor – still trying to catch her breath:

"Jarvis."

He nodded. "Yes, that's it – Jarvis." He scratched his chin and made the same expression – as if playing a game:

"And what was in the envelope?"

"Instructions . . . instructions about how to create some kind of software. I . . . I really don't know how it works – they hadn't gotten it to work when I left to come up here. But . . . but I believe it is to be used to find the chosen of Israel."

"When did you last talk to your husband?"

"He called me last night."

"Did you ask him if the software was finished?"

She kept her eyes to the floor:

"We didn't talk about the software?"

"I want straight answers. Hope for your daughter's sake that I get them . . . her life depends on it."

He leveled the pistol at Molly – her eyes popped open and she began to squirm:

"Mother," Molly whimpered, "please . . . tell them . . ."

"Mrs. McDonald, when your husband called last night, did you ask him if the software was finished?"

Rachael shook her head. Molly had closed her eyes again and was shaking with fear.

Holly's expression hadn't changed. She stared off and didn't blink. She had nothing on under her robe and was coiled up with her knees under her chin – a position that left nothing to the imagination. What could save her now?

Her interrogator gave the other man a knowing look and then turned back to Rachael:

"Tell me, Mrs. McDonald – why *didn't* you ask him if the software was working?"

"I was afraid that your people would be listening."

He lifted his brow curiously:

"*My* people? Who are *my* people, Mrs. McDonald?"

"Niyaq."

"I will call," the other man said with a heavy accent.

The American looking man held up his hand:

"No . . . wait – we need to learn more."

The darker man ignored him and began a conversation on his cell phone in Arabic. When he finish, he cut the phone off but kept it ready.

"I told you not to call," the American sneered.

The Arab's eyes burned with rage:

"You want to learn more? Learn more! My job is to call – to keep control posted. You do your job and I will do mine!"

The other man clenched his teeth and turned back to Rachael:

"How long has your husband known that we knew about the software project?"

"Since Saturday."

"How did he find out?"

"I had a dream and . . ."

"You lying bitch!" He pointed the pistol at Molly. "Tell me the truth!"

"You waste time – find out their plan – she will tell you!" the Arab screamed.

Rachael helplessly looked on as Molly began to crawl towards Holly. By this time her nose was badly swollen and her blonde hair where she laid was a thick red mat – creating a horrific, macabre image.

The young girl crawled on her all fours, slipping and sliding in the syrupy blood. Her fingernails could be heard scratching at the hardwood floor as she made this hopeless, frantic, desperate, attempt to find refuge. As she moaned and gasped for breath, thick particles flew from her mouth.

Rachael lunged at the gunman but was hopelessly overpowered. She felt something impact her head and fell unconscious to the floor. The man then spun around and fired a single shot into the side of Molly's head – killing her instantly.

"Wake the bitch up and let's finish this," the shooter told his partner.

The Arab was numbed. "How do you plan to get the truth now?"

"We've got the other brat," he told the Arab.

The American looked down at Rachael – his eyes burning with hate:

"Oh . . . I'll get her to talk. You do your job and I'll do mine."

"The girl will not respond. I have seen this before," the Arab told him.

"Won't respond? Shit, the little bitch is playing possum. Here . . . watch this."

He bent down, stared into Holly's eyes and put a cigarette lighter to her arm. He held it for a long time – the color changed and the skin began to pop but Holly didn't blink.

The Arab slowly shook his head. "I have seen this before – she may never come back."

The other man shrugged it off. "So . . . we threaten to kill her – big deal – she's still alive."

The Arab started another phone call in Arabic.

The tall man pointed venomously:

"You talk on the phone. I'm getting some water to wake the bitch up."

He returned with a pot filled with ice water. By now his partner was shouting into the phone – still in Arabic.

The American knelt down next to Rachael who was sprawled on her back. Her ear was split from the pistol blow and thin red lines ran down her neck. He looked over to Holly and his eyes took in an image of erotic, pornographic lure. His attention averted back to Rachael:

He cupped her breasts and then squeezed – studying her face for a reaction. He squeezed a little harder and she made a faint groan. He placed the pot of ice water next to Rachael's head, tore open her blouse and pulled up her bra. He began laughing and playfully jiggled her breasts:

"Wake up, princess – it's party time!"

He yanked at her belt and began to pull at her jeans when he felt a pistol touch the back of his head. He instantly froze:

"What are you doing?"

The Arab put a bullet in that back of the American's head and he collapsed on Rachael.

As Rachael awoke she felt something warm in her eyes, and the weight of a man on top of her. *I'm being raped!*

She pulled at the man's hair but it was slippery with blood.

The Arab pulled the man off Rachael and stepped back – still holding the pistol in his hand.

Rachael blinked a few times, wiped her eyes, and crawled toward Molly.

Molly's face was unrecognizable – a large portion of her forehead had been blown away.

Hot bile came up from Rachael's throat – she coughed, her body shook.

She made her way to Holly, gently adjusted her robe, and laid down next to her. When she spoke her voice was high pitched . . . pathetic:

"Holly . . . honey?"

The Arab shouldered his pistol and stood over Rachael.

Rachael looked up at the man.

"Come . . . get up!" The Arab ordered as he pulled her to her feet.

She placed her hand to her injured ear and looked down at her blouse and her undone jeans: "I . . . I've been raped. I've been cut."

She carefully ran her hands over herself – looking for an injury. She then held up her bloody hands and looked numbly up at the Arab.

"No. That is not your blood," he told her.

Dazed and confused, she noticed that her pants were undone.

Rachael looked ghoulish as her head slowly turned. She pointed at the dead American.

"No. You have not been defiled," the Arab told her.

"But . . ."

"I tell you no – as Allah is my witness."

She un-modestly rubbed her hands over her breasts that were covered with the American's blood. "But . . ."

"I shot the American. He was going to defile you."

"Was . . . was he *in* me?"

"No," the Arab said. "You must stop whining. Nothing more will happen to you or your daughter if you tell me the truth."

"Truth?"

"Allah will let you live – you and your daughter – but you must tell me what you know – and tell me fast. You can clean yourself – *after* we talk."

Rachael looked around dazed but made no effort to cover herself:

"But . . . but how will you know if I am telling you the *truth*?" Rachael whimpered

"Allah . . . he will reveal this to me," the Arab said. "It was he who spared your lives." He nervously glanced at his watch:

"The software – they will put it on a disc?"

She nodded.

"And then?" He grew impatient:

"Quick – you must tell!"

Rachael pointed:

"My purse – bring me my purse."

The man jumped up and retrieved it. He dumped out the contents in front of her. She picked up the beacon phone:

"We talk to Jarvis with this. It is also a beacon – Lebeh knows where I am." She pointed:

"See? The beacon is on. When the software is done, they will call with this."

"You know this – this is how it will happen?"

"Yes – I think so. There is also a communicator inside the quiet room. I . . . I think it is on a different frequency. Maybe they will call with that."

"Perhaps they will give a signal in another way? Maybe they didn't want you to know the whole plan?"

"I don't know." She looked around the room helplessly. Her naked breasts were shiny with smeared blood:

"I should be crying – why aren't I crying?"

"What happens after they call?"

"Ah . . . a helicopter will come."

The man stood to his feet and paced about as he spoke on the phone. He then sat down and looked over at Rachael:

"We will give it a few hours. If nothing happens then you and your daughter will have to come with me."

"But . . . you said . . ."

"Allah will keep his promise."

She tried to think. "But . . . Lebeh . . ."

"They will not come for you. The men Jarvis sent to help you are dead – all of them are dead."

"Oh God," she moaned as she glanced around at the carnage.

She knelt down next to Holly and looked over her shoulder at the Arab:

"Do you know what eye drops look like?"

"Yes. We use them – very much in the desert."

She pointed. "There – on the floor – bring them to me.

Holly doesn't blink. I need to get these drops into her eyes and get them closed."

She looked at the bottle:

"Yes, these are for dry eyes."

She put a few drops in each eye and tried to close them. "Darn it!"

"Lift her lids up and squirt some underneath," the man suggested.

"Ah, there we go – good idea. Please – pick her up and put her on the couch."

They got her on the couch but couldn't straiten her legs.

Rachael let out a long sigh and covered Holly up with an afghan that lay on the end of the couch. "I guess we'll have to leave her that way."

Something occurred to Rachael:

"My husband is going to call at eight. What do I do?"

"What do you *want* to do?"

Rachael was panicked:

"I want to talk to him – but if I do he will know I'm in trouble – I don't want to worry him."

He shrugged. "Then *don't* talk to him."

"But . . . I *want* to talk to him," she objected.

The Arab looked at Rachael with disgust:

"Talk to him, don't talk to him – it does not matter. He will die; his Jew friend will die; Jarvis will die. It will not change if you talk to him. It will not change if you don't."

Rachael looked pleadingly at the man. "I don't want to frighten him – but if I *don't* answer the phone he will be frightened *anyway*.

Hey . . . why do you keep going over to the window? Do you have men outside?"

"Of course."

"What . . . what will I do when Marty calls? I know he'll be upset if I don't answer the phone."

Something occurred to the Arab:

"Yes, you are right. We would like to have the disc – it would be good if he finished it."

"So you can find and kill the chosen of Israel," she concluded.

"Yes."

The hardwood floor was very uncomfortable. She glanced at the other couch. No – she would stay next to Holly. The blood on her breast was starting to dry:

"I'm itching . . . and . . . and that smell."

"That is the smell of battle – you will never forget it."

But she *wanted* to forget it.

"What do I do when my husband calls? Tell me what to do."

He looked at his watch. "I need to listen."

Rachael pointed. "Bring me that phone; and then get the portable phone . . . in the kitchen."

She looked down at her breasts:

"I'm going to put on some clothes."

She heard him behind her as she proceeded to Agatha's bedroom. The Arab looked out the window as she scrounged for something to wear. She put on a tee shirt and a loose black skirt, opened Agatha's sock drawer and saw a small handgun:

Rachael froze.

She looked over her shoulder and then back in the drawer. With one eye on the Arab she picked up the gun. It was very light – not much heavier than a wallet. As she pretended to look through the drawer, she tilted the revolver to see if it was loaded. It was – but she had no pocket – no place to stash it.

"Come!" the Arab commanded.

She shut the drawer and turned:

"Let's get some sheets and cover up Molly and Agatha."

"No."

"No?"

"If you want to live you will do as I say." He rudely nudged her towards the door. "Go!"

Rachael followed him downstairs and sat on the floor next to Holly.

After a few moments she pointed to the man who had shot Molly and Agatha:

"He . . . he wasn't a Moslem?"

"He is an infidel that we paid – we paid him much. The Jews . . . the Christians . . . perhaps they would offer him more some day. He got us into places that we needed to go." He sneered and shook his head:

"He could never be a Moslem."

A few minutes passed.

Rachael felt the man's eyes.

"The Christians and the Jews with their slutty women," the Arab grumbled. "Even *now* you tease me."

Rachael looked over and saw the man scowling and looking at her breasts. Her nipples were pronounced through her tee shirt.

"I'll put on a jacket."

Before the man could speak, she bounded up the stairs, retrieved the small revolver from the drawer and dropped it into the inside pocket of a blue jacket. She heard the man behind her and turned around:

"So . . . I'll put this on," she said as she reached in the closet for the jacket. "I'll even button it for you."

10 IT HITS THE FAN

"Martin!"

"Who . . . who's that? Are you an angel? Is Rachael with you? I can't see."

"Why don't you try opening your eyes?"

Martin's eyes blinked opened:

"Jarvis? Gosh . . . what time is it?"

"It's 7:30."

"I slept like a log. I had the best sleep."

Martin smiled up at Jarvis who gave him a cup of coffee. He took a sip and sat up.

Jarvis had a 30 caliber rifle on a shoulder sling – he walked around the room unscrewing light bulbs. He took something out of the socket of the lamp next the bed, opened the window slightly, and tossed it out:

"That was one of Eddie Boy's bugs." He grinned:

"What I did was put a little duck tape on em and stick em to the speakers downstairs. I've got a Christian radio station playing."

Martin laughed. "That's very thoughtful of you, Jarvis."

"Yeah . . . I thought that would be the very *least* that I could do for my little towel-headed buddies. If you see a light bulb that hasn't been unscrewed – unscrew it and check for one of these little babies. You can sprinkle them anywhere; but they will lose their charge if the light isn't turned on from time to time."

"Well . . . do you think you got em all?"

"There's no way to know for sure.

The phone is still on; they haven't cut that yet – and we've got the beacon phone and a cell phone."

"Do you think we should try to call out for help?"

"Well . . . maybe we can and maybe not. But if we got through we would seal our fates. They could easily take us out before any help arrived."

Martin sipped his coffee:

"So . . . what's your thinking?"

"Wait and see what Michael has to say." He motioned towards the rifle:

"What we're going to do is have a crash combat course. Come on – get your buns out of bed."

Martin got up and Jarvis handed him the 30 caliber:

"What kind of pajamas are those?" Jarvis asked.

"They're silk."

"Well . . . maybe you should just wear those – the towels will think you're some kind of crazed fruitcake."

"Well . . . if I had known you were going to visit my boudoir, I would have donned something more gung-ho."

Jarvis laughed. "Oh . . . give me some shit, McDonald; that's probably the manliest outfit you've got."

Martin's eyes narrowed suspiciously:

"You're having a good time – aren't you, Jarvis? I mean . . . you're right in your element."

Jarvis motioned to the backpack on the floor. "Load a 20, put her in battery."

Jarvis watched him. "Put it in full auto. OK . . . take the clip out, eject your round. Now, put in a drum, put her in battery."

"God, this drum weighs a ton," Martin complained.

Jarvis had to show him how to fix the drum:

"OK, now you do it, McDonald."

Martin completed the task and looked up at Jarvis:

"What kind of gun is this?"

"Shit, McDonald – you don't know what that is? It's a good old G.I. Joe M-14. The drums are a new innovation – but the clip is standard military. Its got a scope and heavier barrel; but other than that it is just a good old M-14. In my mind there has never been a better infantry rifle. I'm old fashioned – I still like the idea of knocking the hell out of someone with one shot at 300 yards."

"What kind of rifles do the men outside have?"

"M-16s, and some silenced bolt-action sniper rifles."

"Well . . . that gives us the edge on them."

Jarvis looked disgusted and shook his head. "Don't be an idiot, McDonald; I was the one who equipped those men – they could take on a small army." He took the rifle from him:

"Look, McDonald – until you get the hang of this rifle you need to leave it on semi-auto. You don't have the *time* to get the hang of it . . ."

"So . . . I'll leave it on semi-auto."

"Good – I'll make a soldier out of you yet – but ya gotta get out of those freaking PJs . . . Christ!

OK . . . if someone is close on you remember that a head shot is better. All of these 30 caliber rounds are armor piercing. Use the clips for anti-personnel and save the drums for the choppers – or if the shit *really* hits the fan. If you *do* select full-auto, make your bursts very short or you will shoot over their heads – got it?"

"Because of the recoil?"

"Yeah. They had the same trouble with the BARs." He took the rifle from Martin, still fitted with the drum magazine:

"This is how we deal with the choppers. Aim on the right side of the chopper. Brace the top of the barrel against the bottom of the window about here. Got it?"

"Yeah . . . now what?"

"Make sure you are on full auto. Aim starting on the right end of the chopper – maybe just a bit low. When you touch her off she will drift left – the window brace will keep her level. Let her rake across the chopper from right to left."

"How many shots do I fire?"

"Shit . . . if you're on target you want to empty the drum. I would guess they will come in civilian choppers. These bullets should go though both sides and put a serious hurt on everything in-between.

Ideally, you want to hit the chopper before it lands – the higher the better. After you shoot move to another window – better yet, to another room. These stone walls should stop anything but the big stuff."

"Like 50s?"

"50s will go though this house. 50s will go through any house."

"Well . . . what kind of heavy stuff do the men in the woods have?"

"Shoulder rockets, a big flame thrower, and 2 M-134s. They're not a mobile commando force; they're a fixed position defense force. And they are dug in."

"M-134s . . . they're 50s."

"Thirty caliber."

"Well hell, we got thirties."

"They have Gatling, six barrel mini-guns modified for field service. They only weigh 35 pounds but are devastating. The ones out there are modified to slow the firing rate down to 500 rounds a minute -- but they can shoot as fast as 4000 per minute if they choose to do so. So . . . figure out for yourself what two of those guns can do. And they got a mountain of ammo.

Listen, McDonald, if they let loose with those mini guns – drop to the floor and cover your eyes. If you don't you will be blinded by flying particles."

Martin gestured wildly:

"You expect me to just lay there and get shot?"

"If you don't get shot and they stop firing you will at least have your vision. If they let loose with those mini-guns at that range they'll blow right though these walls. I guess if they get lazy they could just launch high explosives in on us and level the place with one big bang."

"They won't do that."

"Huh?"

"The disc, Jarvis – they want the disc."

He nodded. "That's right – they might try to storm the house. They might be afraid to blow us up or use rockets."

"So . . . how many men are in the woods?"

"I put eight men out there."

"Jarvis, do you suppose that they are *all* Niyaq."

Jarvis considered it:

"Well . . . let's just assume that they are. It takes two men to run one of the minis." Jarvis rubbed his chin:

"If we get into a fire fight they won't have enough men to cover all the windows. So . . . you get some broom handles and put some shirts on em. Stick em up in a window and draw their fire, then move to another window and do the same thing. Just don't get your buns shot off. I'll be downstairs and try to shoot at anything that fires at us or comes out of the woods."

Martin held up his finger:

"Ah . . . wait a minute, Jarvis – I thought you said that those minis could go through these walls."

"Maybe they won't use the minis because of the disc?" Jarvis proposed.

They stared at each other and finally Jarvis made a face:

"You got a better idea, Pajama Boy?"

"Gosh no, Jarvis – what could be a better plan than me giving away my position so that 8000 rounds a minute can vaporize my ass so that you can have the opportunity to fire a few shots. Shit . . . why should I complain about that?"

"Oh . . . everything has got to be just perfect with you, McDonald." Jarvis set his jaw:

"The trouble is that we really don't know *what* is going on out there. All I know is what Wilcox told me yesterday – and he acted strange."

"Strange how?"

"I was in Nam with Wilcox. I know him very well; and I could sense something odd in his mannerisms."

"So . . . Wilcox is Hashmootz?"

"The traitor? Yeah . . . my gut tells me that he is."

"You figure that Niyaq will come in a chopper to pick up the software?" Martin asked him.

"I'm hoping that they do." He grimaced. "The trouble is, we don't know what is going on with your wife."

McDonald swallowed hard:

"I . . . I talked with her late last night and she was OK. God, Jarvis – I'm worried sick about her. Michael said that she was going to be OK . . . but . . ."

Jarvis looked pained. "I shouldn't have mentioned it, McDonald."

"She was searched by the cops when she went to see her sister. They said it had to do with a bomb scare."

"You don't buy that shit do you?"

"No . . . of course I don't; but the point is that Niyaq knows that she doesn't have the disc. They thoroughly searched her person and the car."

"So . . . what's your thinking?" Jarvis asked.

"Maybe they'll still send a chopper in to get the disc and we can clobber it with the drums. Maybe they don't know that we're on to them."

Jarvis took a deep breath and groaned:

"Maybe I shouldn't have fooled with those bugs that Ed planted. That might have tipped em off that we're on to them."

Martin sighed. "I'm not sure it really matters anymore. I'm just worried about Rachael and the girls. The best that we can hope for is to keep Michael out of Niyaq's claws. I suppose if we just wanted to draw attention to the house we could open fire on one of the neighbor's houses – that would bring the cops."

"We'll just have to wait and see what they do," Jarvis concluded. He reached into his backpack and pulled out a radio.

"What are ya doing, Jarvis?"

"I'm pretending that the men outside are friendlies:"

"Jarvis to Dovetail."

"This is Dovetail."

"Is that you, Wilcox?"

"Affirmative."

"What's going on?"

"Nothing – we've seen nothing. The men have been up all night. They're locked, cocked, jacked up on Methedrine and ready to rumble. What's on the inside?"

"We're almost there – not much longer. How far away are the birds?"

"Ten minutes max."

"Stay handy – over and out." He looked over at McDonald:

"Christ . . . wouldn't I love to get my hands on Wilcox."

With that, Jarvis walked over to the window, sat down on the floor and stared out.

"What are you looking at?"

"Michael. He's out there under that big tree."

Martin sat next to Jarvis. "The poor little guy."

"Humph . . . poor little guy? He's the only one that really knows what's going on – he's got one foot in this world and one foot in the next."

McDonald watched a tear streak down Jarvis' face:

"Jarvis? What is it, Jarvis?"

Jarvis wiped the tear:

"McDonald . . . ah . . . I've never been big on saying I'm sorry . . . but . . . I . . ."

"What . . . what is it, Jarvis?"

"What did Michael tell you about me?"

"Tell me? As far as what?"

"Did Michael tell you how I fouled up this whole deal?"

Martin considered it for a moment:

"Well . . . he mentioned that some things didn't go the way that he wanted – but he said that you meant well."

"He was being kind," Jarvis said as he looked away.

"So . . . what are you trying to say, Jarvis?"

He began:

"Michael contacted me because he knew that I was with Lebeh; and he knew that Lebeh had a lot of people in the Bureau."

"Go on."

"Well . . . Michael knew that you were on the list to be contacted for the Phase Three Project; and he wanted me to make sure that you weren't recruited. He knew that if you were recruited, then Niyaq would most likely be on your heels. Well . . . he didn't want that to happen.

Michael wanted to contact you *himself* to help him with the software project. He didn't want Lebeh *or* the Bureau in on it *at all*."

"And?"

"Well . . . Lebeh had just acquired that disc from the professor and hijacked the Sub from the Bureau. So . . . I convinced Lebeh to put me in a position to fudge the Phase Three Deal with you, with the understanding that I would try to recruit you to look at the disc for Lebeh and supply a place to test the Sub. I told Lebeh that I had a man proficient in biblical Hebrew to help you analyze the disc.

They bought into that idea and settled on my request for 150 K in cash. They didn't know who would help you and didn't ask. Lebeh respects peoples' privacy for the most part."

Martin was puzzled:

"I'm not following this at all, Jarvis – I thought you said that Michael didn't want to get involved with Lebeh."

Jarvis looked pained:

"My deal with Michael was that I wouldn't recruit you for *anybody*. The idea was to use Lebeh to put me in a position to fudge the Phase Three deal. The plan was that I would simply tell Lebeh that you weren't interested. That would have been no big deal for them – they already had a number of people analyzing the disc and they would have just tested the Sub somewhere else."

Jarvis searched McDonald's face:

"See? Then, there would be no eyes on you; and Michael could have contacted you on his own."

"But . . . you got shit-faced and got your signals crossed."

"Is that what Michael told you?" Jarvis asked.

"Well . . . something like that." Martin squinted at Jarvis:

"Where are you going with all of this?"

Jarvis took a deep breath and began:

"One of the things that the Bureau found out about you is that your folks pulled a few strings to get you out of serving in Nam."

"Yeah . . . I got a low draft number when they did away with my 2S deferment."

"Well . . . that didn't set very well with me. So . . . in my mind you were a vain, draft-dodging alcoholic with an agoraphobic wife who was hooked on prescription drugs – that was how I was briefed.

When we went out back of your house that day, I concluded that this would be a perfect place to lay a trap for Niyaq – thick woods with no footpaths.

Niyaq pinpointed the location of every one of the Subs; and there was no reason to assume that they wouldn't be on to Lebeh's hijacking.

So . . . I let you think that you were being hired by the Bureau.

I hand-picked the men and they set up motion detectors and cameras before the Sub was brought in. Because of my insistence, the main objective was not the disc – but to use your house as Niyaq bait."

McDonald's jaw hung open:

"You sold my family down the river just to catch a few thugs."

"Yeah . . . that's what I did.

My plan was to talk Michael out of working with you. How was I supposed to know that you were the only one on the planet that he wanted!"

"So . . . Michael came to work with me anyway – even after he found out the risks involved."

Jarvis threw up his hands:

"I couldn't talk him out of it. I tried. Christ, how I tried!

In the Bureau, the guy next to me might have classified information that I didn't have. And, just the same, I might have info that he was not aware of. So . . . it's a liar's game. And . . . it was much the same way in the military. I guess that is why Lebeh wanted me. I was their Dirty Harry."

"So . . . you played the same old game – business as usual, rob Peter to pay Paul."

"Yeah . . . that's about it. I did manage to funnel the 150 grand from Lebeh to Michael for the continuation of your software project."

Martin marveled and looked out at Michael:

"So . . . you screw things up; and Michael sits under his tree, prays and tries to put things back together."

"Yeah. But – if I knew then what I know now about Michael – I would have done it differently."

Martin's brow lifted. "How so?"

"Well . . . I would have just done as I was told and not taken so much of my own initiative."

"Humph. Well, I'm afraid that your spiritual revelation has come a bit late."

"You surprise me, McDonald."

"How's that?"

"Well . . . I didn't think you would take this so easily."

Martin considered it for a few moments and casually shrugged:

"Michael was right. You meant well. You're a soldier and this is war. There has always been a need for good soldiers."

Jarvis was shocked. "Christ, McDonald – you're just making me feel worse. Do you have to be so damned agreeable?"

"I'm ready to die, Jarvis. There's a lot that you don't understand about me.

Right now all I'm worried about is my family. Michael said that Rachael will be OK. I'm trying to believe that – but it's hard." He turned to Jarvis and tried to smile:

"Your apology is accepted." He gave him a playful nudge. "Come on – let's talk about something else."

"Did Michael tell you how he was going to get the software past Niyaq?" Jarvis asked.

"No, did he tell you?"

Jarvis shook his head:

"He just said that the Throne had taken care of it. I don't know . . . I got the impression that it was a done deal. All Michael is worried about is being captured by Niyaq."

"That's my take," McDonald agreed. "Well, we should be able to keep *that* from happening."

They looked out at Michael

"Do you suppose that Niyaq has Michael in their sights?" McDonald asked.

"I would suppose that Niyaq is still pretending to be Lebeh."

McDonald made a sour face:

"Are . . . are they doing it for money?"

"What else?

Lebeh pretends to biblically oriented; and I'm sure there are a lot of good people in the organization. But in the strong arm end of things there is often a mercenary spirit. I thought I could find eight people in the organization that I could trust – but I was mistaken."

They looked out the window.

"I'd better go out and get Michael," Jarvis volunteered.

"No. I'm the one that needs to go. You're better with guns – you need to stay and cover me."

Jarvis laughed. "Cover you? You need F-16s loaded with napalm to cover you. Christ – what a joke!"

Martin sat down on the end of the bed and put on some bedroom slippers. "You like em? They're mink."

"Yeah – they're fine. And that slight shade of red will go well with your scattered remains. Good God, McDonald – you're not going out like that!"

"The idea is to look as unthreatening as possible."

Jarvis cracked up again. "Good thinking. Plus, it's hard to hit something when you're laughing."

"Yeah . . . that's a good point," he said as he considered himself in the mirror.

"What about the detonation device?" Jarvis asked.

"It's a little thing – I'll put it in my underwear."

"Are you sure it will stay there?"

"My undees are pretty tight. I'll change when I get back."

Martin exited from the back patio and casually made his way towards Michael. The statue that Jarvis had destroyed was eighty yards from the patio, and the woods perhaps forty yards past that. *That would make it about 120 yards from the woods to the house – a long way to run in the open.*

It was perfectly quiet and he saw no movement from the woods:

"Hello, Michael."

Michael looked up and smiled.

"Um . . . would you like some breakfast?" Martin asked. "Are you hungry?"

On the way inside Martin heard chopper blades. He looked up and saw a civilian helicopter with three large windows on the each side – large enough to make ample gun ports. The craft was flying low but the tinted glass made it impossible to see the occupants.

Martin and Michael stopped just short of the house and looked up to see the chopper hovering overhead. A voice bellowed from above them:

"You dumb shits! Get inside and get down!"

Martin hustled Michael inside, pushed him to the floor and carefully peeked up at the chopper.

Jarvis concentrated his fire at the pilot; and then raked down the side of the chopper. The chopper leaned and began to lose altitude – disappearing over the treetops. There was no loud crash, but the blades could be heard thrashing in the woods. Thick black smoke belched up against a clear blue sky as small arms fire chattered from the woods.

It had begun.

Jarvis crawled up dragging his backpack filled with ammo. He leaned up against the wall next to Martin and smiled – affectionately patting his rifle:

"Now . . . do you understand why I like this old girl?"

Martin nodded. "Yeah – and the drum is a good feature."

"That's right. I would have had to load four clips. Shit, they might have gotten away."

"The gunfire from the woods has stopped. You . . . you don't suppose that our guys got the best of them – do you?"

"I doubt it – they would have been taken by surprise – five men can take twenty in that kind of situation."

Jarvis' attention turned to Michael. "Come over here with us – and stay down."

Michael got situated and turned to Martin:

"I thought you said 'breakfast.' Did I misunderstand you?"

"Yeah . . . well . . . I didn't know that quick-draw Jarvis was going to start a war."

"I figured that was the only clear shot I was going to get – so I took it."

"Ya did good, Jarvis. So . . . what now? Do you want me and Michael to do the shirt thing and you watch the woods?"

He shook his head. "Find a phone, dial 911, give your address and tell them we are being attacked by Al Qaeda – tell them to call in the military. If the phone is dead use a cell phone, and try the beacon phone as well. Get your gear from behind the couch. And stay down!"

"Mr. Jarvis?"

"Yes, Michael."

"Why do they not shoot at us?"

"Well . . . I'm not sure – maybe they're waiting for reinforcements. I think I surprised them when I downed that chopper."

"That helicopter had Niyaq men in it?" Michael asked.

Jarvis looked away.

"Mr. Jarvis?"

"Well . . . it had to be, Michael – there's no airport around here. I mean . . . what business does anyone have hovering 200 feet above this house. They had to be Niyaq."

Martin crawled up with his gear and a cell phone in his hand:

"No phone, no power." Martin looked disgusted as he glanced over to the sound system:

"Good idea with Eddy's bugs – now they can hear every freaking word that we say."

"Oh . . . everything has to be perfect with you, McDonald," Jarvis blurted. "Why don't you quit whining."

"If you're worried about breakfast – I usually just have cereal," Michael informed them. "I really don't care about a hot breakfast."

"Gee, Michael . . . that's good of you to relieve us of that burden," Jarvis said as he looked over to Martin:

"Can you tell when he's kidding?"

Martin cut his eyes quickly to Michael and then dialed 911 on his cell phone. He shook his head:

"Nothing but static." He tried the beacon phone and shook his head:

"Static – nothing but static."

Jarvis moaned:

"OK . . . put the beacon signal on and forget about it."

Martin looked pleadingly at Jarvis:

"Why isn't anything happening? The sky is filled with black smoke that you can see for twenty miles. And all this gun fire." He marveled:

"When my alarm goes off a squad car is here in five minutes max. We should be hearing sirens by now. Talk to me, Jarvis – what gives?"

Jarvis was preoccupied:

"Give me that lamp next to you."

He moved the shade part of the lamp in front of the window and there was a hail of bullets.

Martin was dumbstruck. "But . . . they don't know where we are . . ."

"Da-ah? That's the whole point, Sherlock. They got every window zeroed."

"So . . . what do we do?" Martin asked.

"You've got the gadget that blows the Sub?"

"Yeah."

"We blow the Sub," Jarvis suggested. "The Sub is in the back of the house. When we blow it the back of the house will catch fire. That will mean we will have a smaller perimeter to guard. Plus, the smoke will give us some cover."

Martin pulled the device from his pocket.

"Wait!" Jarvis exclaimed.

"Huh?"

"Ah . . . I think we need to move. Maybe to the foyer or the kitchen."

"Why?"

Jarvis looked sheepish. "Well . . . I wasn't planning on being here when the Sub blew. Ah . . . I might have put too much plastic down there."

Martin's mouth hung open and he stared at Jarvis. "Spell it out, Jarvis."

"Well . . . I got to thinking that maybe when the Sub was detonated that the disc might be in another part of the house."

Martin looked over at Michael. "The Colonel got to thinking. It layman's terms, this means that we're screwed to the max." Martin closed his eyes and slowly shook his head:

"How much plastic did you put down there?"

"About a thousand pounds – the cabinet against the wall is solid with it."

"I think that we should move to the kitchen," Michael suggested. "There are no windows there – I can get some cereal." He looked at Martin:

"You have cereal?"

"Frosted Mini Wheats."

"Fruit?"

"Yeah – I think there are some raspberries in there."

Jarvis and McDonald watched as Michael crawled toward the kitchen.

"Do you mind if I eat these blueberries?" he yelled from the kitchen.

"They're wild huckleberries; but my wife is saving them to make a pie."

"But . . . I have never had these huckleberries. Could I try just a few of them?"

Jarvis sighed. "Is he kidding – or does he just go retard on us?" He marveled:

"I can't figure it."

Martin yelled back. "Go ahead and eat the huckleberries."

Jarvis shrugged. "I wouldn't mind some raspberries."

"You're not going to hog the raspberries, Jarvis. I'm going to put them on my cereal – you can have what's left."

They found Michael on the floor in front of the sink:

"Look – huckleberries, cream and brown sugar."

After Martin had fixed his cereal he gave the leftover raspberries to Jarvis.

"Are you sure that you can afford it, McDonald?" Jarvis complained.

"Times are tough."

"Maybe you should hock your mink slippers."

"I know what it is," Michael began; "I know why the police have not come."

"Why?"

"Because Niyaq has stopped them." He looked back and forth from Jarvis to Martin:

"I was told that there would be many Niyaq people here – here in this town."

Martin made a face:

"If Niyaq is taking out fire and police, they must know that this will initiate a military response."

Jarvis nodded. "That's right."

"So . . ."

Jarvis held up his hand to stop Martin:

"Listen."

"A jet fighter?"

"That's a Tomcat, McDonald; I can tell by the sound. Those planes don't fly around here – not unless they're called in."

Martin smiled. "The cavalry has arrived."

"But what good will it do *us*? To bring in an air strike you need designated targets. Niyaq knows that – they're not going to give our pilots a turkey shoot."

"You can't see those positions in the woods from the air?" Martin asked

"No."

Martin threw up his hands:

“Well . . . that’s probably because you did such a hunky-dory job with the camouflage.”

“A chopper at tree top couldn’t spot those positions,” Jarvis told him.

Martin stared at Jarvis:

“And proud you should be, Colonel. I would bet that a bloodhound with a turbo-charger fixed to his nose couldn’t sniff out those positions. As we speak, squirrels are nesting in your ecologically sensitive Gatling guns.

Indeed, your plan would be flawless except for the minor fact that *Niyaq* holds those positions.”

Martin was rolling. He directed his attention to Michael who was still enjoying his huckleberries:

“Rambo here says that I complain too much. I’m not a military man – but defending an 11,000 square foot mansion with three people just doesn’t make it.”

Not missing a bite – Michael casually held up two fingers.

Jarvis laughed. “Come on and be a sport Mikey – at least pelt em with a few huckleberries.”

Martin leaned over to Michael and talked in his ear:

“It looks like were losing but we actually got em by the balls. We’re going to blow ourselves to bits – that’ll show em.”

Jarvis spoke up:

“Michael said that Niyaq knew I put a bigger charge down there. That might have been the only thing that I did right. They probably have enough men now to flood in here and take us with small arms; and you can bet your buns they’d do it if we didn’t have our hand on the switch.

They want the disc and they don’t have a plan. And, they are running out of time. The towels are out there shittin green nickels. They don’t have a clue as to what to do.”

“Well . . . there’s that,” Martin agreed. “But . . . what if we blow it and it doesn’t kill us all. Maybe we’ll just get knocked out – or mangled. Niyaq could come in and drag us away.”

“If you’re worried about that we can go to the other end of the house. We can sit right on top of the Sub if you want.”

Martin shook his head:

“Nah – we’d never make it. There are too many windows – tall windows. Niyaq probably has people in trees looking down at us.”

“Oh, quit bitching McDonald – everything has to be perfect with you.” Jarvis looked up:

“Hear that – those sound like attack helicopters.”

“I’ll bet . . .”

"Quiet. That sounds like a big cargo plane – maybe a gunship."
"I'll bet you watch all those Schwarzenegger movies – Don't you, Jarvis?"
"Yeah."
"I'll bet you had an orgasm when you watched 'Blackhawk Down.'"
"No . . . but I did get somewhat aroused – what of it?"
Michael laughed:
"You have become friends. It is very enjoyable to watch you tease each other."
The phone rang.
"I thought the phone was out," Jarvis said.
"Well . . . it was. You answer it, Jarvis; it's probably Niyaq."
"This is Jarvis. Oh . . . Mrs. McDonald . . ."
Martin yanked the phone away:
"Rachael?"
"I'm here."
"Listen . . . you don't have to be careful about what you say. The shit has hit the fan – they've got us pinned down."
"Is Michael all right?"
"Michael is cool – but Jarvis is all bent out of shape. He thinks I squeaked him on the raspberries."
"There are lots of raspberries in the refrigerator. Look in the vegetable drawer."
"Hey Jarvis – my wife says there are more raspberries. Look in the bottom drawer of the frig."
"What are you doing?" Rachael asked.
"We're eating breakfast. We were going to eat earlier, but Arnold Schwarz-a-Jarvis shot down a chopper and we've been dodging bullets ever since. Rachael – who's that in the background?"
"There is a man on the line – a man from Niyaq."
He put his hand over the receiver:
"Niyaq has her! They're listening to our conversation."
Jarvis took the phone from Martin:
"This is William Jarvis."
"Hello, Mr. Jarvis. Please . . . let me speak with Mr. McDonald."
Martin was becoming hysterical:
"What . . . what's he saying?"
Jarvis put his hand over the receiver:
"You need to let me handle this," he calmly said.
"No way! No way!"

"Please, Martin," Michael pleaded, "it is better that Mr. Jarvis handles this."

Jarvis put the phone to his ear. "What's on your mind?"

"I need to talk to Mr. McDonald."

"Ah . . . he's in the shower – can I take a message?"

"Don't get cute . . . I have his wife – would you like to hear a few screams."

"One scream and I blow this place. I mean it asshole! And put Mrs. McDonald back on the line."

"I won't do that."

"Yes you will. I'll give you five seconds. If I don't hear her voice I'll blow this place. And guess what? Niyaq will kill your ass for fouling up this deal!"

"Jarvis . . . it's me."

"I want you to stay on the line, Rachael – OK?"

"OK."

"So . . . where does this leave us, Mr. Jarvis?" the Arab asked him.

"With my hand around your balls."

There was silence for a few moments.

"Rachael?" Jarvis said.

"I'm here."

"What's he doing?"

"Talking on his cell phone."

"What's he saying?"

"I can't understand – he's talking Arabic."

"Stay on the phone, Rachael."

"I will."

He covered the phone. "She's OK, McDonald. The Arab is talking on his cell phone – probably to the people outside."

Martin was shaking uncontrollably.

"Come on, Martin . . . try to calm down," Michael urged.

Martin looked wide-eyed at Michael. "But . . . but you said . . ."

"It will be as I told you, Martin."

"But . . ."

"It will be as I said. Please . . . you . . . you could have a heart attack."

Jarvis spoke into the phone. "Rachael . . . what's going on?"

"He . . . he's still on the phone."

"OK. I'm going to give the phone back to Martin. But if anything starts to happen, make sure he gives the phone back to me. OK?"

"OK."

He handed the phone to Martin:

"Here . . . talk to your wife."

"Honey?"

"I'm here, Martin."

"I'm losing it."

"No . . . don't do that – I'm OK."

"Has that man hurt you?"

"No."

"He hasn't hurt you at all?"

"No."

Jarvis nestled next to Michael and whispered:

"You told Martin, 'it will be as I said.' What does that mean?"

"His wife will live – she will be all right."

Jarvis nodded. "OK – just tell me what to do about Rachael. What do I need to do from this end?"

He shook his head. "Nothing – the angels will look after her."

Jarvis leaned back and sighed. "I'm getting sick of this – I'm ready to get it over with. Michael . . . you *have* to tell me what to do – you *have* to tell me what to do about Rachael."

"I have told you already."

"She's shot him!" Martin cried out. "She shot the Arab."

He handed the phone to Jarvis. Jarvis looked at it and handed it to Michael:

"Rachael . . . what have you done?" Michael asked her.

"I shot him – I shot him in the back of the head. What should I do?"

"What do the angels tell you?"

"Run?"

"Then run, Rachael, run!"

Michael held the phone in his lap and looked back and forth from Jarvis to Martin.

"What?" Martin pleaded

"She is running," Michael softly said.

"Running! Are you insane? Do you think that *we* can run? Jesus God!"

Martin began to shake again – this time more violently.

"He's flippin out, Michael – do something!" Jarvis urged.

Jarvis looked down at his friend who was now spasmodically twitching:

"Come on, buddy!"

Michael shook his head:

"He cannot hear you. Bad spirit has hooked to his fear and confused his mind."

Michael knelt over Martin and placed his hands on the top of his head. There were a few violent jerks and Martin lay still.

"What's happened to him?"

"He is sleeping. When he awakes we need to comfort him and tell him that Rachael is safe. If we do not do that, the fear could come back."

After a few minutes Martin began to stir.

"Hey old buddy – are you still with us?" Jarvis asked. "Wake up, Pajama Boy."

"Martin," Michael began. "Can you hear me? Your wife is safe, Martin."

"Rachael?"

Michael beamed up at Jarvis and then looked back to Martin:

"Yes, Martin – she is safe."

He was still disoriented:

"But . . ."

Jarvis put the M-14 in his lap. "Time to snap out of it, pal – it's towel season."

He looked down at the gun. "Yeah . . . OK."

"Christ, McDonald – I'll bet you sit around the house on Sunday with those fruity slippers on and watch golf."

"Yes . . . well . . . I don't always wear *these* slippers."

Jarvis laughed and gave Michael a knowing look. "I think he's OK."

"Yeah . . . I'm OK. Rachael is safe – I can feel it." He smiled at Jarvis. "I'm OK."

A loudspeaker boomed outside:

"William Jarvis. We want to talk."

Jarvis groaned. "How the hell does he think I can answer him?"

"William Jarvis," the voice sounded outside.

"You guys stay here," Jarvis grumbled as he crawled into the next room:

"You want to talk? Call on the phone!" Jarvis screamed.

"I can't do that, Mr. Jarvis."

Michael and Martin could faintly hear Jarvis mumbling profanities. After a few moments his voice bellowed:

"Send in a man. One man. And the guys gotta be naked – buck naked. Send in one of *my* men."

"You don't have any men out here, Mr. Jarvis."

"You know what I mean, shithead!"

"No deal."

"Then no talk!"

A few moments passed.

"OK, Jarvis, we're sending someone in. You've got ten minutes."

"Send him in the side door towards the front of the house – on the East side," Jarvis bellowed.

"The sliding glass doors? Is that what you mean?"

"That's the South end of the house – you moron!"

"We need to make this clear," the speaker boomed.

"It's a tough world, buddy – get your own compass!"

Jarvis made his way back to the kitchen.

"What are you smiling about, McDonald?"

"What's that old song?" Martin jibed. "Something about lonely soldiers?"

Jarvis made a face:

"I liked you better when you were a demon motel. McDonald, I couldn't let one of those guys come in here with a bomb or a weapon."

"What's your thinking with this meeting?" Martin asked.

He shrugged. "It will buy us some time. If our boys get here before the towels split, then we will get every last one of them. As a general rule, these baby killers are no match for a bunch of pissed-off Marines."

"Well . . . do you think Niyaq will stick around that long?"

"Probably not," Jarvis guessed. "They'll want a quick deal. If they don't get it they'll probably finish us in short order and split."

Martin looked down at his M-14. "I'd like to get just one of them. Come on, Jarvis – put on your thinking cap."

"I was going to kill the traitor piece of shit that they send in here; but I'll let *you* do it if you want."

"That would be dishonorable," Michael objected.

"Come on, Michael, give Rambo a break," Martin began. "Do you think that these guys outside wouldn't do that to us?"

Michael drew tight his lips and glared at Martin:

"I will say this only once. I do not make the decision of what death will count and what death will not count."

Michael's offensive posture was most uncharacteristic. There was silence for a few moments as Martin and Jarvis looked at each other.

Martin glanced down at the gun in his lap:

"You . . . you don't want me to use this, Michael?"

"Yes – you can use that." He looked at Jarvis. "But no deceit and no murder."

"It's a military execution, Michael," Jarvis concluded. "You can look the other way. Sorry."

Michael's face grew long and he placed his bowl of huckleberries on the counter.

Jarvis' expression soured and he looked over at Martin. He then addressed Michael who looked away.

"Michael?"

"What is it, Mr. Jarvis?"

"You . . . you aren't going to finish your berries?"

"I am no longer hungry. You . . . you become like them."

Martin looked down at the floor and slowly shook his head. "I'm confused."

Jarvis took a deep breath. "What do you expect me to do, Michael? This guy betrayed God, he betrayed his country . . ."

"If you believe in God, then you must also believe that it is He that will judge."

"I think we need to listen to Michael, Jarvis," Martin began. "There's a lot more at stake here than your revenge. Do you know what I'm saying, Jarvis? I mean, the Throne is hip to what's happening down here."

Jarvis gritted his teeth and the veins of his neck enlarged:

"McDonald – all I want to do is to get my hands on this guy. That's all I can think about."

"And then you will kill him?"

"Yes – I will kill him with my bare hands."

Martin shrugged. "I don't know, Rambo. You need to imagine that there are thousands of angels hovering around us. Then you got to figure that we'll be dead soon. The last thing they're going to see is you ripping apart this naked guy."

"So . . . you figure that'll turn em off?"

"Well . . . yeah."

Martin and Jarvis looked at Michael:

Michael nodded. "Yes . . . I think that they would find that sort of behavior very disquieting. I want you to treat this man as you would treat a guest."

Martin leaned over and whispered something in Jarvis' ear.

Jarvis' whole demeanor changed:

"You're right, Michael. We will treat this gentleman as our guest. McDonald, you know more about this guest stuff than I do . . ."

Martin perked up and smiled:

"I'll make us a nice cheese tray. Michael, I'll never make it down to the basement wine cellar – so . . . you will have to handle the wine."

"Well . . . that is much better. Yes, of course – I will help with the wine. What kind of cheese do you have?"

"I've got something called 'Saga Baby Blue.' It simply cries out for a dusting red. Michael, we must not let those cries go unheeded."

Michael became enthusiastic. "I am thinking Bordeaux – a very *big* Bordeaux."

"I'm thinking big, I'm thinking velvet, I'm thinking . . ."

"Margaux?" Michael guessed.

Martin lifted his finger. "Bingo." He looked over at Jarvis:

"You find a big picture and fill it with water. I'll start on the cheese tray. Oh – and get four wine glasses – they're over the sink."

When Martin finished the cheese tray he sat down on the floor next to Jarvis and Michael. Jarvis looked puzzled.

"I suppose it would be rude to start without our guest," Martin speculated.

"Perhaps he will find it in his heart to forgive us?" Michael mused as he spread some cheese:

"This is wonderful. Has all the full flavor of blue without the tartness."

"I am glad you're pleased."

Jarvis made a face:

"You guys think this wine is good?"

"You are such a peasant, Jarvis. There's vodka in the freezer and scotch in the frig."

Jarvis got them both and put ice in a glass:

"The cheese is good – I like the cheese."

A loud speaker boomed:

"Mr. Jarvis. Your man is coming in. You have ten minutes."

Jarvis chambered a round into his rifle. Martin sat his wine down and began to do this same.

"McDonald!" Jarvis cried out.

"What?"

"Don't point your gun at me when you do that – moron!"

"Sorry."

Jarvis took a big slug and made his way into the next room.

"It took you long enough to figure out which door to come in," Jarvis yelled from the window. "Hey . . . I bet you were the guy in charge of the map when Moses tried to make it out of the wilderness!"

A tall thin man appeared in the doorway with his hands over his groin. Jarvis crawled towards the kitchen behind him:

"Have a seat, Wilcox."

"Martin," Michael began, "get this man something to cover himself with."

Jarvis sat down and poured some vodka. "Yeah, I think a postage stamp would do it."

"Bad idea . . . I might forget and lick it later." With that Martin tossed the man a shot glass:

"That ought to do it."

Michael handed the man a dishtowel and looked disapprovingly at Martin and Jarvis.

"Look, Jarvis – we don't have time to shit around," Wilcox announced.

"Watch your mouth!" Jarvis raged.

"Oh, fuck off, Jarvis, we . . ."

Jarvis gave the man a quick jab to the mouth. His head flew back against the refrigerator. Dazed and confused, he felt in his mouth for the remnants of his front teeth."

"Jarvis," Michael pleaded.

"Well . . . he was saying bad words." He smiled at Wilcox:

"We invite you for hors d'oeuvres and you say bad words? No, Wilcox – this is bad form and will not be tolerated."

"That's right, Wilcox," Martin began. "You see, the angels are watching us and they are very sensitive."

The man sat up. There was blood everywhere:

"You've gone insane, Jarvis. You need to look at your watch – you got till two minutes after the hour."

"Is Kofax dead?"

"Yeah."

"What about Yeomans?"

"Dead. What difference does it make, Jarvis?"

"How much, Wilcox – how much did they pay you?"

"Half a mil."

"How many, Wilcox – how many turkeyed out on me?"

"Just me and Waterman . . . but more men arrived last night. The men had no reason to think that you hadn't sent them. And, well, you know how Lebeh is – nobody knows anybody else."

"What are they going to do when the time runs out," Jarvis asked.

"Ha! You don't think I'm going to tell *you*!"

Jarvis shrugged. "Why not?"

"Why should I?"

"We're not going to let you leave." Jarvis smiled and threw up his hands:

"You're going to die anyway.

So . . . tell me, Wilcox – how much of that half mil have you spent?"

He shrugged. "So what – my wife has it."

"I can't believe you are such a fool," Jarvis snarled. "They will kill your wife and take the money back. They'll probably rape and torture her – just for fun. Niyaq has plenty of men – they don't need infidels. You were useful – but only for this one thing. Now, they will have no use for you."

Wilcox reached into his mouth and took out a broken tooth.

"I never thought that you would turn towel, Wilcox."

Wilcox looked defiant in spite of his condition:

"Is that right? Well . . . I tried the hero bit and got spit on by a bunch of long haired freaks."

"That's a lame excuse and you know it," Jarvis said as he balled up his fist for another strike.

The man held up his hands defensively:

"Come on," the man pleaded, "cool down."

"Shoot him if he moves, McDonald."

Remembering what Jarvis had told him, Martin trained his rifle at the man's head.

"What are you going to do?" Wilcox asked Jarvis.

"I'm going to have some more cheese and crackers. You bled all over my raspberries."

"You've flipped, Jarvis. You've totally flipped."

Wilcox looked around as the trio enjoyed their cheese and crackers and sipped their drinks. His he was totally perplexed by their relaxed demeanor:

"They can't hear us here in the kitchen – did you know that?"

"I didn't know that," Jarvis casually answered.

"Did you know that most of the men have left already?"

"Talk to me, Wilcox."

Wilcox considered the bizarre behavior of the trio and gathered his thoughts:

"Niyaq is getting out of Dodge. Well . . . they're *trying* to get out of Dodge – it's yet to be seen how many will make it. All aircraft have been grounded. Anything that takes to the air is knocked out – they're knocking everything out of the sky. A lot of Niyaq's choppers have been hit on the ground. Every airport in New England has been taken over – it's total marshal law. All the roads are blocked. I don't think any of them are going to make it out of here."

"What about Lebeh?" Martin asked.

"Niyaq hit em from every direction. I think Lebeh is finished."

"How many are left in the woods?" Jarvis asked.

"Five besides me."

Jarvis looked hatefully at the man:

"That makes no sense, Wilcox. If there is no way out for the men, then what's the point of ordering them to leave their dug in position?"

"No order was given." He studied Jarvis' face:

"There's no way to stop a full-scale desertion."

Jarvis looked at his watch:

"Talk to me, Wilcox."

"When the time is up they're going to fire DP rockets through the windows and light up the minis."

"Why don't they launch explosives at us?"

"There's nobody left that knows how to use the launcher. They have rockets, minis, and that big flame thrower."

Jarvis made a face:

"You don't know how to use the launcher?"

"I was never trained on it."

"Christ – did your brain turn to shit when you went towel?"

"Without the launcher, the explosives are useless," Wilcox explained. "They can't carry that stuff across McDonald's golf course. It would take two men to carry it. They don't have enough men left to provide cover." He looked down at Jarvis' M-14:

"You knocked out the chopper with that?"

"Yeah."

"That fooled em. They're figuring three people with M-60s."

"Do you think the men that are left have cut and run?" Jarvis asked.

"No."

Jarvis looked over at Martin and took a deep breath:

"What do you think, Pajama Boy?"

"It's your call."

Jarvis looked over at Michael who was spreading some cheese.

"Mr. Jarvis," Michael began, "I have no understanding of the things that you speak of."

Jarvis looked at his watch:

"Talk to me, Wilcox."

"How much time do we have?"

"A minute."

"Where are the stairs to the basement?"

Martin pointed. "Right there."

"Come on – the minis and rockets can't get us down there. Quick!"

They scrambled down the stairs.

"What room is the farthest from the Sub?" Wilcox asked at the bottom of the stairs.

"The wine cellar," Martin said as he pointed the way.

"Quickly," Wilcox urged, "in case we have to blow the Sub."

They all sat down on the cold floor.

"Shouldn't we close the door?" Wilcox asked.

"There would be no light if we did that," Martin dryly said.

"So what?"

Martin pointed his rifle at Wilcox. "Da-ah? Why do you think?"

"It's freezing in here," Wilcox complained.

"It's a wine cellar, Wilcox."

"How much time do we have?" Martin asked.

"Right now," Jarvis said.

"I'm confused," Martin admitted. "I . . . I just didn't think that it was going to play out like this."

"Where's the Jewish guy?" Wilcox asked

Michael spoke from the darkness:

"I am back here."

"What's he doing?" Wilcox asked.

"I would guess that he's praying," Jarvis speculated. "He does that a lot."

"Hey, Michael," Wilcox called out. "We're cool – I think we're OK."

Martin gave Jarvis a knowing look.

Jarvis turned to study Wilcox's face:

"You nervous about something, Wilcox?"

"No," he shrugged unconvincingly.

Jarvis' eyes narrowed:

"Just keep quiet, Wilcox."

They waited, and waited, and waited.

Michael emerged from the darkness:

"Mr. Wilcox?"

"Huh?"

"You think that you have tricked us. This is not true. You have not tricked us – we have tricked you."

Martin watched Jarvis' expression turn to rage in the thin light that came through the cellar door. He could sense fear in Wilcox.

Wilcox made a surrendering gesture:

"Hey, take it easy, Jarvis; he doesn't know what he's talking about," Wilcox said with a shaky voice.

Martin spoke up. "Hey, what's that behind you, Michael?"

When Michael turned around Jarvis took his cue and snapped the man's neck like a twig. Michael heard the sound and turned back around. Jarvis and Martin could see Michael's expression with the backdrop of wine bottles – he was calm and thoughtful:

"It was hard to like Mr. Wilcox," Michael casually noted.

"And he said bad words," Martin offered. "I was hoping that Rambo's little Father Duffy chat would have straightened him out, but . . ."

"And he was a terrible fibber," Jarvis concluded.

They sat in silence and let the minutes tick by. Every moment that they could stay alive would bring the Marines closer. Martin suddenly jerked:

"Did you see that?" he asked in a whisper. "A woman just went past the door – I could see her silhouette."

"A woman?" Jarvis asked.

"I saw her too," Michael volunteered.

"I'm confused," Martin whispered to himself.

"I think she was Niyaq – and probably a he," Michael told them.

"Talk to us."

"Lebeh always underestimates Niyaq. You must know that their people would be dressed just like the people of this town – they will not be wearing uniforms."

"I'll shoot her when he comes by again," Martin declared.

Jarvis pulled out an ugly knife:

"Michael – you get behind the door with your hand on the knob. At Martin's signal jerk the door open."

Jarvis' strength was awesome. He handled the person like a rag doll and sent him flying into the wine cellar without a sound. Blood smeared the cellar floor. In the scuffle the man's wig came off.

"God – I *hope* that's not a woman," Martin lamented.

"Yes," Michael agreed, "she would be a wall plant."

Jarvis looked down at the man. "In order to be a wall flower, somebody's got to let you in. This one would never make it through the door."

"What's going on?" Martin queried.

Jarvis looked at Michael:

"What *is* going on, Michael?"

"I only know what I am told. They said that this Wilcox man lied. They do not tell me everything – so . . . I *must* believe that they have told me all that I need to know."

Jarvis turned to Martin:

"What's your take, Sherlock?"

"She didn't even have a rifle. Anyone from above would just think that she was a neighbor coming to see us. Probably nobody's phones work. The whole town could be without power for all we know."

Jarvis nodded:

"Yeah. Niyaq was probably listening to our conversation and knew that we had come down here. Christ – they're probably listening to us now."

"So . . . now what?"

Jarvis reached into his back pack and got an ammo vest and handed it to Martin:

"Ok, McDonald – this is the plan. We're going to take out everything that moves in this house.

You've got some catching up to do, Pajama Boy. You gotta figure six or eight in the chopper, plus Wilcox and the turban dyke." He looked down at the dead man in the dress:

"God – wouldn't you think they'd get a better looking man to play a woman."

"You're not thinking, Jarvis – if they did that, their own men would be hitting on em," Martin pointed out.

"Mr. Jarvis – what should *I* do?" Michael asked with pleading eyes.

Jarvis sighed as he turned to Michael.

Michael glanced back and forth from Jarvis to Martin. He showed no fear; but there was a telling look in his eyes that they both sensed.

"What are the angels telling you, Michael?" Martin asked.

Michael smiled and gently reached out and took their hands. His eyes were soft and filled with love:

"The angels – they do not tell me so much as you think. Most of the time I am just like you. And yes – it is best this way – this is life. Only at certain times do I hear them."

A few moments went by as they silently stared at each other.

He pointed at his heart:

"Me, Michael, would like to say goodbye to my good friends in case they do not return. But know also that I will see you both again in happier times."

Martin's eyes filled with tears and he looked down at his rifle:

"I'm out of the mood for this – I really don't want to shoot anybody."

Jarvis was moved and had to look away:

"Martin, stay with Michael – I'll check the house."

"Is that what I should do, Michael – is that what you want me to do?"

Michael considered it for a moment:

"Perhaps you should help your friend. I will wait in the quiet room.

Martin, I want you to give me the detonation device."

Martin looked over at Jarvis who nodded:

"Give it to him."

Martin held the device in the light so that Michael could see it. Jarvis watched on with wet eyes.

"You move this little thing out of the way . . . and . . . and you just push this switch in the direction of the arrow."

When Jarvis spoke his voice broke with emotion:

"Please . . . please forgive me, Michael. I . . . I didn't mean to . . ."

"It is all right, Mr. Jarvis. The story has an unpleasant climax but a very happy ending." He searched Jarvis' face:

"Is this not what you believe, Mr. Jarvis?"

"Yes . . . I *do* believe that."

"Can we get into the sub without the power being on?" Michael asked Martin.

"Yeah . . . batteries operate the locking system."

Jarvis plodded like a rhino through the basement – wielding the heavy rifle and drum as if it were a toy. Michael and Martin followed along behind.

The Sub was undisturbed.

Jarvis looked under the bookcase and checked the detonation wires and traced them back to the batteries:

"It doesn't look like they've been in here."

Michael sat down and held the device in his lap. He looked up, smiled at his friends, and gently waved goodbye. Martin and Jarvis returned the courtesy and closed the door of the Sub.

Jarvis stopped at the foot of the basement stairs and turned around to Martin. He groaned and rubbed his forehead:

"This is killing me, McDonald."

"Michael knows – he knows we aren't going to make it."

"He . . . he's so innocent – he doesn't belong in this world."

"I know it."

"His pre-battle pep talk left a lot to be desired," Jarvis grumbled.

"I know it."

Jarvis made an off-hand gesture:

"Let's go upstairs – let's go upstairs and get it over with."

The sky was strangely quiet – the gunship that had circled the downed chopper was gone. They searched the house from top to bottom but found nothing. They returned to the ground floor and peered out the window.

"I don't get it – it's almost like everything has returned to normal," Jarvis observed. He pointed:

"Look, there's a lone Cobra off about two miles." He cocked his head. "I hear some small arms' fire – but it's way off. Yeah, lot's of small arms' fire – it seems to be all around us . . . but nothing up close."

"I'm confused as hell," Martin began. "If Niyaq came to town to get *us*, then why aren't they *here*? I mean – what's all this shit going on around us?" He gave Jarvis a curious look:

"Hey, Jarvis, you don't suppose that we could just walk out of here – do you?"

"You got eyes, Sherlock." Jarvis pointed out the window. "What do you see out there?"

"Nothing. The only Arab we've seen is the guy in the dress – and he didn't even have a gun."

"He had a pistol on him but your point is well taken." He cocked his head:

"But . . . listen to it, McDonald – that's a lot of damned small arms' fire."

"So . . . what now?"

"You stay here and I'll go talk to Michael."

"Then what?"

"I don't know. Maybe . . . maybe Michael . . ."

"Has heard from his angels?" Martin speculated.

Jarvis marveled. "What a way to fight a war." He picked up his rifle and looked down at Martin:

"McDonald – don't trust anyone walking up in civilian clothing."

He nodded. "I can recognize my neighbors. If he looks like the 7-11 guy I'll blow his doors off."

"That's the ticket. Don't stay in one place. Go from window to window and stay down."

Jarvis rapped on the door and Michael spied him through the peephole and let him in.

"Hello, Mr. Jarvis."

Jarvis sat down next to him; but kept his rifle pointed at the opened door of the Sub:

“We didn’t find anyone in the house. The planes have disappeared but there seems to be gunfire in the distance.”

Michael lifted his brow:

“And?”

Jarvis took a deep breath:

“Michael, I don’t understand what’s going on. He studied Michael’s face:

“Do *you* understand what’s going on? Have the angels told you anything?”

“No.”

They heard a shot from upstairs.

Jarvis looked sick:

“*Pajama Boy*. Michael – you stay here!”

As soon as Jarvis disappeared, Martin’s courage waned. *I’m not geared for this.*

He went from window to window. He saw something move in the woods to the Southeast and looked through his scope. *A civilian with what looked like an M-16.*

His heart came up in his throat. It was about a 120 yard shot. *Where was Jarvis! Should he take the shot? What would Jarvis do?*

He took aim but the man moved out of sight. Martin panicked. *What if they saw him? What if they open up with the minis?*

He ran to the other end of the house and positioned himself. He saw three men walking towards him – out about 200 yards.

He looked through his scope. They had rifles. He squeezed one off and a man fell as the others hit the ground. He looked out the window again. He heard a swishing sound and something stung his cheek. Jarvis bellowed behind him:

“McDonald – what are you shooting at?”

He turned to see Jarvis approaching:

“We’re surrounded. I saw a guy with an M-16 to the Southeast and just shot a guy out there.”

Jarvis pointed. “Out there?”

“Yeah. There were three of them. They’ve hit the dirt.” He felt his face and looked at his hand:

“A bullet grazed me.”

Jarvis looked out the window:

“What were they doing?”

McDonald was rattled:

"Walking."

"How far out?"

"About 200 yards."

Jarvis looked sick.

"What . . . what is it? What's the matter?"

"They were in the middle of that clearing – just walking?"

"Yeah."

Jarvis took a deep breath and studied Martin's face:

"McDonald . . . are you *sure* they weren't wearing uniforms."

Martin's mouth hung open:

"Oh my God . . ."

Jarvis leaned against the wall, put his head down and groaned:

"Oh . . . you've done it now, Pajama Boy. Now everything in the sky will know that hostile fire came from *this* house – the good guys might have gotten their first confirmed target. Now – what do you suppose is going to happen?"

A voice bellowed:

"Mr. Jarvis!"

The room filled with armed Arabs in civilian clothing. One man held Michael, another stood next to him smiling. The smiling man was Arabic – tall, well groomed, spoke Harvard English, and was very articulate:

"How do you say it, Colonel – 'the jig is up?'"

Jarvis had his M-14 in his lap.

"Don't even think about it, Jarvis."

The man motioned and his men took their guns and frisked them.

"Mr. McDonald, it is unlucky for you that you are such a sound sleeper." He held up the detonation device:

"We cut the wires in this last night as you slept."

He walked over to Martin:

"I must confess that your attire has caused quite a bit of speculation." He thought for a moment:

"We heard a shot."

"Ah . . . Pajama Boy thought he had his safety off," Jarvis interjected.

The smiling man folded his hands in front of him and addressed Jarvis:

"So . . . this is the mighty Jarvis." He looked at his watch:

"Perhaps you have some last words to utter – we have a little time. I didn't think it would be this easy to take you out."

"Perhaps *you* have some last words to utter," Jarvis came back.

"That won't be necessary. You see, Colonel, I'll be leaving in a little while. And I'm taking your friend McDonald and the King Kike."

"The King Kike?"

The tall Arab smiled and looked around at his men who in turn smiled back – still pointing their guns at Martin and Jarvis:

"Actually, we were a bit impressed with the little trick that Jew Boy did with the wine. We have a little sample that we're bringing with us." He scratched his head and knitted his brow:

"Let's see, seems that there was an old legend of another Jew who could do that." He looked around and his men smiled as on cue. He continued:

"Jarvis, it seems like I went looking for silver and found gold. Yes, and I will also take Mr. McDonald with me. Something tells me that he will cooperate and make us a new disc. And, of course, I will kill *you,* Mr. Jarvis.

We have outsmarted Lebeh once again. The town is in chaos – citizens are shooting at each other; and your air-born armada can do little except watch the carnage. Your silenced sniper rifles proved to be very accurate, Mr. Jarvis." He laughed:

"We have beaten you, Jarvis."

"Oh, I get ya – you really believe that you can leave here."

The tall Arab laughed again:

"I *know* we can. You see, we've been planning this for a long time."

"Do you have a name?" Jarvis asked him.

"You don't need to know that."

"Fine . . . I'll just call you Mohammad."

"Moe for short," Martin offered. "You know, Like Curley, Moe, and Larry."

Jarvis nodded. "That'll work."

This time he wasn't amused. "Oh . . . a couple of comedians."

"Well, Moe," Martin began, "you're furnishing us with some pretty good straight lines."

Jarvis blew and made a face:

"Christ, Moe, you don't think that we didn't know about your little kitchen cam."

The big Arab twisted a sinister smile:

"Oh, I suppose that you *meant* to tip us off about Messiah Boy."

"Hell, we figured you turkeys already knew about that," Jarvis jibed. He looked disgusted:

"I knew you towels had shit for brains – but I didn't think you were that thick."

The man's eyes raged. He pulled out a silenced 9mm and put a round into Jarvis' thigh.

Jarvis jerked but didn't cry out. He clutched his leg and blood oozed between his fingers. He spoke with his teeth clenched:

"We went downstairs so I could kill Wilcox without you camel jockeys knowing. Ha . . . you guys thought you had us fooled – not for a minute!"

"That figures – you Christians are well-known for killing each other. You're doing it right now – all around us." He looked around at his comrades and smiled:

"I'm certain that this is all part of your master plan." He laughed:

"Tell me, Jarvis, did you enjoy breaking the infidel's neck?"

"Yeah. And I also enjoyed killing what's his name."

"What's his name?"

"Yeah, the other guy – the towel. It was a learning experience for me."

The man's eyes narrowed. "And how is *that*, Mr. Jarvis?"

"I finally figured out why you folks cover your women's faces."

The man's eyes widened with rage.

Jarvis casually turned to Martin:

"What was that guy's name?"

"Ah . . . Abdul . . . Abdul Transvesti Towel."

Jarvis roared with laughter:

"Good one, Pajama Boy."

The man raged and trained his pistol on McDonald. He changed his mind and put a bullet into Jarvis' other thigh.

Jarvis clutched both thighs in an effort to slow down the bleeding.

Michael appeared next to the man with his hand out:

"Give it to me."

He handed the gun to Michael and watched him go over to the window and throw it out. Michael turned, looked around at the faces and sat down against the wall next to Martin.

There was no telling how long it was before anyone uttered a sound. The men simply glanced around at each other as if they had just seen Moses part the Red Sea.

Their leader was the first to move. He took an M-16 from the man next to him – faked a smile, and looked around at his men:

"We have plenty of guns."

This time, nobody smiled back.

Jarvis was bleeding badly. He knew that he didn't have much more time. His mind raced:

"Well . . . now that you boys believe in magic, I think I will show you a little sleight of hand."

He rolled up both sleeves with his bloody hands and smiled at the numb looking Arabs:

"See, nothing under the sleeves." He looked at Martin and blinked a few times with his left eye – so that none of them could see:

"This works better in the sunlight:"

He held a hand in front of the window and made a variation of gyrations – all the while blinking at McDonald with his left eye. When he was finished he clutched his legs again and turned to Martin:

"Look out the window for a confirm – tell me when you get it."

Martin peered out:

"That's affirmative, buddy – they got it."

"Pajama Boy – tell the towels what I just did."

"Nah – you're on a roll – you tell em."

Jarvis couldn't stop the bleeding – his breathing had become uneven and his eyes drooped.

"I called in a cone – a max cone."

Martin lifted his brow:

"A max cone? Isn't that a bit excessive?"

"Use your head, Mink Foot. Your wife may decide to rebuild – this way she can start fresh. A max cone will dig right down to bedrock."

He considered it and nodded. "Yeah. Or, it might make a nice little lake . . . and then she could put the house next to it." He marveled:

"You're thinkin all the time – aren't you buddy?"

"Yeah . . . well . . . when your strike force consists of a messiah and a guy wearing a parachute . . . with gerbils on his feet . . ."

Jarvis' head began to slump.

Martin looked around at the faces. Fear shown in their eyes – like rabbits in a wolf's den.

"You OK, Jarvis?" Martin whispered to him.

"Well . . . it smarts a bit."

Martin looked up at the men:

"There's a bottle of vodka on the kitchen floor. Somebody go get it for Jarvis."

Their leader seemed as dazed and confused as the rest of the men. He looked helplessly on as a man handed two bottles to Jarvis. Jarvis took a healthy slug of vodka. He wiped the blood off the label:

"One hundred proof. Hey . . . this is Russian – this is commie crap!"

"Mr. Jarvis," Michael began, "does everything have to be perfect with you *all* the time? Will you never be satisfied with *anything*?"

Jarvis was the first to laugh; then Martin and Michael joined in. They laughed – they laughed until tears rolled down their faces.

By this time the Arabs had moved in closer – forming a tight semi-cycle around the trio. Some of them were kneeling down – some standing. Their leader seemed to be lost somewhere in the crowd.

Michael motioned:

"Put some pressure on his wounds."

One of those who had knelt down addressed Martin:

"What is this cone? The max cone."

The room was dead quiet and all eyes were on Martin:

"OK. These gunships are technological wonders. You know the minis that you guys got out there?"

"Yes."

"Well, the *smallest* thing that a gunship would have might be 20mms – and they shoot faster than your minis. Then they got 25s, 30s, 40s . . . the biggest they got . . . ah . . ."

"105," Jarvis offered.

"Yeah." He thought for a moment:

"First the ship takes a position."

"Orbit," Jarvis interjected.

"Yeah . . . orbit. They'll bank at about . . ."

"Thirty degrees," Jarvis muttered through his clenched jaw.

"Do you want to just tell them, Jarvis?"

"Go ahead, Pajama Boy."

"Can I finish the story?"

He took a healthy slug. "If you want to finish you'd better make it fast."

"OK. The cool thing is how the guns work. All the guns can be fired by a single guy. See? It's all done by computer. If they want, they can pinpoint the fire – you know, to dig out a bunker or sink a ship. But, they can also put down a cone of fire – any size that they want. In this case, the cone would be the size of this house. That's a small cone for these babies – very concentrated fire."

"Your leader did not lie to you," Michael began. "You will leave here. That is good news, yes?"

They hung on his every word.

"The messiah cannot lie," someone said.

A man close to him spoke up:

"Tell us, holy man, how will we leave?"

Michael looked around at the pleading faces:

"You will be carried by the wind."

Jarvis spit out a mouthful of vodka:

"That's the best one yet!"

Martin marveled:

"And the timing – it was perfect!"

They heard something drone above them.

"That's a 130," Jarvis said. "They've probably come to airdrop some camel shit so you towels can have a barbecue." Jarvis looked around him:

"If you want to get in any shots, you'd better do it fast."

As the men scrambled to the windows, the trio looked out and watched the huge plane bank into position.

Confusion reigned as the men shouted in their native tongue. Their leader bellowed something in Aramaic.

"What did he say, Michael?"

"He is telling them not to fire.

Mr. Jarvis, is there anything such as a max cone?"

"I made that part up. Hey . . . they're towels."

Michael rested his head against the wall and closed his eyes – his expression was strained.

Jarvis and Martin exchanged glances.

"Michael," Jarvis began, "I keep thinking about that little thing you did with the wine. How'd you do that?"

Michael took the vodka from Jarvis and promptly handed it back. The vodka had turned red.

Jarvis was awe-struck:

"But . . . but this isn't water . . ."

Michael had an impish grin:

"Half water."

Martin took the bottle from Jarvis and took a swig:

"Wow – talk about your fortified wine."

He handed it back to Jarvis who took a taste and nodded:

"It's good. I think I like it better."

Jarvis and Martin stared at each other for a few moments. Jarvis looked at Michael and made a face:

"Nah – it can't be."

Jarvis kept staring. Michael was wearing Reeboks, blue jeans, and a tee shirt that had an ad for a restaurant on the back. He took a healthy slug of his wine and noticed that Michael's hand was on his leg. He had stopped bleeding:

"I . . . I've stopped bleeding."

Martin playfully wiggled his eyebrows.

Jarvis slowly shook his head:

"Nah – it can't be."

The Arabs screeched louder.

Michael sat up and looked out the window:

"There . . . there it goes again."

"No," Jarvis said, "that's *another* gunship."

"Why do they not shoot?" Michael asked.

"They're waiting for orders," Jarvis surmised. "They're not going to light up those babies to take out one sniper. We've got to do something to piss em off."

"Michael, what are the Arabs saying?" Martin asked.

"I could say it better in Hebrew."

"Do your best."

"They are excreting."

"Huh?"

Michael smiled:

"Green nickels."

Martin jabbed Jarvis:

"Look . . . coming up my neighbor's driveway. What *is* that? It looks like a little tank with wheels."

"Yeah . . . it's a little tank with wheels, an LAV."

"What are those boxes on top?"

"Stinger missiles. She's rigged for air defense. That other thing on top is a 25mm Gatling gun."

"The towels don't see it yet – they're all looking up in the sky."

Jarvis pointed:

"Do you see that goofy looking thing over there next to your computer towers?"

"The giant pistol?" Martin asked.

"It's a shoulder rocket. You can learn to shoot one in about two minutes. You see the stuff stacked up next to it?"

"The big pipes?"

"Those are the rockets for it. Look – the pipes have little arrows on them."

"Yeah . . . I see em," Martin observed.

"That tells you which end of the rocket is the front," Jarvis told him.

Martin marveled:

"Wow. It's almost like . . . like they were custom designed for towels."

"Exactly. Also, there's the danger that these weapons would fall into enemy hands. Without the little arrows, the enemy could waste valuable time figuring out how to load them."

"Can they hit the LAV from here?"

The LAV had stopped and taken a position.

"You're a golfer; how many yards out is it?"

"Three hundred – maybe three twenty-five."

"Yeah . . . probably even a towel could hit it. But I would guess they'd have to take it out with the first shot – that 25mm is wicked."

"The towels wouldn't have time to reload?"

"You can figure it yourself, Pajama Boy. Say that the gun shoots two thousand rounds a minute and they got maybe 400 rounds with the first burst and another 600 in reserve."

Martin rubbed the back of his head thoughtfully:

"Jarvis, if the towels had a way out before . . . then maybe they may *still* have a way out."

"Get a grip, McDonald – *there is* no way out."

Martin nudged Jarvis and pointed to Michael:

"Look – he's got that weird look again."

"Michael?"

"The angels . . ."

"What are they saying, Mikey?"

Michael gave Martin a strange look and leaped out the window. Before Jarvis or Martin could think of what to do they heard him whisper:

"Hear – take it."

The silenced 9mm pistol that Michael tossed out the window appeared on the window sill.

Jarvis hid the weapon behind him:

"McDonald, can you see him out there?"

"No."

"Jesus – what does he think I can do with this pistol?"

"Yeshua."

"Huh?"

"They called him Yeshua – not Jesus. Actually, the Jews don't have a J in their alphabet."

"*What* in the *hell* are you talking about, McDonald?"

"Gosh, Jarvis – I thought you knew all about the Bible."

"Oh, I see – this is a Bible lesson."

"In Hebrew, if you put an H after Yeshua, then it would mean salvation. Michael says they are pronounced almost the same and probably a goy couldn't even tell the difference. Cool huh?"

Jarvis stared at Martin – his face totally void of expression:

"Really? Gosh, that's about the most interesting thing I ever heard."

Martin smiled at Jarvis – obviously pleased with himself.

Jarvis kept his eyes fixed on Martin and slowly shook his head.

"You are a *total* dildo, McDonald – do you really think this is the time for Sunday school?"

Michael climbed back in and a half a dozen guns took aim."

"No!" their leader exclaimed.

The tall man came over and stared down at Michael:

"What are you doing?"

"I had to pee."

The tall man trained his M-16 on Jarvis.

"I would rather you did not do that," Michael said.

He shrugged:

"All right. I will do this for you. Perhaps you will see that I am not so bad." He looked down at Jarvis:

"This is your lucky day, Mr. Jarvis."

Jarvis smiled up at him. "If things went any better I couldn't stand it."

The man lifted his brow curiously:

"No insults, Mr. Jarvis?"

"Well . . . I guess I don't feel like *pushing* my luck."

"That's wise," he said as he turned around.

"Moe?"

He turned around and leveled the gun at Jarvis with his finger on the trigger:

"What!"

"I was wondering if you've seen the LAV?"

"You're pushing it, Jarvis."

Jarvis motioned to the window.

The man took a look:

"I don't see anything."

Jarvis pointed:

"There's some brush at the property line. Beyond that you can see a house. Look in the stand of trees to the Southeast of the house."

"Yes, now I see it."

The tall man sat down in front of Jarvis – about five feet away. He kept his carbine aimed and trigger ready. The room had quieted down and the trio could hear him clearly when he spoke:

"The max cone thing fooled them. I told my men you were bluffing. They didn't believe me; but *now* they do. So . . . I am wise and strong in their eyes and they follow me again.

You Christians are always mouthing about how the Holy Spirit tells you this and that. Allah talks to me in the same way. It was he that provided me the insight not to fire at the house. And, as you can see, Allah's strategy is flawless.

You've got guts Jarvis – but you're a dying breed. The good Christians are dying off and our strongest men are being born into the world."

His smile was profoundly sinister:

"Now . . . how do you suppose that things are going to play out?"

Jarvis was weary – exhausted.

By this time a number Arabs had gathered.

The man laughed like Satan himself:

"Well . . . don't blame me – *I* was not the one to prophesy these things." He pointed at Michael:

"It was *he*."

He laughed again his men joined in. He rose to his feet and pointed at Jarvis:

"The holy man – he asked that I spare Jarvis. He did not ask his God – he asked *me*. The holy man is wise – he knew that his God could not save Jarvis – just like his God could not save him from the cross.

Mr. Jarvis. These men around you. You call them towels; and you claim that they have shit for brains. Your book, your Bible – how does it describe these men?

You are silent? But I was told that you read this book often and know it well.

You have lost your spunk, Mr. Jarvis. Perhaps you should make some more signs in the window. Go ahead – I will not stop you.

You bore me, Mr. Jarvis."

He pointed to Michael:

"Then I will direct my attention to this man – the man whose name asks the question, 'who is like God?' the man who cannot tell a lie. Then, perhaps I will get some answers.

Holy man . . . when these men before you reigned on Earth, how were they described – how did Moses describe these men in the Torah?"

"Hanephilim. Hagiborim. Ha'anishy Hashem," Michael answered.

"Yes. They were men of great reputation – the movers and the shakers – mighty men. They were running the show back then. Is this not how it was, holy man?"

Michael stared at the man with contempt. "They were running things, stealing things, killing things."

"Ha! According to who? According to *your* God they we were guilty of *many* things. But, holy man, your book left out some details. True?"

"*All* books leave out details."

He sneered:

"Humph! The Nephilim were running circles around Yahweh's little brats. There was nothing *unfair* about it – Yahweh's spoiled brats were just getting the short end of the stick. The Nephilim were just better at the game of life than Yahweh's bunch and Yahweh couldn't stand it. So . . . Yahweh rigs the game and bounces *our* asses out; and, somehow, it's all portrayed as being *our* fault.

Yahweh does what *Yahweh* wants to do. And, somehow, nobody gets to question *his* motives.

And what are these things – good and evil? It is just a question of individual *style*. Yahweh just doesn't like our *style* and that is all the theology that there is – there is nothing more to add. Indeed, your own book points out this absurd dichotomy.

We are Hagiborim and Ha'anishy Hashem – the mighty men of renown. This is good. But we are also Hanephilim – the fallen ones. This is bad. Why? Because Yahweh doesn't like our *style*. He is afraid that we may take advantage of his defenseless children. So . . . we are not allowed to play. So . . . Yahweh kicks us out of the little sandbox that he made for his little kiddies."

"Yes . . . *'that He made'* – that was your *only* bit of truth," Michael asserted. "You would steal *everything* from Yahweh if only you *could*."

The tall Arab glared down at Michael:

"Time will tell, holy man; time will tell."

"That was your *second* bit of truth," Michael came back defiantly.

"I grow tired of this." He turned and spoke to a heavyset man with an M-60.

"Michael, what are they saying?"

"Something about a 25 . . . and load armor stabbing . . . but only shoot on my signal . . . it is almost time. Something like that."

Martin nudged Jarvis. "So . . . they're probably talking about the LAV."

"Yeah . . . it sounds like they're going to load the shoulder rocket with an armor piercer. And . . . as far as the time . . ."

Michael winced. "We know what that means."

They watched as a man positioned himself in a window with the shoulder rocket. Someone behind him looked at his watch and shouted something.

"He told him not to fire," Michael said as he looked at Jarvis. Fear showed in his eyes:

"They are still planning to leave."

"There's no way that can happen," Jarvis insisted.

"This man that you call Moe," Michael began, "do you think he is stupid?"

"Say something, Jarvis," Martin pleaded.

"There is no way out." He looked at Martin:

"Well . . . do *you* see how they can get out?"

"Moe said they have been planning this *for a long time*."

They turned to Michael.

"The angels told me to give *you* the gun, Mr. Jarvis," Michael said.

The mighty Jarvis looked helpless:

"So what? So what am I suppose to do with this little pistol? Am I supposed to shoot at the tank – take a shot at a gunship – take on the towels?"

"I do not know."

"Well . . . ask your *angels*," Jarvis suggested.

"I have grown fearful," Michael confessed. "I do not want to go with them, Mr. Jarvis."

Jarvis rubbed his forehead and Martin noticed that his hand was shaking.

"You OK, Jarvis?"

"I'm weary, Martin. I . . . I've lost a lot of blood – I can't think."

"Mr. Jarvis – is there not something you can do?" Michael pleaded.

"I can't think! None of this makes sense!"

Martin placed his hand on Jarvis' shoulder:

"Jarvis . . . don't lose it – don't lose it now. Have some of Michael's wine."

"I don't like it."

Michael looked hurt:

"But . . ."

"I didn't want hurt your feelings."

Martin picked up the scotch and offered it to Jarvis:

"So . . . drink some of this – maybe it'll steady you."

"I don't drink that pussy, country club crap."

Michael made a face.

"What is it, Michael?" Jarvis scowled.

"The least little thing goes wrong and you fall apart."

Jarvis looked back and forth at them and snatched the bottle from

Martin:

"You two are a royal pain in the ass."

The three of them watched as the room grew quiet. The Arabs glanced at their watches and looked up at the sky.

"If that towel had his finger on the trigger of that rocket I could do something," Jarvis informed them. "If he had his finger on the trigger, I could shoot him in the arm – he'd flinch and maybe touch one off. That'd be good cause he'd probably be off target enough to miss the LAV at that range."

"And then?" Michael asked.

"And then all hell will break loose. Then you won't have to go with the towels. The little tank will open up and probably the gunships."

"That would be good. I would much rather leave with you and Martin." He smiled at his friends:

"Do not worry – I know the way; and when the time comes you shall see me again."

Jarvis caught Martin's eye, huffed, and shook his head. "This is too weird."

Martin took his cue:

"So . . . what do you think, Michael – will this death count – will this death do it?"

"I will put in a good word for you. How do you say, 'you have heard it from the horse's mouth.'"

Martin took the bottle from Jarvis and marveled. "This *is* getting pretty weird."

"When the hell breaks loose, will the little gun on the funny car go through these walls?"

"Ha! These walls will make it worse. It will be like a thousand grenades going off at once."

"I will watch. I will watch the right hand of the man with the strange gun. When he puts his finger on the trigger I will tell you."

"That's right, Michael – that's the lower hand. Just give me a nudge and I'll whack him."

The Arabs got louder.

"Talk to me, Mikey."

"They say, 'they are coming for us.'"

Jarvis looked out the window:

"It's a military Chinook – one of ours."

Martin's jaw dropped:

"They must be towels. That's how they were going to get out. They create diversions to clear the sky, then they send in that chopper with towels dressed like Marines."

"Yeah. A good plan. But the sky *isn't* clear – not anymore.

Martin . . . in a military action pilots can't act on their own. You can't just fly around anywhere and land anywhere you want."

"Jarvis, for all we know they are in contact with the airships and the LAV. They might have a ruse going that they are coming in here to hunt out the sniper."

"Oh come on, Martin – you watch too much TV. Do you think they have stolen the pilot's identity?"

"Why not?"

"Get a grip! Do you suppose that guy rides around by himself?

Wind from the giant chopper gusted into the window. One of the Arabs shouted.

"Michael," Jarvis cried out, "what is that guy saying?"

"He said, 'the turret is tuning.' The man with the funny gun has his figure on the trigger."

Jarvis put his hand behind his back and grabbed the 9mm pistol. Everyone's' eyes were on the chopper; and he had a clear shot at the man holding the rocket launcher.

A round splashed into the man's right shoulder. He reached over and grabbed his wound with his left hand and the launcher swung to the left. With the noise and wind of the chopper, no one could hear the report of the silenced pistol; nor did they notice the distress of the man who held their fate in the balance.

Jarvis whacked him again and the rocket fired and exploded point blank into the Chinook.

The Arabs scrambled into defensive positions at the windows. All but one:

The tall man that they called Moe looked over at Jarvis; but the Colonel had already taken aim and put a round neatly into his forehead.

Michael peeked out the window and Jarvis yanked him down to the floor. At that moment the chopper exploded like a fireball and flames and smoke came through the windows.

Michael grabbed Martin by the shoulders and yelled in his face:

"Remember what I told you about Zak!"

The 25mm Gatling gun opened up and raked across the house just a foot or so above the floor. The first few rounds could be seen spitting through the wall – dissolving everything in its path. What shortly followed was a thick rolling dust cloud that enveloped everything.

NEW HOPE

11

It had been a month since Brentwood experienced its day of horror. Of the fourteen people who worked at *Threshold,* two had perished that day. Martin – whose body was never found – and another man whose favorite window seat spelled his demise during a business meeting.

Rachael had put *Threshold* up for sale and Sheila Warner had assumed Martin's role. Sheila elected to remain at her own desk and Martin's office had remained virtually unchanged.

Every effort was made to maintain business as usual; but Friday afternoons seemed empty without Martin's "happy lunches."

It was Friday afternoon; and Sheila was staring off into space smoking a cigarette.

Frank Phillips had been with Martin from the beginning. He wandered in like a lost sheep and sat down across from Sheila:

"It's amazing how I get geared to a schedule. I always get out of whack on Fridays – ever since . . ."

"I know it." She gestured towards Martin's office:

"Hey, let's go into Martin's office and have a drink."

"Just you and me?"

Sheila playfully wiggled her eyebrows:

"Why not? Heck – I'm the *real* boss now."

They settled in and poured a couple of Martin's scotches. Frank looked around the room:

"Martin had plebeian taste as far as decorating."

Sheila nodded and considered it:

"Rachael wouldn't let him make any decorating decisions about the house and she made all the decisions when they built this place. So . . . Martin insisted that he would at least decorate *his* office to suit himself."

"I always thought that the Sharps rifle with the bullet bandolier hanging over it was a nice touch," Frank noted tongue-in-cheek.

"He didn't call it a 'Sharps.'"

"No . . . he called it a 50-140. You see, Sharps kept making bigger and bigger rifles. They finally came out with the 50-140 which kicked so bad that *nobody* could shoot it." He made a funny face:

"However . . . Martin, in his wisdom, chose not to tell me *that* until *after* he goaded me into shooting it."

Sheila laughed:

"I remember the time we came back from lunch and you shot that thing?"

"Yeah. I bet Martin that it didn't really fire. I had no idea those huge bullets were real."

"That bet was a brilliant maneuver," Sheila noted.

He shrugged. "Too many cocktails."

Sheila took a sip and smiled:

"We went out back and Martin positioned himself very meticulously with his hands out. Ha – we all thought that he meant to catch *you* if you fell."

Frank belly laughed:

"Yeah. And then Marty catches the rifle and I land on my butt. Marty looks down and says, 'turkeys like you are a dime a dozen – I paid six grand for this gun.' Frank marveled:

"God – what a character!"

Sheila sighed. "Don't I miss him."

"Hey, let's not get melancholy again. This is getting to be a routine for you – you have a couple of pops . . . and you get misty."

"I know it," she said as she fixed another.

"Have you been out to see Rachael?"

She made a face and shook her head.

He lifted his brow:

"You mean, you haven't seen her since . . ."

"No, Frank. If I went out there I would start crying. And then Rachael would ask me if I was in love with her husband . . . and . . . and did I ever sleep with him."

Frank looked at her intently. "Well? That *is* the $64,000 question."

"No, I never did – but do you think she'd believe me if I blabbered away like some lovesick schoolgirl?"

"You should go out and see her, Sheila – it's not right," Frank scolded.

"I know it."

They sat silent for a while.

"Well . . . why don't you go over there?" Frank suggested. "Nothing is happening here. Everybody is sneaking cocktails – the place smells like a distillery."

She looked determined and gulped her drink:

"Tell them they can go home early if they want."

Sheila hadn't been to Brentwood Acres since the incident.

Two HUMVEEs were positioned at the gate of the estate. A Marine approached and she rolled the window down.

"Yes, ma'am?"

"I'd like to see Mrs. McDonald."

"Your name?"

"Sheila Warner."

The Marine called from his HUMVEE and returned:

"You'll have to leave your car here . . . and your purse. I'll ride you up there."

When Sheila got out of the car the Marine carefully looked her up and down.

"Are you going to frisk me?" She jokingly asked.

The Marine was visibly embarrassed:

"Ma'am . . . until we make a positive identification, I will need you to place both hands on the dashboard."

"Is . . . is that a trailer? Rachael lives in a trailer?"

"Yes ma'am."

"But . . . where's the house?" she whispered to herself.

He pulled the HUMVEE to a stop:

"Ma'am . . . just stay like you are and I'll open the door for you."

"Sheila!" Rachael cried out. "Sheila Warner!"

They hugged and tears came to their eyes:

"Come on, Rachael – don't get me crying." She turned to the Marine:

"What's your name, soldier?"

"Corporal . . ."

"No no . . . what do your buddies call you?"

"Tex."

Sheila wiggled her eyebrows:

"Tell me, Tex, is it true that everything that comes from . . ."

"Don't go there, Sheila," Rachael interjected.

Sheila kept her eyes on the man:

"If all Marines looked like you I would join up. Hey . . . are you sure you don't want to frisk me, soldier?" She pointed to her chest:

"I could be packing a pair of 44s in these babies."

Rachael laughed. "You're *already* packing a pair of 44s. Come on, Sheila – you're embarrassing the man."

Sheila's expression changed and she wiped a tear from the soldier's eye:

"What is it, soldier?"

The Marine turned to Rachael:

"Ma'am . . . I've been working up the nerve to tell you something since I started here."

Rachael's brow lifted:

"What . . . what do you want to tell me?"

He swallowed hard. "I was the first to fire on your house."

Rachael was taken back:

"Can you come in for a minute?"

"I've been assigned to guard you and can use my discretion depending on varying circumstances."

"Can you come in, soldier?"

"Yes, ma'am."

"Where do you keep the scotch?" Sheila asked.

"I don't have any, Sheils; but Holly keeps some wine in the refrigerator."

She opened the frig. "Good . . . a box . . . a heavy box."

Sheila brought in the box of wine and they got situated at a table. The Marine looked around awkwardly.

"Tell me about it, soldier?" Rachael urged him.

He took a deep breath:

"I'm a gunner, ma'am. It . . . it was a Monday . . . an officer came in the barracks screaming my name. He said to follow him. We ran out to the airfield and he pointed to an AC-130 that was warming up on the runway. He told me to climb in the LAV, and said that my crew was already inside. The plane was filled with paratroopers and one LAV.

"What does LAV mean?" Rachael asked.

"Light Armored Vehicle."

"Go ahead with your story."

"My Commander was pissed off – really steaming. He said, 'they're going to drop us – drop us with three extra Marines and all this damn equipment. Help us strap this shit down!'"

"Drop you?"

"Yeah . . . parachute us down. The LAV was made for air defense. There are no seats for troops – just for a crew of three. We had six aboard and extra gear in case we landed on our side. If that happened then our weapon systems would be useless and we would be, basically, six grunts with carbines. Well, the Commander didn't like that. And . . . we had to figure out a way to strap in the extra guys. And . . . we had to secure the equipment. God – what a mess.

From the time the officer grabbed me to the time we were in the air was maybe five minutes. All the Commander knew was that we had the GPS coordinates of a downed chopper. Our mission was to get close to the downed chopper; and deploy the three Marines for reconnaissance. We were told to consider civilians as potential hostiles, and to be on the lookout for Arabs in civilian dress." He made a face:

"We were confused as hell. The Commander thought that maybe they just grabbed the first LAV that they saw. We were in an AD model – designed to shoot down aircraft; but our mission seemed to be anti-personnel. We carried 16 Stinger missiles and also had a magazine of armor piercing. With the Gatling gun up top we could take out a battle tank with that ammo. I know because we demonstrated that capability to the brass – with a rig just like we had. But . . . it made no sense to be dropped on a little town with these kinds of weapons. We didn't know *what* to expect.

They dropped us on a dairy farm NE of here. Gear flew everywhere but we ended up on our wheels and nobody got hurt. The radio cracked with reports of sniper fire. A fire truck had been hit with missiles and police cars taken out with machine guns. But, when we rolled into this neighborhood there was nothing going on. The driver looked through the scope and me and the Commander took the side windows. There were little groups of people everywhere. They tried to talk to us; but the Commander ordered us to stay buttoned up.

About a quarter mile from the wreck site we deployed our three Marines and they went ahead. The Commander told them to maintain constant radio contact and to watch out for civilians. Just a few minutes later they reported a man down from sniper fire. They identified the shooter and returned fire but they couldn't confirm a kill." He winced:

"The sniper fire came from a lower window of your house. It was a civilian."

"How could they tell?" Rachael asked.

"They ID'd him through their spotting scope. The way he exposed himself in the window made it clear that he didn't have combat training. Plus . . ."

"What . . . why do you make that face?" Rachael wondered.

"They said that the guy was wearing pajamas and . . . and what looked like an early style ammo vest. They said he had what looked like an M-14 with a scope."

Rachael put her hand mouth. "White pajamas?"

"We didn't ask."

"Did . . . did he have blonde hair?" Rachael asked with a shaky voice.

"Ma'am . . . I don't know."

Sheila noticed Rachael's fearful expression. "What is it, Rachael?"

"Martin . . . he had a bad habit of wearing his pajamas during the day."

"And those goofy mink slippers," Sheila added.

Rachael nodded. "He'd go to the door looking like that – embarrassed the hell out of me." She looked numb:

"But why – why would Martin fire at the Marines?" She looked at the soldier:

"Why?"

"I don't know."

"Finish your story."

He gathered his thoughts for a moment and continued:

"We called command about the downed Marine; and they told us to get into position to fire on the house – but no closer than 300 Yards. They asked how close our men were to the house and we told them 200 yards. They said 'move em back!' By the time we got into position there was a gunship orbiting the house – and then another.

A big Chinook chopper showed up and said that they had orders to set down some Marines. One of the gunship pilots said, 'Orders? Orders from who?' There was some static and they lost radio contact with the Chinook. The gunship pilot kept saying:

'Get out of there! Damn it – get out of there!'

We watched as the chopper settled down. My Commander yelled,

'Those idiots are nuts!'

They landed the chopper so close to the house that I was afraid the blades would hit. I was told to set my range and be ready to put a line of fire across the house – just below the first floor windows." He marveled:

"Then the Chinook blew up."

Rachael jolted:

"Blew up? Are you telling me that my husband blew up the helicopter with . . . with his rifle?"

"No ma'am, I'm not saying that – we don't know *how* it blew up.

I was ordered to fire and emptied my ready ammo. By the time I got in battery again the target was gone. The gunships had opened up and all I could see was smoke.

The Commander gave the order to pick up the three Marines and leave the area. Then . . . someone ordered napalm strikes and the woods lit up. I'll bet the driver got that thing going sixty. He almost lost it a couple of times."

Rachael stared numbly out the window:

"Martin."

"Ma'am . . . there are different levels of classified information. But, when an incident like this occurs . . . well . . . Marines talk to each other."

"And?" Rachael urged.

"The real crew of the Chinook was murdered and the bodies hidden. They were found by accident a couple of days after the incident."

"They didn't die in the explosion," Rachael concluded.

"That's right." He studied her face:

"Mrs. McDonald – you don't seem surprised."

"Well . . . I figured from your account that the men in the Chinook were Arabs. Is it true that Marines in civilian clothing were deployed to hunt down Arabs here in Brentwood?"

"Yes."

"Were any innocent civilians killed?"

"That I don't know, Mrs. McDonald. I was assigned to a LAV-25 after the smoke cleared. I didn't have anything to do with that end of it."

Rachael studied his expression:

"Yes . . . but Marines talk."

The soldier looked intense:

"Yes, they talk – but they talk to *each other*. Shit happens, Mrs. McDonald . . . shit happens."

"Is there anything else that you can tell me?"

"No. I'm sure that civilians talk too. There are lots of stories going around about the incident."

"Do you know what the final death toll was? The news never reported it."

"No ma'am."

When Rachael stood up the soldier did likewise. Rachael held out her hand:

"Thank you, soldier – thank you very much."

He nodded and Rachael and Sheila followed him outside. The Corporal opened the door of the HUMVEE and turn to look at Rachael:

"Ma'am?"

"Yes."

He gave her a curious look:

"Well . . . ah . . . I was at the gate when the President of the United States came here. I was just curious . . ."

"I asked him to please get rid of you boys and that his tanks were ruining our streets."

"Did he ask you what caused all of this?"

"Yes."

"Could you tell me . . . could you tell me *anything* about it?"

Rachael's eyes waxed angry:

"One of the men with the President went to great lengths to emphasize the secrecy of the matter. I told him, basically, to stick it. For God's sake – I had just watched them put my husband into a vacuum bag."

They watched as the man drove back to the gate.

Sheila made a face:

"Vacuum bag?"

Rachael pointed:

"The wind was drifting that way. That's where most of the dust settled. The bigger pieces were under the dust. They came out here with this contraption – like a giant vacuum cleaner. There were some large chunks of metal – I guess that was the chopper."

Sheila marveled:

"Rachael . . . how do you do it?"

"Huh?"

"Well . . . you look good – better than you have in years. And . . . and after all of this."

"I was given a promise by a very special person. A person who cannot lie." She smiled:

"I have hope."

"Michael?" Sheila guessed. "Are you talking about Michael?"

"Yes."

Sheila's eyes lit up in anticipation:

"Do you know where Michael is?"

"Michael is dead."

Sheila gasped. "Dead?"

"Yes. He was our cook. He stayed in the guesthouse."

Rachael studied Sheila's grieved expression. "Did you know Michael?"

"No. But . . . I didn't know that he was *dead* . . . I . . . I didn't know that Martin had hired him."

"I hired him." She thought about it and smiled:

"One day the doorbell rang – I opened the door and Michael was standing there. It was strange. I knew the man from somewhere; but I couldn't place the face."

"So . . . *you* hired him?"

"Yes . . . well . . . there's more to it than that."

"Martin told, me, Rachael – he told me how this man helped you." She sighed and looked at her empty glass:

"Let's go inside."

Sheila exchanged her wineglass for a highball and sat down next to Rachael.

"Sheila, you need to lay off that stuff!"

"Why? My liver is *already* shot."

"That will regenerate – that's what they told Martin."

"I just don't give a shit anymore, Rachael. Martin promised me . . . ."

"What?"

"It doesn't matter. Forget it," Sheila grumbled.

"Gosh . . . you're a barrel of laughs."

"Humph – that's what *everybody* tells me."

A few moments passed.

"Have you found any buyers for *Threshold*?" Rachael asked.

"Two big companies are looking at it," Sheila began. "Frank has been a total angel – he's talked everybody into staying until you get a buyer. Christ – without them, all you would have to sell is a building."

Sheila lifted her brow and caught Rachael's eye:

So . . . what are you going to do after you sell *Threshold*?"

"I'm going to stay right here – at least for a while."

"You're going to rebuild?"

"No."

Sheila looked like she smelled dirty feet:

"You're going to live here? In this little trailer?"

Rachael ignored Sheila's zealous reaction:

"Yes. It's just Holly and me."

"Do you mind if I ask you about something?"

"Try me, Sheils."

"The funerals for your sister and daughter were both closed casket. The newspapers didn't say how they died."

"It's better that I tell you nothing of that," Rachael sadly informed her. "It would probably be better for you if you hadn't come out here."

"You gotta be kidding, Raech! This is probably the safest place in the world." She threw up her hands:

"Rachael – they've made this a no-fly zone. You got an army around you."

Rachael twisted her lips and shook her head:

"They are still here – I guarantee it."

"*What* are you *talking* about? The Marines got em – every one of them."

"They're still here," Rachael concluded.

“I’d better go,” Sheila blurted.

Rachael was surprised:

“Why?”

“I . . . I get into these crying jags.”

“You need to stop *drinking*, Sheila.”

“If . . . if I don’t drink the crying jags hurt *more* – they’re *worse*.”

“Well . . . Holly will be home soon. Don’t you want to see Holly?”

Tears formed in her eyes:

“Yes – I’d like to see Holly.” She forced a pathetic smile:

“I’ll stick around for a while.”

Holly came through the door:

“Miss Warner!”

She gave Sheila a big hug and they talked for a few minutes.

“I’m going to make a sandwich,” Holly said. “Does anyone want one?”

Rachael looked at Sheila:

“No . . . you go ahead, hon.”

Sheila was dumbstruck – as if she’d seen a ghost.

“Sheila? What is it?” Rachael asked her.

“Holly . . . she . . . she’s just glowing.”

“She’s a happy girl,” Rachael concluded.

Sheila stared off at nothing. After a few minutes Rachael spoke up:

“Tell me about this promise that Martin made to you.”

She snapped out of it, gulped her wine and scowled:

“It doesn’t matter now.”

“Tell me . . . please?”

Sheila reluctantly began:

“You were . . . well . . . in pretty bad shape for a long time. Martin told me about that encounter you had with Michael, and how it changed you. To make a long story short, Marty promised that he would introduce me to Michael. And . . . I was hoping that . . . that this man could help *me*.”

Rachael smiled:

“Well . . . it’s not too late for that.”

Sheila groaned.

“No Sheila, it’s *not* too late,” Rachael insisted.

Sheila became hostile:

“Da-ah? Have you lost it? Michael and Martin are both *dead*!”

“I have a story to tell you. Would you like to hear a story, Sheils?”

“Sure. Make it a funny one. A good laugh would help.”

"OK. Holly was catatonic for three days following the deaths of Molly and Agatha. Oh . . . the doctors ran the usual checks – but they really didn't know if she would ever wake up. And . . . if she did . . . .

Anyway. I stayed by her bed for three days. I prayed and I prayed.

On the third day her eyes popped open. She smiled at me and said, 'hi mom,' as if she had just woken from a nap."

"Did . . . did she remember anything?"

"Yes."

"Well . . . tell me!" She urged.

"She remembered being in a huge tunnel. Somehow she knew that good people were above her, and that bad people were below. She was very afraid that the bad people would see her."

"And carry her down?"

"Yes."

"Go on."

"So . . . when she saw a small opening in the side of the tunnel she crawled in there and hid. She said it was like a little cave."

Sheila's eyes were wide with anticipation:

"And?"

"Well . . . she was *very* afraid. Much too fearful to peek out of her hiding place. So she just stayed there."

"And?"

"Well . . . it finally occurred to her to pray to Michael. As soon as she started praying Michael appeared and carried her upwards though the huge tunnel."

"And?"

Rachael smiled:

"And that's the story."

Sheila was confused:

"Well . . . what did Michael say to her? I mean – did she tell you?"

"Yes. But I can't tell you that part. I will say this, Michael prophesied to her – he gave her hope."

"Hope? That's what *I* need."

"I knew you would like the story."

"But . . . what good will it do *me*?" Sheila complained.

"Da-ah? Don't you get it?"

Sheila was disgusted:

"No. I *don't* get it."

Rachael smiled cheerfully:

"Michael isn't gone – not really. You can still pray to Michael just the same as Holly prayed to him."

"Pray to him? You want me to pray to this dead guy Michael?"

"Yes. Tell him who you are. Tell him what good friends you were with Martin; and tell him about the broken promise.

If it worked for Holly then it can work for you. You saw how happy Holly was."

Sheila considered it. "So . . . do I need to sober up first? I mean . . . I am *so* screwed up right now."

Rachael smiled warmly at her. "Oftentimes prayer is most effective when you *are* screwed up."

YOU SAY "GOODBYE"

12

Sheila woke up with a terrible hangover.

She donned her robe and started some coffee. Her hand shook a bit as she poured:

"I think I'll take it with," she said to herself.

She sipped the rum concoction and lit a cigarette. Her mind went back to her conversation with Rachael the day before:

"I forgot to pray," she mumbled as she added another tad of rum. She dialed the phone.

"Hello?"

"Rachael . . . do I need to get down on my knees?"

"What?"

"Ah . . . I'm going to pray . . . I forgot to do it last night."

"Well, Sheila . . . just so it's heartfelt."

"I . . . I want to do it right. I don't want to blow it."

"You won't *blow* it."

Sheila groaned. "Well . . . how do I know if the message gets through?"

"Just have faith."

"Yeah . . . OK."

"Are you all right, Sheila?"

"Yes . . . well . . . I'm a bit shaky."

"Do you need to get anything from the store?" Rachael asked.

"Ah . . ."

"I'm going. Tex is going to take me."

"Tex – the Marine?"

"Yeah."

"Well . . . let me try to get it together a bit. Ah . . . I'll call you later."

Sheila poured some flavored creamer in her mug and added some more rum. She knew that Rachael felt sorry for her; but that wasn't what she needed. Seeing Rachael made her think of Martin and that only led to more tears.

The more rum she drank the better she felt; but the less she felt like praying – if she felt like it at all. She was spiraling out of control and there was no one to help.

She added some ice and some more rum.

"Dear Lord," she began. "Ah . . . I mean – dear Michael. I'm going nuts here . . . it's not just the booze – it's . . . something more serious. I'm . . . I'm a good friend of Martin's; and he promised to ask you to help me. Ah . . . Rachael said that I should pray and ask you if you could *still* help me. I mean . . . I know that you're dead and all . . . but . . . Rachael said . . ."

The doorbell rang.

"Christ – who's that."

She opened the door. A handsome, well-built man in tee shirt and jeans smiled at her.

She knew him from somewhere but couldn't place the face:

"Yes?"

The man looked around awkwardly:

"Ah . . . I've come to help you."

Sheila's heart race:

"Jesus Christ!"

"Not really."

"Huh?"

"Jerry – my name is Jerry."

Her mouth hung open as she stared at the man:

"Wow."

"Wow?"

"That was fast, Jerry."

Jerry gave her an inquisitive look:

"Fast?"

She marveled. "I mean . . . I wasn't even finished praying for you to come."

"Well," the man stammered, "then the timing is good."

"Wha . . . what do we do now?"

The man playfully rubbed his chin:

"Let's see. Now you invite me in for coffee."

Sheila stepped aside and followed the man into the kitchen.

"When did you paint?" he asked.

"Ah . . . a couple months ago. What do you think?"

"It's OK."

"How do you like your coffee?" Sheila asked him.

"Put some of that cinnamon and vanilla stuff in it."

Sheila watched as he sipped his coffee:

"You're peeking," she told the man as she adjusted the top of her robe.

He made an offhand gesture:

"Oh . . . ah . . . I'm sorry."

Sheila's eyes narrowed suspiciously:

"Perhaps we have a misunderstanding."

"How's that?"

"Well . . . I thought you were the answer to my prayer."

His demeanor became serious:

"I see." He thought a moment. "And what did you pray for?"

"Help . . . help of a *spiritual* nature."

The man beamed at her. "Then, my child, I am he whom you requested."

She looked down at her robe. "But . . . you peeked."

"It's my first assignment and your double D's threw me off a bit. Bear with me, my child, I am a man – not an angel."

She rolled her eyes. "Just my luck – to get a holy man on his first assignment."

"Nah, don't worry about it." He pointed skyward:

"They do all the work – there's nothing to it." He continued:

"Actually, I would have gotten here sooner if it wasn't for the road blocks. They finally got rid of them."

She eyed him suspiciously:

"All you have to do is talk to them and they'll let you through."

"Yeah, right," he said sarcastically. "I just tell them that my name is Jerry and I was sent from God to lay hands on Sheila Warner. That would get me on the bus to Belleview." He viewed Sheila and faintly lifted his brow:

"Either that or the guy would tell me that I had to wait till the Christmas party like the rest of the townsfolk."

Sheila laughed but quickly caught herself and squinted at the man.

"Ah . . . I was well briefed," he explained.

"You are not at *all* what I expected," she admitted.

The man lifted his finger to make a point:

"Yes, my child – the Lord works in mysterious ways."

Sheila got up, walked to the sink and poured some rum – thinking that the man wouldn't see her.

"I saw that!"

Sheila winced and turned around. "I'd like to get off this stuff. Can you help me with that?"

"Sure. They can get rid of the *jones*. Whether you start again or not is up to you."

She twisted her lips:

"You sure don't *talk* like a holy man. How do I *know* that you were sent from God? Maybe . . . maybe . . ."

"Maybe I'm from the other side?"

"What other side?"

"Never mind."

"What else do you know about me . . . from . . . ah . . . your briefing?"

"Well . . . apparently . . . this character, Martin, was quite the stud-muffin." He studied her expression and continued:

"You always kind of . . . well . . ."

She looked annoyed.

The stranger tuned to her displeasure:

"So . . . to make a long story short, Martin makes you a promise but turkeys out on it."

"Turkeys?"

"Yeah, he finks out on ya. So . . . his buddy Michael gets on his case about it and . . ." He smiled curiously:

"Here I am."

She pointed at the man:

"Do I know you from somewhere?"

He was caught off-guard:

"Ah . . ."

Her eyes widened. "Aha! A holy man cannot lie. Answer me, holy man!"

"You look for answers that are fast and easy," he dryly concluded.

"Yes or no, holy man – answer me!"

He defiantly folded his arms in front of him:

"I do not have to answer you."

Sheila was taken back. "Why?"

He shrugged. "Ah . . . cause . . . those are the rules."

With that he got up and fixed himself another coffee.

"What do you hear from Rachael?" the man asked.

"I was out there yesterday."

The man's eyes widened in anticipation:

"And?"

His urgency surprised her:

"Ah . . ."

"How is Holly?"

"She's fine."

The man slumped with relief.

Sheila continued:

"But . . . Molly and Agatha . . ."

"I know about them. How's Rachael?"

"She's great. I really don't know how she does it."

The man sat back down, stared off and smiled:

"Has Holly found a new sweetheart yet?" the man asked.

"Sweetheart? She's been going with this Bobby fellow for ages – I don't know of any new sweetheart." She eyed the man:

"Do you know Rachael and Holly?"

"Well . . ."

"Are you going to plead the 5th amendment on me again?"

The man looked a bit peeved:

"Miss. Warner . . . I have come here to help you. I am not getting paid; I do it for its own sake. Please, don't put anything additional on me."

"I'm sorry."

His face remained tense:

"I'll see that you get help; but I cannot allow myself to be questioned by the military or the police."

Sheila became suspicious again:

"Are you some kind of crook?"

The man squared off and glared at her:

"Don't fart around with me, Sheils – if you do I'm out of here. Keep your mouth shut about this – Brentwood is crawling with cops and detectives. I . . . I'm up the creek if they question me."

Sheila's mouth hung opened as she blankly gaped at the man.

His expression softened and he gently took her hand. Sheila felt a tingling comfort run through her; and she knew in her heart that she could trust the stranger. She smiled affectionately at the man:

"Yes . . . OK."

Jerry acknowledged her and rubbed his hands together:

"Are you ready to go?"

"Ah . . . well . . . sure."

"OK. Let's go into the living room where there is some soft carpeting."

Sheila followed the man to the other end of the house.

"Put your hands above your head like this," he instructed her. "That's right. Now, close your eyes and pray about what you want the Lord to do for you."

"Who was that on the phone, mother?" Holly asked.

"That was Sheila."

"She didn't look very good yesterday. Do you think she's alright?"

Her mother sighed and looked out the trailer window in the direction of their old house:

"Come on, Holly – let's go outside and sit for a while."

Holly followed her mother out to a round table. The umbrella had been taken down to take advantage of the waning fall sunlight. They sat for a few moments and looked around at the devastation that was once the McDonald estate.

There was nothing left of the house or the guesthouse. The material had literally been taken away in dump trucks. The lawn was ugly and dead where the dust had laid and the napalm had burnt it. The surrounding woods were bleak, blackened sticks. The legs of the statue that Jarvis shot were the only remnants still standing on its own.

"Mother?"

"Yes."

"I want you to tell me what happened here. I have a right to know."

A hint of sadness showed in Rachael's eyes:

"Honey . . . we've been over this before. It's a closed chapter. You have no knowledge of what caused this; and, for the time being at least, it must be left that way." She studied her daughter's expression:

"You have to trust me on that."

"Mom . . . Tex told me that dad fired on the Marines. He said that he checked around and found out that the man in the window *was* wearing white pajamas, and *was* blonde-headed just as you suspected."

Rachael groaned.

"Did dad go crazy?" Holly asked.

"No. The gates of heaven opened up for your father and Michael. If your father shot a Marine, then I believe that there was a reason for it."

Holly gestured around at their surroundings:

"There was a reason for all this? This somehow has to do with God's plan?"

"Yes."

"I'm having a bit of trouble with that, mom," Holly confessed.

"Some day you will understand," Rachael assured her.

Holly became impatient:

"But, mother, I thought that everything was going to get *better*. I prayed and prayed that you would get over your depression and believed that Michael was the answer to those prayers."

"He was, Holly – just as sure as he answered your prayers when you were catatonic."

"Mother?"

"Yes, Holly."

"Why did God leave you that way for so long?"

Rachael thought a few moments and began:

"I made bad choices; and people have to pay for their bad choices. I was in bad shape for about ten years; but some people never come out of it and stay in a pathetic state throughout their entire lives."

"But . . . things were good for you and dad at first. Right?"

"Your father and I fell in love in the 60's. Your dad was fun-loving and had a great sense of humor; and he was in no way arrogant – but very humble. That's one of the things that I loved about your father – his humility.

For a long time your father had a regular job; but later he decided to start a business of his own; and we sold the house and used the money to start it. We were in debt up to our eyeballs – that's when we rented the little place on Yale Street.

Your father needed me then. He needed me to take care of his girls, and to squeak on everything that we bought from groceries to clothes.

Marty worried a lot about money in those days. Many a night I assured him that everything was going to work out fine; and, if it didn't, we were young enough to start over.

We found a little spirit-filled church to go to. Marty became interested in the Bible and we would read it together at night. Before we went to sleep we would . . . ah . . ."

"I get the picture, mother."

"Yes . . . well . . . and then after that we would pray together and fall asleep.

Neither one of us drank very much in those days; and your dad couldn't afford to join the country club. Oftentimes we would ride through the club and Marty would declare that we would join some day and he would teach me to play golf.

But those were the *good times* – as I was to find out later.

Marty had a knack of motivating people around him and the business grew rapidly. We bought a house of our own and continued to upgrade until we built here in Brentwood Acres."

"It's hard for me to think of dad as humble," Holly volunteered. "It seems to me that he was always the boss, the wheeler dealer."

Rachael considered it:

"After he became – the boss and the wheeler dealer – he began to *lose* his humble characteristics. Your father built a world of his own and he put himself in the middle of it. Unfortunately, he did not leave a place there for me.

At first we bathed in his glory together. I had a respected identity – the wife of a superman who had made a whole lot with very little. It didn't seem like your father knew how to make a bad business decision.

In the beginning, I did everything that was expected of me. I hung out with the girls at the club and attended all of the parties. And, I orchestrated many parties at home. Before the parties would begin, Marty would brief me on people that he was doing a lot of business with, or, people whose business he was trying to get. As time went on there were less and less people that I wanted to see, and more and more people that I was *obligated* to see. Socializing became work; and, as time wore on, less and less of our old friends were invited.

And the booze flowed. The booze always flowed.

I started to feel cynical about my lifestyle and became morose. I began to come up with excuses to avoid some of the social occasions and soon found out that I was more content to stay at home, drink by myself, and watch TV.

One morning Marty called up and asked if I was going to be home at lunchtime. I said that I was; and he informed me that he was coming home.

Well . . . I thought that was great and prepared a nice lunch – hoping that he wanted to fool around afterwards." She smiled as she thought of it:

"That was a weekly routine in the beginning, but waned with time.

But Marty had *not* come home to eat or fool around. It was more like a business meeting. He told me that my only job was to help with the social end of things; and that this was an important aspect of his business. I informed him that I was his wife, and not one of his employees. I then began to cry and confessed that I felt lonely and frustrated." Her eyes became sad as she relived it:

"I was taken back by the lack of concern that Marty showed for my welfare. He said that I needed to get back on the 'band wagon,' and complement his efforts as I had done in the past. I told him that it was his bandwagon that was the *source* of my woes.

So . . . he just motions around at the lavishness of my surroundings and informs me that I am hardly the abused person that I was pretending to be. He accused me of staging my own 'pity party' – a phrase left over from our church days.

He went back to work without us resolving anything." Rachael's expression pained:

"Things only got worse after that. You were there, Holly – I don't have to tell you."

Holly looked frightened:

"You said. 'I made bad choices; and people have to pay for their bad choices.' Are you sorry that you married daddy?"

Rachael shook her head assuredly:

"No, honey, I married the right man. What I meant by that was that *I chose* to see myself as a victim who had no solution to her dilemma.

In desperation I asked Marty if I could work at *Threshold*. I thought if I did that, then I could get back into his life somehow. Of course, Marty would have none of that. And, well, he already had Sheila as his 'Girl Friday.'"

Holly looked sheepish:

"Do you think that she and dad ever . . ."

"I never confronted your father with that. There was a period where I didn't like your dad very much. Actually, there were times when I really didn't care *what* he did with Sheila.

I became a person that people didn't want to be around. Not just your dad – I fell away from my other friends too.

I had placed *too* much faith in your father. I expected that *he* would be my source of happiness; and, when that fell apart, I felt abandoned and alone.

My biggest mistake was that I didn't turn to God for help, and believe that He would find a remedy for my situation. Instead of tapping into God's resources, I blamed Him for my condition. You can't expect God to do everything in a sovereign fashion – sometimes you need to *ask* for help. So . . . I cut myself off from my best avenue of hope.

There were plenty of other things that I could have gotten back into – things that I did before *Threshold* took off. I still had friends that would have helped me if I had only reached out for them. But I *chose* to continue on as a victim; and, in doing so, I isolated myself from anybody or any activity that I might have found fruitful."

Holly smiled:

"And then Michael came."

Rachael's expression softened:

"Yes. He laid hands on me; and when I awoke I no longer had bad feelings towards your father. I could remember the hurt; but it had lost its sting." She marveled:

"In one instant Marty and I were right back to where we started at the beginning:

He joked and clowned and acted the fool to make me laugh just as he had done in the beginning. He even started back with some of his old 60's lingo. Life became an adventure again, like it had been at the start. And, circumstances had changed where Marty needed me again – just like he had when we began together. My simple faith in God returned."

"Just like it had been there at the start," Holly offered.

Rachael nodded. "Yes."

"Why was it that dad needed you again, mom – what had changed so radically?"

Rachael considered it for a moment:

"*Where your treasure is, there will your heart be also.*

All at once, everything that he worked for at *Threshold* became as nothing. He had gotten himself into a very dangerous situation – one that he couldn't control. He wasn't worried about himself as much as he was worried about his family. He realized what he had – that was of *real* value – and his heart softened." She smiled and nodded contentedly:

"And I was there to help him; just like I had been there to help him in the past."

"And then dad is killed by the United States Marines," Holly said curtly.

"Yes."

Holly motioned towards the remnant of their house:

"And then you sit here smiling as you look around at the devastation."

Rachael squinted at her daughter:

"Are you trying to say something?"

Holly took a deep breath and began:

"I ran into Martha from your old church the other day."

"They've been good about coming to see me," Rachael mentioned.

"Yes . . . well . . . Martha seems to think that you need to grieve and move on. She thinks that you are in denial and behave as if dad is still alive and will walk through the door at any minute. She says that you must be in La La Land to sit out here in this trailer in the middle of all this ugliness."

Rachael shrugged it off:

"Well . . . I'm sure that Martha means well."

There stared at each other for a moment.

"What is it, Holly – what's on your mind?"

Holly gestured:

"Well . . . why *haven't* you grieved? I mean – I haven't seen you cry. Did you get that over with before I woke up?"

"You don't understand," Rachael accused.

"I'm listening."

Rachael turned to her daughter:

"Before I came up to Agatha's, I knew that Martin was going to die. And, I suspected that Michael and the other man were going to die as well."

"What?"

"Yes. I knew that your father would die; and I knew the reason behind it.

Before I left the house that last day, Marty and I talked and agreed *not* to say goodbye – because we were only going to be apart for a brief intermission."

Holly pointed an accusing finger:

"So . . . you *are* in denial."

"Is that what you think?"

"Yes."

"So . . . you think I should bid farewell to Marty – say goodbye and move on with my life?"

"Yes."

Rachael was visibly annoyed:

"Holly, deal with Marty's death as it suits *you*," Rachael asserted. "*You* say goodbye to him if you want to. *I'll* deal with it *my way*."

Rachael then smiled.

"What's so funny?" Holly asked.

"Well . . . what do you suggest, Holly – should I find a new squeeze?"

"Well – maybe you should."

Holly glared at her mother as she chuckled:

"I'm not joking, mother. It *is* weird staying out here. You've collected a pot full of money on the insurance and you can sell the land. You don't *have* to stay here."

"But had I not done it that way then you might never have gotten to know Tex," Rachael pointed out.

Holly purposely ignored the comment and continued:

"And . . . and Martha is right – you *don't* act like someone who just suddenly lost her husband. You *do* act like dad is going to walk through the door any minute."

Rachael lifted her brow inquisitively:

"And your advice, daughter?"

"Well . . . you act like you can just sit here in this trailer; and, somehow, something marvelous is going to happen to make you happy. Well . . . things don't usually work out that way. I mean, for something to happen an effort has to be made."

"Your point is well taken. But . . . Michael didn't specifically tell me about the effort part."

"Look, mother – Michael was a great guy and I liked him a lot. And, yes, he laid hands on you and you got better. But they do that sort of thing all the time down at the church where you and dad went."

Rachael sighed. "So, daughter . . . where are you going with this?"

"Well . . . Michael helped you – but that doesn't mean that he knows the future."

"Holly . . . Michael helped you as well; and he prophesied to you. Don't you believe what he said?"

"Mom, he prophesied that I would live long and have many children. Gosh, what's so tough about that? I mean, that's pretty general."

"Holly . . . if you knew Michael very well you would think that was an *extraordinary* prophecy."

"I didn't know Michael very well and I think it's pretty general," she quipped. "That could apply to almost *anybody*."

"And he told you something else . . ."

"Which makes absolutely no sense. Michael was somewhere between worlds when I prayed to him. Maybe I should have prayed to Jesus or God. Maybe then I would have gotten some *usable* information."

"Would you like to hear something else that Michael said about you?"

"Yes."

"He told me that you would find a new sweetheart before you broke off your engagement with Bobby."

Holly's eyes widened:

"Really?"

"Yes."

Holly couldn't hide her enthusiasm:

"Well . . . *that's* pretty interesting."

Rachael twisted an odd smile:

"Maybe?"

Holly looked suspiciously at her mother:

"What are you trying to say, mom?"

Rachael acted nonchalant:

"I'm just repeating what Michael said."

Holly frowned.

"What's the trouble now?" Rachael asked.

"If daddy knew that he was going to die then he should have told you to move on with your life and be as happy as you can. He should have let you go."

"Neither one of us felt like letting go. And, I might add, there was no reason that we should."

Holly glared at her mother defiantly:

"You've got an answer for everything, mom; but they don't make that much sense to me. I mean, if Michael was such a good thing, then why are dad and Agatha and Molly dead; and why are we sitting in a trailer staring at a burnt-out forest? When enlightenment comes does it mean destruction?"

Rachael nodded. "Sometimes that is true. This was one of those times."

Holly looked away and scowled:

"You're making me crazy, mom." She looked back to her mother:

"Tell me this: Is the trouble gone? Are we safe again?"

"Yes . . . I believe that we will be safe for a season."

"Because of something that Michael said?"

"Yes. But after a time there will be trouble again."

"For us?"

"For everybody."

"Everybody where?" Holly asked desperately.

Rachael made a dramatic motion. "Everybody in the world!"

Holly stood to her feet and looked down at her mother:

"I'm glad that you're happy. I'm glad that you're off the booze and pills. But, it would be nice if you made a bit more sense." Having said that, she headed back towards the trailer. Rachael laughed and called out after her:

"Where are you going?"

Holly turned:

"I'm going to go talk with Tex. And . . . and I'll just die if he doesn't make any more sense than *you* do."

Rachael laughed again:

"Come back and talk to me. I want to talk some more."

"About what?"

"Please come and sit down." She smiled at her daughter:

"Tell me that story again. You know, when you talked with Michael . . . when you were catatonic. I love to hear it. No more doom and gloom. OK?"

She reluctantly sat down next to her mother:

"Well . . . I don't remember falling down on the floor at Agatha's house. And . . . it seemed like time stood still when I was hiding in the cave."

"What did Michael look like?"

"He looked like Michael – with that same little smile that he always wore. We went up and out of the long tunnel before I could say anything. He told me that you were fine and that you needed me to come back. At first I wanted to stay; but he told me that you were distressed and waiting next to me in a hospital. When I agreed to return there was a swishing sound and the sensation of speed. I opened my eyes and you were there."

"Tell me again what Michael told you."

"Well . . . he said that I would live a long time and would have many children. He gave me a number and said that I should tell it to no one except the person who knew it. That person would explain things to me and be my guide."

Rachael grew serious:

"That's the part I don't get. What does that mean to you?"

Holly mused for a moment:

"Well . . . I guess that the person that knows my number is someone that I should trust." She shrugged. "I guess that's what it means."

"Did Michael say that you should mention the deal about the number to me?"

"He said that I should mention it to you and *only* to you. Mom, I thought *you* were the one who would know my number."

Rachael shook her head:

"I don't have any idea what that is about.

Did he say anything about your fiancée, Bobby?"

"You're asking because Michael told you that I would find a new sweetheart before I broke up with Bobby."

"Yes – that's why I'm asking."

Holly avoided her mother's stare.

"Holly . . . what's going on with you and Bobby?"

"I think Bobby and I are finished."

"Since when?"

Holly looked disgusted:

"After we discussed calling off the marriage, things just dried up."

"Were you and Bobby sleeping together?"

"Mother!"

"Did you want to get married so you could have sex with Bobby?"

Holly looked away:

"I suppose that was part of it."

"How would you feel if you broke off the engagement?"

"Relieved."

Rachael tried to get Holly to look at her:

"A month ago you were worried that you would *lose* him."

"Yes, I know."

They looked at each other for a moment.

"Mother, there is *so* much that I don't understand." She sighed:

"I think Bobby wants to break it off as well. He won't do it because he would feel guilty. You know . . . with the way things have been."

"You need to straighten it out," Rachael asserted. "You'll feel better and so will he."

"I know it. Every time the phone rings I expect it to be him." She brightened:

"Maybe you and I can drive up there and I can talk to him?"

"I don't know if I want to drive anywhere just yet. To tell you the truth, I've gotten a bit used to having Tex and his buddies protecting us." She studied her daughter's face:

"Why don't you go call Bobby on the phone and get it over with?"

Holly looked off and smiled:

"Tex is one cute Marine."

Rachael lifted her brow and studied her daughter's expression:

"He's noticed you as well."

Holly came alive:

"Really . . . what did he say?"

"Well . . . I promised that I wouldn't say anything to you about it. He made me promise that after I told him you were engaged."

Holly gasped. "You didn't!"

"Well . . . you *are* engaged."

"But *mother*, I didn't want you to *tell* him that." Her eyes narrowed:

"So . . . that's why Tex has acted so distant lately."

Rachael wiggled her eyebrows:

"Well . . . I didn't know that you had taken such a shine to Tex."

"His name is Corporal Richard Maddox."

"Hmm . . . that's got a ring."

"Mother . . . did he say that he liked me?"

She smiled curiously. "A bit more than that."

Holly looked at her mother pleadingly for more information.

"Actually," Rachael began, "he said a *lot* more than that – but I promised . . ."

Holly beamed and looked at her watch:

"It's Saturday morning, and Bobby will still be in the sheets. I'm going to call Bobby – then you can tell Tex that my engagement is off."

"I think it would be better if you did that yourself."

Rachael watched as her smiling daughter emerged from the trailer:

"How did it go?" Rachael asked.

"Very well. He acted awkward over the phone. It was over in a minute."

"Do you think that someone was there with him?"

"Yes . . . but it's alright. I can understand it."

Rachael studied Holly's expression:

"So . . . are you going to go down and tell Tex?"

Holly looked away:

"I'm going to have to work up to that."

"Well . . . Tex is a very nice boy – I've grown very fond of him."

"Thanks, mom."

"For what?"

"Oh, for liking Tex . . . and . . . and for the advice – to call Bobby and get it over with. It wouldn't have been good to drive up there. It would have just brought back bad memories."

Rachael gently took her daughter's hand:

"You don't have to *ever* go back there. There are other good schools."

"Mom?"

"Yes, Holly."

"Why do you keep asking me to tell the story about Michael?"

Rachael attempted to shrug it off.

"Oh . . . I just like to hear it."

"You're looking for something for yourself – aren't you?"

"Holly . . . there were three people in the house when it was destroyed. Michael knew that they would all die; but, he told me that I would experience a time of refreshment – a time of peace and happiness."

"And you can't understand how that will happen without dad," Holly concluded.

"No . . . I *can't* understand it. But I *believe* it and that's what keeps me going." She gently squeezed Holly's hand:

"Sometimes I feel guilty for not insisting that you go back to school. But, I'm glad you didn't . . . and you seem to be happy."

"I'm happy to be with you and . . ."

Rachael wiggled her eyebrows and embarrassed Holly.

"Whew . . . I can't believe that I said that. I mean . . . he hasn't asked even asked me out."

"Why don't you go down and talk to Tex. And, while you're at it, ask him to take us to the store – we need some groceries."

Rachael sat in the back of the HUMVEE and guided Tex to Sheila's house. Holly and the Corporal chatted self-consciously as they rode along.

"Take this next left and it is the second on the right," Rachael told Richard.

Tex got the HUMVEE as close to the front door as he could.

Rachael opened the rear door:

"You two stay here. I'll go see what Sheils is doing."

"I'll need to go with you," Tex asserted.

"No . . . it's better you stay here, Richard."

"I'm sorry, but . . ."

"But what?" Rachael curtly blurted.

Tex glanced knowingly at Holly and then back to Rachael:

"Ah . . . I'm sorry, Mrs. McDonald – but I have orders . . ."

"Are you telling me what to do?"

He swallowed hard:

"I have orders . . ."

"Bullshit!" Rachael cried out.

Before Tex knew what hit him Rachael pulled him out of the HUMVEE by his left ear. She sat down in the drivers set and started messing with the telephone:

"Show me how to work this thing!"

Tex rubbed his ear and looked on helplessly:

"Ah . . . who do you want to call?"

She waved a piece of paper in his face:

"I've got a hot line to the President of the United States. I'm going to call him. I agreed to the protection so long as the military stayed out of my private life." She glared up at him:

"I'm going to have your orders changed, Corporal!"

Tex was disgusted:

"I really don't need this, Mrs. McDonald."

"Neither do I!"

He considered it a moment:

"OK. You go up to the door and make sure that everything is all right. Then . . . come back here and talk to me." He defiantly glared at Rachael:

"Do you understand that, Mrs. McDonald?"

Without saying a word, Rachael pushed passed him and headed for the door.

Tex reached inside the HUMVEE and grabbed his M-16.

Fear showed in Holly's eyes:

"Richard?

"You be quiet and stay down," he barked.

Tex took a position behind a bush close to the door and trained his carbine.

Rachael rang the doorbell a couple of times and waited a few moments. Without looking back she opened the door and entered the house. Tex leaped from his position and grabbed her arm as she attempted to close the door behind her.

Rachael clenched her teeth and jerked her arm away:

"Damn it, Richard – this is getting old!"

"Yes it is!"

Rachael softened:

"OK, Richard – you see if her car is in the garage and I'll check the house."

"No," Richard commanded. "We stay together."

Tex followed her into the kitchen.

"Look, Richard – two coffee cups."

"This one's got booze in it," Tex noted.

Rachael opened the door leading to the garage:

"Her car is here."

They walked into the living room and found Sheila sprawled out on the floor.

"Good Lord!" Rachael exclaimed.

Richard knelt down beside her and put her finger to her neck:

"I . . . I think she's sleeping – maybe she passed out from the booze."

"No, I don't think so. That's not like Sheila."

"To drink?"

"No . . . to pass out – she usually drinks everybody under the table."

"Maybe she took some pills," Richard surmised. "Maybe we should get her to the hospital."

Rachael winced:

"Yes . . . she's been depressed lately. This doesn't look good."

As Tex began to pick her up her eyes blinked open:

"Hey, good lookin," Sheila said as she pulled the Marine's head closer.

"Sheila!" Rachael cried out.

Sheila's attention turned to Rachael:

"Rachael . . . what are you doing here?" She looked around at her surroundings:

"What's going on – where's Jerry?"

"Jerry?"

Sheila sat up and closed the top of her robe:

"Yeah . . . where'd Jerry go? What's going on?"

"You tell us," Rachael requested.

She looked numbly at Rachael:

"The guy's name is Jerry. I prayed and he came and laid hands on me." She turned to Tex:

"You're Holly's new sweetheart, aren't you?"

"Ah . . ." he stammered.

"Yes," Rachael began, "he's her new sweetheart. How did you find out about that?"

"Um . . ."

"Think, Sheila," Rachael urged.

"From Jerry."

Rachael tried to hide her excitement:

"Tell me about this Jerry guy."

Sheila looked around the room:

"He's supposed to be here. I wasn't done talking with him." She looked at Tex:

"Don't tell me you drove up here in that big green thing."

"We call it a HUMVEE."

"You scared him away! He doesn't want to talk with you guys!" She looked at Rachael:

"Why can't you ever drive *your* car?"

Holly's voice came from the doorway:

"Who is Jerry?"

Rachael jumped to her feet:

"What?"

"I just talked with this man Jerry," Holly told her mother.

The Corporal pulled his radio from his belt:

"Give me his description, Holly – he'll never make it out of town."

Rachael jerked the radio out of Richard's hands:

"Don't call!"

"With all respect, Mrs. McDonald – this is a military matter and I have to follow orders."

"Yeah, like you followed orders and cut my house in two and killed my husband."

Rachael turned to her daughter and began in a very slow, calculating tone:

"If you let Tex do this . . . if you allow it . . . then I want you out of my house . . . I want you out today." She turned to Tex:

"You just take my daughter and get her stuff out; and you can scram too. I'll have you reassigned."

"Mother, I guess you'll call the President to get that done," Holly said sarcastically.

"Yes, that's right."

Sheila spoke up:

"President? What President?"

"She's talking about the President of the United States," Holly dryly announced.

"Oh." She caught herself:

"Huh?"

Rachael took a deep breath and collected herself.

"Holly . . . tell me what Jerry told you."

Holly looked for help from Richard but he simply threw up his hands. She turned back to her mother:

"Mother . . . he wants to meet with you . . . alone . . . no police, no military."

"Where?"

Holly turned again to Tex for help.

"Holly," Rachael began, "you don't understand . . . I need to . . ."

"Whose fault is it that I don't understand?" Holly protested.

"I'm trying to *protect* you," Rachael stressed.

"I want to protect you *too*, mother," Holly came back.

Rachael turned her attention to Sheila:

"Tell us what happened with you and Jerry."

"Well . . . I prayed to Michael. You know, like we talked about. And before I was finished the doorbell rang and there was Jerry. I felt like . . . like . . ."

"Like you knew him from somewhere?" Holly interjected.

"Yes."

Everyone turned to Holly.

"That's how I felt when I saw him walk up to the HUMVEE," Holly told them.

"Go on, Sheils," Rachael urged.

"Well . . . I thought the guy was a bit goofy . . . the way he talked . . . the words that he used. But . . . he seemed to know . . ."

"He seemed to know what?" Rachael asked impatiently.

Sheila threw up her hands:

"He seemed to know *everything*. Everything about everything. He knew what happened to Agatha and Molly . . . he seemed to know about Tex . . . he knew that Martin had made me a promise. He told me that Michael got on Martin's case about not keeping it. That's how he put it, 'got on his case.'"

Holly looked knowingly at her mother:

"I know what you're thinking, mother – you think this guy knows my. . ."

"Don't say it!" Rachael interjected.

Holly held up here hands as if giving up:

"Look . . . I can't handle this right now. Why don't Richard and I go to the store. It won't take us long. You . . . you can talk with Sheila."

Rachael caught Holly's eye:

"Isn't there something you want to tell me before you leave?"

"Mother, we'll be right back."

Rachael tugged urgently on the Corporal's sleeve:

"Don't be too long, OK Richard?"

"Tell me which way to go, Holly," Tex said.

"I . . . I think you should pull over."

"Huh?"

"We have some time – I want to talk a minute."

He glanced at the side mirror and pulled over:

"You want to talk about your mom."

Holly was beside herself:

"I'm worried about her. She doesn't act right – I think she's delusional, or, at least, in denial. And . . . I'm not the only one who thinks so. Other people that know her are worried as well.

She . . . she just doesn't make sense sometimes. And . . . she's caught up in all of this biblical prophecy jazz. Now it looks like she's dragging Sheila into it."

"Well . . . she seems OK to me; and I can't blame her for wanting to get the military out of her life. After all – we *were* the ones that flattened her house and killed her husband."

"You don't know her as well as I do, Richard."

"I don't think your mother acts like she's crazy. She's been through a lot – give her a break."

"I've been through a lot too! There are a lot of things that I haven't told you, Richard."

"I just don't agree that your mom is nuts." He shrugged. "Sorry."

Holly looked accusingly at him:

"Richard . . . you didn't buy that presidential hot line stuff?"

"Yeah, I did. The president came to see her in person. Didn't you know that?"

Her brow lifted:

"No, I didn't."

"Well . . . I was at the gate when he came. You hadn't arrived yet."

Holly was visibly surprised:

"I didn't know that."

Richard thoughtfully rubbed his chin:

"The president's hot line thing – do you think that is one of her delusions?"

"Well . . . yeah, I do."

"You think that phone number is phony?"

"Yeah."

Richard studied her a moment:

"Perhaps *you* are delusional."

Holly's eyes flared:

"What is that supposed to mean?"

They sat silent for a few moments and Holly spoke up:

"I guess we're having our first argument."

Richard looked nervously around:

"I don't know what I'm supposed to do. Darn it, Holly – if I had followed orders I wouldn't be so freaked. Maybe we should just go back."

Holly picked up the phone number and handed it to him.

"Go ahead; call the President of the United States."

"Are you nuts?"

She yanked the paper away from him:

"OK . . . I'll call! I'll prove to you that this is just part of mom's weirdness."

"Ha! You don't have the balls."

She smiled at him:

"You hope."

He laughed and then caught himself:

"This isn't funny – how can you joke around?"

"It *is* funny. Poor Sheila was half out of her gourd to start with and mom fills her head with all this weird crap. Then mom manipulates you with this phony phone number."

"You agreed that Jerry looked familiar," Tex countered.

"Well . . . he did," she admitted. "Maybe I've seen him somewhere."

"What about all that stuff Jerry knew?" Richard asked her.

"Mother knew all of that – she could have told it to Sheila. You saw

Sheila that day – God, she was bombed. She's been on the ragged edge for years."

"She looked OK today," Tex offered. "Don't you think so? I mean, maybe this Jerry guy is for real."

Holly was disgusted:

"I'm looking for some sanity here, Richard."

He threw up his hands in desperation:

"What do you want from me, Holly?"

"Well . . . If something goes wrong you can just tell your superiors that mom threatened to call the President if you didn't cooperate with her and disobey orders." She rolled her eyes and huffed:

"That sounds real mature."

Tex looked away and groaned.

"I'm going to call," Holly announced.

"Yeah, right," he smirked. "What are you going to do if you get through to the President?"

"That won't happen."

They stared at each other.

"If the call goes through I'll just say that I'm mom. What's the big deal?"

"Ha! And you call your *mom* weird."

"OK, hot shot – you dial and I'll talk."

Without hesitation he handed the phone to Holly and dialed the number. He sat back with his eyes on Holly.

"Yes . . . I'd like to speak with the President. Ah . . . this is Rachael McDonald." She put her hand over the receiver and looked wide-eyed at Richard:

"He said, 'he's in the air – hold on.'"

"Oh, Christ!"

"Should I hang up?"

"No no no! They'll think something is wrong and swarm in on us!"

"What do I do?"

"Just . . ."

"Yes, Hello Mr. President . . . . No, everything is fine . . . . She's fine . . . I'm still out in the trailer . . . . I really haven't decided . . . . I'm going to sell the company . . . . Actually, I'd like to visit a friend in private . . . and the Corporal's orders don't allow that . . . . Corporal Maddox . . . . M A D D O X."

"Oh, Jesus," Richard whimpered.

"Yes, that's him in the background . . . . OK, I'll put him on."

If looks could kill, Holly would have died at that moment. Richard ever so slowly took the phone from Holly.

"This is Corporal Richard Maddox . . . . Yes, well . . . I didn't know when we left the house that Mrs. McDonald was planning a personal visit. My orders were that I could accompany her by myself on errands; but not to lose contact . . . . Yes . . . . In the future I will do it that way . . . . That's very nice; I didn't know that Mrs. McDonald had mentioned me to you . . . . Here she is."

Extremely relieved, he handed the phone back to Holly:

"Mr. President . . . . No, I feel OK about it . . . . Yes, next time we'll do it that way. Yes, he's a good soldier . . . . I realize that his first obligation is to obey orders . . . . No, I'm not upset with him at all – if anything I respect him for keeping the chain of command . . . . Ah . . . yes . . . that is good news . . . . Goodbye, Mr. President."

Holly hung up the phone and stared off numbly. "Wow."

"What did he say?" Richard asked with total disgust.

"He told me . . . ah . . . I mean, he told mom, that you weren't a chauffeur and that I was supposed to obey your directives because they were given for my own safety." She looked sheepish:

"I guess the President told you how to handle visits where you would be out of eye contact with mother."

"Yeah," he moaned. "I'm supposed to check the building first and then establish a perimeter around it. That ought to set well with your mother." He pointed at her:

"You're going to have to tell your mother about this."

"Why me?"

"Because it was *your* brainy idea – that's why."

"Well . . . OK." She studied his expression:

"You shouldn't complain – you came out smelling like a rose. You should probably thank me."

"Thank you! Have you flipped? Now I'm going to have to disobey the President of the United States if your mother is to meet with this Jerry guy. You want me to thank you for that!"

Holly put her hand to her mouth and tears came to her eyes.

"Come on, Holly," Tex began in earnest, "I didn't mean to make you cry."

"You don't understand, Richard; you just don't understand."

"Well . . . talk to me, Holly – I'm listening."

She stared blankly out the window:

"It's happening all over again."

"What . . . what's happening?"

"When Michael came it was just like this. He came out of nowhere and he laid hands on mother. And . . . he just stayed after that. Everybody seemed filled with some kind of mystical hope and expectation. But it turned soured. Evil people came after us.

Mother and I are the only survivors. I really don't know what they did to mother; but I suspect that she was raped. She won't talk about it."

"And . . . and you think that the same thing might happen again?"

"Yes. And mother . . . she *is* in La La Land. Mom doesn't have a clue. Mom is delusional."

Richard gently took Holly's hand:

"Holly . . . I understand now why you're afraid. But . . . what do you plan to do?"

"I don't know."

That sat for a while and looked out at the trees that had turned a fall crimson color.

"Richard . . . I just want life to be simple. I'm . . . I'm not up for another tragedy."

"I'm not sure that our lives *can* be simple."

"Why?" she pleaded.

"Because of the times that we live in. Things will get much worse before they get better."

"Oh no – you're not into all this end-times prophecy jazz?" She searched his face:

"Well . . . are you?"

"Yes, Holly, I *am* into all this end-times prophecy jazz." Richard looked intently at her:

"When Jesus came all of his close friends were killed. So . . . we shouldn't judge Michael just by that."

"You're as nutty as mom," Holly concluded with total disdain.

"Holly . . . you can't run away from this. I mean . . . what are we going to do about Jerry?"

"I'm confused. Help me, Richard – help me decide."

"OK. When is Rachael supposed to meet Jerry?"

"One o'clock."

"Today?"

"Yes."

He looked at his watch:

"That doesn't give us much time. I thought you said we had plenty of time."

"I wasn't going to tell mother," she confessed.

"Where are they supposed to meet?"

"In the parking lot behind the butcher store. Mom knows where it is."

Richard thought for a while:

"OK. We'll go back to Sheila's. You stay with Sheila; and your mother and I will go to meet with Jerry. I'll park the HUMVEE and let your mother walk the rest of the way."

Holly was terrified:

"What about the President? Aren't you forgetting about your orders? I mean . . . you could get into a lot of trouble."

"This is more important than *orders*."

"Ha! You're caught up with this thing too. Mother thinks that this guy has something for her; she thinks he has something for me; and you and Sheila are the other hopefuls." She made a desperate gesture:

"You've all totally flipped!"

"What's wrong with hope?" Richard objected.

"Hope or delusion, Richard – which is it?"

He shrugged and started the HUMVEE:

"Well . . . there's only one way to find out."

"Take me home," Holly ordered.

"I can't do that. I left with you and your mother. I can't bring you home alone."

Holly groaned.

Tex was visibly annoyed:

"What do you want to do, Holly – crawl into a hole and hide?"

She put her hand to her mouth:

"That's what mom did," she whispered to herself. The image of her cave flashed in her mind and she forced a weak smile:

"OK, Richard – we'll do it your way."

AND I SAY "HELLO"

13

Richard pulled the HUMVEE into Sheila's driveway and shut off the ignition.

"Are you OK, Holly?"

"No," She pathetically whimpered.

Richard managed a reassuring smile:

"Listen . . . things are going to be OK. Just stay here and keep Sheila company."

Rachael anxiously looked at her watch:

"We're a bit early. Maybe you should avoid Main Street – I don't want Jerry to see us riding together."

"You're nervous as a cat," Richard noted.

"I can't help it. And . . . Holly isn't helping. What is *wrong* with her?"

"She's afraid that the same thing is going to happen that happened after Michael came. She's certain that trouble is on the way." He looked over at Rachael:

"She's just not up for it, Mrs. McDonald – she's terrified!"

Rachael sighed. "She thinks I've flipped."

Tex considered it a moment. "Delusional – she thinks you're delusional."

Fear came over Rachael. "Is that what *you* think? Is this a trap for Jerry?"

Richard was taken back by her sudden distrust:

"Mrs. McDonald . . . you know me!"

Her eyes grew wild:

"I've been fooled before and it cost the lives of my daughter and sister."

He managed a feeble laugh: "Come on . . ."

Rachael pulled a small revolver from her purse. "Pull over. Your bullet-proof vest won't protect you from a head shot – don't get any ideas!"

He found a place to park under a big oak in the Town Square, shut off the HUMVEE, and slowly turned towards Rachael:

"What are you *doing*, Mrs. McDonald?"

She glared at Richard and the tiny revolver trembled in her hand. "What are *you* doing; and why is Holly so upset."

Tex threw up his hands in desperation. “I *told* you.”

Rachael didn’t buy it:

“You didn’t want me to go into Sheila’s by myself; and now, you’re going to dump me off to meet a total stranger? And Holly has gotten all freaked. *Something* doesn’t add up.”

Tex was disgusted. “I can’t *believe* this.”

Rachael’s eyes raged with anger. “Do you think I’ve flipped-out, Richard? Is that what Holly convinced you of when you two went for your little ride. Well . . . you didn’t go shopping and you were gone quite a while.”

Tex looked down the barrel of the little gun that was aimed between his eyes:

“Come on, Mrs. McDonald . . . you know me . . . don’t get paranoid.”

“Oh . . . now I’m a *paranoid* delusional. Any other labels you wanna stick on me?”

“Please . . . Mrs. McDonald . . .”

“Well . . . you better come up with something.” She looked at her watch:

“Talk to me, Corporal.”

“I don’t know what you want from me, Mrs. McDonald,” he concluded.

“Why don’t you start off by giving me a reason to trust you?”

Richard swallowed hard and began:

“Do you know that statue in your backyard that is still partially standing?”

“What of it?”

“I’ve dreamed about it many times. I could never figure it out – a statue of just someone’s legs.”

“And?”

“Well . . . I first saw it for real though the scope of the LAV.” He looked off and mused a few moments:

“I knew that something important was going to happen that was associated with your house.”

He had gained her attention:

“Like what?”

“It’s a long story.”

She glanced at her watch again:

“Make it short.”

Richard seemed more relaxed and noticed that Rachael had lowered the gun to her lap:

“There is someone somewhere that knows my number. I‘m supposed to trust that person and he is to be my guide."

Rachael looked as if she'd seen a ghost.

Richard marveled:

"It's you – isn't it? *You* know my number."

She looked down at the gun in her hand:

"Oh, Richard, I am *so* sorry. Forgive me. *Please* forgive me."

"Tell me my number, Mrs. McDonald," Richard said with excitement.

She gave him a puzzled look:

"Your number? Oh . . . I . . . I don't know what your number is."

Richard made a face:

"Huh?"

"I don't understand this number business," she confessed:

"Well . . . maybe Jerry . . . ah . . ."

She lit up. "Yeah, maybe Jerry knows something about this number business."

"That's what I was thinking," Richard agreed.

She put the revolver back into her purse:

"Well . . . we've got 5 minutes or so. Maybe we should ride some more."

"Or I can clean the crap out of my pants."

Rachael laughed. "Really?"

"Well . . . almost. You looked like you were ready to *use* that thing."

"I've used it before."

"What do you mean?"

"I killed a man with it." she blurted without thinking. "God, maybe I shouldn't have told you that. I . . . I wouldn't want to scare you away." She studied his face:

"Do you think I'm nuts, Richard?"

His laugh was genuine:

"No nuttier than me."

Richard found a place on Main Street and parked. He looked over at Rachael and she detected fear in his eyes.

"We haven't thought this out very well, Mrs. McDonald."

"As far as what?"

"What if something goes wrong?"

"So . . . what's your thinking?"

Richard looked around nervously. "I'll wait five minutes and come looking for you."

"Give me ten," she suggested.

"He can *kill* you in ten," Richard asserted.

She shrugged it off. "He can kill me in five. Just in case I'll keep my hand in my purse."

"Yeah, OK," he reluctantly agreed. "Ten minutes and I'm coming for you."

Rachael's heart pounded as she made her way down Main to the butcher shop – nodding politely at acquaintances but maintaining her gate.

She went over the description that Sheila had given her:

Short brown hair, six feet tall, blue eyes, well proportioned, late 40's early 50's, tee shirt, jeans, running shoes.

She walked through the front door of the shop, exchanged a few words with the owner and made her way to the rear parking lot. There were four or five cars but nobody to be seen. She heard a voice behind her:

"Hello, Rachael."

She turned with a start and viewed the stranger wearing jeans and a tee shirt. Time stood still as she stared at the smiling man. She searched his face for a connection – something familiar. He was *indeed* familiar – but in what way she did not understand.

"Well?" the stranger said awkwardly.

"Well what?"

When he spoke his voice broke with emotion:

"I . . . I'm lost for words, Rachael. I had no idea when I left that this was going to happen."

Rachael swallowed hard and kept her hand in her purse:

"Happen . . . what's supposed to happen?"

"I have so much to tell you."

Rachael was nervous and confused. "You do?"

The man frantically nodded – all the while staring intently into Rachael's eyes. "Yes. Let's go somewhere and talk." He pointed:

"That's my car."

Rachael's mind raced but nothing made sense – nothing added up:

"Ah . . . it's not so easy as that. Someone is going to come looking for me in ten minutes."

He panicked:

"Someone? Someone like who!"

"Tex."

"Who is he?"

"He . . . he's my daughter's new boyfriend."

Relief spread over the man:

"Oh, that's wonderful – I can't wait to meet him."

Rachael remembered Sheila telling her that this man seemed to know everything about her family. "You know about Tex?"

He nodded. "Yeah . . . well . . . I knew that he'd come along; I . . . . I just didn't know when. I need to talk to this lad."

"Well . . . this lad is actually a Marine that has been assigned to protect Holly and me."

He smiled. "That's fine – a Marine in the family might be the ticket." He looked down at her purse:

"Why do you have your hand in your purse?"

"I just do."

He smiled and gave her a knowing look. "Ha . . . you just do. Let's see the gun, Rachael."

She stepped back and lifted the gun out of the purse but didn't take aim.

The man laughed good-heartedly:

"Raech – you think I'm Niyaq!"

"Well . . . you must be a mind reader," she said, pretending to be brave.

"Just sometimes. I mean – I don't do it on purpose. Ever since . . ."

Rachael stepped back some more and held the gun with both hands.

He pointed. "That looks like Agatha's gun."

Rachael glanced at her watch and aimed at the man.

"What are you *doing*, Rachael?"

The little gun shook in her hand:

"We're just going to wait till Tex gets here."

"Rachael, I'm not Niyaq!" he pleaded.

Sweat began to form on Rachael's forehead:

"I left this gun next to the Arab's body. The only people that would know that it's Agatha's gun would be the police or Niyaq – and you don't look like a cop."

The man raised his hands in a defensive position:

"Wait a minute, Rachael; I can't allow myself to be questioned by the military."

She held her aim. "Sorry."

The man looked desperate. "How much time do we have?"

"About five minutes."

"That's not enough time! We need to talk! Please, Raech, don't do this," he begged her.

"The name is *Rachael*," she said coldly.

Jerry began to panic again. "Rachael . . . it's me, Martin – I've come back!"

She held the gun out further in a shooting position. "Just stand there and don't move. I'll use this – don't think I won't."

The man's mind raced:

"OK . . . ask me something that only Martin would know?"

"I don't want to play."

His eyes pleaded. "Come on, Raech, we've got a few minutes to kill before you betray the only man you ever loved."

Rachael attempted to glance around without taking her eyes off the stranger:

"All right. Where were we married?"

"Too easy, Raech, I could have been briefed for that one. Madison Wisconsin, we were married by a judge May 12th, 1970."

"What did we do that night?"

"Well . . . we didn't have any money, so I made a deal with Fast Eddie. I let him use my motorcycle and he gave us some money."

Rachael's expression softened and she lowered the gun:

"And what did we do with the money?"

His demeanor became confident:

"We bought a jug of Chianti and ordered a pizza. Double cheese, mushrooms, Italian sausage – and anchovies on your half. Fast Eddie gave us the roaches that he had been saving and we . . ."

Rachael's eyes went back in her head and she fainted dead away.

The man knelt down beside her:

"Oops – this doesn't look good."

"You're right about that!" a voice behind him barked.

He turned, looked down the muzzle of an M-16, and slowly raised his hands:

"Take it easy, soldier."

Tex was angry and determined:

"I'll blow you away! One wrong move and I'll blow you away!"

"She . . . she's just fainted. When she comes out of it she'll vouch for me."

"Spread eagle!"

"Oh, come on," he said with disgust. "I'm not lying down in that grease."

The Marine aimed at the stranger's head with his right hand and pulled his radio from his belt with his left:

"Spread eagle!"

The stranger motioned wildly with his hands:

"Don't use that radio . . . because . . . ah . . . I'm the one who has your number."

Tex froze:

"What!"

Jerry nodded frantically:

"Yes . . . I'm the guy you've been waiting for." He quickly checked out the parking lot:

"Now . . . we need to be cool and not attract attention to ourselves."

Richard looked down at Rachael. "Why has she got a gun in her hand?"

"I knew you were coming – I told her too much too fast. She . . . she just fainted."

A door slammed behind them and the owner of the butcher shop came hustling out:

"What's going on?"

"Rachael has fainted, Henry – bring me a bucket of ice water," Jerry requested.

"Who the hell are you?"

"It's all right – get the water," Tex commanded. He took the revolver from Rachael's hand and turned to Jerry:

"You're just going to throw it in her face?"

"You got a better idea?"

"Well . . . I don't have any of those things with me."

The owner of the shop appeared with the ice water.

"You can go back inside now, Henry," Jerry told him.

Tex nodded in agreement and the man left.

The stranger poured water on Rachael's face and her eyes blinked opened.

"You fainted," Jerry began. "You need to tell Tex not to shoot me."

Rachael sat up and gathered herself for a moment:

"Why are you going to shoot him?"

Tex stood gawking with his carbine in one hand and Rachael's revolver in the other:

"Ah . . ."

"Listen you beanheads," Jerry impatiently began. "I've been in town for less than a day and two people have drawn guns on me. If we draw attention to ourselves we're gunna to be in a world of trouble. And there will be no way out." He looked back and forth from Rachael to Tex:

"Are you two hearing me?"

"Yes," Rachael answered.

Jerry helped Rachael to her feet.

"Tell me my number," Tex requested.

Rachael's eyes widened:

"We were right, Richard!"

"Tell me my number," he reiterated.

"Then will you trust me?"

"Yes."

"And you'll do as I ask?"

"Yes."

"OK . . . you got pen and paper?"

"In the HUMVEE."

The stranger motioned his hands as a signal to calm down:

"Fine. Let's all put on our happy faces and get out of here." He looked at Rachael:

"You make some small talk with Henry and pick up a few steaks. Tex and I will wait for you out front. Oh . . . and get some matches from Henry.

Tex?"

"Yeah?"

"Give Rachael back her gun."

Jerry sat in the front next to Tex and Rachael sat in the back.

"Raech . . . you watch behind us to see if we're being followed." He glanced at Richard:

"Get this thing going, Tex."

"The deal was . . ."

"Tell him to drive, Rachael."

Rachael nudged Richard's arm:

"Let's get going, Tex."

The Corporal pulled into traffic:

"Where are we going?"

"Just drive."

After Jerry was convinced that they weren't being followed he told Tex to find a place to pull over.

"Now you're going to tell me my number?" Tex asked.

"Yeah . . . now we're going to do the number thing. Raech, give me the matches.

OK, Tex – here's how we do it. *You* write down your number on a piece of paper and *I'll* write your number down on a piece of paper. Then, we'll see if they match.

I'll go first."

Jerry took the small notepad, scrawled a number on it, folded it and handed the paper back to Rachael. He then handed the pen and pad to Tex and turned to Rachael:

"Rachael, let me see your purse a minute."

She handed it over and Jerry pulled out the revolver and pointed it at Tex.

"Jerry," Rachael said softly, "you don't have to do that."

Tex froze with pen in hand:

"Oh no . . . not again," he groaned.

Jerry kept the gun aimed at Tex. "There's something screwy in Saint Louie; and I'm thinking it might be youie."

Tex slowly turned to Rachael for sympathy. Rachael managed a feeble smile:

"Just write the numbers, Tex."

The Marine turned back and looked down at the notepad. He heard a faint click as Jerry drew back the hammer of the snubby:

"When you're finished, Tex, put the piece of paper on your right shoulder and place both hands on the wheel. I'm a bit nervous . . . move slow and easy."

He did as he was told and Rachael took the piece of paper from his shoulder:

"It's a match – a perfect match," she cheerfully announced.

Jerry sighed with relief, carefully let down the hammer and gave the revolver back to Rachael.

After a few moments passed, Richard – hands still glued to the wheel – looked over at Jerry:

"Ah . . . can I take my hands off the wheel?"

Jerry ignored him and calmly addressed Rachael:

"Hon . . . we can still blow this thing. I had to be careful. You might know this guy; but I don't."

"I know it. Whew, a few minutes ago I thought that *you* were Niyaq."

"What's Niyaq?" Tex asked.

"Jerry . . . shouldn't you say something to Tex?" Rachael suggested.

Jerry smiled at the Marine and held out his hand. "Welcome to the family, Tex."

He reluctantly shook Jerry's hand:

"What family? What's Niyaq? What does my number mean?"

"Never say the word, 'Niyaq,'" Rachael advised.

"That's right, Tex – that'll get you killed," Jerry confirmed.

“Or worse,” Rachael added.

Jerry smiled at Tex. “You’ve got some catching up to do – be patient.” With that he burned the two slips of paper.

“Please tell me what my number means? I’ve been waiting a long time to find out.”

“All right.” Jerry considered it a few moments:

“It actually means a couple of things. For one, it means that you’re the perfect match for Holly.” He studied Richard’s expression:

“Well . . . you love her don’t you?”

Tex looked around awkwardly. “Ah . . . yeah, I do.”

“OK . . . and you’re serious about marriage, right?”

“Ah . . .”

“Jerry,” Rachael cut in, “Holly just broke up with Bobby this morning – Richard and Holly haven’t even gone on a date yet.”

“Oh . . . well then I guess you need to go on a few dates,” Jerry suggested somewhat tongue-in-cheek. He pointed at Richard accusingly:

“But you stay out of her drawers till you tie the knot. And even after that, I don’t want you to just go blasting in there.”

Richard was stunned:

“You want me to wait – even after we’re married?”

“Yeah.”

Tex attempted to read Jerry’s face:

“Ah . . . how long should I wait?”

Jerry cut his eyes at Rachael:

“I don’t know – a few months or so.”

Rachael laughed. “He’s teasing you, Richard.”

“Is Holly still at Sheila’s?” Jerry asked.

“Yeah.”

“Good. Let’s go over there; I’m dying to talk to her.”

“There’s a little problem with Holly,” Rachael revealed.

Jerry was taken back. “But . . . Sheila said she was doing fine.”

“She was till *you* came along,” Richard interjected.

Rachael nodded:

“That’s right – she thinks there will be trouble like there was after Michael came.”

Pain showed on Jerry’s face.

Richard spoke up:

“Holly told me that this Michael guy came out of nowhere and just stayed – he never left. And now . . .”

“This Jerry guy comes and just stays, and will bring the same trouble with him." Jerry finished.

Richard took a deep breath and huffed. "Is that what you plan to do? If so, Holly is definitely gunna freak."

"Rachael," Jerry began, "I understood that there was going to be a time of refreshment, of peace and love."

"Ah . . . I guess it hasn't started yet."

"Maybe I should split till things calm down a bit," Jerry suggested. "We can still blow this thing."

"No," Rachael objected. "Jerry . . . all Tex has to do is put you on the guest list and you can come to the trailer."

"Well . . . I really do need to talk to you. But what about Holly?"

"Tex can go run some errands with her." She looked at the Marine:

"Some *long* errands."

"That'll work," Richard said. "I'll take you back to your car, go get Holly and drive back to the trailer. You wait about a half an hour and then go visit Mrs. McDonald. By that time I will have left with Holly and your name will be on the guest list."

Jerry clapped his hands together:

"Good – that's the plan."

"I need your full name; you know, to put on the list."

"Jerry Dean Roads."

"Is that spelled with an 'H'?"

The stranger looked a bit perplexed. "Hmm."

Jerry pulled out his wallet and produced his driver's license. "You're right – it does have an 'H' in it. R H O D E S." He looked up and smiled:

"How about that."

Richard methodically put away pen and pad and turned around to Rachael.

She sheepishly smiled. "Welcome to the family, Richard."

The Marine pulled out and headed back to the butcher shop. He became aware of Jerry's continual stare:

"What – is there something wrong?"

Jerry reached over, felt of the man's bicep, nodded, and looked approvingly at Rachael:

"Hmm . . . looks like good stock."

"Don't embarrass the man, Jerry – I really don't think he's in the mood."

Jerry pointed to himself and feigned innocent:

"Me, embarrass the man? Ha."

He kept looking at the Marine:

"So . . . I guess that Tex is your nickname."

"Yes, sir. My name is Richard Maddox."

"I like that. So . . . Holly will be Holly McDonald Maddox. That's got a ring – I like it."

What's your mother's maiden name?"

"McIntyre."

"So . . . you're not Jewish?"

"Ah . . . not by bloodline, sir."

Jerry's brow lifted. "Not by bloodline," he reiterated. He turned to Rachael:

"Did you hear that, Raech? He said that he wasn't Jewish *by bloodline*. How many folks do you know that would have given that as an answer?

That's interesting Corporal – very interesting indeed.

Listen . . . ah . . . about pulling the gun on you . . ."

Richard shrugged it off:

"You don't have to apologize."

Jerry kept his eyes on the Marine. "I've seen what a well-trained Marine can do with his hands, Richard – and you're one big Marine."

"Were you in Nam?"

"No . . . I knew a Marine named Jarvis and I watched him do a few tricks."

"Colonel William Jarvis?"

"Yeah, that's right. You've heard of him?" Jerry asked.

"Who hasn't – they're still telling stories about that guy. He's got to be getting up in years – he served as a Captain in Nam.

Where do you know him from?"

"Well . . ." Jerry started.

"Jerry," Rachael interrupted, "Richard was in the LAV that fired on the house. He was the gunner."

His eyes widened as he stared at Richard.

"Jerry," Rachael pleadingly began, "perhaps now's not the time . . ."

Richard glanced over at dumbstruck Jerry:

"What . . . what is it?"

Rachael chimed in:

"I can tell you about it when you come over, Jerry. Richard is spooked enough already."

Jerry turned around and looked at Rachael:

"Yeah . . . perhaps we're trying to go too fast."

Rachael had taken a quick shower and put on make-up. Her heart raced as she saw Jerry pull up to the gate. She felt like a silly child waiting to go on her first date.

They both acted nervous and awkward.

"Would you like something to drink?" Rachael asked him.

"Ah . . . you got any Coke?"

"No. Holly has a box of wine in the fridge. I'm afraid that's all I have."

"I don't drink anymore, Rachael."

Her brow lifted:

"You don't drink any alcohol? Not at all?"

He smiled at her and shook his head:

"No, Rachael, I don't drink at all. The booze destroyed us once. Let's learn from our mistakes."

They looked affectionately at each other for a few moments. Jerry finally spoke up:

"This is crazy; isn't it?"

"Whew . . . this is *very* crazy, Marty."

"I . . . I guess you shouldn't call me that anymore."

"I suppose not," Rachael confirmed.

Rachael stared off and thought for a moment:

"What is heaven like, Jerry?"

"Ah . . . I really didn't go all the way there; it was more like the Near Death Experiences that we read about."

"Tell me what happened to you," Rachael implored.

"Ah . . ."

"Why don't you start from the beginning – after I left?"

"Alright:

Jarvis and I couldn't figure out *what* was going on. None of it made sense – it was total confusion."

"Do you understand it now?"

Jerry nodded:

"Yes."

"Thank God for that."

Jerry began:

"From the start, both Jarvis and I were in the dark about what the *real* plan was. We were simply acting out our parts as Niyaq looked on and observed our every movement."

"Huh?"

"Jarvis' original deal with Michael was to keep me from involving myself with the FBI's Phase Three Project. Michael knew that if that happened, I would be targeted by Niyaq.

But Jarvis gets this idea for Lebeh to set a trap for Niyaq by putting detection devices and cameras around the perimeter of the house, and have a strike team capable of clobbering anything that came in. You know, after they got em on tape."

Jerry marveled:

"Right from the beginning we were doomed. Jarvis sold us down the river to catch Niyaq people. We didn't have a chance. Jarvis knew that Niyaq would track the Sub, associate the hijacking with Lebeh, and come to find out what was going on.

What Jarvis *didn't* figure on was that his team leader was a double agent. So . . . the detection system is only as good as the person monitoring it. This Wilcox guy enabled Niyaq to come into our house and set up all kinds of cameras and snooping devices."

Rachael looked sick:

"Do you think they even watched us . . ."

"Make love? Yeah . . . I suppose they did."

"How is it that Michael didn't learn this sooner?"

"I would guess that Michael knew it all along. It was actually part of the scheme that the Throne hatched for Michael's people to pull off.

Michael and Zak had the Niyaq disc for a couple of weeks before Michael came here. They learned, among other things, that Niyaq believed that Elijah and Jesus are the same entity. A plan was hatched by the Throne to create the software; and then have Niyaq believe that they destroyed the software and killed Jesus."

"So . . . Jesus is really Elijah – one of the end days witnesses who will prophesy against the Beast?"

"Well . . . I don't know if that is true or not; but that is what Niyaq believes. Apparently, Niyaq had the professor code for that precept."

"Does Zak still have a copy of the Niyaq disc?"

"Yeah. When things cool down a bit, I'm going to get a copy."

Rachael considered it for a moment – attempting to fit the pieces together:

"So . . . Niyaq thinks they squashed the software project and killed their primary latter days foe?"

"Yes."

Rachael nodded and smiled. "But . . . they only squashed the software project and that can be accomplished at another time?"

Jerry lifted his figure to make a point:

"You've got that wrong. You see, Raech," he pointed at himself, "*I am* the software. I know how to build it and test it; and, when the time comes, that I will do."

"So . . . Lebeh put one over on Niyaq," Rachael concluded.

"No. Lebeh is corrupt and inept. This plan was totally hatched by the Throne and put into effect by Michael's people. And, I might add, it worked perfectly."

"So . . . do *you* believe that Michael is Jesus?" Rachael asked him.

Jerry considered it for a moment:

"I don't *think* that he is. But, while he was convincing Niyaq that he *was* Yeshua, he convinced me also." He stared at her:

"Get it?"

"Yes, I get it."

Jerry continued:

"Jarvis was well briefed on me. I'm sure that he shared this briefing with Michael. I believe that Michael knew that I would wonder about the wine, and create a suspicion among Niyaq as to his true identity. It's my view that Michael knew that I collected wine, and that I would know that what we were drinking didn't come in pitchers and wouldn't be served in water glasses on the rocks.

That last day Michael turned a pitcher of water into Margaux – right in front of one of Niyaq's cameras. Suspecting that Michael could indeed be Christ, Niyaq's original goal of stopping the software project was superseded by a new plan to kidnap myself and Michael."

"Capture the Messiah and the man who knew how to make the software," Rachael concluded.

Jerry nodded to confirm:

"Exactly. That's why Niyaq had to be careful when they stormed the house. They wanted Michael and me alive."

"But you and Jarvis didn't know that."

"No . . . we were confused as hell."

Something occurred to Rachael:

"But . . . if Michael wasn't Jesus, then how could he turn the water to wine?"

"Well . . . I never really put much stock in that 'turn the water into wine jazz.'"

"But you do now?" Rachael asked.

"Yep. I would guess that the Throne does the miracles. This time it was done to fool the Nephilim."

"You learned all of this when you were dead?"

"No. I learned it after I came back. Zak told all of this to me."

"Who's Zak?"

"That day that you left – the day that Michael talked to each of us separately – Michael told me that, if I ever woke up somewhere in a strange place and was confused, then I should just pretend to have amnesia. I should pretend that my memory was blank and wait for Zak. And, right before Tex opened up on us, he reminded me of it."

Rachael was hanging on every word:

"Tell me about it."

"Well . . . the last thing that I remember was seeing something that looked like a giant water hose spraying through the walls. Everything in front of it just disappeared. I don't remember any pain – just a sudden jolt.

The next thing I remember was floating over the giant dust cloud that used to be our house. I remembered seeing a blast come from the end of the house; but I couldn't hear the explosion.

The instant that my thoughts turned to you, I found myself over Agatha's townhouse. Somehow I knew that you were in the dumpster behind it; and suddenly I was right next to you.

I tried to talk to you; but you couldn't hear me. I looked inside and saw Agatha and Molly. I got very close to Holly and she seemed to be uninjured.

Then police came through the door and I knew that you and Holly would survive."

Rachael motioned to make a point:

"When the police couldn't get through to the house they checked the phone records of the last calls made. That's why they stormed Agatha's townhouse."

Jerry continued:

"I wanted to stay with you but was drawn away. I went through what was like the tunnel described in some of the Near Death Experiences that we had read about. Through the tunnel I went and into the light. I was surrounded by people that I knew."

He marveled:

"Remember that show called 'This is Your Life,' where the participant is bombarded by many of the people that he has loved throughout his life?"

"Yes."

"Well . . . it was just like that," Jerry revealed. "I never realized that there were that many people in the world that I loved. Then, of course, I realized that I *wasn't* in this world – I was approaching my heavenly dwelling place.

Before I could place one person, another would catch my eye. I was in the presence of incredible love – it was like nothing else that I have ever experienced." He looked wild-eyed and overjoyed:

"It's all true, Rachael! Perfect harmony *has* been established in the heavens. I know that for sure now! Rachael – I am a witness of it!"

Rachael looked back at him for a few moments – not knowing what to say. "Go on with your story," she urged.

He continued:

"These people . . . ah . . . angels . . . that I knew and loved so well . . . they . . . they seemed to be thinking things like, 'oh . . . he is here,' 'look . . . he is back,' 'he made it,' 'he did it.' Then, just as fast as they arrived, they left.

There was only one person left with me. I didn't recognize him; but I trusted him completely:

'Where did everybody go?' I asked. 'Where is Michael?' 'Where is Zak?'

The man simply said, 'you need to rest.'

I saw an inviting bed in front of me and climbed in."

"Then what?"

He shrugged:

"Then I woke up in Jerry's body. He had been in a coma for a couple of days."

Rachael looked confused:

"Well . . . what happened to the *real* Jerry? Where is he now?"

"I don't know," he shrugged. "It wasn't long before Jerry's friends and neighbors came in to see him . . . ah, I mean, me."

Rachael looked concerned:

"Is Jerry married?"

"No. He was a while back . . . he doesn't have any kids and his folks are dead."

Rachael was relieved:

"I see. Well . . . where do his friends and neighbors think that he is now?"

"I told them I needed some time alone. They seemed to understand.

Zak took his sweet time coming to get me. I guess he wanted me to learn a few things about Jerry from the folks who came to see me in the hospital. Zak also signed my name for me when I checked out so that my signature would match Jerry's. They had it all figured out."

"What does Tex's number mean?" Rachael asked. "What is that all about?"

"I got the information about Tex from Zak.

Michael only partially explained the software to me. I guess there was still a chance that Michael's scheme wouldn't work and we would be taken by Niyaq. There was the possibility that you, Michael, and myself could have been taken by Niyaq.

But Zak filled in the missing pieces and furnished me with what I needed to know to continue on with 'The Woman Project.' That's the name of the project that my software program is connected with.

This is the scenario of the software that I created and how it will function in the future:

There is someone out there that has a map of the entire world. This map is broken up into 144 segments and each segment is given a number. Another name for this number is 'area,' or 'pulse.'

Zak told me that millions of people are having latter day dreams and visions; and that many would interpret them falsely and believe that they are part of the chosen of Israel – you know, the folks that will be protected from death and be the ruling elite of the new order. He told me that many well-meaning people would be mixed together with those that have a true calling as one of the 144,000 of the twelve tribes of Israel. He also told me that there would be people among them that *were not* well-meaning.

So . . . that's where this software gadget comes in. It is used to weed out the true elect from the wishful thinkers and wannabe hopefuls. In a way it is a bit disgusting. You go to the left and burn; you go to the right and live.

The true elect will have a number that they received through the Spirit. That number is plugged into the software with the identifying number of the area where they were born. All that is left is to plug in the birth date. The software can recognize valid numbers as they match up with the two other inputs. So, only those who have valid numbers get to go."

"How does the software work?" Rachael asked.

"I really don't know *how* it works except that it has something to do with frequency and harmonics. You see, the Torah itself is the guts of the software – all *I* did, was follow the instructions and hook it up. Michael told me how to run it."

"So," Rachael began, "you won't know if Tex is one of the elect until you re-create the software?"

"Wrong. Zak gave me his number and it matched with the number that Tex received through the Spirit."

"What about Holly's number?"

Jerry was surprised:

"I didn't know that she'd gotten it yet."

"Yeah, she just recently received it," Rachael told him.

“That’s interesting. I used Holly’s numbers to test the discs. I have all of Holly’s numbers.”

Rachael made a face:

“But . . . this makes absolutely no sense. We’re not Jewish. Holly isn’t Jewish.”

Jerry was unaffected by her remark:

“Frankly, I really don’t care if it makes sense or not. All I have to do is do what I am told to do. All I have to do is my little end of it. I’ll leave the theology to someone else.”

Rachael looked annoyed:

“Don’t be absurd – it just doesn’t make any sense.”

“It *will* make sense to the folks who are issued numbers by the Throne – I can guarantee you that!

I’m *not* being absurd with my intentions to obey and do *only* what I’m told. If Jarvis had taken that approach this whole thing would have been a lot easier. Instead, he added his own strategies to the equation; and, in the end, double-crossed us all. None of us would have died if Jarvis had kept his word to Michael.”

Rachael’s brow lifted:

“But . . . if Jarvis hadn’t fouled up, then Michael’s people might not have been able to fool Niyaq the way they did.”

He slowly nodded in agreement:

“Yeah, I considered that. Zak says that things couldn’t have worked out better. The software part of ‘The Woman Project’ is a done deal and Niyaq won’t be looking for Jesus. And, they won’t be looking for me either.

I get confused whenever I think about it.”

Rachael considered it:

“Well . . . maybe you only know what you *need* to know? Maybe you’ve misunderstood something?”

“I’m just going by what Zak said.”

“Maybe Zak is wrong,” Rachael mused.

“You think so? If that’s the case, then how did Zak know Tex’s number?

I’m sure the Throne knew that we would have doubts about Zak; and that the number deal with Tex would calm the waters. Plus, he came to get me just like Michael said he would. How did he know to do that?

All this was done so that we would know who to trust when Michael left us.”

“You’re right,” Rachael agreed. “We have to trust Zak. But . . . I still don’t understand all of the ramifications of ‘The Woman Project.’ Didn’t

Zak explain it to you?"

Jerry considered it for a few moments:

"I guess I always looked at the elect (chosen) of Israel as just a procreation tool to populate the next age; but, according to Zak, they are much more than that.

Zak told me that not everyone in the world will die in the tribulation. There will be pockets of survivors located all over the world. Zak said that there were five primary races in the beginning and that they would be preserved. The elect will be comprised of people from all over the world, and will share race and language with these different nations. Ships carrying the elect will sail from Israel; and these elect will return home to their native lands to carry the law of Yahweh. The people in distant lands will be waiting for them; and will, for the most part, respect their authority. These elect of the twelve tribes will be the ruling elite of the next age. Not only in Jerusalem will the elect rule – they will rule entire world.

According to Zak, these elect will be very special people with a very special faith – possessing in their physical memories a first-hand knowledge of heavenly Jerusalem. They will have images of this perfected habitation in their minds, and will be great teachers who will inspire the world with their knowledge and God-given faith."

Rachael was caught up with his enthusiasm:

"Are you saying that these Jews of different races and languages will sail to the outer frontiers of Earth and settle there?"

"Yes. That is what Zak told me," Jerry replied.

"Do you suppose that Holly and Tex will come back to America to settle?" she asked.

"Yes."

"And . . . then you might have some Chinese Jews going back to China?" she speculated.

"Sure, why not."

"So . . . some copies of your discs will be sent as far away as China?"

"Yep."

She made a face:

"Well . . . what about us, Jerry – where do we fit into all of this?"

Jerry shrugged his shoulders:

"Rachael, have you received a number?"

"Nope. Have you?"

"No, I haven't, Raech – maybe we'll be too old to go with Tex and Holly. Maybe . . . maybe maybe maybe. We'll just have to wait and see.

It doesn't really matter. Apparently I did OK with the chore that the

Throne gave me to do, and was martyred while doing it. Perhaps we can be born into the new world together." He smiled:

"Plus, now we have a little time to relax and enjoy ourselves."

She smiled back. "Where do you plan to stay?"

He pointed at the floor. "Here . . . right here."

"What about Holly?"

He thoughtfully rubbed his chin:

"Well . . . she can elope with Tex."

"But . . ."

Jerry became impatient:

"Rachael, enough of the picky details – we've got the big stuff covered."

"Yeah . . . but who is going to *believe* all of that weird stuff that Zak told you?"

"I don't care *who* believes it. The Throne didn't say that I have to go around preaching it and making a complete fool out of myself.

Plus, this isn't the gospel that needs to be preached to the world; this is a self-sustaining internal process – it only affects a relatively small number of people."

Rachael got up and retrieved a Bible:

"OK . . . show me some of that stuff in the Bible."

"We could be fooling around or something; and you want to read the Bible?"

"Come on, Marty."

"The name is Jerry."

Her lip curled up. "I hate that name."

"Humph, you'd better get used to it."

He stared at Rachael curiously.

"What," Rachael said, "is there something wrong?"

"Ah . . . I was just admiring your outfit."

Rachael looked down at her blouse that was definitely in the "yes" position.

Jerry caught her eye:

"Rachael?"

"Yeah?"

Jerry grinned ear to ear:

"You're dying to know what I'm packing under my shorts, aren't you?"

She turned a bright red and tried to shrug it off:

"Well . . . I guess I wondered a little."

Jerry playfully wiggled his eyebrows and motioned:

"Lead the way to the boudoir."

She pointed at him:

"OK . . . but *you're* going to have to undress first."

"Huh?"

"You've already seen *me*."

He wiggled his eyebrows again:

"Ha . . . you're afraid I'll be too much for you."

She wiggled her eyebrows back at him.

"Oh? Is *that* what you think? Gosh, I hope you don't miss heaven that far."

"How long till Holly gets home?" Jerry asked.

"About an hour."

Rachael smiled. "Well, better that she catches us reading the Bible than . . ."

"Jeez . . . I gotta sneak sex with my own wife."

(A while later) "Show me some things from the Bible, Marty."

Jerry looked at his watch:

"Yeah, we can look at the Bible if you want.

I've had plenty of time to read it – waiting two weeks for the road blocks to be taken down."

"You could've called," Rachael suggested.

"Your phone has got to be tapped. Didn't they tell you it was tapped?"

Rachael nodded. "Yes, they told me that."

"What did you tell the police when they questioned you?" Jerry asked.

"I never talked with the police. Men in suits came with a military escort."

"Were they FBI? CIA?"

"I'm not sure," Rachael began. "The first time I talked with them I told them that the military chopper was probably filled with Niyaq. Ha . . . they didn't have a clue of what I was talking about. But, after that, they found out that the real crew of the Chinook wasn't on board. They found their bodies later.

Then more people came and questioned me. I had to take a lie detector test. Even the President came to see me."

Jerry walked to the window and looked out at where their house once stood:

"There couldn't have been much evidence left."

"True." She pointed at the woods where the first chopper went down:

"Over there, that's where the civilian chopper went down – it had Americans in it. They figured out that much. I told them all that I knew; but I really don't think that I gave them anything useful."

"Did they get any Arabs alive?"

"The papers said that they didn't."

Jerry stared off in contemplation.

"What is it?" Rachael asked.

"God, I'm glad that we got that one Arab."

"Huh?"

"The towels that stormed the house had a leader," Jerry began. "He was . . . *very* formidable – *very* powerful."

"He scared you?"

"He did – he even scared *Jarvis*!"

"What about Michael?" she asked.

"We were all freaked at the end – it looked as though they were going to take us."

Jerry smiled broadly and slowly nodded:

"But . . . it was all worth it, Raech. The whole ordeal was worth it just to see the expression on that Arab's face the instant before Jarvis put a bullet into his brain. I can tell you this much, Raech, it wasn't the look of someone who was about to visit 70 virgins."

Jerry marveled:

"When I look back on it I can't help but wonder how many strings the Throne pulled in the background to make things turn out the way they did. I guess I'll never know."

Rachael gave Jerry a curious look:

"So . . . did you finally prove yourself to the great Jarvis?"

Jerry's eyes narrow accusingly:

"You know how to cut to the quick – don't you?"

"Well?"

He considered it:

"Yeah . . . I guess I *did* want to prove myself to him. I made a big show of not being afraid."

"Did that work?"

"Well . . . it worked until Jarvis and I got separated."

"That's when you panicked and shot the Marine," Rachael surmised.

"That's right. Fooling around with guns doesn't make you a combat soldier."

He tried to shrug it off:

"Yeah . . . I panicked; but when I shot the Marine the gunships came back and the LAV concentrated on the house. Niyaq might have gotten us if I hadn't shot the Marine. If Jarvis hadn't downed that chopper, I *know* that Niyaq would have gotten us. Niyaq had an almost foolproof plan to get us out of there; and it almost worked."

"All's well that ends well," Rachael pointed out.

"Well, it hasn't ended yet. Heck, The Woman Project won't go into full swing until the last seven year period is upon us."

"This Woman Project, this is prophesied in the Bible?"

"Yeah.

In the Old Testament the sealed elect are sometimes called 'those who escaped.'

The Bible speaks of the law going out of Zion and the word of Yahweh going out of Jerusalem.[1] It explains that people will be on the coastlands waiting for the law of Yahweh to arrive.[2]

It is illustrated that the ones who have escaped (the sealed elect), will be sent by ship to distant coastlands – to peoples that do not know of the glory or laws of Yahweh. These travelers shall manifest the glory of Yahweh to the gentiles of these far away lands.[3]

A lot can happen in a thousand years, Raech. NeroCain and his bunch will have no influence upon the thoughts and deeds of man; and Yahweh will choose His *best* to be born *first*. This is how Yahweh will ensure that a life experience is created that is pleasing in His sight, and nourishing for the souls of men.

The slates of the souls of men will once again be filled with the experiences of life; but these will be experiences that will nourish, edify, and heal the souls of men. In the course of time, these experiences will work together to mold their hearts into something finer than the tainted experiences of the last age produced.

And, when the thousand years are finished and the rest of the dead begin to see life again,[4] it will be a better world that they are born into – a school for life prepared by Yahweh and His servants. This is the healing of the Nations.[5] This is the prophecy of the Great God Yahweh and the message of His Messiah. This is the future of mankind."

"And it all starts off with your little disc."

---

1 Isa 2:3
2 Isa 42:4
3 Isa 66:19
4 Re 20:5
5 Re 22:2

"Not *my* disc – Yahweh's disc. All I did was to plug it into electricity."

Rachael took Jerry's hand and searched his face:

"Are we safe, Jerry – are we really safe?"

A deep sadness came over him:

"We've got a little break that the Throne gave us to cool our heels a bit. But *nobody* is safe anymore.

The Nephilim are being born into the world in ever increasing numbers. People marvel when they watch the news – they marvel at the outrageous acts of evil that are being committed in every strata of society. But . . . but they don't put the pieces together – they don't understand why man has suddenly turned to evil in such unprecedented numbers. They don't recognize it as a fulfillment of Bible prophecy. These evil ones are those whose names were originally *excluded* from the *book of life* by Yahweh.[1] They are waiting for *their* messiah to manifest himself. They are readying themselves for world domination.

It is true that of late there has been a resurgence of conservative ideals – a backlash to the success of the cultural revolution that has corrupted the country. While this might give a temporary boost to the Republicans, the die has been cast as far as the final outcome is concerned.

Europe has all but stopped having babies. They must rely on immigration to man their depleted work force. The Muslims are breeding like crazy and are all too happy to leave their depressed situations and fill in the gaps. When the Muslims become the majority, do you think that they will grant the same religious freedom to their host country that was granted to them? I think not. Then, Europe will offer the same quality of life that is currently given to those of the Arab countries. The end is in sight."

Rachael numbly stared off into space. "Boy, aren't *you* the optimistic one."

"Rachael . . . I'm just speaking my mind.

My dad told me that there was an epidemic of Mexican illegals in the early fifties. Well, there were plenty of WWII vets around in those days. They had just seen the world and felt that our country was worth preserving. Ike instigated "Operation Wetback" to send the illegal Mexicans home."

He looked intently at Rachael:

"That outrageous act of political incorrectness was what the country needed to preserve itself. Now we are becoming a country divided. By and large, the Hispanics aren't coming here to be a part of our culture – they are coming here to establish their *own* culture and speak their *own* language.

---

1 Re 17:8

Americans just sit back and let it happen. Why? Because, supposedly, it is the *correct* thing to do. We trade our culture away under the banner of equality as if equality was what made us great to start with. We post signs in Spanish. Not because we have to; but because our cultural revolution has determined the correctness of it. The cultural revolution brings out only the flaws of America, therefore justifying change. Whether the change will be good or bad for our culture in general is a moot point as we have become a people down on ourselves and critical of the heritage that made us great."

"You got something against Mexicans?" Rachael asked him.

Jerry looked disgusted:

"That sounds like something Molly would say.

No, I don't have anything against *Mexicans* – I would just like a bit of sanity to creep into our immigration policy. We sent a boatload of Jews back to Europe to get gassed in WWII – folks that would have made good citizens. Now, we let an army of foreigners come in here illegally and take over. I just want our government to use some common sense. I cite Mexico because they represent what is probably our *biggest* immigration bungle."

"It's all such gloom and doom," Rachael began sullenly. "It's like we're just waiting for the end to come – waiting for the total domination of evil. Michael, he's the lucky one – he can just watch from a safe place." She stared off numbly:

"It's like . . . like there is nothing left for us to do."

Jerry took Rachel's hand. "That's not true, Rachael. Our job is to keep Tex and Holly out of harm's way. They will experience a blessed event that is beyond our imagination. They will sing with the Cherubim of God, and view heavenly Jerusalem. And . . . and there is The Woman Project. There are lots of exciting things on our agenda."

She wasn't convinced:

"But what about the *rest* of the world, Marty – what can *they* look forward to?"

He considered it for a few moments:

"You know, Raech, after I resigned myself to death it wasn't that bad. I mean – it was like I was getting aid from an outside source. OK – I freaked a few times – next time I will do better.

The Bible says that the gospel of The Revelation[1] will be preached to the whole world before the end comes. Let's hope that plenty of folks believe it and put on a good show. Folks need to realize that Yahweh will need lots of help when he battles NeroCain in the heavens. Folks need to know how to enlist – they need to know not to worship the Beast, and to

---

1 M't 24:3-14, M'r 13:3-13, M't 10:38,39 etc.

keep their testimony to Yahweh. There will be plenty to do for Christians and Jews that are willing to get involved.

These precepts *need to be known by man and understood.* And, it is only fair that man is made aware of the consequences of siding with the Beast. Indeed, those that take his mark will share the fate of the Nephilim – the very ones who have caused the bulk of the chaos. Could Yahweh be a just God and exact this kind of punishment without warning? I think not.

In the physical world those who resist the Beast will be viewed, by many, as fools – dead fools. There will not be any evidence to onlookers that these martyrs have just purchased their tickets to the age of peace, and have enlisted to follow the Lamb into war with the Beast in the spiritual realm. Folks will need to have faith in The Revelation gospel – it will be their only hope!

The stronger one's faith, the easier it will be to fight and not side up with the ruler of the world. Folks need to start *now* to build that kind of faith. If folks can really believe that a martyr's death will lead to eternal life in the age to come,[1] then they can do what is required of them. After all, their opponents have this kind of fervor."

Rachael viewed her husband approvingly:

"You put that very well, hon."

Martin was caught up with enthusiasm:

"Listen, Raech. The Revelation says that the Beast will make war with the saints and prevail over them. It doesn't say that the saints give up – it doesn't say that the saints surrender. It doesn't say that the saints are a bunch of joyless wretches that tremble at the sight of the Beast.

There is plenty left to do that is noble and worthwhile. We just have to get pumped up for it. We need to pray more and rely on Him for strength. We just have to look at this as the great holy rumble that it is, and be assured that we will do our best and please God in doing so.

I'll tell you one thing, Raech:"

"What's that?"

"Before all things come to fruition, there will be little doubt about what Yahweh has been protecting man from for all of these thousands of years. There will be little doubt left as to what the consequences would be if Yahweh ever lost control of the tree of life. There will be no doubts left among the righteous as to why it is so important to have a just, moral God directing the course of mankind."

"Whew . . . Michael was certainly right about one thing," Rachael told him.

---

1 M'r 10:30

"What's that, Raech?"

She rolled her eyes:

"I need a break from it all – at least for a season."

"Yes – and you shall have it, my love."

"What about Niyaq, Marty; do you think we are safe from them?"

"Zak says that Niyaq has no trail to follow. I can't imagine that Niyaq would think that we stashed a disc outside the house on the property somewhere. They were watching us like a hawk."

"Maybe I should sell the land just the same," Rachael volunteered.

"Yeah . . . I think maybe you should.

What about *Threshold,* Raech?" Jerry asked her. "What are you planning to do with it?"

"I've got it up for sale," she told him.

"Take it off the market, Raech; we'd be better off to sell part of it to Frank and Sheila and let them run it."

Rachael looked sour:

"Marty, I mean, Jerry . . . you don't plan on working there – do you?"

"Ah . . . well . . ."

Concern swept over her:

"Jerry, you've known those people too long. They'll catch on. I mean, your mannerisms and the way that you talk – they'll figure it out!"

He nodded. "Gosh . . . you're right. Hmm, what'll I do with myself?"

Rachael laughed:

"Why don't you do the same thing that other prophets do when they are laid off?"

Jerry raised his finger to make a point:

"Ha! Go to the wilderness. Perhaps you could come along?"

"What about Holly?" She asked.

"Didn't you say that she was acting rebellious?"

Rachael sighed. "Yes . . . I've never seen her act this way before."

Jerry wiggled his eyebrows impishly and rubbed his hands together as if devising a scheme:

"That's good. She'll show *you*, by running off with *Tex*; which is *exactly* what we *want* her to do."

He looked curiously at Rachael:

"Do . . . do you suppose that Holly is still . . ."

"She's still a virgin," Rachael assured him.

"Wow."

"Yeah . . . we got it on the first night," Rachael pointed out.

Jerry jolted:

"You didn't tell Holly *that* – did you?"

"No . . . of course not."

Jerry's eyes saddened:

"It was *our* generation that fouled up. We spearheaded the downward spiral of the country with our cultural revolution of desolation."

"I know it," Rachael agreed.

Jerry's eyes wearied as he recounted:

"Dad used to try to talk with me about it. Of course, I thought he was a total idiot."

He considered it for a moment and continued:

"We were talking about democracy one day and dad said that the US policy of spreading democracy should really be a policy of spreading the Judeo-Christian values that created the quality of life that Americans experience." He caught himself:

"I suppose a better way to state that now would be the quality of life that Americans *used* to experience.

He said that democracy, without faithful fervor, was merely a vacuum waiting to be filled – an ideal platform to birth an alternate faithful fervor. He also pointed out that the alternate faithful fervor – the one that would fill this empty void – would, most likely, be inferior to the proven fervor of our ancestors.

Dad thought that democracy was OK; but he didn't *believe* in it. He said that a nation with Christian fervor could handle a bad king; but a county without it couldn't control the fate of its own democracy."

He slowly shook his head:

"Dad was right."

Rachael nodded:

"Yes . . . and we were part of the problem – just as your dad accused us."

Martin took a deep breath:

"Well, maybe now we can be part of the solution."

NOTES ON BIBLICAL HEBREW ELS TERMS

The numbers in brackets are reference numbers from *Strong's Exhaustive Concordance of the Bible*. All definitions are from this source unless otherwise noted.

CHAPTER 5 NOTES

<u>Caesar Menorah Report</u>

(1) 2. קסר מנרה (ELS term)

Caesar (is a) Lampstand.

קסר "Caesar." Transliterated as was done in the 666 scenario of The Revelation.

מנרה Noun f (4501). "Lampstand."

(2) 3. שטני קא לי

My adversary (Satan) (is) vomit to me.

שטני Noun m (7854). "An opponent." Also a word for "Satan," arch enemy of God. Noun has pronominal suffix "י" "My adversary."

קא Noun m. (6892). "Vomit."

לי To me.

(3) 4. קין שא בית אש

Cain, suffer to bear the house of fire!

קין Cain (7014). "The name of the first child."

שא Verb "nasa" (5375). "To lift, in a great variety of applications, lit. and fig." Qal 2ms imperative: "Suffer to bear!"

בית Noun m.(1004). "House."

אש Noun c.(784). "Fire."

(4) 5. שם הדלק ים אש

Kindle there the lake of fire!

שם Adverb (8033). "There."

הדלק Verb "dalaq" (1814). "To flame, (lit. and fig.)." Hiphil imperative 2ms (as in Ezekiel 24:10): "Kindle, cause to burn."

ים Noun m. (3220). "A sea...or large body of water:" "Lake."
אש Noun c (784). "Fire."

(5) 6. אבדו שוה מכבש

He brought forth his own destruction from the Lamb.

אבדו Noun m (8). "Destruction." With "ו" pronominal suffix: "His destruction."

שוה Verb "shavah" (7737). "To level...yield, etc." Piel 3ms perfect: "He brought forth."

מכבש "Lamb." Noun m (3532). "A ram (just old enough to butt)." Also rendered as "lamb, sheep." With "מ" prefix: "From the lamb."

(6) 7. תוה לסאי השמיני

Mark for my measure of the eighth!

תוה Verb "tavah" (8427). "To mark out." Piel 2ms imperative: "Mark!"

לסאי Noun f "seah" (5429). "Measure." "as seah, or certain measure (as determinative) for grain." With pronominal suffix "י" "my." With "ל" prefix meaning "for:" "For my measures of."

Note: se'ah is generally cited as a female noun; but is also attested in the male gender as ". . . appar. masc., perh. after anal. of other measures of capacity. . . ." (Brown-Driver-Briggs pg. 684). It is attested as modifying a male noun in two instances in the Tanakh.

Alternate rendering could be:

Mark for My eighth measure (portion)!

השמיני "Eighth" m (8066). Ordinal number. With "ה" prefix: "The eighth."

(7) 8. יהוה הפחם חש

Has YHVH made ready their trap?

יהוה "Yahweh."

הפחם Noun m (6341). "A spring net." With "ה" heh interrogatory (?) prefix, and with pronominal suffix, "ם": "Their trap?"

חש Verb "choosh" (2363). "To hurry." Qal 3ms perfect: "He hastened, he made ready."

(8) 9. קדח ירא בבנה בור הוא שאו

He kindled fear when building a pit that you shall suffer to bear.

קדח Verb "qadach" (6919). "To inflame." Qal 3ms perfect: "He kindled."

ירא Adj (3373). "Fearing." "Fear."

בבנה Verb "banah" (1129). "To build." Qal ms participle, "one building." With "ב" prefix: "When building."

בור Noun m (953). "A pit hole:" "Pit."

הוא Particle pronoun m. (1931). "...this or that."

שאו Verb "nasa" (5375). "To lift, in a great variety of applications, lit. and fig." Qal 2mp imperative: "You suffer to bear!"

(9) נרונקין שנא נזנה

Nero(n) Cain – to hate, we will play the whore.

נרונקין Nero(n) Cain.

שנא Verb "saneh." (8130). "To hate." Qal infinitive construct: "To hate."

נזנה Verb "zanah" (2181). "To commit adultery." Qal 1cp imperfect: "We play the whore."

(10) נרונקין שנאן זנה

Nero(n)Cain – to hate them, he played the whore.

נרונקין "Nero(n) Cain."

שנאן Verb "saneh" (8130). "To hate." Qal infinitive construct with 3fp direct object suffix "ן" "To hate them."

זנה Verb "zanah" (2181). "To commit adultery." Qal 3ms perfect: "He played the whore."

CHAPTER 6 NOTES

(11) לוח בכורי אל ותאמנו אדם

Tablet of (writing of) firstborn (firstfruits) of God; and you have been established, man."

לוח Noun m (3871): "Tablet."

בכורי Noun m (1060). "Firstborn." "י" suffix denotes plural construct: "Firstborns of."

ותאמנו Verb aman (539). "To build up or support." Niphal 2mp imperfect, "ו" prefix tense change: "And you have been established."

אדם Noun m (120). "Man."

CHAPTER 7 NOTES

<u>**War in Heaven Report**</u>

(12) 2. מובא משיח תנו לו וו (ELS term)

The entrance of messiah – give to him a hook.

מובא Noun m (3996). "Entrance."

משיח Noun m (4899). "Messiah."

תנו Verb "nathan" (5414). "To give." Qal 2mp imperative: "Give!"

לו To him.

וו Noun m (2053). "A hook."

(13) 3. תם כחם שמשיח

That messiah will make an end to their strength.

תם Verb "tamam" (8552). "To complete, in a good or bad sense." Qal infinitive construct: "To make an end."

כחם Noun m (3581). "Strength." With pronominal suffix "ם" "Their strength."

שמשיח Noun m (4899). "Messiah." With "ש" prefix: "That messiah."

(14) 5. הה נרו מה חממ בו

Woe to Nero! What aroused them against him?

הה Interjection (1929). "...ah! expressing grief:" "Woe."

נרו Nero. Without silent Greek "N": used for 616 scenario of the anti-christ.

מה Interrogatory (4100). "What?"

חממ Verb "chamam" (2552). "To be hot." Qal infinitive construct, with direct object suffix "מ": "To arouse them...to inflame them." "Aroused them."

בו "Against him."

(15) 6. מדר גוימ נוא

Because posterity of Nations restrained.

מדר Noun m (1755). "A revolution of time, i.e. an age or generation...." "מ" prefix: "Because posterity."

גוימ Noun m (1471). "A foreign nation." Plural: "Nations."

נוא Verb "nuw" (5106). "To refuse, forbid, dissuade, or neutralize." Qal ms passive participle: "Restrained."

Note: Attested in Qal with that meaning (discourage or break), Numbers 32:7; and in Numbers 32:9, with same meaning in Hiphil.

(16) 7. עלת יהוה בהו נכי

A burnt offering of Yahweh (as a wholly consumed obligation to God) (is) the desolation of my attackers.

עלת Noun f (5930). Singular construct: "Burnt offering of."

יהוה "Yahweh."

בהו Noun m (922). "Emptiness, void:" "Desolation."

נכי Noun m "nekeh" (5222). "A smiter, i.e. (fig) traducer." Attested once in Psalms 35:15, **נכים**. Text points to "attackers." Mostly rendered as "attackers or smiters." Sometimes as abjects – despicable rejects. From "nakah" (5221), "to strike." In this form with "**י**" suffix: "My attackers."

(17) 9. לחמים ערו ילה (NE)

Destroy attackers! Let him waste away.

לחמים Verb "lacham" (3898). "To feed on, to battle (as destruction)." Qal mp participle. "Ones attacking," as in Psalms 56:3: "Attackers."

ערו Verb "arah" (6168). "To be (cause make) bare . . . demolish." Piel 2mp imperative as in Psalms 137:7: "Destroy!"

ילה Verb "lahah (3856). "To be rabid...also (from the exhaustion of frenzy) to languish." Qal 3ms jussive: "Let him waste away."

(18) 9. אם מות שם ארה

The mother of death is there gathering.

אם Noun f (517). "Mother."

מות Noun m (4194). "Death."

שם Particle (8033). "There"

ארה verb "arah" (717). "To pluck." Qal fs participle: "One gathering – gathering."

<u>Nod and the Tree of Life</u>

(19) אנה שהי תת עצ החיים נוד מי גנ בוא

Where is my Lamb to give the tree of life? Nod whose garden is to come.

אנה Adverb (575). Interrogatory: "Where?" as in 2 Kings 6:6.

שהי Noun c (7716). "A member of a flock, i.e, sheep or a goat." With "**י**" pronominal suffix: "My Lamb."

תת Verb "nathan" (5414). "To give." Qal infinitive construct: "to give."

עצ החיים From Genesis: "The tree of life."

נוד Noun f (5113). "Nod, The land of Cain:" "Nod."

מי Pronoun. Not interrogatory (4310). "Whose," as in Jeremiah 44:28.

גן Noun c (1588). "Garden."

בוא Verb "bo" (935). "To go or come." Qal infinitive construct: "To come."

Passover to Yahweh

(20) שם רן השביע (Lateral term)

There to sing, "he caused to swear an oath."

שם Particle (8033). "There."

רן Verb "ranan" (7442). "To sing, to shout for joy." Qal infinitive construct, "To sing."

השביע Verb "sheba." (7650). "To swear." Hiphil 3ms perfect: "He caused to swear an oath."

Note: An alternate rendering could be: "The name of the song is 'He Caused to Make an Oath.'"

Who is Cain?

(21) שר איל ראה מי קין

See who is Cain? A ruler of strength. (NE)

שר Noun m (8269). "Ruler."

איל Noun m (353). "Strength."

ראה Verb "Ra'ah (7200)." "To see." Qal 2ms imperative. "See!"

מי Pronoun interrogative (4310). "Who?"

קין Cain (7014). "The name of the first child."

(22) ללוע נרון קסר שמו

Nero (n) Caesar is the name of the one who behaved wildly.

ללוע Verb "luwa" (3886). "To be rash (Strong's)." "To talk wildly (Brown-Driver-Briggs)." Qal infinitive construct: "To behave wildly."

נרון קסר Hebrew transliteration of the Greek, Nero (n) Caesar, 666.

שמו Noun m (8034). "Name." With "ו" pronominal suffix: "his name."

The Fate of Nod

(23) שש לגר בחרי נוד לתם

White linen for the stranger of Nod, chosen by me for integrity.

שש Noun m (8336). "White linen." "White linen."

לגר Noun m (1616). "Foreigner." With "ל" prefix: "For stranger."

בחרי Verb "bachar" (977). "To select." Qal ms participle (one chosen) with "י" pronominal suffix: "My chosen."

נוד Noun f (5113). "Nod, The land of Cain:" "Nod."

לתם Noun m (8537). "Completeness...innocence." "Integrity." With "ל" prefix: For integrity."

(24) הרר תוב כדונ נדו

The mountain (congregation) of your mark – as One judged they wandered.

הרר Noun m (2042). "Mountain."

תוב Noun m (8420). "A mark." With "ב" suffix: "Your mark."

כדונ Verb "diyn or duwn" (1779). "To judge...to strive (as the law)." Qal ms passive participle: "One judged." With "כ" prefix: "As One judged."

נדו Verb "nuwd" (5110). "To wander, flee, disappear." Qal 3cp perfect (as in Jeremiah 50:3): "They wandered."

The Rescue of Hell (Nod)

(25) אברו שאולה ימ קא

I fly Him into hell – a sea of vomit.

אברו Verb "abar" (82). "To soar." Hiphil 1cs, "I fly." With "ו" direct object suffix: "I fly him."

Note. This verb is only attested once in Hiphil in defective spelling similar to the above, Job 39:26.

שאולה Noun c (7585). "Hades or the world of the dead." With heh "ה" directive suffix: "Into hell."

ימ Noun m (3220). "A sea...or large body of water:" "Lake."

קא Noun m (6892). "Vomit."

(26) ימש מצא ראשיתו

Let him depart to find his beginning.

ימש Verb "moosh" (4185). "To withdraw (both lit. and fig)." Jussive 3ms: "Let him depart."

מצא Verb "matsa" (4672). "Find or acquire." Infinitive construct: "To find."

ראשיתו Noun f (7225). "Beginning." With "ו" pronominal suffix: "His beginning."

Where is the Savior of the Waters

(27) איה מושיע המימ

Where is the savior of the waters?

איה Adverb (346) interrogatory: "Where?"

מושיע Verb "yasha" (3467). "To be safe; causative, to free or succor." Hiphil ms participle, "one causing to be saved:" "Savior."

המים Noun m: (4325). "Water(s)." With "ה" prefix: "The waters."

(28) עברני גן עדן

He crossed me over (to) the garden of Eden.

עברני Verb "abar." (5674). "To cross over." Qal 3ms perfect with "ני" direct object suffix: "He crossed me over."

גן עדן From Genesis: "The garden of Eden."

<u>My City Rejoiced</u>

(29) אנשי תבל מהל ששו עירי (ELS term)

He mixed the men of the world; My city rejoiced.

אנשי Noun m (582). "A mortal...a man." Plural construct form: "Men of."

תבל Noun f (8398). "The earth...the globe...its inhabitants." "The world."

מהל Verb "mahal" (4107). This verb is only attested once as Qal passive participle (Brown-Driver-Briggs) and is rendered "mixed" (KJV). Qal 3ms perfect: "He mixed."

ששו Verb "soos" or "sees" (7797). "To be bright, i.e, cheerful." Qal 3cp perfect (as in Lamentations 1.21): "They rejoiced."

עירי Noun f (5892). "A city." With "י" pronominal suffix: "My city."

(30) בתם במוצ ההרים שבע

With integrity against the extortioner, the mountains to be satisfied.

בתם Noun m (8537). "Completeness...innocence." "Integrity." With "ב" prefix: "With integrity."

במוצ Verb "muwts" (4160). "To press i.e. (fig) to oppress." Qal passive participle. "One who oppressed (similar to Isaiah 16:4):" With "ב" prefix: "Against the extortioner."

ההרים Noun m (2022). "Mountain." Plural with "ה" prefix: "The mountains."

שבע Verb "saba" (7646). "To sate, i.e. fill to satisfaction." Qal infinitive construct: "To be satisfied."

ACKNOWLEDGMENTS

Whether the Bible codes are fact or fiction has been a debate that has raged for years. If messages are hidden in the Torah – as I believe that they are – for what purpose did God put them there; and what knowledge is man meant to garnish from these messages?

My fascination with eschatology, and the book of The Revelation in particular, led me to code for the precepts that were discussed in *NEPHILIM: the Fallen Ones*. There are many other avenues to explore; and there are many more researchers like me who are looking for answers in the Bible codes. It has yet to be seen what the full scope of the codes are; and indeed, the possibilities are so vast that it is likely that they will never be fully comprehended.

No man is an island unto himself; and so it was with this book. Several of my friends – also involved in Bible code research – aided me a great deal.

Roy Reinhold is a Bible scholar and long time codes researcher – whose help with the book was indispensable. He was there helping and encouraging me from start to finish.

Kevin Acres, the creator of the CodeFinder: Millennium Edition Bible coding software, has long supported my efforts. On many occasions, Kevin made modifications to his software to help my progress.

If you're interested in learning more about the Bible codes, Roy has an excellent Bible code website, Codes In The Bible at, http://ad2004.com/ Kevin's site is: http://www.research-systems.com/

Barry Roffman also gave me many bits of editing advice for which I am grateful. Barry is an orthodox Jew who is using the Bible codes in an effort to find the site of the Ark of the Covenant.

I wish to thank the big one, the other one, and the woman for all of their help (they insisted on remaining nameless).

These acknowledgments in no way imply that these gentlemen – and the lady – agree with any of the theological precepts presented in the book.

Walter Keith York

You can contact the author directly at: latterdays@ec.rr.com